W9-BOO-599

PRAISE FOR
PATRICIA POTTER:

"One of the genre's finest talents…"
—Melinda Helfer, *Romantic Times*

"…This one *(Samara)* with its eloquent phrasing and beautiful writing style generates a delicious tension that plays on the nerve endings like impending thunder."
—*Rendezvous*

"Ms. Potter has the unique gift of homing into our deepest emotions, bringing reality, hope and the belief that love can heal all wounds in our lives. You will believe good always triumphs…"
—*Romantic Times*

AND
RUTH LANGAN:

In *Highland Barbarian* "the lovers more than hold their own. The first spark of attraction flames into passionate sensual love, a love that surmounts all the villainies and trials. A keeper!"
—*Romantic Times*

"Ms. Langan weaves a spell over her readers with stirring characters that have a unique spirit that allows them to fight through the devastation of their lives."
—*Rendezvous*

"Ruth Langan is a true master at involving your emotions, be they laughter or tears. Her books are definitely worth the time."
—*Romantic Times*

PATRICIA POTTER

Patricia Potter has become one of the most highly praised writers of historical romance since her impressive debut in 1988, when she won the Georgia Romance Writers of America's Maggie Award, and a Reviewer's Choice Award from *Romantic Times* for her first novel. She has received the *Romantic Times* Career Achievement Award for Storyteller of the Year for 1992, and its Career Achievement Award for Western Historical Romance in 1995. In 1996 she was nominated for a Reviewer's Choice Award for best British Isles Romance. Ms. Potter has been a Romance Writers of America RITA finalist three times, and has received a total of three Maggie Awards. Prior to writing full-time, she worked as a newspaper reporter in Atlanta. She has served as president of Georgia Romance Writers, and currently is a member of the board of the River City Romance Writers.

RUTH LANGAN

Ruth Langan traces her ancestry to Scotland and Ireland. It is no surprise, then, that she feels a kinship with the characters in her historical novels. Married to her childhood sweetheart, she has raised five children and lives in Michigan, the state where she was born and raised. Ms. Langan received the Book Rack Award in 1994 for *The Highlander,* the *Romantic Times* Lifetime Achievement Award in 1989, and has been a finalist for many other awards, including the *Romantic Times* Career Achievement in Western Romance and Reviewer's Choice for Best Contemporary. She is the author of over fifty books and short stories, and continues to be one of the Harlequin Historical line's most popular authors.

PATRICIA
POTTER

RUTH
LANGAN

Ransomed Brides

Harlequin Books

TORONTO • NEW YORK • LONDON
AMSTERDAM • PARIS • SYDNEY • HAMBURG
STOCKHOLM • ATHENS • TOKYO • MILAN
MADRID • WARSAW • BUDAPEST • AUCKLAND

HARLEQUIN BOOKS

by Request—RANSOMED BRIDES

Copyright © 1998 by Harlequin Books S.A.

ISBN 0-373-20150-8

The publisher acknowledges the copyright holders
of the individual works as follows:

SAMARA
Copyright © 1989 by Patricia Potter
HIGHLAND BARBARIAN
Copyright © 1990 by Ruth Ryan Langan

This edition published by arrangement with Harlequin Books S.A.

Printed in U.S.A.

CONTENTS

Dear Reader,

I'm delighted that Harlequin Books has chosen to reprint *Samara,* a tale of the War of 1812.

Samara was my third book, and it will always rank among my favorites, perhaps because the heroine has so much of me in her. She's inquisitive, impulsive and adventuresome. And because she is who she is, the book contains a great deal of humor, including one of my all-time favorite scenes in which she and the hero are trying to get each other tipsy without getting drunk themselves: she is emptying her wineglass into his boot, while he is emptying his wineglass into a plant. Neither object fares very well.

My hero is a British privateer, and my heroine the daughter of an American patriot, the hero of my first book, *Swampfire.* Wanting adventure, she stows away on her brother's ship, only to be captured by our hero. It is his downfall, and only the first of many adventures for the intrepid Samara.

I hope you enjoy this second of the O'Neill saga.

Sincerely,

Patricia Potter

SAMARA
Patricia Potter

To my mother and father,
whose love story,
like Sam's and Connor's,
continues

Chapter One

South Carolina, 1812

Dull. Dull. Dull. The refrain sang in Samara O'Neill's mind as she jabbed the needle in and out of the sampler. Dull. Dull. Dull. The words followed each stitch as her frustration grew. Her life was just too dull. Nothing exciting ever happened to her. *Oh, I wish I were a man.*

She looked at the sampler with loathing. She was much too old for such things, but her mother had talked her into it, and her mother was one of the few people she really tried to please. So here she was...on a beautiful day...sitting inside. Her fingers, eager to finish the tiresome task, mistook skin for cloth and red blood spurted over her painstaking work. *Damn.* The oath escaped her mouth involuntarily, and she waited breathlessly for lightning to strike. She had been told often enough that no young man would look kindly upon a lady who took such liberties with her tongue. Not, of course, that she was overly concerned with the young men of her acquaintance. *Namby-pambies, all of them,* she thought with disgust.

"The devil take it," she uttered with defiance as she looked at the damaged cloth, then glanced guiltily around, sighing with relief that no one had witnessed this latest transgression. Samara wished, not for the first time, that tenaciousness was not one of the few qualities about her that could be termed a virtue. She *would* finish the dratted thing. She had a compulsion to finish whatever she started. It was her least favorite virtue because it often meant enduring a lifeless book or seeing through to the finish a task completed only with dogged perseverance.

A noise from the doorway caused her to look up. Conn, the brother closest to her own age, stood there, watching her industry with amusement. She wanted to throw the sampler at his irritating smirk.

"You look wonderfully domesticated, little sister," he commented, as the smirk developed into a full grin. "And just when I was going to ask you to go for a ride to look for Bren. But I wouldn't dream of taking you from such fruitful pursuits."

Samara's chin thrust out and she said in her most dignified tone, "*I* finish what I start...not like other members of this family I can name."

Conn blushed. Samara's tenacity was legendary while his own left much to be desired. Of all the O'Neill sons, he alone had not found a purpose. Bren, the oldest, ran the family shipping line; Marion had just completed medical school in Edinburgh, and Jere was in firm—and maddeningly competent—control of the family's second plantation. But Conn, like Samara, sought adventure and, with the recent declaration of war against England, had enlisted in the militia and was awaiting orders.

He eyed his pretty younger sister. Having grown up the only sister of four older brothers, she had more skill at masculine activities than feminine ones. Samara was competent with a rifle and pistol, as well as being a fine horsewoman. And she possessed a streak of stubbornness a mile wide.

"At least *I* know when to quit," he retorted. She giggled and his quick grin returned as they both recalled what was now known as Samara's "groomsman period."

At age ten, Samara had desperately wanted a horse of her own. She had, she was quite sure, outgrown her beloved but elderly pony and had embarked on a campaign that ranged from tears to tantrums. For once, neither had much impact.

She was quietly informed by her mother that she could have a horse only when she was thoroughly equipped to see to its care.

With her head held high and her mouth unwisely open, she had taken up the challenge and announced to one and all that she could take care of not only one single horse but the entire stable. It had, after all, looked very simple when she watched the groom. All he did was shovel a bit, here and there.

Unfortunately, her father had taken up the offer, and Samara, dressed in her brothers' old cast-off clothes and carrying a shovel much larger than herself, had set upon the task. Her small hands grew blistered and her clothes were a horror to anyone who drew near, but she refused to cry for quarter. To her parents' amazement, she stayed with the stable all day long. She had won her horse, and had learned early not to commit quite so easily to tasks of which she knew little.

"You're sure you don't want to go with me?" Conn questioned. "I salute your diligence," he said with a mock bow, recognizing defeat as he saw the stubborn set of her jaw. "I'll tell Bren you prefer a sampler to him." He ducked as Samara threw a cushion at him and looked longingly at the door as it slammed behind her brother. Reluctantly, she returned to her work.

Dull. Dull. Dull. Samara's hands played with the threads of colored silks as she contemplated the intended verse.

You will mend your life tomorrow still you cry
In what far Country does tomorrow lie?
It stays so long, is fetch'd so far, I fear
T'will prove both very old and very dear.

It was to be a gift for her godmother in the city of Washington and one, Samara's mother promised with more than the usual laughter in her eyes, that Annabelle McLaughlin would appreciate.

Since Samara dearly loved her unorthodox godmother, she had consented easily enough, forgetting how much she hated sewing. Particularly samplers. Such memories had been lost amid her enthusiasm and, once started, no task was too odious to be left undone. Her mother knew her all too well, Samara thought bitterly.

Dull. Dull. Dull. Her fingers fairly flew now. Anything to be done, and outside, awaiting Brendan's arrival. Brendan. Her beloved oldest brother who was to sail for France in two days.

Her eyes caught the verse again. "In what far country..." Oh, how she wished she could go with Brendan and see the wonders of France, taste the adventure of outwitting the British, spend wonderful days at sea. If only she weren't a girl...

She had begged and begged to go with him, but her parents said it was far too dangerous. Indeed, she couldn't miss the concern in their eyes when they spoke of Bren's upcoming voyage. The British had effectively locked up the American ports with their navy. Just as dangerous now were the British privateers, who had expanded their hunting from French to American vessels. *Pirates*, her father called them with no little bitterness. The O'Neill shipping line had lost several ships to the private adventurers who sailed and fought for gold, not for patriotism.

But Samara knew with all her heart that Bren would outwit and outfight any Englishman. He was her god, bright and shining and heroic. Fourteen years her senior, Bren had always taken special care of her; had, in fact, spoiled her shamelessly, according to their mother and father. She loved all four of her brothers, but Bren was special. The room lit up when he walked into it.

Now he commanded his own blockade runner, the *Samara*, which he had named for her, calling her "the only lass pretty enough to give her name to the loveliest ship afloat." And the *Samara* was beautiful. Built in Baltimore, the schooner could outrun any British frigate.

Although told in no uncertain terms that she would not be allowed a voyage, Samara was hoping at least to travel to Charleston with Brendan and visit friends there. She had a standing invitation to visit the Demerest family, and, if nothing else, she could see Bren off and watch the lovely sails of the *Samara* unfurl and send it off to a new adventure. As her needle continued its path, Samara began to plot her strategy with all the skill of a general.

Dinner, as usual, was a gay affair, especially with all four O'Neill brothers home for a change. Bren had finally arrived in late afternoon; Marion was staying home for several weeks before starting a medical practice in Charleston; Jere, who lived at nearby Chatham Oaks, had come with his wife, Judith; and lighthearted Conn completed the foursome.

As always, when Samara was at home with her father and brothers, she compared them to her suitors. The suitors always emerged very poorly indeed. No one could compare with the O'Neill men. She was beginning to think she would never find anyone as wise as her father, as strong and funny as Bren, as sweet and gentle as Marion, as clever as Jere or as much fun as Connor. Everyone paled by comparison.

And then there was the special relationship between her mother and father. She would never settle for anything less after seeing them together. She knew it was very rare. None of the other adult couples she knew acted this way. Their eyes didn't continually linger on each other, nor did they use any excuse to touch each other or laugh and tease one another constantly.

Samara thought her mother beautiful, and often wished she had inherited her blue eyes as well as her lustrous black hair with its peculiar red glow. She disliked her own eyes, never realizing their dark smoky gray sparkled with the hues of the colors around her. She was the only one of the five children with such eyes, and she constantly envied the others, thinking it most unfair that Bren should have golden hair and blue eyes while she remained so colorless.

"Samara."

Her eyes jerked across the dining room table toward Bren. She had been daydreaming and her face held a question as she looked his way.

"How many lovesick swains do you have now? Have any won your heart?" His teasing voice held a slight hint of seriousness.

Samara blushed as she always did when someone mentioned her suitors. They were usually a matter of embarrassment to her…too young, too old, too short, too thin, too dull.

Her mother saved her. "Give her time, Brendan. She's only eighteen."

"And has already broken half the hearts in the parish," he said. "Perhaps I should give her a chance to do the same in Charleston."

Samara couldn't believe her ears. Was it really going to be so easy? Her eyes opened wide. "Charleston?"

"Mother told me how much you wanted to visit Melanie," he said. "And I cannot think of a better good luck charm than your farewell."

Samara's eyes were glowing. "May I, Mother? May I, really?" It would be the first time she had ever been permitted to take a trip on her own.

"I don't know about letting her loose in Charleston," her father said slowly, but a twinkle in his eye told her he was merely teasing.

Samara flew up from her chair and kissed both her parents, then Brendan, in unabashed joy.

"What about us?" clamored Marion, and Samara made the rounds, taking a playful slap here and a sly warning there. Oh, how she loved them all!

She couldn't eat anything else, not the rich pecan pie nor even an apple tart. She was going to Charleston! She would have adventure at last!

It was sometime later during the night that the thought first surfaced. As much as she pushed the unworthy notion down, it would immediately surface someplace else…like a cork bobbing in water.

I can't, she chastened herself.

But Mama did. Mama ran away and rode and fought with General Francis Marion and found Papa, the little demon inside her argued.

But it will hurt them, Samara fought back.

Ah, but you will be with Bren and they know he'll keep you safe. They'll understand; they had their adventures, the sly part of her countered.

Go away, her conscience demanded.

You know you want to go, said her devil. *It would be so easy. You can slip on board just before sailing and hide in the hold.*

Samantha knew she was fighting a losing battle. Her good side always lost to her wayward one. Her father always said an idea planted in her head never needed nourishment. It flourished on its own.

And so it was doing. Like Jack's beanstalk it grew throughout the night, gaining in strength and intensity and complexity.

She was going to France!

As Samara was determining her future, her mother and father were puzzling over it in their own bedroom.

"She needs another girl's influence," Samantha O'Neill reasoned. "She's surrounded by masculine company here."

Connor smiled as his hand played with one of his wife's black curls. "She has you, my love."

Samantha arched an eyebrow at her beloved husband. "I fear I leave much to be desired as a guide for a young woman today."

Connor laughed. He had never been able to cure his wife of donning breeches and flying over the plantation on one of her prize horses or staying up all night with a foaling mare. Nor had he wanted to. He loved her exactly the way she was—unpredictable, untamable. He pulled her to him now, delighting in the feel of her body next to his. He would never lose his enchantment with it, his enchantment with her. His only hope was that his children would find a love as fine, as totally complete as his. She had made every moment of their life together a joy although, he thought wryly, at times provoking. She loved to tease him out of his serious thoughts and lull him from worry.

She was doing that now, her fingers trailing down his furred chest, exciting him just as she had done thirty years earlier.

"Don't worry about Samara," she said. "She'll find someone in her own time, in her own way."

A frown came into Connor's eyes. "She sends everyone away. I think she compares them all to her brothers. She's with them entirely too much." A quick, proud smile erased the worry on his face. "Although I have to admit, they are all rather extraordinary."

Samantha snuggled further into his arms. "Not as extraordinary as their father…"

"Hmm," he said, feeling her hand going lower and lower, feeling the familiar surge of desire. God, would it always be this strong?

"Maybe Charleston is what she needs…a chance to meet new young people…"

"Hmm," was all he could reply as the embers blazed into fire.

"Charleston…that's it," she whispered before losing herself in the beautiful all-consuming union of their bodies.

Samara packed very carefully and was still the first person down to breakfast. The sideboard was already overflowing with bacon, ham, eggs, warm bread and jams. She took more than usual, wondering when her next meal would come. She had invaded the kitchen before anyone was up, stealing two loaves of bread, some cheese and a bottle of wine which she had hidden carefully in her sewing basket.

She gave everyone a sunny smile as they joined her, disregarding their surprised looks at her early appearance and unusually large plateful of food.

Her mother gave her a kiss and a swift embrace. "I'll miss you, Samara, even for a week."

Samara felt a sudden pang of guilt, but her course was set and her mother, more than anyone, would understand. She would worry and perhaps grieve but she would understand Samara's need. Her father…that was another matter. She knew that next to her mother she was her father's heart. He showed it in everything he did, even in his rare, mostly unsuccessful attempts at discipline. Samara went to him now and kissed him lightly on the cheek. "I love you, Papa," she said softly.

"And I love you, little one. Mind you, behave in Charleston and enjoy yourself. We'll see you in a week."

There was no more time for conscience. Brendan was ready to leave.

Leaving only the trunk for Bren to carry, Samara took her own packages out. She didn't want to have to explain any of them. There was a neatly wrapped package that contained one of her dresses but which was disguised as a present for Bren. There was her sewing kit, with the food and Annabelle's sampler. And there was the carefully written note to her parents.

It was a wonderful day as she and Bren, his horse tied behind the carriage, moved swiftly through the countryside towards Charleston. It was fall—still warm—and the air seemed alive with the aromatic smoke-tinged pungency of the season.

Bren had brought Caesar along as a driver and to accompany Samara to the Demerests after leaving him at his ship. He would be late enough as it was…he wanted to leave at dusk, the best time for his dyed gray sails to blend into the sky and sea. His mind was preoccupied with the task ahead of him, and he paid little heed to Samara's behavior.

But he couldn't help notice her unusual silence as they picnicked along the Pee Dee River. He looked at her thoughtfully.

"What mischief are you planning now, little sister?" he asked, his finger on her chin as he stared intently into smoky eyes.

She cast them downward before replying. "I'm just thinking how much I would like to go with you."

"You would be bored very quickly, I think. There's damn little to do on a ship…unless you're hauling sails or scrubbing decks, and I don't think you would like either."

Her chin went up. "Try me," she said impishly.

"Maybe sometime, after this war, I will," he said, remembering the stable episode. He had always respected his little sister's determination.

When they reached Charleston late in the afternoon, the harbor was crowded with small craft and one other blockade runner. The two would both be making the run tonight, hoping if one was sighted, the other could distract it. It was a dangerous game of tag, but one the captains knew well. Their ships were both faster than the British frigates, and the principal danger lay in too early a detection.

Samara had made her plans carefully. She took her sewing basket aboard, saying she would catch a few stitches while her brother saw to some last-minute details, and deposited it in an inconspicuous place. Then, just before sailing, she would tell Bren she'd forgotten his present and run down to fetch it, telling Caesar that one of Bren's crew would take her to the Demerests. Once back aboard, she would slip into the hold, knowing Bren would be fairly distracted. The only part that really worried her was the hold. She would have to spend enough time down there that Bren would never consider returning to port. They would have to be well past the British threat, and that meant maybe two days. She hated the hold. Bren had taken her there once and, even with his presence and a lantern, it had been terrifying—dark beyond imagining and haunted by strange creaking noises. She had put a small candle in the sewing basket, but she knew the danger of fire and hoped she would have the courage not to use it.

She straightened her shoulders in determination as she told Bren she was returning for her package. The distraction in his eyes and quick, almost indifferent, nod told her everything was proceeding to plan. Now to convince Caesar.

Chapter Two

Aboard the British privateer, the Unicorn

Reese Hampton stood at the helm of the *Unicorn*, his bare feet hugging the deck as his lean, graceful body rolled with the same gentle rhythm as his ship.

His loose, flowing white shirt whipped around him and his tawny hair, bleached gold by the sun, tumbled over a face darkened a rich oak color by the same force.

Taking one hand from the wheel, he raked it through the mussed hair, pushing the wayward strands back from his forehead. He kept it shorter than fashion, not wanting the distraction of errant hair during a battle. He cared little for current fashion or the conventions of society. Long ago he had left such trappings to his twin brother, Avery, who had, by right of birth seven minutes earlier than Reese, inherited the Hampton estates and title in England. A fortunate twist of fate, Reese often thought, for Avery had a love of the land while Reese longed only for a life at sea.

It was a day to make the heavens sing. Against a backdrop of pillowy clouds, a bright sun plowed trails of gold against the sparkling emerald and cerulean blue of an ever-changing ocean. Dolphins raced the ship, their playful antics seeming to dare the *Unicorn* to even greater speed. Reese rested his hands on the wheel, feeling the ship's quick response to his every

demand. He often thought of her as a woman, sleek and beautiful and sensitive to his every caress. But much more loyal,
he thought, as a wry smile curved his sensuous lips. He always
knew what to expect from the *Unicorn*.

He had ordered the ship built to his exact specifications.
Although British-built, she was tailored from an American design which he had admired, and he knew every inch of her.
A large schooner with a sleek hull and high, raking masts, she
carried two long guns as well as twenty quick-firing carron-
ades whose grapeshot could tear rigging to shreds.

He had, with his usual sardonic wit, named the ship the
Unicorn. It had amused him to give such a gentle name to a
deadly predator.

And predator she was! Captain Reese Hampton had been a
privateer for five years and had made, and spent, several fortunes off his French prizes. His choice of targets had expanded
with the Declaration of War by America in June of this year,
1812. He had already taken two American vessels and sold
both ships and cargo in Bermuda.

He enjoyed pitting his skill against the Americans. They
were excellent sailors, unlike the French who often sat like fat
sheep ready for the slaughter. And their ships brought excellent prices. For that reason, he preyed on the waters stretching
along America's eastern coastline, close to the ready markets
of Bermuda and the Caribbean.

His watchful eyes swept the horizon. They seemed woven
by the brightest colors of the sea itself, a mesh of startling
blues and greens, sometimes clashing, sometimes melding, but
always reflecting the restlessness and mystery and depths of
the water around him.

Reese saw nothing now but the gentle swells of the sea and
the shimmer of gold across the waves. He felt the gentle caress
of the sun and breeze against his body, and he spread his legs
and threw back his head and roared in a shout of pure joy at
being alive. His outcry expanded into booming laughter which
raked the decks and startled the busy sailors.

Several looked at him and one crossed himself in supplication. It seemed at that moment that their captain, his face

lifted to the heavens and his hair glinting with flecks of fire from the sun, was challenging the gods of nature.

The hold was beyond Samara's worst imaginings. She had barely settled herself when it started to close in on her. Only that streak of iron stubbornness kept her there.

It was black beyond anything in her experience. Nothing in her life had prepared her for this total void, where time was distorted and reality disappeared. The first few minutes seemed like hours and the only way she knew they weren't was the movement of the ship. She could tell from its gentle sway that it was still anchored, although she fancied she could feel its eager anticipation to be free of its tether.

How long must she stay here in this black hole? She had originally thought two days. Two days would put them so far out at sea that Brendan would never consider going back. But now, in the reality of the hideous place, she was rapidly reconsidering. Perhaps once they had cleared the English blockade, Bren would be sufficiently committed to complete his voyage to France. That should be a day...or even less. But how would she know? How could you know anything down here?

Until now Samara's plans had gone exceedingly well. Caesar had readily believed her, knowing the O'Neills' almost fanatical concern for their horses. It seemed most reasonable to him that Master Brendan would wish the tired carriage horses to have care and food as soon as possible, and equally as plausible that he would send one of his officers to accompany his sister. He had handed the package to Samara, never seeing her quick hand planting a letter in the corner of the carriage seat. It wouldn't be noticed, she knew, unless the carriage was searched or another passenger used it. When she turned up missing, she knew everything would be turned upside down for a clue.

After watching Caesar turn the horses, she had run back up the gangplank to the ship. No one had paid any attention; everyone had been at work preparing the ship for departure. The corridor to the hold was empty and she had slipped inside, praising the Lord that it was unlocked. It was filled to almost overflowing, but she had found a little cubbyhole near the door before closing it and extinguishing all light. The upper hatch on the deck had already been closed and locked. Samara very carefully placed her sewing basket, full of food, and her package, containing one dress and a change of underclothing, nearby. They were her security.

In the succeeding long, dark minutes and hours, she finally had time to consider her actions. She tried not to let doubts assault her waning optimism. Her father would be very, very angry. And very hurt. But she had made her decision and once a decision was made...

Bren would understand. He always understood her. He often said they were much alike, with a common love for nature and mischief. He sympathized when she had had to switch to a sidesaddle, and groaned with her as she was forced into stays and petticoats when all she wanted was her brothers' breeches. He would, she thought, appreciate her adventure, perhaps even admire her for it. She did crave his approval. She wouldn't let herself think that he might frown upon her action.

Oh, how dark and warm and frightening it was. She could hear little rustling noises and worried that it might be rats. She gathered her skirts tightly around her legs, hugging them close to her body, making herself as small a tidbit as possible as the rats grew, in her mind, to horrendous sizes.

Samara finally heard the creaking sounds of the ship slipping from its bonds. The movement quickened, dipping and rolling as the wind caught the sails and pushed the *Samara* out to sea.

How long has it been now? It seemed like days to Samara who, in her fear of the tiny furred things that had already touched her legs, remained steadfastly awake. She had found a quick movement chased the animals—mice or rats or whatever—away. Temporarily anyway. The first time she felt the invasion she had almost screamed, then caught her lips with her hand. Not yet. It was not yet time, she knew. How awful to go through all this, then be sent back. Instead, she steeled herself and remained alert to the tiniest little noise.

It was hot, so very miserably hot. She could feel sweat running down the stays in the back of her dress and dampening the cloth under her arms. Think of something else, she scolded herself. Think of Father.

He had spent months and months in chains in a hold like this during the previous war. For the first time, Samara understood why his eyes narrowed and his mouth grew tight when something reminded him of those terrible months. He would not talk of it, not even when she had begged him after seeing the scars on an ankle. For one of the few times in her life, he had been curt with her, saying it was better forgotten. Later, seeing Samara's hurt, her mother had sat down with her and explained how terrible it had been, how the experience had left more scars than those on his ankle. It was, her mother added, one reason why he disliked the English so much and why he was so vehemently in support of this war. He had raged at the continued impressment of Americans by the English as well as England's arrogant restraint of American trade with France.

Samara could now well understand his fury. At least *she* knew she could leave at any time. How terrible to be locked in a place like this, without sun or stars or a cool breeze to refresh you. It was like a tomb, a grave in which you were buried alive…

Only a little while now! The knowledge that she had the ability to leave helped her to stay. Had it been six hours or twelve or twenty? Hunger clawed at her, and she searched blindly in her sewing basket. There was one piece of bread left; the wine bottle felt very light, and as she put it to her lips, she greedily lapped up the last few drops.

A new scurry of feet startled her. Her companions were growing bolder, particularly when they caught the smell of food. It was time, she determined, to take her leave of this place. She started to rise, then sat again, wondering if she was yet ready to encounter Bren's wrath. A nip on her leg decided her. She stood unsteadily, stiff from her cramped position. Now where was the door? She bumped into one crate after another, completely losing her sense of direction. She looked for her sewing box containing the candle, but that too was gone.

Disoriented and frightened, she did the only thing she could think of. She screamed.

Brendan O'Neill was taking his first rest of the voyage. He had not dared leave the helm for even a few moments during the first two days out. Cloudy skies and the accompanying fog had blessedly hid the *Samara*'s gray-painted hull and dyed sails, and the ship had skimmed by the English frigates with ease, her presence no more noted than the numerous seabirds. There was still the danger of encountering a British naval ship or privateer and the ticklish business of defying British ships along the French coastline. But the first major obstacle had been easily overcome, and Bren saw it as a good omen.

He wearily took off his boots and lay his head to the pillow, hoping to catch several hours of sleep. As always, it came easily. He had trained himself on voyages over the past ten years to take rest whenever he could. Even before the war, there had been long storms to fight and the ever-present danger of pirates, and he had often gone for days without sleep.

The motion of the ship aided his intent. The sky had cleared and the ocean was calm. He relished the feel of the *Samara* moving swiftly through the water ahead of the brisk wind. He loved his ship; it was the culmination of everything he had worked for over the past years, the first of a new design of fast merchant ships. Even as a boy he had watched with envy the ships which visited Charleston and he could often be found listening to tales of their sailors. His father had sensed that Glen Woods and Chatham Oaks held no interest for him, and urged his son to follow his heart. Bren had taken the fledgling O'Neill line, formed mainly to transport the plantations' indigo, and had built it into a major shipping fleet. He rarely captained vessels anymore, seldom finding the time away from supervising the building of new ships, negotiating contracts, finding competent crews and managing a major business. But the British blockade had become deadly, and he was reluctant to send inexperienced crews against it. He would be damned if he would ask others to do something he was not willing to do. And, he privately admitted, he hungered for the feel of the sea again. And for the chance of outwitting the British.

Barely had such thoughts been lost to sleep when a pounding on his door awakened him. He slipped quickly from the bed, instantly alert and jerked the door open, his mouth set in a scowl. It deepened when he saw Scotty, his second mate, and someone in the shadows behind him.

"Beggin' yer pardon, sir," Scotty said. "But we seem to 'ave an unexpected passenger." He moved aside, and Bren saw Samara, her gaze uncustomarily downward, her dress soiled beyond redemption.

Bren closed his eyes against the image before him. When he opened them, hoping it had been a nightmare, she was still there—standing just a little more defiantly.

With narrowed eyes and clenched lips, he stared at her in total dismay. "Where was she?" he finally demanded.

"The 'old, sir. She must have 'id there the last day and a 'alf. I guess she got scared. She started screaming as I went by and I found 'er."

Bren couldn't take his eyes from her, nor could he hide the fury growing in them. What an altogether stupid and dangerous thing to do.

"Thank you, Scotty," he said, the glint in his blue eyes belying the calm in his voice. "You may go back to your duties. Samara, come in here."

Samara met his eyes but couldn't comprehend the anger she saw there. She slithered in, trying to make herself as small as possible. She had never felt his rage before, indeed had never realized he possessed such a thing. Bren was the most even-tempered person she had ever known, always laughing, always teasing, always understanding. Until now. *That* she knew instantly.

A muscle throbbed in Bren's jaw as he sought to control himself. "What," he finally asked, "in the hell did you think you were doing?"

"Going to France," she answered evenly, a slight quiver of her lips the only betrayal of her growing apprehension.

"What about Mother and Father? Didn't you stop to think for a moment what this might do to them?"

Her head went up. "I wrote them…they know you'll take care of me."

"And what about the British…do you think they'll appreciate that fact? Damn it, Samara, don't you know how dangerous this is?"

"You're better than all of them…they can never catch you." The words were said with such utter confidence that Bren had trouble keeping his face bent in such censure.

He shook his head. "The fact is, my dear sister, that if anyone sights us we are in a great deal of trouble. The *Samara* is a merchant ship. We don't have the guns to defend her against a warship. We are depending on speed…and luck."

"I don't care," she said stubbornly. "No one can touch you."

"Such faith," he replied wryly.

He held her at arm's length, taking in her tired, smudged face and thoroughly stained dress. "How long have you been planning this?"

"Just since the night before we left Glen Woods," she replied honestly.

"And I played right into your hands by inviting you to Charleston."

Only her eyes admitted the truth.

"Ah, Samara, I have spoiled you much too much. We all have. If I had thought it safe, I would have been delighted to have your company. Now it's just too damned dangerous. We're going back."

"You can't," Samara said, desperation crowding her voice. "You can't go back through the blockade again."

"We won't go into port. I'll slip close to land and have several of my men accompany you back. There's nothing else to do," Bren said gently. "Dangerous as it might be, it's less than what we'll find on the rest of this voyage."

Samara's dream crumbled. Not only had she failed, but she had unnecessarily put her beloved brother in needless danger.

"I'll do anything," she said in a low, pleading voice. "I'll scrub your decks, I'll cook."

"I don't need an extra hand," Bren said. "I should like to keep my sister in one piece. We'll talk about it no more." He looked down again at the dress. "Do you have anything else to wear?"

She looked miserable. "One dress."

"I'll see you get a bath and you can get some sleep. You look like you could use it." His mouth crooked up in a half smile. "Did you really stay in the hold all this time?"

Her gray eyes grew large as she contemplated the horror of her time there, and nodded slowly.

Bren's finger touched her cheek. "Oh, Samara...whatever are we going to do with you?"

He turned to go, the new course change already turning over in his mind, when both of them heard the loud cry from above.

"Sail, ho."

Bren fought back a string of curses. What miserable luck! So much for that first euphoric feeling of good omen. "Stay here, keep the door locked unless you hear my voice," he ordered Samara curtly and bounded out the door and up onto the deck.

Brendan strode to the lookout. "What flag?"

"She's not flying any."

Picking up his glass, he looked out across the distance and cursed again. The ship was a schooner, much like his own but larger and heavily armed. He knew a sudden unfamiliar apprehension.

He turned to Briggs, his first mate. "Let's make a run for it."

The ship turned to the wind and Bren ordered his men aloft to loosen the topsails. The ship picked up speed, but Bren saw that the other ship followed suit, closing some of the distance between them.

In less than an hour, the ship was within firing range and Bren saw the British flag go up, accompanied by signal flags ordering him to turn about.

In those minutes, he had a torturous decision to make, one made more difficult by Samara's presence. Many of his crew were British-born and, under British law, subject to impressment, imprisonment or even hanging if found to be deserters from the British navy—as some were. He would be condemning each and every one of them if he surrendered the ship. And only God knew what would happen to Samara. Since it was not a naval ship, it was obviously a privateer, and none of that breed was much better than a common pirate. He had heard more than one story of their mistreatment and ransoming of prisoners.

Brendan made his decision quickly. They did not have the Englishman's firepower but perhaps a lucky shot would disable their opponent's rigging enough to give them a chance to escape.

"Run up our flag," he told a helmsman. "Prepare to fire."

The next hour was what Samara imagined hell must be like. She could hear the smashing of cannonball and shot into the ship, feel the boom of the *Samara*'s returning fire, smell the smoke of gunpowder. Worst of all were the agonized screams and cries of the wounded which competed with the noise of cracking and splintering wood. Frightened beyond anything in her experience, she did as she was told and stayed in the cabin. She was thrown from her feet when the two ships met and grappling hooks from the privateer locked them together, but she kept her fear contained by convincing herself that Bren was the best. Bren would win. He would never let anything happen to her. Never.

Brendan never saw the shot that felled him. He had continued to direct the firing from the quarterdeck and had taken the wheel when his helmsman fell. The decks were now slippery with blood and the air acrid with smoke. He knew the smell of defeat, but something in him refused to acknowledge it. Just as he took the wheel, seeking to turn the ship and slip from the privateer's reach, a cannonball hit one of the yards above him, splintering it into hundreds of sharp missiles which rained down on top of him. One piece hit his head while another went into his arm and pinned him to the deck. As blood splurted from his wound, he lost consciousness.

With its captain downed, the ship easily capitulated. The crew, badly outnumbered, were mostly peacetime sailors, untrained in the close-in fighting now required of them. They threw down their arms, one by one, and stared in apprehension as a golden-haired blood-splattered giant jumped lightly aboard and took control of the ship.

Reese Hampton's eyes quickly scanned the deck for the captain. He had not expected the kind of opposition he had received and he wanted no more surprises. Only one man seemed to have any authority.

"Captain?" he queried, his voice harsh and demanding.

"No," Briggs growled. "First mate. The captain's near the wheel, badly wounded. He needs medical attention."

Reese strode over to the fallen man. "His name?"

"Captain O'Neill."

Reese leaned over and pulled the piece of wood from Brendan's arm. Ripping a piece of cloth from the man's shirt, he wrapped it tightly around the bleeding wound and gestured to several of his men.

"Take him to the *Unicorn*; tell Yancy to do what he can for him," he said before turning back to Briggs and ordering in a terse voice. "Separate your wounded from the others. We have a surgeon aboard."

He ordered three of his men to search the rest of the ship for any survivors and sent his boatswain to the captain's cabin for his papers. Reese wanted to know exactly what the ship was carrying and whether it had been worth the damage to the *Unicorn*. He then surveyed the damage to the *Samara*, as he wondered briefly about its strange, exotic-sounding name. The ship was salvageable, but it would take a great deal of work. What a little beauty it was! He damned the stubborn American for not yielding sooner.

He was continuing his careful perusal of his latest prize, when his boatswain interrupted him. "Cap'n, the door's locked."

Reese looked at the man with impatience. "Then break it open, Evans."

"Well, sir, it seems to be latched from the inside… someone's in there…I thought you might want to know."

A frown darkened Reese's face. It didn't make sense. Why would anyone be hiding now? Surely it was known the ship was taken. Perhaps to destroy some papers?

"Let's go, Evans," he said, fairly leaping for the hatchway.

Once there, he regarded the door with interest. He briefly thought about ordering the offender to open it but discarded the notion. It would only give him warning and perhaps a chance to shoot. Instead, he whispered to Evans to keep his pistol ready and rammed his shoulder against the door, feeling the wood splinter. Another lunge swung the door open and he heard it bang against the wall as he stared in utter amazement.

Standing against the wall, holding a wine bottle as one would hold a sword, eyes blazing with a mixture of fear and defiance, was one of the loveliest women he had ever seen.

Chapter Three

Samara had known something was dreadfully wrong minutes before the handle of the cabin door rattled. The sound of battle had quieted, but there had been no sign of Brendan. As minutes wore on, fear and apprehension swirled inside her, growing with each second's passing. It turned to terror when she heard footsteps in the corridor and the cabin door being tried. Then there was quiet, as footsteps receded.

Oh, God, where is Bren? He wouldn't abandon her, not unless he was wounded…or dead. The last thought was incomprehensible, but she couldn't drive it from her head. She sank to the floor in total despair. This couldn't be happening. She heard boots tramping above her, heard orders being shouted by strange voices and then a noise at the door again.

She looked frantically around for a weapon…anything. Then the door rumbled and splintered and the only thing she saw was a wine bottle apparently brought for Bren's dinner. Grabbing it, she backed up against the far wall.

She was prepared for anything but what suddenly confronted her.

For a moment, Samara thought she was seeing the devil himself. He seemed a giant, taller than her father, than any of her brothers who usually towered above all others. Even in the darkening cabin, his tawny rumpled hair flickered with streaks of gold and copper. Dressed only in a white flowing shirt and cutoff white breeches, he was splattered with blood…from his two bare feet to his wide shoulders. But even as her mind somehow registered all of this, she felt pinioned to the wall by his eyes. She had never seen any like them. They were a deep, restless greenish-blue which seemed to glitter like a multifaceted gem, quickly changing from anger to amusement to something more complicated. She didn't know exactly what it was, but it sent shivers through her. She tried to back up further, but there was no place to go and, instead, she raised the bottle in bravado.

"I knew I had a rich prize; I just didn't know how rich," the giant said in a deep, lazy voice, and Samara's shivers grew. He leaned against the doorjamb, all strength and grace like a jungle cat, as his strangely brilliant eyes first scoured, then mentally undressed her.

For the first time in her life, Samara wished she could faint at will…anything to get away from those eyes. No one had ever looked at her like this, no one had ever dared. She felt naked before him, not only her body but her mind and soul, as well. She knew he could read her fear and was amused by it, and that shamed her even more than the obvious lust in his eyes.

"Do you really intend to do battle with that bottle?" The question was part interest, part mockery, and she hated him at that moment. She instinctively held it higher. As poor as it was, it was the only thing between them.

His voice softened to the purr of a tiger. "Come now…there are much better things to do with a bottle of wine."

There was something hypnotizing about the invitation in his voice. She sought desperately to break the spell he was spinning. She finally managed a few words. "Captain…Captain O'Neill…is he…?"

The giant continued to lean indolently against the wall, studying her, and Samara felt herself flush under his intense gaze.

Reese was intrigued. She was filthy, her face smudged and dress stained, but it didn't detract from the interesting promise of her willowy figure. The violet color of her dress was reflected in the huge uncertain gray eyes that flickered between fear and an almost touching defiance. Black hair, streaked with a red glow like flame, tumbled down her back and framed a truly lovely face. Who could she be? Not a wife. No captain would take a wife on such a dangerous journey. Nor, he thought ruefully, would they wish to. Most men he knew went to sea to escape such bonds. Mistress? Likely, he concluded. The thought excited him. If she were the captain's mistress, she would, perhaps, not object to becoming his. He was seldom denied any woman's favors.

Already, his blood was warming and, unconsciously, his half smile turned into a full leer.

Samara didn't miss the change in his eyes nor the tightening power of his body. Almost desperately, the bottle went higher. "The captain...where is the captain?"

"He's on my ship," Reese said slowly, wondering how much it really mattered to her. "He was wounded but I think not badly. My surgeon's looking after him."

"I want to see him," she demanded, with a boldness she didn't feel. She bit her lip to keep it from trembling.

His eyes softened slightly and some of the leer left his face as he heard her concern. There was no doubt she cared for O'Neill. But how much?

"What is he to you?" he asked softly, his eyes changing again, puzzling her. The small half smile, which told her nothing, was back.

With her fear for Bren somewhat allayed, she turned her full attention to her captor. He was the most striking man she had ever seen. His face seemed chiseled from stone, each feature strong and clearly defined...from his deep-set eyes to the determined chin. It was nearly bronze from the sun, making his gold hair and glittering aqua eyes startling by contrast. Arrogance and power radiated from him, and she almost gasped at the shaming shivers of her body. She had never been so affected by a man.

He was an Englishman.

And a pirate.

And a thief. He was stealing her ship.
And possibly, her brother's murderer.

Reese Hampton read the confusion in her face, saw the flush as her eyes examined him as carefully as he had her, smiled as she bit her lip in embarrassment at being caught at it.

She looked impossibly innocent...and vulnerable. Reese felt a fleeting moment of compassion but quickly shrugged it aside. She couldn't be as innocent as she looked, not a woman alone on a ship full of men.

She hadn't answered his question about O'Neill. He tried again, bowing slightly. "I'm Captain Reese Hampton. Whom do I have the honor of addressing?"

The bottle came down several inches. Samara's hand was becoming tired and she was beginning to feel very silly. As if the bottle would do any harm to the warrior across from her. But as he stepped toward her, her arm raised protectively once more.

"The bottle." The words were spoken softly, but with a confidence that once more stirred her to a confusing mixture of anger and desire. She flinched as he continued to move, catlike, toward her, his hand held out.

Samara tried to inch along the wall in a vain attempt to place distance between them, but she was suddenly trapped between two long arms, and the bottle was being pulled gently from her fingers and set firmly on a nearby table. She sought to duck under his arm, but one hand caught her chin, cradling it as he forced it upward until her eyes were staring straight into his. A finger from his other hand traced her cheekbone with feathery lightness, and she felt unfamiliar flickers of flame race through her.

"Please..." Her voice was very low, very uncertain.

"Please what, my sweet?" he replied, the warmth in his tone nearly mesmerizing her. "Please continue...or please stop?" He felt confident of her answer. Her body was trembling under his hands as it unconsciously strained towards him.

"S-s-stop."

In answer, his lips met hers, and Samara felt herself whirling as if swept up by a tornado. She had never been kissed like this, had never been touched like this, had never known feelings like this. His touch ranged from a gentle sweetness to fevered want, carrying her progressively from note to note, arousing depths she hadn't known existed until now. In sudden terror at what was happening, she jerked away, her hand instinctively going back and swinging at his face with a force created of desperation. The impact stunned them both, the sound of the slap magnified by the closeness of the room.

Samara looked at the bright red color left by the blow and stood paralyzed, waiting for the retaliation she was sure would come. Her eyes now dominated her face, looking like those of a trapped dove as a hawk attacks.

Reese's first surge of anger quieted under her obvious fright. He had never mistreated a woman, nor taken an unwilling one. He forced himself to relax, but his body did not want to cooperate.

"Why didn't you just tell me no?" he asked finally.

"I...I...I...tried..."

"Not very hard," he said with the former mockery, and she flinched at his words. He was right.

He put his hand to his cheek ruefully. "Your captain should have put you up on deck. Maybe he would have won."

His words brought Samara painfully back to reality. "I have to see him."

"Please," he said tauntingly. "Say please."

For a moment, she felt a surge of satisfaction that she had slapped him. She only wished it had been harder. "Please..."

"Please, Captain Hampton..." he urged, continuing to bait her.

"Please, Captain Hampton," Samara replied sullenly, ready to do anything to leave the cabin...and him...and her shameful, inexplicable reaction to him.

"And who is asking?" He questioned with a mocking insolence that masked his real interest.

Pleading eyes lifted to his glittering ones. "Samara," she said finally, almost hopelessly. "Samara O'Neill."

Reese felt as if he had been kicked. So she *was* O'Neill's

wife. That accounted for the ship's name. His disappointment
startled him. He had a very limited number of rules for himself, but he had vowed long ago that married women were
taboo. It was a decision made after a friend had died in a duel
with an irate husband. No woman was worth dying for, or
killing for, particularly one who betrayed her husband. There
were altogether too many fish in the ocean to fight over one
already netted.

"Captain O'Neill is your husband?" He couldn't resist the
question, even knowing the answer.

Samara looked at him, startled. She had never thought he
would assume that. But she didn't miss the new restraint in
his voice, nor the almost imperceptible withdrawal. It was difficult to believe that this…this pirate would respect marriage,
but perhaps he did. Perhaps that would save her from him,
and she from herself. Even now, she felt strange new urges
tugging at her senses, and she had to restrain her hand from
reaching out to touch him. *He's a pirate*, she kept telling herself, *and an Englishman*. She didn't know which was worse.
But together…

She closed her eyes for a moment, then opened them and
stared him straight in the face. "Yes," she said. "And I would
like to see him…if that's not too much to ask from a pirate."

Reese's eyes narrowed. "I am a privateer, Mrs. O'Neill, and
our countries are at war."

"That's just an excuse for murder and thievery," Samara
said, suddenly brave as she echoed her father's words. Her
terror was gone; she had lost her fear of any physical harm
from the man opposite her. *Don't think about the other. Don't
think about the way he makes you feel.* To protect herself from
him, she planted a seed of anger and willed it to grow. This
man, this "pirate," had attacked the ship named for her and
was responsible for her brother's wounding. He was everything she had been taught to despise, and she loathed herself
for feeling even the tiniest bit of warmth or attraction for him.
The result of all this emotional turmoil was a baleful glare
sent in the general direction of the Englishman.

To her everlasting mortification, it seemed only to amuse

him. The sides of his mouth twitched, and his eyes gleamed with humor. He moved to the table where he had deposited the wine bottle.

"I think I will take your deadly weapon with us," he said, grabbing it with a strong brown hand. "I might need it," he added, deliberately.

She looked up. He was laughing at her. His eyes fairly danced with merriment at her discomfort, and Samara clenched her hands in frustration. She wanted to hit him again but she didn't quite dare. She knew he would be ready this time.

Reese's grin grew wider. He couldn't mistake at least part of her thoughts; he had had much too much experience with women for that. Perhaps rules were made to be broken, he thought with a start. Perhaps she was not so very married. In any event, it should prove to be a very interesting voyage.

With a small mocking bow, he took her arm, completely disregarding her attempt to free it, and steered her out the door and up on deck. This time, she didn't have to force her anger. She could have joyfully murdered him.

The full horror of the previous several hours did not dawn on Samara until she reached the upper deck. Her stomach lurched as she viewed the cluttered wreck that had once been Brendan's well-tended ship. Torn pieces of sail floated like kites over the carnage. Splintered wood and jagged pieces of iron littered the usually immaculate deck. Bright crimson stains looked like a madman's painting, the thick globs forming obscene patterns on a wooden canvas.

Samara couldn't take her eyes from the mayhem, where each sight was worse than the last. She saw some of Brendan's crew, their clothes black with gunpowder, working under armed guards. Others, obviously wounded, were huddled in a corner, awaiting some disposition. The fear in their faces told her they didn't know what it would be—death or salvation.

In still another corner were several bodies. She saw a familiar striped shirt and jerked loose from the Englishman, running to the still form.

She knelt beside him. "Scotty," she whispered, her hand

reaching for his and finding it covered in blood. She had known Scotty for years and he had been unfailingly kind to her. She remembered now how glad she was to see him…just hours ago when he rescued her from the hold.

"Oh, Scotty," she repeated, unaware of the warm tears that had formed in her eyes and started down her cheeks. She had never seen violent death before, never been exposed to anything more than the usually quiet leave-taking of aged animals. Even that had created tears for days; even when she knew death had come gently after a long life.

"Mrs. O'Neill." The pressure on her arm was gentle…but commanding. "Mrs. O'Neill," the voice came again as through a fog, "this is no place for you."

She stood up then, staring at him as her rage grew from a tiny bubble to a boiling cauldron. Samara whirled and faced her captor. "You," she said with cold hatred. "You did this. Damn you. Damn you to hell." Her hand went back, just as it had earlier, but this time Reese was prepared.

His hand whipped out and caught it in midair. His other hand caught her left wrist, and he pinned both of them behind her. "One," he said tightly, "is all you're allowed."

She stood there shaking, tears streaming down her face as he pulled her closer. Then the wetness traveled to his shirt, and she could smell a pungent mixture of musk and blood and sweat. Something wild and primitive inside her responded, and she trembled as her heart beat so loudly she knew everyone could hear. *What was happening to her?* She couldn't seem to move, to breathe, to think. Think about Scotty, she told herself.

With sudden determination she pushed away, surprised to feel his arms fall from her. She forced herself to look at him, prepared to meet his hatefully amused eyes with her own disdainful ones. But his weren't amused, and the warmth and unexpected gentleness she found there almost undid her again. She quickly dropped her own, thinking, knowing she had been mistaken about his sympathy. He was a pirate. He had created all this destruction.

When she looked up again, she knew she was right. His eyes were penetrating. Cold.

"This is no place for you," he repeated. "I'll take you to your husband."

Without waiting for an answer, he steered her to where the two ships remained locked together. A plank made easy commerce between the two, and Reese easily swung her up and leaped up behind her with the same catlike grace she had noticed before. He placed his two hands firmly around her waist.

The feel of his hands sent new fire through her, and she sought to throw them off, losing her balance on the narrow plank in the process. To her humiliation, she started to fall until two arms scooped her up and held her tightly against a rock-hard chest. She knew the touch of his breath, the feel of his heat and the sound of his heart. He held her as easily as she would a feather, and she wondered at his strength. Then they were across, and still he was holding her, his face staring down at her with some strange expression she couldn't decipher.

"You seem determined," he finally said, in the same amused drawl that had angered her earlier, "to wreak even more damage."

Samara glared at him with renewed fury. "Put me down," she demanded haughtily.

"Only if you promise to behave," he said. He raised a questioning eyebrow, and Samara thought he looked more than ever like her mental portrait of a blond Lucifer.

He sounded as if he were speaking to a child, and Samara's outrage continued to flame. How dare he? She wriggled to free herself, only to find her body even more enmeshed in his arms.

She could feel the laughter rise in his chest as he drew her tighter to him, making it nearly impossible for her to move. She steadfastly avoided looking at him, sensing that he would read what his closeness was doing to her. His very touch burned her like a brand, and she couldn't understand it. She should hate him. She *did* hate him! *Bren. Keep your mind on*

Bren. Why, oh why, hadn't anyone warned her she could feel like this?

His arms relaxed, and she was settled, ever so gently, in a corridor before an open door. Too stunned by events to move, she could merely stand there, trying to restore some measure of control.

He was taking her arm again, leading her inside, and somehow her eyes focused on those within. Bren was on a table, silent and still, his usually sun-darkened face pale and set. A man was leaning over him, pulling a needle through her brother's skin, oblivious to his patient's quick withdrawals of breath as the pain ebbed and flowed with each stitch.

Samara forced herself to watch silently, afraid that to disturb them would increase the torment. Unexpectedly, she felt the Englishman's hand on her shoulder, not cruelly or even possessively as before but, once more, almost with gentleness. She looked up quickly, again catching that fleeting glance of something vulnerable. She instantly dismissed it as whimsy and turned back to Bren.

As the doctor tied his final knot, she ran over to her brother. Bren's eyes widened at the sight of her. Everything had happened so quickly, he had almost forgotten Samara. There had been the attack, the thunder of guns, then pain and, finally, blackness. He had regained consciousness just minutes earlier, his head reeling with pain and his arm a fiery furnace of agony.

"My husband...my dear, wonderful husband," Samara said as she rushed to him, leaned down and kissed him.

Bewilderment...total bewilderment...clashed with his pain, as fogged eyes questioned her.

"I was so worried about you," she rattled on, ignoring his incredulous expression. "This...this...pirate," she looked back at Reese, "said I could see you."

All of a sudden, Bren comprehended. For some reason, Samara thought it wise to masquerade as his wife. He didn't question her reason. His eyes told her he understood and his left hand lifted and squeezed hers. He tried to rise slightly, but nausea forced him back down. He could only look helplessly around him.

In addition to the doctor, there were two seamen, apparently standing by as guards. As if he could move, much less fight back. A bitter smile formed on his lips.

Behind them was a tall figure, lounging against the wall in apparent disinterest. But despite the careless pose, Bren sensed something intense and dangerous about him. It was in the narrowed eyes, a certain recognizable tautness that was quietly menacing.

The man approached him now, and Bren feared for his sister. This was no man to play for a fool.

"Captain O'Neill," the voice was low and pleasing, carrying little of the precise English inflection Bren had expected. "I'm Reese Hampton, captain of the *Unicorn*. You and your crew are my prisoners."

"My ship?"

"Afloat. Just barely. We're trying to salvage it."

"And Samara...my wife?"

"She will be safe enough...hostage, as you will, to your own good behavior. Not that she sets a very good example." Bren heard the laughter in his voice, and his fear for Samara quickened.

"If you touch—"

Reese's mouth tightened. "You are in no position to make threats, Captain. But I'll tell you, just once, that I don't make war on women."

Bren had to be satisfied with that. He knew from his captor's face he would get no more. "My crew?"

"Seven were killed. The injured are being cared for. The others will work for their keep."

"On a British ship?" Bren snarled.

"If they want to eat, yes," Reese replied mildly.

"And then?" The words came with difficulty. Brendan O'Neill had no experience as a supplicant, but his concern for his English-born crew members overrode everything else.

Reese's stern expression relaxed only slightly. "If you cause me no trouble, I'll put you and your crew ashore at a neutral place."

"All my crew?"

Reese had little difficulty in recognizing the question's meaning. One of the causes of the war had been Britain's unyielding insistence that anyone born in England, Scotland or Ireland remained subjects of the king and liable to impressment or worse.

"All," he agreed. "I have no particular desire to fill the navy's ranks. I'm more concerned with getting these two ships to Bermuda."

"An English port," Brendan sneered. "Is that what you call neutral?"

A muscle throbbed in Reese's cheek, the only sign of his growing anger. "I'm not accustomed to having my word—or my honor—questioned," he said.

"Honor?" Bren's voice was tinged with contempt. "A privateer? Why should I believe you?"

Reese's voice was silky now. "Because you really have no choice, Captain." He turned to the two seamen. "Take him to the hold with the other officers." He had considered allowing the enemy crew run of the ship, but O'Neill's hostility changed his mind. O'Neill, he knew through years of experience, could be a great deal of trouble. He had also learned long ago to separate the crew from their officers; without leadership, there was usually little rebellion.

"No!" Samara's voice interrupted the silent duel between the two men.

Reese turned to her, both eyebrows raised in mock surprise. "No?" he repeated softly.

Even Brendan's eyes were disapproving now.

"I...I..." she couldn't continue. She only remembered her own frightening hours in the dark hold. She couldn't stand the thought of Brendan, with his wounds, imprisoned there.

Reese ignored her plea and turned his attention back to O'Neill. "Why, under all God's mercy, did you bring your wife with you?"

Bren closed his eyes in frustration. The censure in the Englishman's voice was clear.

"He didn't bring me," Samara broke in, unable to let Bren

assume the blame for her misdeed. "I stowed away. He found me just before you attacked."

Reese couldn't hide his astonishment. So that's why she had all those smudges. They were at least two days from any port. Bemused, he considered the words. It was completely outside his comprehension that a woman would go to all that trouble and discomfort to be with her husband. There must be more between these two than he'd first thought. His eyes continued to dart between the two, sensing a deep affection, yet finding something amiss. He hadn't, he knew, mistaken the girl's reluctant awareness of him, nor the sparks that snapped between them. There was none of that between the two standing before him.

From the beginning, he had noticed she was not wearing a wedding ring. Yet there was no denying the familiarity between his two unwilling passengers, nor the fact that the ship bore her name. One didn't usually name ships after mistresses; it was much too public.

He shook his head to clear it. He had time to solve this particular mystery and solve it he would.

He placed a restraining hand on Samara and repeated his instructions to the two crewmen.

Bren shot Samara a warning look and struggled to sit up. "What about my wife?"

"She'll have my first mate's cabin. Nothing will happen to her, nothing she doesn't want to happen." Reese eyed O'Neill as he made the last suggestive comment. He wanted to take more of a measure of the man. He wasn't disappointed.

"Damn you," Bren raged as he lunged towards Reese, only to find his legs wouldn't hold him. Only the intervention of Reese's two crewmen kept him from falling. "I'll kill you if you harm her."

Reese's steel-like grip on Samara kept her from reaching for Bren. The Englishman, with Samara firmly in tow, stepped back to allow the two guards and their prisoner to leave. Samara could only watch helplessly as Bren, his eyes a mixture of rage and fear for her, was half dragged, half carried away.

Chapter Four

The first mate's cabin was tiny, holding little but a narrow bunk built into the cabin wall, a table bolted to the floor, a chair and a trunk tucked into a corner. It was as spartan as a nun's cell.

Captain Hampton had opened the door and ushered her in, studying her with insolent interest. He bowed slightly. "I beg forgiveness for the quarters but we had not expected so lovely a guest," he said.

"I would prefer to be with my...husband," Samara said, still defiant.

"I'm afraid that's not possible," Reese said, with the grin she was beginning to hate. "He is not the only one there, and I think propriety, if not modesty, would prevent you from sharing their quarters."

She could only glare at him.

"Do you have some other clothes aboard your ship?" he asked as he regarded her critically.

Samara suddenly realized how she must look. Her worst fears were confirmed by the twinkle in those ridiculously blue-green eyes. She jutted out her chin, not realizing that any dignity was compromised by the childlike smudges on her cheek and chin.

"I had a dress...in a package...in the captain's cabin."

"I'll send for it," her tormentor said, "as well as a bath." He said the last as his eyes glided up and down her with what

Samara catalogued as a wickedly lecherous look. The tingles started inside her again even as she fought to subdue them.

"There is no need," she said, trying to put indifference into her voice. "I'm perfectly fine as I am."

"Ah, but there is a need," the Englishman drawled. "I wish your company for dinner and I think I would like to see what you look like after the hold washes away." His hand reached out and touched one of the deeper smudges on her cheek.

"I would rather starve," Samara spat, "than share dinner with a pirate."

"Privateer," he corrected again, then added, "Ah, but would your husband and his fellow officers?" The gleam in his eye belied his mild tone.

Samara looked at him with horror. "You wouldn't?"

The side of his mouth twisted up. "No?"

"I detest you," she said, trying to think of the worst possible way to insult him. "You are no gentleman."

He threw back his head and roared. "There are many who would agree with you on that point. Besides, what else would you expect of a pirate?" He was mocking her again, using her own words against her.

She looked around, hoping for a weapon of some sort. Impotent fury filled her eyes as she found none.

"I'm afraid," he said, reading her thoughts exactly and more than a little intrigued with her seemingly unconquerable spirit, "I dropped your wine bottle on the other ship. Now be a good girl and take a bath." With that, he slipped from the cabin, and she heard the door lock.

Despite her brave words, the bath felt wonderful. A cabin boy and deckhand appeared almost immediately after Hampton's departure, one armed with a bathtub which barely fit inside the cabin and the other with buckets of hot water. The boy, his eyes wide with interest over the new passenger, also carried her package and some towels.

"'ere ye are, mistress," he said. "'ope ye enjoy yer bath."

Samara eyed them both with suspicion until they retreated under her baleful stare. Despite everything, the bath did look inviting. For one used to bathing daily and changing clothes often, she felt horribly miserable under the layers of dirt and dried perspiration.

She tried the door, finding no lock on her side and, instead, propped the chair against it. Eyeing the bath with the intensity of a starving man approaching food, Samara quickly slipped from her dress and into the water.

The warm liquid felt like velvet against her sticky flesh and she slid down further, letting it encompass her like a cocoon. Instantly, she felt guilty at the comfort. How was Bren being treated? She saw Scotty's body again, and the wounded. How were they? Rage flowed through her like hot lava. That she was attracted to the man responsible shamed her to the core. What was she to do now? Captain Hampton had told Bren he would not hurt her, but what guarantee did she have? He had demonstrated his ruthlessness over and over again—in his treatment of her brother, in his threats to starve the *Samara*'s crew. It was obvious he did not take easily to being thwarted in his wishes. And there was no hiding his interest in her. She had never seen such an openly lecherous leer.

If only he weren't... But Samara wouldn't let herself think "if only." It was altogether too dangerous, and only kindled those new, tormenting feelings. The English captain was so arrogantly handsome, so compelling. She had never seen a person completely dominate everyone and everything as easily. A warmth crept through her as she remembered the flashes of heat where he touched her, those strange unfamiliar cravings that surfaced when he had pressed her to him.

"No," she whispered. "He is our enemy. Bren's and mine. He's a rogue and a pirate and he's stealing the *Samara*." And no one, no one could do anything about it.

Or could they? The little voice which had urged her to stow away returned. Her gray eyes lighted as it continued to prick at her consciousness. Only too aware of the consequences of its latest mischief, she tried to shoo the voice away. But, as always, the imp refused to obey.

He's attracted to you, it said. *Use it to help Bren escape.*
But how?
The wine. Get him drunk tonight and steal his keys.

Samara's fertile brain took the idea from there. She sat up abruptly in the bath, splashing water on the floor, her eyes wide with possibilities. She had seen her brothers drunk, much to her parents' dismay, and knew exactly how debilitating it could be.

After living in a family with so many men and eavesdropping on numerous forbidden conversations, Samara knew exactly what to do. *Laugh at my wine bottle, did he,* she giggled to herself. He'll find out how dangerous it could be. She would get him drunk, bang him on the head with a bottle or whatever was handy, steal a weapon—hopefully a pistol; she knew how to use that—and free Brendan and the others. With her usual optimism and customary disregard for realities, she smiled confidently to herself and once more sank down in the cooling water.

Reese felt a curious uncertainty as he discarded his clothes, throwing the blood-stained shirt and breeches in a pile on the floor. He washed quickly and shaved just a little more carefully, rubbing the back of his hand over the now smooth cheek.

What was it about the little she-cat that provoked more than his usual superficial interest? Especially if she was, as she claimed, married. Cat? She was more like a half-grown kitten, spitting one minute, warm and cuddly the next. He hadn't missed that startled response to him, the leap of fire between them which she tried so futilely to quench. He shook his head in frustration. There was an appealing innocence about her that just didn't fit a married woman. Unless, of course, it was all an act. He was plagued with the thought that something was not quite what it seemed.

He burrowed in his sea chest in his usual careless way, finally finding a pair of bucksin breeches and a clean linen shirt. He slipped into a pair of boots, eyed them with disfavor and exchanged them for another, this time a brushed soft leather reaching to his knees. Reese laughed at himself. It was odd that he cared so much about his appearance! He seldom did aboard ship. His smile changed to a scowl. No kitten, he vowed, was going to put her claws into him. Especially not an upstart American. And a married one at that. That was another puzzle that nagged at him. But he would solve the mystery of Samara O'Neill. And wine, he thought as his face lightened, was exactly the way to do it.

Samara had just finished brushing her hair to a fine luster when a knock came at her door. She quickly smoothed out her dress, wishing it were not the plain, sensible day dress she had deemed most suitable for an ocean voyage. The best thing about the dress was its color—a rich blue that reached to her eyes. She tensed at the sound of the knock, preparing herself to face *him* again. Strangely enough, she felt a stab of disappointment to find, instead, an attractive dark-haired man who introduced himself as Michael Simmons, the first officer. He bowed, while eyeing her with no little appreciation. He had been busy when Reese brought her aboard and was just told minutes ago that he had lost his cabin. His first irritation fled as he studied her.

"Captain Hampton asked me to escort you to his cabin," he said finally. "And I need to get a few things from the cabin."

Samara almost apologized for dislodging him before realizing she didn't want to be here in the first place. She was certainly not going to thank her captor for her prison. To Simmons's disappointment, he received only a smoldering glare as she stiffly accompanied him down the corridor, steadfastly refusing his arm.

But her bloodthirsty inclinations receded into stammering confusion when the door to the captain's cabin opened, and *he* stood there in all of his glorious splendor. And, by any standards, he was glorious. Samara's knees swayed under her as her heart seem to pound as loud as any drumbeat.

With the blood removed, he seemed almost civilized. And yet there was something primitive about him. Perhaps, she thought, it was the restless fierceness of those glittering eyes. Or perhaps it was in the chiseled perfection of his face. It reminded her of paintings of the capricious Greek gods she had seen in books. Capricious and treacherous, arbitrary and dangerous—mythical figures who thought of little but their own pleasure.

As if reading her very thoughts, Reese bowed, a sardonic smile on his lips.

"I was right," he said. "There was a beautiful woman under all that grime," his lips twitching at her discomfort.

It was that expression which restoked Samara's faltering furor. Handsome is as handsome does, she silently repeated her mother's favorite homily, and Captain Hampton was as ugly as a wallowing pig. Thus mentally fortified, she looked back up at him, only briefly remembering that her favorite pet was once a pig she had saved from slaughter. She would show no such mercy this time.

The thoughts restored her humor and a quick, delighted smile flashed across her face, catching Reese off balance. She was bewitchingly lovely in that moment, her thickly lashed smoky eyes alive with her own private joke, her lips curved in a slight, enticing smile.

He caught his breath as a raw ache started to grow within him. He looked up and saw his first officer staring at both of them, eyes traveling from one to another in puzzlement.

"Thank you, Michael," he said firmly. "Please tell Davey to serve when the food is ready." He grinned at Michael's baffled expression as his friend left, closing the door gently behind him.

Samara glanced around the cabin with real interest. Surroundings told a lot about a person, and she needed to know as much as she could about Captain Reese Hampton. It was large and comfortably, though simply, furnished. The bed was much larger than her own, and seemed to dominate the room. When she could force her eyes away from it, she surveyed the rest. There were two tables, one apparently a small working desk, the other a dining table large enough for six or more people. An intricately carved chest was pushed into a corner, and numerous maps had been shoved against the wall.

There was a strange, exotic, half-dead plant in one corner and a pair of discarded boots near the table. Whatever else he was, Captain Hampton, Samara decided, was not a tidy man.

The room was clean but cluttered. He seemed to treat it with the same careless indifference that she suspected ruled all but his most important passions. And war, she sensed, was one of those passions. There had been no carelessness there, nothing left to chance. Her eyes then found the books, almost hidden by a wooden bar which held them in place. She walked over to them, her eyes opening in astonishment as she studied the titles. There were the expected military and nautical books, as well as several volumes of history along with Shakespeare and Milton and Donne. But what completely shocked her were Homer's *Illiad* and *Odyssey* in Greek.

Her startled expression stirred him to comment. "Pirates do read, you know," he said with a wry smile. He spoke in the slow, relaxed deep voice that so unnerved her.

"In Greek?" she said skeptically.

Now his eyebrows furrowed together. "You can read Greek?"

"Of course," she said airily, not bothering to mention it was quite her worst subject and that her knowledge extended little beyond ciphering the name of the books. Her parents both had a passion for knowledge and, if nothing more, had wanted their children at least exposed to both Latin and Greek. But Samara, seeing no need for such skill, had nearly driven her tutor to madness by her inadequacy in that particular area. She wouldn't admit to a certain awe, however, that someone other than a tutor could, or would even want to, read such a bewildering language.

"A glass of wine, Mrs. O'Neill?"

Her eyes went quickly to him, noticing the shirt stretched across his wide shoulders and the form-fitting breeches which displayed every muscle of his strong legs. She swallowed. Remember...handsome is as... Remember Bren.

"Yes, thank you, Captain," she said finally, her hands trembling slightly as she took a silver goblet.

"Reese," he said. "Please call me Reese." His voice was mesmerizing.

Samara struggled for control, hiding behind a sip of the wine. It was, she discovered, quite good. She had never had very much, only a glass on special occasions. She hadn't re-membered it being quite so delicious. She took another sip, a larger one, and found it easier to smile brightly.

A wave of something akin to tenderness swept over Reese at her smile. There was something so vulnerable about her, something that stirred in him a mixture of protectiveness and desire. Desire won. He took one step towards her, placing his goblet on the table, then taking hers from trembling hands. He lifted her chin with his fingers, searching her eyes and finding an answering flame. His face moved down, his lips craving the touch of her. Almost in a trance, Samara stretched to meet his tall height, all her reason drowning in a tide of bewildering but undeniable need.

A knock came at the door, and Samara backed away like a terrified animal, horrified at what she had nearly done. Reese swore long and hard under his breath.

When he threw the door open in frustration, the cabin boy entered, his hands holding a heavily laden tray of aromatic dishes. The boy's face flushed when he saw Reese's frown.

"Mister Simmons said now," he stuttered nervously.

Reese's face softened. "It's all right, Davey." He turned to Samara. "This is Davey. If you need anything, you have merely to ask him."

The boy nodded eagerly to Samara who could barely man-age a slight turn of her lips. She had come so close to disaster. It was the wine, she thought, disregarding the fact that she had felt similar urges without assistance. Both Davey and the cap-tain were looking elsewhere, and Samara searched frantically for a repository for her wine. Her eyes settled on the discarded pair of Reese's boots near the table. One foot pushed them a little closer. In went the wine.

And then he was near again, guiding her to a chair, his hand like a burning brand on her arm. He politely pushed in her chair and sat down opposite her.

The smells assaulted Samara's senses. She had had very little to eat in the past three days but until she saw the food the terror and confusion of this day had obliterated her hunger. Now it attacked her with ferocity and she greedily eyed the offerings, her tongue unconsciously licking her lips, a move-ment which did not go unnoticed by Reese.

But as Davey filled her plate with chicken, buttered potatoes and hot bread, she thought of Bren—wounded and hungry and locked in darkness—and she despised herself for selfishness. "I don't want any," she forced herself to say, her fingers itching to reach out and grab, but her heart preventing it.

Reese watched as the conflicting wants and loyalties flick-ered across her face, and was surprised at the sudden ache they created.

"Would it help," he said, almost gently, "if you knew the doctor checked on Captain O'Neill and he's doing fine?" He couldn't bring himself to say husband. "And," he added wryly, "he's been fed very adequately."

Samara brightened. She didn't know why, but she believed him. Even if he was a rogue. She hesitated no longer but plunged into his offerings, only barely noticing that he refilled her goblet...and his own. At the moment, she cared little about her manners or even her plan. She had never known one could be so hungry.

Reese watched her quick fingers and mouth with amused fascination. Once relieved of guilt, she attacked the food with the single-mindedness of a starving wolf. He had never seen a lady eat with such complete abandon. For some strange rea-son, it made her even more attractive. She had been ready, albeit reluctantly, to forego the food despite her obvious hun-ger. For love? For duty?

Another knock came at the door, and Reese bade entry. It was Davey with fresh fruit. Neither of them saw Samara lean over and transfer more of her wine into the boot.

After Reese excused Davey for the night, he leaned back and eyed Samara, who was returning his steady gaze with wide, wondering eyes. He wished like hell he knew what she was thinking.

What, she pondered, is *he* thinking? She was trying to fathom something of this contradictory man, trying, after some of his kindnesses, to renew her conviction of purpose.

He refilled both of their wineglasses, thinking that she must be feeling some effects of the wine. Unfortunately, she appeared perfectly sober. He took a long swallow. "How long have you been married, Mrs. O'Neill?" he asked finally, his eyes searching her face for clues.

Samara gulped. She hadn't really thought about the details. "Two...two months."

He leaned back in his chair. "You must love him very much to stay in the hold for...what was it...two days?"

"I...I...do."

His eyes narrowed. "It gets very dark down there."

Her eyes widened as she remembered. Reese saw the horror flit across her face and didn't doubt that much of her tale.

"Some more wine, Mrs. O'Neill, or may I call you Samara?"

"No...no."

"No what? No more wine, or may I not call you Samara?" The former mockery restored her senses. Remember. Remember the plan. Her eyes saw the wine bottle. It was empty. He would have to rise, and turn, to get some more.

"It would not," she said with as much dignity as she could muster, "be proper for you to call me by my given name. And, yes, I would like some more wine."

As he rose and turned, more to hide laughter than anything else, more wine went into the boot. This time, she could hear it slosh. The fool boot was rapidly filling.

When he turned back to her, a fresh bottle in hand, he refilled both goblets, wondering at her capacity. Even he, who had been known to outdrink the best, was beginning to feel the effects. Perhaps she just didn't show it. He probed again.

"Tell me about your home. Where do you live?"

"South Carolina," she said cautiously.

"And your family...what would they think of this?"

Her family. She had forgotten her family in the past hours. For the first time, she considered their anguish. A sudden pain struck her heart. She had thought of no one but herself, and now she knew not what would happen. Her mother and father would suffer dreadfully if they lost both Bren and herself.

Struck anew by guilt, she could only stare at Captain Hampton
and take a hasty draft of wine. It warmed her and filled her
full of new false confidence. She would save them both. She
took another sip of wine.

Reese watched, thoroughly absorbed by the changes in her
face. He wondered if she had any idea how enchantingly trans-
parent she was. It was obvious that she had some mischief in
mind. He looked at his goblet. Perhaps she was not the innocent she seemed. Perhaps she was trying to get him drunk.
And then? It might be interesting.

He refilled both their goblets, then directed her attention to
the chest in the corner. "I found it in India," he told her as
he poured his wine in the nearby half-dead plant. "You might
like to take a look at it." Samara turned wide eyes toward the
chest while her left hand tipped her wine into the boot. She
wondered momentarily exactly how much a boot held. Her
eyes, all innocence and wonder, turned back to Reese as she
lifted the empty goblet to her lips and pretended to drink.

No sooner did she place it on the table than Reese refilled
it. Damn the woman, he thought. She must have a cast-iron
system.

"You didn't tell me," he reminded her softly. "I asked
about your family."

"Oh, I'm an orphan," she said, crossing her fingers and
asking forgiveness of…whomever.

A raised eyebrow questioned her. He had met orphans, and
none of them had Samara's well-loved look. There was none
of that terrible hunger in her—hunger for love, hunger for
belonging. Despite all her confusion and earlier terror, she had
the confidence of one who had never known real want or hurt.

Samara read her mistake in his eyes. "My uncle raised
me…" With a burst of inventiveness, she added, "Bren is my
cousin. No one thought we should get married; that's why I
ran away to be with him." It was partly true, she justified to
herself. That was what happened to her friend Melanie's parents. She had heard the story often and thought how romantic
it was. Now she took it as her own.

Reese accepted the story. It would explain much, including

the easily familiarity and lack of grand passion between the two. They had probably been good friends and family opposition made marriage attractive. It wouldn't be the first time. Somehow, the thoughts assuaged his conscience.

"What about you?" Samara's direct question startled him. There was real interest in her eyes. "Do you have a family?"

"A brother," he said, a slight smile on his lips. "A twin brother. In England."

There was no mistaking the affection on his face, and it startled Samara. He seemed like a man alone...with few attachments or roots.

"Is he a pir...?"

"A pirate, too?" Reese interrupted, undecided as whether to laugh or be irritated. "You do persist in thinking the worst of me. But no, he is not a privateer." Now he did laugh. The very thought of his dignified, responsible brother being a pirate sent ripples of laughter coursing through him.

Although offended by his continued amusement with her, Samara was fascinated. There was no guile, only interest, when she leaned forward. "Tell me about him."

"He's the Earl of Beddingfield, by grace of being seven minutes older," Reese said, the wine making him more loquacious than usual.

Recalling her first sight of him with bare feet and bloody shirt, Samara was stunned. "*You* are the son of an earl?"

Reese chuckled. "It does seem unlikely, doesn't it?"

Samara tried to remember everything she knew about British nobility. "Does that make you 'my lord,'" she said, with a hint of American disdain.

"Only 'Honorable,' I'm afraid," he admitted, with a raffish grin that was altogether too charming.

The expectant expression and tease in his voice started a rumbling volcano of giggles inside Samara that bubbled and boiled until they burst freely from her mouth. It was, she knew, a humiliating loss of composure, a condition aggravated not a little by the wine. Despite her best diversionary tactics, she had imbibed more than she had intended. As she struggled to control the little explosions, she caught the suddenly boyish expression on his face as he shared her amusement. It was the first time, she thought, that he had laughed with her rather than at her, and she was startled by how entirely pleasant it was. More than pleasant, really. Something magical was happening between the two of them and their eyes met with surprised awareness, hers mixed with dismay, his with a sort of shocked astonishment.

Samara forced her gaze away. She tried to subdue the growing realization that she might actually *like* him. She suppressed the notion quickly. It was bad enough to fight the seemingly unquenchable little blazes that darted from her toes to some mysterious place deep inside. He was an Englishman which, according to her father, was the next thing to a devil, and he was after her soul. And, Samara was mortally afraid, he was not being entirely unsuccessful.

Concentrate, Samara lectured herself. Concentrate on freeing Bren. Concentrate on the plan. Concentrate on the goblet. Concentrate on anything but the vitally alive, magnetic man across from her.

"May I have some more wine?" Samara asked finally, her voice trembling slightly, cringing at the knowledge that he was hearing it, that he must know all the extraordinary things going on inside her.

His crooked smile and teasingly arched eyebrow told her only too well that he did. She had no doubts that he was very aware of the effect he had on women, and her in particular, and that made her angry enough to stiffen her weakening heart. She pretended to drop a fork and reached over, draining the wine in the almost saturated boot. Why, oh why, doesn't he get sleepy, or unconscious, or whatever it is that men do when they drink? She felt tired and giddy and excited and frustrated all at the same time. She put on her brightest and most ingenious smile. "Tell me more about your brother," she said. "Did you resent him becoming the earl?"

"Good God, no," Reese said, and Samara couldn't doubt his sincerity. "This was one time fate did things right. I bless the stars every night that I was the second son...that I am free of the responsibility of so much land, so many people. I was restless from the day I was born. The prodigal son, so to speak."

"And your brother...did he also want to be free?"

"Not as I did. He was always the steady one, the responsible one. Although," he said, warming to the subject, "not dull. Avery is never dull. He's interested in everything—books, politics, new ways of improving the land." Reese didn't know why he was babbling on like this. He had never done it before, particularly with a woman. Perhaps it was the real interest in her face, perhaps the challenge in her eyes. Damn her. Would she never succumb to the wine and say more about herself? She was like a clam, yet she was slowly invading what he had always considered private territory.

"But there's responsibility in running a ship."

Her observation startled him. At first he thought her a very pretty, but very young, piece of fluff. Spoiled. Reckless. Trouble for a husband. Even more trouble for anyone else. He had insisted that she join him for dinner because he had been without feminine company for a very long time, and she intrigued and amused him. He was used to simple prostitutes, experienced courtesans and confident ladies who were only too aware of their beauty and lineage. He had wearied of all three. Samara O'Neill was an entirely new experience and there was something extremely appealing about her little rebellions and the confused awareness in her huge eyes which kept changing color. She stirred something new in him, and he wasn't quite sure whether he liked it.

"Responsibility..." she was saying again, not really wanting an answer.

"Even for a pirate?" he resorted back to his old mockery. "Hasn't anyone ever told you pirates have no responsibility?"

He didn't miss the sudden disappointment in her eyes, something close to hurt. His heart clutched just for a moment, then he willed it released. He owed her nothing, particularly not a piece of himself. He would never let her know how much the *Unicorn* meant to him, how much each and every man in his crew stood in his regard, how much his brother and even the estates were a part of him, or how most of his prizes now went to their upkeep. Best let her think him a pirate, the vilest of the vile. For that, he could tell in her all-too-artless eyes, was what she was, indeed, thinking.

"And you, Mrs. O'Neill," he said, his face sardonic, "would you favor me with more about yourself?"

She looked at him uncertainly. How quickly his moods seemed to change. Like quicksilver. She ducked her head, not wanting to confront those probing eyes with her own guilty ones. "There's nothing to tell," she said sullenly, as he leaned over, inspected her empty goblet and refilled it.

"Well," he said with the old laughter, "I would very much like to know how you can consume so much wine without becoming unconscious."

"Well, you're not," she retorted, again failing to meet his eyes.

"Ah, but I expect I've had more experience than you," he drawled, not wanting to admit that his plant would probably be quite debilitated itself tomorrow.

"It's a god-given talent," Samara answered loftily, with sudden inspiration. She was totally disconcerted when he leaned back and laughed. It was, she thought grudgingly, a very lusty, attractive laugh.

"More like the devil," he finally managed, his sexy chuckle sending goose bumps down her spine.

"*You* should know," she retaliated, her confusion becoming outrage. Would he never take her seriously?

"If you won't tell me that," he continued as if he hadn't heard her, "tell me where your name came from. I've never heard it before."

Samara gulped. "It's a family name."

"And you're an orphan? No brothers or sisters?"

"No," she said defiantly. He saw the flicker in her eye and knew she was lying. He just didn't know why.

And then he saw it. A little red trickle running from his abandoned boot, going first in one direction, then another with each gentle lift of the ship.

"More wine?" he asked softly, wondering just how much of his very fine wine had been diverted this night. He coughed to hide the laughter that was threatening to erupt again. He pondered briefly, with no little humor, whether either his boots or plant would survive this night. The little minx! She was obviously far more complex than he had first thought. But what had she planned? There was only one way to find out.

In the course of the next half hour he let his mouth slacken, his eyes dull and his words slur. With each new sign of debility, her eyes brightened. Finally, he let his head drop.

He somehow kept his eyes closed as he heard her move around the cabin, opening the trunk, looking in corners. He heard a sigh of satisfaction as she found something, then listened to more exploration. A hand reached in one of his pockets, extracted what he knew were keys to the locks in the ship. It was all he could do to keep still, but he wanted to know exactly how far she would go. He could feel, rather than hear, as she hesitated above him, then felt a whisper of air as something was raised. His hand reached out and grabbed her descending wrist as a bottle went skidding across the floor.

Instantly, he was up and out of the chair, his hand still clasping hers like an iron band. He twisted it towards him, making her face him.

"H-h-h-how?" she stuttered as she looked at the anger on his face. Gone was the quiet amusement and the lazy manner. His eyes were like green flames and his mouth was curved in a tight, cruel smile. Samara shriveled, knowing very real fear.

"Tell me," he said in dulcet tones that were more menacing than a roar, "were you planning to kill me or just do substantial injury?"

Samara tried to step back, to tear her gray eyes from his glazing ones, but it was as if she were hypnotized.

"Nei-nei-nei..." she said, hating herself for showing her fear so plainly. "I...I...I just...just wanted...wanted you... you to sleep..."

"Sleep, my sweet?" came his hatefully smooth voice, "with a full bottle of wine? Do you truly not know how easy it is to crack a man's skull?" His hand tightened on her. "Because if you don't, you're a very dangerous child."

Her eyes went wide as she considered his words. She had

truly never wanted to do any real harm. And then his last
words registered. "Dangerous child." Her tempestuous temper
rose, reducing, a degree at a time, her fear.

"I wish I had," she said nastily. "And I'm not a child."

"No...?" His tone told her she had just made a very grave
error. "I think I'll find out..."

Before she could say anything more, his mouth was pressed
against hers. This time there was no gentleness, only a cruel,
punishing savagery. He forced her lips open, and his tongue
darted in like Eve's serpent—malevolent but tempting, beguiling while traitorous. To her horror, she couldn't stop her
body's response, even as she knew it was punishment, not
pleasure, he intended. Every physical part of her rebelled
against her mental anguish. All she knew was how much she
wanted him to continue, to bring her body alive.

His mouth softened as he felt her surrender, and his body
throbbed with need. His hand released her wrist and encircled
her slim waist, pulling her closer. He could feel the tremors
of her body, as it arched towards him, and the ache deep in
his loins. And then he remembered her treachery.

"You disappoint me, Madam," he said now, with icy contempt. "First you try to murder me, apparently for the sake
of your husband; then you're wont to betray *him*. Perhaps my
little entertainment tomorrow will not be as effective as I'd
hoped."

The cold disdain in his voice and expression cut her to the
quick. From his point of view, she supposed she deserved it.
He thought her married, and now she was responding to him
like any courtesan. God in heaven, what was happening to her?
As his words sunk in, her face went white.

"What entertainment?" she was barely able to whisper.

His voice was silky again, but his piercing, burning eyes
impaled her, and his body was taut with anger and frustration.
She couldn't stop the shivers that shook her.

"I shall let you wonder about it tonight," he said. "What
price attempted murder? What price mutiny?"

Samara was stricken by the implications of each deliberately
uspoken word. She had seen many sides of him in the past

twelve hours—some of them warm, even boyish—but this cold, hard stranger staring at her with such contempt froze her to the very core.

"I will take you back to your cabin, Madam," he said now, disregarding the terror in her eyes. His sympathies, at the moment, lay not with her. Those wonderful eyes—those large, pleading, vulnerable eyes—merely covered a treacherous heart. He had been a fool to ever think otherwise. He felt a momentary regret for Captain O'Neill. It replaced the envy that had, sometime during the day, crept upon him.

His hand took Samara's arm with the same strength as earlier but with new cruelty. He didn't care overmuch if he hurt her. For the first time in his life, he really wanted to strike a woman. He knew, if he analyzed his feelings, that it was because none had ever touched him in this way before, and the disappointment at her perfidy was deep and wounding. He half pulled, half dragged her down the corridor and into her room. He did not leave her there, as she had silently pleaded, but entered, filling her full of new apprehension. But he paid no attention to her as his eyes searched the neat cabin, apparently looking for weapons. His hands released hers, but she dared not move, as he roughly searched his first mate's trunk.

When totally satisfied, he turned to her, his brilliant eyes now hooded. "You *will* replace those items in the trunk... neatly," he said, his voice as hard as agates and as unyielding. "You will do, from now on, exactly as you are told." Then he added meanly, as if the word were an insult, "Madam...do you understand me?"

Samara could merely nod her head as she tried to rein in the tears that were gathering in her eyes. She could bear almost anything but this horrible, icy mockery. She could withstand his anger, his rage, but not this complete repugnance. Why did she care? Why did she care anything about what this...this pirate thought of her? But deep inside, she did. Desperately. Could she explain to him that Brendan was not really her husband? That she was not just another unfaithful wife—as he apparently believed. But there was no chance for words as the door slammed closed behind him, and she heard the lock.

Reese Hampton did not go to his cabin but went up on deck, pacing restlessly as he tried to cool his rage. The extent of his anger surprised him.

It was deep night, and millions of sparkling gems made the sky a backdrop of infinite beauty…and apparent peace. But there was no peace in him. What was it about the little she-wolf that had worked its way into his self-contained world. Her fiery spirit had amused and warmed him; her apparent vulnerability had touched him, her unusual dark beauty had stirred him, and her reluctant but very real passion had aroused him to near madness. He wanted her…more than he had ever wanted a woman before. Even now. Even knowing she was not above betrayal. Even knowing that those innocent eyes hid a not-so-innocent heart.

Tomorrow. He would find out more tomorrow. He was not particularly proud of what he was planning, but Samara O'Neill needed a lesson. And he was going to give it to her.

Chapter Five

It was probably the most wretched night in Bren's life. His arm felt as if some demon were sticking red-hot needles in it, and his head ached from the blow. His physical surroundings didn't help. He shared a small room with five of his officers, and they each had just enough space to stretch out. There was no bedding, no chairs...only a slop bucket that cast a fetid odor in the enclosed space. The only light came through a grilled window where two guards stood watch. It had been closed for a time when the rest of the *Samara*'s crew had been marched to another place in the hold for the night. They were then, for those moments, encased in total darkness.

But the physical discomfort was slight compared to Bren's mental agony. He had never known failure before; it was an unacceptable word to the O'Neills. Now he had lost his ship and failed to protect Samara and his men. He had neglected to prepare his crew for what had befallen them. In his blind arrogance, he accused himself, he had thought his ship swift enough, himself clever enough, to elude the British.

At least he and his officers had been spared the additional discomfort and humiliation of chains. He had noticed, in the dim light of the cell, the rings imbedded in the walls. In some contradictory twist of his mind, he partly resented the fact they hadn't been used. Did he seem so weak, so powerless to the Englishman? The thought galled him as he recalled Hampton's insolent stance and arrogant words.

And Samara. Just the thought of his sister in Hampton's not-so-gentle clutches made his hands tighten into clenched fists. He had not missed the man's deliberately provocative words, and he grew sick with worry. Samara, spoiled and protected, was no match for a man Brendan instinctively recognized as very dangerous—and obviously used to getting his own way. The problem, he knew, was that Samara would think she could handle him—as she had so many unwanted suitors—and go blithely running into trouble. Her impulsiveness had frequently amused her family, and there had been a private conspiracy to protect her, without her knowing it, from her own follies. Now Samara was on her own, and the thought tormented him.

They had been amply fed. Brendan had been surprised at both the quantity and quality of the stew given them, but he could eat nothing, the nausea from the wounds and the worry about Samara had stolen his appetite. He had passed his own bowl to the other captives. He knew he should eat to regain his strength, but the very thought of food brought bile rising up inside him and he could not force himself. Instead, he spent the endless hours thinking of ways to even the score with Captain Hampton.

He knew of the passage of time only by the changing of the guards and the temporary closing once more of their tiny window, again, he supposed, as his crew was marched out to work. Hate—an emotion usually foreign to him—swirled inside him. His helplessness fueled its reckless course until he was consumed by it.

When the door opened, he knew no caution, only the need to release the fury inside him. Disregarding the pain in his arm, he threw himself at one of the guards and was hardly aware of the sound of the door slamming shut as he was pulled out quickly, leaving the rest of his officers pounding on the door. He threw himself at one, then another, using his head, his feet, his left arm. And then with agonizing pain, his arms were seized and his hands quickly tied in front of him. He was pushed and pulled down the passageway to a narrow stair, then partly dragged, partly carried, up to the quarterdeck.

He blinked when he reached the top, his eyes barely tolerating the harsh glare of the sun after so many hours in the darkness. He took his time to accustom them to the light, trying to regain some control. Slowly they found Hampton. His enemy's face was inscrutable, his eyes hooded. One hand was on Samara's shoulder, holding her there next to him. Brendan saw Samara's eyes widen as she saw the fresh blood on his shirt, the new bruises, the stubble on his unwashed face. He saw her try to step forward toward him, a move firmly prevented by a tightening of Hampton's hand. He saw the fear and the distress in her face, and he felt his hate expand. He tried to move forward, but his arms were firmly held.

Hampton finally spoke, his voice cold and impersonal. "I told you your wife was hostage to your behavior. She apparently didn't understand that you were also hostage to hers." His hand tightened on Samara's arm as he felt her struggle, and he knew she sensed what was coming.

"She tried, rather unsuccessfully I might add, to kill me last night," Reese continued in the same cool, almost unconcerned tone. "Since I do not feel disposed—at the moment—to punish her, you will take her place."

"No," Samara screamed, trying to jerk away from the Englishman.

Reese completely disregarded her protest and her frantic movements. "Lash him to the mast," he directed the two men holding Brendan. "I think twenty strokes will be sufficient."

Bren closed his eyes but made no struggle as he was led to the mast. His hands were untied, his blood-stained shirt stripped from him, and his wrists retied, this time around the mast so he was hugging it. Neither he, nor the nearly hysterical Samara, saw Reese's crew look at each other with bewilderment. In all their years with him, Captain Hampton had never permitted, much less ordered, physical punishment. Offenses were always met with dismissal from the crew or, in less serious cases, several days in the hold. Since the *Unicorn* was both a profitable and happy ship, threat of banishment was usually sufficient.

Reese, for his part, was ready to end the little charade. He had made his point; he would inform Samara that the outcome would be much different if she persisted in mischief. He was about to order O'Neill released when she tore away from him and ran to O'Neill, throwing her arms around him.

"No," she said, this time her voice strong and determined. "I did it…not Brendan. If anyone is to be punished it should be me. I'm only sorry," she added with defiance, "that I didn't kill you."

The crew's eyes went from one figure to the other. The actions of their captain were incomprehensible. And they couldn't help but admire the girl's courage and spunk.

"Get her out of here." O'Neill's words broke the long, tense silence. "She's my wife. I am responsible. Just get her away from here."

Samara's arms went tighter around him. There was no childishness about her now. She looked back at Reese, her eyes pleading. "I'll do anything," she said quietly, and Reese knew she meant it. So did Brendan.

Brendan struggled against his bonds, and blood flowed anew from his wounded arm. "No," he shouted. "Damn you, Hampton, get her out of here and get on with it."

Reese had never felt quite so small. Self-disgust swept over him in waves. He had meant to teach a lesson and instead had received one, one in honor and self-sacrifice and love. So she did love him. An unexpected pain assaulted him. He whirled around.

"Cut him down," he said curtly. "Take him to the doctor, then to my cabin."

"You," he said to the first mate, whose mouth was agape with astonishment over the proceedings, "take Mrs. O'Neill back to her cabin." Without any additional words, he disappeared, leaving his crew staring at each other in disbelief.

Leaning back in his comfortably curved chair, his legs stretched out lazily in front of him, Reese nursed his brandy as he waited for O'Neill. His indolent pose belied the turmoil inside him. He, like Samara, had drunk more than he had intended the previous night and he felt terrible. But at the moment he needed the brandy, to erase the sorry scene topside from his mind. He was disgusted to find it did little to calm his disquiet. His head sank into the palm of his right hand as every second was repeated, over and over again. He had never mistreated a prisoner before, particularly a wounded one, and he felt shame wash over him. He had made a total fool of himself, and why? Another man's wife. His pride had been wounded last night, but it was nothing compared to what he had done to himself this morning. The devil take the little she-cat.

Damn if she hadn't been glorious this morning. The contempt he had felt last night disappeared in admiration—a feeling that did nothing to ease an unusual ache in his heart. He knew now that she had not been betraying her husband by the kiss but, instead, seeking a way to help O'Neill. He must have imagined her response to him, or else she was a consummate actress. Either way, he would keep his distance.

A knock on the door broke his reverie, and without moving from his chair he bade entry. O'Neill stepped inside, flanked by two of Reese's burly crewmen. Reese's eyes quickly flickered over his prisoner. Yancy had found the man a shirt, but the sleeve couldn't hide the bulky bandage, and the arm was now held stiffly against his chest by a sling. His eyes glittered hatred, and Reese didn't blame him one bit.

"Beggin' yer pardon, sir," one of the men said. "Mister Yancy said to tell you if yer determined to kill this gent, do it all at once 'stead of pieces. Save 'im trouble."

"Tell Yancy to mind his own damn business lest he taste the cat himself," Reese said, a softening around his eyes belying the severity of the words. "Leave us alone."

"Want we should wait outside, sir?" one of the men said.

"No," Reese said softly, and watched O'Neill's body tense with anticipation.

The two men eyed each other warily as the door closed behind the crewmen. Reese had earlier poured a second glass of brandy and placed it on the large round table. Now he shoved a chair forward with his boot and nodded towards it. "Sit down, O'Neill."

It was as if Brendan had not heard him. He continued to stand, swaying a little. He had lost a lot of blood and eaten nothing in the past forty-eight hours. He only hoped he would not disgrace himself by falling. He would show no weakness before this man he now considered a hated enemy.

Reese slowly unwound himself from the chair and stood up, his eyes never leaving O'Neill's. The two men took each other's measure, neither finding a deficiency. They dueled silently several moments without words.

Reese was the first to speak and he did so quietly. An almost imperceptible flexing of a cheek muscle told Brendan how much it cost the man.

"I've never apologized to a man before in my life. I've never thought I needed to," he said slowly. "I wanted to teach your wife a lesson this morning.... I let it go much too far. I'm sorry."

Brendan was stunned. Nothing in the past hours had made this side of Hampton plausible.

His eyebrows arched in question and his hands clenched. "My...wife. She hasn't been harmed?"

A flash of temper crossed Hampton's face. "I told you I do not make war on women. She is unharmed. More so than she would have me!"

"You also told me you would do nothing...that she did not want," Brendan said, wanting to believe this new dimension of Hampton but not quite ready to do so. "There was a certain...shall we say...implication in those words."

"Are you so unsure of your own wife?" Reese taunted, his anger growing.

"She's very young," Brendan answered, his eyes intent on Hampton's face, "and very vulnerable."

"Not as vulnerable, I think, as she would have you believe," Reese said ruefully.

The two men's eyes met again, this time with a new but still wary understanding.

"Samara's very headstrong," Brendan said unnecessarily.

"And very loyal," Reese said. "Recklessly so." This time, there was a warning in the quiet voice.

Bren's legs started to fold, and he put his hands on the table to steady himself.

"I don't usually give orders twice," Reese said. "Sit down."

This time, Brendan obeyed. He was forming a reluctant admiration for the man across from him.

"The brandy might help," Reese offered, noting O'Neill's clenched lips as he fought against the pain and weakness.

Bren ignored his suggestion. "What do you want from me?"

Reese shrugged at the man's renewed hostility, choosing to ignore it. "I have an offer."

Brendan's eyes framed the question.

"I'll give you and your officers free run of the ship...if you promise to give me no trouble."

"And my crew?"

"They will still work during the day...at night they can sleep where they wish."

Brendan hesitated but not for long. There was no way he and his crew could even attempt to retake the *Samara*. They were outnumbered, they had no weapons, they were, most of them, no match for Hampton's experienced warriors. And there was Samara. Free, he would be able to watch over her and protect her.

He nodded curtly.

"You understand you will also be responsible for your crew...and your wife?"

Bren nodded again, his lips clenched. God, he hated surrender. But he saw no other alternative, not with Samara aboard.

Reese threw him a key. "Your wife...she's in the next cabin. You can share it with her." He was careful that his tone was indifferent. It hid the jealousy that was battling his inherent sense of fairness.

Brendan heard the dismissal in Hampton's voice. He rose painfully and made his way to the door. He turned, searching Hampton's face for some clue as to the happenings of the past hour. Hampton remained seated, still looking relaxed with his legs stretched out, the brandy in his hand, his face void of any

emotion, his green-blue eyes dark and hooded. He seemed not
to notice the other man's hesitancy. Brendan opened the door,
went through the opening and closed it behind him. He heard
the sound of glass shattering behind him and surmised that his
glass of brandy had shifted with the movement of the ship and
broken. He gave it no more thought.

Reese continued to sit, the stem of the glass still between
his fingers. The upper part had broken with the unconscious
pressure of his fingers. Some of its splinters sprayed his hand,
giving rise to little streams of blood. They went unnoticed as
he stared, unseeing, at the closed door.

The door to Samara's cabin was locked. Brendan tried the
key, and the door swung open. Samara was crouched in the
corner of the small bed, her face wary and fearful as he entered. It relaxed only slightly as she saw him.

"It seems," he said slowly, "that we, as an old married
couple, are to share this cabin." There was an unmistakable
censure in his voice that Samara had not heard before.

For one of the few times in her life, Samara had no words.
Everything she had done since leaving Glen Woods had ended
in complete disaster. Her large eyes reflected regret too deep
to utter. A simple "I'm sorry" wasn't, she knew, sufficient.
She had wanted to die this morning when she thought herself
the cause of Bren's torment. She had been wrong, so wrong,
when she had run away, when she had hidden in Bren's ship,
when she had so easily let Captain Hampton think she was
Bren's wife, when she had been foolish enough to believe she
could outwit the *Unicorn's* captain. In the past few hours, she
had reviewed all her actions and found them sorely lacking in
both maturity and common sense. She had acted like a child
and been treated like a child. It was a very bitter realization.

Even more vexing were the recurring images of Captain
Hampton that continued to plague her. Eyes, which alternately
went from green fire to green ice, inserted themselves into
every thought—as did the searing heat each time she remembered his touch. His practiced touch, she reminded herself. He
knew exactly what he was doing. She had been completely

helpless under his hands; those damnable, knowing, tormenting hands. His contempt last night had been extremely painful,
but his careless cruelty this morning had been worse. She had
sat huddled in this spot since, locked within—wondering, fearing, hating. And something else. Something she wouldn't admit.

Now she looked at her brother with an uncertain face.
"What happened?" she whispered.

"What happened?" Brendan repeated. "I'm not completely
sure myself. It seems Captain Hampton has a certain reluctant
honor."

"Honor? That villain! That pirate! That blackguard!
That..." She stopped when she saw her brother's raised eyebrow.

"I think the lady doth protest too much," he said evenly,
as anger clouded his eyes. Perhaps he had been wrong to trust
Hampton. He strode over to his sister and took her chin in his
hand, forcing her to look up at him. "Did anything happen
between you and Hampton?"

"No," she said fiercely, conveniently ignoring the fiery kiss
of the previous night. "I hate him."

He regarded her levelly for several minutes, seeking the
truth. Her eyes seemed to blaze with new passion, but it could
well have been hate, after this morning. The scene on deck
had not been pleasant. Nor, he knew, would Hampton have
released him if the man had intentions towards a woman he
believed to be his wife. It would have been very easy to keep
him locked up while he tried to seduce Samara. Another telling
factor was the fact that Hampton apparently accepted the marriage. He obviously had no suspicion that Samara was a virgin.

Brendan released her chin. "You've stirred a devil's pot,
my lovely sister, and now we're trapped in it. How in the hell
are we both going to sleep in here?"

She looked at him miserably. "I'll sleep on the floor," she
offered.

"You would, too, wouldn't you?" he said, his eyes merry
again, more like the old Bren. "I really don't think that's
necessary. But I will take the bed right now, if you don't mind.

I've had damned little sleep in the past four days…and my arm hurts like Hades.''

Samara scooted from the bed and took the chair. "Did he…did he say anything about me?''

Once more, Bren looked at her quizzically. There was more than a little interest in the question. "Only," he said slowly, "that I'm responsible for your conduct. He was, I think, rather annoyed with you. What *did* you do?''

"I tried to get him drunk," she admitted in a small voice, "and then tried to hit him over the head with a wine bottle.''

Bren put a hand over his face, trying to hide the smile. He dared not give even tacit approval, for fear of what she might do next.

"And what, dear sister, do you know about getting a man drunk?''

"I listen," Samara said righteously. "Remember that time…?''

"No…I don't think I want to," he said. "Didn't you think you might get drunk at the same time?''

"I didn't drink very much," Samara said smugly. "I hid it.''

"Where?" Bren asked, now quite fearful of the answer.

"In his boot" came the self-satisfied reply.

Bren sputtered, then coughed, failing, this time, to contain his laughter. He was becoming more and more surprised that Hampton hadn't carried out his threat this morning. The man was rapidly rising in his estimation.

"Aren't you ever afraid of tweaking the tiger's nose?" he asked finally.

"I was this morning," she answered honestly, the mischief gone from her voice.

"Good," he answered quietly, "because I think Captain Hampton is not a man to play with. I want your word that you will behave. No more rescue missions, no more tempting fate. Do you promise?''

She nodded, still remembering the horror of this morning. She had seen a very cold, very ruthless side of the Englishman and even she did not wish to provoke it again. She would stay away from him. If only her thoughts, too, could stay distant from the Englishman's restless, tawny perfection.

Samara's good intentions lasted approximately three hours. Some food arrived: bread, cheese, salt beef. Bren wolfed most of it down, his hunger finally realized and his concern for Samara somewhat quieted. He then took off his boots and, within minutes, was asleep.

Samara sat in the chair, watching him. She couldn't remember seeing a man asleep before. Privacy was a much valued quality in the O'Neill house and her brothers' rooms had been off-limits. She would sometimes sneak in, but they had always been awake. She studied Bren, amazed at how much younger he looked now that the lines of responsibility were erased from his face. His light blond hair, several shades lighter than Captain Hampton's, curled around an unguarded face, and she thought how much she loved him, how good and caring he had always been toward her. Even now when she had caused so much trouble.

She would be ever so good now. She would do whatever he said; would, in fact, be the model young wife. *Wife.* How strange a word. It made her think again of Captain Hampton.

Did he look this boyish when he slept? Did his hair curl in the same mussed way? Did sleep make him look more approachable, wiping away that half-amused, half-sardonic expression he usually wore?

I hate him, she told herself. *He's cruel and he's hateful. A reluctant honor, indeed.* The man had no honor. She couldn't understand why Bren had said such a thing, not after what happened this morning. There had even been a note of…liking? Never. Bren would never succumb to the man's insidious charm. He was their country's enemy; he had killed some of Bren's crew; he had stolen Bren's pride, the *Samara.* He had…he had taunted her, and laughed at her and taken liberties. That she might have assisted in those liberties, she refused to acknowledge.

Samara straightened in the chair, wishing the cabin were a little larger. One could stare at a sleeping brother only so long, even one as wonderful as Bren. She looked at the first mate's trunk. Perhaps he would have a book at the bottom. She had not seen one last night when she had replaced the items so roughly searched by Captain Hampton. Perhaps she had missed something. She had been shaken; shaken and terrified and perhaps even a little tipsy.

But there was nothing there. She wished momentarily for her sewing basket, but the Lord only knew where that was now. Was it only five days ago when she thought her life dull? Did she wish it returned to that stationary condition? Never to have lived through a battle? Never to have seen Captain Reese Hampton? Never to feel the all consuming fire that rushed through her with only a glance...not to mention his touch?

She bit the knuckles on her hand, a most unbecoming and unladylike habit, she knew. But she had to find something to take her mind from the Englishman. Or she would go quite mad. This she knew.

A book. There were many in the captain's cabin, and he would probably be back on the top deck now. She had heard him pass earlier, and he would never miss one wee book.

Her good intentions sublimated by need, Samara crept across the cabin floor and slowly, very quietly, opened the door and peered out. There was no one in the corridor. She hesitated a moment, then taking a deep breath rushed for the captain's cabin, opening and closing the door quickly. She stood just inside for a moment, remembering Reese's almost gentle expression as he had sat there talking of his brother, remembering the sensuous twist of his mouth as he had mocked himself. She shook her head to rid it of the images. A book, she reminded herself. She went to the shelf, her eyes quickly running over the titles again before selecting Shakespeare's *Macbeth*.

So absorbed was she in her search she didn't hear the door open, nor the captain's almost soundless approach. "You *are* a bloodthirsty little thing, aren't you? I thought it was just me who spawned your violence...or do you like mayhem in general? Or," the low, droll voice paused, "are you looking for a different method to dispose of me? Perhaps considering giving up on wine bottles? I would be appreciative since my supply went down considerably last night."

Samara whirled at the sound of his accursed drawl, her suddenly lifeless fingers dropping the volume.

Reese Hampton was leaning against the door, making it impossible for her to flee. He looked incredibly masculine and untamed, his hair mussed from the wind, his tight-fitting fawn breeches hugging his legs, and his feet bare once more. Samara stared at them. She had never thought feet beautiful, but his were. Like everything else, damn him.

He caught her look. "You must forgive my attire, little cat, but during the night my boots were, somehow, filled with wine. Since I don't believe in miracles, I can only assume some human hand erred. I don't know which loss I regret more...the boots or the wine."

His voice was silky now, taunting her, challenging her.

"I'm...sorry," she said, not really sorry at all as she glanced at his icy eyes and twisted smile.

"Exactly what are you sorry about?" he asked, the sarcasm in his voice deepening. "My wine, my boots, or my failure to be your willing victim?"

She could merely stare at him as if she were a trapped mouse. "I meant you no real harm," she said slowly. "I just wanted time to..."

"Time to rescue your love," he jeered, surprised by the depth of his anger. "So now what are you doing here? Where's O'Neill? You have what you want."

"Not the *Samara*," she couldn't help blurting out.

"Not only bloodthirsty but greedy," he said. "Did your husband send you here to ply your wiles? Because if he did, it's useless. Pretty as you are, my love, I wouldn't pay that high a price for you."

Stung and humiliated beyond reason, Samara attacked him. He was ready for her hand but not for her foot which aimed recklessly forward and made contact with his shin. He winced and the pure unexpectedness of it made him drop her hand. It went straight for his face and, with no little satisfaction, she heard a resounding smack.

A long stream of oaths came tumbling from his mouth and he sought to control her again. Hands like steel bands encircled her, and she was being lifted and carried, then set down, her stomach over a heavily muscled thigh.

"It's time," he said, through gritted teeth, "that you learn you can't keep slapping people with impunity."

Samara felt her skirt being smoothed down around her, then felt the slap even through the garment. She struggled for freedom, but his hand was unyielding as the other came down soundly. Once, twice, three times. Never had anyone touched her in anger, and she felt an overwhelming humiliation that he was doing this to her. Even in her dismay, however, some part of her recognized that he was husbanding his anger. There was some hurt, but not much with the layers of clothing protecting her; it was mostly the ignominy of the situation, and she knew that was exactly what he intended. It did nothing to endear him to her.

When he was finally through, he smoothed down her dress and set her upright—almost gently. His finger traced a tear that had escaped her eye, and when she looked up at him, she saw something like wistfulness in his eyes. It was gone so quickly she thought she must have imagined it. They were cloaked again...and as cold as the Atlantic.

"I've never raised my hand to a woman before," he said finally. "But, damn it, you would provoke a saint."

At her incredulous look, he flashed the quicksilver smile that was so devastating. "Not, of course, that I'm claiming sainthood...although you may well drive me to it."

"More like Satan's apprentice," she muttered, just loud enough for him to hear.

He laughed, his eyes warming. She looked so hopelessly lovely with her eyes wide and glazed silver by the tears she was so determinedly holding back. He wanted to kiss her and tell her all was well. He wanted to hold her and protect her from everything. But she was someone else's, and he would not poach, no matter how much he wanted her...and he was astonished at how much that was. In some peculiar way, the situation had, this morning, become a matter of honor.

His smile disappeared. "You may take the book," he said finally. "But the next time you will ask, and Davey will fetch what you need. Is that understood?"

Again, his rapid change of mood confused her. Samara nodded, anger and hurt and wanting and hating all mixed up. She couldn't bear to see him looking at her so coldly, not realizing that he did so to protect himself. Leaning over, she picked up the book which earlier had fallen from her nerveless hands, and, clutching it as if her life depended on its safety, she fled the cabin.

Chapter Six

Time crept painfully along for Samara. Her brother's ship had apparently been patched sufficiently to sail slowly to Bermuda, and crews on both ships were preparing to get underway.

Bren had still been sleeping when she, and her sore backside, returned to the cabin. She was unreasonably resentful that he had slept so peacefully through her ordeal. But when he woke, at Hampton's summons, she couldn't bring herself to tell him of her misadventure. She was, instead, the picture of innocence, sitting where a porthole directed a stream of light, reading intently or at least appearing to read intently. He had not asked, thank the heavens, the source of the book. The O'Neills all had an uncanny ability to find books no matter where they were.

He left the cabin almost immediately to talk with his officers, who had already been freed from the hold, and discuss the terms of their parole. He was then taken to the *Samara*, where he relayed a similar message. An hour later, he returned to the *Unicorn* and watched silently as the *Samara*'s repaired sails were unleashed and his ship rode the sea under the command of another.

Reese Hampton, understanding only too well, allowed the American his privacy. His initial respect for O'Neill, which had started with the fierce and very competent battle, had grown steadily in the past two days, peaking this morning on the quarterdeck. The subsequent interview in his cabin had strengthened that opinion. O'Neill had done what he had to do, and done it with dignity…without harsh words or accusations or meaningless threats. It took courage to do so, as much as it took to fight, perhaps even more. It was a quality Hampton admired above all else, and, he supposed, the reason he had so reluctantly decided to leave Mrs. O'Neill alone. He would have to suppress that rush of blood that flowed so swiftly when he saw her, tame his fascination with her dauntless and unquenchable spirit. Much to his surprise, he found himself wondering if he would, this minute, exchange places with O'Neill. That he would even consider such a trade horrified him. A ship for a woman! His freedom for a pretty face! Yet he couldn't drive Samara's face from his thoughts, and he knew he was smiling when he recalled her various expressions—from mischief to cunning to outrage.

He finally joined O'Neill and stood silently beside him, a curious comradeship binding them.

"I'll miss her," O'Neill said quietly, without self-pity.

Reese knew he meant the ship. "She's a beauty," he acknowledged.

"I designed her," Brendan replied, with no little pride. "Next time," he added ruefully, as he looked over Hampton's *Unicorn*, "I'll add more sail."

"But then you would need more depth and you wouldn't be able to hide in those rivers and shallow waters so easily."

Brendan turned to Hampton with an appraising look. "And I suppose you'll be lurking just outside."

"Probably," Hampton said easily. "I admire your ships."

"I can see that," Brendan replied, noting the similarities between his ship and the *Unicorn*. The *Unicorn* was larger and able to handle the additional canvas and the heavy guns, but it had the same sleek hull—bare of ornaments—and the same high, raking masts. Because of its size, it would not be able to slip so easily into hidden coves, but it could still tack quickly through narrow waters. It had obviously been carefully designed with privateering as its specific purpose.

"And I suppose *you* designed this ship," Brendan said finally. The two men regarded one another with new esteem, both realizing abruptly and with some dismay, that under other circumstances, they would like each other immensely.

Reese shrugged. "As I said, I admire your ships. I'm afraid I stole many of your countrymen's ideas. You do have a unique feel for shipbuilding." He left O'Neill then, sensing the man's need to be alone.

Samara had come up on deck during the last of the conversation. Still humiliated over the scene in Captain Hampton's cabin, she watched the two men from a distance, afraid that if she approached, Hampton would reveal their latest encounter to her brother. She watched the two men carefully, saw their intent expressions as they talked, saw the camaraderie that flashed across their faces. Resentment bubbled up inside her. How could Bren talk so easily with an enemy? With his captor? With the man who had laughed at her and...beat her? Men! She silently cursed them all. With no little anger, she stomped back to their cabin, slamming the door behind her.

Her rage continued but her restlessness kept pace with it. The tiny cubicle was more than she could stand. A tear formed in her eye and she felt Bren's betrayal acutely.

She was still there, her resentment simmering when Bren entered. His eyebrow arched at her sullen expression. He knew her moods only too well.

"I thought," he said cautiously, "that you might like some fresh air...I'll take you topside if you wish."

Samara looked at him rebelliously. "I *was* up," she said. "You were too busy with that Englishman to notice." She spat out the word Englishman.

Bren regarded her interest curiously. Her reactions seemed surprisingly vehement...even for her. Samara never did, or felt, anything halfway. The morning *had* been very harrowing for her, he realized that, but Hampton had attempted, in his own way, to make amends.

"Strangely enough," he said now, "I can't help but like him."

Samara stared at him in disbelief. "He's a pirate," she insisted. "Papa says they're all pirates."

"Then we have a fair amount of pirates of our own," Bren said reasonably. "We have our own privateers, remember."

"That's different," Samara replied, trying frantically to think why. "Besides, it's the *Samara* he's stealing. How can you just talk to him as if nothing's happened?"

Regret shadowed his face. "It was the chance I took, Samara. I knew the risks. I'm sorry that he found us, that he captured her, that you were with us. But I don't hate him for it."

"Well, *I* do," Samara said furiously. "What about Scotty, what about the others?"

Brendan sat down. How could he explain? How could he tell her each had evaluated the risks and chosen to take them. He mourned Scotty's death; the sailor had been with him for several years and had been a good friend. But the war had caused Scotty's death, just as a storm had caused others. Personal blame seemed as senseless against one as the other. He gave up. Samara, particularly in her present mood, would never understand.

"Would you like to go up?" he asked again, ignoring her question.

Part of her did. The other part flinched from seeing *him* again. But she would go quite insane if she didn't leave this cabin. She nodded.

He offered his arm. "We *are* married, you know," he said with a slight smile, trying to rouse her from her unusually dour mood. "I suppose we should act like it."

Samara looked at him banefully. She was in no mood to be teased.

"We could," he tried again, "tell him the truth. Then you could have the cabin all to yourself once more."

The thought was shattering. Without Bren's presence and protection there was no telling what the Englishman would do. Or, more to the point, what *she* might do. Her legs still turned to melting wax when she looked at the despicable man.

"No," she answered almost frantically, causing Bren to look at her once more with puzzlement.

It was worse when they reached the main deck. The sun was beginning to set, and the sky was haloed with what seemed dozens of shades of coral and pink and orange, each weaving its own intricate pattern against pillowy clouds. The sea was darkening with the day, its deep blue catching traces of gold from a faltering sun. Samara turned to look for Reese Hampton and saw him at the wheel, his body at one with the ship, his strong hands resting easily on the polished wood. His feet were still bare and his white shirt, much like the blood-covered one he had worn the day before, was open to the waist. Golden hair shone against a sun-darkened chest and muscles flexed as he easily, oh so easily, turned the giant wheel. A shadow fell across his face but she didn't need to see his eyes to know they were glowing, alive with that great energy only he seemed to have. She shivered as she thought, once more, how like a mythical creature he was. She had wondered about the name of his ship, the *Unicorn*, but no longer. It seemed, somehow, fitting.

Just then, he turned and his eyes fastened on her. She had been right. His eyes blazed with vitality and exuberance and pride. This was so obviously his domain. The ship moved, under his hands, as if it caressed the ocean, and he stood, braced against the wind, his back framed by a multicolored gem of a sky as her heart fluttered, swelled and became a discordant symphony of warring feelings.

His mouth curved into a smile as he watched her, and she knew he was reading her feelings. Conceited oaf, she denounced him mentally. But nothing, she knew with dismayed certainty, would ever erase that portrait from her mind. He was like the wind—free and unpredictable—and who had ever tamed the wind?

Moments later, he joined them at the railing, having given the ship to Michael Simmons.

"I wondered," he said smoothly to Brendan, "whether you would honor me with your presence at dinner, you and Mrs.

O'Neill. Mr. Simmons and the ship's surgeon, Yancy, will also join us.''

Samara's foot reached out to kick her brother, but he either didn't understand or decided to ignore it. He bowed slightly, and Samara wanted to hit him. "We accept," he said, disregarding her frantic attempts to gainsay him. He had not looked forward to an evening alone with Samara's foul temper.

"Mrs. O'Neill?" Captain Hampton's eyes were full of humor. Her reluctance was very evident.

"I find myself overly tired," she said, "particularly after the distress of this morning." The stilted words brought even more amusement to his face.

"I'm sorry to hear that, Mrs. O'Neill," he said. "I'll have something brought to your cabin." He turned to Bren. "You'll still join us, I hope."

Bren glanced from Samara's furious face to Hampton's amused one. Something was going on between the two, and he wished he knew what it was. He was suddenly afraid for Samara; there was an unmistakable current between his sister and the English captain. He would use tonight to search out Hampton's intentions.

Some of the cordiality in Bren's voice was gone when he answered affirmatively.

"Good, then," Hampton said. "My cabin boy, Davey, will call for you." He bowed politely to Samara. "And my sympathies for your…your distress." He was gone before Samara could think of a suitable retort.

Instead, she rounded on Bren. "How could you have dinner with that scoundrel?"

"Forgive me," he said gently, "but I thought that's exactly what you did last night."

Samara turned an unbecoming shade of red. She really didn't want to be reminded of last night. Or this afternoon in the blackguard's cabin. She didn't want to be reminded of him at all. "I was just trying to help…"

"Perhaps," he said even more gently, "that's what I am trying to do, too."

Samara looked up at his worried blue eyes. There were new creases in his face, and his lips were uncharacteristically tight.

"I'm sorry," she said penitently. "I keep saying that, don't I. But I am. I'm sorry for worrying you...for this morning...for my terrible temper."

Brendan studied her carefully. She was no longer a child. He had seen the hunger in her eyes when she looked at Hampton, watched her flustered confusion when he neared.

"Watch yourself, little sister," he said. "I think he probably eats little girls like you for breakfast."

So great was her distress that she failed to respond to "little girl," and Bren knew it was worse than he imagined. He was beginning to understand why she had insisted they remain "married." He would make that relationship very clear to Hampton tonight.

His brother had always told Reese that he could, when he wished, charm the stars from the heavens. For some perverse reason, he wished to do so tonight.

The dinner table included four—Reese, Brendan, Yancy and Michael Simmons. The latter two could only exchange amused and intrigued looks as their captain sought to learn everything there was to know about their American prisoner-turned-guest—and his wife.

Fortunately, Samara had during the day briefed Brendan on all she had said to the Englishman, receiving a very pained look when she told him of her sad life as an orphan.

"Mother and Father will be distraught to hear of your unhappy childhood," he said with a lift of an eyebrow. "You, my dear sister, should write some of those silly novels you read."

She gave him a look of utter disdain. "They are very good," she said, "and maybe if you read some you would know what you are missing and finally take a wife."

He grinned at her. "Well, you seem to have arranged that," he said, "even if I can't have some of the more interesting advantages of matrimony..."

So now he could answer Hampton's questions with some confidence. He remained aware, however, that the man was certainly no fool, that the icy blue-green eyes probed every expression, and quick ears heard every nuance in his words. It was disconcerting to Brendan, particularly since he hated to lie and especially to someone he respected, however reluctant that emotion was.

"And where were you taking your cargo?" Reese was asking now. "I understand France is not much more welcoming than my own country."

Such, Brendan knew, was only too true. The only reason the United States declared war on England and not France was England's seizure of American seamen. Both France and England were similarly arrogant in prohibiting and blocking free trade, but the fledgling nation could not fight both at once.

There was no real reason to withhold his destination from Hampton. He had certainly guessed it by now. "There are some in France who don't like her trade policies," he merely said.

Reese's mouth twisted into a slight smile. "Smuggling?"

Brendan shrugged. "Some might call it that. We need markets for our cotton and indigo. The war between England and France has made them slim."

"And what do you bring back?"

"Guns, of course," he replied. His eyes reflecting a certain playful challenge. "Guns and ammunition and cannon."

The two men smiled at each other in perfect understanding as their quiet dinner companions merely shook their heads.

As they finished an excellent meal of freshly caught fish, buttered potatoes and apple tart, the four shared a bottle of brandy.

"I want to thank you," Bren said slowly, suddenly watchful, the brief companionship gone, "for your courtesy to my wife. She told me what she tried to do. I think you've shown great forbearance."

Remembering the scene on the deck this morning, Yancy and Simmons exchanged questioning looks. Neither had thought the Captain showed any forbearance at all and both privately condemned his action, but neither did they know what had prompted the unusual display.

"As you said," Reese replied easily, "she's very young." And very beautiful, he added to himself. "Have you been married long?"

Bren shrugged. "A few months. I'm afraid she hasn't learned obedience yet."

Nor will she ever, both men thought almost simultaneously, their expressions identically wry.

Bren couldn't miss Hampton's deep interest, despite the man's attempt to conceal it. Damn, he thought to himself. Hampton and his sister! What a match that would be! An English lord…nearly, according to Samara. A man who was probably as much at ease at court as at the helm of a ship. And his fiery little American sister. He couldn't stop the grin spreading over his face. It could well be a repeat of Shakespeare's *The Taming of the Shrew* with Hampton as imperious Petruchio and Samara a marvelously bedeviling Katharina.

He immediately shook the image from his mind. Samara was much too young, too innocent, too unworldly to be more than a passing fancy for Hampton. Their worlds were diametrically opposed. She was instinctively right in her fear, and he would do his best to protect her. But, by all that was holy, it would have been interesting!

Samara threw the bowl of mush against the wall with all the fury she possessed. Which was, at the moment, considerable.

The bowl had arrived with a note from Captain Hampton. She could almost see his roguish grin as he wrote it.

I am desolated that you are indisposed tonight and unable to join us. I had planned a very special meal. But since you are feeling unwell, I thought this might best serve you and your poor appetite. I wish you a speedy recovery.

Hampton

From the moment she declined his invitation, she regretted her action, but pride forbade changing her mind. Even before her sparse meal arrived, she had sat in the cabin remembering all the wonderful food of the previous night and even more devastating, the force of Reese Hampton's personality. Her mind was filled with his raw magnetism and enchanting moments of boyish charm. She shivered as she relived the angry kiss that ended an evening which had swung so erratically between pleasure and pain.

And then Davey arrived with her dinner, if it could be called that, along with the insolent note which mocked her, and anger overwhelmed desire. He was the most infuriating, condescending, overbearing, egotistical knave she had ever had the misfortune to encounter. The bowl, still full of its unappetizing contents, went against the wall, splashing gray puddles over the floor. How could her brother sup with the man? How could he exchange civil words with him? Damn men. Damn them all. Damn their peculiar sense of honor. She saw no honor in what had happened during the past several days.

Unable to bear the small cabin any longer, she opened the door and climbed the ladder to the open deck. She found a little hidden place and sat, letting the wind ruffle her hair as she stared out to sea. She could see the lights of the *Samara* at a distance, and she felt a quiet sadness at the sight. Bren had treasured the ship as little else; it was something he had created completely on his own—without any assistance from his family. It carried his pride.

Reese Hampton had taken it…and, oh, so easily. As he had taken some inner part of herself, a part that would never be wholly hers again. She knew this as surely as she knew the sun would rise in the morning. He had awakened feelings and sensations she hadn't known existed, a craving for some unknown yet irresistible wonder, an awareness of her own vulnerability. She had never thought of herself as weak, but Captain Hampton made her so. She knew she must stay away from him but realized, just as thoroughly, that she could not. Like a lost child, she looked for a star to wish upon. There were millions from which to choose, all of them brighter than any diamond against a flawless, midnight blue sky. How very

lovely it was, she thought. How very lonely. And she did feel
lonely in her confusion and doubt and wanting…wanting the
impossible, desiring the unobtainable. For Reese Hampton was
her enemy, a member of English nobility and, just as bad, a
heartless rogue who obviously valued his freedom.

She finally found her star. *Let me forget him,* she whispered.
Take these feelings away.

The star seemed to wink back at her, but somehow she had
the feeling that it was not her spoken plea it heard, but another
silent one.

She could feel him before she heard a sound. It was like an
approaching storm, when everything seems to come to a stop;
even the wind stills and you can almost taste the peril in the
atmosphere as the elements prepare their assault. She had always felt helpless before such a rampage; she felt the same
now as Captain Hampton approached.

Her hands clenched as she waited for him to speak, sure
that he would goad her again. She stiffened, then stood, prepared to renew the battle. But he stood silently, saying nothing,
and Samara felt goose bumps climbing their way up and down
her arms.

When he finally spoke, after what seemed endless hours, it
was done pleasantly. It was one of the few times she had heard
him without laughter or anger or mockery, and she thought
how warm and deep and pleasurable it was.

"It is beautiful out here tonight," he said simply. "God
must smile broadly when he looks upon what he created."

Samara, who had been trying to look at anything but the
Englishman, turned around and stared at him. He almost
sounded awed. And sincere. But Reese Hampton…talking of
God as if they were on a familiar basis? She suddenly had a
suspicious thought. He was trying to throw her off balance.
This was simply a new tactic to disarm her, to amuse himself.

He didn't give her a chance to retort. He could read the
disbelief in her eyes. He merely smiled.

"You looked very wistful," he remarked in a half quizzical,
half gentle tone.

"I was wishing on a star," she said defensively, not entirely sure what to make of him at the moment. She halfway thought she would like the old teasing Englishman back; at least then she would have some defenses. She had few against him at any time, and even fewer at the moment. She wanted, more than anything on earth, to lean up against him and feel his lips on hers.

Reese thought he had never seen such an exquisitely enchanting creature. Moonlight danced against her long black curls, accenting the red sparks that shone like fire in its glow. Her gray eyes, at first defiant, now puzzled, seemed to reflect the infinity of the night as tiny silver lights illuminated their depths. Her lips were slightly parted, and her tongue unconsciously had moistened them as she stood regarding him with a wondering face.

His heart thumped in a most unusual way and his hands clenched into tight knots of want and frustration. His right hand finally eased and, almost of its own accord, wandered up to touch a dark curl, and he marveled at the softness of it, at the sweet clean smell that intoxicated him. It was as if she was bewitching him...this child-woman of the night...this lovely siren who was someone else's wife. Which was she? Innocent or temptress? At the moment, he didn't care as his head bent, almost unwillingly, towards her lips, unable to break the spell that was drawing him, inescapably, inevitably to her.

Samara was caught in the same magic. The moon glow that touched her embraced Reese, seeming to caress him, showering him with glistening pieces of radiant light. More than ever, he seemed to come from a distant world, some mythical kingdom that she longed to enter. Any resistance she tried frantically to summon melted under his smoldering eyes. She forgot everything else, everything but his approaching lips as she offered hers up for the taking.

Their mouths met, melding together as if destined, his lips wanting, hers needing. Samara felt herself whirling and spinning in a fantasy beyond any commonplace dreams. Every sense was alive, singing with joy, crying for more. Her hands crept up, around his neck, and played with the tawny locks of his hair as her mouth opened and she sought an even greater taste of him. She felt his tongue tease and beguile until she knew she could stand no more of the exquisite pain, the sweet torment that was welling up inside her.

She broke away suddenly, staring at him as if he had stolen an essential part of her. And he had. At that moment, she knew she was lost, that she was his, and would always be his. But with agonizing clarity, she knew it could never be. Their worlds were too far apart, would always be too far apart. With huge, sorrowful eyes, she backed slowly away, then turned and ran.

Reese stayed at the railing, staring at the sea. He didn't know what had just happened. He had felt a moment of complete joy, of rapture, but now there was only emptiness. Heaven and hell. He had never known how close they could be.

When Brendan, fully prepared for a disgruntled Samara, arrived back in his cabin, he found only a broken bowl and splashes of some unappetizing substance all over the floor and walls. He didn't even want to guess what it might be.

A piece of parchment crunched under his boot heal, and he reached down to pick it up, reading it swiftly. He grinned.

He could well imagine Samara's outrage. Reese's impudent note would be like putting a match to tinder. He could see the evidence of the resulting explosion.

Brendan thought about going on deck and searching for his sister, but he hesitated. This day's foul mood of hers had evidently deteriorated into pure fury, and he had no desire to confront her. It would be best, he reasoned, to let her cool off on her own. He did not worry that she would encounter Hampton; he had left the man comfortably ensconced with his first mate and ship's surgeon, and it appeared they would be there for some time.

Brendan knew Samara was badly spoiled. She had come late to her parents' life, the last child, and his mother, he remembered clearly, had had a difficult time in childbirth. After four boys, only their mother believed the fifth child would be the much-wanted daughter. He would never forget that night, never forget his father's tenseness and fear, his mother's screams while he comforted his frightened younger brothers. And then there was joy as each of the boys was allowed a brief glimpse of their new sister. Brendan thought he had never seen anything so small—so small and perfect. She took his finger and squeezed it, and he puzzled over the strength of the tiny being. She had, at the same time, grabbed his heart and had never let it go.

His father and mother both doted on Samara. They loved their sons—each son knew their warmth and affection and, best of all, their recognition and appreciation of them as individuals—but Samara had always been something special to all of them. She had a vitality and mischief and inherent goodness that enchanted them all. She could be contentious and uncommonly stubborn, on occasion, but then so completely thoughtful and sweet that no one could resist her. She was particularly gentle with animals and children and would often beg forgiveness for an erring servant.

All the brothers adored her, teased her, played with her, but Brendan, who was fourteen when she was born, was most often responsible for her. He had admired her spirit, spurred her curiosity, and applauded her independence. And spoiled her. By protecting her, overmuch he now thought, he had made her unaware of the consequences of her often impulsive acts. She had now run into someone who would not tolerate her schemes and who had a will as strong as her own. And she simply did not know how to cope. There should be, he thought, some interesting days ahead! Samara had never known humility. He had the feeling she was going to learn. Perhaps even Hampton might acquire a little. He shook his head at the thought.

Just as he decided to go in search of her, the door opened with a crash, and Samara rushed in, her hair in a tangle, her face white. All his protective urges surfaced again.

"What happened?" he said tightly. "Hampton promised…"

"Nothing," she said, her voice shaking, but she went to him for comfort and he put his arms around her.

"Nothing?" he questioned softly. He could feel her shake.

"What is it like to be in love?" She asked the question fearfully.

He pulled away and stared at her. He couldn't really answer as he had never been there—not like his parents. There had been brief infatuations, but nothing more. He had hoped and waited and wanted, but that all-consuming passion for another human being seemed always to evade him.

"Do you think you're in love with Hampton?" He feared the answer. Despite his momentary fancies that the two would be an interesting match, he questioned whether Hampton could ever be held by one woman.

Her gray eyes were enormous, and tears swam in them, creating little pools of misery. "I...I...don't know...I can't...can't..."

"Did he touch you?" There was anger in Bren's voice.

"He...he...kissed me...I wanted him to...he...knew it."

He swore. Samara was so damned inexperienced.

"Do you want to tell him you're not married to me?" he asked finally.

"No!" The indecision was gone. "I know it can never be." She didn't have to explain the reasons; they hovered silently between them in the air.

Brendan's anger grew. For all Hampton knew, he was trifling with a married lady, with the wife of the man he had just entertained. He had violated his word.

"Go to bed, little sister," he said. "I'll take a walk while you undress."

She merely nodded, for once spiritless. He opened the door, looked back at her drooping shoulders, and quickly strode toward the ladder.

Reese had stayed on deck, hoping that the rising wind would blow away his troubled thoughts. For the first time in his life, he wanted something he couldn't have. And he wanted it desperately.

Samara O'Neill had bewitched him; that could be the only explanation. He had vowed to leave her alone and, in just hours, had violated that vow. He despised himself for that weakness, but he had been unable to restrain himself as she had stood there in the moonlight, an answering desire flickering in her eyes.

Her response had confused him, her flight bewildered him, and he damned himself for a fool. Was she a faithful wife or was she caught in the same inexplicable fire that was consuming him, and too inexperienced to cope? All the signals were mixed and for one of the few times in his life he was totally at a loss. He had always thought marriage a trap. In his class, marriage was usually for convenience: to bind two families, to build a fortune, to consolidate estates or titles. It had been so with his brother. The marriage to Lady Leigh Albarry had been planned when both were children. It had, apparently, turned out much better than most such matches. The most recent time Reese had been at Beddingfield, the two seemed happy enough, and they adored their two children. But Reese had decided long ago that no one would tell him whom to marry. He had doubted, in fact, whether he would marry at all. He had no desire to tie himself to property, home and a demanding wife.

But then Samara intruded into his thoughts once more and he thought how very lovely she was, how challenging. She made him laugh in a peculiarly warm way. She would never be dull, by God. She would lead anyone a merry chase.

Reese heard some steps behind him and turned, only to see a fist come directly at his face. He tried to duck, but he was too late. He went smashing down on the deck.

The blow was not that strong, and Reese knew it had been surprise, rather than strength, that had felled him. O'Neill had used his uninjured left arm.

Reese rubbed his jaw and looked at the American with a wry curve of his lips. He shook his head as several men came rushing up, prepared to seize O'Neill. They dispersed reluctantly at their captain's silent gesture.

He slowly stood up, the same fixed smile on his lips. "I

don't think," he said, "I want to meet you when you have two good arms."

Brendan merely continued to glare at him. "You gave your word…"

"So I did," Reese said with a grimace. He could only assume that Samara had told her husband about the kiss, or that Brendan had suspected something from Samara's distress. He loathed himself intensely at the moment. He liked the American, had given him his word and then quite dishonorably violated it. He turned away from Brendan, for once at a loss for words. His fists found the railing and tightened around it. "Your wife will be quite safe," he said finally. "I would suggest, however, that you accompany her when she comes on deck. My men…all of us…have been too long at sea."

Brendan knew the words were another apology, and he relaxed. He felt a strange sense of guilt himself. Samara still wasn't fully aware of her own beauty or charm, and he could well imagine her impact on the Englishman. He also realized that Samara, unwittingly, had probably invited the kiss. She had created this convoluted situation which was now weaving all of them into a tapestry of lies and deceit. He didn't like it one bit and was tempted, here and now, to tell Hampton the truth. But Samara's misery-clouded face appeared in his mind, and he wondered once more if she was ready to face Hampton on different terms. He would wait and watch. He merely nodded curtly and returned to the cabin, leaving Hampton to muse alone.

Chapter Seven

The next few days formed an unhappy pattern for Samara.

Brendan laid down rules in no uncertain terms and for once in her life Samara obeyed without question. She knew she had caused no little trouble to everyone, including herself. She had never been so unhappy, so troubled, so completely unsure of herself.

Among them was that she was not to go wandering about by herself. She was to leave the cabin only in the company of Brendan or one of his officers. The only exception was Yancy.

Yancy had become one of her several friends among the English crew. She had accompanied Brendan to Yancy's small hospital to visit several of his wounded crew members and found a use for herself. Yancy was extremely busy with wounded from both ships and grateful for Samara's offer of help. Like every other plantation wife and daughter, she knew a bit of rudimentary medicine and didn't flinch at the sight of blood or wounds. After discovering this, Yancy allowed her to change bandages, feed those who could not feed themselves or just try to cheer the most critically injured. Although sorely heartsick herself, Samara was able to summon a smile and that, alone, according to Yancy, was invaluable medicine.

As for Yancy, he remained a puzzle. He apparently had no other name, at least none he would admit to, and Samara couldn't discover whether it was his first or last. He was a taciturn man who seldom smiled or gave a compliment. But

Samara knew he cared about his charges; with them he was consistently gentle, while often irascible with his captain and even easygoing Michael Simmons. She had liked him instantly and sought his approval. Captain Hampton and his damnably amused gaze often made her feel a willful child; Yancy made her feel a useful person.

Working with him gave her something to do other than think of Reese Hampton. She wondered about the surgeon and tried to pry—to no avail. He would say nothing, absolutely nothing, about himself but instead turn the conversation to her. Since she also had a secret past, the conversations were limited in content. But she knew little escaped his wise eyes, and there was interested speculation when he watched her with either Brendan or Reese or both.

She wasn't entirely convinced that just her presence helped the wounded but she did her best, and with the same stubborn dedication she tackled everything. One particular sailor, a member of Hampton's crew who had lost a leg in the battle, became her particular challenge. She would often sit with him and talk about his sweetheart. She tried to convince him that the loss of his leg wouldn't matter; it wouldn't matter to *her*, not if she loved him. The boy had responded eagerly, wanting to believe but not yet quite able, not when the waves of pain assaulted him, and he could feel the agony in the limb that was no longer there. Yancy explained that such feelings were quite common and often persisted long after removal.

When it happened, Samara would hold the boy's hand and avert her eyes from the tears in his face.

She was still clutching his hand one afternoon when he fell asleep. She didn't want to risk waking him, so she remained by his side, her hand around his, compassion evident in her grieving eyes and the bowed position of her body. She felt a gentle hand on her shoulder, and turned, staring up at magnetic green-blue eyes which held no laughter.

Captain Hampton, almost tenderly, unlocked her hand from the boy's and without a word led her into the corridor and up on the top deck. Once there, he released her and stared out to sea.

When he finally spoke, the voice was soft. "Yancy said you've done much for Rob and the others. Thank you."

"What will he do? How will he live?" Samara's voice was broken, her mind still on Rob's pain.

"He'll have enough money from this trip…and others…to buy a cottage, to live comfortably for the rest of his life."

"Comfortably?"

Hampton's lips tightened. "No…I suppose not…but I'll do what I can for him."

"Give him back his leg?" she retorted, angry now. "Why do men like war? Why are they so eager to kill…and maim…and…?" Her voice faltered. It wasn't just Captain Hampton, it was her brothers and her father; they had all been eager for war. She hadn't really understood before; war was something bloodless and distant, something you just talked about. But now there were Scotty and Rob and the other wounded. There was Bren who had come so close to death. She couldn't comprehend why anyone would welcome war or gladly participate in it.

Reese saw the confusion in her eyes, but he had no words. Her devotion to the wounded, particularly to the English sailors whom she claimed to hate, intrigued him. He had stayed away from her, and Yancy's rooms, but his friend had kept him apprised—and with irritating frequency. And then today, as he was passing, he had seen her bowed, unhappy figure and couldn't resist touching her. He didn't know how to comfort her, or even if he should try. That was her husband's privilege.

But she looked so sad, so unlike the vibrant, rebellious Samara that first night aboard the *Unicorn*. They both touched him in different ways. He had known many women, some even lovelier than Samara O'Neill, but none had ever so enchanted him with the spritelike magic he had found at dinner, the compassion she showed toward others and the courage the morning he had threatened to whip O'Neill. She was many different people, and he was fascinated with each one—even when she tried to do him bodily harm. Samara was entirely different from any woman he had ever met: freer in spirit, yet obviously very well educated. She was a mystery, and she had woven some charm around him, one from which he could not seem to extricate himself, no matter how hard he tried. And he *had* tried.

She looked at him now with those splendid eyes, waiting for an answer he couldn't give. How could he explain the exhilaration he felt before and during a battle or the challenge of outmaneuvering an opponent or the way the proximity of death made every moment more exciting and precious? How could he explain that this is what he did best? He belonged to this world as he never had to Beddingfield.

Beddingfield. He had never coveted Beddingfield, but he had coveted his father's attention. It had all gone to Avery, who had been groomed from his youngest years to manage the estate. And while Avery studied and learned, Reese ran free and wild, often getting into trouble and earning his father's wrath. It was a pattern that had continued when he went to Oxford. Reese had a hunger for knowledge and an equal appetite for women and cards, and he was one of the few who could mix the three successfully. His father died shortly after he completed Oxford, and Avery inherited the title and estate while Reese received a large financial settlement. Perhaps in defiance of his father, Reese had promptly squandered the inheritance—much to Avery's dismay. He wenched and gambled and drank and earned a reputation as one of London's most reckless and charming rakes. He had nearly depleted his funds when he met Capt. Amos Kendrick at a club and the two had become friends. They gambled frequently and one day made a different kind of wager. Amos, an American who had made a fortune from smuggling, wanted to turn to the slightly more respectable profession of privateering. He needed the Hampton influence to obtain letters of marque, and he needed Reese on board ship to legitimatize the venture. So the wager was made: a thousand pounds against Reese's presence aboard the *Maryanne*. Reese lost.

At first chagrined and angry, Reese soon found his real vocation. He was challenged by the sea as by nothing else in his life. Seamanship came as easily as breathing; so, he discovered, did leadership. He had a confidence and magnetism that naturally attracted men. Slowly, other latent qualities started to emerge: among them a sense of fairness and justice that kept men loyal to him. When Amos was killed two years later, he left Reese the ship. In the next ten years, Reese Hampton was a merchant, smuggler and privateer, earning and wasting several fortunes on cards and women. He relished the freedom, and money meant little—until he discovered that Avery and Beddingfield were in financial trouble. From that time, most of his funds went to Beddingfield. When the *Maryanne* was badly damaged in a battle, he designed the *Unicorn* and watched carefully as the ship was built—personally inspecting every piece of lumber that went into her.

His lack of funds did little to discourage feminine interest nor attempts to trap him into marriage. They were traps he easily and often arrogantly avoided, and they only increased his cynicism toward the opposite sex. Still, he heartily enjoyed the company of women and their favors. His taste usually ran to blondes and to a certain sophistication; he was thoroughly confused, therefore, by his fascination with a dark-haired hoyden who not only poured wine in his boots but threatened to do him bodily harm.

His hand went involuntarily to the dark hair blowing beside him in the wind, and he touched a curl, feeling its softness in his fingers. The lovely eyes were slightly misted as they searched his face, the endless shades in them changing as her emotions ran from anger to wistfulness to sadness. There was always a certain current between them, and he felt it even stronger now.

"Why?" she insisted, in the low musical voice he had grown to hear even in the silence of his cabin. "Why do you destroy...?"

There were answers, of course, but none he could voice. It would be like giving part of himself away, and he couldn't do that, especially to Samara O'Neill who had already stolen something from him.

Instead, he merely grinned, forcing a gleam into his eyes. "Because, of course, I'm a rogue and a pirate and I enjoy living well." The words and tone were condescending. "And now,'' he added, ''I think it's time to take you back to your husband. I warned him about letting you wander alone. It seems he doesn't value you overmuch.''

Samara's eyes filled with fury. It was always thus. He would lull her into liking him, and then he would turn sarcastic, once again making her feel like a child. She hated him.

She was much too angry to let the words go. ''He thought me safe with Yancy,'' she said through clenched lips. ''It was you who forced me away. Damn you.'' She turned and stalked away.

Reese watched Samara go, her back stiff and unyielding. He knew she was hurt. Why, for God's sake, did she have such a hold on him? Why did he feel, at this moment, like such a bastard?

It was impossible for Samara to avoid the English captain. Especially when, for some perverse reason even he didn't understand, Reese continued to invite the O'Neills to dinner with Yancy and Simmons and, occasionally, other officers. He made the invitation an order for Brendan, and Samara didn't want to give him the satisfaction of her refusal. Mealtimes were all the same—equally horrible. Captain Hampton exuded charm and dominated the conversation, regaling the company with tales of faraway ports. Brendan was wary and reticent, a departure from his normal ebullient nature. Yancy and Simmons usually remained silent, although Yancy occasionally raised an eyebrow. Samara picked at her food, unable to eat much at all with Hampton sitting across the table, his mouth curved into a cynical smile and his eyes always assessing her.

Reese was unfailingly courteous and polite to her. Too courteous, too polite. It was worse than his most scathing derision. When she could no longer keep her eyes from him, his gaze was carefully cool. It sent a red-hot flare of pain stabbing through her. To her complete mortification, she knew Yancy recognized—and pitied—these wayward feelings. She would catch his compassionate dark eyes intent on her, his mouth in a worried frown.

Yancy's age was indeterminable; he could be anywhere between thirty-five and fifty, Samara thought. His light brown hair was laced with gray and his face was creased with worry lines, but his step was lively and he was seemingly tireless. His almost black eyes were, by turns, wise, tolerant, impatient. But there was always a hint of pain in them.

He and Hampton seemed to have an unusual relationship, one that transcended that of captain and crew member. They challenged each other frequently, Yancy having none of the courteous respect that marked the rest of the crew. But no one could miss the affection between them. Samara wondered about the bond.

After dinner, she and Bren would take a walk on the top deck. He was often silent on these strolls, and she knew the inactivity was taking its toll on him. He would stare morosely at the *Samara* in the distance and refight, in his mind, the battle that had lost her.

It was, Samara thought often, an altogether terrible time for both of them. As hard as she tried, she couldn't still the explosive thrill when she saw Captain Hampton, nor the pounding in her heart. It did not help to realize that in a matter of days he would be gone. Forever.

It was the sixth day when the pattern broke.

Samara was helping Yancy when she heard the cry, "Sail, ho." Minutes later, Reese strode into the hospital area and curtly ordered her to follow him to his cabin. After one look at his tense face, she obeyed without a word. Simmons had located Brendan, and both men were already in Reese's cabin.

"It's a British frigate," Reese said without preamble. "They want to board."

Samara saw Brendan stiffen. All his crew were subject to imprisonment, and the British-born members to impressment or worse. He had heard that some taken from American vessels had been hanged as traitors. His eyes searched Reese's face for intent.

The Englishman saw the look and his jaw tightened. "I told you," he said, "that your crew would be safe. Despite what you may think, I *do* put some value in my word." He turned to Simmons. "Tell the crew to share their clothes with the

Americans.'' He turned to Bren. ''Any British officer worth
his salt need take only one look at your crew to know you're
Americans. And you,'' he added to Bren, ''are now a deckhand. I don't want anyone approaching you as an officer. Your
speech would betray you in a minute.''

He turned to Samara. ''And you, Mrs. O'Neill, are now
Mrs. Hampton. No one other than a captain would ever be
allowed to bring a wife. I rather expect our visitors will be
surprised enough that *I* allowed you aboard a warship.''

''How will you explain so large a crew?'' Bren asked curiously.

''With difficulty,'' Reese answered quickly with a disarm-
ing charm. ''But I suppose I can say, disallowing modesty, of
course, that I expected to take a number of American ships
and needed the extra men.'' He saw Bren flinch at the reminder.

Reese became all business, his charm gone in a barrage of
orders. Brendan was told to talk to his men, tell them what
was expected and see to their change of clothing. He told
Samara to bring what few belongings she had to his cabin and
place them conspicuously about.

''I want you to look your best,'' he added to Samara, ''and
join me topside. We will greet them together...Mrs. Hampton.'' With a devilish grin at her discomfort, he turned to Brendan. ''I'm sure you won't mind if I borrow her for a while...
considering the alternatives.''

Samara looked quickly at Brendan, who nodded. She disappeared out the door toward their cabin.

Brendan stared at Reese for a moment before following her.
''You're taking a chance. If they find out you're hiding Americans you could be charged with treason. And what about your
crew? Will they all be silent?''

''They will do as I say,'' Hampton replied curtly. ''And I
very much doubt whether any junior officer will question my
papers...or my loyalties. And don't you make that mistake,
either.''

''But why are you doing this?'' Brendan persisted.

"Damn it, O'Neill. We don't have time to debate my reasons."

"Aye, sir," Brendan said with a slight smile as he turned and disappeared.

The *Unicorn*'s crew was uncommonly sloppy in returning the signals, trimming sail and finally preparing for boarders. Brendan and his crew were busy tending sail when a party of eight, led by a young lieutenant, climbed aboard Reese's ship. Suspicious eyes raked the deck, then settled on the tall commanding figure and the extraordinarily lovely woman beside him.

The lieutenant's salute was perfection. "Captain Smythe sends his compliments, captain," he said crisply. "We have heard of the *Unicorn*."

Reese felt Samara tense, and his hand cautioned her. "Please return *my* compliments to Captain Smythe," he said smoothly. "What can I do for you?"

"I must check your papers," the lieutenant said, almost apologetically now. "And Captain Smythe noticed you have taken a prize." He gestured to the *Samara* which rode the water not far from Reese's ship. "He suggests taking the prisoners off your hands."

Reese bowed slightly. "I am most grateful, but I have none. I took the American vessel near the Carolina coast and set the crew ashore. I had neither the room nor the inclination to trouble with them. Contentious lot, they were. As you see, we're already carrying extra hands for prize crews."

"You are very confident," the young officer said.

Reese merely smiled. He felt Samara wriggle again…in irritation, he rightly guessed. He couldn't resist the next words. "These Americans," he said disdainfully, "they're such easy prey." Only his tight grasp kept Samara at his side.

The lieutenant nodded eagerly. He had, Hampton guessed, not yet encountered an armed American vessel. Well, he would learn.

"Captain Smythe will be disappointed," the young lieutenant said. "We're shorthanded. He was hoping to impress some of your prisoners…there's usually several Irish and Scotsmen amongst American crews.''

''I apologize,'' Reese replied with such fine-tuned sarcasm that only Samara recognized it. ''I shall remember that in the future. In the meantime, perhaps I can moderate his unhappiness with a few bottles of excellent wine. It has been used for far less noble purposes.'' This time, even Samara had a difficult time suppressing a giggle. He was quite incorrigible.

''My wife,'' he continued smoothly, ''will be very pleased to find you several bottles. She's quite inspired in her grasp of wines.''

Samara bit her lip to keep from laughing at his impudence. She gave Reese an irrepressible smile that forgave his earlier comments. ''Ah, my dear husband…you are the source of my inspiration. You always seem to spur me to new…and more creative…accomplishments.''

Reese didn't miss the challenge in the words, and he too couldn't resist a smile, even as he realized they were playing a dangerous game. He was tempted to grab her, then and there, and set his lips on her teasing ones. ''Go then,'' he said with difficulty. ''Davey will help you.''

She knew the reason for his last comment. She had no idea where he kept the wine, much less the quality of the different bottles. Her use had been entirely indifferent to that aspect.

Afraid to say anything more least she give away her brother, she merely nodded and went in search of Davey, leaving an admiring lieutenant.

''You have a very lovely wife,'' he said, envy thick in his voice. ''But I'm surprised you would bring her on such a voyage.''

''My wife has a mind of her own,'' Reese said wryly. ''And we were just married. You can see how difficult it is to say no to her.''

The lieutenant swallowed, and nodded.

''If you will just follow me,'' Reese said, ''I'll show you my papers. I would like to get under way while the wind is still so favorable.''

The lieutenant nodded. Once in Reese's cabin, his eyes

couldn't miss the feminine articles, particularly an undergarment. He gulped, quickly accepted a glass of wine and downed it in one swallow. He barely glanced at Reese's letters of marque. Davey soon knocked, laden with five bottles of wine which he offered for Reese's approval.

"My wife," Reese said to the lieutenant, "did her usually outstanding job. I'm sure your captain will enjoy these." Almost without the lieutenant's awareness, he ushered the man out. "So grateful for your kindness and speed," he said. "My brother, the Earl of Beddingfield, will also be grateful. He's close to several in the Admiralty, you know."

"No...no...I didn't," the man stuttered, all thoughts of a more complete inspection gone.

"And please convey my compliments to your captain...he has a fine officer in you," Reese continued, steering the man to the ship's ladder. He watched as the wine was carefully lowered into the small boat, and the oarsman turned toward the British frigate.

"Let's get the hell out of here," he told Simmons who had come to stand next to him. "I don't want his captain to have any second thoughts."

The two crews were only too happy to comply. In minutes, they were under full sail.

A new harmony fell upon the *Unicorn*. Bren's crew, which had been silent and bitter since their capture, was now somewhat perplexed and grateful for their deliverance. Their captors had nothing to gain and much to lose by their protection of the Americans, and it was difficult to understand why they risked so much. The Americans, better than most, knew the penalty for treason. They decided not to question that which was unanswerable, but instead joined the Britons in their messes, in their games, in their music. Friendships, forged now by shared danger and common interests, flourished.

Brendan sought out Reese Hampton. The English captain was a complete enigma, as seemingly changeable as the sea itself. Hampton was constantly revealing yet another side of himself and no one side stayed long enough to brand him. He apparently acted on whim, completely unfettered by convention or traditional codes. He wished, not for the first time, that they were not on opposite sides. There was something about Hampton, as mercurial as he was, that inspired loyalty and obedience. He had seen it repeatedly in the English crew, but never so much as today.

He found Reese in the sick bay, talking in a low voice to Yancy. He heard only scraps of the conversation, including Yancy's violent oath. "Bastards...bloody arrogant bastards." Bren saw Reese shrug, and he backed away. It was obviously a private conversation and, after this morning, he had no desire to eavesdrop. He waited at a fair distance for Captain Hampton to finish.

When finally Reese appeared in the passageway, the man's face was tense and his eyes clouded. He curtly acknowledged Brendan's presence.

"If you want to continue the conversation we had earlier, don't," Reese said. "I told you before I had no interest in filling the navy's billets."

"Nonetheless," Brendan said with a bow, "My men and I are grateful."

"There's no need. I had my own reasons, and they had nothing to do with you." Some of the tenseness left him and Hampton's mouth stretched into a wide smile. "Your wife is very quick. I think she mesmerized that poor lieutenant. If he belonged to me, by God, I would have him court-martialed. He barely glanced at my papers, much less at the odd number of crew members. Alas. The British navy isn't what it used to be."

Bren could only stare at Hampton's colloquy. Then he saw the twinkle in Reese's eyes and recognized the game. In mocking the navy, he was mocking himself, erasing the debt which he knew Brendan felt. He obviously wanted neither thanks nor gratitude nor even an acknowledgment of what had happened. By orally reducing the risk and belittling its scope, he was attempting to reduce it to nothing.

Brendan nodded and grinned in understanding. He knew deep inside, spoken or unspoken, he would forever be in the man's debt. Not so much for himself but for those crew members whose lives had been saved this day.

Reese turned toward his cabin without additional words, and Brendan wondered whether he would ever cease to be amazed by him.

Samara was likewise mystified. Despite the danger, she had thoroughly enjoyed those few minutes of banter while the English lieutenant looked on. Her arms still tingled from Reese's touch, and she would never forget that warm teasing fire in his eyes. It had been quite glorious to be called Mrs. Hampton. A wife twice, she pondered, and a virgin still. It was unfair. Especially when all these wonderful new urges inside were demanding her attention. Her body tingled with expectation, and her nerves felt as if they had been pierced by hundreds of little pins.

The door opened and she looked at it partly with expectation, partly with apprehension. It was only Brendan, a slight smile still on his face.

"Your captain, dear sister, is a most unusual man."

"He isn't *my* captain," Samara said slowly, wishing right now that he were.

"You looked mighty convincing on deck," her brother chided. "What did he say? I could tell you were trying not to laugh."

Samara recited the conversation, and Bren threw back his head and laughed. He stopped when he saw the sudden pain in her eyes.

"Are you sure you don't want to tell him the truth, Samara?" he asked, knowing it was useless. Once his sister made up her mind, it was impossible to change. He was startled, therefore, at her brief hesitancy.

"It wouldn't matter," she said finally. "He's like a seabird. He will never live as you or I. It's better this way. Better to think of myself as married…better that he believes it."

Her voice was sad and wistful and more mature than he had thought possible. Even he couldn't guess at the pain behind it.

"You may be right," he said slowly. *And you might not*, a

nagging voice whispered. But it was her life, her decision, and
he would never forgive himself if he interfered and it turned
out badly. Still, he couldn't forget how natural they seemed
together earlier, or how they had smiled at each other, mischief
lighting both their faces.

"Think about it," he said finally. But her closed face told
him she would not change her mind. It was that damned stubbornness again, he thought. He shook his head in frustration.

Dinner was even more difficult than during previous nights.
Samara agonized as she played with her well-seasoned
chicken. It had been easier when she had convinced herself
she hated him, that he was ruthless and cruel and dishonorable.
He still was, she tried to insist to her doubting mind. There
must be some nefarious purpose behind his otherwise inexplicable action today. But Brendan certainly didn't think so as
he now conversed ever so easily with the man across from
him. The two men chatted as if they had been friends forever,
comparing notes on sails, debating the world's most treacherous waters and even finding taverns in common. It was dis-
gusting. She caught Yancy's eyes on her, and tried to summon
a smile but it was weak at best. He smiled sympathetically as
if he could read her thoughts. She quickly turned her face
away.

Reese was all proper courtesy and charm, turning to her just
enough to be polite, asking imbecilic questions such as how
she enjoyed her meal. As if he didn't know her stomach was
churning and her senses reeling. Her knees probably wouldn't
hold her up if she tried to stand. She could merely glare at
him impotently, fuming at the amused twitch of his lips.

She would be content only when she saw the last of him.
But curiously the thought brought an aching hurt. Thus in-
wardly embattled, Samara raised her eyes to feast upon him,
and saw his smile falter as he turned to her. No one at the
table could miss the current that suddenly engulfed the two of
them, sweeping them along to some special place of their own.
It was, for a moment, as if no one else existed, as their eyes
met, sparking tiny fires then gently surrendering, leaving tides
of emotion neither could fathom. The air was palpable with

the runaway feelings that seemed to swell, wave by wave, as minutes passed.

Yancy looked at Brendan, expecting anger, and saw only a small cryptic smile which disappeared the second the American noticed the doctor's eyes on him. Yancy raised an eyebrow in question, receiving only a blank look in reply.

Michael Simmons was nearly hypnotized by the scene, his eyes darting from Reese to Mrs. O'Neill, bewildered by the strength of what was passing between them.

"Ahem." Yancy's interruption was forceful. It did nothing to break the spell. "Captain!"

This time the sound reached Reese's mind, but it took several seconds for it to register. He shook his head to clear it, wondering what had happened. Samara's eyes had lowered, but the magic was still there; the invisible cord still bound him as tightly as any ropes.

Reality struck and he slowly took measure of those around the table. Simmons looked both embarrassed and dumfounded; imperturbable Yancy looked interested; and O'Neill...

Brendan O'Neill returned his gaze steadily, his mouth crooked in a position which was neither smile nor frown but something indefinable. Reese had expected anger; he didn't know how to interpret the quiet, inscrutable man across from him. His eyes moved back to Samara, and pain struck him with unexpected impact when he saw tears pooling in her lovely, wistful eyes. Abruptly he pushed away from the table, sending his chair crashing to the floor.

"I have duties to attend to," he said to no one in particular, his voice harsh. Four pairs of eyes followed him as he almost staggered from the cabin.

Brendan paced the small cabin restlessly. Samara was sitting on the bed, her face pensive. He realized now the strength of the attraction between his sister and Hampton—and the fascination. Whenever the two were together the air was alive with tension, as if caught in a summer storm: all thunder and lightning. He could feel the magic between them and could well understand. Samara was a lovely woman, made even more so by her unawareness of the fact. She had humor and intelligence and an innocence that must completely perplex Hampton. And Hampton? Brendan knew he should be worried about Samara, but he couldn't ignore a persistent feeling that the two of them were right for each other. He had hated Hampton originally but in the past days had learned a healthy respect for him. He was the type of man Samara needed, one who would never be ruled by her but who would respect and encourage her spirit. But these were only assumptions, and he wished he knew more of Reese Hampton. What would he do if he knew Samara was free? Would an English aristocrat, even one who apparently had shed the trappings of that kind of life, marry an unsophisticated American, an enemy of his country? Or would he just use her?

With sudden determination, Brendan decided to talk with Yancy and find out what he could about the puzzling Captain Hampton.

His pacing stopped and he turned to Samara. "I'm going to Yancy's cabin," he said. "I want to check on the men."

It was a sign of her distress that she didn't clamor to go but merely nodded in a halfhearted away. He might have been a bothersome fly, he thought as he left.

And at the moment he was. Samara had wanted him to leave and had willed it mightily. She had thought of nothing but Captain Hampton in the hours since dinner, and she had come to a decision. She could not wonder the rest of her life whether she had made a grievous error. She would tell him, this night, the truth. At the thought, her body tensed, and seem to sing with its own anticipation. Reese. She said the name. Once. Twice, three times...testing the sound on her lips. She had always avoided it before, afraid that such familiarity would only increase the yearning of her mind and body. But now it sounded wonderful. Reese Hampton.

Her mind raced on fancifully. When he found she was free, he would embrace her, tell her that he loved her as she now knew she loved him. She would feel those gloriously strong arms around her, that hard body reaching expectantly to feel hers next to it. His eyes would soften and...

She could stand it no more. She quickly reviewed herself. The dress was hopeless. It was, of course, the same one she had carried aboard the *Samara*, and had worn almost constantly, only once changing long enough to wash it. Her only other garment was the stained and soiled one she had ruined in the hold. She had tried and tried to clean and mend it, but it was beyond repair.

She knew her hair was presentable. She had washed it earlier, and brushed it until it fairly glowed. She wore it up at dinner, and now she released it, letting it fall in waves around her shoulders. She pinched her cheeks, bit her lips to give them color and hurried in search of her objective.

Reese was exactly where she expected him to be—at the wheel. He turned, sensing her presence, and his lips tightened.

"I would like some words with you,." Samara said softly, hesitantly. She almost lost her courage when she saw the sudden anger in his face.

"Where is your husband, Madam?" he asked, his voice cold and impersonal. She couldn't know how much control it took to make it that way. His body was rigid with the effort.

"He went to see the wounded, but he's not my..."

She didn't have a chance to finish. "Then why," he said even more icily, "are you not with him?"

"He's not..."

He interrupted again. "Marriage obviously doesn't concern you overmuch." It was a statement, not a question. But before she could retort, he continued. "But then marriage doesn't seem important to many women. Once they trap a man, they apparently feel free to put horns on him." He disregarded the growing distress in her face as he continued, as much for his benefit as for hers. *God, how beautiful she is.* "I vowed I would never marry," he continued in an almost conversational note, realizing from her face that each word was a whiplash, but he had to stop this now! He had to make her understand how impossible it was. He had to make *himself* understand. He *had* to put a distance between them for both their sakes. "Why should I when I can get anything and everything I want without it?'' The voice was suddenly arrogant and the meaning only too clear.

Samara's teeth bit into her lip and it reddened as blood escaped the wound. He obviously had nothing but contempt for her. It was, she knew, because he thought she was married, but she no longer had a reason to disabuse him of that fact. He had made it very clear that he had little respect for marriage, or for women. He had said he would never marry. Her heart felt dead, the anticipation drained, the dream lost.

"Marriage is for fools," he concluded, but the words were lost to Samara who had turned and fled, her pinched cheeks now white with anguish.

Reese gave a sudden jerk to the wheel, wondering why he felt as if he had just tortured a kitten. She had, after all, deserved every word. She had played her games, had, after all, flirted with him while her husband looked on. Damn her. He tried to convince himself that she was not worth even one thought, but every star wore her face, and the moon was dulled by her absence. Damn her!

Yancy heard the knock as he stood bare-chested, preparing to change clothes before looking in on his charges. Believing it to be Reese, he opened it without bothering to cover the scars etched deep in the skin on his back, crisscrossing each other in ugly patterns of malicious violence. They were reminders of agony so great that he tried to hide them even from himself. He allowed only a tiny shaving mirror in his cabin, and he had permitted no one other than Reese a glimpse of the nightmare he had somehow endured. Reese was allowed, because Reese had seen it happen…and Reese had saved him, had patiently rubbed ointment into flesh raw to the bone despite Yancy's oaths and curses and threats. Because Reese had given him the will to live.

But as he opened the door and saw O'Neill, he was half turned, and he knew the American could see at least part of the scars. He knew it from the expression on the man's face. Surprise. Pity. Compassion. Yancy almost slammed the door, then shrugged. The American had already seen his humiliation. Besides the American looked as if he had something important on his mind, and Yancy certainly had some questions of his own. He opened the door wider, allowed O'Neill in and without saying anything pulled on a shirt. Turning back to O'Neill, he simply raised an eyebrow in question.

"Hampton," the American said. "I would like to know more about him."

"Then ask him," Yancy said with an edge to his voice. Almost unwillingly his own curiosity took over. "I don't suppose you would like to tell me why you seem so indifferent to Samara?"

"Indifferent?" Brendan said. "Never."

"You seem to have a certain…shall we say…lack of proprietorship."

"Samara is not someone you own," Bren said simply. "She usually ends up doing the right thing. There seems little reason to get angry because of one look."

Yancy merely gave him a look of disbelief which said more than words could.

"About Hampton…have you been with him long?"

"Almost three years," Yancy said, hoping that if he gave something he would get something in return. He didn't want his friend hurt. "I knew him several years before that."

"Is he always as changeable as he is now?"

"That depends on how well you know him," Yancy replied. "I've always thought him very consistent…" Until now, he added to himself.

It was Brendan's turn to look surprised.

"Reese has his own code," Yancy said suddenly. "It may not be the same as yours, but he has a strong sense of justice…and honor." The older man hesitated a moment before continuing. "I was a doctor near the docks five years ago. His crew brought him in, half dead from a festering wound. He survived, and I didn't see him for another two years.

"One night, I drank too much brandy and was taken by a press gang. The next years were pure hell. I complained once too often about the food and treatment of the wounded. They were complaints the captain took personally. He ordered one hundred lashes, enough to kill. More than enough. We were in Bermuda when it happened, and the captain was halfway through his bloody punishment when Reese boarded to deliver some mail for England. I was already half dead.

"I found out later that Reese literally bought me, and for a tidy sum. I had been a thorn in the captain's side for a long time and he was loath to let me go. Probably wouldn't have except he thought I would die. And I wanted to. But Reese wouldn't let me. He made me so damned angry I lived to get my hands on him."

Yancy laughed ruefully. "And when I was well enough, I still wanted to get my hands on him. I swung. He ducked. And we've been friends since." He shrugged his shoulders at the obvious absurdity.

There was silence. Brendan silently weighed the words. He realized it had been a difficult story to tell.

"I've never told anyone else," Yancy said. "And I never will. But I want you to know I'll never allow anyone to hurt him…not if there's anything I can do to prevent it." There was a definite warning in his voice.

Brendan nodded.

"I asked you a question before," Yancy said. "You didn't really answer."

"I gave you the best one I had," Bren said. "I can give you no more now."

Yancy searched the American's eyes and liked what he saw. Why in hell, of all the women in the world, was Reese so attracted to Samara O'Neill? The whole thing was a puzzle, and he knew no more now than when O'Neill had entered his cabin. But for some strange reason, he felt better.

Chapter Eight

From a distance, Bermuda looked like a muted, multicolored gem displayed on a sea of turquoise velvet. Bathed in a pink glow from the setting sun, the island resembled a fairyland, Samara thought sadly. She wished she could appreciate its beauty, but her spirit had been tapped by days of self-reproach and heartache. Her mind registered the softly muted pastels, but they didn't touch her, not as they would have days ago. She felt a stranger to herself, an onlooker who had ceased to participate in life because it hurt too much.

She stayed in her cabin at meals and ate little. Despite Bren's entreaties, she had refused to budge from the cabin unless she knew Reese Hampton was asleep. She simply couldn't bear to see him again. Samara had told him some of the conversation with Hampton, offering only that Reese apparently had a low opinion of women and had said he would never marry. It was best, she argued, that they continue their hoax. Telling the Englishman now of their trickery might anger him to the point of turning Bren and his crew over to the British navy.

Brendan had dried Samara's tears and reluctantly agreed to keep silent. He didn't want to risk either Samara or his crew if his opinion of Hampton was wrong. But he remained deeply troubled. Her brief account of the conversation with Hampton certainly didn't sound like the same man Yancy had described. He had never seen his sister so drained of enthusiasm and curiosity. The sooner they left the *Unicorn*—and Captain Hampton—the better. He, too, refused any additional invitations from Hampton, and conversations were curt and wary. Both silently regretted the loss of something they had enjoyed, but neither could explain his private reasons for the strain.

Bren's arm went around Samara. He had almost forced her on deck, not wanting her to miss the beauty of the island. He had been there previously...before the war...and never tired of its enchantment.

But it held little charm now for Samara. She suspected Reese would be at the wheel, and she carefully averted her gaze from the area. She tried to summon some enthusiasm for Brendan, but she felt dead inside. She felt his arm tightening as he sensed her unhappiness.

"You have to let it go, Samara," he whispered.

Her only reply was to lean against him, borrowing some of his strength. He had, after all, lost more than she. She had lost only a fleeting dream. She had endowed Captain Hampton with qualities he didn't have; she had been blinded by his charm and his uncommonly handsome features, and by her own fancies. She shouldn't feel so great a loss for something so superficial, so meaningless. *Oh God, help me conquer this ache; take away this emptiness. Let me feel again.* But the yawning hurt only grew greater as the sun exploded into a profusion of golds and pinks and finally crimson. Crimson for blood. Crimson for loss. Her tears soaked Brendan's sleeve. He rested his chin on her head in sympathy, then drew her away. He had hoped the sight of Bermuda would cheer her; it had only deepened her despair.

Reese couldn't keep his eyes from the two. His heart contracted as he saw Brendan's arm go around her, as the American rested his chin intimately on her soft hair. They stood there, washed in the colors of twilight, and he knew a yearning so great that everything in his life paled by comparison. The sea lost its fascination, the sky its beauty, the ship its allure. He would gladly give it all up, this moment, if Samara O'Neill rested herself so trustfully against him. *What in the hell is happening to me? I have to get her off the ship...both of them.*

But how? Bermuda wasn't safe, not for O'Neill or his crew. It would take several days to sell the *Samara* and effect repairs to his own ship. Then another week or more before dropping them off in Florida where they could easily get home. The *Samara*. He couldn't avoid a stab of guilt. He had seen O'Neill's eyes follow the ship. There was much more there than the ordinary attachment of a captain to his ship. But members of his own crew had been killed and wounded in its taking, and he could not simply give back something that was not his alone. But…after it was sold…

An idea pricked his mind. It teased and challenged him, as it expanded. By God, it would solve several problems. His head lifted, and his eyes caught the last splashes of sunlight. A crooked smile touched his lips for the first time in days.

Reese left the shipping offices of Faulk and Henner with more buoyancy than he had felt in weeks. Everything had gone as he planned, and a transfer of funds had already taken place at the island's principal banking house. He had insisted on immediate payment, and Upton Faulk had been sufficiently eager for Brendan's sleek, handsome schooner to readily agree. The ship was a bargain; the cargo alone was almost worth the price agreed upon after long haggling. Reese grinned as he remembered Upton's face. The man had tried to hide his jubilation and greed after he had told him that a family emergency required his presence in England immediately and, therefore, he must sacrifice such a fine prize. Reese had always detested the dishonest Faulk and his partner; the two had tried repeatedly to raid his crew, to overcharge him for supplies, and to delay repairs on his ship. As the largest shipping firm in Bermuda, they could often control such activities. They also were active in the slave trade, a profession Reese abhorred. All in all, they had been a thorn in Reese's side for a long time. He would take great pleasure in diddling them.

Yancy, who knew the plan, was waiting at the *Unicorn's* railing for him. The doctor had no desire to go ashore, not with the harbor overflowing with British naval ships. He quickly saw from Reese's gleeful expression that all had gone well. Perhaps now things would get back to normal, and the captain's irascible humor would be replaced by his usual good nature.

Reese nodded to Yancy as he strode up the gangplank, and the doctor was delighted to see the old puckish light back in his lively green-blue eyes.

"Three days," he said. "I heard Faulk give the yard orders that the *Samara* be ready to sail in three days. He's putting all their resources on it. I told him how profitable privateering can be, even gave him the name of a good captain." He couldn't stifle a laugh. The suggested captain was the most inept man who ever sailed. The man had somehow managed to conceal most of his mistakes from his owners, but crewmen, who spoke freely in front of Reese, were not so easily fooled. The man drank to excess, was unconscionably careless, and his reputation for cruelty kept him from obtaining a competent crew.

Yancy shook his head at Reese's elaborate scheme, but couldn't halt his own spreading grin. Damn if he wouldn't like to see Faulk's face when the *Samara* disappeared.

For the next two and a half days, Reese watched the repairs on the American vessel. He had made sure the two ships were side by side. Many of the *Samara*'s yards were replaced, and new sails took the place of the mended gray ones. Parts of the hull were reinforced. The name was painted over, replaced by *Swift Lady*. Brendan, still dressed in the rough clothes of a seaman, flinched openly as he watched this last sacrilege. Reese, who had moved next to him to watch, saw a suspicious wetness at the corner of the American's eyes and, despite all his conflicting feelings, his hand instinctively went toward him in reassurance.

Startled, Brendan turned and looked at him, all trace of emotion quickly controlled. Reese had been curt, even unpleasant, in the past days. He had ordered the Americans to stay below and posted sufficient guards to make sure they did. One had remained outside Brendan's cabin at all times, and neither O'Neill was allowed on deck without a guardian. It reminded Bren constantly of his status as a prisoner, and he was on deck now only because Yancy had accompanied him.

"You will have dinner with me tonight," Reese said unexpectedly. The abrupt tone made it an order and left no room for refusal.

"Samara?"

"No." Reese continued. "The pleasure of your company will be quite sufficient."

Brendan searched the Englishman's face. There was something different about him today, an aura of mystery, of anticipation. *What in the devil was he up to now?*

"Do I have any choice?"

"None at all," Reese replied in a courteous tone which did nothing to disguise the command. "Until eight, then."

Samara was silent when Brendan told her of Hampton's order. The silence was more unnerving than any tantrum.

"I have to go, Samara. He made that quite clear."

She just nodded, and Brendan wished for the return of the old spirit.

"We're just his puppets," she said finally. "He pulls the strings and we jump."

"I'm sorry, Samara. I have you and the crew to worry about."

"I know," she said in the same listless way. Then for his benefit, she tried to force some life into her voice. "Yancy gave me a new book today, and maybe...since *he* will be in his cabin...I'll get some air."

He suddenly thought of the new name on the *Samara*. He didn't want her to see it. "I don't think that's wise right now, Samara. Stay here tonight...for me. Don't leave the cabin without me."

She smiled at his worried frown, the first smile for several days.

"I wish you *could* be my husband. I'll never find anyone as dear and generous and forgiving. I'll stay here. I promise." She thought of the nights he had slept on the floor, half of his long frame under the table. When she had protested, he had merely replied that it was far preferable to the hold. He had stayed with her when she knew he would rather be topside, and he tolerated her moods patiently.

She contained her curiosity about the dinner, and hid her anxiety. When Davey knocked at eight, she smiled at him with some of the old warmth, and Brendan hoped she was beginning to heal. She was certainly growing up.

Brendan did not believe what he was hearing.

The dinner had been odd from the very beginning. There were only Reese, Yancy and himself, and at first he wondered why he had been summoned since he was virtually ignored as Yancy and Hampton talked, completely ignoring him except for an occasional question as to whether he was enjoying the meal.

"The *Samara* is ready to sail," Reese said to Yancy. "Faulk has taken the cargo and provisioned her for several months."

Yancy shook his head. "I can't believe Captain Hendricks didn't post more guards. Almost anyone could steal that ship....damned careless. He deserves to lose it."

"He's a poor captain by any standard," Reese replied. "It's the night before he sails and I heard he's going to a party." Reese neglected to add it was he who arranged the party. "I plan to be there...and most of the crew. What about you, Yancy?"

"You know the way I feel about the damned navy. I'll stay and keep guard. That way you can let the others go."

Reese pondered the offer. "It's an idea. There's not one who hasn't asked for liberty. And we will be sailing soon. Do you think you can handle it? There's all the Americans...but then there's really no place for them to go." He turned to Brendan. "Is there?"

Brendan's eyes had been fastened on his plate. Now he lifted them. For the first time since his capture, there was real animation in them. "I can't think of a place in Bermuda," he said solemnly, his eyes fairly dancing with hope.

There was no more mention of ships. With little effort, Reese turned the conversation to books and music, and Brendan was startled by the man's knowledge. It seemed he was familiar with almost everything—from ancient philosophy to the new American writers.

But before long he became restless. There was much to do this night. He had learned that Hampton did everything with a purpose, even, apparently, prolonging this evening. Yancy finally left, and Reese offered him a glass of brandy. Not knowing how to refuse it at this point, Brendan accepted.

There was a long silence. Reese stretched out leisurely, putting his booted feet on the chair Yancy had vacated. He sipped the brandy thoughtfully.

When he finally spoke, the words were quietly said, but very, very final. "No one," he said, "is to know about this dinner...or the conversation. It was private, between... friends."

Brendan could only nod. He wished there were something he could say. There was nothing. The way Reese and Yancy had voiced everything, words of gratitude would constitute a betrayal. That Reese believed Brendan would recognize the complicated reasoning was a supreme compliment.

"*No* one." Once again, Reese's soft voice emphasized the insistence behind it, and Brendan knew the Englishman meant Samara specifically.

Brendan nodded again, his eyes troubled.

"I bid you good night then, sir," Reese said as he slowly unfolded himself and stood.

The two men looked at each other steadily, then Brendan slowly bowed. "It's been an honor, Captain," he said and knew he would never forget the wry, rather sad smile that darted rapidly over Reese Hampton's face.

Brendan did not go back to the cabin immediately but stopped and talked to several of his crew members, giving explicit orders to pass on to others. His guard had disappeared, and he watched as Hampton's crew left the ship in twos and threes. Among them were Michael Simmons and Hampton. The English captain never looked back.

Brendan stopped in at the sick bay. Yancy was there, bottle in hand.

"Are Billy and Adams able to take a small stroll?" he asked. "For exercise."

"With some assistance, I imagine," Yancy answered. "But see that they don't exert themselves too much. Your wife should be able to see to their needs."

Brendan thrust out his hands. "On behalf of my crew and myself, I thank you. If there's anything I can ever..."

But Yancy had turned away, his back unyielding in its rejection. He, like Hampton, wanted no acknowledgment of their assistance. Brendan could see why the two men were such close friends; they had much in common.

Yancy made one final comment. "Davey took some of his clothes to Samara for mending. But I think they're irreparable. Reese had intended on replacing them."

For a moment, Brendan would have given his soul if Yancy would, for once, speak forthrightly rather than in riddles. But he rapidly comprehended. The clothes were meant for Samara. The Americans could not risk leaving the *Unicorn* openly, or boarding the *Swift Lady* by the dock. It would put both them and Hampton at risk. They would have to swim to the other ship. It would be difficult for Samara in a dress.

"I'll see," he said finally, "that Samara does everything possible to prolong their life."

A small surprising chuckle rose from Yancy, but he didn't turn, and Brendan sensed his dismissal.

"I'll send some men to assist Bobby and Adams," he said and left.

When he returned to the cabin, Samara was pacing up and down. A pile of torn clothes lay on the bed. "Something strange is happening," she said.

Brendan looked at her with a question in his eyes.

"The guard is gone," she said.

"I think Hampton's decided there's no place for us to go."

Reluctant to think anything good about Hampton, Samara shook her head. "I think he wants us to leave. I think it's a trap. I think maybe he has soldiers waiting in town."

"What would he gain by that?" her brother queried gently.

"He had the labor of our crew…he wouldn't have had it if he turned us over to the navy at sea. Now he probably just wants to get rid of us." The last was said miserably.

"Then we'll fool him," Brendan said, hating himself. He had promised Hampton, and he would not break that covenant. "We'll take the *Samara* back."

Some sparkle came back into Samara's eyes. "How?"

"I noticed there are just a couple of men aboard. Two of us will swim over and take them. The rest of you will follow." His glance took in the clothes on the bed. "What are those?"

"Davey asked me to mend them," Samara said, considerably brightened now that they might, for the first time, outwit the arrogant Reese Hampton.

"Try them on," Bren said. "You'll have to swim, too." He did not worry about that; she had always been an excellent swimmer. He had taught her himself.

Samara nodded eagerly. She would be getting away from the Englishman, twitting his nose. She laughed at the thought of reclaiming the O'Neill ship from him. She laughed to hide the sudden stab of inexplicable grief and loss inside her. *Think of home. Think of safety.*

Brendan left, and Samara changed quickly. She hurried up on deck, meeting Hugh Butler, her brother's third officer, on the way. His face was alive in a way she had never seen before; he was usually quiet and somber. Now he took her arm, hurrying her along, as they met the two wounded men, young Billy Faucette and James Adams.

Hugh warned the others to stay out of sight, as he and Samara looked down at the water between the two ships. She could see her brother's long strokes barely disturbing the water and another man keeping pace with him.

Samara looked at Hugh questioningly.

"Mick," he said, and Samara remembered the tall, loud Irishman who now swam silently beside her brother. Samara watched as the two reached the anchor chain at the rear of the ship. As facile as monkeys, they climbed the chain and disappeared out of sight. Several minutes later, Brendan appeared, signaling success. Ropes were lowered over the side of the *Unicorn* hidden from the docks. Samara knew other ropes were being lowered on the blind side of her brother's ship.

The night was cooperating nicely, she thought. It was cloudy, and only dim light reached the dark water. She watched as man after man climbed down the rope and swam over to the other ship. Those who couldn't swim were given a partner. The two wounded men were lowered by a makeshift sling, then assisted by two swimmers each. Samara was to be among the last to go. If an alarm was raised, Brendan wanted her safely on Hampton's ship.

Samara took a last searching look around the *Unicorn*. It had become home in the past two weeks—home and something else. It held her heart, and behind the shadows she could envision a tall, laughing Englishman who had awakened the woman inside her. *Reese Hampton.* She whispered the name, despising herself as she did so. He cared nothing for her, or for the feelings he had aroused in her. He was, even now, probably with a woman, charming her with his roguish grin and challenging eyes. Her hand caressed the rail, as she had often seen Reese do. Her eagerness to leave disappeared as she considered the reality of never seeing him again. She realized, inexplicably, that she did not want to leave. Yet how could she stay? He might even now be reporting Bren to the authorities. Forget him! He had never indicated any feeling for her…except a kiss. And he probably gave them most freely. She had been a temporary diversion. Nothing more.

When she finally slipped into the water, her tears mixed with salt water, and she looked back, watching the *Unicorn* strain at its tether, as restless as her master. Desolation swept over her as she was assisted aboard the *Samara.* Almost indifferently, she watched two men cut the ropes binding the ship and felt the first gentle movements as the *Samara* inched away from the deserted dock. She half expected an outcry, but the waterfront was empty. The British navy had no idea that the Americans were among them and, unknown to Samara, friends of Reese were hosting several parties. There were few guards, and those left wanted only to enjoy the revelry of the night....

As she stood staring back toward shore, Brendan was at the wheel, guiding the ship toward the open sea. He knew if he escaped the harbor, he could outrun any ship anchored here. Except, of course, the *Unicorn*. A broad smile split his face. A flash of intuition told him he would meet Reese Hampton again. In the darkness of the night, he gave a brief salute to the flickering lights of St. George and to the baffling man who had taken—and given—with such remarkable aplomb.

Chapter Nine

Home! The carriage containing Brendan and Samara turned into the tree-lined road leading to the two-story brick house with its wide verandah and climbing roses. It was near Christmas now and the roses were gone, but Samara held them in her mind. They always seemed so much a part of Glen Woods.

The house was fairly new. It had been built in 1783, replacing one burned by the British some two years earlier. It had been built with love and, accordingly, seemed to radiate warmth and comfort and peace. And that was exactly what Samara needed at the moment. A great deal of peace.

For she had found none on the voyage from Bermuda to Charleston. Every waking moment seemed dominated by a laughing, teasing giant who was gone forever. Sleep, which had always come easily, eluded her. After several restless nights she came to fear even what little came. Because if Reese Hampton dominated her days, he haunted her dreams. She was always running toward him, but as she finally came close he faded away. She would reach out but there was nothing but air and space. And she would wake with a yearning so deep and so painful that it terrified her.

There had been no books on board to distract her and she had no clothes but Davey's torn ones. Dressed in a tattered seaman's blouse and a boy's rough breeches, she had walked the ship, bow to stern, until Bren thought she would wear a path in the polished wooden decking. She volunteered her services, but other than providing minimal nursing skills, she was more a hazard than a help. The ship's cook threatened mutiny after she spilled a giant pot of stew while attempting to season it. She had thought the *Unicorn*'s food far superior to Bren's ship, although she was careful not to mention this galling fact. Then she offered to help with the sails but when one sympathetic sailor permitted it, she ripped her hand open against the rope and Brendan exploded at both of them. She tried to clean Bren's cabin, but he roared when he couldn't find his compass or his charts, and she had forgotten where she'd placed them.

It seemed she couldn't do anything right. So she wandered listlessly, unhappily, in the cooling air as they moved west. The live chickens were killed fifty miles from the Carolina coast. Brendan would be running the blockade in the early dawn and he wanted no crowing to disturb the silence. Samara heard the squawks and shuddered. The cutting off of life. Why did it seem to signify this whole miserable adventure? Adventure? She would never long for one again. Home. That's what she wanted…needed.

As the carriage rolled up the driveway, doors opened and people poured out of the main house, the barns, the neat rows of cabins which housed the field workers.

"Miss Samara…Mr. Bren." The cry went up everywhere. Brendan had dispatched a rider to Glen Woods the moment they'd docked. He had also sent Samara to a dressmaker while he'd seen the harbormaster. She was now, if not elegantly, at least decently clad.

Samara watched as her mother and father came quickly down the wide stairs of the verandah, their faces alight with welcome, and felt a deep guilt for the worry and trouble she'd caused. Before the carriage had come to a complete stop, she jumped from the conveyance and threw herself into her father's arms, tears splashing down her face. She was so glad to see them, to have their comfort. But even clasped tightly in their warmth, she knew something was missing. She had thought she would feel whole again, but she didn't. For some reason, the loneliness that had plagued her these past weeks seemed even greater.

It was her mother who sensed all was not as it should be, and she looked quizzically at Brendan. He could only shrug, indicating he would tell them later.

"Come with me," Samantha commanded her daughter. "We'll get you a nice hot bath." Connor and Brendan exchanged grins. A "nice hot bath" was Samantha's solution to many problems. After quickly dispensing orders, Samantha accompanied Samara upstairs to her room and sat her down.

"What happened, love?" she asked gently.

Samara looked at her mother hopelessly. What to say? That she had fallen in love with a pirate. A scoundrel. An Englishman. A man who despised women and marriage. A man who had probably been ready to betray them.

"Brendan's message said the ship was captured by a privateer but that neither of you was harmed. Was he wrong? Did someone take advantage of you?" Samantha's voice was tender but insistent, and Samara's resistance crumbled.

"No one harmed me," she said softly. "No one but myself."

Her mother said nothing, waiting for her to continue, knowing she couldn't force the story.

Samara looked at her desperately. "What does it feel like to be in love?"

"It can be the greatest joy known to man or woman," Samantha said carefully. "Or the worst torment."

"You and father seem so happy...did...did you...were you...?"

With a slow sigh and a fleeting frown, Samantha reluctantly recalled the worst month in her life. She had wanted to die; oh, how she had wanted to die. And she would have had it not been for the babe she was carrying. Connor had discovered she was the daughter of the enemy he had vowed to ruin and kill. He had discovered that their marriage was a sham, that their months together had been a web of lies.

"Yes," she said softly. "There was torment. Perhaps that's why our love is so strong now...it was forged from a great deal of pain."

Samara was looking at her mother with astonishment. This

was a part of her she had never known. She had known there was something about Chatham Oaks, her mother's plantation, that took the warmth and laughter from her father's eyes. But she had never known exactly what, and neither, she thought, did her brothers. It was one subject never broached in the O'Neill home.

Her mother's voice broke the spell. "Will you tell me what happened?"

"I think I'm in love with an Englishman." Samara said it with such distaste that her mother smiled.

"Not all Englishmen are bad," she said. "And you and Bren are both home, safe, so this one couldn't be too wicked." *Besides*, Samantha thought, *you wouldn't love someone who didn't have a lot of good in him. I know you too well.* She sensed, however, that Samara wouldn't welcome the thought right now.

"How can you say that?" Samara said indignantly. "Father says they're all arrogant bastards and this one certainly was."

Samantha didn't know whether to laugh or scold. She decided a scolding would accomplish nothing at this time.

"Did he take advantage of you?"

"Yes…no…I…"

Samantha's lips tightened and the amusement disappeared. "Yes? Or No?"

"He…he kissed me."

"Nothing more?"

"He…he thought I was Bren's wife."

"He what?" Samantha's stomach lurched. Lies again. Lies were what had almost destroyed any chance she and Connor had. Was history repeating itself in some obscene pattern?

The story now poured out…every last miserable detail. Several times, Samantha had great trouble in withholding a smile. Reese Hampton was either a very great scoundrel as Samara accused, or the most patient man who ever lived. He was, Samantha suspected, something between the two. Well, Connor would be talking to Brendan. It would be most interesting to see how the two tales compared.

In the meantime she soothed Samara, urged her into a hot

tub of sweet-smelling water and then combed her hair as she
had when Samara was a child. Samara, emotionally spent and
physically exhausted from her sleepless nights, finally sank her
head into her pillows and went to sleep. Samantha stood over
her for several minutes, thinking how very young she was...
and how lovely. Could it be that she had found the one man
she would love? For Samantha firmly believed that there was
one man and one man only for Samara...as there had been
for her. She had waited patiently, never pushing, for Samara
to find him. She wanted her daughter to know the same joy,
the same exquisite happiness she had found in marriage. But
had Samara found it and already destroyed it with lies?

"Damned arrogant English."

Samantha sighed with frustration as she rode beside Connor
along the Pee Dee River. Her husband was furious. Brendan's
story was much like Samara's, although her son apparently
couldn't hide a certain admiration for the English privateer.
Because of his promise, he had neglected the exact details of
his retrieval of the *Samara*. He did, however, tell his parents
that Hampton had kept them from being taken by the British
navy. Connor, like Samara, chose to believe the worst, that
the damned pirate just wanted slave labor.

But Samantha had also talked to Brendan and saw something in his eyes that Connor had not. She knew she had not
received the entire truth, just as she knew Brendan had thoroughly liked and admired the man Samara labelled an unprincipled blackguard.

Now she bit her lip as she listened to Connor's diatribe.
Connor was one of the kindest, most just men alive—until it
came to the British. She understood it easily enough; they had
burned his home, killed his father, kept him chained in a ship's
hold for months. Her own father, an Englishman, had killed
Connor's brother. The years had done little to dim the pain,
or ease the lingering bitterness. The recent high-handed tactics
of the British had only heightened his outrage. And an outraged Connor was a very dangerous one. His passionate dislike

had been passed on to his children, at least to all but Brendan and, perhaps, Marion who liked nearly everyone.

Samantha smiled as she thought of her oldest son. Brendan was so much like his namesake, his uncle. Quick to smile and easygoing by nature, he had the same independence of thought, judged each man on his own merit and stubbornly went his own way. Samantha knew he usually judged well.

She tried to soothe Connor. "We have much to be grateful for. He apparently didn't touch Samara or do lasting harm to Brendan. And we have the ship back."

"He damn well did do something to Samara," Connor growled. "She hasn't been the same happy child since she returned."

"She's grown up, Connor. She's no longer a child. And that's not Captain Hampton's fault."

"Isn't it?" Connor, his gray eyes icy, said angrily. "I think it is." He said it with such finality that Samantha gave up. Temporarily.

In an effort to pacify him, she spurred her horse. "I'll race you."

Connor, hearing the laughter in her voice, knew exactly what she was doing. His anger melted as he watched her. She would always be thus, free and enchanting and very knowledgeable about him. He gave his own horse its head, and his laughter joined hers.

If Yancy had thought Reese's mood foul prior to the departure of the O'Neills, it now became close to intolerable. No one could satisfy him, and the raw vitality was replaced with angry tension. That tension exploded the morning the O'Neills left. Badly hung over, he was visited by Faulk and ended up throwing him off the ship.

The man had demanded his gold back, and virtually accused Reese of complicity in the theft.

With bleary eyes and knotted fists, Reese, rage virtually steaming from him, stared at Upton Faulk with undisguised contempt.

"Are you impugning my honor?" he said. "It seems you

were more than a little careless with your property and now you seek to blame it on another. Well it is *your* property now, and not mine, and I'll be damned if I'll give you a farthing for your own stupidity."

Faulk's face grew redder with each passing second and Hampton thought hopefully he might have apoplexy.

"I'm calling the authorities," Faulk blustered.

"Do that," Reese said, "And show yourself to be the biggest fool on the island. At least be grateful you have the damned cargo."

"You bastard..."

"Not exactly," Reese replied, "and I do take offense at that remark. Unless you are prepared to give me satisfaction, I advise you to apologize."

Faulk took one look at Reese's frigid eyes and backed off. "I...I...might have spoken hastily"

"Get off my ship. Now."

Faulk almost ran down the gangplank. He didn't see the amused expressions of the crew who had arrived at various times during the early morning hours to find the ship curiously empty. They knew better than to ask questions, but they could guess. And they all approved, although they didn't know exactly what had happened. They had liked the Americans, and they disliked Faulk and his captains. Quiet chuckles and guffaws were heard frequently during the day.

But when they tried to share the joke with their captain, they received only a curt reply, and the ship set sail that evening. They had expected to return to the American coast, but Reese, instead, charted a course toward Europe. For the moment, Reese Hampton had had his fill of America and Americans.

Two French prizes in tow, the *Unicorn* reached London five months later. Reese's dark mood still pervaded the ship; he couldn't seem to shake it.

Every corner of his ship held the spectre of Samara O'Neill. Though he knew it was impossible, he could have sworn he still smelled the fresh, feminine scent of her in the cabin. And whenever he took a glass of wine, his lips would twist into a smile as he remembered that ridiculous dinner her first night aboard.

He was completely bewildered. No woman had ever affected him like this. None had ever invaded his heart and thoughts so thoroughly. He damned himself nightly as a fool, but still the images remained. He had never known loneliness before; now it ripped into him like a whip, tearing at his insides, filling him with a vast emptiness.

It was time to go back to Beddingfield, back to his roots. And he missed Avery. They had always been close, despite certain differences in their personalities. Perhaps that's what he needed, perhaps that was what his soul was craving. Not Samara at all but home.

Once secured at the London docks, Reese made arrangements for additional repairs and released his crew for three weeks. Dressed elegantly in tight, fawn-colored trousers, a shirt of fine linen, a simply tied cravat and plainly tailored blue coat, he left the ship and joined the throngs on the docks.

He was fascinated, as always, by the sounds and colors that surrounded him, the multitude of accents and the peacock dress of so many dandies. There were small boys shifting through the crowds, looking for purses to lift; and gaudily dressed women, from twelve to fifty, reaching out with filth-covered hands to offer their personal wares. Beggars, many of them former soldiers with missing limbs, held out their hands in hopeless supplication. More than a few coins left Reese's pockets to jump and jingle in a cup or hand and earn him a "God bless ye, sir."

He almost gagged from the smell of dead fish mingled with that of unwashed bodies and human waste carelessly thrown from windows. He had forgotten, perhaps because he wanted to, the filth of the city, the pervading smell of rot and disease.

Wanting to put the turmoil of the London docks behind him, he quickly hailed a carriage to take him to the Hampton home on Grosvenor Square. He very much doubted if Avery would be in residence, but he could take one of the horses the Hamp-

tons had stabled nearby for town use. He would leave in the
morning for Beddingfield.

When the carriage reached the address, Reese paid the
coachman and started up the stairs two at a time, stopping
only at the sound of a familiar voice.

"Hampton...I say, Hampton, slow down."

Reese turned, and his face warmed in greeting. "Jeremy...you devil. It's been a long time."

Jeremy Clayton, Earl of Sheffield, responded with his usual
wide grin. "Too long, Reese. I heard you turned pirate."

Reese groaned. "Not you, too. Privateer, my friend. Privateer."

"Whatever it is, it seems to agree with you," Jeremy said
enviously, looking at his sun-bronzed, heavily muscled, yet
lean, friend. His eyes danced mischievously as he continued.
"I hope you're not planning to stay in London long...none of
the rest of us poor bachelors will have a chance."

Reese's eyes glinted with amusement. Jeremy, with his deceptively innocent face, title and wealth, had bedded half of
London ladies, available or not. What was so amazing to
Reese was that he had remained friends with all of them. It
was difficult if not impossible to get angry at Jeremy Clayton
whose love of the world, particularly the feminine world, was
so uncomplicated. He quite simply liked everyone.

"You mean there's one left that hasn't yet succumbed to
you?" Reese replied now. "Now however did that happen?"

Jeremy's smile was devilish. "There is one...a widow...I'll
make you a small wager."

Reese arched an eyebrow.

"There's a ball tonight...at Tallant's. She'll be there. I'll
wager you can't take her home."

"And the prize?" If she had spurned Jeremy's best attempts, she must be difficult indeed.

Jeremy eyed him speculatively. They had attended Oxford
together and had often competed for the same women. It had
become a game. Neither had ever cared enough about one
particular woman to let it ruin their friendship. But both had

lost substantial sums of money. It was often Jeremy's irresistible likability and title against Reese's superb good looks.

Reese thought rapidly now. Perhaps this is what he needed. A challenge. Perhaps another woman would drive the images of a dark-haired, gray-eyed sorceress from his thoughts.

"A hundred pounds," Jeremy said now, "if you lose."

Reese's eyebrows went higher. "And if I win?"

"One of Sable's colts," Jeremy replied, watching the fire leap in Reese's eyes. Hampton had frequently spoken of purchasing one of Jeremy's prize horses, but the price had always been too high, especially when Beddingfield needed so much and he was so often at sea.

"You must be very sure of yourself," Reese said now.

"I've just missed wagering with you," Jeremy answered, his face wreathed in little boy charm and innocence. "Is it a wager?"

"It is," Reese replied against his better judgement. God, he needed a diversion. And Jeremy's taste always ran to beautiful women. Usually blond hair and blue eyes. It was a taste they both shared. He couldn't think why now. The image of dark hair and thundercloud gray eyes made everyone else colorless and tame by comparison. His fists clenched in frustration. Would his mind never let her go?

Jeremy was looking at him curiously. "Don't you even want to know what she looks like?"

Reese forced himself to grin. "Blond hair and blue eyes?"

Jeremy stared at him with astonishment. "How did you...?"

Reese just laughed, but it had a hollow sound. "I trust I will be welcome...I have no invitation."

"You are always welcome, Reese. You add spice to our poor bland stew...it's been deucedly dull without you. Until tonight, then...my carriage will pick you up." He turned and walked rapidly away before Hampton could change his mind.

Eloise Stanton was indeed a beauty, Reese thought as Jeremy introduced her. Dressed in gold satin which matched the rich color of her hair, she was slim and elegant...and surprisingly cool. Her green eyes held a note of reserve as she examined Reese.

"I have heard of you, Captain Hampton," she said in a low melodic voice. "You have an interesting reputation."

Reese, who was about to deliver a lavish compliment, abruptly closed his mouth. Her comment was as close to polite condemnation as one could get. He could almost hear Jeremy's mirth, and he silently cursed the irrepressible young lord.

He bowed low, knowing that compliments would not be the route to success with this lady. "You must tell me about it, my lady, and give me a chance to defend myself."

"And could you?" she replied tartly.

"It depends on what it is." He smiled genuinely, his eyes flashing with humor. He wondered exactly how much his reputation had been embellished in his absence. He found he liked Eloise Stanton's directness. "I can assure you I do not beat women or children."

"A relief," she answered quickly, a smile finally lighting her face.

"Now that is ascertained, may I have the honor of this dance?"

Lady Stanton tipped her head in thought, but the gesture lacked coyness. Reese knew he would have been most attracted to her months ago but now...damn.

What would Samara look like, dressed in a ballgown with her red-streaked hair set aglow by the hundreds of candles in this room? He imagined her in his arms; he felt his loins ache with the thought.

"Captain!"

He looked back down at Lady Stanton's puzzled face.

"I believe your attention is elsewhere," she said, her eyes clouded with thought.

"I was only thinking how lovely you are," Reese replied.

"I don't think that's entirely true, Captain, but I'll accept it for now. And, yes, you may have this dance."

Reese offered his arm and led her toward the other dancers, briefly glancing back at Jeremy and watching the astonishment on his friend's face. He grinned in reply.

It was a pleasant evening, more pleasant than Reese had thought possible. He monopolized Eloise's time, and she permitted it despite constant bids for her attention. His liking for her increased, along with his guilt over the wager.

As the room grew close with the heat of bodies and the cloying smell of perfume, he asked her outside. They walked in the small formal garden and finally sat on a small stone bench. In days past, he would have started his seduction...a hand on the shoulder, a touch of lips against the hair, the whispering of sweet compliments. But he could force none of them. He liked Eloise, but he wanted Samara. And he liked Eloise too much to play his old games. There was a dignity about her that he respected and had no wish to destroy.

"Your husband?" he said gently.

"Killed three years ago by the French," she said softly.

"You still miss him." It was a statement.

"Every day of my life," she replied. "We had been married less than a year, but he was my heart. I often wonder if it will ever be whole again." There was a small sigh.

"Do you have any family?" he asked, watching curiously as she stiffened.

"My...husband's brother, and a sister. It was my sister who convinced me to come tonight. I'm staying with her..."

Reese noticed the increasing tension in her voice. "She was right," he said quietly. "You're much too lovely to hide."

"And you, Captain? I see a certain preoccupation."

He laughed wryly. "You see too much, Lady Stanton."

"Including a certain wager?" She had relaxed once more, and her eyes twinkled in the moonlight.

Reese was rarely disconcerted. He was thoroughly so now. "How did you...?"

"I know Jeremy," she said, "and I couldn't help but notice his expression when I consented to dance with you." She laughed now. "And I knew there had to be a reason he told me all those terrible things about you today when he called on me. Especially when you showed up together...as friends."

Reese grinned. "He must be apoplectic."

"I hope so," she replied with the first real smile of the evening. "May I ask what you wagered?"

Reese didn't know why he didn't feel uncomfortable at the question. "One of his jealously guarded colts."

"Then we will have to see that he pays it," she said with satisfaction. "What do I have to do?"

Reese raised an eyebrow. "Go home with me...but you can't do that...there's your reputation." He flinched at his newly discovered scruples.

"I know Jeremy," she said. "He won't say anything...he would hate to admit that you succeeded where he did not. And it will be a good lesson. Should we bid him good night?"

"You are an extraordinary woman, Lady Stanton."

"Eloise, Captain. If we are to go to your home together, it's Eloise."

The two reentered the ballroom. Eloise introduced Reese to her sister and said the captain would be taking her home early; she had a headache. Her sister, who had a happy glow of her own as she looked up at her husband, merely smiled, a satisfied look on her face.

Jeremy looked stunned and was, for once in his life, speechless. He could merely nod as Reese thanked him for the introduction. The astonishment gave way to admiration, then sheepishness as he acknowledged Reese's victory with a wink.

Reese took Eloise to his home rather than hers, where servants might talk. He knew the elderly couple that cared for the Hampton town home in the family's absence would be long abed. Once settled in the sitting room, Reese and Eloise sat and talked almost as old friends. Reese discovered that Eloise knew Leigh, his sister-in-law, and had visited Beddingfield several times.

"You're different from what I imagined, from Leigh's description," she said finally. "I think she was always a little afraid of you."

"Probably because Avery and I seem so different. I think she fears my restlessness will infect my brother."

"You *are* different, unusually so for twins."

"Not as much as you think," Reese said thoughtfully. "It's

just that Avery knew from the time we were very young that he had to be responsible, that he would have the title. Sometimes I think he envies me my freedom.''

"And *you*, do you envy *him*?''

"No,'' he said frankly. "I've always been well satisfied.''

Surprise flickered across her face. There was also, he noted, a touch of something like fear, leaving Reese to puzzle. He offered her another glass of sherry, which she refused, and he poured himself some brandy. He studied her.

"Why did you come here tonight?'' he said finally.

"You were kind,'' she said. "I think I had expected something entirely different.'' Her eyes were wide when she looked up at him. "I wanted to teach Jeremy a lesson, and I needed…a friend. In the garden, I thought I might have found one.''

Reese played with his glass. "You are entirely too trusting.''

"Not usually,'' she said, and he knew from her tone she was speaking the truth. "I had heard much about you, not only from Leigh and Jeremy but…''

"I know,'' Reese said dryly. "And most of it is deserved, which is why I still don't understand…''

She looked defenseless as she peered up at him, a departure from the cool demeanor at the beginning of the evening. "I could guess your intentions. I could also see how halfheartedly you were going about it. I suspect there is a lady…?''

A rueful smile touched Reese's lips. "I didn't know it was so obvious.''

She just looked at him quizzically.

"She's married,'' Reese said slowly, "to someone I now consider a friend.''

Eloise smiled in sympathy. Her loss was still too strong for her to be interested in another man. George, her brother-in-law, wouldn't accept that. Somehow, this man—this reputed rake with few known scruples—had recognized it, had respected it. She was grateful.

"What's her name?'' she said now, recognizing his need to talk. How had they become friends? So quickly?

"Samara," he said, the name rolling off his tongue like a poem. She heard the caress in his voice. She was startled at his next words. "She tried to kill me with a wine bottle."

Eloise laughed. "And is that what it takes to capture Reese Hampton's heart? Perhaps I should spread that little secret."

"Good God, no," he said in feigned horror. "It was only because of her ineptness that I am here tonight." His mouth crooked as he regarded her. "But surely she did some damage, since I am here with one of the loveliest women in London, and we are only...talking." The lift of his eyebrow conveyed his mock dismay.

"Ah, Captain," she said lightly. "I believe you are sorely maligned. And it is time to go. If Jeremy followed us, he most surely will be satisfied by now."

Reese regarded her seriously, all teasing gone. There was something troubling her. "If you need anything...anything at all, come to me," he said slowly, "and if I'm not here, go to Avery. I will talk to him."

She merely nodded. "And thank you for a very interesting evening."

After Reese saw her home, he sat brooding as the coach wound through the darkened streets. He could barely believe what had happened this night, that he had been in his own home with a beautiful woman and all he could think about was a dark-haired wildcat. And Eloise? Something was frightening her; he could sense it. He would talk to Avery, do some investigating. Perhaps it would put an end to his recurring dark thoughts.

Chapter Ten

Beddingfield looked prosperous from a distance. The well-tended fields were beginning to show the first of the summer's crop and the cattle and sheep looked fat and content. The manor house, which never failed to awe Reese with its size and majesty, appeared in remarkably good repair amidst the carefully sculptured gardens.

He had not been home in three years but had been spending the bulk of his prize money for Beddingfield's upkeep. Although he cared little about the day-to-day responsibility of the estate, he wanted the lands to remain in the family. Only reluctantly had his brother told him, on his last visit, of financial difficulties. It had taken Reese days to convince his twin to accept his financial help and then Avery would accept it only as a loan. It was money Reese considered well spent. Preferable, he thought now, to London's gambling clubs or greedy mistresses.

Struck suddenly by a flash of joy and pride, he urged his tired gray into a gallop, promising the stallion a well-earned rest. Some of the unusual melancholy that had haunted him the past month lifted; by God, it would be good to see Avery again.

He left the horse in the stables with strict instructions for its keep, knowing all the time it was probably unnecessary. Avery had always selected and trained his grooms with great care. His love of horseflesh equaled and perhaps even surpassed Reese's. His twin would be delighted with Reese's present—Jeremy's prize colt—which was to be delivered in several days by a chastened Lord Sheffield. Reese grinned as he approached the house with impatient strides.

Avery was riding the estate, but Leigh was home and after several flustered moments greeted him warmly.

"Why didn't you let us know?" she asked breathlessly. "Avery will be overjoyed."

"I just arrived in London yesterday," her brother-in-law said with his old mischievous grin. "And I wanted to surprise you." He surveyed her affectionately. Leigh was pretty in a quiet, tranquil way; she had always been shy around Reese, but he had recognized his brother's contentment and loved Leigh for providing it. Now his grin widened. "The prodigal brother returns."

"And he is gladly welcome," she said. "Come inside and meet your niece and nephew."

Even Reese's steps were different, Leigh thought as she led him up to the nursery. They had an impatience that Avery's lacked. She had once thought, fancifully, that while a room was energized with unseen currents when Reese entered, it relaxed when Avery made an appearance. She had always been a little reserved around Reese—not frightened, but not quite at ease either. It was difficult to look into a face so like her husband's and see the restless eyes, the reckless spirit. It sent a quiet shiver through her as she thought her beloved husband might be hiding a similar longing for freedom and adventure.

She shook her head at the nonsensical thought. She and Avery had been married nearly seven years now, and he seemed the most contented and devoted of husbands.

Reese was amazingly gentle with the children, accepting their hugs easily and instantly captivating them with his wide smile. He even further won their hearts by talking to them like tiny adults. Leigh regarded the scene with bemusement; little Catherine was not yet born on Reese's last visit, and young Anthony had been too small to do much but gaze wonderingly at the stranger who looked so much like his papa.

Leigh did not have time to wonder long. A groom from the stable had been sent to fetch Avery and now he stood in the nursery's doorway, his wide smile matching Reese's.

Reese's shorter hair was more golden, bleached by years in the Caribbean sun, but their eyes were the same startling blue-green and now sparkled with the same depths of emotion. Their height and build had once been very similar but Reese, Leigh noted, was now leaner and more muscular from the strenuous activities aboard ship. He looked more than ever like a dangerous jungle cat. She was glad Avery had none of that aura about him.

The brothers eyed each other fondly until Catherine pulled at Reese's hand. "He looks like Papa," she said now, her mouth and eyes like little O's.

"So he does, sweeting," Avery said, then untangled his hand and clasped his brother with both arms, receiving a similar bear hug. They stood there for several seconds, in wordless understanding.

"You're going to stay a while this time, aren't you," Avery said finally.

"Long enough for you to wish my departure," Reese replied. "You know my tendency to interfere in everything."

"Not enough, Reese, not nearly enough. You know I wish you would come back permanently and work with me."

"No estate needs two masters."

Avery's face clouded. He had always felt guilty that he'd inherited, and no disclaimer on Reese's part had relieved that guilt.

"Aren't you going to offer me a brandy?" Reese asked, seeing the familiar shadow. "I want to know how everything goes, how the tenants fare. What about Joe Farley? I didn't see him at the stables."

Thus distracted, Avery led the way down to the handsome library where he poured drinks for both of them, and they settled into two leather chairs.

"Joe," Avery said of Beddingfield's estate manager, "is looking at some new mares for me."

Reese's mouth turned up in a sly smile. "I hope your stables aren't going to be too full. I come bearing gifts. One of Sheffield's colts, out of Sable.''

His brother looked at him with disbelief. "I've been trying to get one of those animals for years. Would you like to tell me how you did it? For future reference?"

"I don't think you want to know," Reese answered, an enigmatic look on his face. It became an amused grin as he considered the very unlikely possibility of Avery resorting to this particular wager. "And I don't think Leigh would want you to try it."

Avery merely looked puzzled. He suspected he wouldn't receive a more substantial answer, not when Reese had the familiar gleam in his eye.

Reese changed the subject. "The estate looks well, prosperous."

"Thanks to you," Avery said, his eyes not quite meeting those of Reese. He busied himself selecting a cheroot and lighting it. He tried to suppress his feeling of guilt. He often wondered why Reese did not suspect him. One twin could usually tell instantly when the other was lying or withholding something. But Reese was obviously preoccupied at the moment, despite his observation about Beddingfield. There was something different about him, something so subtle that Avery thought few others would see it. Partly to change the subject, partly because he was intrigued, Avery started to probe gently.

"Still no ladies…of a serious nature?"

The shadow that deepened the color of Reese's eyes told Avery far more than his almost forced answer.

"In the middle of an ocean? And who can compete with my lovely *Unicorn*?"

"You are missing much, brother," Avery said slowly. "There's a special happiness in sharing your life with someone you love. And Tony and Catherine are little miracles. When they reach for my hand, I feel I'm the richest man in England."

A muscle flexed in Reese's jaw, and his eyes clouded.

"There is someone," Avery said.

"She's married, and she's a fervent little American," Reese

replied, knowing now that Avery wouldn't stop until he knew everything. They had always confided in each other.

Avery raised his eyebrow in a fashion amazingly like his twin's, as Reese slowly related the tale. At its end, he could only shake his head. "What now?"

Reese shrugged hopelessly. "Try to get her out of my mind. Damn if I understand what happened."

"Love," Avery said softly. "Love happened. You appear to have all the symptoms."

"And nothing I can do about it," Reese said. "Rather ironic, isn't it? After all these years of denying there's such a thing, and then an American…a married American at that…"

Avery looked at him sympathetically. He had hoped these past few years that Reese would find love—and some peace. Instead, he had finally found love—and pain. Once more he felt guilt at his good fortune. "Are you planning to go back to the American coast?"

"I thought I would trouble the French a bit more. I seem to have lost my taste for American ships." The wryness was back. "Temporarily, anyway."

"Don't you think your luck might run out one of these days?" Avery asked. "Won't you even consider giving up privateering?"

The old sardonic look came into Reese's face, the one that always frightened Leigh. "I might as well give up breathing," he said.

"That might well be the result," Avery observed thoughtfully. "Beddingfield is doing quite well now; it really doesn't need any more money."

"Even if it doesn't, I wouldn't quit. Not now. Not when England is still at war with France and now America." he grinned. "I'm not as easily tamed as you, brother."

The conversation changed then, and Reese asked about Eloise.

"Any interest there?" Avery inquired.

"I like her," Reese answered quietly. "No more. And she seems troubled. She said she was a friend of Leigh's."

Avery hesitated. He had had the same feeling about Eloise.

"She's been here several times to see Leigh. Now you mention it she did seem quite...almost frightened. I thought it was grief. She obviously loved her husband very much. It was one of the real love matches at court."

"What about her family?"

"There's her husband's younger brother, George Carlton. He's now the Earl of Stanton. I don't think he and Robert got along well, but of course Eloise couldn't inherit the family estate. Robert did leave her the bulk of his own money. She has one sister who's older. That's all, I believe." He looked at Reese curiously. His brother seldom showed such interest in a woman he didn't desire. Reese, Avery knew, had not held a high opinion of the female sex. This newly revealed gallantry surprised—and delighted—him. Apparently Reese had changed more than he'd first thought.

"Why don't you ask Leigh to invite her? Maybe we can find some way to help," Reese suggested.

"You constantly amaze me, Reese. I've never thought you a Lancelot."

"I'll try anything once," Reese retorted, sipping his brandy. Avery merely laughed and lifted his own glass.

The week before Reese's planned departure, the Hamptons and Lady Stanton arrived in London. Feverish preparations were under way for a ball planned in three days' time. Invitations had been sent a week earlier and few were declined. Everyone wanted to see the notorious Reese Hampton, who was said to have amassed a fortune in his not quite respectable profession and who had a reputation as the wildest of rakes. Young ladies' hearts fluttered, while older ones remembered, but no one refused an invitation.

George Carlton, the present Earl of Stanton, was more than a little curious at his inclusion. He didn't know the Hamptons well; Avery Hampton was seldom in London, preferring the quiet life at his estate. But he was known to have friends close to the king and for that reason Stanton planned to attend. Reese Hampton was no more than an adventurer and Stanton had little or no interest in the man.

It was one more mystery. The other was the whereabouts of his sister-in-law. Damn her, anyway. Where had she gone? He had sent out inquiries but, as yet, to no avail. He had had her guarded on the estate, but she'd slipped away. When he followed her to her sister's, she was already gone and Serena had denied any knowledge of her whereabouts. He doubted he would find out anything tonight, but there was always the possibility.

His brother had left Eloise all his money, leaving George with an empty title and entailed land with little income. His own gambling had brought the situation perilously close to disaster. In the past two years, he had courted, then bullied, Eloise, threatening her sister with financial ruin and her friends with harm. He had tried to isolate her completely. If Eloise persisted in her denial of him, he had planned a tragic accident. The inheritance would then revert to him; he had forged enough documents to ensure that eventuality. But she had slipped away before he could implement his plan.

The ball was well under way when he arrived. He felt himself well dressed, not realizing how completely his bright green waistcoat emphasized his pudgy body.

The house was glittering with hundreds of candles, and he envied the richness of the furnishings if not the conservative taste of them. His attention wandered slowly around the room, noting the quality of the guests. There were several members of the royal family, and titles abounded, many far greater than his own. Again, he wondered at his own inclusion. Then his eyes fastened on the two women and two men standing together as they greeted guests, and his heart dropped.

There, standing with the Hampton brothers was Eloise. Elegant in a gold gown, her hair crowned by flowers, she stood close to one of the Hamptons, damn if he knew which one. As he watched, the man's hand went possessively around her waist, and he struggled for control. He approached them warily.

After brief, stilted greetings, Stanton's hand, almost involuntarily, darted out for Eloise. It was stopped midway by

Reese Hampton, whose hard face, glittering eyes and grimly set mouth sent shivers of fear through him.

Hampton's voice was coolly courteous as he bowed slightly. "Eloise wanted you to be the first to know we're betrothed. We plan to announce the engagement tonight," he said in a tone loud enough to capture the attention of many of their distinguished guests.

Stanton blanched. Fury flickered across his face as his overweight body stiffened. "As her closest male relative, and protector, I will not give my consent," he blustered.

Reese now looked amused. "I don't think either of us requires your consent," he said. "Eloise will be staying with my brother until the marriage. Be advised she is under our protection." His voice grew cold and was as clear as a pistol shot in the packed room. "God help anyone who tries to interfere!"

Stanton took a step backward at the open threat, one that he knew many had heard. His face crimsoned as he saw curiosity on more than one face.

"I wish only the best for Eloise," he said. He gathered his courage, and added in a firmer voice, "Your reputation does not recommend you as a husband."

"And yours," Reese shot back, "does not recommend you as a man."

Stanton was now publicly insulted. He glared helplessly from Reese to Eloise, seeing all his hopes disappear. He knew he was no match for a man of Hampton's highly touted abilities. He could only try to extricate himself. As if he hadn't heard the last remark, he bowed carefully to the two Hamptons and to Eloise. "My best wishes," he said stiffly, the words practically choking him. Perhaps, just perhaps, he could arrange a little accident for the interfering pirate. He was, after all, in a very risky business. A word about the bastard's destination to the right ears…the Americans would pay dearly for such information. It would not be the first time he had sold information. Now he would do it for pleasure, as well as gold.

Despite the amused and knowing looks he had to endure during the evening, Stanton stayed, trying to look as unconcerned as possible. His humiliation was dimmed only by his secret plotting—and the knowledge he would soon repay the arrogant pirate. He had to learn everything he could about Reese Hampton: when Hampton was leaving, where he was going.

He was, then, very attentive when he overheard Reese speaking with Jeremy Clayton.

"You're a sly one," Jeremy said. "I never thought to see *you* harnessed. When is the wedding?"

"Not until after my next voyage," Reese said. "I have some unfinished business." During the past few weeks he had changed his mind about American ships. He had grown increasingly angry over Samara's hold on his thoughts. By avoiding the American coast, he was merely giving in to those feelings. Perversely, he thought the way to end them was a direct confrontation...if not with Samara, at least with what she represented.

But he told Jeremy only that he was returning to the Carolina coast...

After the last guest left, Reese and Avery shared a few minutes together.

"She should be safe enough now," Reese said. "She can break the engagement when I come back...or before if she wishes."

"She would make a good wife," Avery said slowly.

"She would indeed," Reese replied wryly, "but not for me. Nor do I have her heart, only her gratitude."

"There have been happy marriages based on less," Avery commented, still hoping that his twin would find the happiness he himself cherished. He flinched at the morose expression of his brother's face.

"But not for me," Reese answered. His voice grew firmer. "I like my freedom." He only wished that he still believed those words.

While the two Hamptons talked, Stanton, who had left shortly after hearing the conversation between Jeremy and Reese, was meeting with an agent of the American government. And several miles away on Fleet Street, a weary printer

was painstakingly assembling hundreds of tiny pieces of type
in preparation for the next day's newspaper. Among the stories
was the betrothal announcement of Reese Hampton and Eloise
Stanton. The news had spread rapidly.

Chapter Eleven

∽⟨⟨∾⟩⟩∽

After her weeks on the British privateer, Samara took a new
interest in the war. Until her ill-fated adventure the war had
seemed a long way off and politics had bored her. But now
her fervor was more personal. She knew how close Brendan
and his crew had come to imprisonment or impressment. She
had heard from members of his crew of the horrors of British
ships, and the impressment issue was suddenly very real to
her.

And now she had a new source fueling her patriotism. Conn
had been fighting the Creeks with the Alabama Militia. He
had been badly wounded in the leg by a British musket and
would always have a limp. His tales of the horrors inflicted
on settlers, and the role played by the British in supporting
and even encouraging atrocities against women and children
infuriated Samara. Similar atrocities by Americans against the
women and children in the Indian villages, and the earlier
wrongs against the Cherokees, were not mentioned or dismissed as aberrations.

There were similar reports from the northwest, and stories
of torture and murder—all at the behest of the British—multiplied. At the same time, there were increasing news items
about the terrible conditions in Dartmoor prison in England—
the holding place for many American seamen and privateers.
It increased the fear of the O'Neill family, for now—at the
request of the navy—Brendan had outfitted his ship with heav-

ier guns and had turned to privateering himself. He had been
gone several months and they had heard nothing.

All this continued to build Samara's rage against the British
and, consequently, Reese Hampton who was a ready target for
her condemnation. She conveniently dismissed Yancy and
Davey and Michael Simmons. They had to follow their captain's commands. And she convinced herself more than ever
that the Englishman had been planning, in some devious way,
to betray them. She could not let herself think anything good
of him, for then she would indeed be even more lost and
miserable than she was now. She could fight the loneliness
only by convincing herself he was the worst kind of blackguard.

Not long after her return home, Samara had ridden to the
family's secret cave. Beset by an anguish she could not understand or quash, she sought the place where she had once
dreamed so happily. The cave held a special place in each and
every heart in her family. It had been where her mother had
found Papa, wounded and near death, and had nursed him back
to health. Each of the O'Neill children knew the story by heart.
Sore-hearted at her failure to dismiss Captain Hampton from
her thoughts, Samara sat in the cave, watching the weak trails
of light that came through the heavy underbrush, and wished
for a knight errant of her own. An American one. But the only
vision that came to her was a tawny-haired, sun-kissed giant
who stood at the helm of a ship, his face toward the heavens
and his eyes searching…always searching. There was an odd
feeling here…as though the cave were waiting for something.
There seemed to be an expectancy that she had never felt
before. Mystified, she allowed herself to dream briefly of
Reese Hampton, remembering the magic of that night on deck
when their lips had touched so hungrily, when the moon had
embraced them lovingly and had made them, for precious un-
forgettable seconds, the only two people on earth.

Fool. She scolded herself. *He's gone, and he probably
doesn't even remember you exist.*

Even worse, chimed in another inner voice, *he could be out there even now, attacking Brendan again, or some other American ship.*

Or it could be Reese himself in danger, came the first voice. Fear hit her like a physical blow. Reese Hampton in danger? "It could never be so," she whispered to the silent walls. "Not him! It would be like stilling the wind."

But even so, she could not dismiss a shiver of premonition. Suddenly cold, she left the cave.

The strange feelings of that day—the expectancy and the fear—stayed with her. Despite repeated urgings from her family, she declined most invitations, thinking them frivolous in this time of peril. She simply had no interest. The men in the district held no attraction, and it was all she could do to even remain polite when they called. Soon, most became discouraged and invitations fell off.

She spent more and more time with her father, talking about the war. Although he worried constantly about her lack of interest in suitors or other matters, he approved of her new-found interest in the war and politics. He was usually damning the Federalists for their continuing opposition to the war, and fuming about the current military leadership. Connor O'Neill was particularly incensed one night at dinner after one major disaster.

"That damned fool William Hull ran and left a column of men to be massacred," he said. "The coward should be hung."

His namesake, Conn, bitterly agreed. General Hull had been sent to Detroit with 2,200 men. Faced by a British-Canadian Army of only 250, he had dillied and dallied until one of his supply columns was massacred. He then surrendered without firing a shot, exposing the whole American northwest to the Indians, and Hull's name was being cursed throughout the country.

"It's no better in the northeast," Connor said. "The *Gazette* said a large force moved to cross the Niagara River into Canada, but part of the army refused, leaving the first troops with nothing to do but surrender. With that kind of leadership, God knows what will happen."

Samara listened intently as she ate. The only good news came from the sea. Though tiny, the American navy was as deadly as any afloat. The captains of the *Constitution* and the *United States* had reported major victories, and the smaller brigs and sloops consistently displayed speed and accuracy superior to their British counterparts. Equally damaging to the British were the American privateers which had become a major force in the conflict. Samara had read only today that insurance rates for British ships had tripled in the past months because of losses.

She usually joined in the dinner discussions but tonight she was silent. As the war grew more bitter, it seemed inevitable that disaster would strike one of the people she cared about most: Brendan, who was now at greatest risk; Conn, who planned to rejoin the militia in Alabama as soon as his leg had healed sufficiently, and gentle Marion, who was attached to the militia as a doctor. And then there was, of course, Reese Hampton. The irony of the situation did not escape her.

The *Unicorn* seemed cursed from the moment it left London. Unlike previous voyages, when luck accompanied every nautical mile, Reese now ran into one disaster after another. The bad luck started at the docks when three of his most trusted crew members, one of them his best gunner, failed to return to the ship; after several days' search, he found that two had been killed in a tavern brawl and the other had just disappeared. Restless and unwilling to spare the time to search for competent new members, Reese decided to sail shorthanded. The *Unicorn* then ran into a series of storms, each one more severe than the one before. Oilskins were useless, and there was not a dry spot on the ship nor a dry rag to wear. The cook had to douse the galley fire, and there was no warm food. Salt water often mixed with the fresh. After three weeks at sail and ten days of continuous storms, Reese was almost numb with fatigue and the ship was battered. The canvas was badly torn, and one of the cannons had torn loose from its moorings, badly injuring two more of his crew.

Usually storms exhilarated him, creating a match of his wits against the strongest and ablest of forces. But now both he and the ship were exhausted and he wished only to see an end to it.

When morning came on the twenty-first day, it was little different from the previous one. The same thick gloom made it barely possible to distinguish day from night; a blinding rain raked the ship and the wind howled like demons as it battered the rigging. Blinding flashes of lightning ran down the conductor and hissed as they leaped into the sea, each accompanied by its own distinctive roar of thunder. The waves were mountainous and played with the ship as if it were a toy, tossing it almost at will and straining every fibre of her frame.

Reese fought the wheel as he never had before; for the first time in his sailing years he was forced to consider his own mortality as the warring elements wrestled him for control.

In late afternoon, the barometer started to rise, and Reese turned the ship over to his first mate as he studied the considerable damage. They were leaking badly, and many of the yards were splintered and useless. The wind had cut through the canvas like scissors.

Reese uttered a small prayer. If he calculated correctly, the *Unicorn* was not far from the Carolina coast—and the enemy. He would have to turn away, head for Bermuda and repairs, and pray to God they didn't encounter any American ships. Several of their guns had torn away from their moorings and were washed overboard. One of his few remaining gunners was badly injured and until extensive repairs were made he couldn't even outrun a whaleboat.

Darkness came much too slowly, and Reese blessed the cloud-filled sky. Portholes were covered and work progressed feverishly on repairs below decks: pumping water and repairing planking. Work above deck was difficult in the almost-complete darkness. No lights were allowed; much would have to wait until the first glimmers of dawn.

McDonald, whose eyes were universally recognized as the sharpest, took watch at the masthead. Reese, who had had no sleep in three days, took a short nap before returning to duty at dawn, just in time to hear McDonald's sharp warning. Both

land and sails were visible. Seconds later he reported at least
two ships.

Reese cursed roundly and took the wheel, ordering as much
sail as possible and heading toward the coast. If he could find
a deep enough river, perhaps he could disappear. If the ships
were enemy frigates, they would have a difficult time following. It was their only chance.

The *Unicorn* was sluggish, and it took all of Reese's
strength to turn it against the wind and toward the coast. What
in God's name had happened to his fabled luck? He tried to
summon it now, praying for a fog to envelop his movements
as the two ships started to close the distance. He had no way
of knowing that the ships had, several days before, been
alerted to his destination and had been actively hunting him.
He only knew that his options were rapidly disappearing.

His desperate gamble proved futile. As the ship hugged the
coast, they could find no openings, and he ordered the crew
to prepare for battle, knowing as he did the severe odds against
him. He knew now that he faced an American frigate with
twice his gun power, and a corvette, a ship slightly larger than
his own and almost as maneuverable.

Reese watched as the American flag was hoisted along with
signal flags ordering him to heave-to. He answered with the
raising of his own flag and a salvo from one of his remaining
long guns. Reese was damned if he would surrender, not as
long as there was the slimmest chance he could still find an
escape.

The American frigate answered with a broadside which
smashed several of the *Unicorn*'s boats and shattered her
spars. The *Unicorn*'s return fire tumbled the enemy's foretop-
mast, but the corvette had circled around and the *Unicorn* was
receiving fire from two directions.

Shot was now raking Reese's ship and he could hear the
cries of his crewmen. A large shell entered the *Unicorn*'s side
only a few inches above the waterline and passed entirely
though it. Knowing any further defiance was useless, Reese
prepared to surrender, when an explosion rocked the ship. He
ordered the ship abandoned, and watched as his crewmen scur-

ried down hastily lowered rope ladders. The wounded were carried and placed in the one surviving boat. Reese watched intently until only he and Yancy were left on what was rapidly becoming a pyre of greedy flames. Boats from the Yankee ships were already picking up the survivors, and Reese ordered Yancy off.

"Not until you go," Yancy replied adamantly, carefully watching the encroaching fire.

"I'm going to swim for it," Reese said. "I might just be able to make it. They're after *me*, and if they think I'm dead, you might have a better chance for exchange. And," he added, "free I just might be able to help you escape...if you're not exchanged."

Yancy knew it was possible despite the distance to shore. Reese was an extremely strong swimmer, and if anyone could survive the strong currents that existed along the coast, it was the captain. He also knew he could not dissuade him, not when Reese had that bright gleam in his eyes. Nor could he go along. He would only doom them both.

"I'll tell them you're dead, that you were killed in the last explosion," Yancy said slowly. He took Reese's hand, and clasped it tightly. "Good luck."

"And to you, Yancy." Reese's grim mouth turned up in a sudden confident smile. Cocky and almost boyishly wicked, it reflected the captain's usual relish for a challenge. That particular smile had been gone for several months, and Yancy had missed it.

The doctor felt a new confidence as he heard Reese's next words. "I'll see you in Bermuda. No later than Christmas."

"Bermuda," Yancy confirmed, and hurried over the side without a look back.

Reese took one last look at the *Unicorn*. It had served him well and little deserved this fate. His hand caressed the mahogany rail as his eyes traveled from the quarterdeck, now nearly consumed by flames, to what was left of the bow. Hidden by the flames, he slipped over the railing and dove into the sea.

The news of the *Unicorn*'s destruction traveled quickly through the Carolinas. In the months prior to the capture of Brendan's ship, the English privateer had become almost legendary as he preyed on American shipping. The fact that the notorious Captain Hampton had seized one of the O'Neill ships, and that Brendan O'Neill had stolen it back spurred tales of a feud between the two captains. Brendan had tried to squelch such rumors, feeling profoundly embarrassed about the heroic image he did not deserve. Yet other than tell the truth, which he had promised not to do, there was little he could say or deny. If truth be told, he felt like a damned hypocrite, and he cursed Hampton often for forcing his silence.

He was in Charleston, back for several weeks after a long and successful voyage, when he heard the news. His own ship, the *Samara*, was tucked away in one of the rivers flowing into the sea. He immediately sought more information and discovered from the authorities that Reese Hampton was considered dead. The English captain had refused to leave the ship and was killed in an explosion; the crew had been taken to Boston where they would probably be exchanged.

Brendan was struck by a deep sense of loss although the news hadn't surprised him. Hampton, he knew, must have been aware he would not be as easily exchanged as his men; from what he knew of the Englishman, Hampton would choose death before surrender or captivity.

But what really tormented Brendan was Samara. Regardless of what she said, or how she had railed against Hampton as an "unprincipled pirate of the lowest order," her eyes always betrayed her. They softened when the man's name was mentioned, and there was a wistfulness about her that nearly broke his heart. He had hoped that one day...

But now that hope was gone, and he wondered how she would take the news. There was no use trying to keep it from her...it was discussed everywhere, including all the newspapers. And Samara now read them all avidly. The only thing he could do was tell her himself and try to soften the blow.

It had been easier than he expected, mainly because she

simply wouldn't believe him. She mourned the *Unicorn*, but insisted that Hampton was "simply too wicked to die."

"And," she added for good measure, "no one actually saw his body."

"The ship blew up, Samara," he answered patiently as if to a child. "They searched for a long time, and everyone agreed that no one could swim that far."

"*He* could," Samara said stubbornly. "Not that I care. It would be what he deserves." Her chin stuck out in an obstinate gesture Brendan knew only too well.

"The currents," he added weakly, but the chin did not retreat.

"He's not dead," she pronounced and marched out of the room, leaving him speechless and his mother, who had been there for support, wondering.

For the first time in months, Samara revisited the cave. Dressed in some of Conn's old clothes, she crawled into the interior and sat there, studying the patterns created by the sun's intrusion through the vines which protected the entrance.

"I would know if he were dead," she whispered. She could feel his energy even now, could sense that incredible vitality. For some reason she couldn't explain, she felt close to him here.

For the first time since she had returned to Glen Woods, she cried. The tears started in tiny trickles...thin trails down her face, and grew to great spasms that racked her body and tore at her heart. She didn't believe him dead, but the news had fired her immense need and longing for him. She cried as if her heart were breaking, and it was. It was shattering into thousands of tiny pieces. She knew now how much he was a part of her, how much he would always be a part of her. And he was out there now, alone and possibly badly wounded, in an enemy land; she was struck with a sudden desperate fear for him. She knew she cried because, for the first time, she consciously admitted she loved Reese Hampton, loved him with all the passion and life within her. And although her instinct believed him alive, she also knew her love was something that could never be. He was the enemy and he came from a life she could never accept...even if, by some miracle, he did want her. Which was, she felt, highly unlikely. Except for that brief kiss on deck, he had mostly treated her like a naughty child.

The tears slowed only because there were no tears left in the empty vessel that was Samara. The sobs quieted, and the spasms no longer tormented the physical body, but a worse agony pierced her mind.

Where is he? Please God, keep him safe. Just keep him safe.

Several days later, she said goodbye to Brendan, who was returning to his dangerous pursuits, and wished him Godspeed.

Before he left, he took her chin in his hand and studied the pensive face. "You have to get on with your life, little sister."

"I know," she said wistfully, "but I don't know how."

"Go out," he said. "For me, if not for yourself. You can't hide forever in a dream."

"He's spoiled everyone else for me," she whispered. "I see him everywhere."

"He's dead, Samara. You *must* believe that. There are so many young men out there who would love to put a sparkle back in those eyes. Give them a chance."

She tried to smile. "Emily Fontaine is announcing her engagement next week at a ball. I thought to refuse but perhaps..."

"For me," Bren said. "Go for me."

She nodded slowly.

"A promise?"

"Yes," she said, and she watched him leave, a slight sad smile on his face.

Samara knew her melancholy was affecting everyone in the house, and she made an effort to cast it aside. Both Conn and Marion, who was home for a brief visit, planned to accompany her to the ball. The event was to celebrate the betrothal of Emily, who was one of her best friends, and she knew of no way of avoiding it, not without hurting Emily and further distressing her family. Reluctantly, she withstood the hours of standing perfectly still while being measured and fitted for a new ball gown. When it was over, Samara barely glanced at the garment so patiently planned by her mother and the dressmaker. Unlike the pastels worn by so many unmarried young ladies, this gown had a satin underskirt of midnight blue and a silver-threaded sarcenet overskirt falling from an empire waist. The low, square-cut neckline emphasized the ivory of her skin and the swell of her breasts. The color of the gown brought out a lovely blue hue in her dark gray eyes and contrasted with the clear bloom of her complexion.

But Samara cared little for the magic of the gown and was barely tolerant as one of the maids brushed her hair until it seemed touched with fire, then wove silver ribbons through it, gathering it in the back and allowing it to fall in gentle curls over her shoulders. A silver shawl completed the costume, and she waited patiently for her brothers to finish their dress. A small trunk had been packed; the three of them would stay overnight.

It was a beautiful afternoon and would be a lovelier night. The sky was a rich deep blue without a hint of clouds. Yet there was a pleasant breeze taking the sting from the usually stifling July heat. Samara blessed the current fashions which were light and cool as she tried to enjoy the long ride. They had discussed going earlier during the day, and dressing at the Fontaine home, but Samara had demurred. She knew her mother wanted to help her dress; originally the older O'Neills planned to attend, but one of Samantha's mares was near foaling, and they'd decided to stay home.

Samara enjoyed the ride with her brothers. Both could be immensely entertaining when they tried, and they were trying now. Some of Conn's bitterness, which had festered since his wounding, dissolved as he and Marion bantered back and forth, trading amusing stories they had heard and recounting some of the most mischievous moments as children. Samara felt her heavy mood lighten, and she regarded them both fondly.

Marion was so kind…kind and thoughtful and sensitive. He had started a medical practice in Charleston before the war, but now served with the militia and stopped frequently by

Glen Woods. Conn was the warrior, the only one of the brothers who had really wanted war, who had been impatient to serve. They were so different, yet so alike with their blond hair, just several shades apart, and their blue eyes.

Darkness came late these summer nights, but the full moon was already high in the sky when the carriage arrived at its destination. It was like a fairyland, Samara thought. Lanterns were strung between giant oaks and cypresses, and the air was rich with the scent of jasmine, magnolia and sweet bay.

Dozens of carriages lined the road. Marion and Conn ceremoniously helped Samara from the coach, and they entered the front foyer, greeting their hosts. Samara spied Emily and the two young ladies hugged each other. They separated, and Emily looked enviously as she studied every detail of Samara's gown. But nothing could dim the sparkle in Emily's eyes. This was *her* night; and she was delighted Samara had broken her self-imposed exile to be there.

"Come with me," Emily said, "there is the most exciting man here...he's, well, he's absolutely magnificent. If it weren't for my Jonathan..."

"Who is he?"

"I don't know exactly. He's an acquaintance of Mr. Samuels, a businessman of some kind, and he is so handsome and...sort of dangerous-looking."

Emily pulled a reluctant Samara along behind her. Samara had had her fill of dangerous-looking men and she really doubted if Emily knew the difference, anyway. Emily usually thought everyone was handsome, including Jonathan, her rather plain-looking but very pleasant fiancé.

Samara tried to see above the crowd, but it was impossible. She was being led through the large dining room past tables overflowing with food and into the large room being used for the ball tonight. Emily stopped suddenly, and Samara's eyes lifted from a blue coat which barely contained the impossibly wide shoulders to glittering blue-green eyes that flared suddenly, then glowed with a fervent fire before going blank.

Emily, in her delight at presenting so great a prize, totally missed the shock that passed over her friend's face. A surge of complete inexplicable joy exploded within Samara. Reese. Alive. Here. All the months of wanting, of suppressing those hurting aches, that longing for something unknown yet irresistible. Her hand started to reach tentatively out for him, but his expression stopped it midway. It was the look one would give a stranger. Then, almost immediately, they conveyed a silent message. Warning or plea? Samara didn't know which.

Emily's next words devastated her. She hadn't known what to think as to how Reese had come to be here, but she certainly wasn't prepared for Emily's introduction nor the name given her.

"Mr. Avery, this is Miss Samara O'Neill, my very best friend. Samara, this is Mr. Thomas Avery."

Reese bowed, and for a moment, Samara couldn't see his eyes. When he straightened, one eyebrow was lifted. "*Miss* O'Neill?"

Emily bubbled on, completely unaware of the currents between the two. "Of course, it isn't for lack of suitors. Samara is the most popular girl in the district."

"I can believe that," Reese answered in his deep drawl. A touch of mischief reached his wary eyes. "It quite defies understanding how such a lovely young lady would escape matrimony."

Samara bit her lip, wishing that she hadn't suddenly become tongue-tied. But her mind was racing ahead, and all the thoughts were damning. What *was* Reese doing here posing as a businessman? And, most worrisome of all, why?

"Mr. *Avery*," she said finally. "You have to tell me about your business and what you are doing in our humble state. I don't think I've heard your name before."

The words were said sweetly. Too sweetly for Reese's comfort. They did not belong to the Samara he knew. But, then, how well did he know her? Certainly not as well as he had thought. The little minx. *Miss.* Damn. And damn Brendan.

The orchestra struck up a reel. Reese bowed once more. "May I have the honor of this dance, *Miss* O'Neill?"

"Certainly, Mr. Avery, although I'm afraid my poor country dancing isn't quite what you're used to."

"I doubt that," he said drily. "But in any event, my boots have probably had worse punishment." A sudden smile lit his face, and Samara melted. For an instant, she didn't care why he was here. It was just enough that he was. She accepted his arm and accompanied him to the dance floor, leaving Emily beaming with the joy of a successful matchmaker.

There was no way to talk during the dance. There were too many nearby ears. Only briefly did Samara whisper, "They said you were dead."

"Did you believe them?"

"No."

Again that smile that made her heart churn. Damn him.

As the dance ended, she leaned towards him and whispered quickly, "There's a giant cypress with great twisted roots at the back of the house. In an hour."

He nodded, his eyes searching hers for intent. He had little choice. He had to trust her.

Reese watched for several minutes, then made his way outside where he lit a cheroot. It had been a damn fool thing to do, coming here tonight. He should have refused, but Samuels had insisted.

He thought back to three weeks ago when his ship had exploded and he had barely made it to shore. There had been minutes, more than a few, when he had almost submitted to the cold and fatigue. But something inside wouldn't let him quit even when he wanted to. When he'd finally made shore he'd crawled up the sandbanks and collapsed under some ancient trees twisted by time and wind. He didn't know how long he had slept. It must have been nearly half a day because the sun was setting over the sea by the time he awoke. There were no sails now, only an empty endless ocean and miles of beach. He knew he was in serious trouble. He wore only canvas sailor trousers, and a now-tattered cotton shirt. He had no footwear, no money, no prospects. He didn't even know where in the hell he was. He did have, engraved in his mind for some such emergency, a list of secret English sympathizers in the Carolinas—a gift from his brother. But how to find them? And how could he travel like this?

Still fatigued from the days of fighting the storm and the long battle through the heavy seas, he decided to get more rest. Perhaps, then, he could think more rationally. He slept through much of the night, rising at the first light of dawn. He started north, hoping to find a farmhouse. He would claim to be a shipwrecked American. Reese was sure Yancy had convinced the Americans he was dead; there shouldn't be any alarm. He didn't worry about his accent; the American navy and merchantmen were filled with Scots, Irishmen and even Englishmen who had deserted. And he had been at sea with so many nationalities that his own speech had developed a unique flavor all of its own.

He didn't know how long he had walked, but he was immensely thirsty and hungry, and even the leatherlike soles of his feet were blistered and burned from the hot sand. It was late in the day, and he had eaten nothing when he finally found what he sought: a small cluster of huts and some small boats, none of them in very good repair.

He found both food and welcome in the tiny community. The inhabitants were people who lived with the sea's tragedies and they were ready sympathizers. They gave him a place to stay that night and shared their food, and even offered clothes they obviously couldn't spare. With a deep sense of guilt and shame for his lies, he refused, thanking them quietly for their hospitality, their food and their good wishes and he renewed his journey. Following their directions to Charleston he stayed off the main roads and through theft and burglary found some rough clothes and enough food to survive. He found Samuels' home one week after the sea battle, and met yet another obstacle. He couldn't get to the house, or even close to it. Armed guards stopped him at the main road as he turned toward the Georgian mansion. He knew he didn't present a very comforting picture. His beard had grown to a thick stubble. His hair had not been combed in days. His rough clothes were sweat-stained and filthy, and his bare feet were bleeding. The son and brother of an earl? Even he had to laugh at that.

Only his ring, a jeweled coat of arms, seemed to make any impact. He had hidden it in a tiny pocket he had made in his shirt, and he now produced it. He was told to wait, and one of the guards took the ring and rode to the house. Almost immediately he was back with a stout, well-dressed figure who studied him intently. "Hampton?" The question was unbelieving.

Reese nodded.

"The newspapers said you were dead."

"That's what I wanted them to think."

The man finally smiled. "I know your brother. You are welcome. Come, we'll get you cleaned up and into some... more suitable clothes."

He had spent the next two weeks quietly at the Samuels' home. The planter had been a Tory during the revolution but had decided to stay while others left for Canada or the Caribbean. In the past thirty years, most of his neighbors had forgotten his loyalties, and he made no issue of them. But he still had a deep commitment to the crown and would arrange Reese's passage on a foreign ship to a port in the Caribbean.

It was not until ten days later that Samuels had requested a favor in return. He had been asked by a Federalist friend to secure information about the sailing of American privateers and blockade runners. Samuels knew the information was destined for the English navy. There were many in this country who wanted to see the war ended quickly, and American defeats could force an early peace. Samuels had no crop ready for shipment, no reason to ask questions. He suggested that Reese pose as a merchant who was looking for shipping contracts. There was to be a ball in the next week and many of the important figures in South Carolina's shipping business would be there.

"It won't work," Reese told Samuels. "I know one of them."

"O'Neill," Samuels said. "I heard the stories. But he left several days ago and won't be back for some time."

Reese tried to refuse again, although not out of fear. He doubted whether Mrs. O'Neill would attend without her husband; perhaps she was even with him. But he didn't like the idea of being a spy.

Samuels' good nature disappeared. He had given his assistance and was risking his life to help Reese. A favor was due. And he was calling it. Reese reluctantly agreed.

Samuels was very careful in the way he arranged the invitation. He told Everette Fontaine only that he had met Thomas Avery at a hotel in Charleston, and that the man was looking for some shipping contracts. It was enough. An invitation was sent to the hotel where Reese was now temporarily quartered, and Samuels arranged for a tailor. At the last minute, Samuels decided it best that he not even attend. Reese was left on his own....

Damn. After the past seven weeks he should have realized this would just be another in one long string of bad decisions and disasters. Reese knew he should probably leave now, but he couldn't. He had to see Samara one more time, especially now that he knew she was free. He knew he couldn't let her go without a word, without knowing how she felt. He had lived with agony for nearly a year. Perhaps she would agree to come with him. He stepped back into the ballroom and searched for her, but she wasn't there. He would have to wait. And, devil take it, he didn't know what was awaiting him. The lady or the hangman.

Chapter Twelve

Dozens of lanterns spread their magic—darting little slivers of silver and gold, intermingling and dancing in the glow of a full moon. Millions of stars hung in their intricate patterns, each contributing to the enchantment of the night and its aura of fantasy. Music, just far enough distant to be haunting, contributed to Samara's fearful expectancy, the weakness in her legs, the hammering of her heart. Reese Hampton. She had thought never to see him again…never except in her dreams, in her thoughts where he was a constant crippling presence. She had not been whole since that voyage to Bermuda. She had thought she would never be whole again. He had left her hollow, a shape without substance.

And now he was waiting for her, and she would betray him. She trembled at the thought. She would never forget the way his glittering jewel-like eyes leaped with what could only be joy when he saw her. Or was it joy? Perhaps just fear. But no, she knew it was not. His mouth had crooked in a small rueful smile when she was introduced as Miss O'Neill, but there was also challenge in his face. She knew he had to consider the possibility she might inform on him, and he was gambling that she would not, at least not until he had had a chance to talk to her. If nothing else, Captain Hampton was as confident, as arrogant as ever. Damn him! Damn him for entering her life again this way! Damn him for making her do something she feared she would regret the rest of her life! But she had no choice. She could not allow him to spy on her country. Brendan's life, and so many others, were at stake.

She saw him then, tall and commanding, his hair like molten gold in the flickering lights of the lanterns. He was standing under the cypress; his face, with its intricately carved features, was captured in all its strength by the moonlight. His lips, wide and sensuous, smiled in warm welcome. How completely beautiful he was, Samara thought, as her traitorous body quivered and throbbed. Knowing full well what she had just done, she wanted to die.

He reached out his hands to her, his eyes bright and mischievous. "Miss O'Neill...Samara...", he said, his baritone voice caressing her as intimately as any hand. "I think you must deal in sorcery for I have not been able to dislodge you from my thoughts. And now I find you free, as I have wished so many times. If I weren't so pleased, I think I would take you over my knee again..."

His eyes, his voice, his words burned into her soul. She had dreamed of this so many times. She treasured the moment, riveting it in her mind, because she knew in moments it would be broken, shattered like a delicate piece of glass.

Struggling to keep some sense about her, she was finally able to meet his eyes.

"Mr. *Avery*?" she said, questions in her tone, accusation in her face.

Some of the smile left Hampton's face. A shadow of the old mockery touched his eyes. "*Miss* O'Neill?" Her question was met with his own.

The terrible irony of the situation kept Samara silent this time. What could she say? How could she explain?

Reese Hampton looked at her quizzically, not understanding her unusual reticence. He had hoped for welcome, had expected questions, had prepared himself for accusations. The smile disappeared completely.

"Brendan is your brother, of course," he said now. It had been easy to guess once Samara was introduced; he had confirmed it through a fellow guest. "May I ask why the masquerade aboard the *Unicorn*?"

But Samara found it impossible to say anything. She had seen the figures, cloaked in shadows, as they moved quietly toward the tree. Her lips trembled, and something like desperation showed in her eyes.

Reese could resist no longer. His head bent down, his lips descended, and Samara was lost in her need to meet them. All reason fled as their lips joined; months of hunger, of wanting, of aching exploded into an inferno of raw desire.

Samara forgot her brothers, forgot her trap, forgot everything but the warm delight of his touch. Hundreds of little conflagrations flared in every part of her being as his lips gently, then urgently, pressed against hers, and his tongue made a fevered entrance into her mouth, teasing her senses and fueling her need. Her body readily gravitated to his, cherishing the hard leanness, the magnificent warmth that reached out and encompassed her. So strong was the bond that she didn't realize, immediately, that his arms had stiffened, that his lips had stilled.

A voice broke the silence, her brother's voice. Conn's voice. It was rough and angry.

"You will drop your arms, English, and move away."

Samara's heart froze at the sound. She had never heard Conn's voice so harsh. He was obviously quite ready to kill Reese Hampton. Her eyes traveled up to Reese's face, and she shivered at what she saw there.

The eyes were icy with fury and naked contempt, the mouth, so tender and passionate moments earlier, was compressed in a tight grim line. She could see him struggle for control.

"Your doing, my sweet?" he said finally, his voice dripping with scorn. She felt, rather than heard, the naked pain in it, the disillusionment, and she thought dying would be too easy.

"You are quite an excellent actress, aren't you?" he continued, now almost conversationally but his eyes reduced her to the status of the lowest insect on earth. "It's really a pity we were interrupted so soon; it would have been interesting to see exactly how far you would go." His hands tightened on her arms in quiet rage as he felt the barrel of a pistol press deeper in his back.

"I won't tell you again, English," the man behind him said. "I could arouse the house, and you would probably hang right now. I don't think this company would be sympathetic to an English spy."

"And my alternative?" Reese's voice was deceptively easy. His mind was racing ahead. How many were there? Exactly what was Samara's involvement?

"You will live a little longer: I won't promise how much."

Reluctantly, Reese let his hands fall to his side. As he did, his eyes moved from Samara, and she knew he was mentally dismissing her.

"Put your hands behind your back," came the next order, and after a brief hesitation and another jolt to his back Reese complied. His wrists were seized and he felt the rough rope as it was secured around them. He tried to flex his wrists to give him some slight freedom, but they were firmly, if not cruelly, pressed tightly together. Reese felt the final tug as the knot was tied and he discovered a helplessness completely new to him. His hands clenched into tight fists as he realized Samara had planned this. What a fool he had been to be so elated when he first saw her tonight. How incredibly arrogant of him to trust her. None of his thoughts showed in his face, however. It was as emotionless as a mask as he considered his position. There were obviously two of them because the gun barrel had remained fixed in his back as his hands were tied. What in the devil did they intend?

He felt a cloak being thrown over his shoulders, and he was pushed towards the line of coaches.

"If we are met by anyone," the faceless voice said, "You will act suitably drunk. I understand you are very skilled at that."

At this further evidence of Samara's betrayal, Reese's fury increased. His body tensed with the effort to bridle the rage until it could be used effectively. And it would be, he promised himself. He could not see her now, but the light fragrant scent told him she was still with them. God, he wanted to get his hands around that lovely neck. One of his captors pushed him towards a carriage; a driver was already in place. The barrel of the gun disappeared from the small part of his back, and he watched as Samara entered the carriage followed by a well built, well dressed man who mounted the seat awkwardly. Only now was he aware of the man's stiff leg. Damn. He had been too angry at Samara's role to detect this weakness. There had to be a way to use it. Reese looked for the pistol, but it seemed to have disappeared.

The man still standing with him nodded to the carriage. "Please get in." It was a gentler voice, polite and pleasant.

Reese's face was cold as he eyed him sardonically. "Please?" His voice was full of mockery.

The man didn't take offense but smiled slightly. "Yes, please. I would highly recommend it before someone intrudes on this rather unusual little scene."

Reese put his foot on the step and started to enter the coach. He turned around and suddenly saw his chance. The softly spoken man was directly below him, a perfect target. It would take the other one several valuable seconds to react because of his leg. By then, he could be into the woods. He didn't think about what he would do then...with his hands tied behind him. He just knew an unreasoning rage that required action. He lowered his head and went pummeling into the man below, knocking him to the ground before feeling the jerk on the rope around his wrists. He was forced up, pain arching through his arms and up into his shoulders.

The man in the carriage had been faster than Reese thought possible. Reese was thrust against the side of the carriage, and the gun, held openly now, was aimed at his heart.

The man looked down at his companion on the ground. "Are you all right, Marion?"

Light from a lantern shone down on the fallen man's face, and Reese knew a certain familiarity. He then looked at his other captor, the man holding the gun, and he saw the same features. Features that had also belonged to Brendan O'Neill. They had to be O'Neill's brothers. And, therefore, Samara's. He slumped against the couch. Brendan had obviously kept his word about their joint conspiracy and the theft of the *Samara*; the hostility of the one brother was too powerful for it to be otherwise. Nor had Samara given him the benefit of an explanation. A slight laugh escaped his lips, but there was no amusement in it. He very likely would hang because of his own magnanimity, his own sense of honor. There was a certain poetry about it, he thought bitterly as he was hustled back into the coach. He saw Samara's wide eyes on him as the brother with the gun gave it to her and then very efficiently tied his ankles together and roped them to the frame of the seat, allowing him no movement at all. His brief moment of rebellion was obviously going to cost him even the smallest comfort. The other brother groaned slightly as he moved, apparently hurting from Reese's blow. At least he could take some little satisfaction in that.

Reese's glittering eyes pinned Samara to her seat. "Very neatly done, Miss O'Neill. I compliment you on your treachery." The agony in her eyes did nothing to appease him. "Do you plan to see me hang in the same expeditious manner?" His voice was almost indifferent, his bitterness too deep, too painful, to allow itself to surface. He would not give her *that* pleasure.

He watched coldly as tears welled up in her eyes, hesitating there, like a light fog on a gray morning. "Tears, Samara? How very thoughtful. A bit late, but…appreciated." Derision dripped from his voice.

"Shut up, English," the man on his right growled. Reese could feel the fist balled up next to him. He shrugged.

On the other side of him, the man he had hit stirred. "It's only because of Samara," the man said softly, "that you're not now in the hands of American authorities." Marion had observed the exchange between his sister and the Englishman with real concern. Samara was obviously shattered; there was much more between the two than he had first realized.

He was also concerned about Conn's temper. His brother's experience in Alabama had flamed his hatred of the English. He blamed them for the Indian atrocities he had witnessed, and his leg had not softened an already fierce thirst for vengeance.

A natural peacemaker, Marion disregarded his own hurts

and tried to soften the explosive tension in the coach. "I'm sorry we had to take...such measures, but we had little choice...unless you preferred the military."

Reese turned to him, his eyes raking over the American. It was hard to dislike what he saw. The eyes were steady and frank, the mouth sensitive but firm. There was something inherently decent about him. But Reese was not in a mood to appreciate such a quality. He had never been so furious in his life.

The problem was, Reese realized, that the anger should be directed at himself. Christ, how could he have been such a fool? He should have left immediately after seeing Samara, but he wanted, oh how he had wanted, to touch her, to hold her in his arms. And he had been deceived by the answering spark in her eyes, the same fierce hunger that shone in her face. He had believed her. Believed what? She had said nothing but to meet her...and he had foolishly assumed..."

Reese turned his head and closed his eyes in denial. He tried to relax his long body against the seat but it was impossible. The carriage was moving fast, and it took all his concentration to keep his balance as it swayed and jolted along the rutted road. His arms hurt like hell, his wrists burned from the rough rope, and his legs were cramping from their unnatural position. But he would be damned if he would let any of them know it. His mouth tightened in an implacable line, and he opened his eyes only long enough for Samara to see their smoldering savagery. They were closed before they saw her answering despair...and plea for understanding.

Reese lost track of time. He was so damned uncomfortable every second seemed liked hours. He cursed Samuels who had lured him into this mess, then himself for further entangling himself. Behind his back, his hands fought against the ropes to no avail, but the pain gave him some distraction from his dark thoughts. His life had not been the same since his first encounter with the O'Neills nearly a year earlier. He had never been free of the dark-haired witch; she had ruined every other woman for him even when he thought her unobtainable. His cherished freedom had lost its luster, and his preoccupation with her had, most likely, cost him his ship…and now perhaps his life. Had he totally mistaken her responses on the *Unicorn*? Had he misjudged her first reaction this evening? He had thought then he saw the same rush of joy he experienced. Had it been just a thirst for revenge instead?

He opened his eyes and studied her. God, she was beautiful. In the light of the lantern hanging from the ceiling of the carriage, the midnight blue of the entrancing gown emphasized the lovely ivory of her skin and intensified the blue shadings in the large gray eyes. The cut of the bodice, even with her lace shawl, gave more than a little hint of perfect breasts straining against the soft fabric. The flame in her dark hair was alive in the flickering light, as curls, caught in the back by a pearl clasp, tumbled around the enchanting face. His eyes, made cold by sheer strength of will, saw her hands clenching and unclenching with…with what. Distress? Fear? Regret?

Reese finally spoke, but his voice was emotionless. "Would it be presumptuous to ask my destination?" He directed his question at Samara. He was not going to let her off lightly.

But it was the brother on the right who answered. "Yes," he growled. "It would."

But Reese continued to look at Samara, his eyes piercing and hard, demanding an answer. As he intended, she was defenseless against him. She could cope with his anger, or insults, indeed would welcome them, but this strangely contained Reese was another matter completely. He was more compelling than ever as his eyes bore into her, undressing her emotions as well as her body. She trembled before the merciless onslaught.

"H-home," she finally said in a small voice.

A familiar arching of a rakish eyebrow commanded her to continue.

"Samara…you don't have to." Again it was the angry young brother.

"No, Conn," she said, her voice stronger. "He has a right to know." She met Reese's eyes now, and the old spirit was back. There was apology and unhappiness but also a firm conviction.

"I'm sorry, Captain Hampton," she said. "I did the best I could. I couldn't *not* say anything...not when you had heard so much at the ball; Emily said you were a shipper, and there was so much talk about when ships were leaving. And how." Samara's voice faltered. "And I...I...I couldn't inform on you, not to the authorities. Not even if you did plan to betray us."

Reese's arrogant features twisted with confusion. "Betray?"

"In Bermuda. You obviously intended us to walk into a trap...why else would you leave the ship unguarded?" she answered quite logically, completely misinterpreting the shock in his eyes for guilt.

A small smile curled Reese's lips. "Why indeed?" he agreed smoothly. He was not going to explain his actions or motives, even if they would be believed. Which, he knew, they would not. Without Brendan, why should they? They would just think he was trying to extricate himself from a very ticklish situation.

He looked at her with real curiosity. "Then why, *Miss* O'Neill, didn't you just expose me? Why go to all this trouble?"

Samara's face clouded. "You *did* keep Brendan from prison."

"No other reason?" he taunted now, as he disregarded the tensing body of the hostile brother. "After all, you apparently think I did that just to trap him later. Rather inconsistent of you."

Samara's eyes were full of confusion. Her hands knotted. "I don't want you to hang," she said now. Quietly, wretchedly.

"Very comforting, Miss O'Neill," Reese replied. "So may I ask what in the hell I'm doing here? And what do you have planned instead?" There was a decided edge in his voice.

"That's enough, Hampton," the brother on Reese's right said.

Reese completely disregarded him as he addressed his next

question to Samara alone. "And who, pray, are your fellow kidnappers?"

"My brothers," she said in a low voice. "Conn and Marion."

"Are there any more like you at home?" Reese asked with obvious sarcasm.

Marion spoke up now, wanting to prevent another explosion from his brother. He had listened with a great deal of interest. The sparks flying between Samara and Hampton suggested something much stronger than antagonism alone.

"Only one," he said with gentle amusement. "Other than Brendan, of course."

Reese twisted in his direction, once again unaccountably drawn to the man. He reminded him of Brendan.

Marion withstood his examination with equanimity. He rarely held a grudge and certainly did not now, despite the aches and pain he still suffered from Reese's attack. He didn't blame the man one bit; he had simply reacted. He now understood Samara's unhappiness and apathy during the past year. Hampton, even trussed as he was, was a very forceful personality. Forceful and magnetic. Marion could see the effort both their prisoner and his sister made to deny the fierce attraction that so obviously passed between them. He sighed. There would be trouble at Glen Woods, no doubt about that. It had taken all of Samara's persuasion to keep Conn from unmasking the Englishman at the ball; his brother had finally agreed to this course only because he felt his father would side with him. Marion wasn't so sure. Their father despised the English, but he also was a very fair man. And he doted on Samara.

"It won't be long now," he said softly, "before we're at Glen Woods. I expect all your questions will be answered then."

Reese merely nodded and once more leaned back awkwardly against the seat, wincing at the sudden pain in his wrists.

Marion saw his expression, and with a slight touch to Reese's arm indicated he should turn slightly. Marion inspected the bonds, his supple fingers loosening the knot slightly, reducing the strain on Reese's wrists while still holding them firmly. He noted the rope burns with dismay, and knew the Englishman was experiencing real pain. He took off his neck cloth and, with the small knife he always carried, cut it into strips. He nudged the ropes on Reese's wrists upward, then wrapped a piece of cloth around the deep bloody depressions in the skin and let the rope drop back in place, around the cloth.

The Englishman said nothing as he moved back against the seat. His eyes were veiled, and only an unwilling movement of a jaw muscle and the barely leashed tension in his body indicated any emotion. They rode the rest of the way in silence.

When the coach rolled to a stop, the driver opened the door and assisted Samara in stepping down. Marion leaned down and cut the bonds around Hampton's ankles; the gun was back in Conn's hand.

Reese stretched his legs, trying to work out the cramps before attempting to stand. He had no idea of the time and could only guess that it was in the early morning hours. Refusing to heed Conn's impatient looks or the jabs in his side, he almost lazily moved his legs, feeling sensation creeping back into them. He had no intention of taking a fall from the carriage for their amusement. When he was finally ready, he stood at the door and looked out. They were at the wide steps of an imposing home. In the light of the moon, he studied the house. It was small by Beddingfield's standards but quite handsome compared to others he had seen in the Carolinas. There was a certain warmth and dignity in the pink glow of the brick and the hundreds of roses that climbed the wide porch. He carefully descended the two steps, moving awkwardly on stiff legs, his usual grace replaced by iron determination.

He was pushed, and his bottled-up anger exploded. He shoved back and Conn, caught unaware, stumbled and fell, the pistol sliding along the ground. The house had been dark, but now faint flickering lights appeared in the windows. Samara and her brothers had not been expected home tonight.

Before Reese could make any further move, several servants came out of the house, and Marion had him firmly in tow. Conn rose, dusted himself off and glared at Hampton.

"I don't like being shoved," Reese said, fury in every word. This evening had been full of indignities, and he was damned if he was going to calmly accept any more.

Conn made a move toward him, but Marion intercepted him. "Go up the stairs," he told Reese, "to the drawing room on the left."

Reese nodded. He mounted the steps with Marion behind him, walked past the astonished servants in the doorway and, with only a moment's hesitation, entered the darkened drawing room. In seconds, servants had lighted the candles, which cast a golden glow over the richly furnished room. After a nod from Marion, the servants disappeared, and the four regarded each other warily.

"What in the hell is going on?"

Reese turned towards the door. The speaker, garbed only in a dressing robe, was nonetheless imposing. He was nearly as tall as Reese, with cool appraising gray eyes that missed little. They thoroughly inspected Reese, quickly noting the arrogant set of his head, the unusually handsome features, the well-fitting clothes on his strongly muscled body. He could not see Reese's bound hands, and he stepped forward, his hand outstretched.

"Sir?"

Reese bowed with no little mockery. "I regret," he said slowly, "that I seem unable, at the moment, to return your courtesy." He turned slightly, showing his bound wrists.

Connor O'Neill's eyes narrowed as they moved from Conn to Marion to Samara, all of whom wore apprehensive expressions. Now they were here, they did not quite know how to explain the situation. Conn looked at Marion. Marion looked at Samara, and Samara looked at the floor.

In the absence of explanation, Connor's humor surfaced. "I know," Connor said finally, a glint of amusement in his voice, "that I've been wanting you to bring a young man home, Samara, but I didn't mean for you to go to this extreme."

Despite the seriousness of his situation, Reese couldn't suppress a smile as Samara's face crimsoned.

"Papa!" she said in complete mortification.

Connor stared at her for a moment, then turned back to the man standing so nonchalantly in his drawing room with his hands tied behind him.

"Since my children seem reluctant to explain, perhaps you would be so kind," he said, his eyes questioning each of his three offspring.

"I seem to be kidnapped," Reese said easily, his anger momentarily lulled by the whole farcical situation.

The older O'Neill now fixed all his attention on Reese. "I rather guessed that," he said drily. "I assume there's a reason."

"He's a spy, Papa." Conn finally found his voice. "He's an English spy."

Connor turned to his guest/prisoner. "Are you?"

Reese sighed. "I'm afraid so." There was really nothing to be gained by denying it.

Bewilderment flashed in Connor's eyes at the frank admission. He turned to his sons. "Why in the devil, then, did you bring him here?"

Both Conn and Marion looked at Samara.

"Samara?" Connor questioned. "Would you like to tell me exactly why you are bringing me an English spy in the middle of the night?"

Once more, Reese had difficulty in suppressing a smile, particularly when he saw Samara's discomfort. In any other situation, he supposed he would like the elder O'Neill.

"He's Captain Hampton, father," Samara said slowly.

O'Neill turned back to Reese, and this time his examination was much more thorough. He had heard the damn man's name more times than he wished to remember. Brendan had mentioned him with respect, and even liking, despite all that had happened. And Samara...Samara hadn't been the same in the year since that ill-fated voyage. He had not missed her wistful looks nor the tears that sometimes filled her eyes without apparent reason. "What do you expect me to do with him?" he asked his daughter. "Other than, of course, what you should have done in the beginning...turn him over to the military?" He observed the sudden tension in Hampton's body.

"You can't, Papa," Samara said. "They will hang him."

"Probably," O'Neill said. "That's what they usually do to spies."

"But he's not, not really. He's a sea captain..."

O'Neill turned back to Reese and eyed him carefully. He was both intrigued and impressed with the man's composure. Except for almost imperceptible tautness in his posture, nothing about his face or manner indicated any worry. There was no appeal, no excuses. He simply stood there as if he owned the world. "Exactly what are you, Hampton?"

Reese shrugged. "My ship was wrecked near the coast. I was trying to get back to Bermuda or England."

Conn's voice cut in. "Then what were you doing at the party, posing as a shipper, asking about shipping schedules?"

Connor O'Neill's questioning eyes also demanded an explanation.

Reese remained silent. How could he explain without exposing Samuels as a traitor? And no matter how much he resented the man for getting him into this, he couldn't do that.

Realizing he would receive no answer, Connor pondered his alternatives, liking none of them. He needed time to think. "It's late," he said. "Too late to make any decisions now...or any sense out of this whole thing." He looked at Reese. "The only secure place on Glen Woods is the storehouse; I'm afraid you'll have to spend the night there." He disappeared for a moment and returned with a set of keys, which he handed to Marion. "And you, young lady," he turned to Samara, "will go to bed now. You can expect a long overdue conversation in the morning."

Samara started to leave but stopped at the sound of Reese's voice. She turned and saw the slow mocking bow.

"It's been very...instructional seeing you again, Miss Samara," he said, "and meeting the rest of your...charming family." When he straightened, his eyes were glacial green, and she knew from his expression he would not forgive lightly.

Connor watched his daughter flinch with every sarcastic word, and he struggled to control his anger. He couldn't miss the anguish on her face as she took one backward look before slowly, reluctantly, disappearing through the door. Samara had proclaimed the man the worst kind of scoundrel in the past months, and now she was acting like a lovesick puppy. He regarded Hampton as he would a leper.

Curtly, he nodded to Hampton. "I won't insult you by bidding you good night. In fact, I hope you have every bit as poor a night as I suspect I will." He turned on his heel and left.

"Captain Hampton," Marion said in his usual quiet voice, "you will accompany us." Conn, for once, was quiet, his truculent mood quelled by his father's disapproval.

As Reese was led to the small storehouse, his searching eyes noted the thick iron grill on the one window. The door was unlocked, and Marion went inside, lighting a small candle lamp which hung on a peg in the interior. He motioned Reese inside. As Conn held his all-too-familiar gun, Marion cut the ropes around the Englishman's wrists and stepped outside. With an apologetic glance, he closed the door, leaving Reese alone.

Reese heard the grating of the key in the lock as he rubbed his sore wrists, trying to restore the circulation. He then studied the room. The flickering light from the candle showed it to be half full of barrels and boxes. He was able to open the shutters at the window, but when he tried the iron grill, he found it well anchored. Discouraged, he slid down in a corner, cursing the perfidy of women and wondered what in the hell he would do now.

Chapter Thirteen

Samantha had barely stirred when Connor left the bed. She had been up nearly the entire night with the mare which had finally given birth to a colt, and the emotional and physical strain had taken its toll. She reached for Connor, and her hand found only emptiness. In the sudden fear that sometimes strikes the half awake, she sat upright—just as the bedroom door opened and Connor entered. The candle in his hand revealed a deeply troubled face.

"Connor? What is it?"

"It's nothing, Sam. Go back to sleep."

Samantha knew from his tone and the use of her shortened name that something *was* wrong. He rarely used it any more. Now with the renewed hostilities with England, it seemed to bring back painful memories.

Her voice trembled. "Is it one of the children?"

He went over to her, putting his arm around her shoulder and holding her tightly. "The children are fine."

"They're home? I thought they were staying...there *is* something wrong!"

Connor grimaced. Samantha was now wide awake, and there was no way of avoiding an explanation. He had hoped to put it off until morning, until he had time to think. Samantha was going to be most aggrieved that she had missed the little drama downstairs, and only the Lord knew what she would do. Even after thirty-four years he sure as hell didn't.

"Samara?" Samantha was insistent.

"*Your* children, madam," he said finally, "brought home an English spy...all neatly tied in one angry package. And I'll be damned if I know what to do with him...or what they want me to do. They just dropped him in the drawing room as easily as they would bring in a neighbor." His voice rose as his outrage increased with every passing second.

Samantha looked at him as if he had lost his wits. "A spy?"

"Hampton," he said wearily, as if that explained everything.

"Hampton...Samara's captain?"

Now Connor returned her incredulous look. "Samara's...? He's certainly not Samara's anything."

But his wife was no longer paying any attention. There was a very strange look on her face. If he didn't know better, he would almost think it glee.

"Captain Hampton," she whispered. "But how?"

"He was masquerading as a shipper or some damn thing, apparently gathering information about ship locations and cargoes. Said his ship had been sunk which, of course, we knew. He never did explain what he was doing at the Fontaine plantation."

"Where is he now?" Her question was soft, belying the intense interest in her sparkling blue eyes.

"In the storehouse...until I can decide what to do with him. Though there's nothing to do but give him to the military."

"What did you think of him?" Samantha held her breath while Connor searched for an answer.

"He's arrogant...he all but dared me to turn him over to the authorities." Connor paused. "He even seemed amused by it all, though angry." A little twinkle came into his eyes. "He said it was 'instructional' to meet Samara's 'charming' family. That after being trussed up like a turkey half the night."

Samantha was out of bed, pulling on the pair of breeches and shirt she had worn earlier in the barn. "I want to meet him."

"In the morning," he said in a soothing voice.

"Now…and besides, how could you put him in the storehouse with no mattress…or food…or water or anything? What will he think?"

"What will *he* think?" came Connor's outraged bellow. "He's a spy, by thunder. He stood there and admitted it. And it's a damn sight better than a prison cell, where," he added with a warning, "he'll be tomorrow."

"Perhaps," she answered obliquely. "But tonight he's going to be comfortable."

Connor uttered an exasperated oath, but he knew he might as well try to stop a cannonball with a pillow. "I'll go with you."

"No," she replied. "You'll just get angry. I'll take Caesar and Marcus. I need them anyway to carry some things."

"They're not to leave you alone with him."

"No, sir," she replied, her lips twitching with impertinence.

"I don't like it. He's dangerous."

"We owe him, Connor," she said quietly. "He could have harmed both Samara and Brendan, and he chose not to do so. In fact, according to Bren, he lied to his own navy to keep our son and his crew safe."

"He put them in that position in the beginning," Connor said angrily. "If he hadn't attacked the *Samara*, they wouldn't have been in danger."

"Nevertheless, Bren got his ship back, and I've always thought it strange that he was able to do so."

Connor glared at her. "What do you mean?"

"Did Captain Hampton strike you as a careless man?"

"He certainly seemed so tonight."

"Perhaps," she said with finality. "But I think Caesar and Marcus are protection enough."

She didn't give him any more time to reply. She was out the door, waking the servants and issuing instructions, leaving Connor fuming. Regardless of what she said, he intended to be within rescue distance. He took off his dressing gown and started pulling on clothes.

Samara reluctantly pulled on a nightdress and blew out the candle in her room. But she knew she wouldn't sleep this night. Instead, she went to the window seat and stood there, staring down at the storehouse with its lighted window. She could see shadows of a figure pacing restlessly, and she felt consumed by guilt. He had trusted her and she had betrayed him. During those first few seconds at the cypress, his eyes had been warm and admiring, his face without mockery, his mouth inviting... It was all her dreams of the past year. And they had been shattered.

She had never seen a face change so quickly, eyes move so rapidly from hot fire to frigid fury as he realized what she had done. And from his icy comments in the coach, she knew he thought she had signed his death warrant.

But she *hadn't*. She *couldn't have*. She had only wanted to stop him from revealing what he had learned that night. Her father wouldn't let him hang. Samara shivered as she remembered Connor O'Neill's words in the library. "That's what usually happens to spies." What in God's name had she done?

"*You had to,*" came the tiny whispered voice within her. "*It was your duty. Remember Bren had just left. It might have meant his life.*

"*He wouldn't have...*"

"*You don't know that...you don't really know him at all.*"

"*I know I don't want him to die...*" Tears slid down her face as complete misery swamped her. She continued to watch the pacing man below, sensing his frustration, knowing his rage. He had shown it clearly in the coach.

I have to do something. Samara closed her eyes, trying to think. If only Bren were here...he would know what do do. But he isn't. Mother. She'll understand. She won't let father turn Captain Hampton over to hang. Her mother could always make father see her side...eventually. But would it be too late?

"I'll have to do something myself." The sound of her words echoed in the room. She had been unaware she had said them aloud. But now she heard them and they gave her courage. With the same diligence she had planned the capture of Captain Reese Hampton hours ago, she now schemed to rescue him. Of course, he would have to promise that all he had learned would be forgotten.

Step one...she would have to steal the keys to the storehouse.

Unaware that he was the principal figure in so many thoughts and schemes, Reese prowled the small room, searching for a way out. The room was hot and stuffy, and he had discarded his coat and waistcoat. His white lawn shirt was open at the throat and chest, displaying bronze skin and golden hair. He had ripped off half a sleeve to staunch the flow of blood from a jagged cut in his hand. He cursed softly as he studied both his injured wrists and his newest wound. He had torn a board from one of the boxes and tried to use it to loosen the grill. It had slipped, and a splintered edge tore though his skin and muscle. How many more things could go wrong? It had all started with Samara so many months ago. Bloody little witch. Bloody damn family. This time he included Brendan. He would flinch forever more at the name O'Neill. If he lived long enough.

He heard noises at the door, the sound of a key in a lock. Locating the board he had discarded, he gripped it in his hands, unmindful now of the pain. He stepped back behind the door. Right now, he didn't care who he hit; he just felt the enormous need to strike back.

Filled with curiosity, Samantha was the first through the door, much to the dismay of Caesar who was burdened with food and a bottle of wine, and Marcus who was carrying a mattress.

She suddenly tensed, all her old instincts returning, and ducked as a board came down towards her. Just as she knew it was about to reach her, it stopped in midair and she wondered at the strength and control it took to stop such a swing. She turned and faced her would-be attacker.

The two stood there, staring at each other with equal amazement.

Just as Samara had a year ago, Samantha was stunned by

the man's height and sheer magnetism. His open shirt and tight
trousers displayed a lean, well-muscled body as he towered
above her, his thick, tawny hair sprinkled with gold in the
candlelight. Furious, shimmering aqua eyes glowered at her,
and power emanated from the now stiff figure, his hand tightening around his makeshift weapon as he reluctantly lowered
it. She now completely understood Samara's bewildering behavior of the past months. Captain Hampton would frighten,
charm and fascinate any woman, much less one as inexperienced as Samara.

As for Reese, he found himself facing an older version of
Samara except for the eyes. His unexpected visitor was truly
beautiful, with lively blue eyes that now challenged him with
unspoken questions. She wore her black hair in a braid, and
her slender body was clothed in men's trousers and shirt. He
had never seen such clothing on a woman, and now regretted
it. The masculine attire showed every soft curve. He tried to
estimate her age, but could not; her face was firm, but there
were little laugh lines at the corners of her eyes. And there
was a maturity and confidence that came only with years—
and happiness. He dropped the board, and his grim mouth
curved into a rueful smile.

"Another O'Neill, I presume. I'm beginning to think there
is no end to them."

Her smile in the faltering candlelight brightened the dim
interior with another kind of light. "I'm Samantha O'Neill,
Brendan's and Samara's mother—and, I'm afraid, also of your
other abductors."

It seemed impossible that this woman was old enough to be
Brendan's mother. He wondered idly whether Samara would
be this striking thirty years from now. His amusement at the
absurdity of the moment asserted itself although there was a
bitter edge to it.

"Welcome to my humble abode," he said, his lips twisting
with irony. "And to what do I owe the honor of *this* particular
visit?"

"I wanted to meet you," Samantha said frankly. "You
seem to have turned my family upside down."

He laughed then, his cold eyes warming ever so slightly. "No less than they have done to me, I assure you," he answered. "I rue the day I spied your son's ship."

Samantha moved then, allowing the door to open. Caesar and Marcus, their dark faces creased with concern, moved protectively around Samantha, each holding their bundles.

"I brought a few items to make your...stay more comfortable. I apologize for my husband's lack of hospitality."

Feeling almost as if he were in a madhouse, Reese watched as a mattress was carefully laid on the dirty floor, and a small table placed beside it. It was quickly covered with food, a bottle of wine and silver goblets.

"Forgive me," he said "if I don't quite understand."

Samantha's eyes twinkled at his confusion. "Whether my husband admits it or not, I think we owe a great deal to you. I will see that the debt is repaid."

One of Reese's eyebrows rose in question, and Samantha was suddenly grateful that she loved Connor so thoroughly. This man could break hearts as easily as...as birds sang.

Her searching eyes found his hand, and the bloody rag around it. She held out her own to him. "Let me see it," she commanded, and Reese surprised himself by obediently giving it to her. She gently unwrapped the ragged cut, frowned, and turned to Caesar. "Get me some water, bandages and brandy."

Caesar continued to stand there. "I can't, Miz Samantha. Mr. Connor say to stay wi' you, not to let you out of my seein."

Samantha turned to the tall Englishman. "You aren't going to ravish or kill me, are you?"

A glint of amusement lightened his blue-green eyes. "I might be sorely tempted on the first," he said in a dry tone, "but I'll try to restrain myself."

"You see, Caesar," she said with a wide smile. "I am quite safe. Besides, you can leave Marcus if you wish. Now go."

"But Mister Connor..."

"I will take care of my husband."

With a frown of great disapproval, Caesar left, leaving Marcus with his hands folded, a protective look on his face.

"You look as though you need a glass of wine," Samantha said, enjoying the confusion their reluctant guest was obviously feeling.

"And Samara told me she was an orphan!" he said now, the humor returning to his face. "I still haven't quite figured out how many brothers she does have."

Samantha was enchanted once more. How quickly his moods changed, how completely engaging he could be when he lowered his guard.

"Four...Brendan's the oldest, then Jere, you haven't met him yet, and Conn and Marion. I'm afraid they've spoiled Samara...we all have." She caught just a slight tightening of his jaw and the glint in his eye. So there was some interest on his part. She wondered how much. She decided to pry, and the best way to get information, she had learned from experience, was to attack frontally.

"Why wouldn't you let Brendan tell anyone you helped him reclaim the *Samara*?" It was a guess on her part, but she knew instantly she was correct. A muscle throbbed in his cheek, and his eyes turned wary.

"I did nothing."

"By doing nothing," she probed further, "you did something. That ship meant the world to Brendan. I thank you."

"Did he—?"

"No. It was what he didn't say." She was sure now.

"You are wrong, madam," he said coldly. "I did nothing, I meant nothing. He was my enemy...as I am yours."

"I think not," she replied, "but I won't debate with you. I suppose you have your own reasons."

He turned away from her, his stance rigid. Even he didn't know why he denied his very small assistance. Perhaps it was pride, the refusal to say something which could be construed as begging, or even bargaining. Perhaps he didn't want to acknowledge that he had indeed helped an enemy of his country. He turned and took the bottle of wine, deftly opening it with his left hand. He looked at Samantha O'Neill in question, but she shook her head. Reese poured himself a glass and emptied the contents in one long swallow before pouring another. He knew she was watching him carefully and, quite casually, without further acknowledgement of her presence, he downed another glass. When he finished, his eyes challenged hers. "Apparently you don't have the same fondness for wine as your daughter."

Samantha laughed. Samara had, red-faced, told her something of that dinner. "I think, by now, I've found more judicious uses for it." She liked Reese Hampton more each moment. If her husband would only give him a chance, she knew they would be friends. They had much in common, including a wry sense of humor.

"What were you doing at the Fontaine party?" she said now, back on the attack. "Didn't you know Samara might be there?"

The question surprised him. Now as he considered it, he wondered if perhaps he did. Perhaps unconsciously he was even hoping she would be present. But he couldn't admit that. Not to the woman in front of him, nor himself.

"South Carolina is a big state," he said, instead. "And I knew Brendan had already sailed. Since I thought, quite erroneously it seems, that she was *Mrs.* O'Neill I doubted she would attend a party without him…if she hadn't stowed away again." Once more, a hint of humor emerged in his voice. "But then I should have expected the unexpected. Samara *is* rather unpredictable." The last words were caustic, and the humor was gone, replaced by something which could be interpreted only as raw hurt.

Samantha's heart caught. There *was* feeling there, a great deal, even if he was making a great effort to conceal it.

"Samara did what she thought she had to do," her mother said gently. "I don't think she realized there might be dire results… She always believes everything turns out for the best."

"Including my hanging," Reese said bitterly. "I trusted…" He stopped suddenly. What was it about Samantha O'Neill that made him say so much more than he intended? He turned away.

"I can promise you that won't happen," she said softly. "I won't let it."

Before he could answer, Caesar returned with the bandages, his face creased with anxiety. Quiet disapproval was evident in his every movement.

"Wait outside," Samantha said. "Both you and Marcus."

"Miz Samantha—"

"Please, Caesar."

Reese's deep voice cut in. "I think he should stay, Mrs. O'Neill...I'm a dangerous spy, remember." His voice was as icy as it had been earlier, and Samantha knew she had lost what small progress she had made in gaining his trust. He apparently was regretting those few unguarded moments.

She nodded, knowing she would get no further tonight. Instead she quickly cleaned his cut, pouring brandy on the open wound. He didn't even wince as the alcohol touched the skin, and she smiled at his iron control. He simply stood there stiffly, barely acknowledging her ministrations, and that only with slight tolerance. Samantha felt a sudden fear for her daughter. Reese Hampton was an extremely complex man. Complex and dangerous and very compelling. Could any woman possibly harness that strength and energy? He was like Connor in some ways—in his pride, in his indifference to pain, in his rugged independence—but did he have Connor's gentleness? And honor? She suspected it was there, lurking behind his cynicism. But what if she were wrong...?

After he left, Reese poured himself another glass of wine and blew out the candle. He sat on the mattress, his back against the wall. The night was at its deepest; the time just before the first rays of a new day penetrated the blackness. He was angry, more at himself than anyone else. He had never before betrayed feelings as he had tonight, and he damned himself for it.

Connor watched as his wife and the two servants returned to the house; he was ready to slip away himself when he saw another shadowy form approach the storehouse. The outbuilding was fast becoming the most popular place in the Carolinas, Connor thought ruefully. It was a disconcerting observation.

He identified Samara almost immediately and debated with himself as she crept toward the window. He could stop her now, or wait and see what would happen next. Remembering the pain in her face earlier, his heart ached for her and Connor decided to wait. Perhaps she needed a few private words with the man. The night was lost anyway. Would his life…would his family's life ever get back to normal? He leaned against a tree and watched…

"Captain Hampton…"

Reese had just closed his eyes when he heard the soft words. He opened them slowly, unable to see in the darkness. But he knew the voice and he immediately felt the electricity that was always there between them.

His anger exploded. "Get the hell away from here."

"Captain Hampton…Reese…I have the key."

He didn't move. "You're a little late. I wouldn't trust you again…ever. God knows what awaits me this time."

Her voice shook. "Please…I'll let you go if you promise you won't say anything about what you heard last night."

"No promises, little cat. Now leave me in peace. I don't think your father would approve." Each word was arctic.

Samara couldn't see his eyes but she knew they were probably just as frozen. Her voice shook as she tried again. Nothing was working as it should. Nothing was happening as she intended. "Please…you have to leave…please promise me…"

He stood lazily now, his eyes adjusting to the darkness. He went to the grill. "Do I detect a note of concern?"

"You have to go," she whispered desperately. "You have to promise…please…"

Reese didn't want to take her help. But he knew immediately his obstinacy was self-defeating. Regardless of what her mother had said, he very likely *would* see the inside of a prison if he weren't fitted with a rope halter. Neither was an attractive prospect.

"You win," he said, not trying to hide the bitterness. He

turned away from her tentative smile towards the door, waiting
to hear the key in the lock. God, what a night.

But when the door opened, Samara was not alone. Walking
soundlessly behind her was her father, and the older man could
not disguise his anger.

Reese knew he should have expected it. After all that had
happened, he was the worst kind of fool to believe his fortune
had changed. He and Connor stared at each other with open
hostility as Samara, suddenly aware of another presence,
turned and saw her father.

Samara stepped back, almost into Reese's arms. She had
never seen such censure in her father's eyes. Her face crumpled. "Let him go, Father," she said. "Please."

"It's too late," O'Neill said. "You should have thought
about the consequences last night. Life is not a game, Samara.
I wonder if you understand that yet."

Samara bit her lip at the sharp rebuke, but her chin jutted
out defiantly. She was determined that nothing would happen
to Reese. "I just didn't want...he promised he wouldn't say
anything..."

"Did he now? You've been telling me for the past months
that he's a blackguard and a pirate. How can you trust him
now?" Connor was immensely angry. He had been prepared
to let Samara talk to their prisoner through the window. He
had not considered the possibility that she would try to free
him. It meant, he knew, that there was much more between
the two than he had first understood. He completely disregarded Reese's stiffening form as father and daughter discussed him as though he weren't there.

"Damn you both," Reese snarled in a low enraged voice.
"I don't care what you do...just grant me the slight courtesy
of a little peace." He turned on Samara. "And I don't need,
or want, your damned pity or help or anything else...except
perhaps to see the last of you." His eyes blazing with green
fire, he turned back into the storeroom, slamming the door
behind him.

Connor stared at the door, dismayed by his own mishan-
dling of the situation. Hampton's angry contempt, he feared,

was only too justified. Sighing heavily, he knew his own prejudice had colored his judgement. He would try to find a solution tomorrow...some way.

Connor relocked the door, and put his arm around Samara's shoulder. "Let's go to bed, little one. And don't worry. No harm will come to your Englishman."

Samara looked up at him, tears swelling in her eyes. "He's not mine, and after tonight, I doubt he ever could be."

It was as close as she had come to admitting her feelings for Reese Hampton, and Connor hurt for her. He remembered the agony he and Samantha had gone through, and he had always wanted to save Samara that pain. He wondered now if it were possible.

Reese tried to sleep; he knew he needed all his wits about him. It was all but impossible. In addition to the sounds of an awakening plantation, he was besieged by a pounding anger. He finally gave up any attempt at rest, finding it hopeless. He was tired and depressed and filled with an unfamiliar dread. He wanted some cold water to wash, but all that remained of Samantha O'Neill's bounty was tepid blood-stained water. The wine was gone, the dregs consumed quickly in the aftermath of Samara's attempted rescue. The very thought of the aborted plan made him wince. Poor Samara. All her rescue efforts seemed doomed to disaster: first, her brother, then himself. Unfortunately, her talents were apparently restricted to successful kidnappings.

As he had done the night before, he paced the floor before finally stopping at the grilled window and staring at the house across the way. In frustration, his hands clenched the ornamental iron work that so completely penned him. And he wondered if his fate was being decided.

"I say we turn him over to Colonel Miller," Conn said, referring to the the local militia commander.

"No," Samantha said quietly, her eyes on Samara's pale face. Her daughter had been unusually quiet, and she wondered if it had anything to do with the long discussion between father and daughter this morning. For one of the few times in his life, Connor had expressly prohibited Samantha from the room, and from the discussion. He had said nothing afterward, but had called a meeting of the family. Caesar had gone to fetch Jere.

When Jere arrived, he studied the room in astonishment. His sister was near tears, his mother was uncommonly solemn, his father looked badly troubled, Conn was furious and Marion...who ever knew what he thought?

His father quickly explained all that had happened and outlined the options. Jere was included because one of the choices would endanger him. "If we keep him here, allow him to stay as a guest, we could all be charged with harboring an enemy.

"Samara?" Jere, a gentle caretaker of the land, looked at his sister. "Bren isn't here, so we have to depend on you. You know this Hampton. Will he keep his word?"

"If he gives it," she whispered, not at all sure he would.

"Mother?"

"Brendan liked him...admired him...and you know your brother is seldom wrong about people. I like him."

Conn couldn't be still. "I don't care if he's the most charming man in England, he's still a damn spy...and it's our duty to turn him over."

Only Samantha saw Samara's and her father's eyes meet, and she knew the decision had already been made. Connor was only going through the motions, trying by patient persuasion for common agreement and support, particularly from Conn. Samantha slipped out the door and told Caesar to take the Englishman some fresh water and food. When she returned, the argument was continuing. Conn rebelliously brushed aside any proposal other than his own.

It was Samara who finally settled things. Her lips trembling, her eyes glistening with tears, she finally turned towards Conn, the brother closest to her in age and in thought. "I will leave this house if he hangs. I will never speak to you again. He was...decent...and fair to Bren and me...more than I was to him last night."

From anyone but Samara, Conn would have considered the

words mere bravado, but he knew Samara. And for the first time, he allowed himself to consider the depth of emotion that must have prompted them. It did not make him feel more charitable towards their troublesome prisoner.

"Samara…you yourself called him a rogue and other names I won't repeat."

"I was angry…and confused…but I knew…I always knew he wouldn't harm me. From the first I knew that. And he and Bren *were* friends. I resented that, but they were. Bren would never forgive you if you do what you propose."

Conn looked around, but his eyes admitted defeat. He finally shrugged. "Do what you want…but I won't be taken in by him…like the rest of you. I want to be almighty sure he doesn't go any place until what he knows is too old to do anyone any good."

"Are you volunteering?" his father asked with a slight smile.

"Good God, no. I'm not going to be a nursemaid to a…"

Connor interrupted before his son could say more. There had been sufficient profanity in front of Samara. "He may not even agree to our terms," he said softly. "Our Captain Hampton may settle matters all on his own." He did not look at Samara; he did not want to see misery in eyes so like his own. "It's agreed, then," he said, and one by one the others nodded.

Reese washed his face and hands in the fresh water brought to him by one of the same servants who had accompanied Samantha O'Neill the previous night. The man offered to shave him, apparently unwilling to trust the suspicious stranger with a sharp-edged instrument. Reese nodded and sat on the small table. His right hand was stiff and sore this morning, but he welcomed the pain. It seemed the only real thing in the past twenty-four hours. The rest was almost a dream. Or a nightmare.

After the servant had gone—he suspected a second stood guard outside—he tried to eat some of the food which came with the water. There were fresh eggs and ham and hot bread. He had no hunger, but ate anyway, knowing he needed his strength. He was almost finished when one of Samara's brothers appeared, the even-tempered one he had tumbled the night before. Reese had been too angry last night to determine who was who. He just remembered names. Conn, Marion, Jere. And Bren. Bren who was on his way to raid British shipping. Dear God, how did he ever get himself in this mess?

"My father wants to see you," the young man said.

Reese merely nodded. He would not be unhappy to leave this room, and he wanted to know what O'Neill had in mind. One way or another, it was better to know.

He accompanied the brother to the house, surprised that he was not bound or given a heavier guard. Marion took him to a room which was apparently the library; hundreds of books lined the walls.

Connor was already seated at the desk and quickly rose as Reese entered. The older O'Neill nodded to his son, who turned around and left, closing the door behind him.

The interview was peculiarly dispassionate, considering the heightened emotions of both men. Reese was wary, still very angry although now more at himself than anyone else. He had left his coat and waistcoat in the storehouse and wore only trousers, boots and his now very soiled and torn shirt.

It might have put other men at a disadvantage, Connor thought, but not this one. Hampton stood straight and tense, but with untouched pride and dignity. Only a slight movement of the man's jaw indicated that this meeting was anything but the most common of occurrences for him.

There was a leashed, almost animal power in his every movement, regardless of how slight; and his flickering blue-green eyes—now cold and hostile—would have daunted men less resolute than Connor O'Neill.

Resentful of the intense inspection, Reese spoke first. "I suppose I am here for a reason?"

Although softly spoken, the words carried a hard, unyielding edge, and Connor felt a surge of admiration. Hampton might be English, but, by all that was holy, he had courage—and an audacity that was surprisingly appealing. Despite his

tenuous position, the man showed no sign of defeat or surrender. Connor thought back to his talk with Samara this morning.
There was no question but that she was in love with Hampton,
and she would never forgive any of them if he came to harm
at her family's hands. His own tragic experience—the death
of his brother at the hands of Samantha's father—made him
realize only too well the explosiveness of the situation. He
could lose his daughter forever, as Robert Chatham had lost
Samantha. Even worse, his merry mischievous daughter would
be dead in spirit—if not in body. He *must* obtain the cooper-
ation of this man who now looked as if accommodation were
the last thing he would consider.

Studying the glowering eyes he started slowly, searching
for words that would not fuel the hostility that still hovered
between them. "You have two choices," he said, "and I doubt
you'll care for either one of them. But perhaps there's some
comfort in the fact that I don't like them any better than you."

All of Reese's attention was now riveted on the man. Almost unconsciously, minutes earlier, he had let his eyes roam
over the extensive collection of books. Books said a lot about
a man, often revealing more than spoken words. He wanted
to know more of Connor O'Neill.

But now he was merely silent, waiting for O'Neill to continue.

"I can turn you over to the military authorities and do what
I can to mitigate the charges. I *do* have some little influence.
I might, just *might*, be able to save your neck, but most certainly you would go to prison and I doubt very much if you
would be included in any exchange."

Hampton's face didn't change as Connor, searching for a
reaction, paused. There was none, but Connor hadn't really
expected one. Even his eyes were veiled.

"Or," Connor continued, "You can accept the same offer
you made to my son. Your parole for the relative freedom of
Glen Woods. You will see no one other than my family; you
will contact no one. When Brendan returns, your information
will be useless, and he can take you where he will. In the
meantime you will be treated as a guest in this house, al-

though, for the protection of my family, a somewhat reclusive one. Servants will talk, and neighbors will probably know we have a visitor. To avoid explanations, we will say you are a distant relative in deep mourning for a deceased wife and wish to see no one. You will not leave this house without having one of us accompany you and still another knowing your whereabouts. That way, we can warn you if we have visitors.'' Connor turned and looked out the window, away from Reese's still impassive face, for several seconds before facing him again.

"And I want to know the name of the person helping you.''

For the first time since Connor started speaking, Reese replied. "No," he said simply.

"Not even if you hang for your silence?"

Reese shrugged with the same apparent indifference he had shown the night before, but his eyes lost their curtain and glittered with restoked anger, and his lips firmed in a tight, grim line.

"I didn't think so," Connor said finally. "But now we know a traitor exists and we'll find him." He went over to his desk and poured two glasses from a bottle of brandy sitting there. He offered one to Hampton who shook his head in refusal.

"My offer was not conditional on that information," Connor said.

"Wasn't it?" Reese said. "It sounded like it."

"I had to try."

Reese relaxed slightly. He considered the offer now for the first time. He hated being pushed into a corner and, in effect, surrendering his freedom. He didn't want to be obligated to Samara or any of the O'Neills; his pride had already taken a severe beating at their hands. But hanging was very final, and prison was no more attractive. He stated his one reservation. "I told my crew I would try to help them…I can't buy my freedom at the continued loss of theirs.''

Connor rubbed the back of his neck in frustration. "I have some friends in Washington," he said finally. "I'll see if I can't expedite their exchange. Now that the ship…and captain…are gone, it shouldn't be too great a problem.''

"Is that a promise?"

"Damn you, Hampton. You're in no position to make demands."

"Is it a promise?"

"Yes," Connor said, wondering whether admiration or aggravation was his dominant feeling at the moment.

"Perhaps, then, I *will* take that brandy," Reese said slowly. He knew he was accepting the terms. He really had no choice and at least he was winning something for his crew. As much as the situation galled him, it seemed he could do more for his crew in this manner than he could dead or in prison with them.

Connor smiled for the first time during the tense meeting. Without actually saying the words, Hampton had, in effect, just accepted the terms—however reluctantly.

Minutes later, Samantha appeared at the door and at Connor's nod visibly relaxed.

"I'll take you to your room," she said to Reese, disregarding the cool hostility in his eyes. "You can use Brendan's."

She led the way up a winding staircase, down a long hall to a closed door. When she opened it, Reese scanned the comfortable interior.

"A luxurious prison, indeed, Madam. The storehouse would have served as well…the result is the same."

Samantha ignored the icy comment. "You can use any of Brendan's clothes. They will be somewhat small, I think, but Angel should be able to alter them sufficiently to serve your immediate needs. Marion will get you some new clothes in Charleston."

"You will be repaid," Reese said stiffly.

Samantha nodded, knowing no other answer would be acceptable. "Marcus will prepare a bath. Dinner is at eight. You might want to rest until then; I think, after last night, most of us will."

She smiled, and Reese wondered at her composure. Nothing

seemed to startle or anger her. She was truly a most unusual woman. Before he could reply, she was gone.

Reese looked around the room slowly, taking in every detail. There were several guns, one an old musket, hanging on the wall. He reached for it, his fingers fondling the fine workmanship. Then they withdrew. He had given his word. Reese suddenly felt more a prisoner than if he were locked in a dungeon, for then, at least, he could try to escape.

He tried to decipher his feelings towards Samara. He wanted to hate her, to dismiss her from his life. But she had stolen a deep piece of him, and despite all that had happened he still wanted her with an intensity that astonished him. But he would not trust her again. Never again.

Chapter Fourteen

How could gray eyes shoot off so many sparks?

He had already seen them in so many moods—from misty wistfulness to thundercloud anger. But now she was furious, more furious than she had ever been, even during the worst of his teasing aboard the *Unicorn*.

Despite his almost feeble attempts to keep his eyes from hers, Reese could not. He was uncomfortably seated across from Samara at this very awkward dinner—his first meal with the O'Neill clan.

Reese had remained icy and withdrawn throughout much of dinner, and attempts to involve him in conversation failed miserably. Some of Samara's guilt turned to defensive indignation…and then outrage. She had expected him to be angry, but she thought he would come to understand that she had tried to protect everyone; that her motives, if not exactly her means, were pure and that she would never—never, ever—let him hang.

But Reese's resentment was fed by the irony of his position. That he had placed Brendan and Samara in this very situation a year ago didn't help. "Until you walk in another man's boots…" The words of one of his tutors, a religious man who had taught him Latin and Greek, echoed in his mind. He was walking in those boots now, and he didn't like the fit. And having the lovely little traitorous face across from him didn't improve his temper.

Even conversation among the family members was stilted—
for the first time in Samara's memory. There were few safe
topics. Talk of the war, which usually dominated mealtimes,
was avoided, both out of caution and courtesy.

In the uneasy silences, heightened by the raw electricity that
so obviously bound the English captain and Samara, any attempt at communication was quickly exhausted. No one at the
table, even the least perceptive, could mistake the strength of
the attraction—or the battle—between them.

They were all there, all the brothers except Brendan, as was
Jere's wife. Reese had them all firmly in his mind now—from
the still glowering Conn to the insouciant Marion and the ear-
nest Jere. Jere's wife, Judith, was very pretty in a gentle way
and she, more than any of the others, sought to defuse the
tension, asking about English fashions and weather. Her attempts at kindness brought the first smile from Reese, and
everyone at the table had a small sample of the considerable
Hampton charm. He took his angry eyes from Samara, and
they lightened with mischief as he discussed, most expertly,
the rising of the empire waist and the lowering of necklines.
Only the sudden twinkle in his eyes indicated he knew it was
not altogether suitable conversation, which was exactly why
he was pursuing it.

Samantha's lips twitched, and Connor's eyebrows quirked,
while Samara's own temper irrationally rose at every additional indication that Reese Hampton had in the past year paid
extremely close attention to women's attire and, Samara
thought bitterly, more likely to their lack of it.

When Reese finished his discourse, he sat back and his eyes
returned to Samara. He grinned at her outraged expression and
felt the first satisfaction since his abduction. It was quickly
squelched when he heard her mother's words.

"Samara will show you the plantation tomorrow," she said
easily, ignoring the immediate tension in both her daughter
and Hampton. "You should become familiar with the boundaries."

The muscles in Reese's jaw flexed with ire. If he was going

to have a guard, by God, the last person he wanted was Samara. "I would prefer someone else," he said evenly.

"I'm sorry," Samantha said gently. "Marion is returning to Charleston, Jere is needed at Chatham Oaks, and my husband will be busy on the plantation. There is no one else, other than Conn, and I doubt he would be agreeable company. You can, of course, stay in the house if you prefer."

Reese knew he would probably go quite mad if he had to stay inside. He nodded curtly.

Marion, amused at his mother's quite obvious ploy, smiled and changed the subject. "Do you have an interest in horses, Captain Hampton?"

"My family raises them," Reese replied with a scowl.

Undaunted, Marion continued. "Then I think you'll be most interested in mother's horses. They're extraordinary. I'll take you to the stables after dinner if you like."

The opportunity to escape the house, and Samara, and most of the confounded O'Neills was appealing. He nodded his head in agreement.

"You will excuse us?" Marion said several minutes later after dessert was finished. Silence had, once more, fallen on the table. At his father's assent, he and Reese rose and made for the door.

The two men said nothing as they walked across the lawn to the stables. Once inside, Reese was indeed intrigued by Samantha's golden horses, especially Sunswept, a large, sleek, beautifully colored stallion.

"I've never seen such a color," Reese said in admiration as he reached to touch the shoulder, then the neck. The horse tolerated Reese's touch, but arched its head arrogantly as if to display its superiority.

"He usually won't let anyone touch him but Mother," Marion said.

As Reese nodded at the backhanded compliment, Marion switched abruptly to another topic. "I understand Mother visited you last night."

The Englishman nodded warily.

Marion grinned. "And Samara and Father, and I don't even

want to guess about others. All after being kidnapped at a ball. You must think us a gaggle of lunatics.''

Reese couldn't restrain a smile of his own. "Something like that.'' For the first time, there was no anger in his words. The two men looked at each other and chuckled, then laughed. Reese could feel the resentment draining away from him.

"Did Samara tell you anything about Mother?''

"Your sister told me she was an orphan,'' Reese complained with a wry smile, his humor somewhat restored. "It was a very tragic tale.''

"The real story was tragic enough,'' Marion said soberly. "Mother's father was a Tory. He killed her fiancé—who was Father's brother—the day they were to be married. So Mother, who was apparently as impetuous as Samara is now, ran away and joined General Marion, taking only a golden horse with her...this fellow's ancestress. She rode with him nearly two years; it was then she fell in love with Father, who was a major with General Marion.'' He paused, then continued thoughtfully. "It's a history we've lived with—Brendan, Conn, Jere and Samara. Perhaps Samara's been most affected by it, since she feels she must live up to Mother. And Mother—she's always been as independent as her horses. Father says he could never tame either of them, but then I don't think he really ever wanted to.''

He was quiet for a moment, then added in a low tone, "Samara's much like Mother, but she's always been protected...perhaps too much. She believes things will always turn out for the best, because they always have. She wished no harm to you, Hampton. She fought for you last night and this morning like a little wildcat. She even said she would leave and never come back if anything happened to you. And she meant it. That's the reason Conn backed down.''

Silence settled between the two men. Reese was reluctant to let go of his anger because it was the only thing that protected him from the little enchantress and all she represented. Commitment. Bonds. Sacrifice of a life he had come to cherish. Or had he? Had he just used it to hide a loneliness he wouldn't admit?

He returned Marion's gaze, his face noncommittal, and Marion sighed. He was beginning to think no two more stubborn people existed than his sister and this stiff-necked Englishman.

Two horses were saddled when Samara, prettily attired in a dark blue riding costume, and an aloof Reese arrived at the stables. He courteously but coolly assisted her into the hated sidesaddle and easily swung up onto his own restless bay mount. The horse was fresh, eager for an outing, and Reese enjoyed the effort it took to control him.

Samara watched as he quickly established his mastery, thinking how startlingly handsome he was. He wore buff breeches and black boots, and a white lawn shirt of Brendan's. Both the breeches and shirt were stretched taut across his muscled body, despite Angel's best efforts with a needle. The shirt strained at the wide shoulders and contrasted with the deep tan of his neck and sun-bronzed face. He exuded masculinity and strength and power, and Samara felt herself turning once more to mush as heat and yearning rushed like molten lead through her. She wished she could stay angry with him, but it was impossible. Not when he looked so magnificent!

Reese turned to her, his head lowered in mocking deference. "I am your prisoner, Miss Samara, and at your direction." His eyes glinted with something she couldn't name.

Her lips tightened at his casual insolence, even as she knew she preferred this mood to the frigid indifference of yesterday. "Follow me," she retorted shortly, urging her horse into a canter. He paced himself behind her, just enough to be tauntingly subservient, and she knew he did it to goad her. There was nothing subservient about his proud bearing or the challenging twist of his mouth.

Some of Reese's ill humor left him as he noted her shoulders straighten in irritation. She was lovely in blue; the color intensified the sheen of the dark hair which now tumbled in curls from a clasp in back. Unlike most English ladies, she wore no hat and her ivory complexion had the slight glow of sun. From his position, he also noted that she was an excellent rider, as excellent as one could be in a sidesaddle. She moved easily and gracefully with the horse, retaining firm but gentle control of a spirited mare.

Almost as if she knew what he was thinking, she nudged her horse into a gallop, and suddenly laughing eyes looked back at him and challenged. He had merely to touch his mount and they were racing along the road, Samara's musical laughter charming him with its mischief. She had made sure she had a considerable head start.

He followed her as she left the road and raced across fields and finally into a wooded area where a narrow path made it impossible for him to pass; he could only take the clumps of earth loosed by her mare's hoofs. Little devil, he cursed, while admiring her horsemanship. She knew exactly what she was doing. She stopped so suddenly that his horse almost ran into her and reared in confusion. It took all of Reese's skill to remain in the saddle, and he swore once more as he saw the provocative defiance in her face.

He calmed his horse and dismounted, striding angrily over to her. "That was a damn fool thing to do. You could have killed both of us." He looked down at his once clean shirt. It was splattered now with great blobs of dirt and mud. And from her amused look, he knew there were similar spots on his face. His dignity suffered several seconds before his sense of humor took over and his lips twitched.

"Ah, Samara," he said in a soft almost intimate tone. It had a quizzical, almost rueful note of surrender in it as he reached his hands for her, and she most willingly slid from her horse into his arms.

They stood there together, indifferent to anything except their raw need for each other, for a surcease of the painful, inexplicable torment that had bedeviled both of them for nearly a year. Samara's face looked upward, toward him, seeking reassurance, a sign that he felt the same mysterious aching, the same fierce want as she. She wasn't disappointed. His face was rigid with effort as he sought to control himself and his gem-like eyes shimmered with the same hunger that consumed her. Heat pulsated in wild spurts, starting at her core and reaching out to claim every part of her body, and some vital irresistible craving made her tremble in his arms as she felt them tighten around her.

She strained against him, feeling his growing hardness, and in that one gesture she offered everything she had.

She felt his hand touch her chin tenderly, and lift her face upward. His lips were gentle but still seared her mouth with their warmth and hunger. They wandered, grazing her cheek, caressing her eyes, whispering in her ears, stroking her throat until she thought she would die with the pleasure and joy of it. Her hands crept up his back and played with the thick golden hair as his lips returned to her mouth and his tongue reached inside, stoking little blazes that flared like freshly lighted candles.

Their two bodies clung together as much as clothes would allow, while his hands busied themselves with the top buttons to her jacket. Samara was barely aware of them, so lost was she in the discovery of so many new sensations, new emotions, new hungers.

His mouth tore away from hers, and he hoarsely uttered her name. "Samara...Samara, my love," and there was no mockery in the endearment, only a sort of wonder. He searched her eyes, her face for fear or hesitation but there was none, only the same desperate desire that racked him.

His hands opened the jacket and the top of the dress beneath it and he slid one hand inside, feeling the taut breast. He freed it from the clothing and his head leaned down, his tongue forging trails of fire before his mouth reached for the nipple. He was engulfed with passion, driven by desires stronger than he had ever felt before. He kept expecting her to cry out, to stop the madness, but her lips were buried in his golden hair, busy with their own frantic pursuit. By instinct alone, her lips moved to his ear, and her tongue tasted the tangy saltiness of his skin, touching nerves that drew a low moan from his throat. "Little witch...my beautiful little witch..."

He was reaching for the front of his breeches, now swollen with his throbbing manhood, when he heard the rustle of an approaching rider. In an almost instantaneous return to sanity, he gently pushed Samara away. Her face was flushed, her hair tangled, her riding costume in disarray. Experienced hands quickly worked the small buttons, but nothing could be done for the heightened color in her face nor for the brightness of her eyes.

He had just finished with her buttons when Conn appeared on a chestnut gelding. O'Neill's blue eyes, so much like Brendan's except for the vivid anger in them, raked over the two faces, noting Samara's discomfort and mussed appearance and Reese's now impassive expression. He glowered at both of them.

"You followed us," Samara accused furiously.

"No," her brother said evenly. "But I thought, as you were gone an inordinately long time, you might be in trouble." His expression told her he felt his expectation correct.

Reese's low drawl interrupted the exchange. There was cold anger in his tone. "And you thought I might have ravished and killed Samara and escaped."

"Why not?" Conn said bitterly. "All we have is your word, and I wouldn't accept an Englishman's word under any conditions. I'm not as gullible as my father. And," he added nastily, "it seems I was partially right." His eyes moved from Samara's tangled hair to Reese, taking in every aspect of his appearance.

"You have no right, Conn..." Samara said with fury.

"I have every right, little sister. I'm not going to let him take advantage of you." He turned to Reese. "Get mounted," he ordered.

Reese's lips thinned at the terse command. He saw the tears begin to form in the depths of Samara's eyes and decided to obey. An unsuspected protectiveness welled up inside him, and he didn't want to cause her any more hurt today. He had allowed himself to get out of control and had almost seduced her. If it hadn't been for Conn...

He went over to Samara, took her now cold hand and helped her into the saddle, ignoring Conn's obvious rage. He then mounted his own bay and without looking back at either of them followed the path back to the O'Neill home.

Days passed with agonizing slowness for Reese. He had decided he would not allow himself alone again with Samara. It was much too dangerous for everyone concerned, particularly himself.

During the long sleepless night after their ride, he knew that he could not allow their relationship to go any further. He had, no matter how reluctantly, accepted the hospitality of the O'Neill family, and he would not abuse it by seducing the daughter of the house.

But the magic was always there, a seemingly invincible need for each other that grew daily, even as they tried to deny it. Each accidental meeting renewed raging fires in them; and mealtimes became ordeals to survive. Reese would charm and tease, but often he would end the farce with his hands clenched in tight fists hidden beneath a napkin.

Several days after the encounter in the woods, Reese was in the library, browsing restlessly through the books when Samara entered. He started to leave, but she placed a restraining hand on his arm, and the touch, even through his shirt, was like a brand.

"Don't go, Reese," she said. "Please. I haven't had the chance to ask you about the *Unicorn*...I didn't want to do it in front of the others."

Her wistful look stopped him and he was startled at her insight. She had sensed he needed time, that he wouldn't want to discuss the *Unicorn* in the hearing of her family. That she felt his pain and respected it served only to strengthen his longing for her. She was such a captivating mixture of mischievous child and sensitive woman.

"Tell me," she pleaded, "what happened...I know the crew was taken. Papa's trying to get them released. But how did you get away? And how was the ship sunk?"

"I don't know, little cat," he said. "The *Unicorn* was hit by one storm after another and after the last she was badly wounded." Samara couldn't miss the way he spoke of the

Unicorn as a person, a beloved person. "And then there were
two American ships...almost as if they were waiting..."

"The crew...Davey and Yancy and Michael...?"

Her face was full of concern and involuntarily his hand
touched her cheek. He was reminded of that day in Yancy's
small surgery when she had comforted one of the sailors. That
quality and her stubbornness despite odds were the two facets
of Samara that fascinated him most.

"They all made it, I think," he said. "That's something
else your father is trying to find out. But I saw the American
boats picking them up. I decided to swim for it and try to help
them later. I knew no one else could make it; I didn't know
if I could. I almost didn't." His eyes clouded as he remembered that long, exhausting swim. "You know most of the
rest."

"At least all you'll tell me," she retorted.

"That's right," he said amiably.

She was afraid to say anything else, lest she ruin the brief
peace between them. "I'm glad you're safe," she whispered.
"I couldn't bear it if anything happened to you."

Her heart was in her eyes, and Reese's breath caught under
her soft gaze. There was so much hopeful child there, so much
passionate woman.

His hand, which had stayed on her cheek, fell. "Under any
other circumstances, little cat..." He turned on his heel and
left before he did, or said, something he would regret.

Late summer turned to fall, and still there was no word of
Brendan. Reese became an accepted member of the family, at
least to all but Conn who still regarded him with suspicion
and dislike. But Conn, his leg as healed as it ever would be,
planned to leave in several days to join General Andrew Jackson in Alabama. Despite a bad limp he felt fit enough to return
to duty, and news of a massacre in Alabama spurred his plans.
The Creeks, unhappy with white incursions on the Alabama
lands, had captured Fort Mims and massacred the inhabitants—five-hundred and fifty three men, women and children.

Jackson had been ordered into Alabama, where he would build forts and wipe out the Indian resistance.

The other war news was better—at least for the O'Neills. Oliver Hazard Perry met and badly defeated a British fleet on Lake Erie, resulting in the British evacuation of Detroit. The American family tried to restrain their enthusiasm out of courtesy to their guest, but the elation was difficult to hide entirely.

In light of the war news, Reese chafed at his restrictions. His natural restlessness and impatience made him edgy; and the fate of his crew was of growing concern. He knew Connor was doing all he could, but his crew was still imprisoned. He had learned that they all survived and were being held in a Boston prison, but he feared that his own reputation had hindered their chances for exchange.

Noting his increasing unease, Connor often asked him to accompany him around the plantation, and Reese always accepted. It placed him away from Samara and he was fascinated with the workings of Glen Woods. He had been astounded when Connor explained that most of the servants and field hands were free men.

On their first ride together, Connor had noted Reese's disapproval as he watched the laborers; it wasn't difficult to guess the reason. Many Englishmen abhorred the practice of slavery, and attempts were already being made in Parliament to outlaw the practice in the British possessions. It had seemed quite odd to Connor, however, that the English persisted in using bond servants and convicts, many accused only of political crimes, in much the same fashion. He was particularly sensitive to the fact that many Irish and Scots had been sentenced to long terms of servitude first in America, then in Australia, for merely defending their rights and land. It was, to Connor, another example of British hypocrisy.

Connor disliked slavery in any form, and he explained that most of the hands on both Glen Woods and Chatham Oaks had been freed. The O'Neills did occasionally purchase slaves but then gave them an opportunity to buy their freedom after proving themselves. Artisans and skilled craftsmen could work outside the plantation and keep their earnings. It was a system that worked well for the O'Neills. Their workers produced nearly double that of other plantations.

Startled, Reese reassessed Connor O'Neill, and respect started to grow. The two often rode together now, and a friendship formed and deepened just as it had with Brendan.

From the window of her bedroom, Samara watched the two men as they approached the stable, and she couldn't bury the envy—and desolation—that buffeted her heart. With his hair glinting in the sun, and his long, strong body resting easily in the saddle, Reese was as breathtaking as he was at the helm of a ship. Breathtaking and forbidden. It was as if he were thousands of miles away instead of sharing the same house. For he had made it quite clear that he did not desire her company.

She would never let him know how devastated she was. She cherished the memories of the afternoon in the woods, cherished and held them closely to herself. From the first moment she had seen him, he stirred feelings inside her she had never known existed. Even when she tried so hard to fight him, she knew that a part of her would never be free of the Honorable Reese Hampton. Honorable. An English nobleman. Why should he care about the country-bumpkin colonial?

And he didn't. He had shown that countless times. He avoided her like he might the black death, or smallpox, or any other wretched disease. Which was exactly what she was beginning to feel like. When he encountered her alone, he bolted like a chicken which instinctively knew it was destined as the main course for dinner.

Damn Conn. He had ruined everything. When he had so abruptly interfered that day in the woods, she knew she had been on the verge of discovering something truly wonderful and magical. And since then Reese's warmth had turned to ice, his passion to amused tolerance. Only rarely did she catch a flash of fire in his eyes that was gone almost instantly, lost in the controlled void that hid his thoughts.

He had been here two months now, and each day carried its own litany of misery—of hope shattered and desire spurned. Soon he would be gone. What information he had no longer mattered, but her father wanted him aboard Bren's ship, bound for a neutral port where he could do no damage to the American cause. And so she waited in torment, wanting him to go, wanting him to stay, loving and hating, hoping and dreading. Nothing was right any more. Nothing had been right since that day—it seemed years ago—when a sampler lured her from safety to a voyage that had shaken her world.

I have to know. I have to know if it's all fantasy. There had been times, both aboard the *Unicorn* and here at Glen Woods, when his guard had dropped and she sensed the same intensity of feeling that so overwhelmed her. But it usually fled so swiftly, she could only wonder if she had imagined it all. But she couldn't let him go without knowing. Once more, she started plotting.

Chapter Fifteen

Samara planned her offensive as carefully as any general prepared for battle. Everything was perfect, everything as she knew it must be for her plan to succeed. Her father had gone to Jere's plantation; Conn had taken his protective, scowling countenance to Charleston in last-minute preparations for his return to the militia. Marion had already been gone several weeks. And her mother was in the stables, enraptured with the new colt.

Samara had planned to trick Reese into accompanying her on some counterfeit errand decreed by her father, and lead him, unsuspecting, to the cave. But when she found him in the library she had neither the heart nor the deceitfulness to implement that which she had plotted.

He was standing at the window, obviously unaware of her presence, and his shoulders were uncharacteristically slumped. She saw his hands move compulsively, clenching in fists, and she sensed his frustration...frustration and a sense of failure. An ache started in her and grew and became a clutching, hurtful thing as she realized *she* had done this to him.

She had realized months earlier that she loved him, but she had fought it because he was the enemy. In the past weeks, he had treated her as a problem to be avoided. Only rarely did those magnetic eyes reflect the warmth she had so wonderfully, and briefly, felt in the woods. More often, she was greeted with a grim mouth and hooded eyes. It was like watching a volcano rumble and steam, never knowing when the final eruption might come. In the past few days, she had sensed the growing pressure, the need within him for release. Samara knew he worried about his crew and considered her home no more than an elegant prison. He had been forced into a powerless position and he hated it; hated his helplessness, his enforced obedience to someone else's will. To a man like Reese Hampton who loved freedom above all, his stay at Glen Woods was becoming intolerable.

Samara knew she could not lie to him, could not deceive him into doing something *she* wanted. With sudden maturity born of recently recognized if not completely accepted love, Samara knew she would not try to manipulate this very proud man.

Instead, she went over to him and stood silently next to him, trying to tell him without words that she understood his anguish.

"You shouldn't be here," he said in a low, husky voice after a long silence.

She said nothing. His voice was somehow wistful, a departure from his usual confident tone. She turned and searched his face, and watched his jaw tense with inner turmoil.

"You shouldn't be here," he said again, as if trying to convince himself.

"I want to show you something," she said.

He smiled then, an incredibly winsome smile, tinged with a trace of irony. "And what might be waiting for me this time?" His hand, almost unconsciously, went to her cheek and touched it. It was so smooth, so silky. And her eyes were like gray-blue velvet, warm and luxurious. And dangerous. He had learned that. She was dangerous in so many ways. Ways she didn't even realize.

"Please," she said now. "Please come with me for a ride."

She saw his searching gaze, his indecision. She held out her hand to him, her eyes beseeching him.

"Little cat." The words were so softly spoken she barely heard them.

"Englishman," she said, and the sound was an endearment.

His mouth crooked in a small wry smile. "I'll always be an Englishman, you know."

"I know," she whispered, "and probably a pirate and a blackguard and…"

"And you, my little American, are a beguiling liar. Married! God, I should have known better."

"I think," she said slowly with a small, tentative smile, "perhaps we deserve each other."

"Perhaps we do," he admitted ruefully, and despite his reluctant reply, Samara felt her heart leap with hope. He *did* care. His mouth was saying it; his eyes were saying it.

The glinting hardness was gone, lost in the swirling blue-green depths that beckoned her. They were so intriguing, these eyes of his with all their mysteries. He hid so much in them, revealing little but his great lust for life. It had seemed dimmed in the recent weeks, and that, perhaps more than anything else, touched Samara and gave her pain.

"You look pensive, little cat," he said now, the grim taut line of his mouth softening. She was lovely, standing in a ray of sun that filtered through the window. Her eyes were large and searching, her mouth pursed in an uncertain smile which affected him in a strange and tender way. He wondered now at that emotion; he had felt many things with women, but seldom this tenderness that reached so deep inside him. Or this protectiveness that was keeping him from taking her here and now and damn the consequences.

He wanted her, more than he had ever wanted anything. Her warm, fiery passion, so uninhibited once aroused, was more seductive, more irresistible than any he had ever known. She was so alive, so filled with optimism and hope and humor. But even more appealing was her indomitable spirit which had led her to stow away on Brendan's ship and fight for Brendan's freedom. God help him, Reese thought with chagrin, it had even led her to kidnap him. Samara, right or wrong, was a fighter who pursued her own ideas of honor. From Reese's somewhat jaded viewpoint, it was a unique quality in a woman, and it fascinated and charmed him.

"Please," she said once more. She felt compelled to take

him to her cave, to the place where she had felt his presence so profoundly.

Reese searched for an excuse, but discovered he didn't want to find one. He told himself he wanted to go for a ride, to get out of the house, and under the rules established by Connor, Samara was at the moment his only means. He nodded, cursing himself for a damn fool.

Samara led the way...across the boundaries of the plantation, along the Pee Dee River, past the giant oaks and cypresses draped with gray shrouds of moss. This land was unbelievably lush, Reese thought, as he rode silently, so different from the manicured fields and gardens of England. There was a wild, untamed beauty about it, and Reese could understand how it produced such independent and unconventional women as Samantha and Samara O'Neill. Would either survive in England with its often brittle and cruel society and restrictive conventions? He thought of Samantha that first night when she had visited him in breeches and shirt. He had seen Samara sneak out in the mornings in the same unusual clothing. The sight had stirred the warmth in his loins more than any ballgown. Even now the image fired his blood. He shook his head to rid it of the thoughts. He must keep his senses about him. He should never have come, but the plea in Samara's lovely eyes had shattered what few defenses he had.

It was time to settle matters. They could not go much longer with so many questions unanswered between them. They were in every look, every glance. He couldn't help but recognize the love that too often shone in her face, despite her efforts to hide it. Nor could he deny his own attraction and hunger. But that was all it was, he tried to convince himself, a natural response to a very lovely girl. So why was there such a painful throb in him at the thought of leaving her?

Samara stopped near the cave, and Reese quickly dismounted and tied the reins of his horse to a tree before offering his hand to her. Remembering too well their first ride, he quickly released her and stepped back, waiting to see what it was she so badly wanted him to share.

She led the way, brushing aside the thick vines around the mouth of a cave and darting inside, leaving him to follow reluctantly. Curiously, he studied the interior which widened from the narrow entrance into a large and deep cavern. There were several signs of use: tattered clothes, candles, a tin cup and pail.

He watched, fascinated, in the dim light, as Samara, oblivious to the dirt and dust clinging to her riding costume, lit a candle. Her face glowed in the light, and her gray eyes sparkled as she searched eagerly for his reaction.

And then he felt it too…a peculiar warmth. The day had been cold and the cave, untouched by sun, even colder. But now he felt touched by a kind of radiance. He immediately dismissed the odd feeling as fancy; there *must* be a very sound reason for it, perhaps some hot spring underneath the earth. But all such reasoning fled as Samara moved towards him— as did all his good intentions. She was uncommonly beautiful in the candlelight, her hair fairly dancing with fiery streaks, her face filled with love and expectancy. He could only groan with his need for her.

"No," he tried to say, but the sound disappeared as her lips reached up for his with the same single-mindedness of purpose he had witnessed before. Her eyes were open, searching for response, for an answering warmth. For she knew she would find the truth here. She had to know it.

And she found it in the sudden violent embrace of his arms, in the tender sweetness of his lips that first barely touched, then caressed, then demanded, searing both of them with a brand they would carry forever, exploding greedy wildfires that surged through their achingly ready bodies.

Reese tried to stop, but Samara's body moved against his, sending shock waves through the core of his being. His manhood throbbed and pounded with its need to become one with her, to feel the depth of the warmth she was offering.

His tongue found its way into the welcoming mouth, and teased and stroked until he felt her shudder with unaccustomed sensations. When he finally withdrew it, they were both tense with raging fires.

Her hand reached up and played with his hair, and she stared at him with wonder. He was so handsome, so completely, beautifully masculine as he stood there, emanating strength and power and animal grace. "I love you, I think" she whispered, unable to keep it to herself any longer.

He backed away, his hands on her shoulders, his steady gaze meeting hers. He watched as her desire changed to hope and hope changed to fear and fear changed to despair. His heart began to crack as her despair turned to misery, and she abruptly turned away before he could see her welling tears. His silence had said more than words could.

His arms went around her, his chest to her back, and his lips touched her hair. God, how he wanted to reassure her, to take her now, to love her. But how could he? He was a fugitive in her country, an enemy to her people. And he was a friend to her brother and father. He should not take her without marriage and marriage was impossible, at least at the moment, at least until he found some way out.

He felt her shaking, and his arms felt the warm impact of her silent tears. He swallowed. She was so completely vulnerable.

Reese Hampton could stand it no longer. He knew suddenly that he could stand anything but her quiet anguish. And in that moment, he also knew he loved her and he would sell his soul rather than hurt her.

He turned her around, and once again his hand lifted her chin to face him. His mouth lowered to touch the tear-filled eyes, and moved down to catch the warm, salty tears.

When he finished, he straightened and his brilliant eyes fastened on her tear-glazed ones. "I love you, Samara," he said slowly. He had never expected to say those words, and they came awkwardly. So awkwardly Samara had trouble comprehending them, and she could only stare at him, bewilderedly.

He smiled a flashing, radiant smile that filled her full of golden awe. How could anyone smile like that? She still could not grasp his last statement, not after the long humiliating silence that preceded it.

"You have to forgive me, little cat," he said gently. "You see, I've never said it before."

His eyes were warm, oh so warm, and Samara finally understood. He *did* love her. Her heart thought it would burst with joy, but her eyes pleaded for more reassurance. *Tell me again*, she demanded silently.

"I love you," his words were as equally silent but just as clear and made even more potent by their delivery.

He took the blanket on the ground, shook it out and placed it next to the wall. Reese then took her hand and helped her sit before reclining next to her. He put his arm around her shoulders and held her close to him, taking pleasure in the feel of her.

"The question, Samara," he finally said, "is what do we do now?"

"As long as we love each other..."

His voice was very gentle. "It's not that easy, Samara. If I'm caught, I could very well hang. I can't stay here, and I wonder if you'd be happy in England."

"I would be happy wherever you are," Samara said, her reason lost in the wonderful euphoria she was now feeling. She would conquer the world for him.

He smiled at the words. They were so typically Samara. She was always so certain, so confident that everything would eventually work out well. "I'll be leaving when Brendan returns," he warned.

"I'll go with you," she announced.

He chuckled now, a deep, rumbling sound that charmed her completely. "A stowaway again?"

"If I have to," she said with determination.

"I think not," he said, but his grim tone was belied by the twinkle in his eye. By God, she would...if she had the chance.

"Then..."

"The war is not going to last much longer. It's not to the benefit of my country or yours. Negotiations are going on, and there's growing pressure in England against it. Until then, you must stay here. It's too dangerous for you to travel."

"But you and Bren..."

"Are soldiers," he completed with emphasis. "I know you didn't believe it then, but when I took the *Samara*, you were damned fortunate I had a few scruples." His soft laughter now held some self-directed mockery. "Damn few that they were, and even then I had a devil of a time holding to them. You are a bewitching young lady, Miss O'Neill, and I don't want you wandering about the seas while the war continues, with or without me."

Her fingers tightened around his hand. There was strength and grace in it, as there was in all of him. She suddenly wanted to know all about him.

"Have you ever been in love before?" she asked in a whisper. She feared the answer.

"Never," he replied solemnly. "And what about you? Your friend Emily said you had masses of suitors, all eager for your hand."

"I wasn't eager for theirs," she retorted with such disgust on her face he couldn't suppress his laughter.

"You never even thought about one...as a husband?" he teased.

"No...not ever," she said. "Not until..." She was afraid to say the word, to say "you."

"I'm doubly honored then," he said gallantly.

"Have you...ever thought about marriage before?" she said. "I heard marriages in England are arranged."

"Many are," he agreed, "but there are also many love matches. And no, even my father couldn't force me into marriage—although he tried hard enough." His eyes pierced her. "I would never marry without love," he said, "and I had never thought to find it."

Samara thought she would die from joy. He wanted *her*, just her. But she couldn't let it go. "You've never been engaged?" She just couldn't believe he had gone through so many years without attachments.

"No," he said, not counting his recent bogus betrothal. "Not," he added with a curious roughness in his voice, "until now."

She stared at him, hope leaping up in her eyes.

"If, that is," he continued, "you want to marry an Englishman, and a pirate and a blackguard—isn't that what you told your father?"

Happy laughter bubbled up inside her as he tenderly mocked her words.

"All of those and more," she replied tartly, just before his mouth hushed her.

Once more, the fires started raging and this time there was no quenching them.

His hands moved gently, but the very lightness of the touch made them more erotic as they traced intricate patterns on her cheek, moving to a sensitive earlobe and following them with whisper-like kisses that sent Samara hurtling into a sensation-filled world. Every nerve tingled with expectancy, and she was filled with an aching hunger as his lips traveled with scorching thoroughness to her neck, and his hands reached for her fastenings, releasing them with stunning quickness.

She knew her breasts were bare to him, and she felt him move to stretch out alongside her. Samara felt his lips making intimate little circles on each breast, then claiming first the right nipple, then the left with his tongue, then his lips, sending shivers of ecstasy dancing through her.

She touched his chest through the opening of his shirt as she had wanted to so many times before. Her fingers caught the golden hair and twisted and played with the enticing curls. Her fingers traced little patterns on his chest as her tongue found his earlobe and fondled it until he moaned. She laughed, delighting in knowing she could reciprocate all the wonderful feelings. The laugh was a symphony to him, filled with love and caring and desire and excitement.

Their eyes met, and their hands stilled. There was so much to say to each other, and it was all being said silently. There was no need for words.

His hands trembled slightly as he started anew on her riding costume, carefully, gently peeling it from her body, then the chemise. He looked in awe at the lovely body before him, the full breasts, slender waist, curving hips. "You are beautiful," he whispered.

Her sudden shyness disappeared at his words. He loved her. He wanted her. He thought her beautiful. And *she* wanted him with all the craving and hunger of her newly awakened body.

She watched him as he undressed…first the lawn shirt, then the boots and finally the trousers. She was stunned by the raw rugged beauty of his hard compact body.

He thought she might be frightened by him, but saw immediately she wasn't. He knelt beside her and Samara held out a hand to him. After a moment's hesitation, he took it.

"You're sure," he said slowly, afraid she would say no, equally afraid she would say yes.

In answer, she merely said, "Lie here next to me." More than anything else on earth, she wanted to feel him near her, to feel his skin touching hers, his warmth mingling with her own.

He did as she asked, feeling small explosions as they touched. Her body fit into his as if designed to do so.

Reese's arms went around her, holding her tightly, allowing her to grow familiar with his body as his mouth kissed her forehead, her cheeks and finally her lips with infinite tenderness. He could feel the sensations building in her, and his body grew taut as he sought to control his own needs. Her body moved compulsively closer to his, seeking an even more intimate union. He marveled at her lack of coyness or fear or modesty. She was open and honest and he rejoiced in it.

Samara, for her part, was too lost in the wonderful feelings to care about anything except satisfying the ache that had been within her for nearly a year, from that first kiss so many months ago. She felt no fear of him, or of what was to come, only a joy at his closeness. He *loved* her. He *needed* her. He wanted *her* as his wife.

She felt his hands teasing and caressing her, and dazzling colors took control of her mind as she responded with a passion so innocent and yet so free that it seemed to Reese a miracle of contradiction, a sensual rocketing of the senses.

He turned her, very slowly, very gently, on her back and leaned over to kiss her, letting his lips linger, glorying in the way she responded to his every touch. His hand reached down between her legs, and she shyly opened them for him while his hand stroked the warm dark curly hair. Each touch of his hand inflamed her more, and he felt her need intensify along with his own.

He kneeled above her, his legs straddling her body, his eyes making love as sensually as his hands. He slowly lowered himself, letting his manhood gently touch and tease her, and he heard her soft cries as she trembled with a yearning for something she did not yet understand.

Then, gently, he entered, his warmth becoming a welcomed part of her. There was a stab of pain, and she couldn't stop the small cry from escaping her lips. She felt him hesitate, but now she arched her body towards him, wanting desperately, despite the pain, to continue this voyage of discovery, to receive all of him, to make Reese one with herself, to bring him so close to her heart he would never go away.

As he probed tentatively, carefully, the pain waned in the exquisite tremors that swept through her. She had never imagined how wondrous this could be! Spasms of pleasure exploded from the deepest core of her body and spread like stars from a Roman candle until she thought she could bear no more. But as he thrust deeper and deeper in sure, controlled strokes, each rapturous second surpassed the last until all of her whirled in an upward spiral towards some magical destination and suddenly all she had ever known was swept away in the fiery eruption that so exquisitely rocked her body.

Afterward, she explored his body with her hands, loving the hard muscular feel of him, unable to get enough. He laughed at her greediness, hiding the desolation which had descended upon him in the aftermath. He had felt a terrible sense of guilt when he saw the blood. Although he had known Samara was a virgin, the red stain vividly drove the fact home. His distaste for himself was only slightly mitigated by the knowledge that his intentions were honorable, that he would marry her as soon as possible. But that might still be months or years, and he could not bear the thought of a child. Not until he could provide for Samara's safety.

"Is it always like this?" she asked in a wondering voice, breaking into his unsettling thoughts.

He forced himself to smile. "Very seldom, love." The endearment was unconscious. He still felt little quivers of pleasure reminding him of his dishonor. But she was so serious, so awed. "In fact, I think it's very rare indeed."

"Just us, perhaps?" she said with pardonable pride and delight at his answer.

Reese smiled at her shining eyes. Lord, she was entrancing. She would tempt a saint. And a saint he certainly was not.

"Just us," he reassured her. "But," he added seriously, "it can't happen again...not until we're married."

"When...?"

"I don't know, love. But if you wish, I'll ask your parents for permission tonight." He gave her his irresistible crooked smile. "I doubt if they'll be very happy."

"If I am, they will be," she said quite accurately. "And I am. Wonderfully, marvelously so...just as Mother said it would happen some day. I think Brendan will be too, though we might have to work on Conn. He doesn't like the English."

"I've noticed," Reese said ruefully.

"Will we live in England?"

"Would you like to?"

"I don't know," she said seriously. "I have never thought about living a long way from Glen Woods. And I don't,...didn't...like the English either...unless they're like you..." she added desperately, as she realized what she was saying.

His eyes twinkled at her awkward admission. And then a low rumble of laughter exploded.

Samara was, at first, offended and then she thought about what she had just said. She had hated him thoroughly in the beginning, especially when he'd inspired all those wickedly delightful feelings in her, and she had told him so repeatedly. To hold him up now as her perfect model for an Englishman was inconsistent to say the least. "Well, I *love* you," she said. "I don't really have to like you." At his wounded look she hurriedly added, "But I do. Enormously, I think."

Mollified slightly, Reese reached over and picked up his shirt and pulled it over his head, then reached for his trousers. "We'd better get back, little cat, or they will be scouring the countryside for us."

"I don't want to leave. I don't ever want to leave." But she reluctantly reached for her chemise. "You know this is where my mother fell in love with Father. She stumbled on him here after he had been wounded and she saved his life."

"Is that why you brought me here?" he questioned gently.

"No, I don't think so. But when Bren said you were dead I came here and, somehow, in this cave I knew you weren't. It was almost as if you were here with me." She stopped. "You must think I'm a fanciful child."

"Not a child, never a child," he answered with tenderness. He looked around. There *was* something about this cave— something almost alive. He shook his head and reached for her hand. "Come, love. We must make you respectable."

As they left, Reese looked back into the interior of the cave. The warmth was gone, replaced by a cold chill, and he was struck by a strange foreboding. He dismissed the idea as nonsense, brought on by Samara's tale.

Nonetheless, as he mounted and rode beside the woman he intended to make his wife, he couldn't rid himself of a certain disquiet.

Chapter Sixteen

Connor O'Neill stood in stunned silence as he listened to the accursed Hampton.

True enough, Connor had come to like and admire the vexing Englishman, but that was because he had been lulled into a false sense of security. He had *believed* the reserve between his daughter and his unwilling guest, and so he had relaxed and truly enjoyed his outings with Hampton. The man was entertaining, extremely intelligent and fascinated with everything he saw. His questions were astute, his opinions knowledgeable and his wit sharp.

But married to his daughter?

Whatever else he was, Reese Hampton was his country's enemy, a man who supported himself by pirating American ships and, worst of all, a would-be husband who would carry *his* daughter off to England.

"No," he said, as he glanced around the library in frustrated anger. He looked first at his wife, Samantha, then at Hampton. Samara had been banished from the room the second he realized the direction of Hampton's request to speak with him and Samantha. "No," he repeated. "You do *not* have our consent."

Samantha sat on the settee in the library, an enigmatic smile on her face. It hid the satisfaction she felt. She did not want to lose Samara to England any more than her husband did, but since her daughter's first reference to Reese Hampton she had recognized that he and no one else was Samara's happiness. She had worried and fretted about Reese's apparent indifference to her daughter and was mollified only by the man's occasional unguarded looks when he thought no one was watching. Now she would let Connor fume, knowing he would soon calm down and accept. It helped immensely that he liked Reese. He had told her so, more than once, in the privacy of their bedroom.

"And how do you plan to support Samara?" he said now. "By robbing her country's ships?"

Reese couldn't resist a slight grin. "As your son robs English ships?" he retorted, a combative gleam in his eye.

"The devil take you," Connor said, but he couldn't completely hide a hint of a twinkle in his eye. The man invented insolence. He remembered that first night when he'd asked Hampton if he were a spy, and his eyes grew even brighter as he recalled the answer. Hampton could charm a tiger into eating tamely from his hand.

Reese thought it time to restrain himself. "I'll seek no more American ships...now French, that's another matter."

"There are so many eligible *local* young men," Connor muttered, half to himself.

"And I have heard from her friend Emily that they are all groveling at her feet. I sympathize with your plight, sir," Reese said solemnly without a touch of sympathy in his voice. He was too old for this nonsense. He looked over at Samantha; his mouth twitched when she winked at him and nodded. There was no question he had her approval.

Connor also saw the movement, and it didn't help his temperament. "You too, Madam? You wish to see your daughter taken to England?"

"I don't think she should go anyplace until after the war," Reese interjected. "And afterward...I am thinking about purchasing some property here or in Virginia. I would not ask her to share my brother's home..." The words were said with a quiet sincerity that completely silenced Connor for a moment. Again he looked at Samantha as he remembered the gulf that had once divided them. He was a Whig; her family was

Tory. There had been so much hate between them. And yet together they had discovered a love which still grew daily.

A slow smile replaced his anger. "You're still English, but, by the saints, I like you and I couldn't say that about any of the young dandies that hung around here."

The interview was over.

Samara, wondering how anyone could possibly be this happy, sat on the riverbank, her back leaning against the hard muscular chest of her intended.

Intended. What a wonderful word! She could barely believe that she would, one day, be this magnificent man's wife. She still did not understand entirely why he wanted her, and somewhere deep inside her there remained a kernel of fear that she was living in a make-believe world that might come crashing down around her. But when she looked at Reese she would banish the nagging uneasiness.

The bright love in her face delighted Reese. She had brought something young and fresh into his life. She was unpredictable and unpretentious, and enchantingly unaware of her beauty. He never quite knew what color her eyes would be; they changed with her mood or with the shades of her dress or the sky—or even the sea. They were smoky blue this afternoon, and as expressive as a painting. A new contentment flowed through him as he saw their quiet joy.

He had not meant to say the words he had uttered in the cave. "I love you." But they had come so easily and the moment they'd escaped his lips he knew he meant them. She had not been far from his thoughts since the day he had met her, and he thought now of those first few minutes. She had been so obviously terrified, so impossibly young, yet she had raised that ridiculous bottle against him. He had, he now admitted, probably fallen in love with her at that very moment.

His right arm tightened around her while the fingers of his left hand played with her silky curls. He could feel her burrow further into his chest, seeking his warmth on this crisp, early winter day. He had been very careful not to repeat the madness of the day in the cave, and had resisted her every attempt to lure him back. Although his body ached with its need to join hers, he would wait until they could be married. He could only hope the war would end shortly, for every day was a form of agony, a supreme challenge.

Their time together was almost over, he realized. The O'Neills had received word that Brendan had anchored in one of the several rivers along the coast. He had sent word that his voyage had been most successful, and that the *Samara* had sustained only slight damage. He would see to her repairs and provisioning before stopping at Glen Woods for a brief visit.

Connor had made the announcement at breakfast, watching the mixed emotions on Samara's face. Happiness flashed at the knowledge that Brendan was safe, but it was almost immediately replaced by the sobering realization that Brendan's homecoming meant Reese's departure. She had argued and pleaded and begged in the past week to be allowed to go with Reese, but both he and her father were united on this question. Neither would put her life in danger again and she knew she would never be able to repeat her earlier escapade.

She had planned this picnic, perhaps their last time alone, with great care. Angel had supervised the packing of a special lunch, and Reese and Samara had ridden out this morning to one of her favorite spots.

She turned her head and nibbled on the golden hairs that peeked from the open neck of Reese's shirt, her tongue tasting the musky skin, her hands tracing the corded muscles in his shoulders and chest. Samara felt she could never feel or taste or love enough of him. Her gaze went upward and she etched each beloved feature in her memory. Reese's hand tightened on a curl he was caressing as his body so readily responded to her touch. There was so much tenderness in her expression, tenderness mixed with warm passion. He had never encountered such a potent mixture. God, how he loved her, how she made him tremble. He leaned down, his lips brushing hers with infinite gentleness, thinking how much he wanted her next to him, her body melding with his. *What in God's name was happening to him?* He had to stop this now.

Reese shook as he took his lips from Samara's mouth, and

his body trembled with the supreme effort it took to pull away from her.

"Samara...my lovely little nymph...we can't let Angel's efforts go to waste..."

"Hmm," she murmured, completely indifferent to Angel's bounty.

He smiled at the sensual purr of her response, his resolve weakening once more. A small chuckle started deep in his throat as he wondered at his complete idiocy where Samara was concerned. He had never believed a little cat, *his* cat, could turn him into a powerless mass of jelly.

He tried again. "I think we should eat..."

"Why?" she whispered, her tongue once more setting his skin on fire.

The little witch was seducing him, and doing it very well indeed. He felt the heat surge through his blood. *Damn her.* It was his last thought before he lost himself in her sweet, fervent sorcery.

Later, they lay in the grass, their hands touching, each still shivering with the aftershocks of their union. He had, in one supreme act of control, prevented his seed from spilling into her, but the pleasure and ecstasy of their joining had been multiplied by the knowledge of their impending separation.

"I don't know if I can bear it," she said, her mouth trembling.

He rolled over, his naked body glistening. He was indifferent to the chill but had covered Samara with a blanket they had brought along.

"I know, my love. I won't fare any better...if that comforts you."

She shook her head miserably. Nothing could comfort her. He would be in Bermuda or in England with dozens of available women—attractive, nobly born, sophisticated women.

He saw the clouded expression in her eyes and correctly interpreted it.

"There has never been," he said slowly, gently, "a woman I've longed to be with day and night, to tease and love and share my life with. There never will be, Samara, except you. You *must* believe that."

Her arms went around him, and she buried her face in his chest, her body heaving with bittersweet tears.

Reese held her tightly, trying to comfort and reassure, unaware of the moisture in his own eyes.

Reese was visiting Chatham Oaks with Connor when Brendan arrived at the O'Neill plantation. The Englishman wanted to learn as much as possible about the workings of the plantation and was particularly interested in Jere's new crop—tobacco. Jere, worried about their dependence on indigo, had recently started experimenting with tobacco on part of his land. He felt the soil was well suited to tobacco-growing—fertile with good drainage. Jere was constantly experimenting with ways to improve crops or the production of crops. He was a natural born farmer who loved the land and had a particular genius for extracting the best from it.

Of the family, only Samantha and Samara were home and they were together, talking, when the first cries came to them: "Mist' Bren—Mist' Bren is home!"

Delight flashed across the faces of both mother and daughter, despite Samara's knowledge that Bren's arrival heralded Reese's departure. It had been many months since she had seen her oldest brother, and she had much to tell him. She suspected he would approve. The unlikely friendship between Bren and Reese, which had once so annoyed her, was now a source of satisfaction. Of all her brothers' approval, she craved his most of all.

The mischief that the five O'Neill children had honed to a fine art while growing up danced in Samara's eyes.

She knew Bren had thought her most fanciful when she had protested that Reese could not be dead. And now, not only was the Englishman alive, but he was living on Glen Woods and engaged to Bren's sister. She would say nothing to her brother, just enjoy his shock when Reese returned. Then she would tell him the wonderful news. She exacted her mother's vow of silence and hurried off to warn the servants, finishing the chore just in time to run, quite happily, into Bren's arms as he dismounted and thrust his reins into a servant's hands.

He hugged her tightly, then pulled back to study her, pleased that the haunted look was gone from her face. The old sparkle was in her eyes, and the piquant face radiated happiness and confidence and an intriguing devilment. It was the old Samara—and more. He had never seen her look quite so delighted with herself, even at the worst of her pranks which were always preceded by that same sly expression.

He grinned and reached for her small waist, seizing it in his two large hands, and whirling her around as she laughed with unrestrained joy.

"You look like a woman in love," he said when he finally set her down, his eyebrows arching in question.

"Yes, oh, yes," she said, and Bren was struck by the complete bliss on her face.

Thank God, he thought. *Thank God, she's over Hampton.* He had been uncertain whether to tell her about the newspaper he had found aboard a British merchantman he had taken. The newspaper had reported the betrothal of Captain Reese Hampton and a Lady Stanton, widow of a British earl. The story had emphasized the lady's loveliness, commenting that the engagement was said to be a love match as well as a most suitable alliance between two distinguished families. The match had been announced at a ball during which the couple seemed quite enamored of each other. Bren had kept the article. He had worried that Samara might still be harboring hopes that Hampton lived. The news that Hampton had been engaged prior to the sinking of his ship might quell any lingering feelings on Samara's part. Although he still felt grief at the man's death, he was relieved that Hampton was in Samara's past— gone, and apparently forgotten.

"May I ask who the lucky man is?" he questioned now, his blue eyes warm with affection.

"You will have to wait," Samara answered playfully. "He will be here for supper."

"That long? At least, tell me if I'll be pleased."

The devil was back in her eye as she grinned. "I think so,

eldest brother,'' she said as she hugged him tightly again. "Oh Bren, I'm so happy."

He leaned over and kissed her forehead. "I can't wait to meet this paragon…I know I'll approve of anyone who makes you this merry."

Bren looked up and winked at his mother who also looked very self-satisfied. He bounded up the stairs to the porch where she waited and flung his arms around her. "And you approve?"

"Wholeheartedly," she said.

"And you won't tell me either?"

She laughed. "And spoil Samara's surprise? Never. You'll just have to rein in that curiosity. Come and eat. We were about to have dinner."

"With pleasure. I'm damned tired of biscuits and salt pork." He looked at Samantha apologetically. "Excuse me, Mother. I've been aboard ship too long."

"I'm just glad to have you home," Samantha said, then asked tentatively, "When do you plan to leave again?"

"Almost immediately, I'm afraid. The ship's already been reprovisioned," he said, his tone quieting. "I'm needed. There are just too few of us. Our navy is so da…infernally small, and Congress won't spend any money on ships. The sea is where the war is going to be won. If we do enough damage to British shipping, their merchant class will demand an end to the war. They won't be able to afford it." His sheepish grin broadened. "I'm sorry," he said again, "I didn't mean to lecture. Come, little sister, tell me more about this mysterious suitor of yours.

"I'm engaged," she said proudly.

Bren spun around, delight etched on every plane of his face. "I wish you so much happiness…you deserve it, Samara. I was so afraid…" He stopped, not wanting to introduce anything which would dampen her spirts, but it was too late.

"Afraid of what?" she asked, a slight smile on her lips, her eyes insistent. She suspected he meant her "infatuation" with Reese Hampton and she thought to tease him more. It would make the surprise so much more delicious.

"Just that—that…"

"I would mourn forever for Captain Hampton?"

He looked uncomfortable, his face admitting the truth.

"You see," she said lightly, "you quite wasted your worries. I'm not distraught at all."

He breathed a sigh of relief. "That's fine because…" Again he stopped himself.

Again she insisted he continue. "Because…?

"It's just that one of the ships we took…had some newspapers. There was a report of Hampton's engagement…"

A sudden perceptible change filled the air. He watched as the joy drained from Samara's face, and it turned white with shock. Puzzled, he looked to his mother and saw disbelief in her face.

Samara finally managed one choked word. "Wh-when…?

Bren looked around in confusion. Something was terribly wrong. Could his sister still care about Hampton when she was engaged to someone else?"

"Samara?" he asked quizzically.

"When, Bren…when did he get engaged? To whom?"

Bren was now thoroughly befuddled. He knew something was terribly wrong. He answered slowly, very careful with his words. "Apparently after we left Bermuda. To a Lady Stanton." He was not going to say it was a love match. Not now. Not when his sister looked as if she would faint, and his mother wore a most untypical stricken expression.

He tried to soften the impact of his news. He didn't understand why she seemed to care so very much. Hampton was, after all, dead and gone these many months. And the two of them—Reese Hampton and Samara—had been at each other's throats more often than not.

His words were soothing now. "You know English marriages—they are mostly arranged…alliances between families, for one reason or another."

But the words had no meaning to Samara. Through the haze of pain that was enveloping her, she knew differently. Reese could never be coerced into a marriage he did not want. He simply would not tolerate it. He had said as much that day in the cave. As he had said so many other things.

She stood there, trembling, as she realized the depth of his betrayal. His soft words echoed in her head. "I love you...you see, I've never said it before..." And later...later he had said he would never marry without love.

Anguish was choking her heart as his words kept repeating themselves. How well she remembered each of them. When she had asked so foolishly if he had ever been in love, ever been betrothed, he had said no. Silent tears formed in her eyes and she turned away, wanting no one to see her agony. Oh Reese, how could you? No wonder he planned to leave her here...he never intended to come back. It had all been a game to him, something to occupy his time while he was forced, against his will, to stay. Perhaps it was even his idea of revenge. What a complete fool she had been! All the doubts that had haunted her, all the fear that she had suppressed now rose and condemned him.

Bren looked at her grief-stricken face, too stunned to react. His unshakable mother was also looking as if she had seen a ghost...a very unwelcome one. He turned to her now, his eyes full of questions.

Even Samantha had difficulty speaking. There *had* to be an explanation. She could *not* have been so completely wrong about someone. She could not have so completely misunderstood the softness and love in Reese's face when she watched Samara. And yet what honorable man would offer for a lady when already engaged?

"Perhaps," she tried, "it was another Hampton."

Again, Bren didn't understand why it was so important.

"No, Mother," he said. "It said he was captain of a ship named the *Unicorn*, and he was brother to the Earl of Beddingfield." He gave her a long, searching look. "Why do you and Samara...what...?"

"Reese Hampton," his mother said slowly, "is the man you were going to meet tonight. The man Samara planned to marry."

"The devil you say!" And then—barely audibly—the

curses came in a long, fluid stream. The outburst was so angry he forgot his mother's aversion to profanity.

Samantha winced, while secretly agreeing with his sentiments.

Bren stopped long enough to ask, "But how?"

"When his ship was sunk, he apparently was able to swim to shore. He ended up at the Fontaine plantation…"

Bren, whose arm had gone protectively around Samara, could feel her tense as her mother explained all that had happened. When Samantha finished, his jaw muscles were working furiously.

All the affection and respect he had had for Hampton disappeared as the story unfolded. Not only had the Englishman acted the spy, he had taken advantage of his father's hospitality and Samara's inexperience. There could be no explanation. The formal betrothal in England took place after his sister and Hampton had met, and not many weeks before the Englishman landed on American soil. Bren shuddered at the thought of his sister reading the newspaper report. Love match. Damn the man.

"The bastard. I'll kill him," he said in a tight, controlled voice.

The slow words, each as cold and hard as steel, aroused Samara from her stupor. Still partly stunned from the gaping wound in her heart, Samara knew she could not let this happen. She did not want Reese dead, and even if she harbored such a murderous thought she could not let her brother sacrifice his life. And that, she was all too aware, would most likely be the result. Even Bren would be no match for the dangerous Captain Reese Hampton.

"No," she said, and Bren was surprised by the strength in the one word. Her face, stained by tears, was suddenly determined. "No," she said again.

Through his rage, Bren felt a flash of admiration. Samara was growing up. But what a hell of a way to do it. He wanted to tear Hampton apart with his bare hands.

"Has he…has he…touched you?" Brendan forced the words through his teeth.

Samara shivered. She couldn't let him know, couldn't let anyone know. They would either kill him, or he would kill them...all of them. Or her father would force a marriage, a marriage that now would be intolerable. She gathered her strength and said, firmly enough, "No. He never...just a kiss."

Brendan looked deep into her eyes, great gray-silver mists, and Samara summoned all the control, all the determination within her to keep from revealing the truth.

"Thank God for that," Brendan said, finally satisfied. "But what now? Damn if I'm going to carry him to safety when he's been playing with my sister's heart."

Samantha shook her head. "Connor gave his word. And," she said hopefully, "there might just be an explanation."

Samara interrupted, her voice cold and lifeless. "There is no explanation. He lied about so many things." She had never felt so deathly cold, so empty. She rubbed her hand against her face, trying to brush away the memories of the cave, the riverbank, of how readily she had thrown herself at him. She had made it so easy. "Little cat...little cat..." Even now the thought of those words, spoken so softly, so seductively, sent tremors through her.

I have to get away. That thought overwhelmed everything else. *I can't see him again. I can't let him know what he's done to me.* Her despair evolved into cold, hard fury and finally into resolute purpose.

"I want to go to Charleston," Samara said with a determination strengthened by pain. If she saw him, she would falter. She simply could not face him again, not ever. She couldn't face the raw agony of him; she would do something terrible. "I can stay with Melanie. Please, Mother. Please, before he returns."

Indecision flitted over her mother's face. "I think we should give him a chance to—"

"He lied to me, Mother. Nothing can explain that. Please let me keep my pride; let him think *I'm* leaving him."

"I don't know..."

Bren interrupted. "If you don't want me to break his neck,

I think that's the best thing for everyone. You two can leave immediately for Charleston with Caesar. Marion's there; ask him to ride back. We'll take Hampton to the ship tomorrow. Hog-tied, if need be. The sooner I get rid of him the happier I'll be. If Father hadn't given his word, I swear I would take great pleasure in seeing him hang.''

"I don't want Father or Marion to know...to know why,'' Samara said. "They would call him out. Please tell them, tell *him* I've changed my mind, that I don't want to marry an Englishman, that I've gone away to avoid a scene.''

Brendan hesitated. He had never lied to his father, but Samara was right. His father *would* call Hampton out. And probably get killed. There really wasn't any other choice. Damn Hampton. And once he had thought him a friend. Barely controlling his rage and frustration, Bren tightened his arms around Samara, then slowly helped her up. "If you're to be gone before they get back, you'd best hurry,'' he said softly. His heart nearly broke as Samara struggled to hide the hurt and pain, walking, ever so slowly, out the door and up the stairs to pack.

Happily oblivious of the disaster that awaited him, Reese threw back his head and laughed at the vivid description of his future father-in-law's marriage to Samantha.

It had been a most satisfactory day, and he had settled several problems in his own mind, the most important of which concerned Samara. Much to Connor O'Neill's pleasure, he had announced his intention to settle in the South after the war. Reese had found he liked Americans very much; he liked their independence and their spirit and their predilection for work. He was also drawn by the fact that there were still vast, unworked tracts of land available, land where he could start anew. Honor forbade him abandoning his country in time of war, but after...

He and Connor discussed the possibility of marrying Samara immediately, before Reese left with Bren, but there were so many problems. He was not, currently, a wealthy man; he had given most of his earnings to Avery for Beddingfield and would have to return to privateering to amass sufficient funds to purchase the land he wanted. "French ships," he reassured Connor with a boyish smile. "Only French." In the meantime, Samara would be safer and happier with her family than in an enemy land with few friends.

And there was another problem in marrying her in South Carolina: Reese's own identity. For a marriage to be valid, Reese would have to use his name, and it was only too familiar in the Carolinas. He was thought to be dead and his resurrection would only put everyone in danger.

In a moment of rare confidence, Connor told Reese of his own most unusual marriage, drawing the laugh that rolled over the fields.

"Samantha," he recounted, "didn't use her real name when we first married. I didn't know we weren't legally married until she was just giving birth to Brendan. She was staying with a friend who," Connor's eyes twinkled, "ran a rather famous brothel. I ran out and kidnapped a minister and dragged him unwillingly into a 'house of sin.' The words were said just before the baby came. I doubt the minister ever quite recuperated, though he did consent to stay and toast the child. Several times. You see, you aren't the first to be kidnapped by the O'Neill family. It seems my sons come by it naturally."

Reese grinned. "You seem to have a way of mollifying your victims."

It was Connor's turn to laugh. He liked Hampton more each day. If only he weren't English...if only this damn war were over.

They learned at the stables that Brendan had returned, and that Samantha and Samara had left in the carriage with Marcus. No one knew exactly where they were going or how long they would be gone.

Reese felt a momentary stab of disappointment. Now that Bren was here, his and Samara's time together would be short. He wanted every minute. His humor was quickly restored, however, by the thought of renewing his friendship with Brendan. There had been few men with whom Reese had felt such a ready bond. As a man who seldom sought approval for any

of his actions, he was startled by how strongly he wanted
Bren's friendship and approval, not only for himself but for
Samara. He knew how close brother and sister were.

Brendan had been pacing the floor in the library, trying to
leash his anger. He had to keep it under control in order to
keep his father and Hampton from discovering the real reason
Samara had left. It would be the most difficult thing he had
ever done.

Much of his rage resulted, he knew, from his own personal
disappointment in Hampton. He had liked and respected the
man and, in truth, owed him a debt. Several of them. He had
known Hampton was mercurial, complex, but never had he
thought the man would take such wanton advantage of someone as innocent as Samara. That one action wiped out everything between them. He had tried to explain, in his own mind,
the man's action. But there could be no explanation. A recently engaged man simply did not so readily offer marriage
to another woman. The fact that Hampton had said nothing
about his previous attachment condemned him. If he had, perhaps, changed his mind about the London betrothal, he should
have explained the circumstances to Samara and her family.
It was also damning that he planned to leave without her.

What game had Hampton been playing? Brendan knew he
must have been furious about his abduction. Had he sought
revenge by seducing his sister? Although she denied it, he
couldn't help but fear the worst. If he knew for sure, he *would*
kill Hampton. It was enough he had dealt Samara a blow from
which she might never recover. For now he had to pretend a
coolness he didn't feel—otherwise, Hampton could destroy the
rest of his family.

Almost eagerly, Reese entered the library, his hand outstretched, a smile lighting his striking face. It quickly faded
when he saw Brendan's glacial expression just before the
American turned away. Reese let his arm drop, wariness creeping into his eyes. There was a restrained violence in the room.

He could smell it, taste it. It was perceptible in every jerky move of Brendan O'Neill's body.

Reese had come in alone while Connor gave the grooms instructions about the horses. His hands clenched now with foreboding.

"You know," he said softly. "You know about Samara. I've asked her to marry me. I had hoped you would be pleased."

"There is no engagement, no marriage," Brendan said harshly, as he turned his icy eyes on Reese. Distaste was written all over his face. "Samara has decided she does not want to marry you. She has left Glen Woods until you sail with me. We leave tomorrow morning."

"You lie," Reese said, his voice practically snarling now.

"I think you're rather adept at that yourself," Bren said brutally. "But in this case you're wrong. She doesn't wish to marry a man of your nationality or your profession or your character."

Reese felt a coldness envelope him. What in God's name had happened? He took a step forward, "Brendan…?" He couldn't hide the pleading note in his voice.

But he could find no softening in O'Neill's face. If anything, it hardened. "Be ready to leave at dawn."

"Not until I talk to Samara." Now the entreaty was gone from Reese's voice, and there was a hard determined edge to it.

"She doesn't want to talk to you. Not now. Not ever. She knows she has made a mistake."

"I don't believe you."

"That's a matter of indifference to me, Hampton. You *will* stay here tonight and you *will* leave with me in the morning, if I have to hog-tie you. My father promised to get you to safety and I will honor that promise. But you are a spy in my country, and I could care less about your comfort."

There was a false ring to the speech, something more to Bren's hostility than Reese's own rather unfortunate and very short-lived career as a spy.

The two men were glaring at each other when Connor entered. Like Reese earlier, his smile quickly changed to a puzzled frown at the obvious tension in the room.

"Brendan…it's good to see you. You know about—"

"Samara has decided she does not wish to continue the engagement," Brendan interrupted. "She just doesn't think she could live in England."

"But Reese has decided to—"

"Samara," Bren interrupted, "has gone to visit some friends for a few days. Mother went with her. I must get back to my ship tomorrow, and Hampton will go with me."

Connor started, "But—"

"It's the way Samara wants it," Brendan said. He was dismayed. He had not been surprised at his mother's affection for the Englishman. He had seen the man's charm at its most potent. But his father…and then he remembered how easily he too had been attracted by Reese's easy friendship. Easy and treacherous.

"I don't understand," Connor said, becoming thoroughly angry. Reese Hampton was a guest in his home, a friend. He didn't care for Bren's tone, his usurpation of authority, or his arrogance. "Where is Samara? She owes Reese an explanation."

"She owes him *nothing*." The statement was explosively bitter, and it stopped the older O'Neill. This performance was totally unlike his son and, like Reese, he knew there was something he was not being told. He did not like that knowledge at all. But he obviously was not going to learn any more in front of Reese.

He turned to Reese. "I want to talk to my son alone."

Reese, whose own anger was barely held in check, merely shrugged in a gesture now becoming familiar to Connor. His seemingly indifferent attitude was belied by the rigid muscles in his jaw and the firm set of his mouth.

"I will not leave without talking to Samara," Reese said, walking to the door. He turned back to the O'Neill father and son, and his brilliant eyes, blazing with fury, challenged them. He closed the door behind him with deceptive gentleness and walked to the front entrance, letting himself out. He stood on the porch, looking towards the bare winter trees, realizing for the first time how lonely they looked without their rich green ornaments. The gray wispy moss only emphasized their bleakness. He swallowed. In less than an hour, all his plans for a future had been smashed.

Rage was slowly replaced by an aching emptiness. Reese felt hollow inside and, for one of the few times in his life, uncertain. He had been so sure Samara loved him and wanted a life together as much as he. Perhaps he had expected too much, perhaps she *had* decided there were too many differences between them. Yet she had placed herself in his hands so freely, so lovingly. There had been no reservations.

She *was* young. She *had* been thoroughly protected all her life, but she had also shown a determined independence. What had Brendan said to her? What had caused the American's bitter animosity? A year ago, they had almost been friends. He remembered Bren's last words: "It's been an honor…"

A hand went up and rubbed the back of his neck in frustration. He walked down the steps and, lost in bitter thoughts, wandered almost aimlessly, only barely aware of the two servants who shadowed him.

"I can't believe Samara would do this." Connor O'Neill's voice was louder than necessary. "I've never seen her so happy."

Brendan turned away and stared at the book-lined wall of the library. He couldn't meet his father's eyes. "I don't think," he said slowly, "that she fully grasped what it would mean to be betrothed to an enemy, to watch him go away and know he was fighting her country, possibly even her own family."

"That's nonsense," Connor sputtered, "and you know it. He has said he would no longer attack American shipping. As for the French, who cares? They've attacked and seized enough of our ships."

Brendan spun around, his face almost accusing. "So he's charmed you, too. Can't you see him for what he is? What do you think he was doing when his ship was sunk…after he met

Samara? Has he told you the names of his accomplices? He had to have help here. What do you really know about him? He could already be married, or betrothed for all we know. Members of the English nobility don't marry commoners, nor do they marry for love. They *make* matches. Have you thought that perhaps, just perhaps, he might be using Samara? Using you all?'' Brendan stopped, aghast at his own words. He had never spoken with such rudeness to his father, nor had he intended to reveal so much. His temper had simply taken over. He had gone much too far. He could see it in his father's furious face.

"I thought," his father said coldly, "he was your friend. You certainly gave me that impression months ago."

"That was before I knew he was a damn spy," Bren said, weighing his words more carefully.

"That doesn't explain Samara," his father insisted. "She knew, and she didn't care."

In a more moderate tone, Brendan tried to extricate himself. "She just wanted more time to think about it...and she felt she had to do it alone."

"It's not like Samara to run away from a problem. To run to one, perhaps, but not away."

Bren frowned. "This one was bigger than most." He played his trump card, "And Mother agreed."

Connor regarded him with sheer astonishment, then disbelief. Samantha had been Reese's champion from the beginning. She had always felt that Samara and Reese were meant to be together. It was one reason he had capitulated. It was only later that he had grown very fond of Reese and considered him almost a member of the family.

"There's something you are not telling me," he said now.

"There is nothing. Any engagement will only hamper Samara now. The war could last one or two or even three more years. Hampton could die, or change his mind or any of several things. It's best to wait until the end. If they both feel the same way...then he could return, and we'll all know he really loves her."

"He won't agree."

Brendan's voice hardened. "I don't care if he does or not. He's put this whole family in danger, not to mention his own fate if discovered. And how would Samara feel about *that*?"

Connor, at least, agreed with that observation. Spiriting Hampton out of sight every time there was a visitor had become awkward. There were also questions in the parish as to why the usually hospitable O'Neills had almost completely isolated themselves. He sighed in defeat.

"Where did your mother and Samara go?"

"Mother's accompanying Samara to Charleston. Both will stay with the Demerests for a few days. They've been invited often enough."

Connor raised an eyebrow. "You've worked all this out rather nicely, haven't you?" He was quietly outraged. As far as he was concerned, his entire family was acting abominably. Unfortunately, there was, at this point, little he could do. Hampton was in great danger here, and his presence endangered every member of Connor's family. He could only try to convince Hampton that Samara's doubts were normal, that she would get over them, and be waiting. It would probably be best if Hampton *did* leave now, he thought reluctantly. For the safety of everyone.

Reese went to the stables. He would take a ride, try to clear his head and think things out. All restrictions on his movements had been lifted weeks earlier. He was only cautioned to stay within Glen Woods for his own protection.

But when he asked for his usual mount, he was met with an apologetic smile. "Sorry, Cap'n...Mr. Bren's orders."

Reese stiffened in anger. So even his word was no longer given credence. He nodded curtly to the groom and walked outside, where he stopped. He leaned against a fence and closed his eyes.

When did it start? What second, what minute, what hour had he begun to lose control of his own life? The instant he decided to attack the *Samara*? When he saw a dirty, dusty bedraggled girl bravely confront him? When she was trying, so terribly ineptly, to get him drunk? It seemed everything after that had led inevitably here: his restlessness in England, his decision to return to the Carolina coast, the Fontaines' ball. One inexorable step after another.

Well, he would break the pattern. Perhaps he was well free of Samara, of her whole damned family, of the bonds that had been tightening so securely around him. He had never needed anyone. He didn't now.

He heard the sound of footsteps, but he didn't turn around.

Connor's voice was deep with regret, even pain. "I'm sorry, Reese. Perhaps after…" His words trailed off. If he had been Hampton, he wouldn't want to hear them.

"I'll be ready tomorrow," Reese said. Despite himself, the tone, the slow words, reflected a deep hurt. He had expected so much of this day. One hand clenched the rail in front of him before he turned to face Connor and added softly, "I know you risked much for me. I will do nothing to make you regret it." His brilliant green-blue eyes met Connor's gray ones, and Connor was struck by the raw pain in them.

With quiet dignity, Reese turned and walked back to the house.

Connor O'Neill watched him disappear and knew an unprecedented desire to strangle nearly every member of his family.

Chapter Seventeen

It was the most wretched Christmas Samara had ever experienced. It was made even worse since, weeks earlier, she had expected it to be the best.

When she had returned ten days earlier from Charleston, Reese was gone, and nothing seemed to matter. She had to force herself to wrap the presents she had so halfheartedly purchased in Charleston...she who had loved Christmas better than anyone. There was one present she didn't wrap; it was buried deep in her trunk, but out of sight did not mean out of mind. She had spent many nights knitting a handsome scarf for Reese, in the hope that he would be able to remain at Glen Woods until Christmas. It had been a labor of love for Samara who so hated handwork. But she had wanted to give him something special.

Fool she chastened herself. Stop thinking of him. If only she could. Where was he now? On his way home to England—and to the woman he planned to marry. Or had he obtained another ship and gone back to attacking American vessels? Certainly not this quickly. He was probably celebrating his freedom—freedom from Glen Woods, freedom from her—in some tavern or worse.

Just thinking of his long, beautiful masculine body next to someone else filled her eyes with tears. She had never cried much before she met Reese Hampton. Her brothers thought it unmanly for themselves, and she could never be less than her brothers. She had never cried at hurts or disappointments. But now the tears wouldn't stop coming, and at the most unexpected times. She would be at dinner or reading a book or riding, and something would remind her of his aqua eyes or his easy graceful walk or the way he dominated a room.

"Samara." Her father's voice broke the trance.

Hastily rubbing the wetness from her face, she reluctantly turned to him, knowing the telltale stains remained.

His voice softened. When Samara had first returned home, he hadn't tried to hide his censure. He had been deeply disappointed with his daughter for the first time in her life. He had thought she owed it to Reese Hampton to face him. He had, in fact, been so hard on his daughter that his wife finally decided to tell him the truth. Reese was gone, after all. The danger of a duel, or any kind of retribution was gone.

To her amazement, her husband had become even angrier— at her, at Samara and, most of all, at his oldest son. She had realized then that Connor had become much closer to the Englishman than anyone had realized. And she had conveniently forgotten how very much her husband hated lies and subterfuge. Connor had always been the fairest—most honest—man she had ever known.

"He was going to buy property in Virginia—for Samara— so she wouldn't have to leave this country, so she wouldn't be so terribly far from us. Does that sound like a man planning to marry someone else?"

"Maybe he just wanted—"

Connor interrupted. "You don't ask the questions he asked, with that intensity, without being very serious. And you don't look at a woman as he looked at Samara without being in love." He paced the floor with more and more agitation. "You, Sam, you should know better than anyone how much damage silence can do."

"You should have seen her, Connor. She begged me."

"I'm seeing her now," Connor said roughly, "and it can't be any worse. For God's sake, why didn't you give him a chance to explain?"

Samantha could only shake her head miserably. "What can we do?" she asked.

"I don't know," he replied wearily. "If I were Reese I wouldn't want any more to do with this family. I'll try to write him in Bermuda and England, but God knows what words I'll use, or when and how he will receive it…"

Now this Christmas afternoon, he sat quietly next to his daughter, feeling her grief. He debated whether to give her the gift he held in his hand, but he had promised Reese. Prior to Bren's arrival, Reese had designed it and asked Connor to have it made by a silversmith. Connor had been given a promissory note in payment. On the morning of his departure, Reese had asked Connor to give it to Samara at Christmas.

Connor handed her the small package. "It's from Reese," he said. "I thought you might like to open it alone." He stood and walked away. Samara held it for several minutes, then carefully unwrapped it. She had thought she could feel no worse. But she knew now she could.

Wrapped securely in a piece of blue velvet was a small silver medal. Carefully crafted on one side was an intricately etched schooner. On the other, a wine bottle.

Her right hand tightened around it. She could almost feel the love in the exquisite small disc. In her mind's eyes, she saw the mischievous gleam in his eye and the soft laughter on his lips.

Not for the first time, she questioned her ready condemnation of him—and her own precipitous action. Had she allowed her own fear and uncertainty to destroy something that was so wondrous? Why had she leaped to such terrible conclusions?

"Was I wrong?" she whispered to herself. "Was I so completely wrong?" She hugged her knees and rocked, her grief so great she wondered if she could endure it.

It had been a nightmare of an odyssey from Glen Woods to Bermuda, Reese thought as he took yet another long swallow of raw rum.

Marion had arrived the morning after Bren's hostile appearance. Reese, sleepless, was at the window of his room.

He had spent much of the night pacing, trying to puzzle out what had happened. But he had no more answers than he had the previous evening.

The three of them—a puzzled Marion, a withdrawn and unsmiling Brendan, and an angry Reese—had left Glen Woods at noon. Reese's only satisfaction was that Connor's farewell to him was much warmer than his to Brendan.

Despite threats, Reese was not bound, but Brendan made sure that he stayed between the two brothers during the long ride. They drank and ate in the saddle and stopped only briefly to water and rest the horses. When they finally reached the river where the *Samara* was anchored, Marion's usual smile was gone. He did not know what had happened to bring about Bren's watchful and hostile attitude toward Reese, nor Reese's tight-lipped silence. He bid Reese a good journey and disappeared, leading the other two horses.

Reese was given the second mate's cabin and told to stay there. He heard a guard being posted outside. The cabin was tiny with only a small porthole, and he felt trapped and confused. It wasn't until the *Samara* reached open sea at dawn the next morning that he was allowed the freedom of the ship. Brendan carefully avoided him, and he ate alone on deck.

At the end of the second day, the captain summoned him to his cabin for the first time.

"We're off the Florida coast," he said curtly, "not far from St. Augustine where you should be able to find a ship. My men will row you ashore." He took a small purse and tossed it to Reese. "There should be enough there for passage to Bermuda and your needs in St. Augustine. I assume you have funds in Bermuda?"

Reese nodded, his eyes searching for a clue as to what had hardened Brendan against him.

"That does it, then," Brendan said. "It ends things between us."

"Brendan...?" The question was soft; puzzled.

Brendan's jaw tightened. It was difficult, if not impossible, to ignore the entreaty in Reese's face. He knew that it must be a very rare sight, indeed, but he was in no mood to be sympathetic.

"Go back to your own world, Hampton. Go back to where everyone knows the rules of the games you play."

"What in blazes are you talking about?"

"Samara," Bren said. "Samara, damn your black heart." His temper boiled over and his fist drove at Reese's stomach. Reese sidestepped and took the blow in his side as his own hands took aim at the American. He put all his fury into the one blow, and Brendan went tumbling to the floor.

Reese stood over him, hands clenching and unclenching as he tried to control himself. Fighting Brendan would solve nothing, but he wanted to strike back.

Brendan came slowly to his feet. He too was suppressing a compulsion to whip the man in front of him. It would be a close match, and he would enjoy every bit of punishment he could deliver. Yet there was danger lurking off the Florida coast, and he dared not tarry for personal satisfaction. "Some other day," he said softly.

Reese nodded. They were the last words they spoke...

He had been rowed to a beach and started walking, thinking of a similar journey months earlier. But this time he had money, and was not in enemy territory. Florida was a possession of Spain, and Spanish fears of American expansionism made the English welcome. He was able to buy an old but serviceable horse and food. In St. Augustine, he found a ship headed for Bermuda...

Yancy was waiting for him on the dock at St. George. Reese's friend had met every incoming ship since he and the rest of the *Unicorn*'s crew had arrived several weeks earlier. They had been unexpectedly, Yancy reported, and very suddenly exchanged after spending three months in a Boston dungeon. Yancy had heard nothing of Hampton and didn't know if he'd survived the swim or the equally dangerous countryside. They looked at each other, smiled and headed for the nearest tavern....

A day later, Reese was still drinking. He was sprawled over

two chairs, his hand resting on a bottle of rum that sat on the floor.

Yancy looked at him with deep concern. For one of the few times in his life he was thankful that the rum was watered, for the captain was finishing his second bottle of the day and his thirst showed no sign of slaking.

Yancy could hear the drunken carolers outside, reminding him once more that this was Christmas day. There were few other signs in the tavern. There certainly wasn't any in the unshaven, unkempt man across from him who bore little resemblance to the usually immaculate Reese Hampton.

"What in God's name happened to you?" Yancy said, watching as Reese took another long swallow. His friend had said nothing about where he had been or how he had escaped.

"Everything that could have," Reese said with a drunken, enigmatic expression.

"And what might that be?" Yancy persisted, thinking that Reese was the only man he knew whose speech got progressively more precise as he drank.

Reese considered all that had transpired in the past months. He had briefly, ineptly, been a spy, been kidnapped at a ball, made prisoner in a plantation storehouse, fallen in love, became engaged, became unengaged, found a friend, lost a friend. Who in the hell knew what had happened? He didn't. It all seemed a crazy nightmare. "Wouldn't believe it if I told you," he said finally.

Yancy shook his head in frustration. "Try me, friend. Perhaps I could help."

Reese opened one of his half closed eyes. "Don't want any help…better this way." He wanted Yancy's companionship but not his advice, not now. He didn't want to think about Samara. Or South Carolina. "'Tis of no matter, anyway," he said very clearly. "'Tis done. Gone. Nevermore." He rolled the last word as if tasting it. "Nevermore," he said again.

Yancy winced at the bitterness in Reese's voice. It was something new, something he didn't like. "Reese," he said, trying to divert his friend's thoughts, "the whole crew's been waiting. They've passed up good berths, even not knowing—"

"If I were dead or alive?" Reese struggled with himself. Yancy's last comment made an impact where others hadn't. Responsibility and loyalty. That's what mattered. Loyalty. There was precious little of that left. Loyalty and trust…and responsibility.

He took another long drink as he considered responsibility. Just as he passed out, he thought of Samara. "You finally managed to get me drunk," he whispered to her…wherever she was.

The next morning Reese wanted only to die in peace. He awoke in a strange room with a head that felt like the inside of a drum. And there was more than one person beating on it.

His stomach felt equally battered and it got worse when he smelled something suspiciously like tea. He cautiously opened one eye.

Yancy was standing there with a wry smile. "It's my turn," he said, "to make *you* better by inflicting misery. Drink this!"

Reese eyed it warily.

"Come on, Captain. You have a lot to do today."

Reese closed his eyes, wishing the doctor away.

"If you don't," Yancy threatened, "I'll tie you up and force it down. And right now you look bad enough that I could do it with one hand."

"You have no respect for your captain," Reese observed, with a pained expression. One hand went up to his cheek and felt the stubble with distaste. He was suddenly filled with self-disgust. He didn't remember much about the previous two days which was, he supposed, probably fortunate. He reluctantly took Yancy's cup, tentatively tasting the bitter brew. There was much more than tea in it, but he wasn't going to question it. He grimaced as he took a long swallow.

"That's a good lad," Yancy said soothingly, barely suppressing a broad smile. Some of the old Reese was returning. Slowly, it was true, but surely. Some life was coming back into the captain's eyes.

"There are a couple of ships you might like to look at," he said, trying to stir some interest. "They're not the quality of the *Unicorn*, but they look fit enough." He was pleased to see the first signs of interest in Reese's face. Perhaps these past two days were what the man needed to get something out of his system. He knew better than to pry. Reese would tell him when he was ready.

As Reese finished the tea, Yancy discussed the men. They had lost three to other ships, but the rest had remained steadfast, waiting for "the best captain on either side of hell." He grinned as he said it, adding slyly, "They didn't see you last night."

"And you aren't going to let me forget it, are you, Yancy?"

"Probably not," Yancy agreed amiably.

Reese relaxed. The tea *had* helped. It was good to see Yancy again. There was a constancy about his irreverence. He could almost believe the past four months had been only a bad dream. Almost. He would make them that.

"About those ships?" he said, immediately turning his mind to exactly how much money he had in the Bermuda banking house. There had been two prizes before he had taken the *Samara*. He should have sufficient funds to purchase a suitable ship and arm it.

Disregarding his discomfort, he and Yancy spent the morning looking at ships and the afternoon talking to his crew. Together, they made their choice and started outfitting her.

They would sail for the French coast in a week.

One of Connor's letters finally caught up with Reese at Beddingfield. It had been waiting there for months, unopened.

The letter was the first thing mentioned by Avery when Reese, taut with weariness and strain, visited while his ship, the *Phoenix*, was undergoing repairs at the London dock. He had been at sea nearly five months and had taken six French merchant ships. He had given his crew a larger than usual share because of their imprisonment—a result, he felt, of his own foolishness. That, plus the cost of repairs, had kept his purse lean.

Avery was in his office, engrossed in the books, when Reese unexpectedly appeared. After a warm greeting, Avery pointed to a white packet. "Who," Avery said, "do you know in

South Carolina?'' Reese had said nothing in his rare corre-
spondence about his adventures in America, only that the *Unicorn* had been lost and he had replaced it. Neither had he
explained the origin of his ship's name, the *Phoenix*, the myth-
ological bird which rose from the ashes.

Reese tensed at the mention of South Carolina, and his face
paled under the bronze color. He glared at the offending letter.

Avery raised an eyebrow.

"You're not going to open it? Leigh has been dying of
curiosity, not, of course, to mention my own brotherly interest.'' Reese looked at the letter as if it were a shark and he a
tempting fish. "No,'' he said shortly, and strode back out the
door, leaving Avery to stare in astonishment, first at the disappearing brother and then the letter.

Despite his long ride from London and the lateness of the
day, Reese ordered a horse saddled and spurred him out of the
barn. He rode as if the devil were chasing him, as he had as
a young boy frustrated by his father's indifference. He rode to
rid himself of the more recent demons that made his life a
misery. He thought he had conquered them, and now this.

Both rider and horse were soaked with sweat when he returned. Avery's face was a study in concern. Leigh was bewildered.

"Would you please tell me what is going on?'' Avery
asked.

Reese looked at the two of them, and felt a twinge of guilt.
His behavior had been erratic, if not lunatic. He bent over and
kissed Leigh on the cheek. "I apologize.''

"You don't ever have to apologize,'' Leigh said quietly.
"Not here, not to us. You know that. Is there anything I can
get you?''

Reese looked down at his dirt-splattered clothes. "I think I
need a bath more than anything else.''

Leigh smiled. "I'll see to it, Reese. You and Avery talk.''
She left, shutting the door quietly behind her.

Avery eyed Reese intently. There was something unap-
proachable about him. A barrier that had never been there
before.

"Is there something I can do?" he asked simply.

Reese's mouth twisted in a wry smile. "No. I thought I had it worked out..." He looked at the letter. "When did this come?"

"Nearly four months ago."

"Ah, blissful ignorance."

"You aren't going to open it?"

"I suppose I have to," Reese said, "or I'll be haunted even more than I am now." He disregarded Avery's quizzical look at his bitter, cryptic words. He took the letter gingerly.

Avery watched his brother's drawn face. "I'll leave you alone." He left, closing the doors behind him.

Reese stared at the parchment, wondering at the strong scrawl. It obviously wasn't Samara; he had seen her handwriting. Connor? Brendan? But surely not Brendan. Reese still smarted from their last encounter.

He slowly opened it.

Anger was his first emotion as he slowly read the letter and crumpled it in his fist.

It was soon joined by a certain anguish that there had been so little trust.

He tried to understand. He was, after all, a member of a class many Americans distrusted and, as it had been pointed out many times, he was technically an enemy of their country. But he had thought, during the months at Glen Woods, that he had gained both trust and friendship. To be condemned without a hearing was extremely painful.

And Samara... Did she have so little faith in him? Could she really think, after that day in the cave, that he would use her so lightly?

He smoothed out the parchment and studied the words...this time with great care. It was from Connor, and the words were obviously very carefully chosen. He wrote that he believed Reese deserved an explanation, one that he himself had not received until after Reese had gone. In short terse words, he relayed the substance of the newspaper report of Reese's engagement and its shattering effect on Samara. In conclusion, he said:

I know there must be an explanation, and I bitterly regret that you were given neither the opportunity nor the courtesy to make one. I believe you loved my daughter and would do nothing to hurt her. I came to consider you a member of my family, and I still do.

I know it is probably presumptuous to write you, to apologize and even to hope you will understand. But Samara, I believe, loves you deeply.

Under the circumstances, I can ask no more of you. But I felt an explanation was required.

With regard,
Connor O'Neill

With a deep sigh, Reese sank into one of the leather chairs in the study. At least, one mystery was solved. He now knew the reason for Samara's defection. Her sudden flight had preyed upon him. He had thought he knew her, and cowardice seemed not in her character. He thought of her now as she had been on the riverbank, so warm and lovely and happy. Seemingly so confident in his love. Apparently, even then there were doubts. There must have been for her to believe so easily that he could be guilty of such duplicity.

He thought of the evidence against him, and with a groan he recalled their conversation in the cave when they had both declared their love. He had teasingly asked her about beaux, and she had queried him in return. He remembered saying there had never been any attachments, and then she had seen the engagement notice!

Reese suddenly understood what had happened. He had instinctively sensed she had always been a little afraid of him—of who and what he was. As much as he had tried, he had apparently never completely conquered that fear. He was everything she had been brought up to distrust, and they had met under the worst possible circumstances.

Could any relationship between them be possible now? He loved her. He had been very sure of that in South Carolina. No woman had ever roused that tenderness in him before. Samara's face stayed in his mind's eye, her passion in his thoughts, her laughter in his heart—despite all his attempts to banish them.

But was that enough? He didn't know. He had offered everything he had, and it obviously hadn't been enough. It hadn't served to quiet the doubts nor provide the trust he needed. His right hand went to his cheek, rubbing it absently.

There was nothing he could do now, anyway. His ship would be undergoing repairs for several weeks. He had arranged, months ago, for a bank draft, along with specific instructions, to be sent to Connor O'Neill for Samara's medal and his own expenses during those lost months. He thought now about writing Connor, then abruptly dismissed the idea. He was still too angry, too wounded. At the moment, he was damned if he was going to explain anything.

"That's wonderful," Samara told Angelique, and the little girl beamed with pride as she settled her primer down on the desk.

"Canty, can you continue?"

The sixteen-year-old boy started, then stumbled as he tried to decipher the next sentence in the book. Frustration and longing crossed his face as his lips moved, but no words came. He bowed his head.

Samara's heart went out to him. He wanted so badly to learn and was terrified he could not. He was being given a chance he had never thought to have, and he was anxious, too anxious.

"It's alright, Canty, you're doing very well," she said gently.

His young, bitter face relaxed, but there was no smile. Samara thought sadly that it would probably be a long time before Canty learned that particular skill.

Her father had bought Canty several months earlier at a slave auction. Samara had been startled because he seldom attended them. He had explained that he had been passing the auction block when one of the slaves caught his attention; a young boy, with pride in his bearing despite heavy chains and a lacerated back.

Connor had brought him home, and for weeks Canty had

displayed only blatant hatred. It had taken time for him to
believe his good fortune: a chance for freedom, a chance to
learn. He had become Samara's most eager pupil, although a
certain amount of distrust lingered.

As she dismissed the class, Samara regarded her small classroom thoughtfully. She had, at first, fought the idea of teaching, thinking her patience limited and her ability to commu-
nicate nonexistent. But her mother had insisted she needed
help, and Samara had quickly discovered she had a natural
talent in the classroom. Perhaps, she thought, it was because
she, in turn, liked children so much. Or perhaps it was a burning desire to be useful. After Reese had left, she had taken
stock of herself and found little reason for pride. She had been
willful and heedless of the consequences. She herself had invited disaster.

The school met three times a week in an outbuilding. Although it was not mandatory, the O'Neills urged all children
between five and eleven to attend along with any older hands
who wished to learn. Freedom without education meant little,
and the O'Neills intended all their servants and field hands to
be free.

Those who attended the school—from the youngest child to
the oldest man or woman—understood and appreciated the
rare privilege, since education for slaves was considered almost treason in South Carolina. They were a joy to teach because they wanted, so badly, to learn. Samara always felt a
certain accomplishment after a morning in the classroom. It
lessened the hurt, but the loneliness never faded.

She hurried to the house, anxious to relate the day's accom-
plishments to her mother. They had always been close, but
now there was a new dimension to the relationship: a mutual
respect and understanding, and a shared passion for teaching.

As Samara entered the dining room, her mother was sitting
at the table, fingering a letter, her face creased with indecision.

"Mother?"

"It's a letter from Annabelle," Samantha said. "She would
like you to come for a visit."

Samantha couldn't miss the sudden glow in her daughter's

eyes. Samara loved her godmother dearly and seldom had a chance to see her. Annabelle lived in Washington with her husband, Joshua McLaughlin, a retired sea captain.

The light in Samara's face, however, died quickly. "I can't leave the school," she said. "Canty's just beginning to gain some confidence…"

Samantha smiled. Samara had matured greatly in the past six months. There was a new sense of purpose about her, a new grace and gentleness. She had been tempered, perhaps, by sorrow. It was a feeling Samantha well recognized, and while she suffered with Samara she also knew pride. She knew now that nothing could defeat her daughter.

Perhaps a trip to Washington would cure some of the melancholy that still seemed to haunt Samara. Annabelle said it was an exciting place, and Annabelle was always in the center of things. Samantha feared Glen Woods still held too many memories.

And Samantha secretly hoped Samara might find another young man. She felt a deep guilt about Reese Hampton after her husband's explosion, and had prayed for some word from him. Connor had sent letters to both Bermuda and the Earl of Beddingfield, but there had been no reply. Either they had not reached Reese or he, quite understandably, wanted nothing more to do with them. She sighed. She had wanted things to be easier for Samara than they had been for her, and she felt at least partly responsible that they were not.

"You forget, little one," she said, "that I've been teaching a lot longer than you. I can take over the school for a month."

"But you have so many other things to do."

"I would love to get back to teaching," Samantha said truthfully. "I've missed it."

"I *would* like to see Annabelle again," Samara said slowly. "It's been two years…"

"Then it's settled. We'll have some dresses made. Your father can take you the first week in July. He can visit Marion then, too."

Expectancy filled Samara. Marion had been sent to Washington with his militia unit, and she had missed him sorely.

Of her brothers, only Jere was in South Carolina. Bren was back at sea, and Conn was someplace near the Florida border with Andrew Jackson.

Connor fell in readily with the plans. He too felt it would do Samara good to get away, and Annabelle was the best tonic in the world.

The day before she was to leave, Samara dressed in some of Conn's old clothes and rode to the cave. She had been there only once since Reese had left, and that was right after Christmas. She had sat there for hours, trying to comprehend what had happened. Reese's gift had shattered her anger. The time, thought and humor that had gone into the silver medal showed he did, in some way, care. But why had he lied? Why had he not said something about the woman in England? She recalled his vivid green-blue eyes as he said he loved her. How warm they had been! She had resolutely buried the medal, trying to bury her memories with it.

Now she dug it up, as she had always known she would. She could not leave it behind. She rubbed it with her shirt until it shone, and felt a pain as sharp and new as it had been the day she ran from Reese. Would it ever dull with time? Somehow, she knew it would not.

Reese's eyes searched for the expanse of the open sea as he guided the *Phoenix* down the Thames, away from London's squalor. He needed the sea now as he had few other times in his life. He hungered for it, for the challenge that would cleanse his soul.

Already the air had changed and the sky was a clearer blue. He felt a sudden pleasure as the river widened and the brown and green earth tones of land gave way to deep blue, sparkling water. His eyes regained some of their usual brilliance and his face lifted to the sun, eager to feel its healing touch. The last weeks had tried his spirits sorely as he brooded about his future. Whatever it was, he knew it did not exist at Beddingfield. He had grown increasingly restless—day by agonizing day—as Avery tried to draw him more and more into the management of the estate. He had listened as they had ridden over every acre, though he knew it well. But Avery needed no help; he had seen that immediately. Apparently whatever shortages there had once been, they existed no longer. Seldom had he seen a better managed property. Although he had no wish to stay at Beddingfield, which was his brother's, he had become increasingly committed to the idea of purchasing property in Virginia after the war. With or without Samara O'Neill.

He had given much thought to the idea of building something of his own. His days of privateering, he knew, were nearing an end. The war with France had ended a few weeks before; he suspected the war with America would not last much longer. In any event, he would no longer attack American ships, and he had little desire to be a merchant or a real pirate—the only two choices remaining if he continued at sea.

Strangely enough, during his rides and conversations with Connor the prospect of farming had become unexpectedly appealing. He discovered that part of him yearned for the stability of a home and land of his own. He had previously mocked the idea, perhaps because he knew he would never have Beddingfield. He had gloried in his freedom, and he now wondered at his motives.

But he would have to wait until the war ended. He wanted that land to be in America. Part of the reason was financial. His limited funds would purchase a much larger tract in the young country than in Britain. But more importantly he was attracted by the energy and independence of the feisty new nation. It suited his temperament far better than England.

Part of that attraction, he realized ruefully, was Samara. After weeks of trying—quite unsuccessfully—to forget Samara and the O'Neills, he surrendered to a compulsion that would not let him go. He could not let her think he had so easily dishonored her. His own wounds were probably equaled or surpassed by those she had suffered. He knew he could write, but he rationalized that no letter could say what was in his heart. And he had feared, after all that had transpired, a letter would not even be believed. His eyes narrowed as he refought the battle within himself: his pride against his all-consuming need for her. He had to see her again!

He had finally told Avery—and Eloise—some of what had happened. Avery urged him to go, and Eloise was devastated at what their small intrigue had wrought. She had made her home at Beddingfield, despite several attempts by her late husband's brother to dislodge her. She now felt safe enough to make a public announcement that the engagement was off, though she would remain at Beddingfield under the protection of Avery and Leigh.

He had gathered Yancy and other members of the crew, warning them that there would be no prizes on this trip and, indeed, that he might well sell the *Phoenix* in Bermuda after a possibly dangerous trip to the Carolina coast.

"We'd sail with ye to hell," said one crewman, echoing the sentiments of most.

"I trust that's not our destination," Reese returned lightly, though his eyes glowed with pride and affection.

Three days later they set sail.

Unlike the *Unicorn*'s earlier storm-swept voyage, the *Phoenix* skimmed over calm seas beneath a radiantly blue sky in record time—less than three weeks. A good omen, Reese thought, as he anchored in Bermuda's St. George Harbor amidst a huge armada of British navy ships. He intended to refill his water and food stores before trying to find a certain river along the Carolina coast. He gave orders to Michael Simmons, who still served as first mate, while he and Yancy went in search of information. They found it at the White Horse Tavern.

The tavern was filled with British officers, many of them boisterously drunk. Reese searched among the faces, his eyes skimming from one to another. With a slight smile, he finally recognized an old school friend. He made his way carefully through the crowded room, apologizing several times to avoid a fight with battle-ready men.

"Longley," he said to an impeccably dressed colonel. "I thought you were with Wellington."

The scarlet-coated officer stood hastily, his hand outstretched. "My God, Hampton. It's been a long time. Join us, will you?"

Reese nodded and introduced Yancy, whose hostility was barely veiled. "Best doctor on the seas," Reese said.

"You should bring him along with us, then," Clifford Longley said. "It seems we're headed for another fight."

"Where?"

"Don't know exactly yet," Longley said. "The Admiralty's still trying to decide. Could be Washington. Could be Baltimore. My bet's on Washington. I understand that's what George Cockburn wants. One thing's for sure, there will be a fight. It's time to teach Madison a lesson." He chuckled. "Chastise, that is. The Admiralty wants him 'chastised.'" He looked at Reese carefully. "Are you still privateering? I heard you took a number of French ships."

"And several American," Reese said cheerfully.

"Why don't you tag along with us," Longley said. "I understand it's open season on the coastal areas."

"When are you sailing?"

"August the first," Longley replied. "Day after tomorrow."

Reese grinned. "We should be ready. I'll follow you at least part of the way. Now tell me about Napoléon's defeat. You were there?"

The next two hours Reese was regaled with the final hours of the war with France. "Even the French were eager to rid themselves of Napoléon," he said. "Paris surrendered, leaving Napoléon with few places to go."

It was late before Yancy and Reese got back to the ship. They stood on deck several minutes, watching the flickering lights on more than a hundred warships—frigates, schooners and transports.

"Are you quite sure about this?" Yancy asked, thinking the question foolish as he saw the determined gleam in Reese's eye. "You can get caught by either side, you know—and hung."

Reese looked around at the ships. "At least we have protection from the Americans part of the way."

"You're a damn fool, Reese."

"Quite possibly," Reese answered with equanimity, "but how do you explain your presence?"

"I'm a damn fool, too. You think you have a monopoly on it?"

"You keep telling me so," Reese retorted affectionately.

Yancy sighed, shook his head and went to his cabin, leaving Reese to his own thoughts.

Reese followed the armada for several days, then grew impatient with its pace and veered on his own toward the American coast, his sails picking up a lusty wind and bringing him closer to the Carolinas. He spent hours in his cabin pouring over charts, looking for one particular inlet and river, the one in which Brendan had anchored the *Samara*.

Although he had been locked in the cabin, he knew the river's general location by judging the number of miles they had traveled by horseback that day. And through the small porthole, he had noted several landmarks. He knew the waterway was deep enough, and isolated enough, to hide his ship for several days. He only briefly considered the possibility of encountering the *Samara*. The odds were exceedingly slim.

It took a day of searching but he finally found the mouth of the river, and he carefully guided the ship upriver far enough to hide its mast among the giant oaks. They anchored; and Reese, after leaving detailed orders with Simmons, slipped from the ship with Yancy who insisted on accompanying him. Reese simply nodded, knowing that Yancy would follow anyway—regardless of orders.

They walked for miles before spotting a small farmhouse. To Reese's delight, he spied several horses grazing in a corral. Telling Yancy to stay out of sight, he rubbed dirt on his trousers and shirt and approached the farmhouse.

He bartered with the farmer and his wife for nearly an hour, saying his horse had thrown him and galloped away. The farmer, back from the field for his meal, insisted on his visitor joining him for some cider. He was reluctant to part with any of his animals, he declared, as he eyed Reese's fine lawn shirt. Finally a bargain was struck, and Reese gained a fairly decent-looking horse for a ridiculously large number of coins. He picked up Yancy and they traveled several more miles before repeating the performance.

Reese took the road leading to Glen Woods with a rare feeling of uncertainty. He didn't know how he would be received—or by whom. If Conn or Brendan were home, there might be trouble. And Samara? What kind of reaction could he expect from her? It had been nearly eight months. His heel touched the side of his horse, and he cantered toward the barn.

"Cap'n." Reese heard Marcus' delighted greeting. "Mighty pleased to see you again, sir…Mist' O'Neill will be, too."

Reese's grim mouth relaxed a little. "This is my friend, Yancy," he said. "Is Mister O'Neill at home?"

"Why, yes, sir, he is. Came in just a few minutes ago. I'll tell him you're here." He called a groom to take the horses. "Come with me to the house."

"I would rather stay here," Reese said, not knowing exactly who was at home or what his welcome might—or might not—be. "Would you ask him to come out here alone?"

"Yessir, be mighty glad to, Cap'n." With a broad smile, he hurried away.

"It seems you have one friend here," Yancy said drily.

"That might well be the sum total," Reese replied with a skeptical smile. Despite what Connor had said in his letter, Reese had learned to expect the unexpected from the O'Neill family.

Reese took Yancy inside the barn and showed him Samantha's horses while they waited. He wanted to be out of sight of the main house.

The barn door opened, and Reese heard Connor's confident steps and his soft, low voice. "Reese?"

Reese stepped into the sunlight and stood there, waiting, his compelling eyes wary.

"It *is* you," Connor said, his eyes lighting, then he noticed Yancy. His mouth crinkled at the sides. "Another spy, Reese?"

"I'm neutral this time, Connor," Reese said, his mouth relaxing. "And my friend even more so. I suspect his sympathies lie with your countrymen. This is Yancy, my ship's surgeon. I think I mentioned him to you.''

"You're welcome, Yancy." Connor turned back to Reese. "My God, I'm glad to see you. I had hoped...come up to the house."

"Samara?"

Connor's face clouded. "In Washington. With her godmother..."

"Washington?" Reese's response was dagger-sharp, but Connor attributed it to disappointment.

"She's been there a month, plans to stay another few weeks. Annabelle's husband is ill and Samara seems to feel she's needed. I'll write to her, of course, and let her know..."

"I can't stay, Connor," Reese said, his stomach churning. He had learned Longley's supposition was right. The British were headed towards Washington, and it was very likely they would destroy the city—or try to. He felt sick inside. There was no telling what Samara might do if confronted by British troops. And the officers he had talked to in Bermuda were of no mind to be gentle. They blamed American stubbornness for prolonging the French-English war. He and Yancy exchanged unhappy glances.

"Stay at least a few days," Connor was saying. "I...we have much to talk about."

Reese's expression was bleak as he realized the trap he was in. Even if Connor wrote Samara today, it might well be too late. The British navy was probably already near the mouth of the Chesapeake. And he couldn't betray British plans to Connor or even to Samara. He could not play the traitor. Leadenly, he followed Connor to the house, his mind searching frantically for a solution.

In the library, Connor poured them all a glass of brandy while a servant was sent for Samantha.

Connor looked at Reese closely. "You received my letter?"

Still reeling from the shock of Samara's whereabouts, Reese merely nodded.

"Is that why you're back?"

"There was...is...some unfinished business," Reese said

slowly. "I wanted you to know what happened, and I didn't think I could do it by letter." Liar, he told himself. You wanted to see Samara. The muscles in his jaw tensed. "I didn't want Samara to think...I didn't care."

"Do you? Still?" Connor said gently.

Reese started pacing. "I don't know," he said, knowing it a lie as he mouthed the words. "If there's no trust, then there can be little else."

He started to speak again, but the door opened and Samantha stood there, a dawning of hope in her face. "Reese?" she said as her lovely blue eyes searched his face for an answer.

Reese bowed slightly, but his face remained grim, and Samantha's tentative smile faded.

"This is my ship's surgeon," he said only. "Yancy."

Samantha turned her charm on Yancy. "I've heard much about you from Samara. Thank you for being her friend."

Yancy was as stunned as Reese had first been on meeting Samantha. He couldn't imagine this small, energetic woman with the lively blue eyes having five children, one the age of Brendan.

"It was my pleasure, ma'am," he replied with a small smile.

Samantha turned her attention back to Reese. "I think...my husband believes...I owe you a very great apology."

Reese turned away, but it wasn't rudeness—more of a need to gather his thoughts. "Perhaps," he said slowly, "it was my fault. Perhaps I should have mentioned Eloise, but I saw no need. It held no importance to me."

He turned around and faced the couple.

"I was betrothed in name only, to protect a lady I knew and respected. It was not a true engagement, only a charade to keep someone from threatening her friends and family. I didn't mention it because it meant nothing to me. To tell the truth, I didn't even think of it." His voice turned bitter. "It could have been easily explained had I been given a chance."

His last words were like slaps to Samantha. She had given in to both Brendan and Samara against her better judgment— and she might have ruined Samara's life in doing so.

"I'm sorry," she now whispered.

Reese's face did not soften. He had suffered the agonies of hell in the past eight months, first from Samara's almost incomprehensible flight and her loss and later, after Connor's letter, from a deep biting hurt at the O'Neills' lack of trust.

Connor understood only too well. He too had suffered, probably similarly, when Samantha had refused to trust him—or their love—thirty-odd years earlier.

"You could have explained in a letter," he said now, searching Reese's intentions. "This is a long way to come—not to mention how dangerous it is—to say something which could be conveyed by letter."

"Would Samara have believed it?" Reese retorted harshly. He turned to Samantha. "Would you? It seems my words are worth little."

Connor regarded him calmly. "Not to me," he said in a deep voice. He hadn't mistaken the depth of pain in Reese's voice. "Will you stay until I send for Samara?"

Reese looked at him, his eyes bleak. He shook his head slowly. "I'm sorry. I can't. We'll leave this afternoon."

Connor's expression was puzzled. Reese Hampton had come across the Atlantic to see Samara and right things. He didn't understand the Englishman's haste in leaving. "Samara? What should we tell her?"

"That I will be back. I don't know when. I don't know how, right now. But I'll try to get back." If I don't see her first, he thought privately. Damn.

"Are you going back to England?"

Reese hesitated. He wanted no more lies, no more misunderstandings, but he could not tell Connor of his intentions to join the British invasion of Washington...if only to see that Samara remained safe.

Instead, the question was avoided with a brief shrug, and Reese asked about Samantha's horses. Connor noticed Reese's clever attempt to avoid an answer and a cold shiver ran through him. Reese had once said he would no longer participate in the war, but perhaps he no longer felt that obligation.

After all that had transpired, he felt he could say nothing nor question him further.

After eating dinner with Samantha and Connor, Reese and Yancy took their leave. As Glen Woods disappeared from view, Yancy turned to Reese.

"I take it we're heading for Washington."

Reese merely nodded, and both men spurred their horses into a gallop.

Chapter Eighteen

Washington was in a panic. British troops, battle-hardened after years of fighting in Europe, had moved up the Chesapeake and were only a few miles away.

A messenger from Samara's brother, Marion, had ridden in the night before, advising Samara and Annabelle to leave the city. The British had defeated American troops at Bladensburg and were moving toward Washington. The American troops were in shambles and unable to stop them; they had been ordered to retreat to Georgetown, leaving Washington undefended.

But Joshua's health was failing rapidly. He was past eighty, and old wounds aggravated his heart condition. Annabelle was afraid to move him. And Samara would not leave them.

After a sleepless night, Samara and Annabelle discussed what was to be done. One of the most important issues was the stockpiling of the medicine and sleeping draughts that Joshua required. If the British did invade Washington, there was no telling what would happen to the city's medical supplies.

The streets were in chaos. Buggies filled with household goods mingled with swarms of American soldiers escaping the oncoming British. A horseman rode by, shouting warnings of redcoats and rape. Samara made her way down the road to Dr. Ewell's home, only to find the doctor gone. She decided to continue on to her friend Julien's store.

Julien had been one of her earliest friends in Washington and the two had grown closer in the recent tense days. Samara knew that Julien, the son of French emigres who now owned a mercantile store, was half in love with her, but as hard as she tried she could never consider him more than a friend. Her thoughts of Reese were too strong.

The store was closed and shuttered against looters, and Julien was standing outside watching the frightened retreat of both citizens and soldiers. As one bumped her, Julien hurried over and took her arm, guiding Samara to safety.

"You shouldn't be here," he said protectively.

"I can't just sit and wait at Annabelle's. There is too much to do. What have you heard? Has President Madison left yet? Where are our troops going? Where is General Winder?"

"Whoa," he said. "Slow down. I don't know any more than you. No one's seen President Madison—he was at Bladensburg with the army. I understand Dolly Madison is preparing to leave and I don't know what General Winder's going to do."

"Are you leaving?"

"Mother and Father are still French citizens, and they are neutrals now that Napoléon has surrendered," he replied. "They think they will be safe enough and feel they can protect the store. You can't imagine how many people are seeking out the French minister, Louis Serurier, for protection. You and Mrs. McLaughlin should go."

"We can't," Samara said. "Joshua can't be moved. Annabelle is afraid it will kill him."

"Then I'll stay with you," he said, his hand tightening on her shoulder.

She smiled her thanks, grateful for his help. She was beginning to feel the first twinges of fear as she watched the fleeing troops. "I'm trying to find Dr. Ewell," she said.

"Wait until I tell Father," Julien said. "Then I'll go with you."

They searched in vain in the confusion. Rumors were running wild, and more and more people were fleeing. They heard that General Winder was in full retreat to Georgetown, and that Mrs. Madison, clutching a portrait of George Washington, had left the White House.

Samara and Julien went back to Annabelle's to check on the couple. Joshua was raging, furious that he could not fight, and it was taking all of Annabelle's persuasion to quiet him.

Dusk fell, and Samara and Julien decided to try once more to locate Dr. Ewell before the British actually entered the city. As they left the house, they could hear the explosions. Powder trains at the navy yard were being destroyed by retreating American troops, and they watched as the flames and smoke gushed upward, casting a red glow over the city. Samara shuddered with apprehension, imagining she could feel the heat. Terror battled with purpose, but her concern for Joshua won. The young couple started toward the Ewell home, only to meet a detachment of scarlet-clad British soldiers. An officer, eyeing Samara appreciatively, asked their destination and ordered one of his soldiers to escort them there. All civilians, he announced, were to stay in their homes.

"To be burned in our beds?" Samara asked with open rage. These were invaders!

The lieutenant looked at her more carefully, obviously admiring her courage. "We have orders not to burn any private residences," he said slowly. "Not unless we're fired upon. You will be safe enough if you stay inside."

Samara stood there, despite Julien's attempts to draw her away. "What are you going to burn, then?" she demanded, noticing the torches in some of the soldier's hands.

"'Tis none of your concern, little miss," he said. "'Tis only government buildings."

"The White House," she said tightly and, at his reluctant nod, added, "*That's* a private residence."

The stern-faced lieutenant grinned at her impertinence, but then saw a senior officer glaring at him. The smile faded.

He turned to Julien. "You'd best get her off the streets, and rein in that mouth." Detailing yet another man to accompany the two, he turned in the direction of the President's House.

Flames now danced heavenward throughout the city, as more and more government buildings were torched. Samara noted that she and Julien were the only civilians on streets filled with British troops. She eyed their unwelcome escort with scorn before turning to Julien. "Come on, Julien, we had better get back to Annabelle." With her chin up, Samara turned and led the way home as two embarrassed privates followed them.

All night, they could hear sporadic firing and small explosions. Julien volunteered to stay since there were only two elderly manservants in the house for protection. Annabelle had armed herself, as did Samara, and they sat at the windows watching the destruction, wondering if one of the many fires would reach their home.

The hours crept by and Samara thought the night would never end. By dawn's light, British soldiers prowled the streets, rifles ready. The small group in Annabelle's house ate their breakfast, wondering aloud what the day would bring.

"Julien and I will try Dr. Ewell's again," Samara said. Annabelle, growing increasingly worried about her husband, agreed. The night had not helped Joshua's agitation.

The two set out, passing British soldiers who ignored them. Samara had deliberately dressed in an unbecoming shapeless frock and hid her rich hair in a bun covered by a cap.

When they reached Dr. Ewell's home, Samara was dismayed to see the number of British soldiers around the building. She gathered her courage and went to the door, noting the broken panes in the front windows. As she reached up to knock, it swung open and a tall British colonel almost collided with her. His hand went out to keep her from falling, and his lips curved into a warm smile.

"Colonel Clifford Longley at your service, miss," he said with a courtly air. "May I help you?"

Samara's brows drew together in confusion. "Dr. Ewell. I was looking for Dr. Ewell." Her voice gathered strength as new anger flooded her. "This is Dr. Ewell's house. What have you done with him?"

Longley's eyes flickered with amusement at the angry little American. Despite her unbecoming dress, his keen eyes didn't miss her beauty. "Why nothing at all, miss. He invited General Ross and his staff to use his home as headquarters."

"I don't believe you," Samara hissed through clenched lips. "He would never willingly have *English* in his home." She might as well have said snake or something worse. The insult was all too apparent in her tone.

"You wound me, Miss…Miss…?" The question hung there.

It continued to hang. Samara had no intention of giving this man the courtesy of her name. Her chin went higher, and her gray eyes were dark thunderclouds. Her hand clenched in frustration. "Where is Dr. Ewell?" she demanded.

"I'll see if I can find out for you," the British colonel said in a clipped accent that was strangely attractive. *Perhaps he reminds you of Reese*, she thought miserably. Although Reese's speech had been softened by years at sea with men of many nations, he had, in times of anger, reverted back to his native accent. *Don't think about him. Think about Joshua.*

She followed the colonel into the house and stood uncomfortably in the drawing room as men rushed back and forth. Colonel Longley asked her to wait in the drawing room while he checked to see if anyone knew of Dr. Ewell's whereabouts. Most of the officers, including General Ross, were still asleep. Perhaps the doctor was, also. As she and Julien waited impatiently, her eyes wandered about the room and rested, fascinated, at the open door leading into the doctor's library. From where she stood, she could see Dr. Ewell's desk, its usually neat surface cluttered with papers.

"Julien," she whispered with excitement in her voice, "watch at the door for that officer." Before he could catch her, she had run into the study and leaned over the desk, her eyes eagerly scanning the papers. There were maps of Washington with targets pinpointed, maps of the countryside with routes apparently marked. She couldn't take those; their absence would be noted too quickly. But she could try to remember them. Her eyes then spotted a thick leather case. Drawing a deep breath, she ransacked it, singling out another map. She couldn't miss the bold circle around the city of New

Orleans and other strange markings around its perimeter. "Good Lord," she mumbled to herself. Her eyes studied it intently, and she realized it must be an invasion plan of some kind.

Samara stuffed the map and several other interesting-looking papers in the garter holding up her left stocking, and hurriedly put the case back where she had found it. It seemed like hours, but she knew it couldn't have been more than several minutes. At Julien's frantic gesture, she rushed from the library back into the sitting room.

She was all innocence as the colonel and Dr. Ewell walked in. Tapping her toe impatiently, she even managed to hide her breathlessness. Dr. Ewell, his eyes bloodshot and clothes mussed, had apparently been roused from bed, and Samara said a silent prayer of thanks. So that's what had taken the colonel so long. She couldn't believe that she and Julien had been left unguarded like this, but then the British hadn't expected Americans in their headquarters, and they had had a very busy night—burning the President's House, the Capital and who knew what else. The thought angered her once more, and she glared at the offending colonel. "I would like to talk to the doctor alone," she said quite haughtily.

The officer looked chagrined at her continued hostility despite his best efforts to be helpful. "As you wish," he said, retreating into the library Samara just left. She winced, hoping he would not check the case. The sooner she could leave, the better.

"Doctor," she said, "Joshua needs some more sleeping powder. Annabelle's afraid *they*," she threw a nasty look at the study door, "will steal it all."

Dr. Ewell shook his head. "It's a bad business, this. But I must say General Ross has been very courteous and has promised not to bother the surgery or confiscate any of my medicines."

"I can't believe you're letting them stay here...like guests."

The doctor sighed. "My dear, I had no choice. They chose

this house and at least as long as General Ross is here I know it's safe. I don't think they plan to stay long."

"Now that they've practically destroyed Washington, why should they?" Samara asked bitterly. Then she remembered her urgency. "I must get back quickly, or Annabelle will worry."

"And we can't let that happen," the doctor said gently. He too was a friend of Annabelle's and was distressed he couldn't do more for Joshua. "I'll go fetch the medicine."

Several minutes later, he was back, his hands holding several small bottles of liquid. Samara took a handkerchief from the small reticule she had brought with her, and carefully wrapped them before settling them inside the small handbag and attaching it to her wrist.

"Thank you," she said, and she and Julien fled out the door.

They almost made it, and would have if the papers hadn't started to slip from her garter. Samara ducked behind a house, catching the papers just as they started to fall. She tucked them in, this time more firmly.

As she came out from the shadow, her eyes widened. Julien was struggling in the grip of a British soldier. When he saw her, he suddenly jerked loose and started running, apparently to distract his captor. Samara saw a rifle go up, heard the loud explosion and watched as Julien crumpled to the ground. Mindless now of the papers, of anything, she ran to the fallen body and cradled Julien's blood-soaked head in her arms. She was completely unaware that the papers had once more slipped and were lying in the street.

Reese hardly noticed the disturbance at the end of the street. His eyes caught an image of a woman bending over a man, her head close to his, but the face was hidden from his view and a cap covered her hair. He thought briefly about seeing whether he could be of assistance, but already a number of soldiers were gathering around, and there would be little he could do. Besides he had a more urgent matter.

His ship had met the main British fleet at the mouth of Chesapeake Bay and he had sailed the *Phoenix* down the Po-

tomac River to Alexandria. His ship was allowed to go no
further, so he hastily found and purchased—once more at an
exorbitant price—a horse from one of the local Tories. Guilt
raked him as he passed the burned-out shipyard and several
other torched buildings. His sympathies, he feared, were inch-
ing toward the Americans. He was, at least, out of it now. He
would fetch Samara, take her home, and try to reach an understanding between them. He only hoped that the British invasion of Washington hadn't created a further schism between
them.

He stopped to ask someone the location of Joshua Mc-
Laughlin's home and was quickly given directions. His momentary spurt of optimism was stilled by the tragic scene in
the street. Perhaps a wife, perhaps a lover...

The McLaughlin house was graceful, with fine classical
lines and a small yard covered with flowers of every description. Unlike the manicured gardens of England, American
flower beds bloomed riotously in a profusion of colors and
shapes. He smiled to himself; it reminded him of Samara.

The door was quickly answered, and Annabelle and Reese
stared at each other, each caught in sudden recognition.

Reese felt as if he knew Annabelle. Samara had talked frequently of her unusual godmother who had apparently defied
convention most of her life. She stood there with warmth and
curiosity in her lovely green eyes.

As for Annabelle, there was no mistaking the tall Englishman. Samara had described him, but even her goddaughter's
wistful words hadn't prepared her for the splendor of the man.
No man should have eyes like his, eyes that looked like the
sun-kissed aqua waters of the Caribbean. He was one of the
most striking men she had ever seen. He grinned and she
couldn't help but smile in unrestrained delight. He was everything Samantha and Samara had said. And more. Much more.

"Captain Hampton," she said, stating a fact rather than asking a question.

He looked pleased that she knew him. "And you are Annabelle. Samara has told me much about you."

"I fear to ask what," she said, her twinkling eyes taking

inventory of his now slightly soiled lawn shirt, tight-fitting buff trousers and scuffed but obviously expensive black boots.

"You needn't," he laughed down at her. "If she hadn't already claimed my heart, I am afraid you might. I loved her stories." His warm eyes told her it was no extravagant compliment.

Samara, Annabelle thought, *how lucky you are. He is exceptional. Like Connor. He is so much like Connor.* The wound in her heart reopened. She had loved Connor O'Neill for fifty years; indeed, would always love him. But it had not been destined, and over the years it had been enough that he was her friend and was so completely happy with Samantha. It was all she had ever wanted: his happiness. And now Samara's.

She was *not* going to let Samara throw it away.

"Come in, Captain," she said. "Samara's gone out on an errand. She should be back any time."

"Has she…said anything…?"

"Quite a bit," Annabelle replied with a wry smile.

"Now *I* fear to ask what," he said with a touch of rueful laughter. "Although I could guess at some of it. Pirate, blackguard, spy. Englishman. That's the worst, I think. She could tolerate almost everything else." His smile disappeared. "I'm afraid the past few days probably haven't helped."

"Samara loves you, Captain. I don't doubt that for a second."

"I have," he admitted, with a wistful little smile that touched Annabelle's heart as little else could. "She doesn't give her trust easily."

"There was nothing to the story of your betrothal?"

"No…and she would have known had she asked…had she believed."

"I think," Annabelle said slowly, "she loves you too much. It frightens her. It frightened her mother years ago…Samantha also kept running away."

"How do I make her stop?"

"I don't think you can. She has to do it herself. And she will. She has bitterly regretted leaving you last Christmas."

"But now...with this damned attack?"

"'It won't make it easier, but then I suspect you don't mind a challenge," Annabelle looked at him appraisingly.

"And you...? You don't object to an Englishman in your home?"

"I think it depends on the circumstances," she replied with a smile. "If you are here to rob and plunder something other than my goddaughter's heart, I might take my rifle to you. And I'm a very good shot."

"I don't doubt it for a second," Reese said, feeling very comfortable with this unusual lady.

They talked for another hour before Annabelle started to worry.

Reese, too, was becoming restless. Samara shouldn't be wandering the streets with so many British troops about. As well disciplined as most of them were, there could always be trouble, particularly with a girl as pretty as Samara and, he admitted, one as outspoken.

"I'll go look for her," he said. "I have a friend..." He stopped in mid-sentence.

"Don't worry, Captain," she said. "Of course you have friends in the British army. Use them, by all means."

He nodded, thankful for her understanding. He only wished Samara shared some of Annabelle's tolerance.

Reese finally found Cliff Longley up the road at the Ewell home. At first, an apprehensive corporal refused him entrance. "He's in a high temper, he is," the soldier explained apologetically, after Reese used his brother's title.

"He's an old friend," Reese soothed, "and I have urgent business with him."

"'Tis on yer head, not mine," the soldier said, as he opened the door to the drawing room and pointed towards the library.

Longley, Reese noted, had lost his usual air of indifference. His lips were pressed tightly together, and his face radiated anger. His eyes did not look up as Reese hesitated at the door but remained on papers lying in front of him.

"What the devil? I said I wanted no interruptions."

"Not even from an old friend?"

Longley looked up and the grimace eased. "Perhaps from an old friend," he said. "Perhaps you can give me some advice. You seem to know a lot about women."

"Not lately," Reese muttered to himself, but an eyebrow raised in question.

"It's a nasty business," Longley said. "And I could well be booted from the army for it."

Reese's eyebrow went up further.

"A young lady came looking for the doctor who lives here. I left her outside in the drawing room while I hunted for him. She apparently got into some papers I was keeping for General Ross. Some very important papers."

Reese's body tensed, his eyes becoming very alert. The moment Longley had mentioned a young lady, he knew. "Her name?" he asked softly.

"Dr. Ewell very reluctantly identified her as a Miss O'Neill."

Reese felt himself go numb, even though he had expected that answer. He struggled to keep his expression bland while he, who had never feared anyone, felt terror rip through his body. "Are you quite sure that she was actually spying?" he asked calmly.

"Caught red-handed. Had a map on her person—and some other papers."

"Where is she now?" Reese managed through clenched teeth.

"The Washington jail. Until some decisions are made." The grim look on Reese's face finally made an impact. "Why the interest?"

"We were...going to marry."

Now it was Cliff Longley's turn to stare. "But she was with a man...he was shot trying to escape."

Reese closed his eyes, suddenly remembering the scene on the street. Samara? He had wondered...a wife? A lover? The woman had certainly appeared devoted to the wounded man. "Just down the road?" he asked tensely.

Longley nodded.

"What happened to the man?"

"He'll live to hang. It looked worse than it was."

"And the girl?"

Longley looked sympathetic. "We can't let her go, Reese. She stole a map with one of our most important plans. We can only assume she knew what it was."

"You wouldn't...?"

"That's up to officers more senior than I. But she will surely go to England...at the very least."

"Cliff..." Reese's voice was pleading. "I didn't tell you this in Bermuda, but when my ship was sunk off the coast I located a Tory, a friend of the King. He asked me to get some information for him, and I was discovered trying to do so." He noticed Longley was watching him with intense interest. "Samara O'Neill's family protected me, kept me at their home for more than four months. They risked their lives for me— despite the fact they support the war and three of the sons are fighting. I owe them a great deal."

"I understand," Longley said softly, sympathetically. "But I don't know what I can do."

"I could marry her," Reese said, once more in a soft but intense voice. "I could take her to England myself. Now. As my wife."

Longley nervously rubbed his hands together. "She's a little wildcat. When my soldiers tried to separate her from the man, she scratched the hell out of them."

"That sounds like Samara," Reese admitted wryly. "She tried to kill me when I first met her."

"And you want to marry her?"

"Odd, isn't it?" Reese admitted. "But yes, I suppose I do."

"Even if she doesn't want you?" Longley eyed his friend with astonishment. He couldn't imagine the sophisticated, arrogant Hampton with the fiery American.

"She did," Hampton said now. "And I think I can persuade her again." But his mouth tightened as he further questioned Longley about Samara's accomplice. He felt an excruciating pain as he did so. Regardless of what Annabelle had said, it apparently hadn't taken Samara long to forget him. "The man with her...do you know anything about him?"

"She told my sergeant he was just accompanying her, that he had no part in it. But he attacked one of my soldiers, and I don't really believe he knew nothing of the documents. They were here together and they certainly seemed fond of each other." His eyes searched Hampton's face for a reaction as he added, "They're trying to protect each other."

"Can you do anything for him?"

"I can talk to General Ross. I suppose we could take him back to England, but he would certainly end up in Dartmoor Prison. Why your concern?"

"Because Samara would never forgive me—nor the entire British empire—if he hangs. Would you try?"

Longley shook his head in disbelief. "I thought she was making my career a shambles. It's nothing compared to what she's doing to your life, my friend. Are you quite sure about this?"

"Will you talk to Ross?" Reese insisted.

Longley shrugged. "All right, though I can't promise anything. General Ross is generally inclined to be lenient, however, particularly if there's a pretty woman involved."

"Thank you, Cliff."

"Don't thank me. I would be only too delighted to get her out of sight," Longley said with the first smile of the conversation. "Maybe everyone will forget about it. I can't believe it. I had a promotion due...but who would suspect a pretty little thing like that?"

"Who indeed?" Reese agreed with a rueful half smile.

Reese waited restlessly while Longley conferred with General Ross. His thoughts jumped from one question to another. Who was the man with Samara? How much did she care for him? A cold chill crept into him. Why had she bent over the American so tenderly? Had Annabelle been so mistaken about her feelings? And would she agree to the terms being offered? He wasn't sure he wanted a forced marriage, but he owed the O'Neills and, as much as he hated to admit it, he loved Samara and knew he always would. He despaired at the thought of her captivity in British hands—and the very real possibility of prison, if not death. A marriage, no matter how reluctant, might be the only way to save her. But what kind of marriage would that be...? How different than the one he had imagined at Glen Woods! A darkness engulfed him as he considered the possible tragedy that was in the making. He had already felt so much anguish and turmoil from loving Samara. He didn't know if he wanted to open his heart again. Not yet. *I can't let her know how I feel. I can't give her that weapon.*

Thus strengthened by resolve, he watched as Longley returned, a slight, satisfied smile on his face.

"General Ross was rather fascinated by your proposal," he said. "He agrees that it is one way out of a very difficult situation. Damned if he wants to be accused of hanging a woman...nor does he want to take her as a prisoner aboard ship for weeks. If she agrees, you'll be married straight away by our chaplain and escorted to your ship. We require your word that you sail immediately, that she has no chance to contact anyone."

"You have it," Reese replied quickly. "And the young man? I doubt she'll agree to anything without reassurances about him. If nothing else, she's stubbornly loyal." He winced at the last words. Loyal, apparently, to everyone but him.

"He'll go to Dartmoor," Longley said. "It's the best I could do."

"Thank you, Cliff."

"Not yet. There are several conditions. I want to talk to her first. We want to know if she has any accomplices or whether..." his smile faded, "she just took advantage of an opportunity." He didn't need to add that it was an opportunity he had carelessly given her.

Reese nodded. He very much doubted whether it had been planned. He knew Samara's impulsiveness only too well.

"I would like to be there."

"I'm afraid not, Reese. I've gone as far as I can. If you're here, she might feel protected." He almost laughed at the suddenly fierce expression on Reese's face.

"Don't worry, I don't plan a thumb screw. Just a preview of her prospects, and that of her friend." He looked at Reese quizzically. "You are sure you want to go through with this?"

Reese nodded curtly. "There's nothing else, is there? You won't release her?"

"No," Longley admitted. "And *you* are to keep her silent for at least four months. Do you understand? It's essential."

"I know what's at stake," Reese said. "And I know you don't question my loyalty to England." There was an edge to his voice.

"No," Longley said. "Of course not, or I would never have agreed to this insane scheme."

"When will you bring her here?"

"In a few hours. General Ross suggested, and I agreed, a few hours in a cell might loosen her tongue."

"Damn it, Cliff. She'll be terrified."

"I hope so," Longley said grimly. "I sincerely hope so."

Samara huddled on the small bench in the nearly black cell. It was the only furniture, other than a bucket in the corner. The smell of her small space was indescribable. It reeked of sweat and dirt and fear. Her fear.

The cell was windowless except for a small grate in the door which allowed only a fraction of light to penetrate. She knew, from occasional scuffling noises, that a guard remained outside. She had asked, nay demanded, that someone contact Annabelle. But to no avail. She had not been roughly treated, but the soldiers and, now, guards were firm in their silence.

What had she done?

She had seen the papers in Col. Longley's case and reacted instinctively. And perhaps had condemned Julien in doing so. At the moment, she was too miserable to care about her own plight. She kept seeing Julien's ashen face, the blood dripping down it and the ugly jagged wound at the side of his head. *Julien, I'm sorry. I'm so sorry.* No one would tell her anything, even whether Julien had lived or died.

She fingered her reticule. Strange how they had left that with her, although they had checked inside. She had pleaded to be allowed to keep the medicine, and a stern-faced sergeant had permitted it. She didn't know he had a daughter her own age, and that he pitied her.

The little bottles of sleeping draught were all still there, but she despaired of ever having a chance to deliver them to Joshua. Poor Joshua. Poor Annabelle who must be worried half to distraction by now.

A scurrying sound made her press closer to the stone wall. It was hot, without even the smallest stir of air. And no water. She wet her lips, feeling their dryness. From fear or thirst? She didn't know.

She forced herself to think of something wonderful. Her mouth curved in a small smile as she recalled the last time she was in such darkness. It was in the hold of Brendan's ship, but then she knew she could leave at any time. Not like now. The smile disappeared as the walls seemed to press in on her, and it took all her courage to keep from screaming.

Reese. Think of Reese. Of the warm days and tender smiles. Of him sitting so confidently on the big bay stallion or standing so free at the wheel of his ship. She could almost see the wind rustling his golden hair and hear his laughter. The bold buccaneer laughter that had both delighted and frightened her. A lump formed in her throat as she remembered their last picnic. "Where are you?" she whispered. "I need you. Oh, God, I need you."

And then she remembered. He was probably in England, perhaps already married to an English lady. She buried her head in her hands as she felt a grief too great for tears.

The hours of anguish in the dark cell did not serve to cow Samara when she was, at last, taken by closed carriage back to British headquarters. Her imprisonment, contrary to the colonel's expectation, had merely served to fuel an outrage which, in the dark hours, alternated with remorse and misery.

They were the invaders. *They* were the arsonists. *They* were the murderers and now *they* had Julien's blood on their head. *They* were bloody Englishmen.

She regarded Longley with no less distaste than she had shown in the morning. It was strangely effective considering

her sorry state. Her drab dress was coated with filth and blood,
her face was smudged with dirt and her hair was wild and
tangled from the struggle with British soldiers as they had
forced her from Julien's side.

"Miss O'Neill, sit down," the red-coated officer said
coldly. Longley's face was hard, his eyes like steel, and there
was none of the previous friendliness. His face was so somber,
in fact, that Samara wondered if it was the same man she had
encountered earlier in this very same house.

She sat, her body stiff, as her hands nervously fingered each
other and the reticule she still carried, now for courage more
than anything else. It was an object on which to focus, something familiar to give her hope. But though her hands trans-
mitted fear, her eyes did not. They were like great angry thun-
derheads, ready to launch lightning bolts.

Longley had difficulty concealing his admiration, and for
the first time stopped questioning Reese's judgment. Under the
dirt and grime, she was a truly beautiful woman with both
courage and spirit.

His plan to dominate the interview was quickly squashed
when she angrily demanded to know about Julien Devereaux.

He leaned forward in his chair, intentionally taking his time
in answering. His eyes bored into her before he said, almost
nonchalantly, "He'll live to hang…as you well could." The
very casualness in his voice did more to instill fear than anything else. He sounded as if it were an everyday occurrence;
nothing to be bothered about, except, perhaps, by the victim.
In that minute, she did not doubt that both Julien's and her
lives might be forfeit.

Her chin went up defiantly. She *had* to save Julien. She had
led him into this. Her stormy eyes went bleak as she remembered his ashen face.

"It was all my doing," she said, almost desperately. "He
did nothing…I just happened to see those papers, and I…"
She stumbled. "He's innocent. He was just trying to protect
me."

His expression was glacial. "You didn't *just* happen to see
anything," he said. "Those papers were packed away."

Despite herself, guilt flooded her face as she searched for an explanation. There was none.

"But it was *me. Only* me," she finally managed. "I saw those papers on your desk, then the case and I...Julien didn't have anything to do with it."

"Are you're sure you're not just trying to protect your Mr. Devereaux because you believe we won't hang a woman? If you do, you're badly mistaken. We hang spies...whoever they are."

"But Julien's not..."

"And *you* are?" the voice was unrelenting. Longley hated himself for what he was doing, but he had to find out. "You're admitting it?"

She stared at him, some of the defiance seeping away. Her hands tightened against each other. He was making it her or Julien. And she would not give him Julien.

"Yes," she said softly. "Now let Julien go. Please."

"You were alone...? It will go easier if you tell me about the others."

From the shock on her face, he doubted very much if there were others. It was, as she said, an impulsive act which had had dire consequences for a number of people, including himself. He could not forget his own blame; he had almost invited it through carelessness.

Samara bit her lip at his hard stare. Did he believe her? She didn't want to die, but she could never live with herself if Julien died in her stead.

"There's also the possibility of prison," the British officer said now. "You had a small taste of it today. Believe me, British prisons are worse." He could see her shudder, and his distaste for himself rose. "You still hold yourself solely responsible?"

"Yes," she whispered, thinking what a living hell it would be. For a moment she thought death would be preferable. But only for a moment. Death was very final.

"There might still be another alternative," he said cryptically, as he nodded to a soldier in the doorway.

Her large gray eyes quickened with hope. But it faded almost immediately. What terrible thing could he offer instead? Because she was afraid to hear it, she spoke, asking the question that had been nagging her.

"How did you know about…that I had…?"

"I didn't," Longley said. "I sent those men to accompany you home safely. Apparently your friend thought you had been discovered and attacked them. To protect you."

A familiar soft laugh came from behind her, and Samara whirled around, half rising. She remembered it well…as she remembered the mocking voice that followed it.

"It seems, my love, that you and I are the two most inept spies on this good earth." The corners of the inviting, sensual mouth she had dreamed of for nearly a year, were pulled up into a bitter smile and his eyes were green ice. "You see we *do* have much in common. It must be a match created in heaven. Or hell."

He was in the open doorway, leaning casually against the doorjamb, his eyes glittering. Samara recognized his mood. Whenever he spoke this quietly, there was a hard tension behind it, a taut anger barely held in check. The first bubble of joy, which had risen spontaneously on hearing his voice, burst with immediate realization.

He had been there all the time! He had listened while she was threatened, terrorized and humiliated. And he had said nothing. Not only that, his presence here in British headquarters was damning. *He* was one of *them*. Her small hands knotted compulsively and her eyes swam with a humiliating mist as part of her heart died. But she resolved not to release her tears. Not for *him*. She would not give him that satisfaction.

Instead, the words came without thought. Her quiet sincerity made them even more explosive. "You bastard!"

Longley looked shocked, then grinned. The famous rake who had won and discarded any number of hearts in England was being repaid in kind. But Reese's face did not change unless, perhaps, the eyes grew colder. Longley wondered how that was possible. His eyebrows raised as he waited for Reese's reply.

It was several seconds in coming. He had heard part of her

interview with Longley and every mention of Julien Devereaux had twisted a knife deeper inside him. He suddenly wanted to hurt her as much as he had been hurt.

"It seems," Reese finally said, "that we've played this scene before." The side of his mouth turned upward slightly. "You looked like an urchin then, too."

The derisive reminder infuriated Samara. She itched to punch him, but with new insight she knew he was trying to provoke her. He was obviously furious, and she searched for the reason. She was the one who had cause for anger.

With all the willpower in her slim body, she turned to Colonel Longley. "Does he have to be here?"

"I'm afraid so," the colonel said with an amused smile. "You see, he's your third alternative."

The words gradually penetrated, and Samara looked from the colonel's obvious enjoyment of the situation to Reese's masked expression.

"I don't understand," she said nervously.

"Our good captain has offered to marry you and take you safely away...where you will have no chance to divulge the information you so inconveniently stole from us."

Samara was stunned into silence. Her eyes flooded with confusion before she understood. Or thought she understood. They were playing with her. Reese was already promised...if not married. She would not be part of their ugly game. Despair overwhelmed her because, despite all he had done, she wished nothing more than to run to him, to bury herself in those strong arms which had once held such comfort. But she couldn't. She would not surrender the only thing she had left. Her pride.

"I would rather hang," she said quite succinctly, her eyes matching the chill in his. Her stubborn chin lifted in determination.

Reese showed no emotion. "And would your friend?" He watched her closely now, looking for an indication of her feelings. He was fighting desperately to hide a raging jealousy and sense of betrayal.

The angry red in Samara's face paled. "What do you mean?"

"We're not just discussing your fate, Miss O'Neill," the colonel broke in. "Your companion is involved, as well."

"But I told you..."

"Do you really think I could let him go, knowing he might have seen those papers?" Longley said with the first sympathy he had shown during the interview.

"But he didn't," she insisted, as her face froze.

"I'm sorry. That's not quite good enough. I can't be sure...nor can I be sure you didn't tell him."

"I promise you I said nothing."

"And can I trust you, Miss O'Neill? As I did when I left you alone in this room?" Longley's calm remark told her he wouldn't change his mind.

"What are you going to do with him?" she asked fearfully, tears hovering in the gray depths of her eyes. Her hands trembled as she sought to control herself.

She didn't see Reese's face, nor the sudden intense pain that clouded his expression. She only heard his voice. It was at his sarcastic worst. "Such concern, Samara. You didn't show this kind of solicitude when you were playing with *my* neck."

Samara stood and took one step toward him, an arm outstretched in supplication. "*He* did nothing...except try to protect me. You can't, Reese, you can't let him hang."

"Oh, can't I?" he said, now angered almost beyond control. He had thought of nothing but Samara for a year. And now she was apparently in love with this young puppy. Why else would she offer her life in exchange for his? "Why?" he asked tightly. "Because he's your lover?"

Incensed at his perfidy, at his mocking indifference, at her own treacherous longing to be in his arms, Samara sought to even the score. "Yes," she said flatly, her gray eyes meeting his angry expression defiantly.

They were now both oblivious to Longley's presence.

"You love him?" Reese's voice was so soft she barely heard it.

"Yes," she said with reckless abandon. "He's gentle and kind and..."

"Everything I'm not," he finished for her, his heart filling with pain. "But, then, perhaps he had more cause to be gentle and kind."

The words bit into Samara as she stared up at him. There was a kind of wistfulness in his eyes, a hint of vulnerability she had never seen before. But then they were instantly hooded again, and she knew she had been mistaken. His voice was hard and merciless when he spoke again.

"Your answer, Samara?"

She looked bewildered. Surely they hadn't been serious.

"But you...are already..."

At this juncture, he had no wish to explain himself nor the sham engagement. This obviously would be a marriage in name only. Samara no longer loved him, if indeed, she ever had. Bitterness welled up in him as he regarded her coldly. He owed Connor this. He could never live with himself if anything happened to Samara. The marriage could be dissolved later by quiet divorce or annulment.

"It is your only alternative, Samara," he said now, "and your friend's. I have been assured that if you cooperate he'll be sent to England and imprisoned. If not," he shrugged, "he'll hang."

"But why?" she asked, through clenched teeth. "I hate you." She looked at his strong, handsome face, now creased by lines of tension, and knew the statement for a lie. She could never hate him. Oh God, don't let him know how much I love him, how much I want to touch him.

"Why?" she asked again, bewildered.

"I owe your father," he said curtly.

Her last hope died. He was doing it only for what he felt he owed her father. Not for her.

She thought of Julien and knew she could not condemn him to death. She bowed her head and surrendered. "Yes," she whispered. "For Julien." She would never let him think it was for any other reason.

"Very well," Reese said, in a harsh voice Samara didn't recognize. "The wedding will take place this afternoon." His eyes studied her critically. "I'll get some of your clothes from Annabelle."

"I want to see her. And Julien."

"I'm afraid that's quite impossible, Miss O'Neill," Longley said from behind them, reminding both he had heard the humiliating exchange and reluctant marriage plans.

Reese felt so painfully drained he didn't care, but Samara did. She hated the British even more for so successfully forcing her to their will.

"Why not?" she challenged Longley. She had nothing more to lose.

"Because, my dear future Mrs. Hampton," he paused, a slight smile on his lips at her infuriated expression, "we will give you no opportunity to pass on any information. You will be married here, by our chaplain, and escorted to your husband's ship." He obviously delighted in taunting her.

Samara looked from one man to the other, finding no sympathy or help in either. In all her conflicts with Reese, she had never seen his eyes colder, nor his reserve greater. Hopelessness flooded her. She was being forced to leave her country and family with a man who obviously detested her. That he was also the man she so unwisely loved did nothing to make the situation easier. Every time she looked him, she would remember his touch, the softness in his eyes, the teasing laughter as her body surrendered so wholeheartedly to his. Could she bear seeing those cold eyes and grim mouth and knowing they were bound to each other by hate, not love?

She pulled her courage together and returned Reese's glare. "You will tell her what happened?"

"I'll explain that you decided to marry me in England, that I had to leave immediately, and you send your best wishes and assurances of happiness," he said wryly. "I see no reason to worry your family."

"You are so kind," she said bitterly. "But Annabelle won't believe you...not without me."

"I think so," he drawled. "Annabelle and I met this afternoon and got along rather well. And you will write a note, explaining the somewhat unusual circumstances and adding that you are most happy with the arrangements.''

"No," she said rebelliously. "I won't lie."

Her vehement denial of him inflamed him once more.

"Yes you will." There was steel in his voice. "Or else the marriage is off. I will not have your family thinking I dragged you off unwillingly."

"Which is exactly what you are doing," she said furiously. "I don't want to marry you."

"Think of Julien," he taunted softly.

"Damn you. Damn you to hell."

She didn't hear his words as he left, slamming the door behind him. "You have already done that, my little cat."

Her first note was rejected by Colonel Longley who could barely contain a smile as he read it. There was a pointed reference to a concern about a brother in New Orleans. The second, which was unenthusiastic at best, was rejected by Reese whose patience was wearing thin. "I will dictate, Samara, and you will very carefully copy my words."

Exhausted and numb, Samara agreed. As he started to leave, she remembered Joshua's medicine. "Wait," she said, unable to force his name. As he turned, she rummaged in her damaged reticule and took out several bottles. She held them out to him. "For Joshua."

Reese took them slowly, his brilliant eyes assessing her woeful face. His mouth twisted against the consoling words that part of him wanted to speak. The other part, the angry wounded self, kept them frozen inside. He merely nodded coldly and left.

Samara was taken upstairs to a bedroom to rest. She heard a key in the lock and when she went to the window she noted a guard beneath it. Defeated, she sank down on the bed.

Several hours later, two soldiers brought in a bathtub and steaming pails of water. Lastly, they brought in a dress—her favorite—along with her combs and brushes.

"I was told, Miss," one said with embarrassment, "that you are to be ready in an hour."

When they left, she looked at the water she once would have welcomed joyously. Now it brought nothing but dread for it meant she was one step closer to the farce of a marriage. He would hate her for taking his freedom, for keeping him from his betrothed in London. And she...

A tear, waiting all day to be released, trickled slowly down her cheek. So, now all the dreams would end.

Chapter Nineteen

It should have been the happiest day of her life, Samara thought, as she and Reese stood in front of the British chaplain. Instead, it was the most miserable.

As she stole a glance at Reese, he stood there stiff and unyielding, his mouth in a tight, grim line, his eyes framed by lines of strain. A muscle throbbed in his cheek, and she could feel him flinch when they were told to join hands.

Her own hand was miserably cold, she knew, and it reflected her heart. She was afraid to feel, afraid to think. A small seed of hope, which had persisted despite all reason, flickered and died when she saw Reese's face at the small gathering of British officers just prior to the horrible ceremony. He had been easy to find as she had come down the steps; he loomed above everyone else. He had turned cold, bitter eyes upon her, and the mouth, which had always smiled so easily, did not even offer a mocking twist. He had merely nodded, his eyes skimming over her appearance with neither approval nor disapproval.

Samara had tried to look her best, but she had neither assistance nor accessories. It was a matter of pride to her that she did not appear defeated to the hated enemies below. She would not admit, even to herself, that perhaps she wanted Reese to think her beautiful—as he once had said she was.

She had washed her hair, and brushed it until it glimmered

with fiery red highlights. Since she had no clasps or decorations, she let it fall freely down her back.

Annabelle had sent her favorite dress—a pale blue cambric muslin which gave a blue glow to her eyes. Its low neck did little to hide the swell of her firm breasts, and the small puffed sleeves emphasized her creamy white skin. The narrow, gored skirt displayed her slender figure to perfection. But despite the admiration in the eyes of the British officers, she saw only indifference in Reese's.

She barely heard the words of the chaplain and was unaware of her own responses. It was as if someone else were speaking them. It couldn't be her, not like this, not in the midst of all these soldiers dressed in scarlet, not with this icy-eyed stranger whose cold lips touched hers in a kiss as frigid as a winter wind.

Ironically, champagne followed the ceremony. How ludicrous, Samara thought, to celebrate, but she took a glass and then a second to dull the raw pain. She felt Reese's arm around her, muttering something and then she was being guided outside to a closed carriage. Reese courteously assisted her inside and closed the door, leaving her alone. As it started in motion, Samara's best intentions shattered. She wanted to display the same indifference as Reese, but she longed for his comforting presence, to be assured that all would be all right. But he cared nothing for her, in truth he gave every sign he hated her. The tears fell silently in steady rivulets down her face.

His thoughts black, Reese settled himself in the saddle and rode in front of the coach, away from the armed escort that surrounded it. Unlike General Ross and Longley, he had no fear that Samara would try to escape, not with Julien's life at stake. The thought only deepened the emptiness inside him.

He had thought about accompanying her in the coach, but had checked himself. She obviously wanted no part of him; that much was clear at the wedding. She had not looked at him during the entire ceremony, and her lips had been cool and unresponsive when he'd touched them in a brief formal kiss. She had jerked her hand from his as soon as possible, and had spoken not a word other than the necessary responses.

It had been all he could do to keep his face impassive, to keep from touching the lovely face with tragic eyes. But they were eyes longing for another man, and he knew his touch would not be welcome. Not now. Nor, for his own sake, could he allow himself that weakness. It would be hell aboard ship. He remembered how much he had resented being captive, and it was much worse with Samara because he had used the life of her young man to bend her will.

With a raw anguish deeper than any he had thought possible, he recalled her response to his proposal, "I would rather hang." His legs tightened against the sides of his horse, and the stallion responded with a confused dance step. He absently stroked the mount's neck, realizing his hands and legs were giving conflicting instructions.

His hands loosened on the reins, and his legs once more tightened, this time giving the horse his head. Together they raced for his ship.

He had sent word ahead to Michael Simmons and Yancy, and as he approached the *Phoenix*, Reese saw the ship was ready to sail. A longboat was waiting at the shoreline to take them aboard, and Yancy, his lively eyes even more inquisitive than usual, was sitting on the riverbank when Reese, his horse lathered with sweat, arrived.

"You look like the devil's been chasing you," Yancy said.

"He has," Reese answered shortly.

"Where's the bride?"

"Behind me. I should warn you, Yancy, she's not very happy."

Yancy, who had been told nothing of the circumstances in Reese's note, arched an eyebrow.

"She was caught spying. The marriage was the only way to save her." Reese's explanation was curt, his face shuttered. It was enough to stay any additional questions.

Reese made arrangements with a British officer to sell the horse, and he and Yancy sat and waited for the carriage. Yancy could feel his friend's tension but said nothing, offering only quiet support.

When the carriage rolled up Reese reluctantly approached it, disregarding the cavalry escort. When he opened the door, he saw Samara huddled in a corner, her eyes red and swollen. It was the first time he had seen her tears and, despite every warning bell in his head, his heart ached for her. He entered and sat, his hand reaching out to her. At first she flinched, but as his hand—ever so tenderly—traced the dried tears on her face, she looked up at him and saw compassion. And something she couldn't define. When he held out his arms, she buried herself in them, new sobs shaking her body. She felt his hand soothing her hair, heard his soft whispers, telling her all would be well. And still the tears came, until she wondered how there could be any more.

When her shudders finally quieted, Samara felt his lips on her forehead. Softly. Gently. Not as a man in love, but as a comforting friend. And that hurt her more than anything.

She forced herself to draw away. "I'm sorry," she said in a small, choking voice.

His voice was warm and kind. "You need never be sorry, little cat. It's been a day to try the strongest of soldiers." Reese's hand fingered one of her curls. "You've been very brave. And everything will be all right. I promise. We'll get an annulment in England, and you can return…" He couldn't finish the sentence.

The bright flare of joy in Samara's heart faded. He was merely being kind. She forgot that she had accused him, recently, of being bare of that particular virtue. She straightened, wiping her face like a child, looking incredibly defenseless in her fruitless attempt to appear strong. "I'm all right," she said. "Truly."

He nodded, his admiration for her rising. As was his longing.

He opened the door and stepped out, turning to offer his hand. After a second's hesitation Samara took it, feeling its warmth sparking fires throughout her body. She hesitated at the edge of the seat, looking intently at Reese. He was still dressed in his wedding clothes, a somber but attractive mixture of grays. A dark gray dress coat and slightly lighter, silver-embroidered waistcoat contrasted with a snowy white lawn shirt. Light gray pants emphasized his muscular thighs, and glistening black knee-high boots encased his strong calves. Her husband. Her very reluctant husband. Once more, waves of wretchedness swept through her.

Seeing her eyes cloud again, Reese reached out his arms and took Samara in them, wondering at how light she seemed. He placed her gently in the longboat and signaled to the sailors to push off. When they reached the ship, he helped her climb the ladder and stood on the deck with her as Michael Simmons piloted the *Phoenix* slowly down the Potomac. He remained next to her as she stared at the shore, saying goodbye to all she had known.

The day passed under bright blue skies and a fair wind. Reese's anger had receded under the weight of Samara's grief. It was replaced by an enormous sense of loss and a burning, hurting ache, a bruising pain which intensified every time he looked at her. For that reason, he studiously avoided her, finding a reason to leave the top deck when she appeared.

He gave her Michael Simmons' cabin, treating her with courteous politeness. He ate alone in his cabin while Samara dined the first night with his officers.

Reese's temper with his men rose with his level of frustration, until it reached legendary peaks. Sensing the bubbling tension, Samara stayed in her cabin as much as possible until she thought she would perish with loneliness. She sought out Yancy, saying little, but the wistfulness in her eyes spoke volumes.

Yancy observed both—Samara and his irascible captain—first with bemusement, then concern. He couldn't believe they were both so idiotically blind. When one thought the other wasn't watching, his or her eyes shone brightly with need—and love. But then when the object of their gaze turned, eyes fell, hiding again in reserves that seemed unreachable. He wanted to knock their heads together, yet he knew his interference would not be welcome, and it went against his lifelong philosophy to meddle. Besides, they had weeks ahead together. If he knew anything about human nature, they would solve the problem...perhaps with just a *wee* bit of help.

After dinner on the second night out, Yancy took Samara up to the main deck to watch the sunset. He didn't miss the way her eyes went compulsively to Reese who stood at the wheel, barefoot once more with the wind rustling his tawny hair.

Samara had gone reluctantly. She was sick of her cabin, but even the barest sight of Reese filled her with fresh misery. His politeness was more devastating than anger. She longed to throw herself in his arms, to nestle in their warmth. But he no longer wanted her, and that knowledge kept her own feelings bound tightly. But as she and Yancy reached the upper deck, she couldn't keep her eyes from Reese, no matter how hard she tried. She could feel her heart hammer and her throat going dry. He was magnificent with the wind blowing the lawn shirt against his broad chest and the tight breeches displaying every muscle as he stood braced against the movement of the ship. Reluctantly, she turned her eyes away...to the sunset which seemed trivial compared to Reese Hampton. The huge sun was bright red as it almost touched the dark blue of the sea. Paths of gold and scarlet and pink trailed across the rippling water as if daring the *Phoenix* to follow them to some magical kingdom.

She heard Yancy's voice. "I have to go down for a moment. You stay here."

"I'll go with you," Samara said, a touch of panic in her voice.

"No...stay here. I *will* be back shortly."

Entranced by the sorcery of the setting sun, Samara agreed. For a moment she fancied being a bird, swooping in and out of the wondrous colors and climbing up into the cloudless sky. How wonderful to be so free.

"It's glorious, isn't it?" Reese's deep voice interrupted her reverie.

Lost in her thoughts, Samara had not seen Michael Simmons relieve Reese, nor the intense gaze of the *Phoenix*'s captain as he watched her lonely figure in the last golden glow of the sun.

Her hand tightened around the railing as she turned toward him, every defense gone in one bewitching moment as he too became part of the evening's radiance. All she knew was the nearness of his lips, of his eyes which were filled with warmth. Without a word, she moved toward him, unable to stop herself. She felt his hand reach for hers, and knew the soft promise of his lips, their urgency and the subsequent fires that swept her body. Her hands moved up, inch by inch, touching, loving. She was unaware of her tears as she sought that which she wanted most and had thought gone forever. She wanted his love, for she knew—beyond any doubt—that her heart was his. Yet she was afraid to say the words, afraid she would destroy this tenuous moment.

His lips traveled from her lips upward, and touched her hair before holding her tight against him, her face pressed against the golden fur of his chest. With deep pleasure, she smelled the rich aroma of musk and sea and her tongue darted out to lick his salty skin. She heard him groan and felt the swell of his manhood as he drew her even closer. "Little cat," he muttered, as if in pain.

She moved back to look straight up into his eyes and was startled by the naked pain there. Her hands entangled themselves in his hair, and her lips reached once more in a command he couldn't resist. The gentle whisper-soft meeting turned into a tempest, as both sought to quiet their doubts and questions in the nearness and warmth of each other's bodies.

Samara felt him slowly, very slowly, draw away, his lips reluctantly leaving hers. He took her hand and turned toward the sun which had now dipped below the horizon, leaving a spreading red halo in its wake.

"We have much to talk about," he said slowly. His low, warm voice made Samara's legs weak; the touch of his hand sent shudders through her now fully awakened body.

Reese looked at her expressive face. Her heart was in her eyes, and some of the emptiness left him.

"I went back to Glen Woods," he continued. "I was there several weeks ago. Your father said you were in Washington and I had heard that the capitol was to be taken. That's why I was there…to make sure you were safe."

"You weren't there…with *them*?"

"No, Samara," Reese said, a small smile on his face. "I went there to save you from yourself…and apparently just in time." His smile disappeared. "I was going to ask you, again, to marry me. I didn't mean it to happen as it did but circumstances, and anger, took over."

Her hand clutched his as she tried to understand. "Anger?"

"Your…apparent fondness for the young man…your lack of trust…your immediate assumption that I had violated my word—not once but several times."

Agony stabbed Samara's heart as the words penetrated. She *had* rushed to judgement, repeatedly. She had never once considered there might be another side. She had been too afraid of loving him. "But the announcement…?"

"That's why I went to Glen Woods. When I left last Christmas, no one would tell me why you disappeared so suddenly. Apparently they didn't tell your father, either. When he found out, he wrote, knowing there must be some explanation."

Samara's voice was very small. "And was there?"

His right hand caught her chin and forced it up, until her eyes met his. "Yes. A very simple one, had you waited to ask." His voice was bitter now, and she winced at the sound.

He let go of her hand and turned toward the sea, but not before Samara saw the bleakness in his eyes. She felt the pain in the next question. "You have never trusted me, have you, Samara?"

She couldn't lie now, not when there was so much at stake. "No," she said slowly. "I suppose I didn't. You are so different from everything I know. I was afraid I loved you too much. I couldn't understand how you chose me. I knew there must be beautiful women, more sophisticated women. When Bren…"

"You little idiot," he said, thoroughly angry now. "Have you no idea how completely lovely you are? I fell in love with your spirit and your humor and your courage—misguided as it often is. And those qualities are very rare. As, I hope, is your damn stubbornness.''

Samara's eyes brightened and hope filled her. ''You mean...you still...you didn't marry me just because of Father? You said you wanted an annulment.''

''Because I thought that's what you wanted,'' he said slowly. ''Because you said you loved that young American.'' His eyes were questioning.

''Only because I thought you were in love with someone in England, and I was so angry...''

Reese's eyes glittered with humor. A chuckle started deep in his throat and spread upward as his mouth widened into a grin. He put his hand to his mouth, trying to stop it, but laughter erupted, rich and strong and lusty. Every crew member on deck, each of whom had been darting glances at the oblivious couple, stared in amazement. It was the first real laughter they had heard from their captain in months.

Even Samara looked as if he were mad, before the infectiousness caught her and she too giggled.

When he was finally finished, his eyes twinkled. ''We make a fine pair,'' he said ruefully. ''When I was speaking of stubborness, I should have included myself. I was too damn proud to tell you about that engagement, then you were too stubborn to tell me about Devereaux, and that only made me more angry...''

Her hand went up to touch his face, longingly, lovingly. ''If only you knew how much I wanted to run into your arms...but you were so cold.''

''And you were so angry.''

''And frightened...so very frightened...''

''And beautiful and brave...''

''And I loved you so much and thought you hated me.''

''We were at cross purposes, it seems,'' he admitted. ''It's over now, Samara,'' he said, leaning down to kiss her lightly. He chuckled again. ''I think we've probably given the crew enough to talk about. I have a perfectly good cabin, and I think we've wasted enough time...''

Samara delighted in the look he gave her. "Much too much," she agreed, "particularly since we've been married two whole days." Laughter trailed them, as Reese picked her up and strode quickly to his cabin.

Finally alone, Reese and Samara stood for several seconds, their eyes feasting on each other's faces, their hands clutching together almost desperately. Then Reese lowered hungry lips, his tongue eagerly seeking the softness of her mouth. And she just as hungrily welcomed him and the wondrous sensations that started to build inside her. She felt her body tremble with anticipation, with physical and emotional need for him. Her lips played gently with his, telling him in many different ways that she loved him. Tenderly. Sweetly. Hungrily.

Reese's hands sought the fastenings on her dress and un-hooked them, deftly sliding both it and her chemise off her shoulders. He looked at her as she stood before him, her eyes bright as silver and her face flushed with love. He had missed her. God, how he had missed her. He started to take off his shirt and was stopped by her hands.

"Let me," she whispered.

She led him over to the bunk and made him sit while she pulled the white shirt over his head, her hands tickling and playing with bronze skin and golden hair. She knelt at his feet and undid the lacings of his breeches. Her hand touched him with awe and she heard him groan. "Samara..."

His one hand pulled her up beside him on the bed as the other finished discarding the restrictive clothing.

She marveled once more at the raw beauty of his body, but she had little time to study it. His mouth was on her breast, his hands tracing intricate, fiery trails on her body until the whole of her was inflamed.

Samara drew Reese to her as her hands traced the strong muscular planes of his back and her lips nibbled his ear. She heard him gasp and felt his lean hips above her. Her body arched up toward him as she was swept into a rocketing world of spinning sensations. She grasped him greedily, drawing him deeper and deeper, rejoicing in each strong thrust that brought him closer and closer to the core of her being. And then everything erupted with one shattering explosion.

For minutes they lay together, their bodies trembling from the aftershock of their union. His lips brushed hers gently and he laid his cheek against hers.

"I love you, Reese," she whispered. "I've always loved you. Since, I think, the first moment you laughed at me."

She loved the rumbling in his chest that heralded his laughter. "Does that mean I should do it more often?"

"You already do it quite enough, thank you," she replied. "Besides," she added seriously, "I don't think I could love you any more."

"I wish I had known that earlier, my sweet," he said ruefully. "It would have saved us a great deal of trouble..."

"You weren't very forthcoming yourself," she retorted.

The rumble started again. "Perhaps...but I'll make up for it."

He drew her tightly to him, and she felt the embers in her flare into bright flames. Her body eagerly reached for his.

Samara spent the night in his arms, rejoicing in his nearness. Several times she woke and stared at him with wonder, her fingers touching him to assure herself that he was real.

As several days passed, Samara and Reese spent an inordinate amount of time in Reese's cabin, much to the amused satisfaction of Yancy and Michael Simmons. The captain, in his rare appearances on deck, was a different man, his voice often raised in song or a merry whistle. Everyone stopped to watch when the pair came on deck together. They were so in love. For some, it revived memories, for others, hope.

Only one cloud darkened Samara's horizon, and that was the information she carried in her head; the information she had obtained at British headquarters. She tried to dismiss it, knowing there was nothing she could do. The *Phoenix* was on her way to England, but all the same it was information that could mean life and death to hundreds of Americans, possibly even Conn who was in the general area of New Orleans.

She was sharply reminded of it when she transferred her few belongings from Michael Simmons's cabin to Reese's.

Her blood-stained reticule was among them, reminding her of that fatal morning when she had clung to it with a desperate compulsion. Inside, she discovered one remaining bottle of sleeping medicine that had somehow escaped her notice that tumultuous day and she tucked it in a corner of a trunk, not quite ready to dispose of it.

Some of Reese's elation faded as the ship's pace slowed to a crawl. The winds, which had been slight since their departure from Washington, were now almost still, and he felt far too close to the American coast for comfort.

His worst fears were realized on the fourth day out when he heard the lookout cry "Sail ho," and the ship galvanized into activity. He hurried to the fo'c'sle and took the spyglass.

"What flag?" asked Yancy, who had come to stand beside him.

Reese's face tensed. "American," he replied curtly, "A schooner...privateer, I imagine."

"What are you going to do?" He knew Reese had sworn off American ships, and his still-fragile relationship with Samara would not be aided by an exchange of fire.

"Run like hell," he said. "If the damn wind will freshen." But it didn't, and during the day the American ship, with its additional sails, crept closer. For one of the few times in his life, Reese prayed earnestly. As the long day wore on, the American ship continued to shorten the distance. Samara joined him on deck, her face apprehensive.

"What are you going to do?"

"Whatever I must, Samara," he said as a muscle throbbed in his cheek, betraying a tension he tried to hide.

"You won't consider surrendering?" she said in a small voice, already knowing the answer.

His hand went to her face, touching it tenderly, almost as if afraid it would be the last time.

"You know I can't do that, Samara. I made a promise to get you to England."

"You made a promise to me, too."

"That I wouldn't attack, not that I wouldn't defend." He turned back to stare at the approaching ship.

When he looked once more through the eyeglass he saw the cannons being primed, apparently for a warning shot.

"Yancy, tell Michael to ready our cannon."

Yancy looked from Reese's set, determined face to Samara's anguished one. "Aye, sir," he said with unaccustomed deference.

"Go below, Samara," Reese said quietly.

"No."

His voice was tired. "I don't want to do it, but I'll have you tied if I must. Now go!"

"Reese..." It was a cry of pain. She was going to lose, whatever happened.

An identical pain was in his eyes when he turned to her. "I'm sorry, Samara. I have no choice."

Her hand started to reach towards him, then fell in defeat. "Be careful," she whispered.

"Aye, little cat," he answered with a crooked smile before turning his attention back to the approaching ship. As he heard the first cannon boom and saw the eruption of water just short of the bow, he called Yancy. "Take Samara down."

Without further protest, she went with Yancy. She didn't doubt for a moment that Reese would have her bound if she didn't obey.

She accompanied Yancy to his cabin and helped him prepare for the wounded, setting out bandages and surgical instruments. She felt the ship rock with its first return of fire, then heard the explosion as a cannonball hit the *Phoenix*. Her hands clasped together until they were white. She wanted to flee on deck, to assure herself that Reese was all right, but she knew she would only distract him. Gone was her concern over the American ship: she only wanted Reese to survive. She couldn't bear to think of a life without him.

"He'll be all right," Yancy said, correctly interpreting her thoughts. "He's indestructible. I think that's why his ship is so popular with seamen. If he can't be touched, then they can't."

"I love him so much, Yancy."

"I know," he said softly. "And he loves you." He shook his head, remembering. "I've never seen anyone so miserable after he left South Carolina. He's been a different man the past few days."

The reminder of those terrible days, of her distrust, magnified her torment. She had never given him trust or support or even understanding. She had been so wrapped up in her own personal conflicts that she had ignored his own. Samara felt very small, very unworthy.

"Reese," Yancy said with understanding, "isn't very good at explaining his actions. Part of the fault is his."

"I should have trusted him...believed..." The words stopped as she heard another explosion on deck, and then suddenly men, blood-splattered and powder-blackened, were pouring into Yancy's small sick bay, and neither had time for more words.

Busy with the injured, Samara didn't notice as the explosions sounded further away nor the gentle movement of the ship. Not until Reese appeared at the door, a lopsided smile on his face. Approval spread over his face as he watched her with the wounded. He shook his head as her eyes widened at his blood-covered shirt. "It's nothing," he said, "just a splinter. See to the others first."

"What happened...?"

"Jules's cannon found their mainmast and toppled it. They're dead in the water. And the wind, God be praised, finally blessed us. We're well out of range."

"The *Phoenix*?" Yancy lifted his eyes from the wounded man he was tending as he asked the question.'

"Battered. The rigging and spars are damaged, but overall I would say we were very lucky." Reese's tone quieted. "We'll have to go back to the American coast for lumber. We won't make England or even Bermuda with what's left, not if there's a storm."

That night, Reese held Samara tightly in his arms. The possibility of loss had made them frantic with need to possess each other completely. When Reese entered her warm welcoming core, she sought to bring him deeper and deeper as if to keep him there forever, to make him so much a part of her that he could never leave. Their passion increased in ever-growing swells, magnified by lingering fear, until they became a tidal wave of sensations. She gloried in the feel of his warm seed rushing through her, hoping that it would take root deep inside. Samara now wanted his child—desperately. The fear had not left and she was so afraid she would lose him. After, they lay together, still shuddering from the intensity of their union, unwilling to move. They stayed, wrapped in each other's arms, during the night.

The *Phoenix* made its way sluggishly toward the coast. Despite the ever-present danger, Reese and Samara enjoyed a contentment and happiness greater than they had imagined possible. They clasped each moment, treasuring it, as if it were the last.

The ship anchored in a small cove off the coast and Reese took a work party ashore. Before he left Samara in Yancy's care, he cupped her chin in his hand and studied her face. "Would it do any good to ask that you stay aboard ship?"

The misery in her face answered him.

His fingers caressed her before he turned to Yancy. "Don't let her out of your sight. Lock her in the cabin if you must." He leaned down and his lips touched hers lightly. "Stubborn," he muttered, and grinned. Then he was off.

Samara watched as the boat reached the shore and the men disappeared along the beach. She turned to Yancy. "I know," she said, "you want to get back to the wounded. I'll go with you."

"Your soft words do more doctoring than my poor efforts," he said, trying to coax a smile from her, before continuing in a lower voice. "Don't try to get away, Samara. Reese will forgive a lot of things, but I don't know if he'll forgive you making him a traitor. He gave his oath he would get you to England."

Samara looked at him in surprise. "You know?"

"Some of it. You gave each other a merry chase."

"Not so merry," she replied somberly. "Not very merry at all."

"Don't ruin what you have between you," he warned.

"My brother is in danger," Samara answered. "My country is in danger. How can I forget them? How can I choose between them and Reese?" She couldn't hide the heartache.

"He is your husband. England is your country too, now."

"No...not England," she denied.

Yancy sighed. "As he said, you're not to be out of my sight."

The afternoon passed into evening and finally the work party returned, the boat making several trips loaded down with wood. Yancy, true to his word, had made sure Samara was with him each moment. When she'd begged a few moments of privacy, he'd waited patiently outside Reese's cabin.

Reese was exhausted, but he managed to supervise repairs throughout the night. When he was finally satisfied, he told Samara there would be one more trip to shore in the morning and then they would leave.

He took her down to the cabin and allowed her to undress him and bathe the sweat from his body. He groaned with pleasure at her pampering as he gratefully took a glass of brandy. When he felt clean again, he drew her down to the bed and held her close, too exhausted to answer the invitation in her eyes. He closed his eyes, then opened them again, fixing them on Samara. "I sleep very lightly, my pretty little cat, and you will sleep on the inside tonight."

He did not miss the shiny brightness in her eyes, but in his growing drowsiness he attributed it to the sparks that always flew between him. He would ignite them, he thought dreamily, later.

Samara waited until she was sure he was thoroughly asleep. She knew that once Joshua took several drops of the sleeping draught nothing would wake him. She only hoped that the same would be true of Reese and his officers. She had doctored the crew's coffee earlier, and had given Reese a small amount in the brandy. Between the draught and wine and exhaustion, he should sleep for hours. She sat up, watching him.

A lock of golden hair had fallen over his forehead and a small smile curved his mouth as if he were dreaming of something quite wonderful. He looked so vulnerable, so handsome. And she loved him so much. How could she leave? She remembered Yancy's warning. "He will forgive much, but…"

She could not live with herself, if she did not at least try to get her information to the authorities. What if Conn died? Or if Britain won a decisive victory, enough to seize American lands? Her hand stroked her husband's cheek and buried itself in his hair, wanting him to wake and stop her from doing what she knew she must. "I love you," she whispered. "Please never doubt that I love you." The words caught in her throat. She gently climbed over him and covered herself in one of his shirts. She had already written the note in her head, now with the light of a small candle, she put it to parchment.

Samara took a few gold pieces, knowing she would need them, and slipped out the door. After the ship had been damaged, she had ransacked the ship's locker and found some sailor togs that fit. She had been afraid to put them in Reese's cabin for fear he might find them. Now she gathered them from their hiding place and quickly drew on the trousers, lacing them tightly.

There would be two lookouts, she imagined, both looking seaward. She crept up on deck and made her way to a railing that was protected from sight. Quietly lowering one of the many ropes, she slid over the side and swam for shore.

Chapter Twenty

Not for the first time during the long, wet, miserable journey through southern England, Reese Hampton wondered exactly why he was subjecting himself to it.

Like so many other times during the past two years, he had been seized by a compulsion he didn't understand.

He needn't go to the grim fortress that housed American prisoners of war. Yancy had already been there several times on his behalf, and had reported that Julien Devereaux, if not very comfortable, should at least survive the war.

After hearing tales of the deplorable conditions at Dartmoor, Reese had sent Yancy to check on the man. Devereaux's imprisonment was partially due to the fact he had tried to protect Samara, and Reese hadn't saved the man from a hangman's noose to see him die in squalor in an English prison.

At least, that was what he told himself as he shivered in the cold February drizzle. Even his heavy cloak could not protect him from the pervading chill, and he wondered how the American prisoners were faring. Yancy had reported they had few blankets, little heat and less food. The doctor had done what he could, supplying Devereaux with heavy clothes and blankets and bribing the guards to supply more food, but it was always questionable whether their promises were carried out. Only Yancy's use of the formidable Hampton name might have produced compliance.

Reese shifted his position against the leather seat of the

coach. He would have preferred riding, but he knew, from Yancy's description, that Devereaux would probably be too weak to travel on horseback. In the opposite seat lay a package of clean, warm clothing, a basket of food and a leather case containing the American's release papers.

The war had tentatively been over for more than a month, but the peace treaty, signed Christmas Eve, had not yet been ratified. Prisoner exchanges were also delayed, and Reese had to use every ounce of the Hampton influence to win Devereaux's early freedom, especially after the news of the British disaster at New Orleans reached London. Ironically, the battle had taken place on the eighth of January, two weeks after the signing of the peace treaty. England was stunned by the magnitude of the defeat: three British regiments decimated, with more than two thousand dead—including the commanding general. There were very few American losses.

Reese had heard the news and wondered just how much his own blindness had contributed to the debacle. He doubted that American authorities would have acted on the word of one young woman, but it would have given strength to other intelligence. In any event, Andrew Jackson had been waiting for the British....

The memory brought back, with all its pain, the September morning when he had awoken, groggy and alone, in the cabin. As comprehension dawned, he had the ship searched and then sent a boat to look for tracks along the beach. They had apparently been washed away by the tide, which meant Samara had been gone for hours. He knew immediately it would do no good to search. She had the advantage of nearly a night's head start.

Reese had almost gone after her, anyway. Until Yancy and Simmons finally convinced him that he would only endanger his ship and crew, and that he could not do. They had been too loyal to die or risk imprisonment once more for his own folly.

He did not read the note Samara left him. He did not think he could endure it. It wouldn't make any difference—in any event. She knew he had given his word, his oath, that he would see her to England. She was his wife, yet she had sacrificed his honor for her own. She had made her choice.

No words could repair the damage this time. He placed the letter over the flickering flame of a candle and watched it burn, unaware as the heat scorched his fingers. His heart turned to ashes with the parchment....

Reese looked out the window as the grim stone fortress of Dartmoor Prison took shape. Even at a distance, it seemed desolate and menacing.

It was worse inside. He nearly gagged at the odor as he looked with pity on the ragged scarecrows confined within. The guards were little more than ruffians who carried clubs and used them freely. After seeing the captain in charge, he was led reluctantly down a stone corridor to a cluster of iron doors, each with a small grated window.

"These are special pris'ners...troublemakers, spies and such scum," the burly guard said, as he stopped at one door. He gave his lantern to Reese while he took out his keys. "I don't know why a gent such as yerself concerns hisself."

"You don't have to," Reese answered, in his most intimidating voice. His contempt was obvious. "Open the door."

The door creaked open, and Reese stepped into the dark space, lifting the lantern to throw its full light on the man who was rising before him. The cell contained nothing but filthy straw and a noxious bucket. The man, dressed in rags, placed his hand over his eyes to shield them from the sudden brightness.

As the guard approached him, he shied away as if to avoid a blow, and Reese stepped between them. "Get out!"

The guard hesitated, taking a look at Reese's face, and touched his forelock in resentful obedience. "I'll be outside."

Reese's mouth hardened into a deep frown as he regarded the American. His skin above the beard was very pale, making his blue eyes appear unusually large and bright. His hair was a dull brown with dirt. His clothes were little more than rags, yet his bearing was proud.

"I thought Yancy brought some clothes?"

Julien stared. His visitor was impeccably dressed and one

of the most imposing figures he had ever encountered. "You must be Reese Hampton," he said finally.

Reese nodded. He had not seen Julien in Washington, had not wanted to.

"I think I have you to thank for being alive...you and Dr. Yancy. He told me you sent him."

"Yancy always talks too much. He was to provide you with some clothes."

"Others needed them more."

"And the food?"

Julien gave him a wry look. "Don't think it wasn't appreciated. I'm afraid your countrymen do not share your generous nature. It was...spread around."

Reese stood for a moment, finding it difficult to speak. "I've obtained your release," he said abruptly. He shifted the package he had been carrying. "Some clothes. You might like to change."

"I don't understand," Julien said with a slight tremor in his voice.

"The war is over. It's only a matter of a few formalities. I've managed to expedite your release. There's a carriage waiting outside. I'll take you to London, and see to your passage home."

"Why?" came the blunt question.

"Ah, American directness," Reese said without amusement. "Perhaps I feel a little responsible for you being here." His half-smile faded. "Or perhaps it's the fact that we are bound by a young lady who led us both into disaster," he shrugged.

"What about the rest of the Americans?" Julien asked.

"They should be released in a matter of weeks. You were all I could manage."

Julien looked at him curiously. "And I imagine that took some persuasion. I've been made to understand I'm considered somewhat special." He flinched as he said the last words.

"It's over now," Reese said in an oddly gentle tone. "I'll wait outside while you change clothes."

"I'm so damned filthy."

"We'll stop at an inn, and you can bathe for hours if you wish."

He started out, but Julien stopped him. "I still don't quite understand all your trouble..."

"I don't, either," Reese answered with a slight smile. "Let's both just accept it as some sort of aberration. I would suggest you hurry before someone changes his mind."

Julien grinned for the first time. "A matter of seconds, Captain."

It wasn't much longer than that before they were hurrying out the stone walls, Reese's strong arm lending support to the weakened man. When they reached the carriage and Reese opened the door, Julien peered in at the rich exterior and drew back, his face red with embarrassment.

"I'll ride on top...I don't want..."

Reese understood immediately. Despite the clean clothes, the American must be infested with vermin as well as the prison odor that clung stubbornly to him.

"I didn't get you out to have you die of pneumonia," he said shortly. "The carriage can be cleaned easily enough."

As the American continued to hesitate, Reese's mouth curved into an easy smile. "Besides there's wine and food inside, and I would be most unhappy to see it go to waste.

Though his face still conveyed humiliation at his condition, Julien needed no more urging.

Once both men were inside, the carriage moved off quickly. Reese leaned over and opened the basket sitting beside his guest. He took a bottle of wine, motioning Julien to help himself to the contents of the basket.

Julien looked at it in amazement. It had been six months since he had seen so much food. The very sight and smell made him dizzy. He looked at Hampton, wondering if it were all a dream, or a nightmare from which he would wake just as the food reached his mouth.

"It's real," Reese said with a slight smile. "No one will take it away."

Julien forced himself to eat slowly, carefully, savoring every bite. As he sipped the wine offered by Hampton he turned his attention back to his benefactor.

"Yancy told me a little about what happened," he said. "That you married Samara..."

Reese's smile turned bitter. "An event which will hopefully be remedied by divorce," he said softly. "You can tell her when you return."

Julien's face questioned. "She loves you, you know. I realized that in Washington. I knew there was someone she couldn't forget...or let go."

Reese's face hardened, his eyes growing as cold as a distant arctic sea. "I would debate that point...if I cared enough," he said shortly, "which I no longer do."

"Then why are you here?" Julien said quietly. "I don't think it's entirely me."

"A debt," Reese said frigidly. "Nothing more."

"All right," Julien said. "I'm too grateful to argue. But I remember reading one of your poets, something like 'I could not love thee half so much, loved I not honor more.' I think that might pertain to women, too. At least to Samara."

Reese looked at him with sudden interest. "Lovelace," he said. "Richard Lovelace. He also wrote 'Stone walls do not a prison make, nor iron bars a cage.' I wonder if you would agree with *that*?"

Julien laughed for the first time. "I must beware of fencing with you. I'm afraid I come off poorly." With that observation, he relaxed with the soothing effect of the wine, settling against the comfortable leather cushions of the carriage.

They stopped several hours later at an inn and Reese engaged two rooms, ordering a bath and pails of steaming water for one. He also asked one of the maids to take Julien's clothes and boil them, leaving a set of his own for the American's temporary use.

Reese went to the taproom and ordered a brandy and set himself down in a corner, his demeanor warning off intrusion. He sipped his brandy slowly as he pondered Devereaux's words. Honor. What a curious word. Particularly when it meant so many different things to so many different people.

He had never thought much about it. He had, quite simply, been compelled to do certain things: some to his liking, some not. And if it were the former, then why could he not accept Samara's actions? Because his pride had suffered? Because he had not realized how strong her loyalties? Because he could not bear the thought of how much that mistake had cost him? If the situation had been reversed, would he not have done much the same as Samara?

She, after all, had not given her oath not to escape…as he had to the O'Neills months earlier. And he knew her knowledge was far more crucial than anything he had gathered. Escape! God, how that word hurt. Escape from him!

Reese took another careful swallow, welcoming the burning liquid which he hoped would dull his pain. He had done nothing about a divorce. He seemed unable to make a decision, a condition totally foreign to his nature. In desperation, he had spent several months in London, halfheartedly pursuing some of his former vices, but the zest was gone. So he'd returned to Beddingfield, full of discontent.

He had even thought about courting Eloise once his marriage was dissolved, but there was no spark between them, only friendship. He would not destroy her life in some fruitless attempt to rid himself of personal demons.

When the war had ended, he had found himself consumed with curiosity over the young man who sought to protect Samara and nearly lost his life in doing so. Perhaps by finishing the whole sorry business, he could obtain some peace of mind. He no longer believed, as Samara had declared in Longley's presence, that she loved the American, but he couldn't shake the strange bond he felt with the man.

And he had found, during the carriage ride, that he liked Devereaux. Despite his youthfulness, there was a maturity and dignity about him. He had been quietly grateful without being obsequious. It had been difficult to tell much about his appearance with his long, ragged hair and beard, but the blue eyes were bright—even after months of deprivation.

At a sudden noise, he looked up and found the object of his thoughts standing at the table. The beard was gone, leaving a pale but pleasant face. Devereaux looked smaller than before, his thin body nearly dwarfed by Reese's clothes. A slightly abashed expression acknowledged the misfit.

"I never thought to be clean again, nor to have a full belly," Devereaux said with a faint smile.

Reese nodded for him to sit and called a barmaid, ordering wine and food for his companion.

As in the carriage, Julien Devereaux was careful to eat and drink slowly as his eyes studied Hampton. When he had completed his meal, he asked quietly, "What now?"

"We'll go to London while I secure passage for you. I assume you would prefer a non-British ship."

"You're very perceptive," Julien said, again with a wry smile.

"You have a family waiting?" Reese asked.

"A mother and father," Julien said, his face finally relaxing. "And a young sister. I will be very glad to get home. And I will repay you." Julien's eyes found the wine goblet, and his hand moved it around absently. "Come with me," he said suddenly. "Talk to Samara."

Reese smiled inquisitively. "An American peacemaker?"

Julien's grin was infectious. "I hope so."

Reese was unexpectedly moved by the generosity inherent in the man. He knew from the expression in Devereaux's eyes when Samara's name was mentioned that the American had been in love with her. Despite his efforts in the past few months, Julien Devereaux had no reason to like him nor any Britisher after the hell he had obviously suffered. Over the past two years, Reese had learned a healthy respect for Americans—for their independence and tolerance and seemingly unquenchable spirit. But it was too soon, the hurt still too deep.

He shook his head. "Not now," he said. "I have business matters to attend to."

Julien merely nodded, not willing to intrude further.

Three days later, Reese took him by carriage to a Danish ship and saw him comfortably aboard.

Feeling somehow cleansed, he left London in the afternoon for Beddingfield, resting at night in an inn and reaching the

Hampton estate at midday. He immediately went in search of Avery.

"I'm going to America," he announced when he found his brother overseeing the preparation of the fields.

Avery's eyes twinkled. "I wondered how long it would take that stubborn pride to bend to good judgment. Then what?"

"I would like to buy some land in Virginia... It might take some time. I'll sell the *Phoenix*. That will give me a start."

Avery's mouth twitched. He knew how much the ship meant to Reese. If he would sacrifice the last vestige of his vaunted freedom, he was indeed serious about settling down. "Perhaps," he said slowly, "that won't be necessary."

Reese darted a confused look at him, but Avery only laughed. "I'll race you to the stables," he said, and any questions were lost in their frantic maneuvering for position.

A triumphant Reese claimed victory...and a drink. After the glasses were poured, Avery went to his desk, hesitated a moment, then pulled out several packets. Uncommonly somber, he studied his brother's face. It was more relaxed than he had seen it in months. Knowing the next few moments might well test their close relationship, he chose his words carefully.

"Your Samara wrote me several months ago. She sent you a letter in my care and she asked me to wait before giving it to you. She said I would know when the time was right." He handed the letter to Reese, who could only stare at his brother. Both anger and bafflement showed brightly in his eyes. "You shouldn't have held it," he said, raw fury starting to cloud his eyes.

"There's something else," Avery continued, pretending not to notice. "The money you've been sending for Beddingfield. I found I didn't need it. I've been investing it for you...in something other than gambling. You have a small fortune, enough to buy as much land as you wish...and still keep your ship." His steady eyes didn't flinch as he saw Reese's rage mount and his hands clench as if itching to hit him. Avery prepared himself for the blow. He had, he knew, unforgivably interfered in his brother's life.

The blow didn't come, but neither was there a change in

Reese's angry look. Reese held up the letter from Samara.
"And do you also know what is in here? Since you apparently
know more about my life than I do?"

"No," Avery said softly, "though I can guess. She's a very
unhappy young lady...and very much in love with you."

Reese glared at his twin. "May I now have the unique courtesy of a little privacy." Avery merely nodded and left the
room.

Reese's hands held the white parchment for a moment. His
eyes found Samara's small, neat handwriting, and his fingers
shook as he broke the seal and opened it. He could barely
restrain a smile at the greeting.

Beloved Englishman:

I asked your brother to give this to you when, perhaps,
your anger had faded and, very hopefully, you had come
to miss your wife.

For I consider myself such...and always will. Although
if you wish it, I will agree to a dissolution. I would agree
to anything to compensate for all you have suffered
through me. But for once, there must be no misunderstandings.

I love you. I have always loved you and always will.
You are my heart, and I feel empty with its loss. You
have given me so much, so many times, and in return I
have given you only pain. That knowledge haunts me day
and night.

Please understand why I left the ship that night. It was
the hardest thing I have ever done. But I would not have
been able to live with the knowledge that I could have
saved my brother...and helped my country...had I chosen to do nothing. I did not betray you, my love; I chose
not to betray myself.

I will abide by your decision. But with all my heart
and soul I hope and pray you will find it within you to
understand. I cannot ask you to forgive. Given the same
circumstances, I would make the same choice. I do not

apologize for that, but grieve for the pain I know it caused—no less, I believe, to me than to you.

I will love you all my life.

Samara

"Avery," Reese roared as his fingers tightened around the letter. He grinned as he saw his brother's apprehensive face. "Don't look so glum…I'll forgive and forget this time…but if ever, ever, you feel like interfering again…" He let the threat dangle as his eyes filled with laughter. "If ever…then feel quite free." A similar grin tugged at his brother's mouth, and they both fell on each other, their laughter exploding over the house.

Three days later, Reese and Avery rode together to London and visited Avery's banking house, leaving with a large draft. Avery returned to Beddingfield while Reese went to work, gathering his crew and supplying his ship. On the first of April, 1815, the *Phoenix* set sail for America.

In and out. In and out. Samara's fingers fairly flew over her newest sampler. She was sitting in the library, the early March sun casting a golden haze through the wide windows and catching the red fire in her hair.

She was intent on her work, a design she herself had fashioned. It was a guardian angel, who strangely resembled a golden-haired Englishman who was more devilish than heavenly. Nonetheless, she had been unable to tame her fingers to make it look otherwise.

One hand left the sampler and touched her swelling abdomen as she felt the child inside her move. *Oh Reese, I wish you were here. I wish you could feel him.* Her yearning for him never ceased. It tormented her at night, and kept her gazing hopefully out the window by day. The loneliness, even here with her family, was unrelenting. Her only solace was the babe. And even that carried its own torture.

She had not told Reese. She had known when she wrote his brother and included a letter. After all that had happened, she would nor force him into a marriage and fatherhood he may not want. And so she prayed daily that he would read her letter and understand, that he would come for her, out of love. She could not bear it if he came out of duty.

She took the last stitch and looked at the sampler critically, wondering how Reese would respond to the likeness of himself bearing wings. A giggle escaped her. He would probably be appalled.

"You're smiling." Brendan's voice broke the spell, and Samara looked up into his blue eyes.

She turned the sampler to show him. "I was thinking of Reese's reaction to being an angel."

"The pirate, the blackguard, the *Englishman*," he teased lightly although his eyes clouded. He had not forgiven himself for his interference or his treatment of Reese Hampton. He had been more than ashamed when he had learned the truth and offered to take Samara to England, but Samara had refused. She forbade him to write Reese about the child or say anything about her. It had to be Reese's decision alone.

"I'm going to England," he said abruptly. "To see your husband."

Samara sat up straight, feeling the baby object to the sudden movement. "You promised."

"I'll say nothing about the babe," he said. "If that's what you truly wish. But I think you're wrong. He has a right to know. By God, it's *his child*."

Tears filled Samara's eyes. "I won't use the child to bring him back."

"Then go with me, Samara. Talk to him. Don't make the same mistake you made before...that *we* made before." His voice broke. "We didn't trust him then...and we were wrong."

"What if he can't forgive me this time...?"

"You still owe it to him, more than ever, to tell him. You can't keep running away."

"I'm not running," she said softly, a tear rolling down her face. "I just don't want to do him any more injury. If he wants to marry someone else...someone he can trust..."

He took her face in one hand and wiped away the tears with the other. "Samara, you have to at least give him a chance."

"But he hasn't written, hasn't tried to contact me...he probably never wants to hear my name again. The kindest thing," she said, "is to let him forget me."

"You are married," Bren reminded her gently. "An annulment will not be easy...not with evidence that the marriage was consummated. Not even if you state the marriage was forced." He looked at her enlarged figure. "And it must be soon. Next week at the latest."

"I'll think about it," she promised.

"Do," Bren said. "Or you will always regret it."

Samara weighed Bren's words carefully over the next few days. He was right, and a letter would not suffice. Reese deserved to know about his son...and legal heir. And face to face, she would know whether he wanted her. Reese. The mere thought of seeing him filled her with joy.

Both Connor and Samantha supported their daughter's decision, Connor most vehemently. Samantha worried about childbirth, but was mollified when Brendan promised to take a doctor along on the voyage. Connor thought Reese should know prior to the child's birth. A birth, he declared, was a marvelous event and should be shared by both parents. Samantha thought about accompanying her daughter but was gently dissuaded. It was time Samara fought her own battles, and Connor shuddered at the thought of a gaggle of O'Neills descending upon unsuspecting Hampton.

Brendan easily found a competent doctor as well as several additional passengers. All had relatives in England and were eager to see how they had fared during the war. Communication had been rare. The *Samara*, proudly flying the American flag, sailed out of Charleston Harbor the last day of March.

Chapter Twenty-One

The voyage was quiet and enjoyable for Samara. It was comforting to look out over the ocean and see the sails in the distance without fearing them. For the first time in many years, the world was principally at peace.

Despite her growing bulkiness, she would stand at the railing for long periods, watching the sky and sea blend together. In those moments, she could almost feel Reese's presence beside her, hear his elated laughter in the sound of wind filling the sails and feel his gentleness in the touch of the sun against her face.

Now she had made her decision, she felt well content with it. She rejoiced with every movement of the baby, and realized she could finally offer Reese a gift of great value. Every rush of wind brought him closer. Each day, it blew strong, sending the *Samara* skimming over the waters. In the eventide, when the sun erupted into a rainbow of colors, she would turn toward the wheel and in the magic of the twilight she could see him there, bare feet set apart, head thrown back in challenge, eyes sparkling with mischief.

When the driver of the coach announced they were approaching Beddingfield, Samara leaned out the window, her eyes missing little. It was a beautifully maintained estate, and that surprised her. Reese had mentioned financial difficulties, and she had anticipated a more unkempt entrance. But everything was perfect, every hedge trimmed, every garden sculptured. And the house! If it could be called a house. It seemed more a castle to her amazed eyes. She stared in awe at its imposing beauty.

As Brendan descended, he told the coachman to hold the conveyance in readiness. Neither could anticipate their reception, after all that had transpired. He gave Samara a hand, squeezing hers tightly as he felt its chill and saw her tremble with anxiety. He carefully helped her down just as the huge manor door opened and a very dignified individual approached them. The man's face appeared expressionless, though there was a slight sparkle in his eyes.

Seeing Brendan's well-tailored clothes and Samara's quite obvious condition, his eyes held a question.

"Is Mr. Reese Hampton in residence?" Brendan asked awkwardly, not quite sure of the titles or protocol.

"No, sir," the man said, watching Samara's face fall and wondering who she was.

"Then his brother, the Earl of Beddingfield?"

"I believe he's at dinner," the man said quite formally. "May I give him your card?"

Brendan, sensing Samara's distress, became impatient. "This is Mrs. Hampton, Mrs. Reese Hampton, and I'm her brother."

The stern face was suddenly wreathed in smiles. He bowed slightly. "Mrs. Hampton...Mr....?"

"O'Neill."

"Mr. O'Neill, please come with me."

Samara and Brendan followed the servant through a great hall lined with paintings, and then through a large, richly decorated room hung with tapestries.

"Wait here, please," the servant asked.

Samara clung to Brendan's hand, all her optimism fleeing in the opulence that surrounded her. Never had she felt more out of place.

The feeling persisted until the door opened. For a moment she thought the servant must have been mistaken. It seemed as if Reese were standing there, a delighted and welcoming smile on his face. Then she noticed the differences. The hair was not as golden nor the eyes quite so brilliant. But the face was the same, and it was regarding her with no little interest.

"Samara," he said, as he smiled warmly at her. He strode over and took her two hands, looking at her, particularly at her enlarged middle. He grinned happily. "You didn't mention anything about a new member of the Hampton family."

"I didn't know if...Reese would be pleased."

"He will be delighted and awed, as am I, Samara. Welcome to Beddingfield." He turned to Bren. "And you are...?"

"Brendan O'Neill."

"I've heard your name," Avery said, a quick flash of mischief in his voice. "I'm Avery Hampton, Reese's brother." His eyes went back to Samara. "Come, sit down."

"Reese...? Where is he?"

Avery fought between pity and amusement. "I'm very much afraid, my pretty sister-in-law, you probably passed each other on the ocean. He left some four weeks ago to find you."

Samara was stunned. "He...he was coming for me?"

Avery's eyes met Brendan's in ironic amusement. "He took your young friend...Devereaux was it...to London. When he came back he had decided to return for you and when I gave him your letter there was no delaying his plans."

"Julien? What did he have to do with Julien?" Samara was becoming more and more confused, her emotions running riot. Joy at the knowledge that Reese wanted her, grief at missing him and confusion at this new information about Julien.

"He apparently felt responsible for him...tried to do what he could. He obtained his release and found passage for him."

"He did?"

"Does that surprise you?" Avery asked gently.

"No..." Her smile was suddenly brilliant and Avery understood why his brother was so bewitched. She was lovely, and her smile would brighten the heavens.

Samara turned to Brendan. "We have to leave. Now. This afternoon and return to Charleston."

Avery shook his head as he took her hand. "I don't think that would be very wise." He looked at her large figure. "I doubt if you want to have your child shipboard. Besides, if I know my impatient brother, he'll also turn back immediately. You might well pass each other again." He couldn't restrain another smile. "I don't know if I could withstand his temper if that occurred. It was bad enough when he knew I had withheld your letter according to your instructions."

Samara impulsively leaned over and kissed his cheek. "Thank you," she said.

"You were right," Avery added. "He wasn't ready to read it…not until he saw Devereaux and worked some things out in his own mind. He *can* be rather obstinate…but then I suppose you have discovered that."

"I'm afraid," Samara said ruefully, "it's a quality we share. It has caused us no end of misery."

"Perhaps now you are both ready for it to end," Avery said gently. He turned at the sound of a door opening behind him and reached out his hand as a very pretty woman approached. "This is Leigh, my wife. Leigh, this is Samara Hampton, the young lady who's been driving Reese to distraction."

"And about time, too," the woman said softly, a warm welcome in her smile. "How pretty you are, but I didn't know…"

"Neither does Reese, apparently," Avery said wryly. "He has several surprises in store for him. In the meantime, Samara will stay with us." He turned to Brendan. "And you, Captain O'Neill, will you also be our guest?"

"I don't know if your brother would approve. Our last meeting was not friendly."

"Of course, he would," Avery said. "Your presence here already says much. We are grateful that you brought Samara to us safely."

"Then I accept. I have amends to make."

Avery's mouth twitched. "I look forward to hearing more about the O'Neill family. Reese was rather tight-lipped."

Brendan's rigid posture relaxed and a fine smile broke the harshness of his expression. "I can well understand why. Between the lot of us, I think we inflicted every sort of mayhem on him."

"*That* I would be eager to hear," Avery said. "He has thought himself immune too long. But first, I think your sister needs some rest. Leigh will show her to her room, and both of you...please consider this your home." When Leigh and Samara disappeared, Avery turned back to Bren. "I think we could both use a brandy."

As the *Phoenix* approached the mouth of the Thames, Reese felt as though he had ploughed a permanent trail into the Atlantic during the past three years. He had been at sea two months on this expedition, and his frustration was about to boil over.

There was a small sense of satisfaction in knowing that Samara had sought him out. But that was almost buried in his overall sense of vexation. Had any two people ever been so star-crossed? Their unique courtship had encountered one disaster after another. Now he was little more than a day away from her, and he couldn't help but wonder what new hindrance might appear. Avery most certainly would have welcomed them and insisted that Samara remain. That they might have passed each other again was more than he could endure.

He felt Yancy's presence beside him and took comfort in his quiet support.

"Will you be coming to Beddingfield with me?"

"I think it's time you and Samara had some time alone...at least as much as you can get in that palace you call a home."

"If she's even there," Reese sighed. "I'm beginning to think it is not meant to be."

"But, of course, it is," Yancy said. He grinned. "If you two have survived everything so far, it must be love."

"Brendan could still be there."

"Probably," Yancy agreed noncommittally. "How do you feel about him?"

"I don't know. He was protecting Samara. I can't really quarrel with that." But there was doubt in his voice. He still felt stung from that final meeting. It was, he knew, his damnable wounded pride.

"Well, it shouldn't be long now."

As the *Phoenix* turned into the vast London docks, his eyes swept the several hundred ships anchored there. It would be pure luck to find Brendan's ship among so many, but he searched nonetheless, seeking reassurance. He didn't find it, nor did the men he questioned on the dock know of such a vessel. There were simply too many of them. Feeling more and more uncertain, he nonetheless turned the ship over to Simmons, located a horse and spurred the sleek chestnut on to Beddingfield.

Oblivious to the young maidservant in the room, Samara sat on the window seat, gazing out over the long driveway into Beddingfield. Her breasts still tingled from feeding her son, who now gurgled happily in the nearby cradle. Her frown eased as she glanced at him; he was incredibly beautiful, she thought, with his dark hair and very blue eyes. Her hand reached out to touch him with a sort of wonder. He was so small, so perfect. And, finest of all, he was half Reese Hampton.

She looked back down at the road as she had nearly every day for two weeks…except for the day she had given birth to Reese's son and the day after, when the Hamptons had demanded she rest. It had been an easy confinement, and she resumed her vigil on the third day, despite protestations. No one could coax her from her post for long.

The gardens were just beginning to bloom and the first flowers danced in the breeze, the hundreds of bright shades glimmering in the sun. Samara watched as her niece and nephew played below her under their mother's close scrutiny, and her heart swelled with love. They had all been so kind to her. In the past month, Avery and Leigh and their two children had become almost as close as her own family.

Her eyes lifted from the children and once more met the road. There was a dot that hadn't been there before. She watched intently as it grew larger and she made out a horseman. Even without seeing the face, she knew. No one else sat so proudly, so arrogantly. And then she saw the sun glint against golden hair as the beloved face searched the windows.

She waited no longer. She was running, running at last to meet her love.

Three weeks later...

The christening took place in the small chapel at Beddingfield.

Samara and Reese stood, hands clasped tightly together, as the clergyman baptized Tristan Adrian Hampton. Leigh and Brendan stood proudly as godparents, as Avery regarded the proceedings with a gleam of approval. It was by his suggestion that Brendan served as godfather. It was only fitting, Avery said, that the child have a godparent from either side of the family.

Brendan took his role very seriously. He held the infant carefully, looking on him with unabashed affection. When the ceremony was over, he flashed his quick, open grin at Samara and Reese, grateful for the honor.

It was, Samara thought as she squeezed Reese's hand possessively, the third happiest moment in her life. She couldn't rank the other two. One was the birth of Tristan. The other was that glorious moment three weeks ago when she had run, skirts and hair flying behind her, to Reese.

When he had seen her, he cantered his horse to her side, reached down and swung her up in his arms, holding her as though she were the rarest treasure in the world. Then he pressed her close, and she could feel the beat of his heart as his mouth reached down so eagerly for hers.

Her arms had wrapped around him and they had held each other with frantic need, each seeking to bind the other so tight they could never again be separated.

The horse shied under such unaccustomed movement, and Reese laughed—his lovely, lusty laugh which seemed to reach the skies. "I love you, Mrs. Hampton."

"And I adore you, Mr. Hampton."

He regained control of the horse and leaned back, his eyes feasting on each delectable feature. His lips then gifted her with the sweetest, most wondrous kiss; it was as if he were openly presenting his heart to her. And her hands, in turn, touched his face with such tenderness, such love that he knew, at last, her own heart was unquestionably his.

"I have a gift for you," she had whispered shyly.

"You are gift enough," he had answered. But his eyes sparkled with inquisitive interest at the quiet intensity of her statement.

But she was not to be coaxed into an answer. "You must come with me."

"Must I? I think I would rather hold you."

"Ah, but would the horse?" she questioned with mischief, as she looked with delight at his wicked expression.

"You have," he teased a trifle ungallantly, "gained a few pounds—very prettily so. You look radiant." He studied her face once more. There was, he thought, something different about her. Whatever it was, her face glowed with a beauty greater than he remembered.

She giggled. If only he had seen her three weeks ago! She wriggled in his arms, and he carefully set her down before joining her and tying the horse to a post. She took his hand and pulled him toward the house, ignoring the dignified Holmes who had opened the door. Giving Reese no time to return the servant's greeting, she pulled him, laughing, up the steps, hurrying him along, her face alight with anticipation.

Samara opened the door to her room and before permitting Reese inside dismissed the servant who had been watching the child. She reached once more for Reese's hand, unable to stop herself from lifting it to her mouth and touching the hard, callused skin with her soft lips. His head was cocked to one side, watching her curiously.

He heard a small cry, then a larger bellow. He saw Samara's smile widen. "Your son sounds like you."

Stunned, Reese simply stared at her, then in three large strides reached the source of the sound. From the door, Samara watched his changing expressions—from disbelief to wonder to shimmering, glowing joy. He looked back at her, his face begging confirmation.

Samara reached his side. "May I present your son, the

youngest Hampton. I was waiting on you to choose the rest of his name.''

His mouth trembled and a suspicious wetness filled his eyes as his arm went around Samara and he gazed at the tiny little being who, at the moment, had quieted and was looking toward his father with a kind of solemn regard...

The christening over, the family retired to the study for champagne, a prelude to a number of farewells that would be said in the next few days. Brendan would leave first, then Reese and Samara planned to sail the following week. Eloise would accompany them. Much to Samara's satisfaction, Brendan had found himself quite attracted to Eloise and asked her to stay with the O'Neills for a visit. When he first mentioned the possibility, Reese devilishly arched an eyebrow in warning, sending Samara into a fit of giggles. At least, she thought thankfully, he was philosophical about his rather unorthodox encounters with her family.

She was also delighted that he and Brendan had renewed their friendship. They had greeted each other warily at first, then disappeared together into the library. They had so much in common, including their deep love of little Tristan. The naming of Brendan as godfather only sealed the bond between them.

It had been decided Eloise would travel with Reese and Samara, both for convention's sake and because Eloise felt she could help with the baby. It would also give Eloise and Samara feminine company. After an initial hesitation, the two women had grown quite fond of each other.

Each day and night were a joy for Samara and Reese, who made their plans wrapped in each other's arms. Their passion flamed and their spirits soared as they rejoiced in each other's nearness. Their trust in each other had finally become absolute.

The morning they were to leave, Reese tenderly watched his son nurse, sucking hungrily as his tiny hands flailed.

''American impatience,'' Reese said fondly.

''British greed,'' Samara retorted with a smile.

"Ah, the best of both worlds," Reese said with the wickedly self-satisfied smile of an English pirate.

Samara opened her mouth to protest, only to find it completely sealed by his teasing lips. Quite contentedly, she surrendered.

* * * * * *

Dear Reader,

Like many of you, I've always been in love with the Scottish Highlands. Romance. Mystery. Political intrigue. Highlanders always seemed larger-than-life. The Highland warrior was the original superhero. The history of the Highlanders is a rich tapestry of life and death, of passion and betrayal.

My hero, Brice Campbell, stands accused by his own countrymen of atrocious crimes. He is a desperate man. Desperation makes him dangerous. Meredith MacAlpin is a woman with both courage and cunning. She will prove a handful, even for a man such as Brice Campbell.

Ah, but there is more. A young queen, determined to lead her country to freedom. And men who would betray not only their monarch, but their own people, as well.

As a storyteller, I hope, as you follow Brice and Meredith's adventure, you will fall in love with them just the way I did. That is my wish for each of you. For love is, after all, the grandest adventure of all.

If you can't get enough of Highland lore, I invite you to read the other titles in my Highland Series for Harlequin Historicals—*Highland Heather, Highland Fire, Highland Heart, The Highlander,* and *Highland Heaven.* In each one you will find yourself caught up in the magic and mystery of love in the Highlands.

HIGHLAND BARBARIAN
Ruth Langan

To my mother, Anna Beatrice Curley Ryan,
In case I've forgotten to tell you lately
how much I love you

And, of course, to Tom.
Always to Tom

Chapter One

Scotland
1561

The line of mourners stretched as far as the eye could see. The men, women and children of the MacAlpin clan waited patiently to pay their respects to their fallen laird, Alastair MacAlpin. Dressed in simple peasant garments of rough wool, their hands callused from lifetimes of hard labor, they had left their fields and herds and trudged for miles to the manor house of their chief.

Seventeen-year-old Meredith, his eldest daughter, sat beside his body to greet her people. Her thick dark hair, the color of mahogany, had been brushed into silken waves that fell to her waist. Her green eyes occasionally misted with tears that were quickly blinked away.

Beside her sat the younger ones, sixteen-year-old Brenna, with hair the color of a raven's wing and eyes that rivaled the heather that bloomed on the hill, and fourteen-year-old Megan, whose copper hair and gold-flecked eyes gave her a glowing radiance that shamed even the sun. Though it was Brenna's nature to be serene in the eye of the storm, it was the first time Meredith had ever known her youngest sister, Megan, to be so subdued.

One by one the people paused to offer their condolences and to pledge their loyalty to Meredith, the new clan chieftain.

"You had a fine teacher, lass." The gnarled old man, Duncan MacAlpin, wiped a tear from the corner of his eye and placed a bony hand on the girl's shoulder. "You've learned your lessons well. You'll do the MacAlpin proud."

"Thank you, Duncan." Meredith steeled herself against the pain. There would be no public display of weakness. What her people, and especially her younger sisters, needed to see now was strength, dignity, hope. Later, when she was alone with her grief, she would give in to the overwhelming need to weep.

The clatter of horses' hooves sent the chickens squawking and clucking in the courtyard. The door to the manor house was opened to admit Gareth MacKenzie and a dozen of his men. The MacKenzie land adjoined the MacAlpin land to the north, then stretched for miles until it met the river Tweed.

"My condolences, Lady Meredith." Gareth MacKenzie bent low over her hand, then turned to study the still form of the MacAlpin. "You know, of course, who murdered your father?"

"Aye. Cowards. Highwaymen who struck under cover of darkness and hid behind masks. Duncan here said there were more than a dozen."

"You saw them?" Gareth turned a piercing gaze on the withered old man.

"I was bringing Mary back from a birthing at our nephew's farm. By the time I realized what was happening, they were gone. And the MacAlpin was drenched in his own blood." The old man choked back a sob before adding, "Mary and I brought him here in our wagon. But even my Mary's medicines could not save him."

"Did you get a good look at any of their horses?" Gareth's hand hovered inches above his sword, and Meredith was touched by the vehemence in his tone. Though their lands had been adjoining for generations, she had never before been witness to Gareth's concern for her father's welfare.

"Nay." The old man's voice broke. "It was too dark, and my eyes are growing dim. But my arms are still strong enough to wield a broadsword with the best of them. A few minutes sooner and the MacAlpin would still be alive." He touched a hand to Meredith's shoulder and added softly, "Or I'd have died alongside him where I've always been."

"Don't dwell on it, Duncan." Meredith stood and wrapped her arms around the man who had been her father's right hand since they were lads. "You and Mary did all you could."

"Those were no highwaymen," Gareth said in a voice loud enough for all to hear.

A murmur went up among the crowd.

"What are you saying?" Meredith turned to study him while keeping an arm around Duncan's shoulders.

"It was the Highland Barbarian, Brice Campbell."

Meredith stiffened. The very name Brice Campbell sent terror through the hearts of all who heard it. He was a Highlander, and rumored to be the most feared warrior in all of Scotland. The Lowlanders, and especially the Borderers, found themselves under attack by both the English and their own neighbors in the Highlands.

"Everyone knows he and his men come down from the Highlands and strike, then disappear into the hills before anyone can catch them."

"But why would the Campbell attack Alastair MacAlpin?"

"The land." Gareth noted the hush that had descended over the crowd. "How many times have your borders been attacked in night raids in the past year?"

It was common knowledge that MacAlpin land had been attacked half a dozen times. Eight men had been killed and two boys under the age of ten. Crops had been destroyed, cattle stolen. And each time the looters had disappeared without a trace.

"'Twas the English. Everyone knows they are the ones who loot and pillage."

Meredith frowned. "My father never mentioned the Campbell."

"Not to you, perhaps. But he said as much to me."

She was stung by his words. For as long as she could remember, she and her father had shared everything. With the death of her mother and then the murder of her little brother, Brendan, father and daughter had forged a bond of love and trust. Why would he have kept such a thing from her?

As if reading her mind Gareth said, "You're young, lass.

Alastair thought it too much of a burden to place on your shoulders. And so he confided in me and suggested that if anything should happen to him, he wanted to be assured that the MacKenzie clan would look out for you.''

''I can look out for myself.'' She drew herself to her full height and turned away, dismissing him.

''I would not presume to intrude on your grief unless I thought it of the utmost importance.'' Gareth touched her shoulder and drew her around to face him, knowing that the crowd of onlookers overheard everything. ''But those under the protection of the MacAlpin must be assured that they will have a strong leader. If it is indeed Brice Campbell who killed your father he will not be deterred by a lone woman. Your father would expect you to form a strong union immediately.''

He saw her eyes narrow fractionally as she gave him a withering look. ''You would speak to me of marriage before my father is even in the ground?''

As she started to turn away he said, ''I speak of a merger of our two lands, our two clans, in order to fight the common enemy. It is a small sacrifice to pay for the safety of those who depend upon you.''

Meredith saw the looks that passed from Duncan to Mary, from one villager to another. Though no one spoke she could sense the fear that had suddenly taken hold. A seed had been planted. A seed of fear and rebellion. And she felt powerless to stop it.

''I am not suggesting that you marry me,'' Gareth said, pressing his advantage. ''Though as the eldest, it would be my right.'' He saw her shiver and knew that he had touched a nerve. From the time they were children Meredith had sensed something unsettling about Gareth that she could not name.

Gareth dropped an arm about a young man's shoulders and thrust him forward. The two were the same height, and the same coloring, with golden hair and tawny skin. ''My younger brother, Desmond, has always been a friend to you. As husband, he would pledge the strength of the entire MacKenzie clan to your protection.''

Meredith saw the way the young man blushed. Desmond, dear, sweet Desmond, hated being made the center of attention. But he had always deferred to his older brother's wishes.

"As my husband, Desmond would also acquire all the MacAlpin land." Her voice was low, challenging.

Desmond always stammered when he was agitated. "Think...think you that the MacKenzies need your land?"

Meredith felt a wave of shame. It was well-known that the MacKenzie holdings were so vast that only Campbell land could compare. Still, the MacKenzie ambition was well-known. If not Desmond's, then at least Gareth's.

"I will speak of this no more until after my father has had a proper burial."

Gareth smiled and stepped forward to lift her hand to his lips. "That is as it should be. On the morrow we will return with a marriage offer that will bring peace and prosperity to our borders."

He seemed pleased when Desmond followed his lead and lifted Meredith's hand to his lips. Moving smartly, he marshaled his men from the house. With a clatter of hooves they left the mourners to whisper and gossip among themselves.

"Stand still, lass. A bride should be calm and serene on her wedding day." Morna, the old woman who had been with Meredith since her birth, fussed with the hem of the gown.

"Serenity is for Brenna."

"Aye. You've always preferred to be in the thick of battle." The old woman stood back to admire her handiwork. "Oh, lass. Your father would have been so proud."

At the mention of Alastair MacAlpin, Meredith's eyes clouded. Oh, Father, she prayed, looking out over the crowd that was hastily assembling, is this what you would have wanted? Am I to give myself to a man I do not love, in order to protect those I do?

She thought of Duncan, who along with his aged wife, Mary, had privately urged her to accept the MacKenzie offer. "Not for myself, lass," he had said fervently, "but for my children and grandchildren. There's been enough fighting among the clans. 'Tis the English we must fear. With enough strength we can stand up to their raids. If the MacKenzies can promise us peace and prosperity, we ought to at least consider it."

There were others. They came in clusters of two and three to speak confidentially to their new chieftain, hoping to persuade her that there should be no more death and destruction. It was the look in the eyes of the old women that finally convinced Meredith. They had buried husbands and sons. Must they be condemned to bury grandsons as well?

The mere thought of giving herself to a man who did not hold her heart was appalling. But Meredith MacAlpin, whose ancestors could be traced to Kenneth MacAlpin, the first King of Scots, had been trained from infancy to put the needs of others above her own. This day she was determined to make the supreme sacrifice. She would marry Desmond MacKenzie. And she would find a way to love the sweet boy who had been her childhood friend.

She glanced at her two sisters, dressed in identical gowns of palest pink. She would do this for them, so that they could, for a little while longer, be young and carefree. So that the young men they fancied could grow to manhood and give them the lives they dreamed of.

"It is time." As the strains of the harp lifted on the spring breeze, Gareth MacKenzie slipped his mantle from his shoulders and fastened it about his brother. "Wear the plaid with pride, Desmond."

The two brothers embraced, then Gareth strode to the back of the church toward Meredith, a smile of supreme confidence lighting his features. "I would be honored to walk with you to my brother's side."

"I fear that honor is reserved for my father's dearest friend," Meredith said softly.

Ignoring Gareth's outstretched hand she placed her fingers lightly on Duncan's sleeve. The old man beamed with pride as Morna thrust a bouquet of heather and wildflowers into Meredith's arms.

Brenna and Megan walked slowly, tossing flower petals along the floor of the cathedral.

As the music swelled, the old man and the beautiful young woman began the long walk up the aisle toward the young man who stood waiting at the altar.

The ancient stone cathedral stood in a green meadow. The nearby loch was swollen from spring rains. The sun was just rising above hills still silvery with dew. To the east, the Lowlands were smooth, with only an occasional hill marring the vast expanse of green. To the west, the Highlands rose up, stark and wild and primitive. More than a million years ago the ice age dragged glaciers across the land, forming sharp hills and steep valleys. Only the hardiest of souls dared to live in such a harsh environment.

As the strains of the harp echoed in the morning mist, eerie figures formed a ring around the cathedral. Some led horses, others were on foot. All carried longbows. One, obviously their leader, tossed a rope to the highest point of the spire. Testing its strength, he slung the longbow over his shoulder and began climbing. When he reached the high open window, he pulled himself silently inside and stood on the stone ledge.

The bishop intoned the words of the service, then turned to face the young couple. Lifting his arms in prayer and supplication, he gazed heavenward. The words died on his lips as he let out a gasp.

An arrow sang through the air. The young bridegroom seemed to stiffen for a moment, then fell forward. With a shriek Meredith fell to her knees beside him and watched in horror as an ever-widening circle of blood stained his mantle.

As the crowd came to its feet a deep voice rang out. "Any man who reaches for his sword shall die."

Meredith turned and felt a dagger of fear pierce her heart. The man on the ledge above them was taller than any man she had ever seen, with shoulders wider than a longbow. He wore a saffron shirt beneath a rough tunic and, like a savage, was bare legged to the knees. His feet were encased in brogues and there was a mantle of dark homespun tossed rakishly across his shoulders. His dark hair was thick and shaggy.

Dozens of men dressed in similar fashion stepped into the cathedral. All of them held bows and arrows at the ready.

"I am Brice Campbell," their leader said, and she was certain he smiled at the fearful murmur that erupted. His name was known throughout all of Scotland and beyond. Only rarely was he referred to by the name Brice Campbell. Those who feared him called him the Highland Barbarian.

"I have come to avenge the blot on my good name inflicted by Gareth MacKenzie. It is not I who raided your lands and slew your sons and brothers. And now that I have silenced the liar's tongue, I declare this feud ended."

Meredith gave a little gasp as she realized that Brice Campbell thought he had killed Gareth. As she touched a hand to Desmond's throat and found no pulsebeat, she saw a movement from the corner of her eye. Turning, she watched Gareth duck behind a wooden pew and shamelessly pull Brenna in front of him as a shield.

Meredith's heart leaped to her throat. Her beloved younger sister was the only thing standing between Gareth MacKenzie and certain death.

"So that you will all remember that Brice Campbell is a just man," the voice from above intoned, "I will spare the life of Gareth MacKenzie's bride."

As the menacing Campbell turned to take his leave, an arrow sang through the air, fired from the protection of the pew. It narrowly missed its mark, sailing through the open window mere inches from the man's head. Instantly Brice Campbell's men unleashed a barrage of arrows, which brought down more than a dozen men on both sides of the aisle. MacKenzie and MacAlpin clanswomen became widows in the blink of an eye.

Meredith's gaze searched wildly about the sanctuary until she spied both her sisters unharmed. Megan had taken refuge behind the altar, where she was frantically searching for a weapon. Brenna lay on the floor, where she had been roughly pushed aside by Gareth MacKenzie.

"Fool!" the man at the window ledge shouted. "This feud was to have ended. But one among you has seen fit to carry it on. Now shall you all rue the day you crossed Brice Campbell. The lady's blood is on your hands."

Before Meredith could move, the man soared through the air, dangling from a rope, and caught her up with one arm.

Looking into her face, Brice Campbell felt for a moment as if all the air had been crushed from his lungs. Her hair, lush and dark, intertwined with ivy and wildflowers, fell to below her waist. The scent of wildflowers surrounded her like a

spring meadow. Her skin was as flawless as fine porcelain.
Her lips were pursed as if to issue a protest. Her eyes, as green
as the Highland hills, were wide with fear. She blinked, and
he watched them darken with sudden fury.

He stared at her heaving breasts, modestly covered by a
gown of pristine white. The cloth was so soft, so fragile, it
could have been spun by angels. His fingers tingled as he
pulled her to him.

Meredith felt hands as strong as iron lift her as effortlessly
as if she were a leaf. Cradled against his massive chest she
felt his muscles strain as he pulled both their weights against
the rope. Together they swung through the air and landed on
the stone window ledge. As he set her on her feet she felt
herself slipping. Her hands reached out for him, clutching
blindly at his mantle. But before she could utter a cry he was
holding her firmly against him.

"Touch one weapon and you shall watch the lady die by
my hand," he called to the assembly.

Meredith felt the anger ripple through him, though he strove
to control it. Through narrowed lids he studied the crowd below until, content that no one would offer further resistance,
he turned. Still clutching her to him Brice grasped the rope
and leaped through the open window. He landed on the ground
and in one swift movement scooped Meredith up into his arms
and climbed onto the broad back of a horse.

His men backed from the cathedral, then scrambled onto
their horses. Before the people inside could even begin to get
to their feet, the horses were galloping toward the hills. Once
there, they disappeared into the rising mists, into the forests,
into the feared Highlands.

Held in Brice Campbell's arms, Meredith felt her heartbeat
keeping time to the pounding rhythm of the horses' hooves.

The man who held her captive was the strongest, most fearsome man she had ever seen. In the morning light his skin
was ruddy. His hair held the hint of sun in the dark, burnished
curls that kissed his wide, unwrinkled brow. The muscles of
his arms were as thick and hard as twisted ropes. She stared,
fascinated, as he urged his mount forward, holding her against
his chest as effortlessly as a child holds a kitten. But it was
his eyes that captured her gaze. Dark, piercing eyes that fas-

tened on hers and held her gaze when she yearned to turn
away.

"So, my lady. It seems you've been made a widow before
you were even given the chance to savor the MacKenzie
charm. A pity that you'll spend your wedding night in a hovel
in the Highlands."

Meredith bit her lip and lowered her head so that this barbarian would not see her terror. She had just been stolen by a
savage. A Highland savage. And if even half the stories she'd
heard about the Campbells were true, she would never see her
beloved Borderland or countrymen again.

Chapter Two

A faint rosy glow spread across the horizon. The hills were washed with pale light.

All through the day and night they had ridden, and when darkness cloaked the hills and forests, Meredith had sensed the change in the landscape. They had been climbing steadily from the beginning of their journey. The terrain was littered with rocky crags and steep pinnacles and frigid waters. The surefooted animals picked their way over the obstacles with the skill of those born in the Highlands.

Now, with the dawn light breaking through the mist, Meredith had her first glimpse of the Highlands. Though close to exhaustion she could not fail to be moved by the glens and fells, the rushing streams and waterfalls. The wild, primitive beauty of the land thrilled and terrified her. Like the man who held her, mile after mile, in his arms. Splendid. Frightening.

After his first murmured phrases, he had spoken not a word to her. At times he had called out to his men in the darkness. They had shouted their responses. Some of the men cursed. More than a few curses had come from his own lips when his mount stumbled, or when tree branches scratched and clawed. Meredith trembled in fear at the depth of passion in the man. He was quick to anger, she realized. Would he be as quick to strike out at others? At her?

A few of their curses had him chuckling, low and deep in his throat. That sound caused strange feelings to curl deep inside her. Feelings that were most unsettling. He was a rough, unlettered man, born and bred for cruelty and killing, she reminded herself. Not the kind of man to cause a ripple of feelings in her.

She heard the change in his tone when turrets could be seen rising above the mist. "At last. We are home."

Home. She had a sudden desire to weep. Would she ever see her beloved home again? Or would she be condemned to die in this strange wilderness?

As they topped a rise Meredith stared at the sprawling structure of stone, standing between two towering peaks. Though not as heavily fortified as the Border castles, for they were constantly being attacked by the English, it was a solid fortress surrounded by wooded hills. What was more, it was luxurious, even opulent.

In her mind she had pictured these rough people living in hovels. Had her captor not said as much? But the roofs she saw among the trees were of solid, sturdy houses. A few even resembled the English manor houses.

The sound of voices could be heard in the forest. The voices of women and children coming to greet their men. The distant sound of hounds baying.

While she watched, the men saluted their leader and veered off the path toward their own homes. Women laughed and children shouted as they were lifted in brawny arms and hugged fiercely. Within minutes horses and riders had disappeared into the forest, leaving Meredith and Brice Campbell in a small enclosed courtyard that led to the castle's entrance.

Half a dozen hounds surrounded their horse, leaping and baying as their master called each name.

The door was thrown open. The first one through the doorway was a thin youth with fiery hair spilling about a wide forehead. A sprinkle of freckles danced across an impish, upturned nose. His arms and legs were as thin as a girl's, though the beginnings of muscles could be seen beneath the clinging sleeves of his saffron shirt. His sparkling blue eyes filled with joy at the sight of Brice.

Servants hurried out to catch the reins of the lord's horse as he dismounted.

The lad threw himself into Brice's arms. "You've been away so long I was beginning to fret."

"Over me, Jamie lad?" Brice tousled his hair and wrapped him in a great bear hug. "You know better. I'll always return to Kinloch House."

"Aye," the lad said with feeling. "And I'll always be here waiting."

"Until you're old enough to ride with me," Brice muttered with a grin. "Which will be soon from the looks of you." He held the lad a little away from him and studied him with a critical eye. "You've grown at least an inch since I left."

The lad laughed, then glanced shyly toward the vision in white who sat astride Brice's horse.

Seeing the direction of his glance, Brice reached up. Meredith was hauled roughly from the saddle and handed over to a bewildered serving wench who stared mutely at her master's captive.

"Take the woman to my chambers. I will deal with her later."

Meredith shivered at his tone. Her mind whirled as she was whisked inside and herded up great stone steps. She had a brisk impression of tapestries and banners lining the walls of the staircase before she was ushered into a chamber on the second floor.

"There's fresh water, my lady," the timid servant said. "And I'll fetch warm clothes if my lord approves." She backed from the room and closed the door.

This was obviously a man's private domain. The furniture was massive, like the man who lived here. A log burned in the fireplace and Meredith hurried to stand in front of it. She had been chilled clear through to the bone. The gauzy gown intended for her wedding had offered little protection from the cold. And though the warmth of her captor's body had offered some protection, she had been buffeted by the raw elements. Perhaps, she thought, she would prefer death by freezing to whatever torment Brice Campbell had in mind.

What did he have in mind for her?

Meredith turned, keeping her back to the fire while studying the sitting chamber. The walls were hung with tapestries and furs. The cold stone floors had been softened with fur throws, as were the chairs and settles.

She needed a weapon with which to defend herself. Sooner or later Brice Campbell would discover that he had killed the wrong man. She would be useless to him. And he would be forced to dispose of her. When that time came she would have to be prepared to fight to the death.

She moved about the room, searching for anything that might be used as a weapon. When she found nothing she entered the bedchamber. The flames of the fireplace cast the room in a soft glow.

A rough-hewn frame of logs supported a huge bed littered with pallets of down and fur. Meredith's gaze fastened on a shelf above the bed where a dozen swords and daggers lay strewn about.

She studied the weapons and selected a small dagger that would fit beneath the waistband of a gown. Clutching it to her, she ran a finger gingerly along the blade and was pleased to find it honed to perfection.

She glanced down at her waist. The filmy confection she was wearing could hardly conceal a weapon. She would have to hide the dagger until more suitable clothes were given her.

Kneeling beside the bed Meredith began searching among the linens for a place to hide her treasure. Her fingers encountered the softness of fur. She closed her eyes a moment, resting her cheek against the velvety smoothness. How drained she was. There had been so little time to rest in the past few days. First there had been her father's death and burial, and then the marriage plans. Marriage. She felt tears sting her lids. There had been no time to grieve for her father or for her husband of less than a minute. She pressed her cheek to the soft bed coverings and choked back a sob.

Though she was an excellent horsewoman, she had spent too many hours of the day and night in the saddle. Her muscles protested. How she yearned to rest her aching body. Oh for a few moments of respite from the fear that lay like a hard knot in the pit of her stomach. She sighed. A minute longer, and then she would get to her feet. She must be prepared when the barbarian came for her. She would rest only a short time. She could not afford to let down her guard. Against her will her lids flickered, then closed. With one hand holding the dagger, the other curled into a fist at her side, she slept.

Brice finished the last of the mutton and washed it down with a tankard of ale. His hunger abated, he leaned back and stretched out toward the warmth of the fire. The dogs at his feet stirred, snatching up the scraps he tossed them, then settled back down to drowse.

He was in a foul mood. Now that he had eaten his fill, he would have to give some thought to the woman.

If he was cold, the woman had to be much colder. The thin gown had afforded her no protection from the chill of the night. But she had brazenly rejected his offer of a warm cloak. What arrogance. He felt the beginning of a grudging admission of respect before brushing it aside. What foolishness.

She was a most unusual woman. Not once had she cried or complained. And not once, when they had made brief stops, had she climbed from his horse and demanded a moment of privacy.

A bride and a widow within minutes. And yet she had not shed a tear. Remarkable.

What was he to do with her? His hand atop the table clenched and unclenched. It had not been part of his plan to steal the woman. In fact, it bothered him more than he cared to admit. But the fool who had defied him and fired the arrow would have to bear the guilt. The terms had been clearly stated. One among the MacKenzie clan had no conscience.

Across the table Jamie MacDonald watched in silence. He had learned to hold his tongue when Brice was in one of his black moods. Jamie did not see Brice's bouts of temper as a flaw. Any man who carried the weight of responsibilities that Brice Campbell carried had every right to moments of doubt. If someone had suggested that Jamie was turning a blind eye to Brice's faults, he would have fought them to the death. He adored Brice Campbell. His devotion to the man was absolute.

Brice looked up as the door was thrown open. The dogs rushed to the door and sniffed, eager to greet the visitors who carried a familiar scent. Angus Gordon, Brice's most trusted friend, burst into the room. Behind him strode Holden

Mackay, whose clan had recently joined forces with the Campbells in the feud with the MacKenzies.

One look at Angus's stormy features told Brice that something was very wrong.

"You've killed the wrong man, Brice."

"What are you saying? You saw him fall at the altar, Angus. It was Gareth MacKenzie."

"Nay, Brice. 'Twas his younger brother, Desmond. Holden and I stayed behind to learn the name of the one who had fired the arrow at you."

"And did you?"

At Brice's arched brow Angus nodded. "Gareth MacKenzie. He would be the only one fool enough to continue the feud after you had announced it over." His tone lowered. "Holden tried but could not get to him. There were too many MacKenzie men. And the kirk was crowded with women and children."

For a moment Brice could only stare from one man to the other. Suddenly scraping back his chair, he raced up the stairs toward his chambers with Jamie, Angus, Holden and the hounds on his heels.

"Woman." The door was slammed against the wall, the sound reverberating along the hallways of the castle. He gazed about the empty room. "Do not try to hide from me."

In quick strides he crossed to the bedchamber and kicked in the door. Jamie, Angus and Holden remained in the doorway, watching, listening.

The dogs circled the figure by the bed.

In that one instant before her head came up, Brice saw her kneeling beside the bed, her hair spilled forward like a veil. He could read her confusion when her lids flickered and lifted. Eyes as green as the shimmering Highland lochs watched him as he strode toward her. By the time he reached her she was on her feet, prepared to meet her fate.

The dogs growled low in their throats. But not one of them made a move toward the woman. They would wait, forever if necessary, until their master gave them the signal to attack.

In her hand was a dagger. A very small, very sharp dagger. Though Meredith's heart pounded painfully in her chest, her hand remained steady.

It was a giant who faced her. A giant whose rough clothes and speech sent terror racing through her. He stood, feet apart, hands on hips. On his face was a scowl that gave him such a fierce look she wanted to flee. But though her heart was nearly bursting, she reminded herself that she was now the MacAlpin. The MacAlpin was no coward. Meredith lifted her chin a fraction and met his look with one of defiance.

He saw the look. Even in his anger he admired her for it. There were not many in this land who could face Brice Campbell without flinching, be they man or woman.

The dagger? Though he had no doubt that he could best this small female in a battle, it irritated him that she would dare to draw a weapon against him.

"Put it down."

Her eyes widened at the icy command.

"If I am forced to disarm you, my lady, I assure you I will not be gentle."

She stared at the muscles of his arms, then lifted her gaze to the challenge in his dark eyes. For a moment longer she held the knife. Then slowly, with no change in her expression, she let it drop from her fingers. It fell to the floor and lay there among the furs, glinting in the light of the fire.

"Your bridegroom," he said, watching her through narrowed eyes. "Was he not Gareth MacKenzie?"

She wanted to hurt him as he had hurt her. She wanted to twist the knife, while he writhed in pain. If not the dagger, then the words that could cut as surely as any blade.

A half smile touched her lips. "Nay, my lord. It was not."

His eyes narrowed fractionally. Damn the woman. She was enjoying his confusion. "The man I killed. Who was he?"

"Gareth's brother, Desmond."

She saw the way his lips pressed together. A little muscle began working at the side of his jaw.

"You lie, woman. Why would the younger brother be allowed to wed before the eldest?"

Especially to one as lovely as the woman standing before him. For the first time Brice allowed himself to see, really see, the woman he had captured. With that wild mane of hair falling in tangles to below her waist and that gown of gossamer snow revealing a lush young body ripe for the picking, she was stunning.

"Because Gareth knew that I would never consent to be his wife. He offered Desmond instead."

"Consent?" Brice Campbell threw back his head and laughed. "And why would he need the consent of a mere girl? Why did he not go to your father and offer for you like a man?"

"I need the consent of no man," she said in a haughty manner that had him lifting an eyebrow in surprise. "Now that you have killed my father, I am the MacAlpin, heir to my father's land and protector of his people."

"I killed your father?" Brice took a menacing step closer and saw the way she watched him with the wariness of a doe in the forest. "Who accuses me of such treachery?"

"Gareth MacKenzie."

He clamped his mouth shut on the curse that rose to his lips. "At least the lie was spoken by one who does not matter to me."

"He matters so little," she said with a look of fury, "that you invaded the sanctity of the kirk to try and kill him."

At her sarcasm Brice felt his temper rising. But just as quickly, her next words had him feeling contrite.

"And succeeded in killing an innocent lad in the bargain."

"I regret having killed Desmond MacKenzie," Brice said with sudden honesty.

For a moment Meredith found herself astounded by his admission. Could it be that the barbarian was almost human?

"But the next time I will succeed," he added in a tone of pure venom. "From this moment Gareth MacKenzie is a dead man."

"And what of me?"

He took a step closer until they were almost touching. The hounds, taking a cue from their master, inched closer, sniffing the hem of her gown.

To her credit, Meredith did not back away, but stood facing him. He reached out a hand, intending to catch her roughly by the shoulder. The instant his fingers encountered her skin he felt the heat. Heat that raced and pulsed until he felt as if he were on fire.

"I haven't yet decided just what I'll do with you." He stared down into her eyes and was astounded by the sexual pull.

"What is your name?" His voice was a mere whisper.

"Meredith." She was surprised at how difficult it was to speak. At his touch her throat had gone dry. All the blood seemed to have rushed to her brain, leaving her feeling weak and light-headed.

"Meredith MacAlpin."

"Meredith." An unusual name for an unusual woman. He had to remove his hand or he would be burned. He clenched his fists by his side and took a step back. "Daughter of Alastair MacAlpin?"

At her nod he said simply, "He was a good man. And a fair one."

His mind began working feverishly while he studied her. "Perhaps I'll use you as the bait in a trap."

He saw the way her lips pursed as she started to protest. The words died on her lips as he added, "If Gareth MacKenzie sees your land slipping away, I'll wager that he'll do anything necessary to get you back."

"Are you suggesting that Desmond was ordered to marry me only to enlarge the MacKenzie holdings?"

He saw the sparks in those green eyes and nearly laughed aloud. So he had struck a nerve. Swallowing back the smile that threatened he murmured, "Was there any doubt?"

He watched the way her features darkened with fury. Aye, a nerve. God in heaven. What a temper. What a fascinating, fiery little creature.

"Oh, Gareth MacKenzie will come for me." She faced him, hands on hips, eyes blazing. "But not to enrich his estate. He will come for me because he is a gentleman. A man of honor. And not a—barbarian."

He did laugh then, a deep, joyous sound that sent little tremors along her spine.

"A barbarian, am I?" His smile faded. In its place was a look of pure venom. "Aye. That is what I must be if we are to believe that Gareth MacKenzie is a gentleman."

He stooped and retrieved the dagger before crossing the room to remove all the weapons from the shelf above the bed.

"Angus," he shouted. "Holden."

Instantly his friends were at his side.

Brice handed them the weapons. "See that these are kept away from the lady." He emphasized the word "lady."

Angus nodded toward Meredith. "Angus Gordon, my lady."

Meredith studied the man who stood beside his friend. Smaller by a head, sandy hair fell in a riot of curls over his freckled forehead. His blue eyes danced with the promise of laughter lurking just beneath their clear depths. In her state of anger Meredith refused to acknowledge him, except for a slight nod of her head.

"Holden Mackay," Brice said by way of curt introduction. "Of the clan Mackay to the east."

Meredith studied the burly man. At first glance he appeared to have no neck. His head seemed to rest upon his massive shoulders. His upper arms, like his chest and shoulders, were corded with muscles. As he lifted several weapons with the ease of a seasoned warrior, he turned and, for the first time, stared directly at her.

"My lady." He inclined his head slightly. "Your stay at Kinloch House should prove to be most interesting."

Meredith shivered at the suggestion in his words. But it was his eyes that frightened her. They were cold, lifeless. Like his soul? she wondered.

"I will join you below stairs," Brice called to his friends.

When the two men left, Jamie continued to stand in the doorway staring with fascination at the beautiful woman who was Brice's captive.

"Jamie. Be gone, lad."

The boy blushed clear to his toes before rushing from the room.

When they were alone Meredith lifted her head a fraction and faced her captor.

Again he felt the pull and had to force himself to step back, away from the heat of her.

He deliberately turned his back on her and walked to the adjoining sitting chamber.

"I will have food sent to you. My servants will see to your comfort." At the door he turned toward her with a look that struck terror in her heart. His eyes were dark, dangerous. "If you try to leave this room you will find yourself most uncomfortable."

"Do you think I fear death at your hand?"

He gave her a chilling smile. "Perhaps it is not death I have in mind, Meredith MacAlpin. Perhaps it is something far worse for a lady such as you. At the hands of a—barbarian like myself."

His words sent a shiver along her spine. She had been prepared to die. But the thought of being used by him like some tavern slut sent her into a state of near hysteria.

He called to the hounds and they ran eagerly from the room.

When the door closed, Meredith began to pace the length of the room and back. She must find another weapon with which to defend herself.

With a feeling of desperation she searched every inch of the room. She was not a woman who accepted defeat gracefully. But defeated she would be without a weapon. As she turned dejectedly toward the bed, she spotted a rough cloak dropped carelessly in the corner of the room. Beneath it she found a dagger, small and sharp. With trembling fingers she concealed it beneath her gown.

This time her captor had not even bothered to disarm her—had merely ordered her to drop her weapon and she had. Now he would think her too puny, too insignificant, to dare to defy him. Hopefully he would not bother checking her for a weapon again.

She strode toward the fireplace and stood, deep in thought. The next time Brice Campbell came for her she knew what she must do.

Chapter Three

When the door to the sitting chamber opened, Meredith's hand automatically moved to the dagger at her waist as she swung around to face her captor. In her eyes was the look of a warrior.

"I brought you food, my lady."

Upon seeing the serving girl Meredith let out a long hiss of breath.

The girl was nearly as tall as a man, with blond hair neatly plaited and twisted about her head. As she set the tray on a table near the fireplace, Meredith noted that her hands were large and work worn.

"What is your name?'

"Cara."

"Have you served Brice Campbell long, Cara?"

With ease the girl pulled a massive chair in front of the table and waited for Meredith to seat herself. "I was born here in Kinloch House while my lord Campbell and my father were in France. When my father died in France, my lord arranged for my mother and me to stay on here."

"And you do not object to being forced into service?"

"My lady, it is a fine life for us. If my lord Campbell had turned us out, where would we have gone?"

"Have you no family?"

"My mother has two brothers, but both had already taken wives. We would have become a burden to them, and in time they would have resented us. Knowing that, my lord Campbell provided for us.''

Meredith noted the warmth in the girl's tone whenever she mentioned Brice Campbell's name. "How can one so cruel elicit such devotion?''

"Cruel?'' Cara gave a sweet laugh. "My lord Campbell is a good and fair man. I have never known him to be cruel.'' She lowered her voice. "But he is cursed with a quick temper. Mother has often said that Father told her he would ne'er be the one to cross swords with him in battle.''

Meredith recalled his curses in the darkness, low and savage, and felt herself shiver. Aye, the man had a temper.

"But he is quick to forgive and forget as well. A kinder, fairer man there is not in all of Scotland. His kindness even extends at times to his enemies.''

"I do not understand.''

Cara gave her a level look. "Jamie MacDonald's father was a Lowlander.''

"I had thought the lad to be Campbell's son.''

"Son?'' Cara smiled at the thought. "Ian MacDonald and his wee son were all that was left of a clan that had been burned and looted in the dark of night. Blaming Brice Campbell, Ian MacDonald journeyed to the Highlands to seek his vengeance.''

"What happened to Ian?'' Meredith asked softly.

"He was killed in battle. When Brice learned that there was no one left in the Lowlands to raise the lad, he took him in. And Jamie MacDonald is like a son to Brice.''

Cara swallowed suddenly, dismayed at the looseness of her tongue. "I pray I have not betrayed a confidence by telling you this, my lady. But let no man call Brice Campbell an unjust man.'' She avoided Meredith's eyes, fearing that she had overstepped her bounds. "I will leave you to your meal. When you have finished I will return with warm clothes.'' She stared pointedly at Meredith's gown. "Though there is nothing wrong with the clothes you wear. You look as lovely as a bride.''

The food, which only minutes ago had seemed so inviting, now tasted like ashes in Meredith's mouth. She pushed the plate aside. "I was a bride. For a moment.''

Seeing the bleak look on Meredith's face, Cara cried, "Oh, my lady. What happened?"

Meredith's voice held a dreamy, far-away note. "He was hardly more than a lad. Doing what his family ordered. As was I." Her tone hardened. "He was killed at the altar." Meredith scraped back her chair and crossed the room to stand in front of the roaring fire. She was suddenly cold. So cold. The scene played once again in her mind and she gripped her hands together so tightly they were white from the effort. "Killed by an arrow from Brice Campbell's longbow. The same Brice Campbell you claim is an honorable man."

"I am sorry, my lady."

Meredith was so deep in thought she didn't even hear the door close as the serving girl took her leave.

In the great hall Brice paced back and forth before the fireplace while Angus and Holden emptied their tankards. Though Jamie MacDonald's eyes were heavy, he resisted the urge to go to bed. The need to be close to Brice, to hear all that had transpired in the Lowlands, was more compelling than the need for sleep.

The hounds lay in a circle before the fireplace, their eyes firmly fixed on their master.

"How could I have made such a blunder?"

"The MacKenzie brothers are nearly identical. From so great a distance it was a natural mistake." Angus added softly, "Do not fret, old friend. We will kill Gareth next time."

"Next time." Brice whirled on his friend, his eyes blazing. "Do you think I can ask my men to risk their lives going down to the Borders again, just to honor my good name?"

"Why not?" Angus shrugged. "You know they would carry your standard anywhere."

"They have wives and children to consider. I will not place them in danger for the sake of my reputation."

"Then you and I will go." Angus grinned. "You know I like nothing better than a good joust. Especially with the likes of Gareth MacKenzie."

"And I will ride with you," Jamie said, jumping to his feet. "I have no need to stay here."

Brice's temper cooled. "Aye. We're three of a kind." His frown turned into a smile. He could never resist Jamie's enthusiasm.

"Then we'll go back down and make good our promise?"

"You have a duty to stay here and grow to manhood," Brice murmured gently to the boy. Circling the room, Brice clapped his hand on Angus's shoulder. "I'll ponder your offer and give you an answer on the morrow."

"What of the girl?" Holden asked.

"Aye, the girl." Brice tried not to think about the way he'd felt when they had touched. The mere thought of it brought a rush of heat. He shrugged. "I'll think on that as well." He crossed the room, then paused on the stairs.

The hounds circled his feet, eager to accompany him to his room.

"Pray she's asleep," Brice muttered. "I'm near exhausted. All I want is a chance to rest this tired body."

"Aye." Angus followed him up the stairs and turned toward his rooms on the far end of the hall. "It's been too many hours since last we slept. I will see you on the morrow."

"You are both fools," Holden hissed. "Do you not know what to do with a warm, soft woman's body on a night such as this?"

Brice turned on him with a look of fury. "Do not talk so about a Scotswoman. Especially in front of the lad."

"I've heard such talk in the stables."

"But not in this house."

"Think of her as the spoils of war," Holden said with a sly smile. "And enjoy this gift you've been given."

"We'll talk no more of it." Brice's tone was low and commanding. "Until I decide what to do with the woman, she is to be treated with civility."

"Aye." Holden laughed. "I will be most civil with Lady Meredith MacAlpin."

Brice recognized the sarcasm in Holden's tone but was too weary to argue further. With a lift of his hand he dismissed his friends and made his way to his chambers.

Meredith heard the door close and was instantly alert. She listened to the slight shuffling sound as Brice crossed the room. She heard the occasional scratch of dogs' paws as they walked to the fireplace and settled down for the night.

The dogs. She had not planned for the dogs to be in the room.

Brice tossed another log on the fire and the flames danced and leaped as they licked at the dry bark. The room was suddenly bright from the glow of the fire.

At the foot of the bed Brice removed his tunic and shirt and she heard them whisper through the air as he tossed them on a nearby chair. The pallet sagged as he sat and tugged off his brogues.

When he pulled down the linens her heart began a wild hammering. Was the man actually going to sleep in the same bed with her? She had thought, nay, hoped, that he would be gentleman enough to sleep on the settle across the room.

The dagger in her hand was damp and slippery.

She was wearing only a sheer night shift, which Cara had brought earlier. Her gossamer gown and kid slippers had been taken away at Cara's insistence. On the morrow they would be clean and ready for their mistress. But their mistress, Meredith thought with a smile, would be miles from here. She would borrow a cloak and boots from Brice Campbell's wardrobe.

Patience, she counseled herself. Despite these unexpected changes in her plans, the dogs, the man in bed beside her, she must bide her time. She must wait, pretending to be asleep, until Brice Campbell relaxed his guard. If he had any warning, all would be lost.

From the warmth of his breath on her cheek she knew that he was facing her. She dared not chance a look at him. If his eyes were focused on her, he might detect the slight flickering of her lids. She would have to wait until the fire burned low and his breathing became even.

Her lids were heavy. Her body begged for the blessed release of sleep. But though the urge to sleep was nearly overpowering, she resisted. Her only chance to escape would be to plunge the dagger into Brice Campbell's heart and disappear into the dense Highland forests.

He shifted slightly and his thigh came into contact with hers. She lay perfectly still, willing herself not to move.

How strange to be lying, not in her marriage bed, but in the bed of a brute who had taken her captive. How warm his flesh where it pressed hers. The thought left her shaken. She must not allow herself to think of him as a man. He was a cruel savage, who would rue the day he had tangled with a MacAlpin.

He sighed and moved a foot. Before she could recover her wits he brought his foot down, dragging the fur coverings from both of them.

From beneath veiled lashes she chanced a quick look around. The dagger was clearly visible if he would but open his eyes. She held herself rigid, afraid to breathe, afraid even to swallow. By the light of the fire the dagger's blade glinted ominously. There was no place to hide it.

He moaned and dropped an arm about her waist. Her gaze flew to his face. His eyes were tightly closed. Gathering courage, she allowed her gaze to scan him.

God in heaven. The man was practically naked. She was so stunned she started to push away before she realized what she was doing. At the movement his fingers closed around her waist, dragging her closer.

The hand holding the dagger was slick with sweat. She clutched it between herself and him, praying that she would not drop it in her nervousness.

Sparks shot from the fireplace, sending a tiny explosion of light into the room. Reflexively he moved, bringing himself even closer to her. His face rested just beside hers, his lips brushing a tangle of hair at her temple.

The nearness of the man was driving her to distraction. All her carefully laid plans were unraveling. With his lips pressed to her temple she was unable to think, to even move. Saliva pooled in her mouth and she forced herself to swallow. The sound seemed overloud in the quiet of the room.

He murmured something in his sleep and tightened his grip on her, drawing her firmly against him. Never in her life had she been this close to a man. Even one with all his clothes on.

With each breath his hair-roughened chest brushed against her breasts, creating a tingling sensation deep inside her. She

was achingly aware of his hips touching hers, of the thigh that
rested against hers. The hand at her waist was warm, so warm
that she felt as if her flesh were on fire. The heat spread,
radiating a warmth that threatened to engulf her.

Despite the thundering of her heartbeat she forced herself
to listen carefully to the sound of his breathing.

Soft. Even.

It was time. Before she forgot who she was and why she
was here. Before she forgot that he was a monster who had
killed Desmond MacKenzie and carried her off like a prize to
be claimed. Before she allowed herself to be frightened by the
presence of his dogs. It was time to buy her freedom even at
the price of his life.

Her fingers closed around the hilt of the dagger. Wet, slippery fingers. For one moment she allowed the knife to slip
from her fingers while she wiped them on the bed linen beneath her. Then, picking up the dagger, she clutched it firmly
and raised herself to her knees.

She lifted her arm and brought the dagger down with all
her might. At the last second she closed her eyes. She could
not bear to watch the blade pierce his heart.

Brice was dreaming. A beautiful woman dressed all in white
was running toward him, her arms outstretched, her long dark
hair streaming behind her on the breeze. He caught her and
lifted her, pressing his lips to hers. Slowly, languidly, she slid
down his body until her feet touched the ground. He could
feel the press of her breasts, her hips, her thighs. His hands
spanned her waist as he drew her closer. Suddenly she was
pulling away from him. Her smile twisted into an evil leer.
Her hand snaked out. Instead of caressing him, she slapped
him. Hard.

Brice awoke, twisting away from the dark, angry vision.

Meredith felt the mattress shift as Brice rolled aside. The
dagger caught the edge of his shoulder, barely biting into flesh.
Blood spurted and ran down his arm. She pulled the dagger
free and lifted it again, intending to take better aim. But before

she could once again plunge the blade her hand was caught and pinned in a grip of such strength she cried out.

He swore, loudly, viciously, as he crushed her small hand in his. "You will drop the dirk or I swear I'll break every bone in your lovely body."

"Nay. I'll not submit to you." She was still on her knees, straddling his prone body, struggling for control of the dagger.

"Submit?" The word was a snarl as he rolled over, pinning her beneath him. "You'll do more than submit, woman. You'll die unless you give up the weapon. Now."

He pressed a thumb to her wrist until the bones threatened to snap. With a shriek of pain she let her fingers go slack until the knife dropped from them.

He picked up the knife and tucked it beneath the bed linens, then stared down at the figure pinned to the mattress beneath him.

"I thought it was a dream." His voice was low, dangerous. "Had I not awakened in time, you would have killed me."

"Aye. You deserve to die for what you did." She felt the sting of tears and tried to blink them back.

Her hand was so numb she had no feeling in it. Had he broken it? She tried to move her fingers and felt searing, burning pain.

"What I did was avenge my honor." His hands continued to hold her roughly. "Gareth MacKenzie has made false accusations against me, attributing crimes to me that he knows I could not have committed."

"What has that to do with me?"

"Nothing." His tone was abrupt, cutting off her protest. "My fight is not with you. You just happened to be a minor obstacle in the path of my justice."

"Justice. What you have done is far from just."

"Aye." He looked down at her and felt his anger continue to stir him, though it was already beginning to diminish. "I had not intended to involve you in this, lass. It just happened."

"Then you are honor bound to release me." She felt a moment of hope before his next words dashed it.

"The MacKenzies do not respect honor. They respect only strength. I have already told you. You will be the bait that lures Gareth MacKenzie to my lair."

Her heart plummeted. Was there no reasoning with this madman?

From the floor he lifted a shirt and tore a strip of fabric. With an economy of movement he wrapped the cloth about his wound and turned to her.

"Tie this. 'Twill stem the flow of blood."

She fumbled with the cloth and managed to secure the dressing. It was incongruous that moments ago she had been prepared to kill him. Now she was bandaging his wound.

A million hot needles pierced her hand as the feeling returned. He noted the way she tentatively wiggled her fingers.

"It's broken." Her voice was flat. "You've broken it."

He stared down at her hand in silence.

Her tears started, and though she made a valiant struggle, they flowed freely.

She knew it was not only the hand that caused her to cry, but the knowledge that she had lost her chance to escape.

Moved by her tears he caught her hand in his and expertly ran his fingers over hers. His tone was gruff. "Not broken. But probably badly bruised. If you lift a weapon against me again I will be even harder on you."

Without realizing it he continued holding her hand. So small. So soft. How could one small hand hold his life in it? The anger inside him merged with other, newer emotions. Instantly his touch gentled.

"Such lovely bait. How can Gareth MacKenzie resist?"

She saw the look that came into his eyes and felt a new terror grip her. She was too vulnerable. He was too dangerous.

"As you said, Gareth has no feeling for me. He will not be ensnared in your trap."

His voice was suddenly harsh. "I think you place too little value on yourself, woman. There are not many men who could turn away from your obvious charms."

Her heart leaped to her throat. Aye, he was far too dangerous.

He lowered his face until their lips were inches apart. She felt the heat of his breath as it mingled with hers.

Damn Holden Mackay, he thought. He had planted a seed in Brice's mind this night. And now, with the woman so near, the thoughts expressed by Holden were taking hold of Brice's will.

"I fear I shall have to sample the bait."

"Nay." She tried to pull away but was held fast.

His lips brushed hers.

She felt the first rush of heat and turned her head, avoiding the lure of his lips.

With a muttered oath he placed a hand on either side of her head, holding it firmly as he brought his mouth over hers.

In that first instant he felt a jolt, like a blow to the midsection. Her lips trembled and he knew that she felt it, too.

He was so startled by his reaction he lifted his head a moment, staring deeply into her eyes. Wide, shimmering pools of green stared back at him. He could read surprise there. And innocence.

Innocence. God in heaven. A virgin?

But she had been betrothed. Could it be that she and Desmond MacKenzie had never known each other?

He studied her face, mesmerized by her beauty. Beneath the beauty, beneath the innocence, he could read something more. There was fire there. He was nearly consumed by the heat.

Slowly, seductively, he touched his lips to hers and thrilled to the feelings that poured between them. With a sigh he took the kiss deeper, savoring all the sweetness, all the innocence he could taste.

Meredith had been kissed before. There had been lads waiting to steal a kiss along a darkened lane. There had been wedding banquets, where the young people were allowed to taste the brew. Such things often led to the first stirrings of youthful desire. She had once been kissed by Gareth MacKenzie. It had frightened and repulsed her. She had sensed something dark and unsavory in Gareth's manner. From that moment on she had avoided him. She had kissed his brother, Desmond. But they had both been children and the kiss had been no more than a touching of lips to lips.

But this. This was something so new, so breathtakingly sensual, she could hardly contain her heart. It was hammering so painfully in her chest she was certain he could hear the sound.

The hands that cupped her face were rough and callused,

and strong enough to break her in two. Yet their touch was so unexpectedly gentle, she felt herself melting into him.

Brice felt the gradual change in her as he lingered over her lips. Though she was still tense and frightened, she was responding, like a woman awakening from a deep sleep.

If he held her here long enough, she would be his.

The thought startled him. And disturbed him. If he was right, she had never been with a man. He had not expected this. Had not expected one so innocent. Had not expected to want her. It complicated matters. He knew he had to end it.

Still he lingered for a moment longer, unwilling to break the contact. Never had he felt such a desire to lie with a woman and take all she had to give.

The need to take became a need to give. Unless he ended this now, he could very well find the situation out of control and not at all to his liking. It had never been his way to take a virgin.

He lifted his head and drew back.

Meredith lay very still, watching him. Her breathing was ragged, her heartbeat erratic.

"A very nice sample," he whispered.

"May you be damned to hell."

He smiled, but the feeling curling in the pit of his stomach was still there, still prodding him to take what he had no right to.

He thrust her away from him. "Go to sleep." His voice was rougher than he'd intended.

He saw the look that came into her eyes. Relief. Gratitude. She had thought she'd have to fight him.

"I'll not sleep in the same bed with you."

He gave a careless shrug of his shoulders. "Then sleep on the floor. But beware the dogs."

He pulled the furs over himself and rolled away from her. His pulsebeat was as wild as if he'd just led a charge of brigands through the Highlands. His hands, he noted, were certainly not steady enough to hold a broadsword.

Meredith rolled away, curling herself into a tight little ball at the edge of the mattress. What choice had she been given? The floor or the bed—with him in it. But then what had she expected from a lout like Brice Campbell?

She would never be able to sleep in the same bed with this brute. If she dared to fall asleep, he might take advantage of her weakness.

As her eyes grew heavy she was forced to admit that it was not she who had ended the kiss but Brice Campbell. If he had wanted to take advantage of her, she would have been powerless to stop him. Powerless. The feeling enraged her. She had been powerless to refuse the marriage offer between herself and Desmond, despite the fact that she had not loved him. And now she was once again powerless to escape this barbarian who held her prisoner in his Highlands.

She would be powerless no more.

She thought about wrapping herself in a fur and sleeping with the dogs in front of the fireplace. But she was so weary. So drained.

Before she finally fell asleep, she spent a very troubling night wrestling with the dark thoughts that plagued her. And all of them centered on the man who slept as peacefully as a bairn beside her.

Chapter Four

Meredith clung to the safety of sleep. Outside the windows a breeze whispered through the trees. A chorus of birds filled the morning with song. Water splashed. A nearby waterfall, Meredith thought, rolling to one side. Her hand encountered a warm spot among the bed linens. Instantly she opened one eye. The place beside her was empty. But the warmth of Brice's body still remained. She fought a sudden chill. She had spent the night in his bed.

The splashing grew louder. A waterfall inside the room? She looked up to see Brice washing his face and arms in a basin of water. Her gaze fastened on his muscular shoulders and she felt her throat go dry.

He was terrifying. He was magnificent. Never had she seen a man to match him. His shoulders were wide, corded with muscles. His waist and hips were narrow beneath the bit of cloth tied about his lower torso. She watched as he lifted his head and shook it, sending a spray of water into the air before pressing a linen square to his face. He turned. She studied the mat of dark hair that covered his chest and disappeared below the cloth tied at his waist.

He caught her watching him. God in heaven, she was lovely. Her dark auburn tresses spilled across the pillow and framed the most beautiful face he'd ever seen. Though she had modestly pulled the bed linens to her chin, he could still recall the lush young body beneath the sheer night shift.

"I trust you slept well."

"Nay." She avoided his eyes. "I am not accustomed to sharing my bed with a man."

She saw the frown on his lips before he turned away and began pulling on his tunic. He did not bother to add that her presence in his bed had cost him more than a little sleep as well. He'd been forced to wage a terrible battle with himself over her.

The hounds had been sitting, watching Meredith from across the room. Now they began timidly approaching the bed. One by one they pressed their noses to her. And though she told herself they were big ugly brutes, she found herself scratching behind their ears, rubbing their thick coats. Two stayed beside the bed, enjoying her tender ministrations. The others turned away, having satisfied their curiosity about this strange female.

"Cara has brought your clothes." Brice indicated the neatly folded pile of garments. "I will leave you to your privacy. We will break our fast as soon as you join us below stairs."

Meredith watched as he pulled on his brogues and tossed a length of plaid over his arm. His strange manner of dress, leaving his limbs bare, was appealing to her. The sight of his muscular legs was oddly arousing.

"Will I dress for traveling?" she called to him.

He paused in the doorway. The dogs milled about his feet. His tone was sharp. "Where would you be traveling?"

"Home." She tossed aside the fur throw and sat up. He caught a glimpse of thigh before she slid the night shift down modestly. "I had hoped that you would return me to my people."

"And why would I do that?"

"Last night you said that I had no part in your plan for revenge."

"Aye. But I also told you that now that you are here, you will become the bait."

He saw the frown that darkened her features. She clamped her mouth shut on whatever angry words she was about to hurl.

When the door closed behind him, Meredith sprang from the bed. If he would not take her out of this wilderness, she would find a way to go by herself.

Meredith crept down the stairs. In her arms she carried a coarse woolen cloak and a fur throw. Both would be needed for the arduous journey home. She might be forced to wander through these mountain forests for days before finding her way out. She had decided to borrow a few warm things from Brice Campbell's own closet.

At the foot of the stairs she paused to listen. Judging by the voices, the refectory was at the far end of a dim hallway. Casting a furtive glance around, she hurried in the opposite direction and pushed open a door. Inside was a cozy room where a fire had already been prepared in the fireplace. There was a large desk and several oversize chairs, as well as a settle draped with fur in front of the fireplace. Atop the desk were books and ledgers.

Meredith stared around the room with a sense of wonder. This library was even more magnificent than her father's. Did this mean that Brice Campbell could read? She had thought all the Highlanders, and this man in particular, were vulgar and uneducated.

Locating a tall armoire she thrust her bounty inside and quietly latched the door. Then she made her way back down the hallway and followed the sound of voices to the refectory.

She paused outside the door and listened.

"...to the Borders alone." It was Brice's voice, low, calculating.

"But why can I not go along?"

Meredith peered inside. Angus and Holden sat across the table from Brice. Angus was arguing with his friend. She could not see his face, but she could hear the note of protest in his voice. "The MacKenzies are not the only ones who will kill you on sight. Do not forget, old friend, that you have incurred the wrath of the MacAlpin clans as well. You have their woman."

"Their leader," Brice corrected.

"Leader?" It was another man, tall, red bearded, who had ridden with Brice on the morning raid.

Meredith saw Brice's head nod. "With Alastair MacAlpin dead, she is now the MacAlpin."

There was a murmur among the dozen men at the table. Jamie, seated on Brice's left, looked impressed. "Why, she's no bigger than I am. How can a helpless female be leader of her clan?''

"Helpless?" Brice gave a mirthless laugh, recalling her attack of the previous night. "Never let the looks of a woman deceive you, Jamie lad. The lady is far from helpless."

Though Brice's words were more amused than irritated, Meredith was more impressed by what she'd heard before that. She stood back, pondering all that had been said. Brice Campbell did not sound like a man who had knowingly murdered her father. Nor did it sound as though Angus or the others had anything to do with that terrible act.

Obviously Gareth MacKenzie had been wrong. But why had he seemed so certain that Brice Campbell was guilty?

When she returned home she would confront Gareth. But for now, there was only one thought. She must elude her captors and make her way back home.

Brice and the others looked up as she entered. The hounds circled about her ankles, then settled down once more by the fire.

Beneath the bulky shawl, she was wearing the filmy white confection. Her wedding gown. Brice felt a swift pang of remorse. How she must hate him for altering forever the course of her life.

He stood and held a chair as Meredith seated herself beside him.

"You may serve, Cara," he called.

The young serving wench came forward with a tray of steaming meats, followed by other servants bearing trays of warm bread and biscuits and platters of sweet puddings.

Meredith's stomach was in knots. The very thought of what she was about to undertake had her hands trembling, her insides turning over. But she must eat all she could in order to sustain her energy for what lay ahead.

Brice watched as she loaded her plate with meats and breads. Each time he looked away, she slipped some of the food onto her lap and hid it among the folds of her gown.

Jamie, busy feeding the hounds who lurked beneath the table, thought it amusing that the lady's hands were also working beneath the table. Odd that she had befriended the hounds so quickly.

"So ye be the MacAlpin now, lass?" A burly man in coarse woolen garments addressed her.

"Aye."

"Alastair MacAlpin withstood many an attack from the English," he said, tearing off a strip of meat with his hands. "He was a clever warrior."

"You knew my father?"

"We met from time to time. He sat on the king's Council, as did Brice's father. The Campbell clan and the MacAlpin clan were part of the king's own guard."

She knew that. Knew also that there had been little trust between the Highlanders and the Borderers. She'd been raised to believe that the Highlanders were a breed apart from other Scots.

"Then you know that my father was a man of peace."

"The English who raided his lands would not agree with you, lass. The man was the devil himself when his land or people were threatened."

"Aye," Brice added. "He wielded a sword with the best of them. But the lass means that Alastair MacAlpin argued for peace among the clans. He said it was our only weapon against the mighty English."

"Some would call his cry for peace a cowardly act."

Meredith's hand balled into a fist. "What would you know about the world beyond your fortified mountains? Do you know what it is to live on the Border? To be raided constantly by hordes of English hoping to steal your flocks, your cattle, even your women?"

"More meat, my lady?" Cara stood beside her with a tray. In her eyes Meredith could read a warning.

Meredith bit down on the words that she had been about to hurl. What good would it do to goad these savages?

Without a word she filled her plate. Beside her, Brice bit back a smile. The lady was not above speaking her mind.

He marveled also at the amount of food the lady was capable of eating. Just moments ago her plate had been piled high with bread and meat. Where did such a tiny little lass put all that?

"You were blessed with a healthy appetite, my lady."

"Mayhaps all the Borderers are taught to eat quickly, before the English can steal it," Angus said.

She heard the thread of laughter in his tone and bristled.

"If I must remain a prisoner in your castle, my lord Campbell, then at least I shall indulge my palate."

"By all means. Would you like some pudding?"

She shook her head a little too quickly. The thought of sticky pudding running down her gown nearly caused her to choke. "I thank you but I have had sufficient."

Out of the corner of her eye she saw Jamie watching her. She rolled the excess material of her gown around the food and prayed that she could escape the room without being caught.

When they were finished Brice pushed back his chair. "Angus, you will be responsible for the woman until I return."

Meredith was careful to grasp the folds of her gown, hugging the food to her bosom. The ends of the shawl were the perfect cover. "I implore you one last time," she said softly. "Take me with you."

"You will remain here." His eyes were cold, his manner implacable.

As he turned away she muttered, "You will regret that decision."

He turned back and caught her by the arm. In that instant he felt the jolt and cursed himself for his foolishness. To touch this woman was to invite feelings that had no place in his life. Abruptly he dropped his hand to his side.

"I already regret having brought you here. But here you will stay until I decide to return you to your people."

Meredith wondered if the trembling deep inside her was caused by his touch or by the fear of having her plot discovered.

They all looked up at the sound of horses. While Brice and Meredith stared out the window, his men took up their weapons and prepared to defend the castle.

Peering through the opening, Meredith saw a company of riders led by a dainty, auburn-tressed young woman. On her wrist perched a falcon. Behind the woman there were at least a dozen men and women in elegant dress.

Meredith glanced at Brice in time to see his grim look melt

into a warm smile. What a truly handsome man he was when he was not glaring at her. She was startled by the wave of alien emotion that washed over her. Jealousy? What nonsense. How could she possibly be jealous of the effect this stranger had on Brice Campbell?

He seemed not to notice Meredith. With a laugh he motioned for his men to put away their weapons. And then, as the woman was being helped from her mount, he was rushing out the door with Jamie and the dogs at his heels. His men followed and came to attention, forming two columns on either side of Brice and the woman.

Meredith lingered only a moment longer. This was the perfect opportunity to make good her escape. While the others were occupied with their visitors, they would never notice that she had slipped away from the castle. Perhaps, if the Fates were smiling upon her, she would be miles from here before she was missed.

She hurried along the dim hallway and pushed open the door to the library. Opening the armoire she pulled out the heavy woolen cloak and filled the pockets with the bread and meat she had secreted among the folds of her gown. She slipped her arms into the sleeves of the cloak. Because it had been made to fit Brice, it engulfed her, the sleeves completely covering her hands, the hem dragging upon the floor. She pulled up the hood, covering her head and leaving her face in shadow.

She stooped and lifted the fur throw from its place of concealment, folding it over her arm. No matter what weather she encountered on her escape, this would afford more than enough protection.

She closed the armoire and crossed to the door of the library. At the sound of voices she froze in her tracks. God in heaven. The voices were coming this way. With a cry of dismay she raced across the room and pulled open the armoire. Just as the door to the room opened, she leaped into the cupboard and pulled the door shut. With the door to the armoire closed, she was in total blackness.

"I cannot believe you are here." At the sound of Brice's voice, Meredith gritted her teeth.

"Nor can I." The young woman's voice was low, with a trace of an accent.

Meredith heard the dogs sniffing at the door to the armoire.

"Why did you not send riders ahead to announce your arrival? I would have prepared a more fitting welcome."

"I wanted to surprise you. Besides, just being here at Kinloch House is welcome enough."

"How did you manage to slip away from your brother?"

"James has other things on his mind these days." The sound of feminine laughter drifted across the room. "He is enamored of Agnes Keith. I hope it will soften him somewhat."

In the armoire Meredith crouched in a most uncomfortable position. She could neither sit nor stand, but was forced to stoop. To add to her discomfort the woolen cloak was so heavy it weighted her down. The warmth from the cloak and the fur draped over her arm, combined with the heat of the fireplace, left her soaked with perspiration. And still the dogs sniffed. When would they settle down before the fire? Why had they taken this occasion to pay her any interest?

"Ah, yes. Agnes, his new bride. How do they fare?"

"At least he has someone other than me to bully."

"Has it been terrible?" Brice's tone was tinged with concern as he crossed the room and cuffed the hounds' heads. "Off with you now."

With a whimper the dogs moved away a few paces before renewing their sniffing at the armoire.

"Oh, Brice. The tales I could tell. The last days in France were worse than the torments of hell."

"Poor Mary." Meredith could hear the sound of footsteps and sensed that Brice had crossed the room to the woman's side.

Peering through a crack in the door, Meredith watched as Brice drew the young woman into his arms.

"I know how much you miss Francis."

"My darling François. Aye, I miss him terribly. But it is more than that. It is this place. It is so forbidding. All the gaiety, the laughter, seem to have died since I returned." Her voice lowered. "And all because of that horrid little man who preaches fire and brimstone."

"Ah. Knox. He has caught the ear of the people."

"He watches and waits, Brice."

"For what, madame?"

"For me to slip so that he can publicly humiliate me."

There was silence in the room and Meredith watched as Brice and the young woman strolled to a window overlooking a vast expanse of forest.

The dogs did not follow their master. Instead, they continued sniffing at the armoire.

The heat in the tiny space was becoming unbearable. Soon, Meredith thought, she would suffocate.

"Be very careful not to offend him, Mary. He could cause you great harm."

"I am only now learning that." The young woman gave a deep sigh. "I long for the dancing, the singing, of France. I long to give elegant parties, to laugh, to—flirt. Oh, Brice. I am eighteen years old and no longer have a husband, nor any sort of life. It is terrible. Terrible."

Meredith detected a note of unspoken laughter in Brice's tone. "You are too beautiful, Mary, too full of life and laughter, to be condemned to a life alone. What man in his right mind would not lose his heart to you?"

"Did you?" It was the voice of a coquette, warm, inviting.

"You know I did. We all did while we were with you in France."

"Oh, you. I know better. Brice Campbell, you were the only Scotsman who never let himself be swept away by the charm of France."

"Only because I yearned for the Highlands. I feared it would be too easy to be seduced by the life you offered us."

"Is that why you left so abruptly?"

"Aye. I had to return to my home. Or be lost."

"Poor Brice. Has it all been worth it?"

There was silence. For long minutes the only sound Meredith could hear was the hiss of the fire. She staggered and leaned heavily against the door to the armoire. If she did not slip out of this heavy cloak soon she would faint from the heat. While she listened to the growing silence she wriggled out of the cloak. When she had managed to free one arm she sighed and began the struggle to free the other.

She was so engrossed in her struggle to free herself from the cloak she did not hear the sound of footsteps.

"So."

The door to the armoire was yanked open, causing Meredith to fall forward into Brice's arms. She would have slumped to the floor if he had not held her firmly.

Instantly the dogs circled around, yelping and baying.

"Why are you spying on us?" Brice's tone was low, menacing.

Meredith's cheeks reddened. She was mortified as she faced the haughty young woman who stared at her as if she could not believe her eyes. How she must look. Like some sort of ragged beggar. The cloak hung from one arm, dragging behind her on the floor. The fur throw was caught about her feet, threatening to trip her. Jagged scraps of bread and meat spilled from the pockets of the cloak. The hounds leaped up, snatching at the scraps and dragging them from her pockets.

At the sight Brice's eyes narrowed. "Are you ready to explain what this is all about?"

She swallowed. She was caught. There would be no use trying to lie. "I—intended to run off while you were occupied with your guest."

"Run off?" The young woman took a step closer, studying Meredith with open curiosity. "And why would you do that?"

"Because I'm being held here against my will," Meredith cried.

"Brice." The young woman turned wide eyes toward her host. "Is this lass telling the truth?"

Meredith's heart soared. Surely this young woman would insist that Brice return her to her clan at once.

Brice continued to hold Meredith by the arm. His fingers tightened their grip. He could feel his temper rising.

"She is. This is Meredith MacAlpin."

"Oh, how exciting. I heard about the—incident at the cathedral. You must tell me everything." The young woman's eyes danced with mischief. "This is so…" She spoke in rapid French for several minutes, while Brice's eyes darkened with anger. Then, reverting to English, the young woman continued, "Such a dashing, romantic adventure. My heart fairly bursts with the thought of it. You are a devil, Brice Campbell.

A rogue and a devil. And you, Meredith MacAlpin. What a thrilling story you will one day tell your grandchildren.''

"You are daft." Meredith kicked the fur throw from her feet and shrugged out of the confining cloak. Around her feet the dogs slathered after the last of the food scraps. "I am being held captive by a barbarian and you suggest that I should faint for joy."

At her insulting words the young woman's laughter faded. She tilted her head at a regal angle and regarded Meredith with a look of contempt.

"You do not have permission to speak to me in that tone. Kneel at once and beg my pardon."

Meredith's mouth dropped open. For a moment she could scarcely believe her ears. She turned toward Brice and found him grinning. That only served to further enrage her.

"Of all the vain, arrogant, pigheaded…"

Brice's fingers fastened upon her arm. In a tone tinged with laughter he said, "Hold your tongue, woman. Have you not yet realized who our visitor is?"

Meredith gazed upon the haughty young woman who continued to watch her through narrowed eyes.

"Kneel, Meredith," he murmured. "And pay homage to your queen."

"Queen?" Meredith's throat went dry. For long moments she studied the woman. Then, with a gasp, she fell to her knees. "Oh, Majesty. Forgive me."

She had heard the stories, of course. All of Scotland had heard that the young queen, having recently buried her husband, Francis, the Dauphin of France, had been returned to her birthplace to assume the throne.

She was kneeling before Mary, Queen of Scots.

Chapter Five

"Vain? Arrogant? Pigheaded?" The queen enunciated each word with great care.

Meredith, kneeling before her, flinched as though lashed by a whip.

"She goes too far. This time, Brice," the queen said haughtily, "you have found a woman with a temper to match your own."

"Aye." He seemed not at all concerned that the queen continued to glare at the lass who knelt abjectly at her feet.

"I could have you publicly flogged for your disrespect of the queen's person."

Meredith lowered her head, afraid to meet the queen's eyes.

"Would you like the flogging to take place here?" Brice inquired, struggling to hold back his laughter. He knew that the queen was far too tenderhearted to ever follow through on her threat. "Or will you have her dragged back to Edinburgh?"

"You mock your queen?" Mary arched an eyebrow and glowered at Brice.

"Nay. In fact, I will send Angus to fetch a whip from the stables."

As Brice turned away the queen caught his arm. "Wait. You are too eager. I have thought of a better punishment for this disrespectful subject."

Meredith braced herself for what was to come. Whatever

punishment was meted out by the queen, she had certainly earned it. How could she have been so foolish as to express herself in such forceful language?

"Rise, Meredith MacAlpin, and face your queen as you learn the consequences of your actions."

Meredith stood on trembling legs. She glanced at Brice's face but could read nothing in his hooded gaze.

"I will give you a choice," Queen Mary said. "A public flogging or..." She bit back the smile that twitched at the corners of her lips. "An opportunity to entertain your queen. You must relate to me and my ladies-in-waiting every detail of your—encounter with this rogue, Brice Campbell. From the first moment you saw him."

The queen burst into laughter at the look of astonishment on Meredith's face. Even Brice could not contain his laughter.

"That is all that you require, Majesty? A simple narrative?"

"Not simple," the queen corrected. "Every little detail must be included. I want to know everything." She turned to Brice. "And you, scoundrel, must leave us alone for at least an hour. This is woman's talk, you understand. And when she has finished, your servants can provide us with a banquet before we return to Falkland."

The queen clapped her hands, summoning the women of her hunting party. "Oh, Brice, this will be better entertainment than any poet or musician. I am greatly in need of such excitement. My life has been so drab since returning from the gaiety of France."

Brice lifted the queen's hand to his lips before departing the room. "Your loyal subjects are most happy to oblige." He shot Meredith a warning look. "Beware what you say in the presence of your queen. The next time you might not fare as well."

Within minutes Meredith found herself surrounded by five women named Mary. The young monarch introduced her four closest friends, Mary Beaton, Mary Fleming, Mary Seton and Mary Livingstone. The four Maries had been with the queen since early childhood. And like all best friends, they shared everything, even their most intimate secrets.

While servants poured tea and passed around biscuits, the women arranged themselves in chairs and settles in front of the fireplace. When the servants left the room, the queen commanded Meredith to begin her story.

While the others listened in awe, Meredith detailed her father's tragic murder and her agreement to marry Desmond MacKenzie in order to assure protection for her people.

"Those of us who live on the Border know the danger of invasion by the English."

"My beloved cousin, Elizabeth of England," Mary said through clenched teeth, "assures us that she is doing all she can to protect our land and people. And while she sends us messages of assurance, her soldiers continue to plunder."

Meredith was surprised at the queen's outburst. Was the young monarch always so outspoken? Was she not aware that even in the presence of her friends her words would not be kept secret? A queen, more than any other, must guard her thoughts carefully.

"Go on with your story," the queen commanded.

"Did you love Desmond MacKenzie?" Mary Fleming interrupted.

"What nonsense, Flem," the queen interjected. "What woman has ever been allowed to marry a man for love?"

Stunned by the queen's comment, Meredith openly studied the young monarch. It was common knowledge that Mary Stuart had been betrothed to Prince Edward of England when both had been mere children. But his death had released her from that bondage. The rumors had been that she was fairly happy with the young, fragile dauphin, whom she had married at the age of fifteen. But his mother, Catherine de' Medici, had been more than happy to be rid of the headstrong Queen of Scotland upon his untimely death.

"Well? Did you love him?"

Meredith studied the toe of her kid slipper. "We were friends when we were children."

"Were you eager to wed him?" Mary Seton asked.

"Or bed him?" Mary Fleming added.

Meredith's face flooded with color.

It was the queen who came to her rescue. "This lass has not been exposed to such bold discourse. Hold your tongues and allow her to tell the story."

"I—was reluctant to wed Desmond. I do not think I would

have ever loved him the way a woman wants to love a man.
But I knew that the union would assure my people the protection of the MacKenzie armies. I would do anything for my
people."

"Spoken like a true Scot." The queen smiled warmly at
Meredith. Despite her earlier insult, the queen admired the
girl's spirit.

"So you were willing to wed him though you did not love
him. Was he as handsome as Brice Campbell?"

Meredith felt her cheeks growing warmer by the minute.
"He was fair of face and hair. Not much more than a lad."

"Brice Campbell," the queen said with a smile of appreciation, "is no lad. He is all man." Seeing Meredith's
embarrassed flush she said with an impatient sigh, "Pray go
on with your tale."

When Meredith described the murder of her husband at the
altar, and the deception by his brother, Gareth MacKenzie, the
women gasped.

"Did Gareth not realize that he was placing your life in
danger by defying Brice Campbell's orders?"

"I had not thought about it," Meredith said. "It all happened so quickly. When Gareth fired the arrow I saw this giant
glide through the air and take hold of me. And then I was in
his arms and soaring over the heads of the people in the cathedral."

"How exciting."

"How terrifying."

"How romantic."

"Did you cry?"

"Nay." Meredith lifted her chin, nearly overwhelmed by
these outspoken women. "I would not give Brice Campbell
the pleasure of seeing me cry."

"Oh, how wonderful." Queen Mary clapped her hands and
urged the others to silence. "That would infuriate a man like
Brice. Now you must tell us everything that happened to you
since your momentous meeting with Brice Campbell."

"Aye. Momentous." Meredith described her abduction, the
tedious journey to the Highlands, and her attempt to kill Brice
in his bed. During the entire narrative the queen's eyes glit-

tered with a feverish light, as though she were living each incident in her mind.

"Brice Campbell is the strongest man I have ever met," the queen said with a trace of awe. "It is known throughout Scotland that there are few men who can best him in a fight or a duel. I have heard many a man declare that he would wish to have Brice on his side in a battle. And yet you dared to attack him."

"In his own bed," Mary Fleming said with a knowing wink.

"I was desperate to return to my own people, Majesty. In my place, would you not have done the same?"

The queen nodded her head. "How did you get into his room while he slept?"

Meredith looked away, too ashamed to meet the queen's eyes. "I was being held prisoner in his room."

The queen turned toward her friend, Mary Fleming, who was watching in silence. "What say you, Flem?"

"Pray, continue with the tale," Mary Fleming said without much enthusiasm. She seemed distracted. While Meredith proceeded to struggle through the story of her abduction, Fleming studied the queen and then allowed her gaze to scan the young woman seated beside her.

Suddenly she blurted, "What a remarkable similarity."

"What are you babbling about, Flem?" The queen arched one brow in a regal manner.

"You and Meredith MacAlpin bear a strong resemblance. You could be sisters."

Meredith felt herself flushing as the others began to study her with great interest.

The queen stood and walked a few paces, then turned and watched the others. "Do you think so?"

"Why, of course," Beaton said. "Look at the hair."

The three women caught at strands of Meredith's hair, lifting it and examining it in the sunlight.

"It is the same color as Your Majesty's. If we were to plait Meredith's, or brush Your Majesty's loose, they would be the same," Seton said.

Queen Mary was obviously intrigued by this unexpected turn of events.

"And both are small of stature, delicate in appearance."
Fleming caught Meredith by the hand and led her to the center
of the room while the others circled about her.

While the others laughed, the queen stood apart. On her face
was a look of intense concentration. Suddenly she took a step
closer. "The gown you are wearing. Is it your wedding
gown?"

Meredith nodded. There was an inflection in the queen's
tone, of guarded excitement, that puzzled her.

"Have you no others?"

"I had no time to choose a wardrobe, Majesty. You will
recall that I was abducted at the altar."

"So Brice and the others have seen you only in this?"

Meredith waited, knowing that the queen was leading to
something.

"Fleming and Beaton. Help me out of my clothes."

The women stared at the queen without moving.

"And Seton and Livingstone, you will help Meredith off
with her gown. Oh, what a fine joke we shall play," the queen
said, twirling about like a little girl.

"I do not understand."

"It is the sort of game we could have enjoyed in France,"
Mary said, her face animated. "We will change clothes and
see who discovers our little deception first."

When Meredith began to shake her head the queen said,
"How many people really look at others? If they expect you
to be in the clothes you have been wearing since your arrival,
they will expect that the woman at the table wearing a white
gown is you. And since I arrived in this hunting outfit, they
will believe that the woman wearing it is the queen."

When Meredith continued to shake her head the queen motioned to the others. "Hurry. Brice promised us an hour. It
will soon be time to sup with the others."

In a daze Meredith stood helplessly as the women, caught
up in the queen's plan, removed her gown and kid slippers
and replaced them with the queen's jeweled burgundy velvet
hunting outfit and high kid boots. While Mary Seton laced the
boots, Mary Livingstone brushed Meredith's hair and dressed
it in the identical fashion to the queen's.

Meanwhile the queen was dressed in Meredith's white gown

and kid slippers. Her plaited hair was brushed loose, falling in crimped waves to her waist.

When both women were ready, they walked to a looking glass, where they stood side by side and examined their appearance.

"Something is wrong," Mary Fleming said softly.

"It is the eyes. Anyone seeing Meredith's green eyes would know that she was not the queen."

"A veil," the queen muttered.

"Of course." Fleming removed her veiled hunting toque and placed it upon Meredith's head.

The dark weblike netting veiled her eyes and most of her upper face.

"Perfect." The queen studied the girl beside her, then stared at her own reflection. "Do you not feel regal in my garb, Meredith?"

It took the young woman a moment to respond. "Aye. It is a strange feeling to know that my queen is wearing my clothes and that I am wearing hers."

At a knock on the door they turned. Cara entered and curtsied before Meredith. "My lord Campbell announces that a banquet has been prepared for Your Majesty."

Meredith was so stunned by the servant's reaction that she gave a little gasp and stepped back in surprise. The women around her giggled. Beside her the queen, dressed in the wilted wedding gown, was nearly doubled over with spasms of laughter. The poor girl, confused by the unexpected response to her announcement, bowed her way from the room, keeping her gaze lowered.

"You see," cried the queen. "She never even looked up at you. She saw the gown, the auburn tresses, and believed that she was in the presence of the queen. Come," she called to Meredith and the others. "We will enjoy Brice's feast and see who discovers our little joke first. Seton," she said suddenly. "I am betting a gold sovereign that our deception will not be discovered until after the first course of our banquet."

"Aye, Majesty," Mary Seton said softly. "I will take your bet."

"Majesty," Mary Fleming said discreetly. "If you are to be believable, you must stand back and allow Meredith to lead the way. And you must assume the mannerisms of a hostage and set aside your usual strong will.''

"Dear Flem. How clever of you." The queen stifled a laugh and stepped aside, allowing Meredith to take the lead.

Brice frowned, deep in thought, as he changed into clothes more appropriate for entertaining the queen. He had planned on returning to the Borders this day to search for Gareth MacKenzie. Once he rid the land of that villain, he would be free to return Meredith to her people. The sooner that was accomplished the better. She was proving to be a stronger distraction than he had anticipated.

It was odd how his plans were constantly being changed by the whims of others.

At a summons from a servant he strode from the room.

The women were already assembled in the great hall along with Brice's men and the men from the queen's hunting party.

When Brice entered, Mary Fleming nudged Meredith. "Your Majesty will want to lead us to the banquet tables. Perhaps our host will be gracious enough to accompany you."

Brice offered his arm to his monarch and felt the small hand on his sleeve. As they led the merry group to the table he murmured, "Did you find Meredith's tale entertaining?"

"Very," the voice beside him whispered.

"I hope you and the others did not shock her overmuch."

"And why would you say that?"

He placed a hand over hers and squeezed. "Do not play the queenly role with your old friend. I know you and the other Maries better than anyone else could possibly know you. You say and do the most shocking things just to see the reaction of others."

When the woman beside him remained silent he studied her bowed head and was puzzled. From their earliest days together he had never known the queen to be at a loss for words, especially when being taken to task for something.

He brought his lips close to her ear and whispered, "Just what have you and the others done this time?"

"Done?" With her head lowered she murmured, "I fear I do not understand."

The queen was behaving in a most strange manner. Brice knew her well enough to know that it meant she was up to one of her tricks.

"Come," he urged, pausing while the others caught up. "Tell me, for I shall surely discover your game soon enough."

"There is no game. I am merely overcome with hunger."

Brice, giving up for the moment, gave her a smile. "Then you shall enjoy a feast fit for royalty."

At the head of the table he held her chair, then seated himself at her right hand. As always the four Maries flocked around their monarch, interspersed with the men from their hunting party. At the far end of the table Brice noted that Meredith was seated between Angus Gordon and Jamie MacDonald, and though she kept her face averted, there was a smile on her lips. Odd. Until now, she had done nothing but scowl at him.

Crystal goblets were filled and Brice lifted his, exclaiming, "To Mary, Queen of Scots."

"To Mary," repeated the entire company before lifting the goblets to their lips.

At the head of the table, the object of their toast nodded her head slightly and drank.

In the silence that followed, the young woman at the far end of the table spoke. "When you leave, will you take me with you—Majesty?"

Everyone gasped at the boldness of the hostage's words. Angus placed a hand on her arm as if to warn her, but she shook it off as though no one had ever before dared to touch her in such a way.

Beside him, Brice saw the queen's head nod slightly. He felt a rush of seething anger at Meredith's crude attempt to escape from Kinloch House with the queen's blessing. When the others left he would deal with her harshly. For now, he would keep a tight rein on his temper and deal with her more diplomatically.

"It is not proper to address the queen unless she first invites it."

"May I speak, Majesty?" came the bold reply from the far end of the table.

Again Angus tried to stifle her outburst. Ignoring him, she opened her mouth to speak.

"Nay. We will eat." Brice held up a hand to silence her.

At his signal, the servants began circulating among the guests, offering from trays of steaming deer, rabbit, goose, pheasant and partridge. There were breads still warm from the oven, as well as steamed puddings.

From the far end of the table, the woman in the white gown called, "Such fine food, my lord."

Brice's eyes narrowed. Was it Meredith's intention to dominate the conversation? Perhaps she hoped to continue to call attention to herself in order to invite the queen's protection.

"There are those who say the Highlanders live like royalty while many in the Lowlands starve." All eyes turned toward the woman in the white gown who sat beside Angus. With a wide, innocent smile she added, "Is that not true, Majesty?"

Brice heard a slight choking sound from the woman beside him. "Aye" came the voice. Then, with just a trace of French accent, she added, "'Tis said that many covet the holdings of the Highland lords. What say you—Meredith?"

Brice turned to study the woman in the burgundy velvet gown. Though the gown and hair were that of the queen, the voice, though similar, was not hers. He and Mary had been friends for too long. He had heard her when angry, happy, ill and well. He would know her voice anywhere.

He strained to study the face beneath the veil. Why would the queen wear a hat and veil to a banquet? A hint of a smile began at the corner of his lips. To hide behind? His smile grew.

"Do you remember that time when you and I and the dauphin went riding in Paris?" he asked.

Beside him the woman went very still.

"Surely you have not forgotten, Majesty. We had a race. I believe the bet was one hundred gold sovereigns."

Still the woman beside him remained silent.

"Unfortunately for you, I won by several meters," Brice said with a trace of triumph.

From the end of the table came the thunderous response. "How dare you, Brice Campbell! I won that race. And the bet was five hundred gold sovereigns. By the time you caught up with me I had turned my mount over to a groom and had retired to my rooms. You threatened to have your horse drawn and quartered for stumbling and losing the race.

Around the table there was stunned silence.

Brice threw back his head and roared with laughter. "And how does my captive, Meredith MacAlpin, know of such things?"

At the foot of the table the queen stood, shocking those guests who had not yet caught on to the joke.

"You knew all along, did you?"

"Nay, Majesty." Brice wiped tears of laughter from his eyes. "Not until I heard the poor imitation of your French accent beside me."

"Ah. Then it was Meredith who gave it away."

"It was the boldness of the one who pretended to be my captive. You have a very—regal presence, Madame. A trait that does not allow you to blend in with a crowd. How much did you have riding on this little prank?"

"A mere gold sovereign." The queen gave him a wide smile. "It is worth losing this bet to Flem just to put you in your place, Brice Campbell." She looked around at the others. "Let no one at this table think that any Highland lord can best his queen in a race. Shall I challenge you again, Brice?"

"Perhaps another time, Majesty."

While the others chimed in the laughter at the queen's prank, Brice turned toward Meredith. In a voice the others could not hear he whispered, "Well done. For a few moments you managed to fool me, little wildcat."

Beside him Meredith merely smiled. Why in the world should Brice's words please her? He was, after all, still the same barbarian who had captured her and held her against her will in the Highlands.

Or was he?

Meredith thought about the loyalty of his people, so unexpected in one of his reputation. And the library of books and ledgers. Did that not indicate an educated man? And what of his friendship with royalty?

So many questions. And yet, long after the queen left, she would be forced to remain here and perhaps learn the answers.

She glanced at the far end of the table where the queen was

accepting the congratulations of those who admired her latest trick. Had not the queen herself brought up the question of what would be done with her? Perhaps she could yet persuade the queen to take her with her. At least then she would be free of Brice Campbell. After all, was that not what she truly wanted?

At the far end of the table, Jamie MacDonald remained rooted to his chair. He was sitting beside the queen. And he had just been privileged to witness one of her renowned pranks. Could life be any more wonderful than this?

Chapter Six

When the feasting was over, the queen insisted upon summoning her musicians who had traveled with her. When they
took up their instruments, Brice brought Jamie before the
queen.

"The lad plays several instruments, Madame, including the
lute. He would be honored to join the royal musicians."

"They would be honored to have him."

Jamie felt his cheeks redden as he picked up the lute and
joined the musicians. At a nod from Brice he began to play.
Within minutes he forgot his nervousness as the music flowed
through his fingers.

"I have not danced since I left France," Mary said with a
pretty little pout, "seeing that dancing has been forbidden here
in Scotland, as has anything else that brings pleasure. But here
in the Highlands," she said, brightening suddenly, "that horrid
John Knox cannot hear even a whisper of scandal about our
adventures."

"Or misadventures, knowing you," Brice added with a
smile.

"Hush. Now that I am once again gowned as your queen,"
Mary said with a glance at the burgundy hunting outfit that
had been restored to her, "I command you to show a little
respect. Further, I command you to learn the latest dances
from Paris."

"I am your obedient servant, Madame." Brice bowed over her hand and escorted her to the center of the room.

From her position between Angus and Holden, Meredith was forced to watch as the queen and her friends taught Brice and the others the latest dances.

It was almost scandalous to see the way the women directed the men to hold them close while the music played. Their feet moved in perfect rhythm, their bodies swaying gently. One shocking new dance even ended with a kiss.

Meredith watched in stunned silence as the queen lifted her face to Brice. Their lips brushed. The men and women around them clapped their hands and called out encouragement.

Young Jamie MacDonald watched in stunned silence. Brice was actually kissing the queen.

"Ah," Mary said, smiling. "You have not lost your touch, Brice. You are still able to make my heart leap to my throat with a single touch."

"And you, Madame," he said with a smile, "are still the most outrageous flirt, as well as the finest dancer in all of France or Scotland."

"You flatter me."

"Nay, Mary," he said, offering his arm and leading her across the room. "Your love of the dance is obvious. You move like a leaf in the wind."

"The heart of a poet beats in the breast of this warrior," the queen said to the others with a laugh.

"I believe it is my dance, Majesty."

The queen turned into the arms of one of the men from her hunting party and together they twirled away. Over her partner's shoulder Mary called, "Dance with your hostage, Brice. I think it only fair that you teach her the dances of Paris."

Brice's smile remained in place until he turned away. At that moment Meredith saw the little frown of frustration that was gone as quickly as it had appeared. He held out his hand and Meredith was forced to accept it.

"I do not dance, my lord."

"Your queen has commanded it."

He saw her bite her lip as she moved into his embrace.

As his arms encircled her the feeling was swift, immediate. It was not at all a pleasant sensation.

Against her temple he growled, "You might try smiling. Learning the dance is not quite as painful as a public flogging."

"Are you so certain? I did not see you smiling a moment ago." She tried to ignore the feeling that curled deep inside.

"I was thinking that I should first search your person to determine if you carried a knife."

She gave him an exaggerated, beguiling smile. "If I did, my lord, it would not be in my hand. It would be in your back."

She felt his hand tighten at her waist as he led her through the intricate movements of the dance. Their bodies moved together, stiffly at first. But as the music of the harp and lute washed over them, they began to relax in each other's arms.

There was warmth along her flesh where his hand rested. Meredith could feel each of his fingers at her back, and was alarmed at the prickly sensation his touch aroused. His breath was warm against her temple. In the crush of dancers he drew her closer, until she could feel his lips pressed to a tangle of her hair. The hand holding hers was strong and firm as he led her with ease. She felt a trembling inside that had nothing to do with the fact that she was disobeying the law of the kirk by dancing. Nay, it was not the dance that was her undoing; it was the man holding her.

As Brice turned her, he was acutely aware of her breasts crushed against his chest. Her thigh brushed his and he felt the heat. Her hand, so small and soft in his, showed the bruises from his show of force the previous night. He felt a trace of remorse at the way he'd been forced to treat her.

"I had hoped to return to the Borders this day and finish this business between myself and Gareth MacKenzie. Then you could be restored to your people."

"Instead you dance to the queen's musicians."

"It cannot be helped."

"Aye. So many things, it seems, cannot be helped." Her eyes grew stormy. "You could not help killing Desmond. You could not help taking me prisoner."

There was heat now of a different kind as Brice held her in his arms. He was not proud of having mistakenly killed an innocent. Nor was he happy about having taken her hostage.

She had hit a nerve. He wanted to shake her. He wanted to throttle her.

Meredith fought back the feelings that simmered inside her. She had hoped that by insulting him, by reminding herself who this man was, she could sweep aside this insidious reaction to his mere touch. But nothing, it seemed, could save her from her weakness.

"The dance is ending," the queen called. "We must all kiss."

Meredith pulled away but she was no match for Brice's strength.

Brice bent, determined to casually touch his lips to hers. This was, after all, not really a kiss. It was nothing more than the latest silly fashion from Paris.

It was the merest touch of lips to lips. It lasted only the briefest moment in time. And yet, in that single second, she felt the fire and reacted as if she'd been burned. The moment his lips brushed hers, she flinched.

Brice felt it as well. He forced himself to absorb the shock with absolutely no expression on his face. The hands at her waist remained still as he commanded them not to draw her closer. But he could not control his pulsebeat. It throbbed at his temples, causing his blood to heat until it was a raging fire.

"Thank you for the dance, my lady." He lifted his head. "Angus." His voice was a low, angry growl.

Instantly his friend was on his feet and moving toward them. Meredith happened to glance over Brice's shoulder toward the place where Holden Mackay was sitting. On his face was a look so dark, so filled with fury, she nearly trembled.

"Dance with the lady," Brice said, handing her over to the surprised Angus.

Without another word Brice turned away and left the room.

Behind him, Meredith lifted her chin, determined not to watch his retreating back. But against her will her gaze locked on him, following his every move. In silence she endured the dance with Angus Gordon.

Jamie, too, watched as his hero retreated. There was nothing the man did that Jamie did not wish to imitate.

Across the room, the queen saw the way Brice stormed

away. She saw also the way Meredith's gaze fastened on him, following him until he was out of sight.

And while the queen watched with avid interest, a slow smile of understanding touched her lips.

By late afternoon the queen and her company prepared to depart. Before leaving, she sent a servant to fetch Meredith.

The queen received her guest in the cozy library and Meredith was reminded of her earlier embarrassment when she had fallen out of the armoire into Brice's arms.

Her cheeks took on a becoming shade of pink. "You have decided to take me with you, Majesty?"

The queen shook her head. "I would not impose my will upon an old friend. Whatever Brice Campbell has in mind, I trust his judgment."

She saw Meredith's face fall at the news. "But at the table..."

"At the table, I was having fun at Brice's expense." To ease Meredith's pain she added softly, "But know this. Though his quick temper and skill with a broadsword are legend, Brice is a fine and honorable man. Although he bears a grudge against the MacKenzies, he will see that no harm comes to you."

No harm? What of the feelings he aroused in her? Feelings she had never even known existed within her? She trembled just thinking about the way she had nearly melted into his arms when they danced. And that kiss. It was no more than the brush of a butterfly's wings. And yet it had caused her heart to pound so loudly in her chest she had feared the others must surely have heard. God in heaven, what was to become of her?

Meredith felt a sudden wave of despair. Was she to be left to languish in this prison forever?

"I wish to go home, Majesty."

"Aye. Home." Mary Stuart heard the plea with a woman's heart. Did she not still think of France as her home? And did she not yearn to return to the opulence, the gaiety, of the French Court? The grim tone of Scotland since the popularity of John Knox was depressing to a woman like Mary. "I have no doubt that you will soon be returned to your home, Meredith. But until Brice makes that decision, I am loath to intervene. Your future lies in his hands.''

Mary stood, effectively dismissing Meredith. And although the young woman yearned to throw herself into the queen's arms and beg for her intercession in this matter, her pride would not allow it. She stood, head held high, spine stiff, as the queen summoned Brice to escort her from the castle.

With her hand upon Brice's arm, the queen swept along the hall and into the courtyard. Behind her trailed the men and women of her hunting party. And behind them Meredith walked between Angus and Jamie.

As Brice helped the queen into the saddle, she stared over the heads of the crowd until her gaze came to rest upon the young prisoner. ''I think, Brice, that you have captured more than you bargained for. In that one, you may have a wildcat by the tail.''

She saw the thoughtfulness lurking in Brice's eyes behind the smile, though he said nothing.

Queen Mary gave a knowing look. ''Farewell, my friend. I hope to see you soon in Edinburgh.''

''The name of Campbell is not well received these days in the Lowlands.''

The queen's eyes sparkled. ''You are also the Earl of Kinloch. That makes you the queen's protector and a member of her Council.''

''That title was my father's,'' Brice said softly. ''It died with him. I am simply Brice Campbell.''

Her tone was soft. ''You are—simply one of my dearest friends.'' Her voice grew firm. ''Despite what others say, a Campbell is always welcome in the home of the queen.'' Mary urged her dancing steed into a trot.

With a clatter of hooves the queen's hunting party followed their monarch across the courtyard and along the forest path. When they were no longer visible, Brice turned to find Meredith watching their departure with a look of naked hunger in her eyes. He felt her pain, sharp and swift, for he knew what it was to miss his home.

''Come,'' he said in a tone softer than he'd intended. ''They could be the last visitors we shall entertain for a long time.''

"Do you not find it lonely here in the Highlands?"

Brice offered his arm and she placed her hand upon it. Instantly he felt the rush of heat and marveled that this woman could be the cause of such discomfort.

"I have never felt lonely here."

He led her to the library and instructed a servant to bring two goblets of wine. Pulling the settle close to the fire he indicated that she should sit, while he chose to stand beside the fireplace. His arm rested along the mantel.

"Have you never known loneliness?" Meredith asked.

"Aye." He accepted a goblet of wine and sipped. "I accompanied the queen to France. Those were the loneliest days of my life."

"Why did you go?"

"My father feared for the safety of the young queen. He wanted her to be surrounded by friends who would remain loyal. Also, he argued that I could get a better education in France than I could here in Scotland." Brice gave a bitter laugh. "I did receive a fine education at the French Court. I learned that not all animals stalk the woods. Some dress in fine clothes and pass themselves off as aristocrats. And wait for a chance to attack unknowing prey."

Meredith heard the venom in his tone and wondered about it. What had happened to him in France to make him so bitter?

For long minutes he stared broodingly into the flames, before pulling himself from his dark thoughts. He set down the goblet on a low table and summoned a servant.

"Accompany the lady to my chambers," he said. "And fetch Angus and Holden to stand guard over her until I return."

Meredith turned, about to protest his latest order. But one glance at the tight set of his mouth convinced her to hold her tongue. Brice Campbell was in no mood to answer to her. Or to anyone.

The aroma of wood smoke mingled with the lingering scent of roasted meat. Two men lounged outside the door of Brice's chambers.

"'Twas truly a banquet fit for the queen," Holden Mackay said thoughtfully.

"Aye."

"Plovers and partridges by the dozen," Holden taunted, watching his friend's mouth water. "Not to mention rabbits, geese, venison. But the plump partridges were my favorite."

"I wonder if Mistress Snow has any partridge left," Angus said, stretching out his long legs.

"You cannot be thinking of food after all we ate this day." Holden grinned. It was common knowledge that Angus Gordon, thin as a rail, was always hungry. The mere mention of food made him salivate. Besides, the young widow Snow, who worked in the kitchens along with Cara's mother, was as appetizing a little morsel as the food she prepared. Angus spent an inordinate amount of time in her presence.

"I could eat a bite or two. But Brice wants us here until he returns."

"Brice will probably be gone until dawn. You saw the look on his face. When those black moods come upon him, he rides the woods for hours."

"Aye." Angus stood and began pacing. "But I intend to be here when he returns. I have faced his anger before when his orders were disobeyed."

Holden leaned back on the bench, stretching his hands above his head. "Mistress Snow makes a fine pudding. And her scones are the envy of every woman in the Highlands."

"Stop talking about food." Angus turned and paced the other way.

"If you wish, I will stay here and keep watch." Holden glanced at the closed doors. "There has been no sound from within for an hour. I'll wager the girl has fallen asleep."

"Aye." Angus stifled a yawn. "'Tis late enough. If I do not eat something soon, I'll not be able to stay awake."

"Go then." Holden was on his feet and turning his friend in the direction of the stairs. "Coax some food from Mistress Snow. And when you've had your fill—" he gave an evil leer "—of both partridge and Mistress Snow, come back here and we'll keep watch together."

"You do not mind?" Angus paused at the head of the stairs.

Holden shook his head and waved him on. "Nay. Go, old friend."

With a laugh Angus was gone.

When the sound of footsteps died, Holden peered about, then walked to the door of Brice's chambers. With his ear to the door he listened intently for several minutes. Then, taking a last glance around, he pressed a shoulder to the door and entered without a sound.

Meredith had decided to take matters into her own hands. Since Brice had seen to it that guards were posted outside the door of the chambers where she was being held, she would simply have to find another way out of her prison.

She knelt on the floor tying strips of linen together. Because there were still servants moving about the courtyard below from time to time, she was unable to drop the rope of linens from the window of her upper room to test its length. But she had determined that when these last three strips were attached, she would have enough to at least get her close to the ground. Under cover of darkness, with the servants snugly in their beds, she would slip from the window to the courtyard. If the rope was too short she was prepared to drop the rest of the way and pray that she broke no bones in her fall.

In preparation for her escape she had removed her soiled wedding gown and, having rummaged through Brice's wardrobe, had donned tight breeches and a shirt of lawn. On the floor beside her lay a tunic and warm cloak, which she intended to pull on just before she made good her escape.

As she knotted the linen strips her hair swirled forward in a wild tangle of curls. There was no time to plait it. With one hand she brushed the tangles aside and continued working.

The only sound in the room was the occasional hiss and snap of the burning logs on the grate. It was not until a shadow fell across her that she looked up in surprise.

"So. What is this?" Holden reached down and snatched the linen from her hands. Studying the knotted rope he arched a brow and looked down at her with sudden respect.

Meredith sprang to her feet with the agility of a cat. Another chance for escape was slipping through her fingers.

"Give it to me," she cried, her voice low and husky. As she made a grab for it his fingers closed around her wrist, holding her still.

"Brice's anger will be a fearsome thing when he sees this."

He studied the way her hair streamed down her shoulders and across her bodice. His gaze fastened on Brice's saffron shirt fastened snugly against her high, firm breasts. Even if he had not been sufficiently aroused, the strange sight of a woman in tight breeches was more than he could endure.

"By all that is holy you are the most beguiling woman I have ever seen."

At the look of hunger in his eyes she was gripped by a sudden, paralyzing fear. She tried to step back but he kept his hand firmly around her wrist.

"Perhaps," he said in a voice meant to seduce, "Brice need never know what you had planned."

"You would keep this from him?"

In one quick movement he looped the linen rope about her neck and drew her roughly toward him, until their faces were nearly touching. "I could be persuaded."

Meredith's heart lurched. There was no mistaking Holden's meaning.

While he held the rope with one hand, his other hand moved to the fasteners of her shirt. When she resisted, he caught at the collar and pulled. With a ripping sound the fabric gave way and tore open, exposing a delicate lace chemise beneath.

"Please. I've…" She swallowed down the hard lump of fear. She must not scream. That would bring the entire staff of servants down upon her. And there was still a chance that she could break free and escape. "I've never been with a man."

She saw the light that came into his eyes as he regarded her. "All the better." He twisted the rope until he heard her sudden intake of breath. With mock seriousness he whispered, "Forgive me, my lady. Am I choking you?"

Her hands clawed at the rope but he only twisted it more until her eyes swam with tears.

"Please." She struggled for a breath. "I cannot breathe."

"Would you like me to loosen it, my lady?"

She nodded her head and clutched at his hands but he only

laughed and gave the rope a final vicious twist. "Do not fight me, Meredith MacAlpin. Soon you will lose consciousness. And when you awaken, you will find out what it is that men have enjoyed from the beginning of time."

"Nay." She felt the floor tilt and the room begin to spin and still he would not relent. Though she kicked and fought and clawed at his hands he never loosened his hold on the rope.

She heard a strange buzzing in her ears, and tiny black specks seemed to float through the air. Though she fought the feeling, she was slipping, slipping. Her hands went limp and she felt her knees buckle.

As she slid to the floor he knelt over her and loosened the rope, then reached both hands to her torn shirt.

In some dark corner of her mind she heard the ripping sound as the shirt was torn from her.

Chapter Seven

Though she was barely conscious, Meredith continued to fight her attacker. She felt a sense of outrage as strong hands tore at her breeches. With no weapon, she used her fingernails to scratch and gouge at the offending hands. And when Holden ignored her feeble attempts, she sank her teeth into his hand, drawing a spurt of blood.

He was stunned by her determination. Though he had seen traces of her fire and spirit, he had convinced himself that this female would be cowed by his superior strength.

"Stupid wench."

He slapped her so hard her head was snapped to one side. Pain danced through a haze of bright stars before she fell back defeated.

As Holden's hands reached for her, a voice from the doorway caused him to pause in midair.

"Step away from the woman."

Holden turned to see Brice facing him. By the flickering flames of the fire, Holden could see the glint of a knife in Brice's hand.

Meredith's attacker felt a trickle of sweat mingle with the blood that oozed from his wounds. He recognized the look of fury that darkened Brice's features. There were many men he would fight for a beauty such as this one. But never would he wish to fight Brice Campbell. Especially in a temper like this.

Thinking quickly he said, "The wench called out to me.

And when I entered your chamber she acted the part of a temptress. Look how she is dressed.''

He scrambled quickly to his feet, stepping a little away from Meredith. Brice saw, for the first time, the tight breeches, the gaping shirt.

Meredith opened her eyes and felt her head swim as she tried to sit up. At a glance she took in Brice, dagger in hand, facing Holden. She felt a momentary rush of relief. Safe. Now she would be safe from her vicious attacker. It was Holden's words that sent her hopes plummeting.

"The wench thought if she could seduce me I would be persuaded not to tell you that she was trying to escape. But I remembered your orders, Brice. Though she put up a fierce struggle, I was able to keep her from slipping out the window.''

Meredith thought about protesting. But why would Brice Campbell accept her word against that of one of his own men? With a feeling of desperation she lay back, prepared for even more punishment from the man who should have been her protector.

Brice took a step closer. "Aye. I see the tunic and warm cloak folded atop a fur throw in preparation for travel. Woman, there is no denying that you intended once more to attempt an escape.''

His gaze locked on the knotted rope of linen that trailed the floor. "You are a clever lass. You even prepared your escape from a dangerous height.''

Suddenly his gaze followed the trail of linen rope from the window, to where it was still coiled loosely about her throat. Dark purple welts were already forming on her flesh. From the way her shirt fell open he knew that it had not been merely unfastened by a woman about to seduce. It was rent nearly in two. And the torn breeches were further indictment.

His gaze lifted to Meredith's face. He saw the dull pain that glazed her eyes. And something else. Terror. Sheer terror.

His fury bubbled dangerously close to the surface. He felt the warmth of the dirk in his hand and fought a surging desire to bury it in Holden's massive chest. What chance did a fragile, unarmed woman have against an animal like Holden Mackay?

In the blink of an eye the anger and guilt transferred from Holden to Brice himself. Who had left the lass in this brute's hands? Who had foolishly thought that a man, far from the comfort of his own clan, could be trusted with the care of a prisoner as beautiful as Meredith MacAlpin?

Had it not been for his own complicity in this, Brice would have killed Holden Mackay for this ugly deed.

In a tightly controlled voice he rasped, "Mackay, you will leave us. You have violated someone under my protection. Return to your people. You are no longer welcome in Kinloch House."

Holden experienced a wild surge of relief. He had feared, from the savage look in Brice's eyes, that he would have to battle him to the death. But just as quickly the relief disappeared, to be replaced by a growing sense of wrath.

"Aye." Holden's eyes glinted with sudden anger. "Turn on your old friends from the north for the sake of a wench who has bewitched you. But the day will come when you will regret this. On that day, when you need the might of the Mackay armies, we will remember this night and take up arms with your enemy."

"So be it."

Holden thought about killing the man who all but ignored him while he studied the woman. Brice's head would be quite a prize to take to his people. The name Brice Campbell still brought fear to the hearts of men in the Highlands. But Holden was aware of the barely controlled fury in the man, and knew that with Brice in such a rage he had no chance to win. Without another word he turned and fled.

Brice fell to his knees and touched a finger to the bruises about Meredith's throat. "The lout choked you."

At the intimacy of his touch she flinched and tried to back away from him. "Do not touch me."

"I must examine your wounds." When he tried to subdue her she mistook his intentions and began wrestling for control of the knife still held firmly in his other hand.

He saw the raw emotions in her eyes and cursed himself for his clumsiness. Tossing aside the dirk he lifted both palms to her to prove that he meant her no harm.

"I am unarmed, my lady. I wish only to make amends for what has been done."

At his submissive gesture Meredith felt the prickle of tears against her lids and blinked furiously. She must not let him see her weakness.

"Do not touch me. I can—take care of myself."

The more she tried to be brave, the more helpless Brice felt.

With a savage oath he yanked the rope free and tossed it aside. Then he lifted her in his arms and strode across the room. Kicking open the door to the bedchamber, he crossed the fur-strewn floor and laid her gently upon his bed.

The room was dim except for the flickering flames of the fire. His voice was as still and hushed as the night that seemed to have wrapped them in its soft, dark cloak.

"Forgive me, Meredith. It never occurred to me that one of my own men would be the cause of such pain."

When she did not respond he whispered, "I regret that I must cause you further discomfort." As he spoke he reached his hands to the waistband of her breeches. "There is blood upon your clothing. I must find the source."

"Nay. Nay." Though she tried to fight him, he managed to remove the torn clothing.

Beneath the breeches and shirt her ivory chemise bore more traces of blood. But when he untied the ribbons that laced the chemise across her breasts, she cried out so sadly he was forced to stop.

He sat on the edge of the bed and leaned close, placing his hands on either side of her head. "Holden has hurt you, Meredith. You are bleeding. Let me help you."

At his gentle concern she felt some of the terror dissipate. Perhaps it was not his intention to harm her. Perhaps he was merely trying to help.

"I am not bleeding," she whispered.

Her breath was warm against his cheek. So warm he had to resist the urge to turn his mouth to hers.

"There is blood on your garments."

"Holden's blood," she whispered.

"Holden's?" He drew closer, staring intently into her eyes. "But you were unarmed."

"Aye. But I had my hands. And my teeth."

"You bit him?" He felt some of his fury begin to melt. In its place a hint of laughter bubbled.

"Aye. I bit him."

"Then I suppose I need not remove your chemise in search of more blood."

"Nay."

"A pity. I was prepared to do my duty no matter how unpleasant."

How could it be that only moments ago she had suffered the terror of the damned, and now, with Brice as protector, she was able to smile and even respond to his silly joke?

"If you should think about removing my chemise, my lord, think about this. If you try, you will need the queen's own physician to repair the damage these teeth will inflict upon your hands."

"These are noble warrior's hands, my lady. They must be ever prepared to protect the weak and suffering."

"They will be exceedingly damaged warrior's hands if they are found where they are not wanted."

He gave her a long, lingering look. "What an amazing woman you are." He saw the hint of color that touched her cheeks. "You are truly unharmed, Meredith?"

The tenderness in his tone was nearly her undoing. He felt her tremble.

"Aye, my lord." Her voice trailed off as she fought a shudder that passed through her body. "I have survived. I am fine."

His voice was suddenly gruff. He recognized the shock and fatigue that was beginning to overcome her. "You are indeed a fine woman. But you are far from recovered. You will sleep now."

He pulled the bed linens over her and added a fur on top of them, smoothing it until she was warm and snug.

Meredith caught his hand. "You will stay with me? You will not send someone else to guard me?"

"If you wish."

"Aye." She clung to his hand. "I wish."

He stared down at the small hand upon his. At this moment he would move heaven and earth if she but asked it.

"I will be right beside you."

"All night?"

"And late into the morning if you desire."

He pulled a chair beside the bed and dropped a fur across his knees. While the fire burned to embers he watched her as she slept.

Thin morning sunlight filtered through the windows, sweeping away the night shadows. Beneath the covers Meredith lay very still, replaying in her mind the events of the previous night.

She recalled clearly the attack by Holden and the tender way Brice had carried her to his bed. Less clear in her mind were the dreams that plagued her as she slept. Several times she had cried out. And each time Brice had been there beside her, soothing, holding. The last time she had sobbed as though her heart would break and it had been Brice who held her in his arms, rocking her as tenderly as if she were a wee bairn.

Brice. She opened her eyes and stared at the chaise drawn up beside the bed. It was empty. She felt a swift stab of disappointment. He had broken his word and left her.

A movement beside her in the bed startled her. Turning she found herself face-to-face with Brice.

Without a word he touched a hand to her cheek. The sweetness of the gesture brought a lump to her throat.

She studied the stubble of beard that darkened his chin, and had to clench her hands into fists to keep from reaching out to him. The nearness of the man did strange things to her. Her throat was dry. Her heartbeat was wildly erratic. And she was suddenly far too warm.

As she sat up and swung her feet to the floor he closed a hand around her wrist.

"You should stay abed, my lady."

"Nay. I have a need to be up and about."

He watched as she crossed the room toward the basin and pitcher. Pouring a little water she began to wash her face and arms.

He sat up. From this vantage point he could admire her Creator's handiwork. How truly lovely she was. The sheer chemise clearly emphasized every line and curve of her body.

As she bent to splash water on her face, he studied the dark cleft between her breasts and felt a rush of heat. His gaze traced the waist so narrow he was certain his big hands could easily span it, then moved lower to her flare of hips. Her legs were long and shapely, her bare feet as dainty as a child's.

She dried her face and began to run his brush through the tangles of her hair. Tossing her head, she brought the hair forward over one breast and continued brushing until it was sleek and shining. Then she tossed it back and allowed it to cascade down her back like a shimmering veil.

She crossed the room to a stool and picked up the crumpled white gown. He watched her with a smile of appreciation. It was then that he spied the bruises on her throat.

He was across the room in quick strides. Without a word he caught her chin in his hand and lifted her face.

Meredith was about to protest his rough actions until she saw the pained look in his eyes. "What is it, my lord?"

"I should never have allowed him to walk away." Brice's nostrils flared as he gently examined each bruise. "I should have killed Holden Mackay for what he did to you."

"I will heal." Embarrassed at his scrutiny she brought a hand to her throat.

"If I but had it in my power," he said, bending his lips to the bruises on her throat, "I would willingly take each of your hurts upon myself."

She stood very still, absorbing the waves that shuddered through her at his touch. Never before had a man dared to press his lips to her throat. And yet the touch was so tender, so loving, she was helpless to step away.

He glanced down at the soiled gown in her hands. "Do not put that on," he said in a low tone of command.

"But it is all I have." As she made a move to pull away he yanked the gown from her hands and tossed it in a heap on the floor.

"I will send Cara up with something more appropriate."

He turned away and pulled on a tunic before leaving the room. It would never occur to him to admit, even to himself, that the gown offended him because it reminded him of the marriage she had almost been allowed to consummate, and the husband who would have bedded her.

Cara helped Meredith into the gown provided by the young widow, Mistress Snow. Though not a perfect fit, it was far more comfortable than the white gown that she had discarded.

The fabric was the color of heather, with deeper purple ribbons banding the bodice and hem. The sleeves were full, then gathered at elbow and wrist with shirring. The color was a lovely counterpoint to Meredith's green eyes and brought a bloom to her cheeks. Best of all, the high ruffled collar hid the bruises that marred her throat.

"Oh, you look lovely, my lady," Cara said as she finished dressing Meredith's hair with matching ribbons.

"Thank you. And thank Mistress Snow for me."

"I will, my lady." Cara crossed the room and held the door. "If you are ready, the others are waiting to break their fast."

Meredith followed her from the room and made her way to the great room, where the rumble of masculine voices alerted her that the others were already assembled.

She took a seat between Brice and Jamie and accepted food from the servants in silence.

Beside her, Brice cleared his throat. Odd. When they were alone, he had no trouble conversing with her. Now that they were with the others he felt the old awkwardness returning.

"You look lovely," he murmured in a voice meant for her alone.

"Thank you, my lord. I would like to go to the scullery later to thank Mistress Snow."

"I will take you myself."

They continued to eat while the conversation swirled around them. There was talk of the queen's visit, which led to a discourse on the scandalous marriage feast the queen had given her brother, James and his wife. The guests had openly danced, knowing they violated the laws of the kirk. The discussion then turned to the latest invasion of the Borders by English troops.

Beside Meredith, Jamie fidgeted. He had heard the whispers and rumors this morrow. Brice had banished Holden Mackay from the castle. Some said the lady had seduced poor Holden, while others whispered that Holden had forced himself on her. No matter what the truth of the rumors, Jamie was unnerved by them. He had witnessed glimpses of Holden's cruel vengeance. He would not wish to endure the man's wrath.

He glanced uneasily at the beautiful creature beside him. Though he was only ten and two, he was already as tall as she. And stronger, he suspected, risking a quick glance at the delicate hand resting beside her plate.

She was very quiet this morrow. But since her arrival he had heard her say very little. Her voice was unusual: deeper in timbre than most females, and as whispery soft as a lullaby. It was the voice he imagined his mother would have had, if he could but recall his mother who had died when he was a bairn.

Meredith sensed the scrutiny of the lad beside her and turned to give him a shy smile. He returned the smile before coloring and turning away quickly.

It mattered not to Jamie what the others whispered about the lady. He knew in his heart that she would never attempt to seduce a man like Holden. To Jamie, Meredith MacAlpin embodied all that was good and fine and noble.

No one mentioned the absence of Holden Mackay, and Meredith fretted that word of her attack had already been whispered about the castle. She frowned and quickly dismissed such thoughts. She would not dwell on somber things.

After their meal, she followed Brice from the great hall and through the maze of dimly lit passageways to the scullery.

The air was thick with the aroma of fresh bread baking in the ovens. A small deer was slowly roasting on a spit, in preparation for the evening meal. Servants were busy fetching buckets of water, while more servants scurried about, scrubbing, cleaning, cutting and preparing.

"Mistress Snow," Brice called.

A small, thin woman looked up from a floured table where she was kneading dough. Seeing the lord of the manor she quickly wiped her hands on a linen square and hurried forward.

Her dress of pale pink was covered by a soiled apron. She touched the end of the apron to her brow as she walked. Dark hair was pulled back from a pretty oval face. Little tendrils of hair clung damply to her forehead and cheeks. Blue eyes danced with laughter as she studied the way her best gown looked on the beautiful woman beside Brice Campbell.

"Lady Meredith MacAlpin came to thank you for the use of your gown."

"It looks far more beautiful on you, my lady, than it ever did on me," she said with a slight bow.

Brice took a moment to study Meredith while she faced the young servant. Indeed she did look beautiful in the heather gown. But it was the exchange between Meredith and his servant that he found most fascinating.

Meredith caught Mistress Snow's hands in hers, ignoring the dusting of flour that clung to her skin. "It was very kind of you to entrust me with the use of your gown. I shall find a way to repay your kindness."

"I desire nothing of you, my lady. It is enough to know that you are pleased with my simple gown."

"I am more than pleased. I am most grateful. Thank you, Mistress Snow."

As they turned away, Brice was aware that the entire staff of servants had watched and listened to this exchange. It was a rare thing to see a highborn woman who would take the time to thank a servant for a kindness.

When they left the scullery they were aware of someone who appeared to be waiting for them. Brice's hand went to the dirk at his waist. Meredith's hand leaped to her throat in a gesture of distress.

Angus Gordon stepped from the shadows and put a hand to Meredith's arm to stop her.

"My lady," Angus said, his face turning a bright scarlet. "Forgive my boldness for approaching you in this manner. But I must beg your forgiveness for leaving my post last night. I am shamed by my lapse of duties."

Now it was Meredith's turn to blush. The young man seemed truly contrite.

"It was not your fault, Angus," she said, avoiding his eyes.

"Aye, but it was." Angus took a step closer, forcing her to look up at him. "Brice had ordered me to guard you. I ignored his orders, and allowed harm to come to you. If Brice had not returned, I shudder to think what would have happened to you at the hands of that coward, Holden Mackay."

"It is forgotten," she said in a tone that left no question of her feeling. "I would ask only that you never mention the name Holden Mackay again."

Angus bowed slightly over her hand. "As you say, my lady. The man no longer exists."

She shivered as Angus accompanied them along the hall. If only Angus's words were true. But the fact was that somewhere in the forest surrounding Kinloch House, Holden Mackay dwelled. And in his heart he could very well be nursing anger and a desire for revenge.

If she ever managed to escape this fortress, there would be another danger added to the elements. A man who would show her no mercy.

Chapter Eight

In the courtyard a dozen horses were being readied for a journey. But though the men awaiting Brice were familiar to Meredith, they were no longer dressed like Highlanders. Instead of being bare legged, they wore trews, the long hose of the Lowland clans. Many wore breeches, as did Brice, and shirts of gray and dun instead of saffron. The colorful belted plaids they usually wore had been exchanged for simple wool cloaks. All the men wore daggers fastened to their belts. Most carried swords and had longbows slung over their shoulders. But though they were dressed in the garb of the Lowlanders, nothing could hide the fierce pride or the rawboned strength of these Highland warriors.

"You are leaving with your men?"

"Aye."

Brice saw the fear that leaped into Meredith's eyes. "Would Holden Mackay dare to return while you are away?"

His eyes narrowed. "This fortress is nearly impenetrable. But to assure the safety of those inside, I leave a dozen men capable of withstanding any attack."

At his words of reassurance she took in a long, steadying breath. "Where do you go?"

"We ride to the Borders."

"Then you must take me home."

He saw the eagerness in her eyes and wished he did not

have to be the one to dash her hopes. "Nay, my lady. We ride on a mission of revenge."

Her heart sank once more. "Gareth MacKenzie."

"Aye." He draped the cloak across his shoulders at a rakish angle and pulled himself into the saddle. "When the MacKenzie is dead I will return you to your people."

"And if you die instead?"

"Would that please you, my lady?"

When she remained silent he gave her a rare, heart-stopping smile. "If I oblige you by being killed, I would suppose the MacKenzie would come for you. That is," he said with a sweep of his plumed hat, "if he still desires to align your two clans."

"He will come for me," she called.

But Brice did not hear her words above the clatter of hooves. Or if he did, he chose not to answer.

"Jamie," he called to the lad who watched their preparations from the doorway. "I leave the lady Meredith in your care until I return."

The boy's cheeks flamed until they matched the color of his hair. "Aye, Brice. I'll see to her."

With shouts of eagerness the men whipped their horses into a run. Within minutes they had disappeared into the surrounding forest.

Meredith sat by the window watching the path of a shooting star. How strange life was. So often, when she got what she had wished for, it turned out to be not at all what she wanted.

She had wished for Brice to leave her alone long enough so that she could slip into the forest and make her way back home. But now that Brice had finally left her, she was unable to leave. Someone now lurked in the forest beyond Kinloch House who wished her even greater harm than could befall her at the hands of Brice.

And so she sat, alone and lonely.

Lonely? She did not miss Brice Campbell, she told herself firmly. How could she miss the quick temper, the cold, dark looks? Why would she care about the absence of the low, taunting voice, the occasional burst of teasing laughter?

At a knock on the door she looked up. Jamie MacDonald stood poised in the doorway. At his feet were several of Brice's hounds.

"Come in, Jamie," she called.

He took a step in and glanced about uneasily. He had never had occasion to enter a lady's room before. The hounds, following his lead, proceeded cautiously.

"I—wanted to see if you needed anything, my lady." His Adam's apple bobbed up and down with each halting word.

Meredith smiled. "How kind of you, Jamie. I was just sitting here feeling lonely. I would treasure your company for a little while." She indicated a chair pulled before the fire. "Sit awhile."

He crossed the room and perched on the edge like a bird ready for flight. The hounds circled the room before settling at his feet.

"What do you do while Brice and the others are away?" she asked.

"I help in the stables, and sometimes go with the men who keep watch along the trails."

"What do they keep watch for?"

"Surprise visitors," he said with a trace of a smile.

Meredith was reminded of another's smile. "Do you miss Brice Campbell when he is away?"

"Aye. Kinloch House is never quiet when Brice is in residence. But when he goes away, it is as if everyone lies sleeping, waiting for Brice to awaken them."

What an oddly accurate description, she thought.

"And the hounds? Do they switch loyalties when their master is away?"

Jamie reached a hand to the head of one of the dogs. Instantly the dog sat up and rested his chin on the boy's knee, staring sorrowfully into his eyes.

"Nay. The hounds follow me and allow me to pet them. But they leave no doubt as to their loyalty. They love only Brice Campbell. As do I," he added fiercely.

Meredith was moved by his simple statement.

"Cara told me how you came to live here. Do you miss your home in the Lowlands?"

Jamie shook his head slowly. "I no longer remember it, my lady. I was but a babe when my father and I came here."

"Do you not feel disloyal to your clan when you swear allegiance to a Highlander?"

Jamie stood and crossed to the window where he stared in silence for several minutes. When at last he spoke, his voice was as soft as a night breeze.

"I know that it could have been Brice's arrow that slew my father. And I know here," he said, touching a finger to his temple, "that I should avenge my father's death. But here," he said, touching a hand to his heart, "I know only that Brice gave me shelter when I had none. He gave me food and clothing, and has taught me to read, to chart the stars, to ride and handle a weapon like a warrior. When he scolds me, I know it is because he expects me to grow to be a man of honor. And when he praises me, my heart swells with pride. Though I am a MacDonald from the Lowlands, Brice Campbell is my father now. I would do nothing to dishonor him."

With a lump in her throat Meredith crossed the room and touched a hand to Jamie's shoulder. "I have a little sister," she said softly, "named Megan. She is near your age. And much like you."

"A sister?" Jamie tried to picture a younger, smaller version of the woman beside him.

"Aye. Two sisters, in fact. Brenna, with dark hair and eyes to match the heather. She is a gentle girl who would never harm a living creature. And Megan," Meredith said with a laugh that bubbled forth just thinking about the child. "She is fair as the sun and as wild and free as the breezes that blow off the river."

Meredith stared at the darkness beyond the window, knowing that Jamie's loneliness was as acute as her own.

"Sit and tell me about your life here," she said.

He smiled and followed her back to the chair. He couldn't think of any place he would rather be at this moment than right here, in the company of the most beautiful woman he had ever seen.

They talked and laughed for nearly an hour before looking up at a knock on the door.

Cara entered, carrying a tray of tea and biscuits.

"Mistress Snow thought you might be hungry." The serving girl placed the tray on a low table in front of the fire.

"When the men ride to the Borders," Meredith asked softly, "how long do they usually travel?"

"Oh, my lady, it could be days. There's no telling how long they'll stay away this time."

Days. Meredith's heart fell. She glanced at Jamie and saw that he, too, was dismayed. As she poured two cups of tea she had a thought. "Is there cloth here at Kinloch House? Enough for a gown?"

"Aye, my lady. There is fine cloth in the storehouse."

Meredith smiled suddenly. "Tomorrow, Cara, after we break our fast, I would like Jamie to show me the storehouse."

"But why, my lady?"

Her smile grew. "I owe Mistress Snow a gown. There is no better time to start than now."

"And when you tire of sewing," Jamie said with a wide smile, "I shall be happy to show you the stables. Brice said I can handle the horses as well as any of his men."

"I would like that."

Together Meredith and Jamie passed another pleasant hour before they bid good-night. And when at last Meredith drifted off to sleep, she felt more relaxed than she had at any time since her shocking abduction.

The line of mourners stretched around the manor house and up the lane for as far as the eye could see.

An old man, slightly stooped, with a walking stick in his hand, joined the crowd and moved slowly toward the house. A rough, shapeless cloak fell from his shoulders to his ankles. When someone in front of him asked his name, the old man cupped a hand to his ear and strained to understand the question.

"He's likely from the MacKenzie clan," one of the women called from behind him. "With Gareth MacKenzie spending so much time on MacAlpin land these days, the MacKenzie clansmen are everywhere. So many strangers," she complained. "There was a time when we knew everyone who passed us on the lane."

"What do you expect?" cried a thin youth. "With old Duncan MacAlpin and two wee lasses the only ones left to lead the clan, the MacKenzies have a free rein in MacAlpin affairs."

"Aye," another responded. "First Alastair, and then Meredith. Both were born leaders. But the younger lasses have not the heart for it. And Duncan is a beaten man."

The crowd moved along and the old man struggled to keep up. Those around him, intent upon their gossip, ignored him.

"Some say old Duncan and Mary will never be the same now." A plump woman with a baby at her hip spoke to the crowd.

"Aye. The murder of an only grandson is too hard to bear," said a ruddy-cheeked man.

"Especially since Duncan's son, William and his wife, Margaret, can have no more bairns." It was a young, pretty woman speaking. Her coloring was similar to Meredith's, since they were distant cousins. "Young William was the light of their lives."

"Aye. Especially Duncan's. He doted on the lad. He and Mary had depended upon young William to help with the chores." An old woman lowered her voice slightly as she addressed those around her. "Gareth MacKenzie himself witnessed the murder of poor William. When he tried to stop them from beating the lad, he took a dirk in the arm from one of them."

"Something must be done to stop the killing."

The crowd murmured its approval.

"Aye," said the ruddy-cheeked man. "And from what I've heard, something will be done."

"What have you heard, man?"

"Gareth MacKenzie is planning to lead an army against the man who would murder even children in his lust for power."

"The filthy, murdering coward," someone in the crowd spat.

"Aye. Brice Campbell must be stopped before he manages to kill the entire MacAlpin clan."

At that the shabby old man stopped in his tracks. Then, keeping his head bowed, he plodded slowly along with the others. When they reached the manor house he studied the faces of the crowd, nodding occasionally when his gaze met that of someone familiar, partially hidden beneath similarly shabby attire.

As they passed the simple wooden casket, the old man paused to study the lad who was being mourned. Young William, grandson of Duncan and Mary MacAlpin, dead at the tender age of ten and five. On either side of the casket stood the parents and grandparents, as well as the three pretty granddaughters who were openly sobbing.

Beside them were two young lasses who stood together, heads high, hands linked. The old man paused to study them carefully. Though their coloring was distinctly different, he knew them to be sisters. The younger sisters of Meredith MacAlpin.

The older of the two, with coal-black hair and eyes more violet than blue, stared above the crowd, drawing into herself to keep from feeling the pain. The other, with hair the color of the sun, eagerly scanned the faces in the crowd as though expecting at any moment to see the one she sought.

Meredith, the old man thought, noting the intensity of the gaze. The younger one had not yet accepted what the older one knew to be fact: that Meredith was not free to return to them in their time of need.

The old man's eyes narrowed as he noted Gareth MacKenzie standing just behind the two lasses. Around him were a dozen or more of his most trusted men, all of them bearing arms.

As always, Gareth set himself up in a position of importance and made certain that the crowd of mourners heard every lurid detail of the lad's murder.

"'Twas Brice Campbell," he said loudly. "And at least two dozen of his cowardly men. I saw and heard everything. They asked the lad's name, then began beating him with their fists."

"Dear God, stop." Duncan dropped an arm about his wife's shoulders as she started to cry.

"When was this?" the shabbily dressed old man asked in a voice that quavered with age.

"On the day before last," Gareth said. "I leaped from my horse and tried to go to the lad's aid, but one of the cowards plunged his dirk into my arm while another held me down and took my knife."

"'Twas Gareth's weapon they used on my William," Duncan said through trembling lips. "It was found, caked with dried blood, beside his body."

Gareth continued his story, eager to feed the crowd's appetite for gossip. "When the lad was no more than a bloody heap, they let me go."

"Odd they did not kill you as well," the shabby old man said haltingly. "Why would you suppose they let you live?"

Gareth shot a cold stare in the direction of the speaker, then shrugged off his comment as being unworthy of a response. The shabby old stranger was probably just another of the MacAlpin clan. Gareth's voice rose. "I call on all men of goodwill, be they MacKenzie or MacAlpin clan. It is time to show the Highland Barbarian, Brice Campbell, that he can no longer murder our young and helpless and then hide in the forests yonder. He captured your leader, Meredith MacAlpin, and holds her captive in his Highland fortress. Who knows what unspeakable things are being done to her this very day."

Out of the corner of his eye the old man saw the two lasses tighten their grips on each other's hands. Neither made a sound. Neither showed any sign of emotion, except for a tightening of their mouths.

In the corner of the room a woman began sobbing.

Still other women gasped before turning into their men's arms and crying silently.

Gareth waited, judging the mood of the crowd. With a voice of triumph he shouted, "And Brice Campbell has murdered another MacAlpin. What say you?" Gareth looked around as a hush fell upon the crowd. "Who will join me in putting an end to his reign of terror?"

For a moment there was only silence. Every man here was aware of the reputation of the man they called the Highland Barbarian. There were none eager to risk their lives at the end of his sword. Still, the sight of the young lad in the casket and his grieving family left them too outraged to dwell on the risk.

"With enough force we can storm Campbell's fortress and save the woman who was to wed my brother. With Meredith

MacAlpin at my side, I vow to unite the Border clans and stand against any attack.''

The room was rocked with shouts and calls as the men hurried forward to shake Gareth's hand and offer their arms.

''In the days to come,'' Gareth shouted above the din, ''I will raise up an army of men. And we will ride to the Highlands and rid ourselves of this scum.''

''Aye. Here's to the death of Brice Campbell.'' Fists were raised in a salute as the men, their blood hot for revenge, surged forward.

''And just to tempt you further,'' Gareth MacKenzie shouted, ''I will offer a price of one hundred pounds sterling to any man who brings me the body of Brice Campbell.''

While the rooms of the manor house rocked with the fury of the crowd, the shabby old man nodded to several others before making his way slowly from the house. In the lane he continued hobbling until he came to a stand of trees. He glanced around, and seeing no one behind him, stepped into the shelter offered by the trees. Several horsemen greeted him. He pulled off the shabby cloak, and with an agility that belied his stooped appearance, pulled himself into the saddle.

''Well, Brice,'' one of the men said softly. ''What news have you?''

He nodded to the others who had accompanied him to the house. Once they reached the safety of the trees they also shed their shabby cloaks and pulled themselves onto their waiting horses.

Brice's tone was as grim as their faces. ''By all accounts I have lived up to the name these Borderers have given me.'' His eyes narrowed fractionally. ''I have just discovered that on the very day I was dancing with the queen, I was also here in the Lowlands murdering young William MacAlpin.''

''That is an amazing feat even for a Highland warrior,'' one of the men said with a laugh.

''Aye.'' Brice's eyes narrowed as he added, ''And Gareth MacKenzie has put a price on my head. One hundred pounds sterling for any man who brings me to him. Alive or dead.''

''MacKenzie,'' Angus spat. ''Come, Brice. Let us kill him now.''

''Nay, friend.'' Brice turned his mount and motioned for

the others to follow. "Already he surrounds himself with too many men. Think of your women and children waiting for you in the Highlands. Within days there will be dozens of men riding through the forests hoping to cut down anything that moves."

"What will we do now?"

Brice slowed his horse until Angus caught up with him. As they rode side by side Brice murmured, "We will do what our ancestors have done for centuries, old friend. We will take up arms and fight anyone foolish enough to dare to enter our Highland forests."

"And what of our families?"

"They remain at our sides," Brice said. "We will bring them inside the protective walls of Kinloch House. And there they will stay until the siege is over."

"And the lass, Meredith MacAlpin?"

A little muscle worked in the side of Brice's jaw as he urged his mount ahead. Aye, he thought. What to do about Meredith? If he were to return her to her people, she would prove the lie that Gareth MacKenzie had spread. That could, once and for all time, clear his good name. But it would be impossible for him to remain with her forever. And left at the mercy of Gareth MacKenzie she would soon be conveniently murdered, as the others had been.

But, Brice reasoned, if he kept her with him, she would be forced into a life of hardship and deprivation while the invaders were repulsed. Yet for now, he could think of no other solution.

Over his shoulder he called, "The woman stays with me at Kinloch House."

"Oh, my lady. This is far too grand for me to wear." Mistress Snow studied her reflection in the looking glass. "I look like the lady of the manor."

"And well you should." Meredith stood beside her, proud of her accomplishment.

It was Brenna, the sister who was younger by a year, who sewed the finest seams. And it had always been Brenna who

could add a bit of ribbon or lace and make the plainest gown
look splendid.

Meredith had taken great pains with this task. And it had
served its purpose well. The long hours alone in Brice's chambers had passed far easier than she had expected. And when
she wasn't sewing she was visiting with the servants. She had
learned the names of all of them, as well as their family his-
tories.

Like a shadow, young Jamie had been constantly at her side,
watching, listening. And though he felt strangely disloyal to
his idol, Brice, he found himself becoming enchanted with the
beautiful young woman who was being held prisoner in their
home.

"I think," Mistress Snow said, interrupting Jamie's mus-
ings, "that I should take back the simple gown I loaned you,
and give you this one."

"And I think," Meredith said with a smile, "that Angus
Gordon will not be able to stay away from the scullery when
he sees you in this."

"Oh, my lady." The young widow blushed furiously before
burying her face in her hands.

Jamie stifled a giggle. He had repeated a litany of gossip
during the days that he and Meredith had spent together. Apparently the lady had paid more attention than he'd thought.

They all looked up when they heard the clatter of horses'
hooves entering the courtyard.

"The men have returned." Mistress Snow raced to the door,
then seemed to remember her position. Holding the door for
Meredith and Jamie, she followed them down the stairs.

Men and horses milled about in mass confusion. Many of
the men stood in a circle, listening intently as Brice spoke in
low tones. Others trudged to the storehouse and began carrying
an assortment of supplies toward the main door of the castle.
As Meredith watched, the circle of men broke up. Most of the
men mounted and rode away, while others joined the group
carrying supplies.

Brice spoke quietly to Angus and another man, then looked
up to see Meredith standing in the doorway with her hand on
Jamie's shoulder. For long moments their gazes met and held.

It was strange to see this woman, his captive, standing protectively beside the boy he loved more than his own life. Strange and—pleasant.

Meredith felt the hypnotic pull of his gaze and couldn't stop the tremors that coursed along her spine. How odd that the man she wished to escape from was also the man who could cause such wild stirrings deep within her.

Brice said something more to Angus, then strode impatiently toward her.

She studied his grim features and waited for him to speak. Instead, he stopped before her without a word, then called out orders to the men in the courtyard.

It was vexing to be ignored in this fashion. In a snappish tone she asked, "Have you extracted your revenge?"

He shook his head and turned to speak to one of his men.

"Then what news do you bring? Am I to be returned to my home?"

He turned toward her but kept his gaze on the procession of men and arms. "Jamie," he said in a patient tone, "go and help the men carry supplies to the main house."

"Aye." Jamie gave Brice a long, questioning look before turning away.

"As for you, my lady," Brice said, still watching the progress of the men, "I fear it will be a long time before you see home and family again."

Meredith swallowed down the knot of fear that leaped to her throat. "What are you saying?"

"We will soon be under siege, my lady. These forests will be teeming with men bent upon my destruction."

She felt a flare of hope. "Gareth MacKenzie? He comes for me?"

"Nay, my lady." Brice turned and met her gaze squarely. "He comes for me."

"Surely Gareth MacKenzie would not be fool enough to bring his men into the Highland forests where they would be outnumbered."

"He and his men do not come alone. They bring the MacAlpin clan with them."

She brought her hands to her hips in a fit of outrage. "My people do not fight in the Highlands. They understand the folly of it."

"They fight when they are persuaded that the life of their leader is threatened."

"You have threatened my life?"

"Nay. But your people believe I have. And," he added tersely, "they agreed to fight when the grandson of Duncan MacAlpin was murdered by the Highland Barbarian."

"What are you saying?" Her hands balled into fists as she turned on him. "You killed William?"

He caught her fists in his big hands as easily as if they were no more than wispy flowers blowing in the wind. "Nay, my lady. The lad was killed on the very day I was dancing with the queen."

"I do not understand."

"The ones who killed young William wanted the murder to be blamed on me."

"Why? Who would benefit from such a thing?"

"Aye. Who indeed?" He studied her in silence for long minutes. "Did I mention that Gareth MacKenzie has offered one hundred pounds sterling for the Highland Barbarian?"

Several men pushed past them, their arms laden with the supplies of war.

When she continued staring at Brice in openmouthed surprise, he said softly, "It could mean that Gareth MacKenzie is so incensed by the death of one of the MacAlpins that he would lead his own men into certain danger." His lips curved into a smile, but his eyes, she noted, were dark and unfathomable. "Or it could mean that Gareth MacKenzie hopes to silence the Highland Barbarian before the truth can be revealed."

"It could also mean that Gareth is determined to avenge the senseless murder of his brother."

Without a word in his defense Brice swung away and strode toward the storehouse.

While she watched the frantic preparations for war, Meredith felt a growing sense of dread. This feud was growing into something far more dangerous than vengeance. Someone was going to a great deal of trouble to ruin Brice Campbell's reputation. Someone who would stop at nothing, even the murder of the young and helpless.

Young William. She felt as if a knife had pierced her heart.

She had watched the tenderness between Duncan and Mary and their young grandson. His death would be a heavy burden.

And what of her people? They were being dragged into a war not of their making. If they were persuaded to leave their homes and follow Gareth MacKenzie, they left their own families open to attack by the English across their border. They lacked strong leadership. And all because she'd had the misfortune of being captured by the Highland Barbarian.

Chapter Nine

"I can handle a broadsword, Brice."

Meredith looked up at the sound of Jamie's pleading voice.

"Nay. I'll not allow it." Brice grasped the weapon, yanking it fiercely from the lad's hands. "'Tis not fit for close combat. It takes two hands to wield, leaving no protection of a shield. Besides, I expect you to play the pipes when I give the command."

"Bagpipes." The lad's face mirrored his disgust. "That is a task for children and old men."

"Is it now?" Brice crossed the room and ran a hand lovingly over the bagpipes resting on the mantel above the fireplace. "When I was no younger than you my father ordered me to play these when we were attacked by the powerful Murray clan. When I saw him about to be attacked from behind by Cedric Murray, I dropped the pipes and reached for my sword. But my father ordered me to continue playing. He said it was what gave him the strength to go on."

It was plain to Meredith that Jamie felt a thrill of pride at being compared with Brice.

"But how could you play while all around you men were dying?"

"I did what my father commanded," Brice said simply. "I knew that it meant more to him to hear the sound of the pipes than to hear the sound of his son's clumsy attempts at a man's work." His voice lowered with feeling. "He knew there would be time enough for that."

"But what if I am attacked?"

"Here." Brice handed the youth a small, deadly dirk. "When fighting a man within these walls, this is your best weapon."

"What about this?" Meredith asked.

Two heads turned toward her. Both faces held puzzled frowns. She was standing in the doorway holding one of Brice's swords in a menacing fashion.

Brice walked toward her until he was the blade's length from her. "It is never wise to take up a weapon unless you know how to use it."

"You think I do not know how to defend myself?"

"Stick to women's work," he said softly.

"Women's work." There was a note of contempt in her voice.

"Aye. Mistress Snow tells all who will listen about your skill with a needle."

"I made her a gown because she had loaned me hers. But that does not make me less skilled in the ways of battle. I can handle a sword as well as you, Brice Campbell."

"Can you now?" Without warning he reached out and yanked the weapon from her hand. He sent it crashing to the floor before taking a step closer and facing her. "So much for your skill with a sword." With a smile he half turned toward Jamie and winked. "How will you defend yourself now, my lady?"

"With this." With a look of triumph she reached into the waistband of her skirt and removed a small, sharp dagger.

"So. You dare to conceal weapons. When you are within these walls, under my protection, you have no need of such things."

She gave him a chilling smile. "It would seem that you forgot to tell Holden Mackay."

Brice flushed. Caught off guard, he advanced toward her.

She lifted the knife in a threatening gesture. "I think you should be warned. I learned such skills at my father's knee. Though I have no wish to harm you, I will not back away from a fight."

At the incongruous sight of the small, delicate figure facing down a giant of a man like Brice, Jamie burst into gales of laughter.

"What will you do now, Brice? Do you risk hurting Meredith just to prove you are the stronger, or do you let a Lowland lass bully you with a dirk?"

Brice studied his opponent. She was perfectly composed. There was no hint of fear in her eyes. The hand holding the dagger was steady. About her lips there was the merest hint of a smile.

"So, my lady, do you think, like Jamie, that you have me at a disadvantage?"

Her smile blossomed. "Aye, my lord. I do. I think it is time to persuade you to release me to my people before they reach the Highlands and engage you in battle."

He moved so quickly she had time only to blink. With one hand he caught her wrist and swung her around. Both his arms came around her, crossing her arms beneath her bosom and pinning her to the length of him. The knife slipped from her hand and clattered to the floor.

His breath was hot against her temple as he pressed his lips to a tangle of hair and muttered, "Now, my lady, I believe the advantage is mine. We will speak no more of releasing you to Gareth MacKenzie."

Her breath came out in a hiss of air, and although she struggled, she was held fast.

"It is not Gareth who will claim me. It is my own people."

His voice was low with anger. "Who are now in league with the MacKenzies."

"If I am free, my people will follow me."

"A woman of strength and leadership, of course. As you have often pointed out to me."

Across the room Jamie laughed and clapped his hands. "Now what say you, Meredith? Do you admit defeat?"

She stopped fighting. The tremors that rocked her had nothing to do with combat. They had everything to do with the man who held her imprisoned in his arms.

"Aye, Jamie." She lowered her gaze, afraid the lad would see the fire that burned inside her at the nearness of her captor. "Defeat perhaps. But only for the moment."

Against her temple Brice murmured, "I will settle for even a fleeting moment of victory over you, my lady." He allowed his lips to linger while he inhaled the soft scent of her. His thumbs brushed the underside of her breasts and he was startled by the rush of desire caused by even that slight contact.

He was aware of the tension in her and felt a thrill. Could it be that he was the cause of such feelings? Or was the lady merely tense at the thought of the battle yet to come?

With a smile he dropped his hands and stepped away. When she turned to him he gave a slight bow. "I look forward to our next round of combat, my lady."

Meredith watched as he crossed the room and continued with Jamie as if they'd never been interrupted. How could he be so calm when her heart was near bursting?

She waited a moment longer until her heartbeat returned to normal. Then she stalked from the room, unaware that Brice watched her every movement. But Jamie noted that Brice seemed distracted as he took up the weapons for another lesson in the art of defense. And long after she was gone, Brice stared at the closed door, deep in thought.

"Riders approach."

It was what Meredith had been fearing for days. The word was passed from men perched atop high, rocky crags to others who concealed themselves in trees or behind boulders. Runners carried the warning to the guards posted at the door of Kinloch House.

Bands of Highlanders had roamed the forests for days, encountering only scattered clusters of armed Lowlanders. The bulk of Gareth MacKenzie's army stayed close together, knowing there was safety in numbers. Their number made it impossible for the Highland warriors to attack. Instead, in groups of three and four, the men loyal to Brice Campbell watched and waited, and made their way back to Kinloch House, where their families awaited their safe return.

Inside the castle all was in readiness. Entire families had been ensconced in every room and made as comfortable as possible. No one knew how long they would be forced to endure such close quarters. Even the sheep and livestock were brought inside the compound, to protect them from being slaughtered by the enemy. It was Brice's intention that the enemy, denied all food save what they had brought with them, would soon be forced to withdraw and return to the Lowlands.

The women shared the duties of cooking and caring for the children, while the men honed their weapons to a fine edge and went out in clusters of twos and threes, attacking small bands of Lowlanders and then returning to the protection of the castle before dark.

Chores were assigned to everyone except the youngest. Provisions had been stored in the dank dungeons below the castle, in case the women and children were forced to spend a prolonged time within its safe confines.

Meredith had hoped that Brice would relent and allow her a chamber of her own. She yearned for a few moments of privacy, away from this man who seemed to dominate her every moment, both waking and sleeping. But now that the others had taken over the rooms of the castle, there was no hope for such a luxury. She was forced to share Brice's sitting chamber and bedchamber. At her insistence, she was allowed to sleep in a settle pulled before the fireplace rather than share Brice's bed. But it did nothing to ease the tension between them. She was still achingly aware of the man whose soft breathing punctuated the darkness between them.

Their close quarters did allow her to see how carefully Brice prepared for the anticipated attack. His weapons gleamed atop the mantel. The broadsword, a two-handed weapon with terrible killing power, had been honed until it was capable of severing a man's head with a single blow. A second weapon with a shorter blade and a basket-shaped hilt of gold encrusted with jewels, also displayed a razor-sharp edge. A longbow and quiver of arrows stood at the ready. And though Brice possessed more than half a dozen dirks, each one had been sharpened to perfection.

At the call to arms, Brice glanced across the room to where Meredith stood. "You will go below now with the women. I have assigned two of my warriors to guard the door. They will protect all of you with their lives."

She felt the rush of anticipation that had always flowed when her father's castle had come under siege. As the eldest daughter she had been assigned the task of seeing to the safety of her sisters. She had been trained to fight. And although there was a knot of fear in the pit of her stomach, she would never back away from the fight.

"For the last time I beg of you, Brice. Set me free. Send me forth to meet my people. They will turn away from this battle, if only they see that I am free."

"We will speak no more of this thing. My decision is made."

She decided to try a new course of persuasion. "If you will not set me free, then let me at least stay here." Her glance strayed to the weapons atop the mantel, then back to where Brice stood facing her. "I could assist those who are wounded."

A hint of a smile touched his lips. "Indeed? Help them die faster, perhaps?"

"I cannot stay in the dungeons, Brice. As leader of the MacAlpins I claim the right to be present at the battle."

"Do you think I could concentrate on the battle at hand, knowing you are vulnerable to attack?"

"The men who ride with Gareth would never harm me. They are my own people."

"Are you so certain of that?" Brice studied the way the sunlight streamed through the windows, turning the ends of her hair to flame. He longed to touch it, to feel the silken strands sift through his fingers. Abruptly he pushed away such thoughts. "What if the men of the MacKenzie clan do not recognize you, and in their lust for blood slay the very one they have come to free?"

Such a thing had never entered Meredith's mind. Though she felt a moment of uncertainty, she persisted. "I am the reason for this attack. If you show my people that I am un-harmed, and allow me to return to the Lowlands with them, your life can go on as before."

"Aye." His tone hardened. "And as before, more innocents will be murdered, and their death blamed on the Highland Barbarian. Who is to say that even you will be safe on the journey back to your people?"

She stiffened. "Are you suggesting that there are those who wish my death?"

He saw the pain in her eyes and regretted his sharp words. If only they had time. Time to discuss the suspicions he had begun to harbor about those around her. Time to share his thoughts about Gareth MacKenzie and his dead brother. But there was not even time to prepare her for what was to come.

He crossed the room and caught her roughly by the shoulder. "We will speak no more of this."

"But..."

His gaze focused on her lips. With no warning he lowered his mouth to hers and kissed her with a savageness that left her stunned and reeling.

He took the kiss deeper, filling himself with the taste of her. God in heaven. What was wrong with him? Never before had he allowed anyone or anything to distract him from the task at hand. Never before had he been forced to wage such a difficult battle with himself. This female, who should mean nothing to him, was intruding too often upon his thoughts. He was worried about her safety. And that worry could mean the difference between living and dying. In a battle to the death, even the simplest distraction could cost him his life.

He lifted his head and stared down into eyes that glittered with a strange light. The woman was bewitching him.

He experienced a wave of self-loathing. In a voice low with fury he whispered, "Go now and join the women and children below the castle."

He shouted for one of his men. Angus Gordon opened the door and stood awaiting his orders.

"Take the lady below. And see that she does not leave."

Meredith backed away from Brice's touch and gave him a look of pure venom. "Aye. I shall go below while you and the others settle this thing."

She moved past him and hurried to the door. With her hand on the door pull she called, "But though you fancy yourself a mighty warrior, be warned. Do not turn your back on your attackers, my lord. Or you may find a MacAlpin dirk buried between your shoulders."

He watched as she flounced away beside Angus. As he bent to his weapons, the taste of her was still on his lips.

Chapter Ten

Dust plumed in great clouds as the horsemen crowded through the entranceway and milled about in confusion. Above the din of horses' hooves in the courtyard there was a great roar of men's voices shouting encouragement to one another as they prepared the attack on Kinloch House. The door to the castle was rammed. And although the massive door had been braced by thick timbers, it eventually sagged and gave way beneath the assault. Swarms of men poured through the doorway of the castle, their voices a chorus of cursing and screeching.

At the sudden mournful wail of bagpipes they seemed to fall back for a moment before regaining their momentum.

Brice saw the looks in the eyes of his men. They had expected no more than a dozen or more Lowlanders. But there were ten times that number. And many of them, though dressed like Lowlanders, had the look of the Highlands about them.

A warning bell rang in his mind but there was no time to fathom it. Something did not ring true about the men attacking them. There was something very wrong here.

In that one brief moment of confusion the Highlanders returned the attack with a vengeance. The air was filled with the sound of sword clanging against shield, of fierce battle cries, of the moaning and shrieking of the first to fall in battle.

In the light of candles set in sconces along the walls, the bearded faces appeared wild and frightening. And because Brice Campbell, the most feared of all men in the Highlands, had a price of one hundred pounds sterling upon his head, he found himself at the point of dozens of swords.

He had been raised with the sword. From his earliest days he had known that there would be men eager to challenge him. But though he willingly accepted the challenge, he took no joy in killing. It was something that had been thrust upon him as leader and warrior. It was his death or theirs. And in his hands rested the fate of his people.

There was no time for fear. He parried each thrust with equal skill, matching move for move. But though he was a skilled warrior, the endless fighting was wearing him down.

As the hour stretched into two, and then into a third, he glanced around at his comrades and felt a heaviness around his heart. This day many good men had fallen. And many more would never again rise up.

Below the castle, in the flickering light of the dungeons, the women rocked their babies and sought to comfort the crying, frightened children. Their eyes mirrored every emotion, from absolute terror to quiet resignation. The battles were as much a part of their lives as eating and sleeping. They had been the daughters of warriors. Now they were the patient wives of warriors. And every woman there knew, like a knife thrust to the heart, that they were also the mothers of future warriors.

Meredith stood with her ear pressed to the heavy door. When she heard the sound of the guards outside the door being engaged in battle, she clenched her hands at her sides and strained to make out the voices muttering savage oaths and barely coherent phrases. A scream pierced the air and she heard the thud as a body dropped to the floor just outside the door. The fighting went on for what seemed an eternity. She heard a second body fall. Then she detected the sound of footsteps receding.

For long minutes she continued listening with her ear pressed firmly to the massive door. There was only silence outside the room. But from the upper floors she could hear the distant sounds of battle.

How much longer should she remain here with the women? This room offered shelter, a safe haven from the battle. But those were her men fighting, dying. And they were here to rescue her. Regardless of Brice's words, Meredith knew in her heart that she had no choice. She must show herself to her men and order them to cease this battle at once and return with her to the Lowlands.

She lifted sweating palms to the latch that secured the heavy door from inside. Behind her the women lifted pleading eyes that spoke of their disapproval.

"Please, my lady," Cara whispered. "There is only death beyond this room."

"I must go. I have the power, the authority, to stop this slaughter."

"Nay, my lady," Mistress Snow said, coming to place a restraining hand upon her arm. "My lord Campbell ordered us to stay here where we are safe. He is the only one who has the authority to end this battle. I beg you, please do not disobey him."

Meredith lifted her head a fraction. No one, not even these well-intentioned servants, would dissuade her.

With her shoulder to the door she pushed it open an inch and peered about. Two men lay in pools of slowly congealing blood. She recognized the two as men who rode with Brice and her heart went out to their widows still waiting bravely just beyond the door. At least for a little while longer she would spare them the gruesome sight of their loved ones.

Motioning for Mistress Snow to latch the door behind her, Meredith slipped out and hurried to kneel beside each of the fallen warriors in turn. Both were dead. Judging by the bloody swords beside them, both had fought furiously before giving up their lives.

She lifted her head and listened to the sounds of battle being waged above her. Lifting her skirts she ran to the stairs and began to climb.

The great hall was littered with the bodies of the dead and dying. Blood spattered the walls and tables. The hulking forms of men writhed and twisted as they moaned or choked back sobs. Pain and death were everywhere.

Meredith walked among the fallen men, kneeling to whisper a word of comfort, to offer a tankard of water. Not one of them, she realized was a MacAlpin. All except Brice's men were strangers to her. Brice. She studied each face, and though she was not aware of it, her heart sought only one. When a search of the entire room did not reveal him, she let out a long sigh of breath. Brice had survived the first wave of attack.

Meredith heard the sound of the pipes from the direction of the courtyard. When she reached the door she looked out at a scene of such carnage it took her breath away.

The storehouse had been burned. Black acrid smoke filled the air. Animals, free of their pens, milled about while swordsmen battled all around them. Chickens, ducks, geese, were trampled in the melee. Goats bleated and ran about, seeking to escape.

Young Jamie, standing alone in a corner of the courtyard, struggled to play the bagpipes while all around him were fallen comrades. Meredith saw tears streaming down the lad's dirt-streaked face, but he continued to play, though she was certain he no longer knew nor cared what the song was. He played because Brice had ordered it. And he would go to hell and back for his beloved Brice.

Seeing a flash of saffron sleeve, Meredith cried out Brice's name and watched in horror as a tall man fell to the ground. His hands pried in vain at the blade of a sword buried in his chest. But when the man's head lolled to one side, she realized he was not Brice.

Her gaze scanned the swordsmen who milled about the courtyard. There were twenty men for every one of Brice's. Where had they all come from?

Hearing a cry from above her, Meredith looked up. A man was pushed from a balcony and hurtled past her, landing with a terrible shudder on the hard-packed earth of the courtyard. A bushy red beard covered his chin. He proudly wore the garb of a Highlander. His vacant eyes stared heavenward.

Meredith looked up toward the balcony. Peering down from his position of victory toward the fallen man was Gareth MacKenzie. On his face was a smile of supreme confidence.

Meredith was certain that Gareth had not yet spotted her. He was still staring intently at the man he had defeated.

Scanning the faces of the crowd, Meredith felt her heart lurch. Brice. Did he lie even now in a pool of his own blood?

She ducked back inside the castle and raced up the stairs toward Brice's chambers.

Outside the door she came to an abrupt halt. Brice, his sleeve hanging in shreds, his shoulder bleeding profusely, faced three opponents. His left arm dangled uselessly at his side. In his right hand was the gleaming broadsword. By the light of the fire the jewel-encrusted gold handle winked with brilliant color.

While she watched, all three men attacked.

Meredith longed for a sword. Though the men fighting Brice were MacKenzie clansmen, and therefore considered her protectors, she chafed at the uneven odds. With a weapon she could at least make the battle a bit more even.

As she watched the dueling swords she heard the sound of running feet. Dropping to her knees, she hid herself in a little alcove. It was a terrible thing to be forced to listen helplessly to the sounds of battle and be unable to join in. Nor could she any longer witness the outcome.

"So." The voice of Gareth MacKenzie rang through the hall. "At last we have backed the Highland Barbarian into a corner. Let us now show him how the Borderers fight scum like him."

Meredith got to her feet. She would show herself to these men to prove that she was truly alive and unharmed. And then she would demand that Gareth's men join her and follow her back to their home in the Lowlands. Though Gareth would insist upon taking Brice prisoner, she would at least see that he was kept alive.

As she began to step from her place of concealment, she heard Gareth's voice, low with fury.

"You men. Join these three and pin the Highlander against the wall. I want it to be my thrust that ends his life."

Meredith sprang from her place of concealment and stood in the doorway.

Five men held their sword points against Brice's chest while Gareth MacKenzie faced him. Brice's sword lay gleaming at his feet.

Seeing the flicker of movement in the doorway, Brice's eyes narrowed. God in heaven. Not now. Meredith must not be seen. If these animals caught sight of her, all would be lost. For there was no doubt in Brice's mind that Gareth MacKenzie was an evil man, bent upon destroying everyone who stood in the way of his lust for land and power.

"And when you have killed me, where will you lay the

blame for your next murder? When innocent lads and old men are cut down in the night, whose name will you curse?''

"When I have taken over your land, and that of the Mac-Alpins, there will be no further need of deception," Gareth stated. "It will all be mine."

"And what of the woman?" Brice's lips curled in a hint of a smile. "What if Meredith MacAlpin refuses to be wed?"

"She will be given no chance to refuse. And I will see to it that this time she is not snatched from my clutches at the altar."

Meredith took a step forward, then froze at Gareth's next words to his men.

"Without her clan here to give witness, I will personally see to the woman. I want Meredith MacAlpin wed and then dead. We will take her body back to the MacAlpins for viewing."

"Why are the MacAlpins not here with you? It is, after all, their leader you fight for." Brice's voice was low with fury.

"They feared that their mistress would be harmed in battle. They favored bartering with you for her safe return."

"Then who are all these men who fight alongside you?"

Gareth gave an evil leer. "I have an unending supply of warriors. It seems the Highland Barbarian has incurred the wrath of many Scotsmen." With a low, mirthless laugh he added, "Now, if viewing the body of Meredith MacAlpin is not enough to secure the loyalty of the MacAlpin clan, the rest of my plan will be more than enough." He studied the bloodied foe who faced five of the MacKenzie's most skilled swordsmen. "I intend to place your sword through the heart of Meredith MacAlpin for all to see."

The men surrounding Brice burst into words of encouragement and taunting laughter.

"Every man on the Border will swear allegiance to me in our fight to rid the land of all Campbells."

"So you admit that it was you who killed the helpless and laid the blame on me."

"Aye."

"Then hand me my sword and fight one who is not helpless. I seek to clear my good name."

"Who would believe the word of a barbarian?" Gareth laughed and lifted his sword until the blade was pressing against

Brice's flesh. "Especially a dead barbarian." To his men Gareth shouted, "I will strike the first blow."

Meredith saw the flash of blade as Gareth plunged his sword. Then, as the others attacked she leaped back into her place of concealment just as Gareth strode from the room. She pressed her hand to her lips to keep from crying out. And while Gareth seemed to take forever to descend the stairs, she was forced to listen to the sound of his men's crude laughter as they continued to thrust their blades into the already fallen Highlander.

When at last Gareth was out of sight, the battle was over. Five bloodied swordsmen strode from Brice's chambers and made their way to join their leader in the dungeons. One of them carried Brice's bloody sword, which he laughingly declared to his comrades would be used by Gareth to plunge into Meredith's heart.

On trembling legs Meredith crept from the alcove and made her way to Brice's sitting room. The fur throws that lined the walls and floor were stained crimson. Against a far corner of the room lay a crumpled form.

With tears streaming down her cheeks Meredith stood over Brice's body. Blood oozed from so many different wounds, she could not count them. And when she knelt and placed a hand to his throat, he did not move. In her overwhelming grief she could not detect a pulsebeat.

At the sound of footsteps on the stairs, Meredith looked up. From the rumble of voices, there were several men. Brice's men? Or Gareth's?

Her heart nearly stopped when she heard the deep, familiar voice. Gareth. But why was he returning? What more could he do to the man who lay dead upon the floor?

Racing to Brice's bedchamber, she grabbed a dirk from the mantel. She watched as a shadow fell across the entrance to Brice's sitting chamber. The sound of footsteps ended.

With the blood pounding in her temples, Meredith crawled beneath the bed. She heard the sound of booted feet scuffling about the other room.

"Campbell is dead."

"As I knew he would be. Did I not pierce him with my sword?" The sound of Gareth MacKenzie's voice sent tremors racing along her spine.

"What of the woman?"

"Search every room."

"We have already done so."

"There was no sign of her?"

"Nay, my lord. All of the women and children were below."

There was silence. Gareth swore. "The witch must have escaped into the forest during the battle. We must find her before she makes her way back to her people."

"Surely you do not think that one lone female can survive the Highland forests?"

"We will see to it that she does not. Come. Let us fetch our dead and wounded and be done with this place."

"What will we tell the MacAlpin clan? They trusted you to return their leader to them."

Gareth paused, considering this new obstacle. "We will tell them that she has been spirited away by one of Campbell's men. I will order them to remain in the safety of their homes until my men and I can rescue her."

"But then you will not be able to blame her death on Brice Campbell."

"Even if Campbell's sword does not pierce her heart, I can still convince her people that it was his fault that their leader died. Was she not attempting to elude his grasp when she fled into the forest?"

One of the men nodded in agreement. "Will we burn the castle, my lord?"

Meredith's heart stopped. She forgot to breathe.

"Aye." Gareth's chilling words rang through the hall. "We have killed their leader. Now we will destroy his stronghold and scatter his clan. But work quickly. Let us waste no time in finding the woman."

Meredith heard the shuffle of feet and waited until she was certain they had gone. She lay under the bed and fought back the tears that threatened to choke her. She must do something. But what?

She pulled herself from her place of concealment and crawled to the other room where Brice lay. The tears that she had been fighting now spilled over, running in little rivers down her cheeks.

Brice. Her strong, angry, giant of a man was dead. She

brought her hands to either side of his face and studied his proud, handsome features.

"How wrong I have been about you. You are not some cruel savage. You are a gentle giant, surprisingly fair with me, generous with your friends."

The tears began anew, and she struggled to hold them back. "You were even right about Gareth. And I have been so wrong. Gareth is evil incarnate."

Tears streamed down her cheeks and she made no move to check them. "What a fool I have been. If I had not been prevented by fateful circumstances from marrying Desmond MacKenzie," she said, pressing her forehead to Brice's, "I would already be dead, and my land and people would be in the clutches of the cruel Gareth.

"Oh, Brice. I see now that it was because of you that I have been given a chance to discover the awful truth about the MacKenzies."

The tears came harder now, and she struggled to subdue her emotions.

She felt a tingling at her fingertips and studied Brice's face, so handsome in repose. She thought she saw a flicker of pain cross his face. Impossible. Brice was dead. And then she felt the tingling again. A pulsebeat? She touched a finger to his lips and thought she felt a slight breath. With a last flicker of hope she pressed her fingers to his throat a second time. Aye. A pulsebeat. Feeble. Thready. But a pulsebeat all the same.

Alive. Brice was alive.

With a little cry she began to cut away the blood-soaked tunic. Tears sprang to her eyes and she quickly blinked them away. There was no time for tears now. There was work to be done. She would stem the flow of blood. She would warm him, with her own body if necessary. And she would keep him alive until he was strong enough to fight his wounds.

And then, together, they would fight Gareth MacKenzie, the brute who sought to subdue her people and steal her land.

Chapter Eleven

So great was Meredith's determination to save Brice's life, she forced herself to ignore the smell of smoke that crept up the staircase and invaded his chambers.

She added a log to the fire and placed a large kettle of water to heat. While it came to a boil she cut away Brice's garments and examined his wounds.

From the courtyard below she heard the sound of men being summoned, of horses being readied for travel. The sound of Gareth's voice calling out to his men set her teeth on edge. She forced herself to shut out all sound. For now there was only this room and this man. She would not leave his side, she vowed, until she was certain he would survive.

And what of the fire that threatened? One glance at the man on the floor told her that she could never drag him to safety. She would remain here and defy even the raging flames to save his life.

She stared down at his bloodied, battered body and felt a tremor of fear. If a giant of a man like Brice could be cut down, could anyone survive?

She thought briefly about the men below who had died in this bloody battle. And about the many more who still lay wounded. What of the women and children? Had Gareth and his men terrorized them, brutalized them? Or had they simply searched among them for the one they sought and then left them? She whispered a prayer for their safety, then bent to the task at hand.

There was no time to think about whether or not Brice would be caused further pain by her ministrations. For now, she would be forced to inflict some pain in order to properly care for him.

Tearing a strip of cloth, she dipped it into the rapidly heating water. With gentle strokes she sponged the blood that oozed from Brice's shoulder. Though the wound was deep, it did not appear to be life threatening, and she breathed a sigh of relief. When the shoulder was cleansed, she tied a clean cloth around it to stem the flow of blood, then moved to the next wound.

Blood flowed freely from a gaping hole in Brice's side. The tip of a sword had pierced cleanly through, then had been brutally withdrawn, tearing the flesh in jagged shreds.

Working quickly, Meredith washed the area, then pressed several thicknesses of clean cloth against the open wound and bound it tightly. It would be important to keep this wound clean. But for now, the most important thing was to stop the excessive bleeding.

She moved on to other, less serious wounds, where sword and dirk had pierced the flesh of Brice's hand, arm and both legs. He was a mass of bloody flesh. Yet none of these wounds appeared mortal. Why was he so near death? Why the pallor, the feeble heartbeat? Something had sapped his strength. One of his wounds was carrying him to death's door.

She heard a great cry from below and recognized the voices of Brice's men and servants as they battled the fire that threatened to destroy Kinloch House. Black acrid smoke filled the air as buckets of water caused the flames to sputter and smolder.

As Meredith sponged, her hand paused in midair. She noted the dark stain that slowly spread across the fur throw beneath Brice's body. For a moment she could only stare at it in dread. Then, struggling to roll him to one side, she discovered the small deadly knife still buried between his shoulders.

"God in heaven."

She thought of her final words to him before the battle had begun and felt a shiver pass through her. "Do not turn your back on your attackers, my lord. Or you may find a MacAlpin dirk between your shoulders.''

Her gaze was riveted on the bloodstained hilt. It was little satisfaction to note that it was not a MacAlpin dirk that had gravely wounded him. It bore the mark of the MacKenzie clan.

The blade could not have pierced the heart or he would already have expired. But this wound was mortal.

There was no tenderness in her touch as she reached for the dirk. It must be removed, and the wound repaired quickly if she would save his life.

With both hands she pulled the knife cleanly from his back.

She looked up as the door to the sitting chamber was shoved roughly open. Smoke billowed inward and swirled like fog above a river. Wreathed in smoke, Angus Gordon, blood streaming from a wound to the head, stood framed in the doorway, leaning heavily upon the arm of Jamie MacDonald. Both of them were coated with soot from the raging fire they had been battling. Their hands were bloodied and raw from handling heavy buckets of water and beating out rapidly fanning flames. Their clothes were scorched. The pungent odor of burning wood clung to them.

Both of them stared at her, then at the bloody dirk in her hand.

Though he was obviously weak from loss of blood, Angus lifted his sword and faced her, his accusing eyes dark with fury, his lips a thin line of hatred.

''So. You would take your revenge even upon a dead man.''

Before she could respond, he shouted, ''Step away from Brice's body, my lady, or I will be forced to kill you where you stand.''

''You do not...''

With tears streaming down his face, Jamie rushed at her, knocking her to the floor. Once on top of her his grimy fingers locked about her throat. His young face was a twisted mask of fury.

''Was it not enough that the MacKenzies killed him?'' he sobbed. ''Did you have to stick your dirk in his back to make certain that he is dead?''

''Jamie, listen to me.''

With a cry of rage he closed his hands about her throat and

squeezed. "I heard Brice say he had never meant to kidnap you. He vowed to see that no harm came to you. And this is how you repay him. How could you? How could you?"

Though the lad was young, he was bigger than Meredith. And surprisingly strong.

"Step away from her, Jamie." Angus staggered across the room and bent a hand to the lad's shoulder. "You've no stomach for killing. Least of all a woman. I'll see to it."

"You do not—understand." As Jamie was pulled from her, Meredith gingerly touched a hand to her bruised throat and took in long, choking breaths. "Brice is not dead. I was cleansing his wounds when I discovered the dirk."

"Oh, aye. And you thought you could bury it in his back rather than toss it away." With his sword lifted, Angus hovered over her, prepared to aim for her heart.

Jamie glanced at the still form of Brice, hesitated, then turned back to her. His look of fury had turned to one of question.

"Could it be that she speaks the truth?"

"She would say anything to save her life." Angus sneered.

"Perhaps. But see for yourself if you do not believe me."

As Angus brought his sword higher to strike, Jamie fell to his knees beside Brice. He ran a finger over the clean dressings at Brice's shoulder and side. Surely no one but Meredith could have applied them. And then he saw the river of blood that gushed from the wound in Brice's back.

"She speaks the truth," he whispered.

"What?" Lowering his sword Angus fell to his knees beside the still form of his friend. In a glance he took in the clean dressings, the kettle of water. "This cannot be. I heard Gareth MacKenzie tell his men that Brice Campbell was dead."

"Aye. He thought so. As did I." Meredith sighed. "But there is a pulse. Feeble, but a sign that life still flows within him."

Angus brought his fingers to Brice's throat and held them there for several seconds. Then he turned back to Meredith, who still knelt where he had left her. In her hand was the bloody knife she had pulled from Brice's back.

"Forgive me, my lady," Angus sputtered. "I thought..."

"It matters not," Meredith interrupted. "We must stem the flow of blood at once, or it will be as Gareth MacKenzie has said. Brice Campbell will be dead."

"Tell me what to do."

Angus offered a hand to her and helped her to her feet.

She shot him a look of gratitude. "Fetch some servants. I learned from my mother how to prepare potions for healing. But we must work quickly."

"Aye."

"You're not strong enough, Angus," Jamie said. "I'll go."

The lad seemed relieved to be able to be of some use. While Angus dropped to his knees beside Meredith and stared helplessly at his old friend, Jamie rushed from the room.

Within minutes he was back, followed by several smoke-darkened figures.

Though she had not allowed herself to dwell upon the fate of the others, Meredith was so relieved to see Cara and Mistress Snow alive, she felt the sting of tears in her eyes. She blinked them away.

"Were the women and children harmed?"

"Nay, my lady," Cara said softly. Soot smudged her face and hands. "Gareth MacKenzie flew into a rage when you were not found among us. He seemed intent upon finding you. He and his men were more than happy to be done with us so that they could scour the forests for a sign of you. But what of my lord Campbell?" The young serving girl glanced across the room and fell silent at the sight of Brice's still form.

"Jamie has explained what has happened here. Tell me what you desire," Mistress Snow said gravely. "And it will be yours."

Meredith noted the charred hem of the woman's gown and the raw, blistered flesh where she had battled the flames.

"Has the fire been contained?"

"Aye, my lady."

Meredith gave a sigh of relief, then spoke quickly, listing tubers, spices and fermented malt. After that she ordered Cara to fetch more clean linens.

"Should we not move him to his bed?" Angus asked.

"I fear it would only cause his wounds to bleed more freely.

For now he will have to sleep here, before the fire. Bring me a pallet and several furs,'' she ordered Jamie.

When Mistress Snow had dispatched servants to find everything Meredith had requested, she returned. Though she struggled to keep her gaze averted from the man who knelt beside Meredith, she could not resist a quick glance at Angus's drawn features.

They had all been through hell this day. Yet they had survived. That alone was a bond that would not soon be broken.

"Is there anything else I can do, my lady?"

Meredith turned to glance at the housekeeper, then at Angus, kneeling beside her. His eyes, dull with pain, were set in an ashen face.

"Aye. You can take this man to his bed and see to his wounds."

Though the servant's face betrayed her pleasure, Angus seemed surprised. "My wounds are nothing, my lady. I cannot leave the side of my friend."

"You have been so concerned about Brice, you do not even know that you have been wounded." Meredith touched a hand to his shoulder in a gesture of kinship. "Brice will not mind that you have left him. He is in another world now. And it will be a long time before he decides whether to join his ancestors or return to us."

"Will you send for me the minute he awakens?"

If he ever awakens, Meredith thought sadly. Please, God, grant him the strength to fight this weakness. Then, brushing aside such emotional thoughts she nodded. "The very moment he is alert, you will be told."

With the help of Mistress Snow, Angus got slowly to his feet. He hesitated a moment, staring down at the woman who knelt beside Brice's still form, the woman who had been captive and was now healer.

"Forgive me, my lady, for doubting you."

"You had every right to think what you did, Angus." She gave him an encouraging smile. "I trust Brice Campbell is worthy of the love and devotion you have exhibited."

"Aye, my lady. He has more than earned my loyalty. And the loyalty of all who proclaim Brice Campbell their leader."

Meredith studied the man who would surely sacrifice his life for the one on the pallet.

"Rest now, Angus," Meredith said, as he leaned heavily on Mistress Snow's shoulder.

"If there is anything I can do, you must tell me."

She touched a hand to Brice's throat and felt the pulse that, though thin and halting, continued to beat.

"You can pray."

Meredith spread the poultice over the festering wound before covering it with fresh dressings. Then she pulled up the bed linens and sat back on her heels, studying the quiet figure on the pallet.

He was so still. So very still. As though his life was slipping away, breath by breath.

He had not moved since she had first found him. Nor had he moaned or cried out, despite the depth of pain he must be suffering.

The servants drifted into the room whenever they found time, as did all Brice's men who were able to walk. They would stay for a few minutes, studying his pale face, watching the woman who worked tirelessly beside him. On each face Meredith saw the love, the concern, for this man. It was evident in the way they studied him, with a kind of reverence, and the way they spoke, in hushed tones usually reserved for the clergy.

The light through the windows had long since faded into darkness. The only illumination in the room was the fire in the fireplace and a single candle beside a basin on a small table.

The sounds of activity in the castle had ceased. The dead had been removed to the burned-out shell of the storehouse until proper graves could be dug and the grieving families could see to their burial. The wounded had been ministered to and carried to beds and pallets.

Meredith continued mopping the sweat that beaded Brice's forehead. Her shoulders drooped in exhaustion. Her eyes blurred and she wiped a hand across them, blinking away the desire to shut them tightly.

Meredith looked up at the sound of the door being opened. Jamie crossed the room and knelt beside her. His gaze fastened hungrily upon the still form of Brice.

"You should be asleep," Meredith whispered.

"I cannot sleep."

She saw the fear lurking in his eyes. With great tenderness she brought her arm about his shoulder and drew him close. "When Brice awakens he will have you scurrying about fetching so many things you will have no time to rest. Then you will yearn for the luxury of sleep."

"Do you believe that, my lady?"

"I must," she whispered. "And so must you."

She felt the lad tremble. And then, in a burst of anguish, he cried, "I am so afraid, my lady. If I dare to fall asleep, I'm afraid Brice will slip away. And I will never have the chance to tell him how much I love him."

"Oh, Jamie." Meredith gathered him into her arms. Against his temple she whispered, "His fate is no longer in our hands. We have done all we can. But I promise you this. I will stay here beside him. And if he should need anything, anything at all, I will see that he has it."

The lad shook his head from side to side. "I am afraid to leave him."

"Then stay with him," she said softly. "Sleep here beside him."

"Here?" The boy seemed astounded by her offer. Never would he presume to sleep beside so great a man.

Meredith lifted the folded bed linens that Cara had left in case her mistress desired to rest. She would have no need of them since she would never be able to leave Brice's side this night.

Fixing a pallet beside Brice, she lifted a corner of the blanket and motioned for Jamie to climb inside.

"Brice will not mind?"

"I think he would be pleased," Meredith murmured, tucking the linens about him.

As she so often did with her younger sisters, she bent and brushed a kiss over the lad's cheek. "Sleep well, Jamie, along with Brice, in the hollow of God's hand."

The boy lay very still, absorbing the shock of her gentle kiss.

For as long as he lived he would never forget her kindness this night.

For long minutes he lay listening to the sound of Brice's shallow breathing. And though he struggled to stay awake and will life into the man who lay beside him, sleep at last overtook him.

Chapter Twelve

Brice awoke in the inferno he had always known would be his destiny. All around him drifted the acrid scent of fire and brimstone. And his own flesh felt seared beyond redemption.

So this was what it felt like to be doomed to an eternity of punishment. Pain throbbed until he writhed and twisted. And though he thought he moaned, no sound issued from his parched throat.

He knew why this punishment had been meted out to him. He had been so consigned to this penance for failing to save Meredith. In that brief moment when he had seen her in the doorway to his chambers, he had realized that if he did not succeed in fighting off MacKenzie's soldiers, all would be lost. Meredith, the innocent victim in all of this, would be forced into marriage with Gareth MacKenzie. Once married, he would claim her land and people. And once MacKenzie had what he wanted, Meredith would no longer serve a useful purpose. She would be conveniently disposed of.

That was what had distracted Brice and caused his downfall. It was the presence of Meredith there in the doorway that had made him lose his concentration. Never before had five or even ten opponents worried him. He was a warrior, born and bred for battle. His own mortality had never caused him a moment's worry. But that was before Meredith. Since meeting the fiery little beauty, everything had changed. The thought of what MacKenzie had in mind for her was more than he could bear. That moment's distraction had cost him the battle.

Now it had all come to pass. Brice felt an overwhelming sense of despair. He had lost. MacKenzie had won. Even now Meredith was no doubt standing at the altar of a small village kirk, surrounded by MacKenzie men, forced to speak vows that would seal her fate.

Brice was consigned to an eternity in hell.

The pain came again in waves, causing him to arch his body and roll to one side and then the other. There was no escaping it. The flames of hell licked across his skin and stabbed deep into his back. A fire raged inside him.

Something cool touched his face and he clutched at it, holding it to him when it would pull away. In his delirium he imagined that it was a small, delicate hand. Meredith's hand. But that was impossible. Meredith had been captured by Gareth MacKenzie. She was lost to him forever. Still he clung to the hand, needing to feel it, small and safe in his.

A voice sounded from so far away he could not make out the words. But from the soft, muted tones, from the low, husky whisper, he knew it was Meredith's voice. Calling him. Calling out to him from a lifetime away. He lifted a hand and tried to reach her, to answer her, to tell her that he was sorry he had failed her, that even now he would find a way to come for her. But his hand dropped weakly to the linens that covered him. He would rest awhile, to gather his strength so that he could plan his escape from this eternal damnation. One thought burned in his mind. He dare not rest until Meredith was safely away from MacKenzie and returned to Kinloch House. There she would be safe. There she would be loved.

Loved.

Aye. Though he would never have admitted it in life, he loved her. Loved her as he loved Jamie. Loved her more than he had thought it possible to love any woman. More than himself.

A dipper of cool water was forced between his lips. He swallowed and accepted another before turning his head away. A cool damp cloth was pressed to his forehead and he felt a moment's respite from the burning heat.

His lids flickered open and he found himself staring into green eyes the color of a Highland lake.

"Meredith."

His lips formed the word though no sound issued from his throat.

She smiled and he thought there would never again be anything as wonderful as her smile. As dazzling as the sun on a summer's afternoon. As warm and comforting as a fireplace on a cold winter's night.

A hundred questions danced through his brain, begging to be answered. How had she escaped MacKenzie's clutches? Was the attacking army still here at Kinloch House, holding her prisoner in this very room? His heart stopped. Or was she also dead? Had she been allowed this one visit before entering heaven?

Though his lips moved, the words were scrambled, making no sense. All he could manage was a weak croak.

"Rest now," she whispered, touching a hand to his cheek.

She was merely a vision, he realized. A lovely, ethereal vision.

His lids lowered. Though the fire raged on, he felt at peace. Anything could be endured, even hell, as long as he was granted an occasional glimpse of Meredith's beloved face.

"How does he fare?"

Angus tiptoed into the chamber and peered over Meredith's shoulder as she changed the dressing on Brice's back.

"He seems to slip in and out of this world," she whispered. "I fear he does not as yet comprehend where he is or who is with him."

"He is a strong man, my lady." Angus touched a hand to her shoulder and was reminded of how small, how frail, she was. Yet beneath her frailty he had witnessed enormous strength of will. Everyone in Kinloch House spoke in admiring tones of the way Lady Meredith MacAlpin tended their leader, refusing to leave his side even to take her meals. She slept curled up beside him, and ate whatever the servants brought her. And all of her waking moments were spent applying fresh poultices and changing his dressings, and seeing to his every need.

Jamie MacDonald had become her most loyal admirer. To the lad she was more than a great lady; she was a saint. He had told everyone who would listen how Meredith had encouraged him to sleep beside Brice for the first two nights, until he was convinced that his hero would not succumb if he left him. And although Jamie had now returned to his own chambers, Meredith encouraged him to drop by Brice's chambers as often as he wished in order to chart the progress Brice made.

"Brice will not easily give up his life, my lady. If he is fated to die he will not do so without putting up a fight."

She gave Angus a tentative smile. "How can you be so certain?"

"I know him, my lady. As well as I know myself. Brice is a warrior."

"Aye. And from the looks of both of you, there was great damage inflicted upon the other side. How do your wounds heal, Angus?" She glanced at the fresh dressings that bound his head, a sign of the loving care administered by Mistress Snow.

"The pain has nearly subsided. Now it only feels as if someone has buried an ax in my head."

Meredith laughed and Angus was pleased to know that he had managed to bring a smile to her lips.

What drove the lady? What caused her to stay by the side of a man who had taken her away from everything she loved? Was she suffering guilt because her own people had taken sides with the MacKenzies? Or was there some deeper emotion involved?

Angus glanced at the man who lay upon the pallet. So still. So pale. The two had been inseparable since childhood. Angus had never questioned the goodness of Brice Campbell. He had been privileged to witness Brice's kind deeds a thousand times. But this woman? What did she know of Brice and his way of life? How was it that she had, after only a glimpse into Brice's life, decided to trust him, to care for him?

"Do not fear for him. Brice will respond to your tender

ministrations, my lady. That other life that tugs at him will give up its hold over him. He will come back to us.''

Meredith gave Angus a grateful look.

At a knock on the door they both turned and watched as Mistress Snow entered, followed by a serving girl carrying a tray.

''This is the broth you ordered, my lady.'' Mistress Snow directed the servant where to set the tray, then turned to study Meredith, noting her pale features, accentuated by the dark circles that rimmed her eyes. ''If you do not soon rest you will be joining my lord Campbell in a sickbed.''

''I am fine.'' Meredith knelt and tasted the broth before nodding her approval to the servant. ''Are the wounded below stairs beginning to heal?''

''Aye, my lady.'' The housekeeper chanced a glance at Angus before adding softly, ''Though it has been a difficult task to keep some of them in bed long enough. Already some,'' she said, staring meaningfully at the man who faced her with a grin, ''are determined to begin repairs on Kinloch House before their wounds have even begun to heal.''

''I heard the sound of axes in the forest and trees being felled. I thought perhaps only necessary repairs were being made.''

''Necessary.'' Mistress Snow gave a hollow laugh. ''If Angus had his way, the castle would be as good as new before Brice had a chance to view the destruction left by the MacKenzies.''

''It will cause him pain to know that his ancestral home has been burned by Lowlanders,'' Angus said softly. ''I would spare my old friend any more suffering. And now I must go below and see to those repairs.''

When he left the room, Meredith glanced at the housekeeper, who was staring at the closed door with a look of concern. ''I know that you fear Angus is pushing himself and the others beyond their limits. But it is how a man deals with his feelings of hopelessness. With their leader cut down, and the enemy beyond their reach, they have a need to do something that is physically punishing.''

''How did a sheltered woman like yourself learn such

things?'' The housekeeper watched as Meredith dipped the spoon into the bowl of broth.

"My father was a peace-loving man. But he was also a warrior.'' Meredith held the spoon to Brice's lips and watched as he swallowed the first trickle of broth. "Each time he was forced to recover from battle wounds inflicted by the English, he quickly undertook a difficult, draining task. My mother explained that it was a necessary part of healing.''

"Your mother was a wise woman.'' Mistress Snow gave a loud sigh. "As for me, I would prefer to take Angus to bed and find a gentler way of healing.''

When she realized what she had revealed, the housekeeper blushed to the tips of her toes. "Oh, my lady. Forgive me for my lapse.''

Meredith's laughter rang through the room. "Oh, Mistress Snow. If you could but see your face.''

"I—must see to the scullery,'' the woman said, hurrying to the door to escape her humiliation. "I will send Cara to see to your needs.''

When the door closed behind her, Meredith shook her head and continued to laugh. Then, filling the spoon with more broth, she cradled Brice's head in her lap and forced a small amount of the liquid between his lips.

It was the sound of Meredith's laughter that seemed to penetrate the fog that shrouded Brice's mind. The sound trilled like the gentle warble of a bird. There was no mistaking it. It was truly the beautiful Meredith, come once more to visit him in this place of misery.

He felt his head being lifted gently, as it was placed upon her lap. He inhaled the steaming broth as the spoon was placed to his lips. He tasted its delicate flavor as the liquid slid down his throat, warming, soothing. His parched throat was eased and he gratefully accepted a second spoonful.

From beneath slightly open lids he watched as she cradled his head in her lap and bent over him, intent upon her task. Her hair swirled forward, the silken strands brushing his hand. As she dipped the spoon once more in the bowl, she leaned forward slightly. He felt the imprint of her breasts and experienced a rush of heat that left him flushed and weak.

Now it was no longer the fragrance of the broth that filled his senses. It was the clean delicate fragrance of pine and wildflowers that seemed to surround her. He inhaled, filling himself with her scent, wishing he could fill himself with her.

She brought the spoon to his lips and he opened his mouth, accepting the broth. When he swallowed, the warm liquid snaked through his veins, giving him precious strength.

Again and again she fed him, grateful that he no longer fought her. It was the first time he had willingly accepted nourishment. When at last, unable to take more, he pushed her hand away, she glanced down and realized that he was watching her.

The spoon dropped from her hand, clattering to the floor. It lay there forgotten.

"Oh, Brice. At last you are awake."

"Am I?" On his face was a dreamy half smile. "I was afraid you were a ghostly specter, my lady."

"I am no ghost."

He glanced around, trying to focus his blurred vision. "Where are we?"

"In your sitting chamber at Kinloch House."

"Truly?"

"Aye. Truly." She laughed and laid his head back against a pillow of fur.

He wanted to tell her that he preferred to have his head in her lap. But it was proving difficult to keep his thoughts from scattering. And even more difficult to put them into words.

After a prolonged silence he murmured, "I dreamed I was in hell. And there were flames all about me."

"There was a fire. Gareth MacKenzie ordered his men to set torches to your home. But after the invading army left, your people were able to put out the flames."

"And you." Brice lifted a hand to her cheek. Even that small effort cost him. But it was worth it to satisfy himself that she was truly here and not just a vision. "I feared that MacKenzie had spirited you away and had forced you to wed him."

"Nay, my lord. I hid myself from view. Had I been braver

I would have faced him with naught but my dirk. But like a coward I hid beneath your bed until he and his men were gone.''

"You? A coward?" At her words he wanted to laugh, but his throat was too raw. He lay there letting strong new emotions wash over him.

"And I have been here with you since. Even though I feared I had lost you.'' She felt tears fill her eyes and spill over onto her cheeks, but she made no effort to wipe them. Instead she cupped his beloved face in her hands and studied him through the filmy haze. "Oh, Brice. I am so relieved that you have come back to the land of the living.''

"Are you? Did you miss me?"

When she merely nodded he felt his heart soar to the heavens. "Maybe that is what saved me. Knowing that it was you I was coming back to.'' He caught her hands and held them in a death grip. "Do not leave me, little firebrand. Promise me that when I again awaken you will be here.''

She would promise him anything at this moment. Anything. "I will not leave you, Brice.''

His lids flickered, then closed. The hands holding hers slid down and dropped heavily against the linens. His breathing became soft and easy.

For endless minutes Meredith merely knelt beside him and watched as he slept.

Alive. Brice was alive. Truly alive. And for the first time since he had sustained his mortal wound in battle, she was convinced that he would not only survive but return to his former strength.

Suddenly she was exhausted beyond belief. The rush of energy she had experienced when he had first spoken was now slipping from her. All the long days and nights of nursing Brice through his ordeal were now beginning to take their toll. Her limbs were heavy. She felt light-headed. Her eyes yearned to close. She was drained. Drained of all strength. Drained of all thought.

With a sigh that welled up from deep within her Meredith curled up beside him and joined him in sleep.

Chapter Thirteen

Brice lay very still, fighting a wave of pain. His shoulder throbbed. His side ached. And something that resembled a flaming torch pierced his upper back.

He tried to roll over but there was a heaviness in his right arm and for one breathless moment he thought it might have been severed in the battle. His eyes snapped open and relief flooded through him as he gazed in wonder at the figure curled up alongside him.

Meredith lay facing him, her head pillowed on his arm, her hands resting lightly at his chest. Her hair spilled across the linens, a dark splash of color against stark white. Her breathing was slow, steady.

In these few moments before she awoke he took the time to study her. When had this fierce little woman taken over his life? How had she come to mean so much to him?

His men, on their frequent visits to his chambers, had relayed how she had ignored the threat of fire to stay with him, how she had stood up to Angus and Jamie when they had suspected her of aiding in his murder. Even the servants never seemed to tire of praising the way Meredith had protected him as fiercely as any she wolf during his recovery.

He had kidnapped her only as an act of defiance against the MacKenzies. It had been his intention to use her to flush out Gareth, and then to return her to her own people.

But now? Now he could not imagine being without her. Her

presence filled these rooms, his home, his very life. And though he knew that her heart lay in the Lowlands, he yearned to change her mind.

If she returned his feelings, he reasoned, she would choose to stay here with him always.

If he truly cared for her, a little voice within him whispered, he would want only her happiness.

He did not love her. He could not. She was a lady, born and bred for the gentle life. And he was a Highlander, a barbarian.

But he did love her.

Love. Why was it never simple?

He had not meant to love her. And surely a woman like Meredith MacAlpin could never love the man who had stolen her freedom.

Meredith's lids flickered, then opened. For a moment she was strangely disoriented. The eyes staring back at her were dark, narrowed in thought.

Brice watched as the last clouds of sleep were blinked away and reality set in.

Brice. She had fallen asleep practically in his arms. And though she was fully clothed, he had little more than a strip of cloth for modesty. As she realized where she was, Meredith pushed herself away from him and sat up.

He studied the flush that colored her cheeks, and noted the guarded look that came into her eyes. Wonder of wonders. This same bold woman who had stripped him of his clothes and tended to his wounds with all the skill and care of the queen's physician, was now suddenly shy with him. Her reaction was oddly appealing.

Her hair fell in a tangle of curls and she dragged a hand through, pushing it away from her face.

"How do you feel this morning?" She tried not to stare at the dark mat of hair that covered his chest, or at the corded muscles of his arms and shoulders. For days he had been a mortal wound to be healed; today he was much more. Today he was a man.

"Like any man who just awoke with a beautiful woman in his arms."

"I did not mean to... I had not intended..."

"Meredith." He chuckled, low and deep in his throat, and reached out a hand to her chin, forcing her to meet his dark gaze. "It brings me comfort to know that, despite my grave wounds, my manhood is still intact."

Her face flamed. Scrambling to her feet she retorted, "I will see about some food. You have grown extremely weak in the days you have been recovering."

"I feel far from weak at this moment. And it is not food I crave."

She turned at the door. Arching a brow she shot him a haughty look. "I will speak to Mistress Snow about sending a Highland wench to see to your needs. There may be an old crone about the place who will not find you too offensive."

As she flounced from the room Brice lay back and gave in to a roar of laughter. The woman had fire. It was one of the many things he loved about her.

"Where are you off to?" Brice lay weakly against the cushions and watched as Meredith drew a warm cape over her gown.

"I ride with Angus to view the repairs being done to the homes nearby."

He nodded, oddly pleased that Meredith would take such an interest in the fate of his people. When she left in a flurry of cloak and bonnet he lay back and closed his eyes, annoyed at the weakness that kept him from taking charge as he had always done.

Angus had told him about Meredith's many kindnesses to the Highlanders who had been made homeless by Gareth MacKenzie's invaders. While the men repaired the burned-out cottages, the women and children had been made comfortable in Kinloch House. Meredith had given Mistress Snow permission to use whatever was left in the burned-out storehouse to see that everyone was given enough food and clothing. The refectory had become an open kitchen to all.

Brice lay back, listening to the sounds of activity. The forest rang with axes felling trees for new cottages. Below stairs was the bleat of a newborn babe. In the courtyard the women called to one another as they hung their clothes to dry. The halls resounded with the barking of the hounds as they romped with the children who seemed to fill every room. The sound of their joyous laughter was everywhere.

Because of Meredith's kind concern, his people shared his home, his food, his supplies, until they could once again see to their own needs.

Meredith had taken this cold ancient castle and had filled it with love and laughter. She thought it a simple feat. He found it amazing. Home. She had made his house a home.

Meredith's frequent forays into the forest were always a source of amazement to her. Every Highlander had a story about Brice Campbell. And every one of them was eager to share the story with Meredith.

"When I lost my husband in battle," Mistress Snow said, riding along beside Meredith, "the attackers began burning our cottages. I hid, along with my babe, in the forest. And when the invaders had gone, I returned to the burned-out shell that had once been my home. That is where Brice Campbell found me. Sitting on a pile of rubble, rocking my babe in my arms."

"What did he do?" Meredith asked.

"He lifted me onto his horse and brought me to Kinloch House. Everyone there was so kind. And when I was strong enough to take charge of my life once more, I realized that I would rather stay at Kinloch and see to the running of the castle than return to live alone in my cottage in the forest."

"But what of the babe?" Meredith could not recall seeing a child.

Mistress Snow's eyes misted. "The babe had been dead for days before Brice came along and found us. In my grief I could not bring myself to bury her. She was all I had left of my husband, and I knew that when I consigned her to the earth, I would be completely alone."

"Oh, Mistress Snow." Meredith caught the woman's hand and pressed it between her own. "How you must have suffered."

"Aye. It was four years ago and the pain is with me still. But," the woman said softly, "I have learned that life must be lived. And each day the pain diminishes a bit more. Because of my lord Campbell's kindness and patience, I know now that I can survive anything.''

It also explained to Meredith why, despite the fact that Angus was attracted to the housekeeper, and she obviously returned his affection, they made no move yet to wed. Mistress Snow needed time. And Angus, in his great love, understood her need.

Meredith stored Mistress Snow's story away in her heart. And when every family in the forest told of a similar experience at Brice's hand, she began to realize the depth of his goodness. She knew now why his people loved him so.

How strange, she thought, to discover so many mysteries about the man. She had believed the myth about the Highland Barbarian. If she had not been forced to learn of him for herself, she would never have discovered the wonderful, flesh-and-blood man beneath the myths.

His goodness was one more reason why she loved him so. Leaving him would be heart wrenching. Knowing that, she no longer made secret plans to escape. For now, her prison had become a haven.

''What is that damnable noise?''

Meredith looked up from the tunic she was mending.

Now that Brice's wounds were healing, he was beginning to show signs of resisting his confinement.

For days she had ordered Mistress Snow to prepare his favorite foods. She had encouraged Angus and the other men to visit Brice's chambers frequently, in order to pass the hours of inactivity. Jamie, too, spent long hours with his hero, reading from the precious books in Brice's library, telling and retelling the tales of heroics of Brice's men during the attack by the MacKenzies.

In time those same stories would be woven into the fabric of which legends were made.

But Angus and the others, having repaired the nearby cottages, were engaged in rebuilding the castle. They had little time to spend amusing their leader. And though Mistress Snow had the servants working overtime, Brice showed little interest in the special food they prepared for him.

"Your men are replacing the beams in the great room that were destroyed by fire."

"How can I be expected to rest with that pounding?"

"They are doing this for you." She bit through the thread and set aside his tunic. "They plan to have Kinloch House restored by the time the laird of the manor is up and about once more. They wanted to spare you the sight of all the destruction."

With a sigh he squirmed about his pallet. "I have remained idle long enough. The men need my direction."

"The men are doing fine under Angus's leadership."

She had no idea that her words only inflamed him further.

"Inform Mistress Snow that I wish to sleep in my own bed tonight, and not this miserable lump on the floor."

Meredith stood, obviously stung by his sharp words. "I will inform her immediately."

As she passed him, Brice caught her hand. She looked down at him and saw his look of remorse.

"Forgive me, Meredith. I have never before been a man who complained about discomfort." He sighed and ran a thumb across her wrist. Instantly her pulse leaped. "It is just that I have never before been forced to lie about while others cared for me. Though it may be the dream of many a man, it does not sit well with me."

She smiled and dropped to her knees beside him. "I know that, my lord. But I do not think you understand just how close to death you were. We feared each minute would be your last. Now that you have survived, we enjoy taking care of you. We all feared that you would not return to us from that other world that held you in its grip."

"Had I not returned, would you have grieved, my lady?"

The words were spoken lightly, but Meredith was aware of the way he watched her while she responded to his question.

"Aye. I would have grieved, as would all the others who— care for you."

Her reply gave a sudden lift to his spirits.

"Help me up, Meredith."

"You wish to walk to the window?"

"Nay." He flashed her a smile and she felt her heart stop for a moment. "I wish to go below stairs and see what causes my men to disturb my rest."

"You have not attempted the stairs yet, my lord. The effort may sap your strength."

"It is high time I tried. Give me a hand."

As Meredith leaned toward him he wrapped his arm about her shoulder and got to his feet. Though she felt the jolt at his touch, she forced herself to behave as though nothing had happened.

"Stand very still for a moment," she cautioned. "It is only natural to feel light-headed when you first stand."

"And I thought it was because of the nearness of you."

She turned her head and was aware of his wicked smile.

"Be warned, my lord, that if you tease me beyond my limits, I shall be forced to take action."

"Will you put a potion in my broth?"

She laughed. "Nay, my lord. I will simply let you go. Without me to lean on, you are as helpless as a bairn."

"You would be so cruel to a man who has returned from death's door?"

She shot him a sideways glance and began to walk slowly toward the doorway, with Brice clinging to her. "You will only discover the answer to that if you overstep your bounds."

At the entrance to his chambers he bowed slightly, then caught her arm once more. "I will be the model of a Scots gentleman."

"That you most certainly shall. Or you will be forced to make a very ungentlemanly appearance at the foot of the stairs. In a heap."

With a laugh he made his way down the great stone steps. leaning heavily on her strength.

The stench of charred wood still clung to the lower rooms of the castle. Along the walls the rich tapestries, many of them woven a century earlier, hung in tatters. The fur-draped settles lay in a broken heap beside the fireplace, to be burned as needed. Blackened beams crisscrossed the ceiling, while soot-covered windows blocked all but a few jagged rays of sunlight.

A dozen men, stripped to the waist, strained beneath the weight of the trunk of a giant tree that was being lifted, by a series of ropes and pulleys, to the ceiling, where it would replace a beam destroyed by fire.

When the men spotted Brice they called and shouted their greetings. Those not engaged in the effort at hand crowded around him and clapped him on the shoulder or embraced him warmly.

Angus, in charge of a work crew, shouted a few orders before hurrying forward to greet his old friend.

"We had hoped to have all of this completed before you had a chance to see the damage."

Staring about him, Brice's tone was almost reverent. "From the looks of things it is a miracle that all was not lost. How did you manage to save Kinloch House, old friend?"

"Everyone helped," Angus said modestly. "The servants worked alongside our men until they could no longer stand. I saw men beating out the flames with their bare hands. And I saw women remove their skirts and use them against the fire. But in the end, we won."

"And now you labor to restore what was destroyed."

"It is good work. It has brought all of us together for a common goal. The anger we feel toward Gareth MacKenzie drives us, feeding our energy."

Brice cast an admiring look at his old friend, then turned to where Jamie and several men were planing a second timber.

"I thought it was time the lad learned other than battle skills," Angus said quietly.

With Meredith's assistance, Brice walked closer.

Jamie gave him a wide smile. "Bowen says I will soon be able to work alone, with only a bit of assistance from him."

"Then you must be doing a fine job. Bowen is the most skilled woodsman in our company."

Jamie beamed at the praise. Though he continued working, he often looked up to watch as Brice moved about the great hall. Leaning on Meredith's arm Brice walked slowly about, stopping often to talk with the men.

When Mistress Snow announced that their meal was ready in the refectory, the men set down their tools and pulled on their tunics before following their leader from the room.

It pleased Meredith to see Brice join his men at table. Servants passed around steaming bowls of soup and freshly baked bread. Joints of mutton and breasts of pheasant rounded out the meal, along with tankards of mead and ale. Although Brice ate sparingly, he seemed to gain strength just being a part of this jovial company.

When the others finished their meal, Brice stood and leaned heavily on Meredith's arm.

"Would you like to continue to watch the men, my lord, or would you prefer the solitude of your chambers?"

"It was good to join my men once more. They have renewed my vigor." He leaned closer and murmured, "But I believe the silence of my room will not seem nearly as confining as it did earlier."

As they climbed the stairs Meredith was surprised at the strength in him. In no time he would be well enough to sit a horse and wield a sword.

She experienced a stab of momentary regret. For these long days and nights she had been given a special gift. She had been forced to watch him lie helpless, had gloried in his healing, and come to learn a great deal about the Highland Barbarian. He was a true warrior, who would not give up even when all were against him. He was a man of high moral principles, despite the legend and lies that had sprung up about him. He was a man much loved by his people. And he was a man who had come to mean a great deal to her. When he was strong enough to return her to her people, she would miss him.

That thought shocked her.

She pushed open the door to his chambers and took his arm. "I asked Mistress Snow to prepare your bed."

They crossed the sitting chamber, then entered the dimly lit sleeping chamber. A fire had been set in the fireplace. Candles had been lit in the sconces set along the wall. The snowy linens had been turned down in preparation for his return.

She eased him down until he was sitting on the edge of the bed.

"I will be in your sitting chamber, my lord. If you desire anything, you need only call to me."

"Do not leave me."

When a look of pain touched his features, she knelt before him, her brow furrowed with concern.

"You are unwell. Where does it hurt, my lord?"

"Here." He touched a hand to a spot on his chest.

"But you were not wounded there." As she reached up he caught her hand and pressed it to his heart.

"Can you feel it?" His voice was low, hushed.

"Feel what?"

"The way my heart thunders when you touch me."

"My lord…"

As she tried to pull away he caught her hand and held it, palm flat against his chest. Though he held her as tenderly as a fragile flower, she could feel the carefully controlled power in his grip.

His words were softly seductive. "You said that if I desire anything, I need only call you."

"Aye, but…"

"I desire you, Meredith. You are the first thing I see when I awake, and the last I see before I close my eyes. Even in my dreams you are there, touching me, arousing me. All these long days and nights I have wanted you. And now that I am strong enough, I want to show you how I feel."

"You must not…"

"I cannot let you go, my lady."

"I believe I have something to say about that."

"Nay." His voice was gruff. "You do not."

He pulled her firmly against him. She brought her hands to his chest as if to hold him at bay. But it was already too late. His mouth covered hers.

This was no tender kiss, no gentle brushing of mouth to mouth. With an urgency that stunned them both, Brice poured out all the longing, all the needs, that had been building inside him for so long.

What was even more shocking, Meredith returned his kiss with a passion that left them both reeling.

Where had it come from, this need, this hunger? How long had it been growing inside them?

When they should have pulled apart they continued clinging to each other, his mouth avid, seeking, her mouth hungry for more.

"I want you, Meredith. God in heaven, how I want you."

At his words she went very still. For days now, while she had hovered about his still form, praying that he would find the strength to recover from his wounds, she had known. No other man would ever mean as much to her as Brice. No other man could touch her with a single word, a single look.

But wanting someone was not enough. If she gave herself to the Highland Barbarian, she would be sullied in the eyes of every other man in Scotland.

And yet, her heart whispered, even that would no longer matter. There was no other man in all of Scotland who could ever own her heart. There was only this man. Her love for him crowded out all other thought.

She continued to kneel, trapped between his knees, while he rained kisses on her upturned face. His lips skimmed the corner of her lips, her cheek, her temple.

The need for her was an ache far worse than anything he had experienced during his long recovery. The need for this woman clawed at his insides until he was nearly mad with the pain.

He had to have her. Or die trying.

Standing, he caught her hand and brought her to her feet. With his hands on either side of her face he studied her in the glow of the candles.

"I want you, Meredith. I love you, little firebrand." His love was the one thing she could not fight.

With a little moan she offered her lips to him.

"And I love you, Brice." She moaned.

Her words, murmured inside his mouth, filled him with such emotion he could only stand and hold her while he gloried in her surrender.

And then his arms were around her, holding her so close that two heartbeats thundered as one.

Chapter Fourteen

Needs shuddered through Brice, driving him farther and farther toward the edge of madness. But the woman in his arms needed time, needed patience and care. As much care as she had shown toward him in the past days and weeks while he'd healed. He would see to her needs and bank his own.

The lips on hers were gentle now, the kiss coaxing, seductive. He longed to plunge his hands through the tangles of her hair and take her here, now, on the fur before the hearth. Instead, he forced himself to go slowly.

He sensed her fear, her hesitation. But he was certain enough for both of them.

"Don't be afraid, love," he murmured against her cheek. "Think of it as a journey. A slow, easy journey we will travel together."

His lips skimmed her face, pausing to trace the gentle curve of her brow. How beautiful she was; how perfectly formed. He ran light kisses over her closed lids, then followed her cheek to the corner of her lips. With his tongue he traced the outline of her lips until she moaned and her lips parted for him.

With his tongue he explored the intimate recesses of her mouth, savoring all the sweet, wild flavors that were hers alone. And all the while his hands moved along her back, drawing her closer, then closer still, until she was pressed firmly against him.

She was aware of his arousal; aware, too, of the thundering of his heart. Its unsteady rhythm matched her own.

How long had she dreamed of being held like this, of being taken on a wild flight to the heavens and beyond? As his lips held her enthralled she flew high, then higher still, until she felt herself break free of earth. Now she was soaring, now gliding.

As his fingers reached for the buttons of her gown she struggled to settle her feet on steady ground. But then his lips grazed her throat and she was helpless once more, held powerless by the sensations that ripped through her.

Her gown drifted to the floor about her feet and lay forgotten. Now the only barrier between them was a thin ivory chemise. With deft movements he untied the ribbons of her garment and slid it from her shoulders.

For long moments he studied her. The sight of her beauty left him breathless. In the light of the fire her skin was as white as alabaster, her eyes as green and shimmering as a Highland glen. With a sense of reverence he ran his fingertips lightly across the slope of her shoulders. She quivered beneath his gentle touch. With a sigh he brought his lips to her throat. Arching her neck she moved in his arms and thrilled to the sensations that skittered along her spine.

Never, never had she known such feelings.

He brought his lips lower to the soft swell of her breast. As his mouth closed over her nipple she heard a low, guttural moan. Hers? Or his? It no longer mattered. They were caught up in such waves of passion they could no longer think, only feel.

Her knees trembled and she feared she could no longer stand. It was as if he was in perfect harmony to all her senses. In one swift movement Brice scooped her up into his arms and carried her to the bed, settling her among the snowy linens. His clothes joined hers on the floor and he lay beside her, gathering her into his arms.

His hands, his lips, moved over her, leaving her body a mass of nerve endings.

The heat between them rose up in shimmering waves. A weakness seemed to invade her, leaving her limbs heavy, her mind blank. She drifted on clouds of sensation that sapped her strength, stole her will.

She was helpless, caught up in feelings that she had never even known existed. She was once again kidnapped and held hostage. This time to passion.

As his hands and mouth worked their magic, she moved in his arms, loving the feel of his work-worn fingertips against her soft flesh. How agile his mouth. How clever his hands.

She longed to touch him as he was touching her. And yet, in her fear and innocence, she was afraid. Would he think her a wicked, wanton woman?

Tentatively she reached a hand to his cheek. He moved against her palm slowly and she saw his eyes narrow fractionally.

Growing bolder she brought her hand to his chest and allowed her fingers to skim along the mat of hair. His nipples hardened as her fingers grazed them and she lingered, stroking until she heard his sigh of pleasure.

As her fingers moved lower she encountered a series of raised scars on his flat abdomen.

At her arched look he murmured, "So many old battles. So many old wounds."

Without thinking she pressed her lips to the flat plane of his stomach, tracing her lips across the scars. "I cannot bear to think of you being wounded."

Instantly she felt his stomach muscles contract violently. She experienced a wild thrill at the realization that it was her touch that had caused such a reaction.

She had the power to make this strong warrior flinch. One touch of her hand could leave him as weak as she had been just moments ago. Drunk with her new power she grew even bolder, pressing her lips to his throat while her hands roamed his muscular shoulders, his hair-roughened chest, his stomach.

His chuckle of delight turned into a moan of impatience as her hands moved lower, exploring, arousing.

"Witch."

He rolled on top of her and began an exploration of his own, allowing his lips, his fingertips, to move seductively over her until she writhed and moaned and gasped his name. It took all of his willpower to keep from taking her. This was her first time, he cautioned himself. He wanted it to be everything and more.

"I love you, little firebrand," he growled against her lips.

His fingers found her, moist and ready, and before she could realize what was happening, he took her to the first shuddering crest.

"And I want you more than I have ever wanted anyone, anything."

Her breath was coming so fast she could hardly get the words out. But her hands clutched at his shoulders as she felt herself tumbling out of control. Madness. She had slipped over the edge of madness.

"Oh, Brice. I—love—you." The words were breathy, barely coherent. She arched her body to meet him, needing him with an urgency that matched his. "Please. I—want you."

Her plea ripped through him, shattering his careful control. He slipped inside her, struggling to be gentle. But the moment they came together, he threw caution to the wind. With a savageness that surprised him she moved with him, matching his rhythm, mirroring his strength, until together they gave in to the madness and soared to the moon.

He was enveloped in the scent of wildflowers, and he recalled that she'd had wildflowers entwined in her hair that first day he'd seen her at the altar of the cathedral. Their fragrance filled him until all he could smell was Meredith lying in a meadow of wildflowers.

Higher they climbed, then higher still, until they reached the velvet heavens. A wild, primitive cry was torn from Brice's lips. And a million stars exploded and shattered into shiny silver fragments.

In that moment she gave him her heart. Her honor. Her innocence.

They lay, still locked together, unwilling to break the fragile, intimate contact. Levering himself on his elbows Brice studied the way she looked, her face damp with sheen, her eyes moist.

"Tears, firebrand? God in heaven." With his thumbs he wiped the tears from her cheeks. "I've hurt you."

"Nay." She turned her head to hide her weakness. "It was just—so wonderful."

He rolled to his side and drew her gently into the circle of his arms. "Aye. It was beautiful." He pressed his lips to her eyes and tasted her salty tears. "And it is perfectly natural to cry at something so dazzlingly beautiful."

"You do not think me a foolish child?"

"Nothing you do or say would seem foolish to me. And," he added with a tender smile, "you are far from a child. You are the most beautiful, desirable woman I have ever met."

She sniffed. "More beautiful than the women you met at the Court in France?"

He bit back a laugh at her artless attempt to be reassured. "No woman at Court could match your beauty, my lady, including the queen herself."

"Her ladies-in-waiting thought I resembled Queen Mary."

He caught a strand of her hair and watched as it sifted through his fingers, catching and reflecting the light of the fire. "Your coloring, perhaps. And the fact that you are both small and slender. But you are a rare beauty, Meredith. And far more lovely than our queen."

She grew silent for a moment, gathering her courage for the next question. With a swallow she asked haltingly, "Is it always like this?"

"Loving?"

She seemed relieved that he understood. "Aye."

With his index finger he traced the line of her brow, the curve of her cheek. His voice was low with feeling. "I fear that many people are never blessed with what we have just discovered."

"Why?"

His finger moved over her lips, still swollen from his kisses. Though it seemed impossible, his desire for this beguiling, bewitching creature was beginning to build once again. "They are afraid to give themselves completely to another."

"What is it they fear?"

"Losing control, I suppose. Or perhaps it is the fear of letting another witness their needs, their weaknesses."

"Have you any weaknesses, my lord?" she asked with a smile.

"I have discovered one." His tone was grave, although his lips curved into a hint of a smile. "One very beautiful, very obstinate firebrand that can make me weak with a single touch."

"Like this?" With her finger she traced a pattern across his chest, then lower to his stomach.

He felt the heat as he became aroused. Before he could reach for her she surprised him by rolling on top of him.

Her hair swirled about him, tickling his chest, brushing over his fingers. Her eyes burned brightly, reflecting the light of the fire. She smiled as she began to move over him. Every touch, every movement, aroused him further.

"Firebrand, I am a man still recovering from battle wounds. You will be the death of me."

"Then I shall simply have to leave you alone to rest and recover."

As she made a move to roll away he caught her and dragged her against him. His hands, his lips, began weaving their magic.

Against her throat he growled, "You are the only medicine I need. Stay with me, firebrand. Love me."

With murmured words of endearment they slipped into a world of endless delight. A world where only lovers can go.

Meredith lay in the midnight blackness and listened to Brice's steady, even breathing.

Did he know what he had given her? Did he have any idea how much she'd needed his quiet strength, his calm assurance of his love?

So much had happened in her young life. So much chaos. The murder of her father. Desmond's shocking death at the altar. Her kidnapping.

There had been little time for reflection. Certainly no time for love. Until now.

Brice's arms tightened about her and she felt a quiver of apprehension at the strength in him. Did he have any idea what power he wielded? It was not physical power she feared. Despite his strength, she would have found a way to escape him in time. The power he wielded was emotional. She needed his approval, desired his love forever. Without this Highland warrior, her life would be as before. Empty. Waiting. Yearning for something she could not even give a name to. Until now. Love. That was what she had been waiting a lifetime to share.

With a sigh Brice drew her close and pressed his lips to her temple. She sighed and snuggled close, then was startled by his deep voice.

"Awake again, firebrand?"

"Aye. This is all so new to me. So exciting. I fear I will never be able to sleep."

"Nor I." He nibbled the corner of her lips until she turned her head and gave him full access to her mouth.

His lips were warm and firm and with one easy movement he drew her fully into the kiss.

"Oh, Brice," she breathed against his mouth. "Will you some day grow weary of me and tire of our lovemaking?"

He chuckled, low and deep in his throat, and the sound sent tremors along her spine. "Never, my lady. It would take an eternity and beyond to even dim the love that shines within me for you."

She relaxed against him and lost herself in the kiss.

"But I have a better way to prove my love," he muttered, shifting until he hovered over her. "Far better than words."

Brice lay very still, unwilling to disturb the woman who slept so peacefully in his arms.

All night they had loved, slept, then loved again until they were sated. And still he had not had enough of her. Nothing would ever be enough. A hundred times. A thousand years. He loved her. Body and soul. Completely.

He thought of the beautiful young woman he had watched from the tower of the cathedral. Clothed all in white, her spine rigid, her head held high. Even then he had sensed the strength in her, the determination. And when he had first looked into her eyes he had read the goodness there.

He dared not lose. He wanted the love they shared to be sanctified and blessed by the kirk. He wanted the entire country to know that the Highland Barbarian was loved by this beautiful Lowlands woman. He wanted to shout of their love from the highest mountain.

He glanced at Meredith and saw the slight flicker of her eyes. Sleep was leaving her now. Within moments she would awaken. His woman.

The decision was made instantly. He would send a messenger to the Lowlands to learn the fate of her people. He would wed her now, as soon as it was possible to prepare a wedding feast. And then, with the might of his Highland warriors behind her, she would return triumphant to her people. With the combined strength of her armies and his, Gareth MacKenzie would not dare to continue his litany of murder and lies.

They could bring a renewed sense of peace between the Highlanders and Lowlanders. Perhaps, because of their love, the Scots lairds could cease their endless fighting and join forces to combat their true foe, the English invaders.

Meredith's eyes opened and she found Brice watching her. On his face was a smile of such contentment, she answered with a smile of her own.

"You look rather pleased this morn, my lord."

"Aye. How could I be less than pleased with the woman I love lying in my arms?"

She sighed and drew her arms around his neck. "I feared I would awake and discover it was all a dream."

"It was no dream, my love," he murmured against her lips. "Nor is this."

His kiss was hot, hungry. His lips persuasive. And because he had spent the night learning all the secret, intimate places of her body, he was able to arouse her instantly.

"If it be a dream," she breathed inside his mouth, "pray do not wake me till it is over."

Chapter Fifteen

Locked in the arms of her love, Meredith drifted on a cloud of contentment. For days now they had closeted themselves in Brice's chambers, leaving their private haven only occasionally to inspect the work being done on the great hall.

Though everyone at Kinloch House, servants and soldiers alike, whispered about the lovers, Brice and Meredith remained blissfully unaware of anything except each other. Wrapped in a safe cocoon of love, it mattered not to them that they were the object of much speculation.

When Mistress Snow realized what was happening, she instructed the servants to respect the privacy of the laird of the manor and his lady. Their meals were announced, then set up quickly in the sitting chamber. Fires were laid, tapers lit in sconces, linens replaced with as much haste as possible.

Even Angus conspired to keep young Jamie so busy with the carpentry work that the lad had almost no time to visit with Brice and Meredith. Or to disturb their bliss.

Through it all the young couple was so absorbed in their newly discovered love for each other, they never noticed what went on around them.

In the great hall Brice moved among his men, stopping often to admire the work being done. In the doorway Meredith paused to watch. It was so good to see Brice move without the stiffness that had marked his movements immediately after the battle with the MacKenzies. At last his health was completely restored. His full strength had returned.

At the clatter of arriving horses in the courtyard she turned and made her way to the door. Alston, the red-bearded warrior who had long fought beside Brice, dismounted and handed over his mount to a stable boy before striding across the courtyard.

Glancing at the lathered steed Meredith remarked, "You have ridden far, Alston."

"Aye, my lady." He shook the dust from his plumed hat and paused. "I come from the Lowlands."

Home. The thought was poignant, fleeting. She quickly dismissed it.

"Was there a reason you rode so far from your Highlands?"

"Brice set for me the task of gathering information about the MacAlpins and the MacKenzies, my lady."

She was oddly touched by Brice's concern. "And how do my people fare without me?"

"They continue to be plagued by night riders and highwaymen who steal their sheep and cattle, and even murder those unfortunate enough to be out after dark."

Her smile faded. "And Gareth MacKenzie?"

He seemed to hesitate for a fraction before saying softly, "Gareth MacKenzie rides to Holyroodhouse to have the queen declare you dead."

"Dead!" Her eyes widened in shock. "But why would he do such a thing?"

"Since you have not been seen, he and his men are convinced that you perished in the Highland forests." His voice softened when he saw the pain that crossed her features. "By declaring you officially dead, your next of kin will become the leader of your people."

"My next of kin."

Alston stepped past her with a bow. "My pardon, my lady. I must report my findings to Brice."

As he strode down the long hall, Meredith suddenly leaned against the heavy door as the realization sank in. Her next of kin was her sister, sixteen-year-old Brenna. Sweet, shy Brenna. She would be no match against the charms of Gareth MacKenzie. He would convince her, as he had once convinced

Meredith, that they must combine their land and forces if they would stand against the unseen Highland monsters who attacked in the night. The MacAlpins, old Duncan and his wife Mary, as well as all the others, would be so weary of the killings, they would urge poor Brenna to accept Gareth's offer and unite their people against a common enemy. And once wed, Gareth would claim Brenna's land and easily dispose of her, should she prove to be a burden.

And what of the youngest, Megan? Impulsive, headstrong Megan. Would the same fate befall her in time?

Meredith felt a sense of horror and revulsion. She shivered and realized that her hands were as cold as ice. While she was safely ensconced in the Highlands, secure in Brice's love, her little sisters were in grave peril.

Her first thought was to run tearfully to Brice and plead with him to go to their assistance. Then she recalled the extreme hatred Gareth nurtured for Brice. For now, Brice was safe only because Gareth thought him dead. As long as Brice stayed in his Highland forest, he could not be harmed.

The same was true for her. But there was a difference. This was her personal battle. She could not possibly stay here, safe and warm, while her family was in grave dan ger.She must show herself to her people. And she must unmask Gareth MacKenzie as the lying murderer she knew him to be.

The MacAlpins would rally round her. Though it would be a bloody battle, they were warriors. Had they not held back the English invaders along the Border for centuries?

The decision was made instantly, with no thought to her own peril. She would return to the Lowlands. She would assemble her people. They would drive Gareth MacKenzie from their land and wrest back control of their own destinies.

With quick strides she hurried to Brice's chambers. Before he returned from his inspection of the great hall, she had much to prepare.

Brice was in a festive mood. The work in the great hall was moving swiftly. In no time it would be restored to its former elegance. Even now, as the charred beams were replaced, and the windows scrubbed of smoke and soot, carpenters labored to make new settles, tables and chairs. Hunters returned with animal hides to replace the ones that had gone up in smoke. And although many of the tapestries had been burned beyond repair, the women of the clan had already begun work on new ones, depicting the Campbell ancestors, their victories, their lineage. These new ones, Mistress Snow had informed him, would also include his own life history, and any wife and children to follow.

So they knew, he thought with a smile. The entire household knew that he and Meredith were lovers. And if the household staff knew, and his men knew, then the entire clan, sequestered in the surrounding forests, had been informed as well.

That thought pleased him. He wanted everyone to know that he loved Meredith MacAlpin. He wanted his friends to rejoice with him. And as soon as the work on the great hall was completed, they would join him in a feast to celebrate his marriage to the beautiful Meredith.

He was also pleased by the news Alston had brought this day. If Gareth MacKenzie believed that Meredith was dead, she would be safe from any further attempts on her life. At least, he reasoned, until such time as she proved to the Low-landers that she was indeed alive. It would take time for Gareth to travel to Holyroodhouse and seek an audience with the queen. By that time Brice and Meredith would be wed. To-gether they would lead his men to the Lowlands to secure Meredith's birthright. By the sheer numbers of MacAlpin and Campbell soldiers, they would thwart any further attempt by Gareth MacKenzie to take by force what was not his.

Peace. Love. Brice had never dared hope that either would be experienced in his lifetime. And now both were within his grasp.

He gave Mistress Snow his request for a very special meal, then made his way to his chambers. Tonight, if the time proved right, he would reveal his plans to her. And he would ask her hand in marriage.

Meredith looked up from the wardrobe. On her cheeks were two bright spots of color. When she saw him she gave a little cry and ran to his arms.

The kiss she gave him sent his pulse rate soaring.

"Firebrand," he murmured against her lips. "Have you missed me so much?"

"Aye."

He marveled at the way she clung to him, as if they had been apart for days instead of mere hours.

Leading him to a long covered bench pulled up in front of the fire, she curled up beside him, still clinging to him as if to a lifeline.

"Do you know how much I love you?"

"Not nearly as much as I love you, my lady. I would die for you," he murmured against her temple.

Instantly she touched a finger to his lips to silence him. "Never say that again. I do not wish you dead, my lord. Not even for me."

"But what good would it do to live if you were not here to live with me?"

"You are important to your people," she said, pulling away slightly. "So many people depend upon you. You have a duty to be here for them."

"And so I shall, little firebrand." He pulled her into his arms and rained kisses across her forehead. "We shall both be here for them." He kissed the tip of her nose. "And we will spend our days having wee bairns and taking them for picnics in the forest." He pressed a kiss to her lips.

His words tormented her. She allowed herself to savor the kiss for long moments before whispering, "Such a lovely dream, my lord."

"It is no dream. We shall live it. We shall have it all."

"Oh, Brice. If only it could be." With tears burning her eyes she wound her arms around his neck and clung to him, burying her face against his throat.

"Trust me," he murmured against her temple. "There is so much I want to tell you. So much I want to share with you."

"Hush, my lord." She blinked away the tears and drew his face down for her kiss. "Not now. I cannot bear to hear mere words. Show me."

With a tenderness he had never known before, he lifted her in his arms and set her on the fur throw spread before the fire.

As he reached for the buttons of her gown, she caught his hand and stared up into his eyes.

"I want you to know this," she said, her voice trembling with emotion. "No matter what happens, I love you, Brice Campbell. For all time. And wherever I am, you are there with me."

He was moved, as much by the intensity of her words as the words themselves. Though this serious little woman often made him laugh, there was now no hint of laughter in his words.

"And I love you, little one. I will love you for a lifetime and beyond."

Bathed in the glow of the fire, they lost themselves in the wonder of their love. Brice marveled at the depth of her passion. Never before had she shown her love so intensely. Never had their love burned brighter, or ignited such fire between them.

Meredith looked down at the sleeping form of her love. It took all her willpower to keep from crying. She must not weep. She must be strong, not only for Brice, but for her sisters who needed her.

"Please understand," she whispered as she scrawled a message on a parchment scroll and set it on a table near the bed.

From his wardrobe she withdrew the things she had prepared earlier. Shedding her delicately embroidered night shift, she pulled on a pair of Brice's breeches, tucking them into tall boots. Over the saffron shirt, a symbol of the Highlander, and dark tunic, she secured a heavy cape. At her waist dangled a sword. Tucked into her waistband was a small, sharp dirk. She tucked her hair beneath a plumed hat and draped a fur throw over her arm. In a small pouch she had stuffed the remains of their supper.

She paused beside Brice's bed and cast a last loving glance at him as he slept. He had whispered love words to her all the while they had savored Mistress Snow's wonderful meal. And while they had sipped wine, he had smiled and hinted that he had important plans to share with her. Plans that would change both their lives.

How she loved him. How she would miss him in the days and weeks to come.

But her home beckoned her. Her clan needed her. She had no choice.

In the doorway to the sitting chamber she paused and peered through the dim light. No one stirred. Satisfied, she closed the door and strode quickly down the stairs.

She avoided the courtyard, choosing instead to leave by a rear door in the scullery. Crossing around to the stables, she chose a great black stallion. Ignoring the sidesaddles, she tossed a man's saddle over the animal's back and rolled and tied the fur behind it.

Because she knew Brice's men patrolled the paths leading to the castle, she led the horse through brambles and dense undergrowth. When she was certain she was far enough away to ride undetected, she pulled herself into the saddle and spurred her mount on. By the time Brice awoke and alerted his men to what she had done, she promised herself, she would be miles away.

Brice drifted on a misty cloud, half awake, half asleep.

What a beautiful night he and Meredith had shared. What a wonderful surprise she was. That fiery, innocent lass he had brought to Kinloch House was a constant delight. Each time he peeled away a layer he discovered an even more exciting creature beneath.

The child in her brought out all his fierce protective instincts. The imp in her made him laugh. The woman in her made him ache.

He rolled to his side and reached for her. He had been too distracted last night by her beauty, by her almost desperate lovemaking, to share his plans with her. Today he would officially ask for her hand in marriage. And then, when she accepted, he would tell her of his plans for their future.

The rest of the bed was empty.

From beneath half-closed lids he noted that the sun was already streaming through the windows. Why did she have to be up and about when he was feeling lazy, and more than a little eager to hold her, to love her as he had last night?

With a sigh he moved to her side of the bed and breathed in her fragrance. Within minutes she would return, mayhaps with a tray laden with Mistress Snow's warm biscuits. They would have a lazy morning of lovemaking, and then he would take her into his confidence.

The bed was cold where she had lain.

Suddenly alarmed, Brice sat up and looked around. The fire had long ago burned to ashes. No one had tended it. Few remains of their supper lay on a tray near the fireplace.

Meredith's night shift lay on the floor. In the open wardrobe her gowns could be seen, hanging neatly on pegs beside his tunics. None of the gowns appeared to be missing.

Crossing the room Brice lifted her night shift. It was unlike Meredith to leave it there. Draping it over his arm he turned and spotted the scroll. In quick strides he walked to the small table and read the message.

Dearest Brice, I go to my sisters who need me. You must not follow. Gareth thinks you dead. Your secret is safe with me. Know always that I love you. M.

A cry of anguish was torn from Brice's lips. Slumping on the edge of the bed he buried his face in Meredith's night shift. It still bore her scent. Inhaling deeply he sat there for long minutes filling himself with her.

Then he stood and tossed the garment aside. There was no time to waste. She was somewhere deep in the Highland forests. There were many dangers out there. Not all of them wild animals.

He must find her before the wrong people did. Or she would be lost to him forever.

Chapter Sixteen

It had been raining steadily for hours. The raindrops filtered through the leaves of the trees, drenching horse and rider as they plodded through the forest.

Across a ridge of the mountain a mist rose up, eerie, ghostlike. Almost hidden below the mist Meredith recognized a lake they had crossed on her journey to Brice's fortress. At least she was heading in the right direction, she consoled herself. But if the weather continued to work against her, the journey would take twice as long as she had anticipated.

On a high rocky crag she brought her mount to a halt and turned to study the trail she had just taken. There was no sign that anyone was following her. Still, she felt a tingling sensation at the back of her neck, as though someone was watching. Brice? Though the day was shrouded in darkness, she guessed that Brice would have awakened less than an hour ago. It would be impossible for him to have come this far in so short a time. Also, she had implored him in her note to stay where he was safe. She prayed that he would listen to the voice of reason and remain in the safety of his Highland home.

If Brice was watching, he would show himself. She felt a tremor of fear and looked over her shoulder. If she was truly being watched, it was not Brice, but a stranger. The thought brought a quick, jolting rush of fear in the pit of her stomach.

She drew the hood of the cloak over her head and tried to shake off the feeling of gloom. She was merely lonely, she consoled herself. She had never dreamed she would feel so lonely. All her life, growing up with loving parents, she and her sisters had known only love and security. And hard work. Growing up in a clan of warriors along the Border, she had been groomed in the art of battle. She knew what it was to take up a sword at a moment's notice when the English soldiers attacked.

Her gentle mother had encouraged all her daughters in the art of nurturing their people. And when they engaged in battle, the entire MacAlpin clan was taken into the manor house for safekeeping until the battle was over. The families, along with their animals, stayed within the compound until it was safe to return to their outlying homes. Always they had stood together, a proud, strong family.

Now, with her parents gone and her sisters' lives in grave peril, the burden of responsibility lay with her alone. Though she felt equal to the task, she sorely missed her parents' quiet strength.

"If only Brice could share this burden with me." To stave off loneliness she talked to her horse.

Why was she torturing herself with such thoughts? Venting her frustration, she nudged her mount with more energy than necessary, sensing its reluctance to plod onward through the mist. But her mind would not give her any rest.

"How did it come to pass that one Highland warrior could mean so much to me? When did I stop thinking only of myself and begin thinking of the two of us as one? When did I begin to put his well-being ahead of my own?"

The horse whinnied in response. Despite her discomfort she smiled.

"It had happened long before we came together in love," she whispered.

During her earliest days of captivity she had discovered that the man who held her hostage was not the man she had thought him to be. The cruel barbarian was a myth, created by legend and the acts of those who would besmirch his good name.

Rain pelted her face and ran in little rivers from her eyelashes to her cheeks. She blinked as she thought of her own father, known throughout Scotland as a fair and honorable man. That thought brought a sense of pride to her. What if someone had blamed him for the acts of another, sullying his good name? Her hand tightened on the cold leather reins. She would search to the ends of the earth for those responsible, and she would give her life if necessary to clear her father's name.

Though she detested war, she realized that Brice had that same right. Gareth MacKenzie must be made to recant his lies and restore Brice's good name to him. Even if it took a war to force his hand. The thought caused her to tremble.

As horse and rider plunged deeper into the forest the tingling began anew. Someone—or something—was watching her. Although the trail was treacherous she dug in her heels and urged her horse into a trot. As the rain-shrouded branches closed in around her she pushed away all thoughts of fear. She was being foolish. How could anyone find her in this dense forest?

Like any true warrior, Brice often had to face down his fears. He had always known that he had as much chance to survive as his opponent.

This time it was different. It was not his life hanging in the balance, but Meredith's. The thought left him terrified.

His first moments of panic had been replaced with rage. Wild, seething rage. He tore through the castle shouting orders at Angus and the others, sending all the inhabitants of Kinloch House and the surrounding forest into a frenzy of activity.

Within an hour the men had prepared their battle gear and were saddling their horses in the courtyard. Mistress Snow and the servants had prepared enough food to allow them to ride without stopping for several days. After that the men should be safely back in the Highlands. If not, they would be forced to hunt for their food.

"What is our plan?" Angus worked feverishly beside Brice, saddling his mount.

"I have none."

"No plan?" Angus turned to study his friend. Always Brice Campbell had been the cool warrior, prepared for any event during battle. But this was a new Brice, a Brice Campbell paralyzed by love.

Brice's first wild, frenzied feelings were now carefully banked. But beneath the icy calm Angus sensed a slow, simmering rage. A rage that still clouded his thinking. The man was spoiling for a fight. Woe to any enemy who crossed his path this day.

"We ride until we find Meredith." Brice pulled himself into the saddle and glanced around at the dozen or so men who followed suit. They were skilled warriors who had ridden at his side in countless battles. He could count on them to come through for him. And this time, more than ever, he would depend on them. "We will ride on to the Borders and rescue Meredith MacAlpin's sisters from MacKenzie's clutches. And we will bring them all back to the Highlands, where they will remain safe."

"That sounds simple enough," Alston shouted, fighting to subdue a headstrong mount.

"Aye."

As Brice led the way into the forest, his mind was awhirl. So simple that it must be flawed. But at the moment he could think of nothing except Meredith. Sweet, beautiful Meredith. Would that God keep his woman safe until she was back in his arms.

Hunched inside the warm woolen cloak, Meredith searched for a familiar landmark. Though she possessed a keen sense of direction, she had ridden this trail only once. And then much of it had been traversed in the dark.

For hours the feeling persisted that she was being followed. But though Meredith stopped often and scanned the surrounding woods, she saw no trace of another human. Had not her mother often accused her of having a vivid imagination? Though at the time it had seemed a blessing, she now realized it was a curse. She was conjuring up dangers where there were none.

From a nearby wood a bird called, its shrill tone piercing the silence. Her hand flew to the dirk at her waist and she peered about, prepared to do battle. When the bird lifted off from the tree and soared heavenward, Meredith wiped her damp hands on her breeches and felt a wild rush of relief.

Moments later she heard the rustle of leaves as a deer, frightened by her appearance, darted behind a boulder. For long minutes her heart pounded in her chest. She swallowed and, calling herself a timid fool, turned her mount toward a ridge of rock to the east.

The rain had finally stopped, although the ground remained moist and spongy. Meredith allowed her mount to pick its path along the trail, trusting the animal's instincts more than her own. Several times the horse stumbled, but each time managed to regain its footing within seconds.

At last they reached the top of the ridge. Stiff from her long hours in the saddle, Meredith slid to the ground. Grasping the animal's reins she led the stallion to the edge of the ravine and peered below. At the sight, she caught her breath.

The spires of trees gently lifted their limbs to the heavens as if in prayer. But hidden beneath their soft thick canopy, she knew, the mountainous trail below her was a maze of winding rivers and steep mountain crags.

There would be no rest if she were to reach flat land by nightfall. The trail below her was every bit as treacherous as the one she had already traveled.

For a moment she pressed her hands to her back to ease her cramped muscles. Then, tossing the reins over the horse's head, she wearily prepared to pull herself back into the saddle.

A strong, muscled arm closed around her throat, pulling her off balance. As she was about to scream a hand closed over her mouth, cutting off her words.

A voice she recognized sent a ripple of terror through her veins. The voice, unmistakably Holden Mackay's, trembled with the excitement of the hunt.

"So, my lady. How convenient of you to leave the safety of the Campbell's bed and come to me. It seems we will have time after all to finish what we started at Kinloch House."

How could she have forgotten this most mortal of all enemies? She cursed herself for her carelessness. The concern for her sisters had erased all reasonable thought.

She pried at his offending hands but could not budge them.

With a laugh he tightened his grip on her throat until dark spots danced before her eyes.

In desperation she gripped the hilt of the sword at her waist. With the pressure at her throat it took all of her strength to pull the sword from the scabbard. But when the blade flashed dully her attacker took a step back, releasing her.

She sucked in several long scalding breaths before turning to face him. "Had I a sword at Kinloch House, Mackay, I would have killed you then."

Though he was startled, he threw back his head and laughed. "Do you think yourself a match for me, my lady?" He laughed again. "Remember, woman, I am a Highland warrior. I was born by the sword."

"Then prepare to die by it as well," Meredith called, lifting the point of her sword to his heart.

He leaped aside, surprised by her boldness. He had expected her to weep and to plead for her life. He had not expected her to fight him.

He reached for his own sword and drew it out. As the blade danced through the air, she lunged, pressed and dodged, with all the skill of a trained swordsman.

Holden Mackay wiped a hand across his forehead to erase the sheen of sweat. His own skill was not with the thin sword designed for thrusting, but with the heavier broadsword. It was unheard of that a woman could best a man at any warlike skill. It was just that she had managed to catch him by surprise, he told himself.

With his sword pointed at her heart he lunged. She stepped aside and brought her sword up, catching him in the shoulder. A scarlet stain bubbled to the surface and spilled across his cloak.

He swore viciously and lunged again. This time he almost caught her, but at the last moment she ducked, bringing the point of her sword singing past his temple.

His eyes narrowed. She was good. Very good. And he was being made to look a fool.

Again he lifted his sword and again she dodged the tip of his blade and watched as the blow meant for her fell harmlessly against the branches of a low bush.

"The forest should fear you, Mackay," she taunted him

with a laugh. "With your wild parrying you may cut down a valuable tree."

"It is you I will cut down to size. When I finish with you, wench, you will wish you had never been born."

Meredith didn't bother to respond. With agile steps she backed him against the trunk of a gnarled old tree and brought the tip of her sword to his throat.

"Those are the last words you will ever speak."

"I think not." A smile slowly spread across his features, giving him the sinister look of a deadly snake. He pressed a hand tightly to his wounded shoulder but blood quickly oozed through his fingers, dripping onto the damp earth and staining the rocks at his feet. "You will hand over your sword to my men who stand behind you or they will cut you up in little pieces and feed you to the wild animals that roam these mountains."

"Do you think me foolish enough to turn away from you for even one moment? I know your little trick. You think to render me defenseless while I am distracted."

His smile grew. "Take the lady's sword."

Meredith felt a hand at her shoulder and turned, prepared to do battle with another. Half a dozen men faced her, swords drawn. From the looks on their faces she knew that they would have no qualms about killing her where she stood.

From behind came Holden Mackay's evil laughter. "Drop your sword or my men will run you through."

He watched as her sword slipped from her fingers and dropped on the moist ground.

"Now, my lady, I believe we have a score to settle." To his men he shouted, "Bind her and toss her over my saddle. The lady is mine." He leaned close. His breath was hot on her cheek as he gave a hollow laugh and added for her ears alone, "To do with as I please."

Brice and his men rode in single file along the path worn into the earth by Meredith's mount. When it was raining it had been an easy job to trail her. Now that the rain had stopped, he prayed they would find her before the earth dried up and the trail was lost.

None of the men spoke, and though they were weary, not one of them complained of the long hours in the saddle. They knew how much their leader loved the woman they searched for. They would travel to hell and back for Brice Campbell.

As they topped a ridge Brice suddenly reined in his mount and slid to the ground.

"There were men and horses here." Brice pointed to the churned up earth. "And there was a scuffle."

He walked several paces before stooping. He touched a finger to the small footprint imbedded in the soil. "No man's foot could leave so small a mark."

Angus swallowed, reluctant to agree.

"Do you recognize the horses' marks?" Though Brice studied the other prints, his gaze kept returning to the small print that he knew had been made by Meredith's booted foot.

Angus called to Alston, and together the two men went over every mark on the ground. While they did, Brice walked about, careful not to obliterate any of the prints.

"They were Highlanders," Alston called out. "Six or seven of them."

"They rode from a northerly direction," Angus called. "And when they left, they headed north again."

"Mackays," Alston said softly.

Brice felt as if a dagger had been plunged into his heart. Holden Mackay. In his mind he could still see the scene in his chambers, when Mackay had nearly succeeded in taking Meredith by force. He thought of the bruises he had seen on her throat, and the fear he had read in her eyes.

Angus swallowed, aware of the pain Brice would be enduring at this moment. All the fear, all the rage, at last had a focus. "It had to be the Mackays," he said in a near whisper.

They stood and began to walk to where the others waited with their horses.

"God in heaven."

At Brice's exclamation, Angus and Alston hurried to his side. Brice was kneeling near the trunk of a gnarled old tree. At the base lay a discarded sword. His sword, which had been missing along with his clothes and stallion.

He brushed his hand over the damp earth, over the small boulders at the base of the tree.

"Blood."

Angus and Alston looked at each other before Angus said softly, "Aye. 'Tis blood. But we cannot be certain it was the lass's."

"And we cannot be certain it is not." Brice pulled himself into the saddle. His face was a grim mask. "By all that is holy I swear that if Holden Mackay harms her in any way he is a dead man."

He turned to his men. "We ride north. To confront the devil himself."

Chapter Seventeen

Meredith fought back a wave of panic as she was forced to ride, hands tied, astride Mackay's horse.

It had been humiliating enough to be bound and lifted like a sack of grain. But to be held firmly in his arms, his hands brushing the undersides of her breasts while his horse broke into a trot, was almost more than she could bear. She had to swallow back a rush of nausea.

She must not give in to the panic that threatened to reduce her to weeping and hysteria. It was exactly what this monster would want. Instead, she must appear calm, no matter what he said or did.

His men fell into line behind him, their spirits high. Their little foray into the forests this day had brought them an unexpected bonus. For weeks, since their leader had returned from Brice Campbell's castle, he had been brooding and sullen. Now, with the discovery of this lass, he had come alive again. It was obvious that there was a simmering feud between these two. And though the men had no idea what had occurred earlier, Holden Mackay now had someone on whom he could focus his anger.

When the skies once again opened up, Meredith hunched deep into her cloak. But the cold seemed to seep through to her very bones. It was not only because of the weather, she realized. It was because she was already replaying in her mind the scene in Brice's chambers, when Holden Mackay had come dangerously close to taking her by force. She knew what awaited her at the end of this journey, and though she tried, she could not blot it from her mind.

They rode for nearly three hours, often leaving well-worn paths to plunge into the dense forest. There was little said between the men now, but Meredith sensed that they passed signals among themselves. Could there be someone on their trail? Or did they take these evasive routes routinely to avoid running into anyone along the path?

She thought about shouting for help. But who could hear her in the forest? And to invite Mackay's wrath was to invite pain. It would probably please him to have an excuse to silence her with as much force as possible.

With the surefooted ease of horses heading home, the animals picked their way across a swirling river. Meredith studied the depth of the water, nearly to the horses' bellies. If she managed to break free of Holden's grip, how far and fast could she swim before being caught? Worse, could she swim with her hands bound? Or would she risk being sucked beneath the swirling waters? At the moment, drowning seemed a better fate than the one contemplated by her captor.

As if reading her mind Holden Mackay tightened his grip at her waist and gave a low grunt of laughter.

"Thinking of slipping through my clutches, my lady?" He bent toward her, his voice sending chills along her spine. "My men would spear you like a fish by the time you hit the water."

"At least my death would be quick."

"Aye. But far less satisfying for me."

A tremor passed through her. She bit back the words that threatened to spill from her lips. Now was not the time to goad him. She would wait. And watch. And listen.

Up ahead through the mist loomed the Mackay fortress. Though not as graceful or elegant as Brice's, it was every bit as well fortified. Built into the side of a rocky crag, there was only one way in or out. Its massive twin doors were surrounded by a courtyard. On either side of the doors stood armed guards, their swords at the ready. They saluted their leader as the door was thrown open and servants hurried out to assist the tired men.

The servants did not seem surprised by the presence of an unknown woman, and Meredith found herself wondering whether Holden Mackay often brought other unfortunate females to his fortress.

A sullen-looking woman stepped forward. Her dull gaze, Meredith noted, remained downcast, as though afraid to look directly at her master. How many beatings had she endured at the hands of this man?

"Shall I take the woman to your chambers, my lord?"

"Nay. No one touches the female. She will go with me."

He lifted Meredith effortlessly from the horse and set her on her feet. And though she swayed a moment he made no effort to steady her. Catching her bound hands he led her roughly across the courtyard and up great stone steps to the upper floor. He paused outside a door and threw back a heavy timber that barred it. Opening the door he revealed a small windowless room.

Thrusting her inside he set a taper in a sconce along the wall and growled, "You will stay here until I am ready for you."

She saw the smile that gave him a cruel, feral look. He withdrew a dirk from his waistband and advanced toward her, watching her eyes.

Meredith noted the blood that still oozed from his shoulder. Did he intend to retaliate for the wound she had inflicted? She thought of the dirk at her own waistband. In close hand-to-hand combat, Mackay would have the advantage. He was twice her size and weight. And she had already tasted his strength.

He saw the flicker of fear in her eyes as he moved closer. But though she was bound to be afraid of him, she lifted her chin in a defiant gesture and faced him boldly.

Damn the woman! Why did she not beg, or at least flinch?

He stood before her, the blade of the dirk glinting in the candlelight. Without a word he caught her hands and brought the knife cleanly through the rope that bound them.

Though she felt a rush of relief at his gesture, she prayed that no emotion showed on her face.

"If you are wise you will sleep. For you shall have little of that tonight."

He turned away and strode across the room.

She watched as the door closed. She heard the timber being thrown into place. And with her ear to the door she listened as Mackay's footsteps receded.

She began an immediate search of the chamber. Apparently it had been a storage room of sorts. Though it contained several pallets and mounds of furs, there was little else. The room was cold. There was no fireplace. And except for the door, which was bolted by a heavy timber, there was no other way out.

Wrapping herself in several layers of fur, Meredith fell upon a pallet to fight off the chill that rattled her teeth. Despite her best intentions, she gave in to an overpowering weariness and slept.

Brice rode at the head of his line of men, setting a brisk pace. Though tree limbs snagged at his sleeves and raked his face, he could not slow down. One thought drummed through his mind. Meredith. His beautiful, beloved Meredith was now in the hands of a brute. A brute who would take delight in causing her pain and humiliation.

"We must not take a direct route to Mackay's fortress," Angus advised.

"And why not? We know who has Meredith."

"Aye, old friend. But has it not occurred to you that Mackay might expect you to follow?"

"I will follow. To the ends of the earth and back to rescue my woman."

"It is what Mackay hopes for. Then he will have it all. Meredith to abuse, and you to kill when you attack him in a blind rage."

"What would you have me do?" Brice slowed his mount as they approached a boulder-strewn ridge. "Leave Meredith to that monster?"

"Nay." Angus put a hand on his friend's shoulder. "All of us know what you are suffering. If it were Mistress Snow who found herself in the clutches of Mackay, I would move heaven and earth to save her."

Brice shot a look at his friend. It was more of an admission than Angus had ever volunteered before.

"But I would hope that you and the others would keep me from doing something foolish."

Brice took a long breath, then nudged his horse into a brisk walk. "How then do you propose to keep me from doing something foolish, old friend?"

"While we ride north we must come up with a plan. 'Twould do no good to ride blindly into a trap."

Brice nodded. "I will think on it."

Angus smiled. "Think with your head, Brice, not with your heart."

Meredith heard the sound of the heavy timber being scraped back. She sat up, instantly alert. The door was pulled open. Holden Mackay strode into the room. He wore clean, dry clothes. At his shoulder was a fresh dressing covering the wound Meredith had inflicted with her sword.

Mackay was followed by a figure in a dark hooded cloak. Upon closer inspection Meredith realized the figure was a woman. A short, stooped woman.

Her cloak was damp, which indicated that she did not live within the walls of this fortress. She had been brought from somewhere outside Mackay's home.

"Well? Is she not a prize?" Holden Mackay's voice bounced about the small room. The stench of ale clung to him.

"I cannot tell, with all those clothes."

"Soon enough you will see her without them." Mackay grasped Meredith's arm and hauled her toward the open doorway. "Come. We will retire to my chambers."

Meredith was led down a long hallway and into a cavernous room. Several servants moved about, stoking the fire in the great stone fireplace, setting out an assortment of beautiful gowns on a fur-covered bed. At Mackay's command the servants hurried from the room and closed the door behind them.

Meredith stared at the huge basin of water in front of the fireplace, then at the array of gowns spread out on the bed. At her arched look, Mackay gave her an evil leer.

"You are here to amuse me, Meredith MacAlpin. I want

you to look like a lady when I take you. Not," he added, pointing at her breeches and tunic, "like some muddy stable boy."

"Rowena," he said to the stooped woman. "You will bathe the lady and wash her hair in scented water."

"Aye, my lord." The woman tossed aside her cape and walked toward Meredith.

"Do not touch me," Meredith said sharply. "I am capable of undressing myself."

Instantly the woman paused and glanced at Mackay, awaiting his orders.

"We are not barbarians here." His voice was low with seething anger. "I can give you everything that Brice Campbell gave you. Especially servants to assist you. You would not know it to look at her, but Rowena was once an assistant to royalty."

Meredith studied the woman. Despite her crooked spine there was a look of elegance about her. And the gown she wore beneath the damp cloak was expertly tailored.

What would it hurt to allow her to assist? Meredith wondered. It would certainly buy some time. She was away from that horrid storage room and into a room with doors and windows that afforded some means of escape. That was a first step. But she needed time to formulate a plan.

While Mackay crossed the room Meredith took a moment to peer about. There were two windows, which apparently led to balconies. A possible means of escape. Unless the guards were still posted below in the courtyard.

Mackay peered at the gowns spread out on his bed. He lifted a shimmering white satin gown, encrusted with pearls, and ran his hand suggestively across the bodice. "She will wear this one," he said to Rowena.

Then to Meredith he added, "It will remind me of the bride Brice Campbell abducted from the altar. The woman who will now be my bride." He threw back his head and roared with laughter at his own joke. "At least until I tire of her."

"Surely you do not intend to watch while I undress her and bathe her?"

The laughter was gone. His voice was low and dangerous.

"And why not? I am her captor. I will do whatever pleases me."

He sat in a chair stretching his long legs out in front of him. "Remove her cloak."

The woman seemed to hesitate, then stepped forward and slipped the heavy cloak from Meredith's shoulders. It dropped to the floor.

Meredith forced herself to show no emotion as the woman reached for the tunic and removed it. Beneath the tunic Meredith was wearing one of Brice's saffron shirts.

"'Tis a man's shirt." Rowena's voice was low, cultured, reminding Meredith of the women who surrounded the queen.

"Aye. And not fit to cover a woman's body." Mackay pointed a finger. "Remove it."

Before Rowena could reach for the buttons of the shirt, Meredith stopped her. "It is a shame—" she spoke directly to the woman, ignoring Holden "—that your lord Mackay cannot be with his men in the great hall, drinking ale and sharing stories of their exciting hunt this day."

Mackay's eyes narrowed. "What game do you play with me, wench?"

"Game?" Meredith gave him an innocent smile. "I merely thought you would be more comfortable with your men than here with women, sharing women's talk."

To Rowena she said in a conspiratorial tone, "Did you know that my lord Mackay hunts humans in the forest? Female humans are his favorite game. Because most of them are helpless. Most," she said with meaning, "but not all."

Out of the corner of her eye she saw Holden Mackay rub a hand over his stiff shoulder.

"How many females have you captured in the past year, my lord?"

For one long minute Mackay could only stare at her. Then he leaped up with a look of fire in his eyes. "I need some ale." He stepped to the door, intent upon calling to a servant. From below he heard the sound of laughter drifting from the great hall, where his men were gathered before the fire.

Below stairs, his men would not make him feel foolish for having nearly been beaten by a woman. Below stairs, there was the comradeship of men who had gone to battle together and had tales of bravery to share.

As a servant stepped forward, Mackay shook his head and sent her away.

For one long minute he turned and stared at the little female who taunted him, who infuriated him. With a look of menace he hissed, "Much as I would enjoy watching you bathe and dress, I would enjoy a tankard or two with the men more." He strode to the door, then turned with a gleam of laughter in his eyes. "Besides, my lady, I will have the pleasure of undressing you myself in just a very short time. And then we shall see who is the victor and who the vanquished."

He pointed to the white gown on the bed. "Remember, woman, I want her to look like the bride Brice Campbell abducted from the altar. The bride Brice Campbell will never have for himself."

His words brought a terrible shaft of pain. But she must not let him see how easily he could hurt her.

Mackay gave a hollow laugh and turned away.

Through narrowed eyes Meredith watched as the door closed behind him. In that brief moment she had noted the guards, whose presence would make her escape more difficult. But she was not about to despair. There were still the windows. And if that attempt failed, she would find another means of escape.

As Holden Mackay's booming voice rang through the hallway, she vowed that he would never hold her in this prison of horrors.

She touched a hand to the dirk hidden at her waist. And no matter what, she would never again allow him to sully her with his touch.

Chapter Eighteen

Brice and Angus lay on their stomachs on a ridge that afforded them a view of Holden Mackay's fortress. For nearly an hour they had noted every sign of movement outside the castle.

They had watched with great interest as a horse and rider approached the courtyard. The rider, a stooped old crone in a dark, shapeless cloak, had slid from the back of the horse and had been greeted warmly by the guards. A bundle had been removed from behind the saddle. Within minutes the doors to the castle were opened to admit the rider and bundle.

While Angus continued to lie and watch, Brice got to his knees and kneaded the stiffness in his shoulders.

"I tell you the best way to attack is simply to storm the courtyard and kill the guards." Brice's tone was harsh with determination.

Angus grimaced. "The doors will be braced from within. 'Twould take a battering ram to force them open."

"Every minute we wait is another minute of agony for Meredith."

"Aye." Angus noted his friend's drooping shoulders. "Do you think I do not know? But there are only ten and two of us. There could be many more times our number within the castle walls. If we can surprise them, we have a chance. But if the guards have time to shout a warning, all is lost."

"Aye." Brice stood, running a hand through his hair. "But with every passing moment I grow desperate."

"I know."

Just then both men looked up as Alston hurried toward them. "Two riders approach."

"Are they headed for Mackay's fortress?"

"Aye, Brice. They are just below us on that ridge. See?" He pointed and the two men followed his direction.

Brice's eyes narrowed thoughtfully, then he turned to Angus and saw that he was smiling. Both men had come to the same decision.

"They are the perfect foil," Brice said. "At all cost we must intercept them before they reach the fortress."

Alston's lips curved into a smile beneath his bushy red beard. "Leave them to me."

A few moments later, as Brice and Angus watched, the two riders were suddenly knocked from their mounts. There was a brief sound of a scuffle. And then the riders' clothes were being removed.

Within a matter of minutes Brice and Angus had exchanged clothes and horses with the dead men.

"You will watch until you see us enter the doors to the fortress," Brice instructed his men. "Before the doors can be closed, you must disarm the guards and storm the castle. Else, all is lost."

"Aye. Have no fear." Alston looked around at the others who nodded and indicated their eagerness to attack. "It will be done."

Meredith stood facing Rowena. She had managed to get rid of Holden Mackay. Now the only one who stood in the way of her freedom was this hunchbacked woman. She would bide her time and watch and listen. And when the time was right...

Rowena dipped a hand in the water. "Disrobe, my lady, and I will wash your hair and see to your bath."

For the moment, Meredith decided to go along with the woman's wishes. Slipping the dirk from her waistband she buried it beneath her folded cloak, then removed her shirt and breeches, carefully folding them as well.

As she crossed the room Rowena studied her with a professional eye. "You have a lovely body, my lady. 'Twould please me to create gowns for you."

"Did you sew all these?" Meredith swept her hand to indicate the gowns that littered the bed.

"Aye. These are a sample of my wares."

"Yours is a fine talent."

Meredith saw the woman beam at her compliment. As Rowena helped her into the water and began lathering Meredith's hair she said, "I was once the royal seamstress."

"You sewed for Queen Mary?"

"Aye." The woman's tone grew dreamy. "I was but ten and three when I accompanied the infant queen to France. Because of my deformity, 'twas determined that I would never marry. So I was taught from childhood how to sew. When the queen mother, Marie de Guise, saw my work, she insisted that I would spend my life dressing her child."

"How wonderful. Did you enjoy your time in France?"

"At first. It was so gay there. There were so many balls and state dinners. I was kept so busy I hardly had time to sleep. I was given a little room filled with bolts of silks and satins and a clean bed of my own. Though it was drafty, and far from the queen and her ladies-in-waiting, it was heaven after the humble cottage I had been born in here in the Highlands."

Meredith leaned back in the water, loving the feel of the woman's strong hands against her scalp.

She had been cold, so cold, on the long journey from Kinloch House to this ancient fortress. The warmth of the bath, the fingers at her scalp, threatened to lull her into a false sense of security. She cautioned herself to stay alert to any chance at escape.

"It all sounds wonderful."

Meredith heard the note of pain that crept into Rowena's tone. "Aye. It was. For a time. But when the young queen married the dauphin, his mother, Catherine de' Medici, stated that I was an embarrassment at Court. She insisted that I be sent back to Scotland at once."

Meredith's sense of fair play overcame her earlier dislike

of this woman. "Was the queen not able to use her influence on your behalf?"

"Influence." Rowena gave a hollow laugh. "As long as Catherine de' Medici lives, there is no other influence in France save hers."

"But Queen Mary has returned from France." Meredith sat up as the woman wrapped a linen about her damp hair. "Perhaps you should entreat her to reinstate your position and once again use your talents."

Rowena toweled Meredith's hair vigorously, then picked up a cake of fragrant soap. Her tone was one of resignation. "I am a humble Highlander. The queen is surrounded by important people, her time taken up with matters of state. By now she has forgotten her childhood dressmaker. There is no way I could ever approach her."

"What of your lord Mackay? Could he not use his influence as a Highland chief to intercede with the queen?"

"My lord Mackay," Rowena said with a note of contempt, "would never act as an intermediary for one of his clan. He is a cruel leader who thinks only of his own pleasures."

"Then why do you assist him in this?"

The woman looked away, unable to meet Meredith's steady gaze. In a soft voice she whispered, "I must survive, my lady. To refuse Holden Mackay is to invite death."

Meredith fell silent for a moment. She had not given a thought to the many people who were at his mercy.

"What made him so?"

Rowena handed the soap to Meredith, then lifted a kettle of hot water from the fire. As she emptied it into the bath she said, "It is rumored that when he was born, his father, Douglas Mackay, was engaged in a terrible battle with English soldiers who had stormed their Highland fortress. One of the soldiers ran his sword through the swollen stomach of Douglas's wife, Genevieve, who was close to her birthing. Genevieve died, but a servant delivered the bloody bairn and placed it in Douglas's arms. He scarce looked at the babe before turning it over to be suckled by a village woman who had also recently given birth."

So caught up in the story was Meredith that she barely took time to appreciate the luxury of her bath. In minutes she stood and wrapped herself in the linen offered by Rowena. Seated before the fire she listened while Rowena dressed her hair and continued the tale.

"Douglas Mackay was gone for two years, locked in terrible battle with the English. When he returned, he stopped at the village and claimed his son, who was still living in the cottage of the woman who had nursed him. Father and son were never apart after that. When Douglas Mackay died, Holden Mackay became obsessed with amassing as much land and power as he could."

"But the death of his mother at the hands of the English and his own cruel birth should not be sufficient reason to be cruel to his people."

Rowena's voice lowered to a murmur, as though fearing that at any moment the object of their discussion might come through the door and overhear her words.

"There are those who say that Douglas Mackay's son was too frail to live, and that the village wench gave up her own son in order to ensure that he would be laird of the manor. Others even whisper that Douglas Mackay's son was murdered by the woman in order to place her own son in the laird's castle. Whatever the truth, she carried it to her grave. But until the day she died, Holden Mackay was devoted to her. It was she who was his adviser; she who taught him greed and avarice and spurred him on to achieve even greater wealth and power than his father before him."

Meredith was too stunned to speak. That might explain Mackay's cruelty. If he was raised from birth to lie and steal another's inheritance, he would become the kind of man who would stop at nothing to succeed.

"Why did Holden Mackay ride with Brice Campbell?" Meredith asked suddenly.

"My lord Mackay boasted that it was his intention to befriend the Highland Barbarian and discover his weaknesses. In that way, he could overthrow Brice Campbell and claim his land and titles."

"Titles?"

"Aye, my lady. Did you not know that Brice Campbell is also Earl of Kinloch? His father was held in highest esteem by King James, until he fell into disfavor just before his death.

Despite the blot on his name the queen considers Brice Campbell to be a noble man.'' Her voice lowered. ''But there are those who would disgrace him and force the queen to award his land and titles to others.''

Meredith sensed the hand of another in all this. ''Could it be that Gareth MacKenzie and Holden Mackay have joined forces in order to destroy Brice and divide his wealth between them?''

''There are many who covet the land and titles of Brice Campbell, my lady.''

Meredith was aware of the warmth in Rowena's tone when she spoke of Brice.

''Do you know my lord Campbell?''

''Oh, aye,'' Rowena said softly. ''He was one of the few at Court in France who treated me with kindness.'' Her tone betrayed her pain. ''There are many who fear those who are different. And many more who are merely offended by my appearance.''

Meredith felt a wave of compassion for this woman. If only there were some way to erase her pain.

''When Catherine de' Medici ordered me returned to Scotland, it was Brice Campbell who gallantly offered to accompany me. And when I first returned to the Highlands, Holden Mackay promised Brice Campbell that I would be taken care of as befits a royal seamstress.'' Rowena's voice hardened. ''But when Brice Campbell returned to his own castle, I was told that the only thing I would be given was the humble cottage where I was born. I have been forced to accept whatever scraps my lord Mackay tosses to me. I am no better than a beaten dog. It is the way Holden Mackay keeps all of his people obedient to his every wish.''

Meredith's earlier resolve returned. She must escape this madman. At any cost.

''Here, my lady,'' Rowena said, lifting the white gown in her hands. ''You must hurry and prepare for your laird. He will be coming for you soon.''

When the woman crossed the room, her eyes widened in surprise. In Meredith's hand was the small, deadly dirk.

''My lady...''

''Be still.'' Meredith moved closer, lifting the knife in a

menacing manner. "Put down the gown and remove your clothes."

"My..."

"Quickly."

When Rowena had removed her clothes, Meredith pointed to the white gown. "Now put it on."

"But my lady, it will never fit."

"Do it."

Meredith watched as the woman, with trembling hands, pulled the gown over her head.

"You will sit there," Meredith ordered, pointing to a bench in front of the fire.

When Rowena was seated, Meredith hurriedly pulled on her shirt, tunic and breeches, then stepped into her boots. "With your cloak to hide beneath, the guards will not stop me."

"Perhaps. But they will know that I am not you," Rowena protested.

"Aye." Meredith paused, then lifted a lacy shawl from the bed and placed it over the woman's head. With her hair covered, and the folds hiding the slight hump on her back, the guards would be fooled if they were given only a glimpse.

"Hold out your hands," Meredith commanded.

"My lady, there is no reason to tie me," Rowena said softly as Meredith tore the ribbons from her chemise to use as cord. "I would gladly take your place in order to help you escape this prison."

Her words came as a surprise.

"I thank you." Meredith looked into the woman's eyes and could read her sincerity. "But think about your own safety. If it looks as though you gave me aid or comfort, Holden Mackay would have every reason to kill you. If, however, he finds your hands tied and your mouth covered, he will believe that I overpowered you." She smiled. "As I nearly overpowered him in the forest."

The woman nodded at the wisdom of Meredith's words.

"Forgive me," Meredith whispered as she tied Rowena's hands. "And thank you for not fighting me." She smiled then, and Rowena realized how truly lovely she was. "As desperate as I am to escape Holden Mackay, I know that I could not have used this dirk on you."

"Godspeed."

"Thank you." Meredith tied a strip of cloth across Rowena's mouth, then fixed the folds of the shawl until she was satisfied that the bindings could not be seen from the doorway.

She tucked the dirk into her waistband, then bundled up the gowns that were strewn about the bed. When all was in readiness she drew the hood of the cloak about her head, took a deep breath, hunched herself over and pulled open the door.

The guards caught a glimpse of the woman, gowned in white, sitting quietly on a chair before the fire. As Meredith pulled the door shut behind her and started toward the stairs, she could hear the guards laughing and speculating about the fate of the poor wench.

With her heart pounding and her palms damp with sweat Meredith descended the stairs. Just as she reached the bottom she found herself face-to-face with Holden Mackay.

His steps were slightly unsteady as he approached her. In his hand was a tankard. He reeked of ale.

"Have you made the wench ready for me?"

"Aye, my lord."

As she began to move past him his hand snaked out, forcing her to stop. Her heartbeat began hammering so loudly in her chest she was certain he could hear it. He had seen through her disguise. She had not hunched herself over far enough. Perhaps a strand of her hair peeked out from beneath the hood. Something had given her away.

"Ten gold sovereigns," he said. "The sum we agreed upon."

"Aye." Her throat was so constricted with fear that the word came out as barely more than a croak.

She opened her palm and prayed that her hand would not tremble. He dropped the coins with hardly more than a glance, then stalked up the stairs.

It took all her willpower to keep from running. But if she was to fool the guards at the door, she must behave as Rowena would.

With halting steps she approached the huge front doors. A servant removed the bracing timber and pulled the heavy doors open. When the guards outside spotted her, one of them retrieved her horse, and even secured the bundle of gowns behind the saddle.

With the guard's assistance, Meredith pulled herself up and nudged the horse into a trot.

As she rode across the courtyard she spotted two riders approaching. Again her heart began a painful hammering in her chest. If Holden Mackay had already reached his chambers, he would discover Rowena in her place. And if he were to call out now, these two riders would seize her and return her to certain death.

She nudged her horse into a run. As she passed the two riders, she kept her face averted.

The two, intent upon their mission, barely noticed the old hunched crone who passed them in the courtyard.

Chapter Nineteen

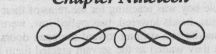

As the hunched woman approached on her horse, Brice felt a prickly feeling at the base of his neck. Something was very wrong. Something he couldn't quite place. Then, as horse and rider drew nearer, a name came into his mind.

Rowena. Of course. The young hunchbacked seamstress who had been cruelly banished by Catherine de' Medici had been from the Mackay clan. He had accompanied her from France to her home in the Highlands, where Holden Mackay had promised to see to her care. Brice felt a momentary stab of regret. He had been too busy to see if Mackay had lived up to his promise.

Rowena had always been an open, friendly woman. That would explain her warm reception by the guards in the courtyard. The soldiers, if they were a decent sort, would take the time to chat with her, assist her.

With hasty movements he pulled the plumed hat low on his head and kept his gaze downcast. If she was familiar with all the soldiers at Mackay's fortress, she might recognize that he and Angus were imposters. Worse, if she were to recognize him from their days at the French Court, she would call out his name. All their carefully laid plans would be for naught.

From the corner of his eye he watched as horse and rider galloped past. She had not even given him so much as a glance.

For another moment he continued to feel that tingling sensation, as though something was not quite right. He shrugged it off. The worst thing a warrior could do before going into battle was to allow himself to be distracted.

He and Angus approached the guards. He experienced the rush of energy he always felt just before battle. Their plan was going to work. He knew it. He felt it.

As their horses drew near, one of the guards called out to a servant inside the house, announcing their arrival. The timber bracing the doors was thrown aside and the doors swung open. Even as a stable boy was reaching for the reins of their horses, Brice and Angus, heads lowered, hats pulled low, were swinging from the saddle and striding toward the open doors.

Once inside they waited as the servant greeted them and began to close the heavy doors. A movement in the shadows of the courtyard alerted Brice and Angus that their men were in place and already overpowering the unsuspecting guards outside.

Drawing a dirk from his waist Angus held the blade to the servant's throat.

"Step away from the door," he ordered.

The wide-eyed servant obeyed.

"Where is your master?" At the man's momentary silence Brice pulled his sword from the scabbard.

The servant stammered, "My lord Mackay has gone to his chambers."

"Where?"

The servant pointed up the wide stone stairs.

"And the woman?"

The servant blinked, then stared transfixed at the sword in Brice's hand. "With my lord Mackay."

Brice's hand tightened about the sword. He would kill Mackay. With his bare hands if necessary. "And where are his men?"

"In the great hall, my lord." The servant pointed again, then trembled in fear as Brice's men poured through the open front doors.

"Go to Meredith," Angus whispered. "We will take Mackay's men."

"Aye." With his sword drawn, Brice started up the stairs.

Just then the door to the great hall opened and several of Mackay's men, obviously drunk, stumbled out. For a moment they simply stared at the dozen strangers who advanced on them. Then, with a shout, they drew their weapons.

Within minutes the rest of Mackay's men spilled through the door of the great hall and joined the battle. Though Brice longed to go to Meredith's aid, he knew that his men were greatly outnumbered.

Without a thought to his own safety, he leaped the several steps that separated them and joined in the fighting.

The air was filled with the sound of sword striking sword as every man fought for his life.

Two men advanced on Brice. With flashing blade he disarmed the first, then traded thrusts with the second soldier, backing him to the wall. As the soldier brought his arm high for the final thrust, Brice was a step quicker, and his blade pierced the man's heart. Clutching his chest the man dropped to the floor. Before Brice could catch his breath the first man, now armed with another sword, took up the fight. Again Brice was forced to defend himself.

This man was a far better swordsman than the other. It took all of Brice's skill to evade his thrusts. But at last he left the man gravely wounded.

Turning away, Brice found himself facing three more opponents. As they fought, Brice felt his energy flagging. The wounds from which he had so recently recovered had left him too drained. Had he possessed less skill with a sword, he would have joined the others who lay on the floor of the great hall, writhing and twisting in pain.

"Behind you," Brice shouted to Angus.

Angus turned to find a swordsman about to land a deadly blow. With agile steps Angus managed to evade the man's blade. With one quick thrust, the man joined his comrades who lay dead and wounded.

"My thanks, old friend." As Angus turned his head he saw two swordsmen behind Brice, about to attack while he fended off a third.

Immediately Angus leaped to Brice's aid. But even while he and Brice fought the three, he could see what a terrible effort this battle was costing his friend. Though Brice's thrusts with the sword were still straight and true, there was a sheen on his forehead and his eyes were glazed with pain.

Two men cut between them, dueling until one of them fell. The other quickly joined in the fight against Angus, and he found himself unable to worry any longer about Brice. It would take all of his concentration and skill just to stay alive.

While Brice continued fighting off the attack of two men, a tall, massive figure filled the doorway. While Brice stood, sword to sword with his opponents, he glanced up and saw Holden Mackay, his sword at the ready, a look of murderous rage in his eyes.

All feeling of weakness vanished. For Brice there was only a wild, churning hatred for this vicious monster. With a few skillful thrusts Brice disposed of his opponents and advanced upon Mackay.

"What have you done to Meredith?"

For a moment Mackay could only stare at Brice with hate-glazed eyes. Could it be that the fool did not know? His lips curled back in a sneer of contempt. "I do not answer to the likes of you, Campbell."

He raised his sword and brought the blade down with a vicious swipe, tearing open the shoulder wound that only days ago had finally mended.

With blood seeping through his tunic Brice stood his ground, exchanging thrust after thrust with Holden Mackay. And although the man was not the swordsman Brice was, he had size on his side, and the wound that was draining Brice of precious strength.

"I warned you that one day you would rue the day you banished me from your castle." Mackay advanced, again and again, until Brice felt the cold stone wall at his back. "You should not have tried to keep the woman for yourself. The spoils of war should be shared by all." He thrust his sword and watched as Brice dodged, and the blade pierced only the fabric of his tunic. He pulled his sword back and advanced again, determined to pin Brice. "Now," he said through gritted teeth, "I will have it all. Your titles, your lands and your woman."

In an unexpectedly agile move, Brice leaped aside and turned, pinning Mackay to the wall. With his sword pointed at Mackay's chest he hissed, "What are you talking about, man? What is this nonsense about titles and lands?"

Holden Mackay's eyes narrowed. "I will tell you, if you promise to let me live."

"I make you no such promise. Now," Brice said, bringing the point of the sword closer, until it pierced Mackay's tunic and shirt and drew a faint thread of blood, "tell me what nonsense you speak."

Mackay began talking quickly, as if hoping to postpone the inevitable. "Gareth MacKenzie offered to share half your land with me, and give me all your titles, if I would but penetrate your castle and discover your weaknesses."

"MacKenzie. So you have been in this with him from the beginning."

"Aye." Mackay's eyes glittered. "I have long coveted the title Earl of Kinloch."

Brice thought of his own disdain for such things. "The title was my father's. He earned it. What good would it do another?"

"It would make me a titled gentleman. I would be as acceptable at Court as you."

"All the titles in the world will not make you what you can never be, Mackay." He ignored the man's look of hatred and pressed the tip of his sword over his opponent's heart. "What has any of this to do with Meredith?"

"Nothing," Mackay snapped. "The woman was a personal prize that I decided to steal from you the way you stole her from MacKenzie."

Brice's eyes narrowed. "You knew all along that I killed the wrong MacKenzie?"

"Aye." Mackay threw back his head and laughed. "You killed the puny brother, Desmond, whose only crime was obeying his eldest brother."

Brice felt a terrible urge to plunge the sword through this monster's heart. But he cautioned himself to hold his famous temper in check. He still did not know the fate of Meredith.

"Is the lady in your chambers?" Brice asked softly.

Mackay's eyes suddenly burned with a feverish light. By the gods, the man did not know. What a wonderful irony.

"The lady is someplace where you will never find her."

"You will tell me or I will make your life a living hell." As Brice shouted, Mackay suddenly brought his hand upward, revealing the razor edge of his sword. He would have severed Brice's head had Angus not stepped in and thrust his blade through Mackay's heart.

A look of shock crossed Holden Mackay's face as he realized he had been mortally wounded. As Angus pulled back his sword, Mackay slumped to the floor. A great gush of blood spilled down Mackay's tunic, the brilliant scarlet spreading in ever-widening circles. His face grew ashen.

With a sense of horror at the turn of events, Brice knelt beside Holden Mackay and whispered, "Before it is too late, tell me what you have done with Meredith."

Mackay's lips curled into a smile. His eyes stared straight ahead. And when Brice touched a hand to the man's throat, he realized there was no pulse.

"May you burn in hell," Brice whispered.

With a growing sense of desperation he raced up the stone steps, Angus just paces behind him. In the great hall, the last of Holden Mackay's men joined his comrades in death.

Rowena sat in the middle of the floor and tasted her own blood. Dazed, she wiped a hand across her mouth and stared for long minutes at her bloodstained hand. Slowly, stiffly, she drew herself to a chair and sat, staring at the flames of the fire, seeing nothing.

The lady Meredith had been correct to tie her and cover her mouth. That alone had probably saved her life. When Holden Mackay had discovered Rowena in place of Meredith, he had demanded an explanation. Once he realized that his prize had eluded him, he had flown into a murderous rage. Never, never had Rowena seen anyone in such a fury. He had picked up a chair and hurled it against the wall where it shattered into a thousand pieces. Still not satisfied he had lifted Rowena from the chair and slapped her, beat her, pummeled her, until she begged for mercy. It was only her plea that she had been overpowered that had saved her from certain death. That, and the sound of battle below stairs. When Holden Mackay left the room to join the fighting, he had been gripped by a lust for blood.

Rowena knew that she should escape while there was yet

time. But she seemed gripped by some sort of lethargy. And so she sat, listening to the sounds of battle, staring into the flames of the fire.

That was how Brice found her.

He raced into the chamber, with Angus just a few paces behind. Both men came to an abrupt halt at the sight that greeted them. The room looked more like a battlefield than the laird of the manor's sleeping chamber.

With eyes dulled by pain Rowena glanced up. In a trembling voice she whispered, "My lord Campbell."

He was shocked at finding her here. "Rowena? Did we not pass you some hours ago outside Mackay's fortress?"

She stared in silence, not seeming to comprehend.

Seeing her shocking condition he went to her and knelt before her. He took her hands in his. They were cold. So cold. In her eyes was a glazed look, such as he had often seen in men after battle.

In a tone meant to soothe he said softly, "You are safe now, Rowena. Holden Mackay is dead."

He watched her shoulders slump as she seemed to let go of the terrible tension that had held her in its grip. A sigh rose up from deep within her.

"What has happened here? Where is the lady Meredith?"

Rowena stared into his dark eyes. He had always been so kind to her. She wanted to return the favor. But it was hard to think.

"Holden Mackay sent for me to dress the lady." She stared down at the bloodstained gown she was wearing. "He chose this gown. He said he wanted her to look like the bride you would never have."

Brice's eyes narrowed. In his jaw a little muscle began working.

"Did he touch her?" His hand curled into a fist. "Did he harm her in any way?"

She shook her head.

"You are certain?"

Rowena met his gaze, then slowly nodded.

He felt as if a band around his heart had suddenly been removed. With a rush of relief he asked softly, "Why are you wearing the gown, Rowena?"

Why indeed? She shook her head, as if to erase the pain of Holden Mackay's fists. Slowly, haltingly, her mind cleared.

"When we were alone, the lady Meredith asked me to change clothes with her. I put on her gown."

"Why?"

"So that when she opened the door, the guards outside would think that she was still seated by the fire."

"Why would they not recognize her when she opened the door?"

"The lady Meredith was disguised as me."

Brice could only stare in silence as the meaning sank in.

"The lady wore my cloak and carried my bundle of gowns."

Brice turned to Angus, who stood listening. "The old crone outside the fortress."

Angus let out a moan. "Brice, she is hours ahead of us on the trail."

"Aye." Brice glanced down at Rowena. "And this dazed, bloody creature has taken a beating for her kindness."

"Had it not been for the lady Meredith's thoughtfulness, I feel certain I would not have survived."

Brice's eyes narrowed. "Why do you say that?"

"Because the lady kindly bound my hands and covered my mouth, saying that unless Holden Mackay was convinced that I had been forced into this, he would kill me."

Brice and Angus surveyed the rubble that had once been Holden Mackay's sleeping chamber.

Brice's tone was low with wonder. "From the looks of all this, the lady made a wise decision." He turned to Angus. "Assemble the men. We ride to the Lowlands. And pray we catch up to Meredith before Gareth MacKenzie gets news of what has happened here this day."

Rowena caught Brice's hand. Her eyes brimming with tears she whispered, "Tell the lady Meredith that I send my gratitude. And my love."

Love. Brice felt a sudden shaft of fear that left his blood like ice. Love was what drove him. It was what caused him such pain.

"Pray I do not fail her," he murmured. "Or I may as well join Holden Mackay in the fires of hell."

Chapter Twenty

Meredith was hopelessly lost.

The route from Kinloch House had been difficult enough to follow. But now that she had managed to escape Mackay's fortress, she could locate no familiar landmarks. Plunging blindly through thickets and woods, she urged her mount onward, praying that eventually she would find a river or stream that would point the way homeward.

The only thought that gave her the strength to go on was the knowledge that she had persuaded Brice to remain in his Highland home where he was safe. Whenever she felt the fear begin to engulf her, she would cling to her belief that Brice was out of harm's way. She closed her eyes, trying to picture him as she had so often seen him, lounging in a chair drawn up before the fire, a tankard of ale in his hand, his men clustered about him and Jamie hanging on his every word.

She experienced such a crushing sense of loss, she felt tears mist her eyes.

As she passed beneath a low-hanging branch, it clawed at her cloak and snagged her hair. She ducked low in the saddle, then noted over her shoulder that the bundle of gowns had pried open. Bare branches suddenly bloomed with brilliant scarlet satin, rich ruby velvet and shimmering blue silk. A breeze caught the rest of the gowns, blowing them into the brush where they were caught and held by jagged stalks and thorns.

"I leave them to you, Mistress Tree." The strange sight gave her sagging spirits a lift. "May you look fetching for years to come."

The sound of her own voice startled her. She had been alone on the trail too long.

Spotting an open area just ahead, she dug in her heels and urged her horse into a run.

Night had long ago fallen and still Meredith continued on. The land had gentled, from steep rocky crags to rolling hills. Though she was not yet asleep, she was no longer alert. The whir and chirp of night creatures and the steady even gait of her mount lulled her until her head bobbed.

When the horse came to the banks of a river, he lowered his head and drank. The sound startled Meredith. She was instantly awake.

For long minutes she merely stared at the narrow ribbon of water glistening in the moonlight. Then she let out a cry of pure delight. Wonder of wonders. They were standing on the banks of the river Tweed. It meandered through gently rolling countryside. Looming in the distance were the Cheviot Hills. Beyond that, England. And there, on the opposite shore of the river, its many turrets shimmering in the silvery moonlight, stood MacAlpin Castle.

Home. There were so many times when she had thought she would never see it again. Now that she was so near, the tears would not stop flowing.

She slid from the saddle and knelt on the bank of the river, drinking her fill. Removing her cloak, she folded it carefully. Then, pulling herself once more into the saddle, she urged her mount into the shallows. Soon the water was deep, and the horse began to swim, while Meredith gamely held on. By the time they had crossed to the far shore, both horse and rider were shivering from the frigid waters. She bundled herself into the cloak and, bending low over the horse's neck, urged him into a trot. The night air danced through her hair as her horse's hooves ate up the final miles.

How Meredith longed to cross the courtyard at breakneck speed and toss the reins to a stable boy as she had done hundreds of times in her young life. How she yearned to hear old

Bancroft, the aging doorkeeper, announce her to those assembled. How desperately she desired to throw herself into the outstretched arms of her sisters and hug them to her. But all that must wait.

First she must ascertain that Gareth MacKenzie and his men had not already taken over MacAlpin Castle, hoping to ensnare her in a trap.

Leaving her horse in a stand of trees, she crept toward the rear tower of the castle. Shivering as she crouched behind a row of shrubbery, she studied the darkened windows of the upper floor.

Meredith and her sisters had often horrified their mother by climbing to the upper balconies. They knew every stone, every indentation, along the wall. Now such childhood games would stand her in good stead. Tossing aside her cloak she reached up until she located the jagged edge of a stone with her fingertips. Pulling herself up, she probed with the toe of her boot until she found a foothold. Stretching, she found another rough stone and pulled herself up farther. Again and again she repeated the process until she had reached the upper balcony of her old room. With her last ounce of strength she pulled herself over the edge of the balcony and slumped to the floor, taking in great gulps of air.

As her breathing grew more steady she paused to listen. There was no sound of movement within her old rooms. Crossing the balcony she stepped into the sitting chamber. The room was cold. No fire had been set in the fireplace.

She crossed the room quickly and listened at the door before throwing it open and striding quickly down the hall. She passed several doors before pausing to listen once again.

She pushed open a door and stepped inside. In the sitting chamber a fire crackled invitingly. From the sleeping chamber beyond she could see the movement of shadows. Someone was preparing for sleep.

She crept silently across the room and peered through the open doorway. When she was certain that the persons inside were friendly, she stepped into the light.

Meredith drank in the sight of the slender young woman with coal-black hair that fell in waves to below her waist. Her blue-violet eyes widened for a moment. Then Brenna was racing to her, arms outstretched.

"Meredith. Oh, Meredith."

The two young women fell into each other's arms, laughing and crying.

"They told us you were dead."

"You can see for yourself that I am not."

"Oh. Let me look at you." Brenna held her older sister at arm's length, then drew her close again, trying to swallow the lump that seemed stuck in her throat. "You are so cold. And wet."

"Aye to both. My horse and I swam the river."

"Here." Brenna began removing Meredith's wet clothes, then wrapped her in an ermine-lined cape.

Across the room an old woman stared at Meredith as if seeing a ghost. When at last she was able to gather her wits about her she hurried across the room and began fussing with the cape.

"Ye'll catch the death. Out of those wet boots now."

"Morna." Meredith caught the old woman's hands and held them when she tried to pull away. "There's no need to fuss."

"But I…" Her old nurse found that she could not go on. With tears streaming down her wrinkled cheeks she drew the girl into her arms and clung to her.

"Oh, lass. I thought I'd never see you again."

"There now, Morna. You see, I'm fine. Just fine." Meredith patted her shoulder, then held her a little away.

Brenna, watching the reunion between Meredith and their old nurse, whispered, "I must tell Megan."

Meredith caught her arm and held her when she tried to turn away. In low tones she said, "Only Megan. You must tell no one else that I am here."

Brenna studied her sister for a moment, then nodded. "I will tell no one."

Within minutes Brenna had returned with their youngest sister. At ten and four Megan was already as tall as Meredith and still growing. Her hair the color of ripe wheat and gold-flecked eyes in a small oval face promised a rare beauty when she grew to womanhood.

She pulled her arm free of Brenna's grasp and stamped her foot. "What is it you cannot tell me?"

"This." Brenna stood aside and allowed the youngest to peer into her sleeping chamber.

Megan's eyes grew round before filling with tears. In quick strides she was across the room, locked in her sister's embrace.

"Oh, Meredith. We thought you dead."

"Aye. I have heard the rumors of my death. Though I must confess there were many times when I thought they would be true."

"Why must you keep your presence here a secret?"

"I am here to unmask Gareth MacKenzie as a liar."

Megan turned to stare at sixteen-year-old Brenna, who looked stricken.

Seeing her shock and pain Meredith placed an arm about her sister's shoulders. "What is it, Brenna? What have I said to cause such pain?"

"Gareth has been—courting me." Brenna thought of the uneasy hours she had been forced to spend in the company of Gareth MacKenzie. "Thankfully I have never been alone with him. Old Morna saw to that," Brenna said with a smile. Her smile suddenly faded. "Gareth has already sought the approval of the clan to wed me when he returns from Edinburgh."

"He is not here then?"

"Nay."

At her words, Meredith felt a wave of relief. At least for now she was safe.

"He left only yesterday with a large party of MacKenzie men to seek an audience with the queen. He intends to ask Her Majesty to declare you dead."

"And to declare you the next of kin." Meredith stroked her sister's hair before asking, "Do you love Gareth MacKenzie?"

"Love him?" Brenna trembled and Meredith drew her close. Against her cheek the young woman murmured, "I do not love Gareth. I fear him. But Duncan and the others urged me to accept his offer of marriage in order to secure our borders."

"They said Brenna could do no less than you, Meredith, if she were truly the MacAlpin." Megan's tawny eyes flashed. "We knew that you did not love Desmond. Yet you agreed to wed him for the sake of the clan."

"Aye. Poor Duncan," Meredith said softly. "He was so certain that Gareth would be as good as his word. He is like all

the others. Fooled by Gareth's charm, and unable to see what
he really is."

"Enough about Gareth MacKenzie. How did you manage to
escape from the Highland Barbarian?" Megan asked.

Meredith suddenly realized how much had happened since
her abduction at the altar. Her own sisters did not even know
about the man who had stolen her heart.

"Come," Meredith said, catching Megan's hand. "Find me
a night shift. We will all climb into Brenna's big bed and whisper and giggle as we did when we were children. I will tell you
everything."

"I will go below stairs and fetch some biscuits. I've heard
those Highlanders eat raw meat." Morna studied the slender
girl and added, "It's a wonder you haven't faded away in that
barbaric place."

Meredith laughed at her old nurse's words. But as Morna
started for the door, Meredith's words stopped her. "Not a word
that I am here."

"Not even to Bancroft?"

"Nay. Not even to him. For a little while longer no one must
know that I am still alive. Do you understand?"

"Aye."

Morna put her hand on the door but Meredith again stopped
her. With the beginnings of a smile she added, "Bring meat
and cheese as well. And mayhaps a goblet of ale."

"Ale?" Brenna turned to study her sister.

Meredith laughed. "Aye. Ale. I have learned to like the taste
of it. Besides it will warm me."

"I will fetch a night shift," Megan called.

"Hurry back. There is much to tell."

Already the horrors of the past months were slipping from
her. How good it was to be home. What a joy to be able to
share with her sisters all that had happened since last they were
together.

"And he loves you, too?"

"Aye."

"It is all so romantic." Brenna sighed.

"But I do not understand," Megan interrupted. "He is a Highlander. A barbarian. And you are the MacAlpin."

"He is an educated, cultured gentleman," Meredith said. "And a trusted friend of the queen."

"If Brice Campbell loves you, why did he let you come alone to clear his good name?"

"Because now that everyone thinks him dead, he will no longer be hunted. If he shows himself, he will once again have to fear for his life."

"But he is the Highland Barbarian," Megan persisted. "He is the strongest, bravest man alive. All my life I have heard songs sung about him, legends whispered about him. If he is so fearless, why would he be afraid to be hunted?"

Meredith was growing weary of her sisters' questions. Brenna had wanted to know everything, from the moment she had been abducted at the altar, to the moment she climbed the wall of the MacAlpin Castle. Megan, on the other hand, was only interested in the reasons why.

"Do you think he will come for you?" Brenna asked, stifling a yawn.

"Nay." Meredith was annoyed to feel tears spring to her eyes. She tried to blink them away but they continued until they clouded her vision. "I begged him to stay where he would be safe."

"But if he loved you he would care more about your safety than his own."

Megan turned to study her oldest sister. "Are you crying?" In consternation she turned to the middle sister. "Brenna, I have never before seen Meredith cry."

Brenna, the most tenderhearted of the three, shot her youngest sister a warning look. "Our Meredith is merely overwrought. It has been a long and difficult journey for her. She has a right to cry."

"I am not crying." Meredith wiped her eyes with the back of her hand and rolled to one side, pulling the linens over her head. With a sniff she said softly, "Well, perhaps I am. It is just that I am so weary. You are correct. It has been an arduous journey. But it is not yet over."

"What do you mean? You are home now." Brenna yanked the linens aside and peered at her sister.

Meredith sat up. "I mean that on the morrow I must ride to Edinburgh and gain an audience with the queen before Gareth has a chance to have me declared dead."

"But that is not why you are crying," Megan said matter-of-factly.

"Nay." Meredith caught her youngest sister's hands. "I am crying because I miss Brice. And I fear I will never see him again."

Megan's lips curved down into a frown, instantly hating the man who was the cause of Meredith's tears. "If Brice Campbell truly loved you, he would want to know that you were safe."

"But I begged him not to follow me."

"Aye. But how can the man claim to love you and not know if you survived the journey from the Highlands to your home?"

Sixteen-year-old Brenna wrapped an arm about Meredith's shoulder and glared at her younger sister. "Meredith has been through enough. We will not add to her burden." To Meredith she whispered, "You must sleep now. On the morrow you will feel better about everything."

"Aye. It is sleep that I need."

Meredith kissed her sisters, then lay back against the cushions and closed her eyes. But sleep would not come. Megan's questions echoed in her mind. It was true that she had begged Brice to remain where he was safe. And she truly thought that was what she wanted. But now the nagging thought slipped unbidden to her mind. Did Brice love her enough to risk his own life? Or had he already put her out of his mind, while he and his men filled their hours in the Highlands, rebuilding Kinloch House?

When at last she fell into a restless sleep, she was plagued with dark, sinister dreams, in which a stranger stalked her. At times the stranger had golden hair and tawny skin. She knew that he was truly evil. But at other times the stranger was someone more familiar to her. His hair was dark, burnished, his eyes compelling. There was about him an aura of danger as well, which she strove to ignore. But each time she ran to him he melted into the shadows and disappeared into the Highland mist.

Chapter Twenty-One

"You must not go to Edinburgh."

Meredith faced her two sisters. Though it was not yet dawn, the first hint of light could be seen on the horizon.

Over their protests she had pulled on her breeches and tunic and Rowena's heavy hooded cloak. While they begged and pleaded, she had insisted upon hurrying to the wooded place where she had left her horse.

Brenna was close to tears. Megan was indignant.

"Would you rather have me declared dead by the queen and have Brenna forced to wed Gareth MacKenzie?"

"Nay." Megan tried another tactic. "But in Edinburgh you will have to face Gareth MacKenzie alone. If you stay here, we will call all the MacAlpins together and plot to kill him when he returns."

"I must stop Gareth from meeting with the queen. If she declares me dead, how do I prove that I am not?"

Megan shook her head in disgust. In the darkness her blond tresses were a sliver of light.

"Then if you must go, we must ride with you."

"Impossible."

Brenna, who had wisely remained silent during most of this argument, jumped on Megan's suggestion. "Aye. We must go together."

"It is a long and difficult journey," Meredith said as patiently as she could. "If something were to happen to me, it would give me comfort to know that my sisters are here to carry on.''

"But it will give us no comfort to wonder what has happened to you, or even whether or not you succeed. We must ride together."

Meredith pulled up her hood and took up the reins. If necessary, she would remind them who was in charge here.

"I am the MacAlpin," she said with quiet authority. "And I declare that I shall ride alone to Edinburgh to gain an audience with the queen. As my sisters, you shall remain here at MacAlpin Castle and carry on in my absence."

"Carry on." Megan sniffed. "We will wilt on the vine while you have all the excitement of Court."

"There is danger and intrigue at Court," Meredith said sternly. "And I will not have my younger sisters exposed to it. You will do as I command."

Brenna and Megan stared at her in sullen silence. Never before had they seen Meredith use such overbearing tactics. It was beneath her.

Suddenly she opened her arms and both sisters flew to her. Against their cheeks she murmured, "Forgive me. I love you both too much to see you harmed. Besides, if I am to arrive in Edinburgh before Gareth MacKenzie and his men I must ride quickly and I must ride alone."

"If any harm comes to you," Brenna worried aloud, "I will never forgive myself for staying behind."

"If you are killed," Megan said menacingly, "I will hate you forever."

At her outburst, Brenna and Meredith stared at her in stunned silence. Then they fell into each other's arms in a fit of laughter. For a moment Megan could only stare at them. Then, joining in the laughter, she hugged her older sisters when they regained their composure.

"Godspeed," Brenna whispered.

"Hurry home," Megan said.

Meredith pulled herself into the saddle and spurred her horse into a gallop to hide the tears that spilled from her eyes, staining her cheeks. At the crest of a hill she turned and waved. Below her, the two young women, tears blurring their vision, waved until she disappeared from view. And even then, though they could no longer see her, they stood shivering in the predawn chill, unable to tear themselves away.

"Summon a groomsman," Megan said suddenly.

"What?" Brenna stared at her younger sister in surprise. "Why?"

"Because we must hurry if we are to stay close to Meredith on the trail to Edinburgh."

For long minutes Brenna regarded the young girl whose amber eyes glittered with a strange light. Then she did something completely out of character. With a delighted little laugh she lifted her skirts and began running toward the stables. Over her shoulder she called, "We will need travelling clothes. Oh, and our finest gowns for our first meeting with the queen."

Brice had never pushed himself so relentlessly. Though he was near exhaustion from the battle at Holden Mackay's fortress, he gave himself no time to rest.

He and Angus moved among the men, dressing their wounds. Six of their company had suffered wounds severe enough to force them to return to their homes. Brice assigned the other five of his men to return with them, knowing that the wounded could still encounter small groups of Mackay's men in the forest.

That left Brice and Angus to follow the trail left by Meredith.

"We will travel faster alone," he remarked when Angus grumbled about their lack of additional men. "We know where the lady is headed. Now we need only catch her before she can fall into any more danger."

"If there is danger," Angus muttered, saddling both their horses while Brice tended to his own shoulder wound, "you can be certain the lady will find it."

Brice looked up with a frown. "Aye. The lady Meredith does seem to have a gift for getting herself into trouble."

Seeing that his old friend was having trouble with the dressing, Angus dropped the reins and finished tying the strip of cloth about Brice's shoulder.

"Thank you, my friend. Now let us catch the lady. Before she manages to surprise us again."

"MacAlpin Castle?"

Brice and Angus sat astride their horses at the river's edge. To the east the sky was aflame with the first rosy slashes of dawn light.

"Aye." There was a softness in Brice's tone as he thought of Meredith, asleep in one of the upper chambers. "There is no time to waste. We will surprise her by entering before the household is awake."

Leading the way, he urged his mount into the icy waters, with Angus following. Once on the other bank they dug in their heels and raced across the last miles that separated them from MacAlpin Castle.

At the courtyard they took note of the saddled horses and the packhorses laden with provisions.

"We have arrived not a moment too soon." Before Brice could slide from the saddle the heavy door was opened and two young women, dressed for traveling, emerged.

At the sight of him both of them fell back in alarm.

"I am Brice Campbell," he said, studying them through narrowed eyes. "And from your sister's description of you, I feel as though I already know you." He turned to the sweet, shy beauty whose raven hair had been coiled about her head in a regal style. Her blue-violet eyes were ringed with black lashes. "You are Brenna, whose talents for cooking and sewing are legend. Meredith claims that men from both Scotland and England would beg for a kind look from you. And you," he said, turning to Megan, "are determined to never submit to any man. But with hair the color of gold and eyes like a cat, I suspect you will break many a man's heart."

The sisters' mouths opened in surprise; their eyes widened as he bowed before them.

"I come for Meredith MacAlpin."

How splendid he looked, with his skin tanned and leathery from the sun and his burnished locks tumbling about his forehead. Meredith had boasted about his muscled arms and thighs, his superior strength. And neither girl had forgotten the way he had looked at the cathedral when he had appeared out of the mists to abduct their sister.

Brenna and Megan turned to each other. On Brenna's lovely face was a look of real pleasure. The romantic in her had devoutly prayed that her sister's lover would overcome all obstacles to claim what was his.

"So you are Brice Campbell." She began to take a step forward but Megan caught her arm, holding her back. "We have heard all about you."

At that Brice's brows lifted. "So. Meredith is here. Take me to her at once."

As he slid from the saddle, both young women realized just how tall he was. They had not been prepared for such a fearsome man.

It was Megan who now took charge. "Meredith is not here."

"Do not lie to me, girl." He used his most forceful tone, hoping to intimidate her. "Your sister just admitted that she was here."

"She was. But she is no longer."

His eyes narrowed. "Where has she gone?"

Megan caught Brenna's hand and shot her a warning look. When they remained silent Brice turned to Angus, who had remained in the saddle, watching with interest. "As you can see, these two do not intend to cooperate with us." He winked. "We shall just have to stay here and watch and wait."

"But you cannot," Megan said, stamping her foot. "If we wait any longer she will get too far ahead..."

Brice's eyes crinkled as the smile touched his lips. "So. You intend to follow Meredith. Without her knowledge, apparently. Where does she go?"

Megan and Brenna turned to each other, then clamped their mouths shut.

Brice crossed his arms over his chest and leaned against the packhorse. "A pity you will not need these supplies. I suppose in a few hours it will be too late."

"Tell him," Brenna whispered.

Megan shook her head.

"Tell me." Though Brice kept his tone low, he wanted to throttle the young girl who displayed a cool manner remarkably like her eldest sister's.

"Only if you agree to take us along."

"What?" Brice's hands dropped to his sides, the fists

clenched. He took a step closer, his eyes narrowing in sudden anger.

"I will tell you where Meredith is headed. But you must agree to take us along."

"I have had enough." Brice turned to Angus. "Come. We will follow her trail."

"It will take you too long," Megan said. "But if you take us with you, we can save you the trouble of searching for a trail."

"You will slow us down. Your sister's life depends upon finding her before Gareth MacKenzie does."

"We will not slow you. We promise. And as for Gareth." Megan shot a look at her sister, who gave her an encouraging nod. "We know where he is, too."

Brice gave a sigh of impatience. "You are testing me, woman. Tell me. And quickly."

"First you must promise to take us along."

Brice gritted his teeth, then nodded.

With a smile Megan said, "Meredith rides to Edinburgh, to seek an audience with the queen before Gareth has her declared dead."

Reluctantly Brice helped the two girls onto their horses before pulling himself up into the saddle. "Angus, take the reins of that packhorse. We ride to Edinburgh."

"To see the queen." As they urged their horses into a trot, Brenna and Megan shouted the words in unison.

To the two young women, it was to be a grand adventure. To Brice, it was a race against time.

Meredith sat astride her horse and drank in the sights of the capital city of Scotland. She had traveled across High Street, surely the cleanest in the world. Channels had been dug on either side to drain off the rain. There were stone houses with their wooden galleries, and farther on, the grand houses and gardens of the Canongate, which led to Holyroodhouse. In Market Cross, with its stocks and pillories, men and women in somber dress bustled about. People gathered to talk, to shop, to discuss the events at Court. Goldsmith apprentices from Elphinstone Court and tinsmiths from West Bow were here, along with stall holders from Lawnmarket. And while they discoursed about the queen, they also discussed the one who ruled Edinburgh and all of Scotland with even more power and persuasion than the queen. John Knox, leader of the Kirk, had spoken openly about his contempt for petticoat government. He waited and watched and vowed that this Catholic queen would feel the wrath of God, as had her mother, as had her young French husband.

Meredith studied the dark, menacing fortress that was home to the queen. Its towers and battlements were not unlike Brice's Highland fortress. And yet it lacked the warm setting and opulence of a Highland castle.

Brice, she thought as she made her way to Holyroodhouse. If only Brice were here with her. She resented the heat she felt at the mere thought of him. She resented the way her body betrayed her, going all weak and soft when she needed to be strong. She would put aside all thought of Brice Campbell. For now she needed a clear head, a steady heartbeat.

She straightened her spine and urged her mount on, past Tolbooth Prison. How many were incarcerated there, she wondered, whose only crimes were gaiety and laughter? She thought of the love, the laughter, she had discovered at Kinloch House. How far away seemed the Highlands. How far away her love.

With every clatter of her horse's hooves she drew nearer and nearer to Holyroodhouse. And farther away from any chance to escape Gareth MacKenzie. For surely Gareth was already here in the capital city, awaiting an audience with the queen.

With fear and trepidation she approached the gates of the palace. There were perhaps two dozen people milling about, awaiting notification of an appointment with the queen. Many of them grumbled that they had been forced to return each day for more than two weeks.

Meredith's heart fell. Two weeks. She had not thought about where she would stay in Edinburgh if the queen would not see her immediately.

And what of Gareth MacKenzie? Would he not also be here, or one of his men? Unless, she thought with a jolt, he had been granted an audience immediately. Then, of course, she would already have been declared dead.

She studied the faces in the crowd. There were men and women in their finest clothing, looking extremely uncomfortable. There were clan chiefs, noblemen and a few common citizens who had matters of interest to discuss with the queen. But there was no sign of MacKenzie men. Meredith gave a sigh of relief when she did not see Gareth. So far, her luck was holding.

As the gatekeeper approached, she made a sudden decision. With so many important people waiting for an audience, the queen could not be expected to remember one insignificant Highland wench. But there was one whose name would open doors.

As the gatekeeper asked her name and the purpose of her visit she replied in a clear voice, ''Meredith MacAlpin to see the queen. At the request of Brice Campbell.''

Her words were recorded and the gatekeeper withdrew. Slipping from the saddle she led her horse to a trough where he drank.

Within a matter of minutes the gatekeeper returned and in a loud voice called, ''Meredith MacAlpin.''

She was aware of the sudden interest of the crowd. Men who had hardly glanced her way now studied her with open curiosity. Women, aghast at the sight of a woman wearing men's breeches and tunic, and flaunting the Highland saffron shirt, watched her with looks that ranged from contempt to amazement.

As she pushed her way to the front of the crowd, the gatekeeper opened the gates and waited until she and her mount were safely inside.

As the heavy gates were closing he bowed slightly and said, ''Welcome to Holyroodhouse, my lady. The queen will see you now.''

Chapter Twenty-Two

The sky was an angry black cauldron that boiled and bubbled. And when at last the billowing black clouds opened up, the downpour was sudden and drenching.

Seeking shelter for the women, Brice found a small hay barn. Inside they inhaled the sweet moist fragrance of dry hay.

Brenna drew her cape about her and found a spot in the corner where she could sit and observe. From what she had seen, this man who had won her sister's undying love was nothing more than a tough, demanding warrior who drove himself and everyone around him to the point of exhaustion. What was it about him that endeared him to Meredith?

Megan, shaking the raindrops from her cloak, paced about, curiosity causing her to peer into every nook. Satisfied, she perched on a mound of hay in the middle of the room and watched as Brice and Angus led the horses in out of the rain. She was clearly fascinated by this man who had stolen her sister, and then captured her heart.

As was her nature she blurted out what was on her mind, without regard to sensitivities.

"Why did you let Meredith undertake such a dangerous journey alone?"

Brice rubbed a rough cloth over his horse's quivering flank, choosing to remain silent for several minutes while he completed his task. "Your sister gave me no choice. She slipped away after I had fallen asleep."

"It seems to have taken you a good deal of time to catch up with her."

"We had..." He glanced toward Angus. "An unexpected diversion."

"What diversion?" Megan demanded.

If he found her questions impertinent he gave no indication. "Meredith was abducted by a Highland chief."

He saw the girl's mouth drop open. His words were clipped, his description sparse to save Meredith's sisters from undue suffering. "When my men and I went to her aid, we found ourselves badly outnumbered."

"Not for the first time," Angus said dryly.

"Aye." Brice chuckled. "It seems to be a habit with us of late, old friend."

Brenna noted the affection between the two men. It warmed her to know that Brice Campbell could inspire such devotion. Perhaps there was something endearing about him. For her sister's sake she hoped so.

As he worked Brenna noted the way Brice favored one arm. "Could that be where you were wounded, my lord?"

"What wound?" Megan asked.

Surprised, Brice glanced up. "You are very observant, Brenna. I thought I hid it rather well." He touched a hand to the tunic that covered the dressing at his shoulder.

"You were wounded?" Megan studied him a moment, deciding that she liked the idea of a wounded man continuing on, in the face of pain. "But you managed to best your enemy." Megan's eyes danced with the thought of the battle. Like Meredith she would not hesitate to take up a sword. "If you were fighting to save Meredith, how did she manage to elude you?"

Brice's smile grew. "Your sister seems to have become a master of disguise."

At the incredulous look on the faces of the two young women he added, "She pretended to be a hunchbacked seamstress, and slipped past everyone."

"Even you?" Megan asked.

"Aye. I confess I did not recognize her."

"And now she is ahead of you again," Brenna said thoughtfully.

"Not for long." Brice strode to the door and peered at the darkened sky. "Already the clouds are breaking to the west. Within the hour we will be once more on the road to Edinburgh."

"Do you make haste because you love Meredith?" Megan asked boldly. "Or are you merely angry that a woman has bested you?"

Brice stood by the door, illuminated by a flash of lightning. At that moment he looked as fearsome as any barbarian. "You have the right to know my feelings for your sister. And so I will tell you." He turned toward the quiet, regal Brenna. "Both of you." In a voice that managed to be both tender and fierce he said, "I love Meredith."

"If you love her as you claim," Megan demanded, "why did you not immediately return her to her home?"

"I did not trust Gareth MacKenzie. I feared for her safety here in the Lowlands."

"And so you placed her in even more danger in your Highlands."

"Sometimes, little one," Brice said to Megan, "we are asked to choose between the lesser of evils. I thought that by keeping Meredith with me in the Highlands, I could be close enough to always come to her aid." He turned to study the progress of the storm. His face was ruggedly handsome in profile. His eyes narrowed thoughtfully. "I have learned that I cannot always be beside the woman I love, to protect her from every harm. I pray the Fates are there to guide her hand and her sword."

"You are a patient man," Brenna said with quiet conviction.

"Nay." Brice almost laughed at the thought. "I am far from patient. But I have had to learn a valuable lesson. When we love someone we are sometimes called upon to make terrible decisions. Decisions that cause pain for one while offering great rewards for the other."

"I do not understand," Megan said.

"He means," Brenna said softly, "that by allowing Meredith to return to the Lowlands to clear his name, he risks losing her."

At her words Brice's hands balled into fists by his side.

"My lord," Brenna said softly.

He turned to her.

"Would you pay any price for my sister's happiness?"

"Aye. Any price." His tone was low, vibrating with feeling. "I would even risk losing her if it meant her happiness."

Brenna shivered. The intensity of his words frightened her. She prayed that neither her beloved older sister nor this fierce Highland warrior would be forced to pay the ultimate price.

Dusk was settling over the city when Brice led his tired party through the streets of Edinburgh.

"It is too late to approach Holyroodhouse this evening. We will have to wait until the morrow to arrange an audience with the queen. For now I will see about lodging."

Leading the way down a narrow lane near the Canongate, he stopped before a tidy inn. Leaving the women with Angus, Brice went inside. Within minutes he was back to help the women dismount. Lifting their supplies from the packhorse, he led the way to a suite of comfortable rooms.

"Angus and I have the rooms across the hall," he explained. "The innkeeper will provide us with a meal. As soon as you have refreshed yourselves, you may join us below stairs to sup."

Megan and Brenna were grateful for the chance to wash away the grime of the journey. Running a brush through their tangled curls, they smoothed their gowns and draped shawls of delicate lace about their shoulders. Then they made their way to the dining room.

Brice and Angus were standing before a roaring fire, enjoying tankards of ale. Their conversation was low, muted. They looked up as the two young women entered.

"We will sit here." Brice led them to a table set with fine linen and china.

Under the direction of the innkeeper a serving wench offered goblets of wine to warm them. She passed around whole roasted goose, suet pudding and sweetbreads. With tea there were biscuits warm from the oven, spread with clotted cream and jam.

At last they sat back, content, replete.

"I do not remember when a meal tasted so lovely." Brenna sighed.

"Aye. 'Twas a difficult journey. But you were true to your word," Brice said, emptying his tankard. "You neither complained nor slowed us down."

Megan voiced the fear that none of them had been willing to put into words. "What of Meredith? Do you think she is as fortunate as we are, Brice?"

He glanced at Megan, then at her sister, and read the fear on both their faces. "Aye. Somewhere in Edinburgh she is sitting before a roaring fire, enjoying a fine meal." He could not allow himself to think about the alternative. He would not allow himself to think about his beloved Meredith prowling the darkened streets in search of decent lodging. And in the process, running into Gareth MacKenzie and his men.

Brice escorted the young women to their rooms, then returned to his own suite and reached for his sword and scabbard.

"Where do go you now, old friend?"

Brice turned to Angus. "Stay here and see to the safety of Meredith's sisters."

"And you?"

"I cannot sleep, knowing that Meredith is somewhere here in Edinburgh, possibly in grave danger."

"The city is too large to find one lone woman."

"Mayhaps. But I must try."

Angus watched as his friend stalked across the room. He listened as Brice's footsteps faded on the stairs. There would be no rest for Brice Campbell this night. Or any night until he once again held the woman he loved in his arms.

"Now where have you hidden away that rogue Brice Campbell and his beautiful hostage, Meredith MacAlpin?"

At the familiar majestic tones Meredith sat up and rubbed her eyes. God in heaven. She had fallen asleep in the queen's own chambers. How she must look with her hair in wild disarray and her clothes soiled from the long journey.

Her clothes. Meredith glanced down at the breeches and

tunic and the faded cloak and let out a little gasp. This was not how she had planned on meeting the queen.

As she swung her legs to the floor the door was thrown open and the queen, followed by her ever-present Maries, strode into the room.

"Now where is that rogue?"

"Brice Campbell was not with her," Mary Fleming said gently. "Although the gatekeeper mentioned both names, the young woman was alone."

"It is true then. Brice is dead."

"Majesty." Meredith curtsied and kept her head lowered as she explained, "Brice is not dead."

She did not see the look that crossed the queen's face. A look of relief that slowly became a look of pleasure.

"I used Brice's name because I knew you would not remember me."

"Not remember the woman who pretended to be me at dinner?" The queen gave a musical laugh. "How could I ever forget you, Meredith MacAlpin?"

"I am honored, Majesty." Meredith dared to lift her head and realized that the queen was studying her carefully.

"Such an extraordinary traveling costume, Meredith."

"Aye, Majesty." Meredith blushed clear to her toes. "The breeches and tunic are Brice's. The cloak belonged to a wonderful seamstress who befriended me."

"Surely you have not ridden all the way from the Highlands?"

"I have, Majesty. But first I made a stop at my home on the Border."

"I have been hearing tales of murder along the Border," the queen said, taking a seat and indicating a chair for Meredith.

"There have been many murders, Majesty."

"'Tis said they are committed by the Highland Barbarian."

"You know that cannot be true." Meredith leaned forward, praying that the queen would allow her to speak frankly.

"And how would I know that?"

"You know Brice Campbell to be an honorable man."

"Aye. I do. But I did not think you shared my opinion. The

last time I saw you, you were begging to be saved from his clutches.''

Meredith saw the gleam of laughter in the queen's eyes and smiled. ''So much has changed since last I saw you, Majesty.''

''So it would seem.'' The queen signaled for wine. When it was poured, she lifted a goblet and waited until Meredith and the Maries did the same. ''You must tell me everything that has happened between you and Brice since I left.'' The queen's eyes glittered with a strange light. ''And you must leave nothing out.''

''Oh, Majesty.'' Meredith took a sip of the wine, allowing its warmth to soothe. ''There is so much to tell.''

''We have all the time in the world.''

While Meredith began, the servants brought in a sumptuous meal.

''So,'' the queen said as Meredith recounted the attack by Gareth MacKenzie and the resulting injury to Brice, ''you found yourself fighting alongside Brice's men for your very life.''

''Aye, Majesty. And when the battle was over, Kinloch House was burned and many of its inhabitants wounded. Among them Brice. We feared he would not live.''

''And that is how the rumor of his death came about?''

''Aye. Gareth and his men found no heartbeat. Nor did I upon first examination. But finally I found a pulse, weak, feeble, but a sign of life nevertheless.''

''And you bravely brought him through the crisis.''

Meredith glanced toward the queen to see if she were jesting. But there was no hint of a smile on her face.

''Aye. He survived. Thanks be to God.''

''Why did you leave him?''

''When I heard that Gareth MacKenzie intended to seek an audience with you and have me declared dead, I knew that I had to journey to Edinburgh and fight for my rights.''

''Once again you have proven your mettle, Meredith MacAlpin. You make all Scotswomen proud.'' The queen allowed her gaze to linger a moment on Meredith's face before she turned to Mary Fleming. ''Is it not Divine Providence that has sent her to us?''

Fleming nodded and spoke rapidly in French to the others, who began laughing and nodding.

"What is it, Majesty?"

The queen stood, drawing herself up to her full height before staring down at Meredith. "You are privileged to write history, Meredith MacAlpin. Because of your strong resemblance to your queen, and the fact that you have been sent to me at my very hour of need, you will provide a great service to your queen."

Meredith glanced uneasily around the table, puzzled by the tension she could feel.

"Tomorrow at Court, Meredith," the queen said somberly, "you will be me."

"You, Majesty? But where will you be?"

"I will be—indisposed," the queen said enigmatically.

"But why?"

The queen clapped her hands and began to laugh. "I cannot keep this a secret from you, Meredith. Tomorrow I am to be kidnapped by a secret admirer."

"Kidnapped." Meredith was thunderstruck.

"Aye. Is it not the most romantic thing you have ever heard of? Ever since I heard your story, I have yearned to experience such a thing. And now it has come to pass. A certain—nobleman desires to be alone with me. And since the queen can never be alone with a gentleman, I must arrange to be kidnapped. But, of course, if I were not to appear at Court, there would have to be a reasonable explanation. We had thought that I would plead one of my famous headaches. But now that you are here, I need not be absent from Court at all. Is this not truly exciting?"

"But, Majesty, there are affairs of state to be determined each day at Court. How can I handle such issues?"

"Simple. Whatever you decree, it is the decree of the queen."

"Majesty!" Meredith felt a sense of hysteria bubbling dangerously close to the surface. But the queen blithely went on making her plans.

"Flem will help you with names and faces. And Seton and Beaton will sit on either side of you for assistance. Because of you, your queen will experience a day of freedom, Meredith.''

Feeling desperately alone, Meredith glanced about the room. Candles flickered in sconces along walls hung with rich French tapestries and gilt-framed mirrors. On the floor were elegant carpets. The table, the chairs, nearly all the furniture in the queen's sitting chamber, had been brought from France. The women seated around the queen giggled and made comments in French, and Mary responded rapidly in the same language.

As she sat in their midst, watching, listening, it occurred to Meredith that they could just as easily have been in the French Court. In fact, she realized with sudden knowledge, that was what Mary had created here in Edinburgh. Dismissing the somber landscape beyond the walls of Holyroodhouse, denying the tension created by John Knox against her, Mary had created a pale imitation of the Court in France, which she so desperately missed. The man she planned to meet secretly would take the place, for a while, of the husband she still mourned. And the women around her, wishing to see to her happiness, were part of the game.

It was all a game, Meredith thought with a sense of panic. The palace, the Court, the petitioners who awaited the verdict of their queen. All a terrible, awe-inspiring game. And on the morrow, she would become a key player in this deadly game. A game that as yet seemed to have no rules.

Chapter Twenty-Three

Brenna, Megan and Angus looked up from their early-morning meal as the door to the inn was thrown open. When Brice stepped inside Angus hurried to him. There was no need to ask the question that sprang to his lips. One look at the tight, hard set of Brice's mouth told Angus all he wanted to know.

"You did not find her."

"Not a trace." Brice ran a hand over the stubble of dark beard that covered his chin. "I inquired at every inn and stable. There has been no sign of her."

"Perhaps she was delayed along the way."

Brice's eyes were bleak. "Or ran into Gareth MacKenzie's company."

"Come, old friend," Angus said gently. "Break your fast with us."

"Nay. We must hurry to Holyroodhouse and demand a private audience with the queen." He brushed past Angus. "I will make myself presentable and then we ride."

Brenna and Megan turned to each other with a growing sense of dread. They had not known until this moment that Brice had stayed out all night searching for Meredith. They pushed away from the table, feeling a hard knot of fear in the pit of their stomachs. What had happened to their beloved Meredith?

Within the hour the four were riding through the city to the queen's residence. The keeper of the gate of Holyroodhouse accepted a message from Brice, then withdrew. After what seemed an eternity he returned, along with a soldier who rolled the heavy gate open. The gatekeeper motioned for the four visitors to follow him.

Brice's look was impassive, his fears carefully hidden behind the mask of a proper nobleman. Behind him, Brenna and Megan could hardly contain their excitement. Despite their fears for their sister, one thought was uppermost in their minds. The palace. They were actually inside the palace and were going to meet the queen.

A servant drew open the heavy draperies, allowing the morning sunlight to stream into the room. In the ornate bed Meredith awoke from sleep as one drugged. After her exhausting journey from the Highlands, her body had begged for rest. And despite the fears that plagued her upon the queen's announcement the previous night, sleep had claimed her the moment she had lain her head upon the pillow.

"Meredith. Meredith." A hand tugged at her shoulder. The voice of Mary Fleming sounded urgent. "You must wake and dress quickly. You have visitors."

"Visitors?"

Fleming's mouth curved into a mysterious smile. "I think you will be pleased. Now make haste."

Next door, in the queen's chambers, Meredith could hear the sound of that familiar, haughty voice and the frantic activity of servants as they prepared their monarch.

Like one in a daze Meredith allowed herself to be bundled into one of the queen's own cut-velvet robes. Her hair was quickly brushed. Meredith was led into the queen's sitting chamber, where Mary, surrounded by her Maries, was being hastily prepared to receive visitors.

At least a dozen servants bustled about the room setting up a morning meal that could have fed an entire village.

When the queen was properly coifed and gowned, she nodded to Mary Seton. "Show our visitors in."

With a puzzled frown Meredith turned toward the door. For a moment she could only stare at the two young women who stood nervously together clutching each other's hands. Then with a shout, they rushed forward and fell into her arms.

"Oh, Brenna. Megan." With tears streaming down her cheeks Meredith caught them to her and hugged them fiercely.

"How in the world did you two get to Edinburgh? And however did you talk your way inside the castle?"

"We had help," Brenna said softly.

As she drew aside, Meredith became aware of the tall figure framed in the doorway. For a moment her heart forgot to beat.

"Brice? Oh, is it truly you?" She started toward him, her arms outstretched. Then, remembering where she was, she stopped and clutched her hands together, drinking in the sight of him.

"You look—fatigued. You should not have attempted so long a journey."

"I am fatigued because I spent the night searching for you, firebrand. And thinking you dead. Or worse." For the first time he allowed himself to smile as he crossed to her in quick strides and brought his hand to her cheek.

He studied the pallor of her skin, the dark circles beneath her eyes. "Are you truly all right, Meredith?"

"Oh, now that I see you and my sisters—" she turned and caught their hands "—I feel wonderful."

"Would you care to greet your queen now, Brice Campbell, or do you intend to stand there all morn and devour that maiden with your eyes?"

With a laugh Brice broke contact and crossed the room. With a deep bow he caught Mary's hand and brought it to his lips. Then, with a laugh, he lifted her out of her chair, swung her around and kissed her on each cheek before setting her on her feet.

"Rogue." She sighed, touching a hand to her cheek. "You are the only man who would ever dare to do such a thing."

"The only man, Majesty?"

Mary blushed furiously. "What have you heard?"

"Rumors." Brice's voice lowered, for her ears only. "The Border Earl of Bothwell is a virile, amorous man, Mary. But beware. A kingdom is at stake here."

Mary became noticibly agitated. With high color she turned

to meet the two beautiful young strangers. "Who are these lovely creatures? Come greet your queen."

Meredith performed the introductions. "Majesty, may I present my sister, Brenna."

The dark-haired beauty curtsied, keeping her gaze lowered.

"And my youngest sister, Megan."

The blond imp curtsied as she had been taught, then boldly studied the queen.

"So there are two more like you. I can see that they will soon be breaking hearts across Scotland. Welcome to Holyroodhouse."

"And you know my old friend, Angus Gordon," Brice said, clapping a hand on Angus's shoulder.

"Of course. Welcome, Angus. Come," Mary said, taking Brice's hand and leading him to the table. "We will break our fast. And you will tell us why you have surprised us with this visit."

Though Brice managed to respond to all the queen's questions, he could not keep his eyes off the beautiful woman who sat across the table. How he longed to carry her away from the noise and babble, away from prying eyes, and share with her all the love that was stored inside his heart. It was not enough to know that she was safe. He needed to touch her, to gather her to him, to hold her.

"...several days?"

Brice tore his gaze from Meredith and turned to find the queen looking at him with a knowing smile.

"I am sorry, Majesty. I was—distracted."

"So you were." She smiled. "If you are not careful, my friend, there will be rumors."

He chuckled. "But there is no kingdom at stake."

"No, my dear rogue. Merely a pair of hearts." The queen stood, and everyone at table got to their feet.

"I have a long and exhausting day ahead of me." She could not stifle the smile that tugged at the corners of her lips. "You will excuse me. Brice," she added, "we will talk again on the morrow."

"As you wish." Brice bowed over her hand, then signaled for Angus and the others to follow him. At the doorway Mary called, "Meredith, you will stay awhile. We have business to attend to."

Meredith kissed her sisters' cheeks, then touched her hand to Brice's. Instantly she felt the heat and yearned for some time alone with him. There was so much she needed to tell him. So much she wanted to ask.

She watched as a servant led Brice and the others to a nearby chamber, where their every comfort would be taken care of.

When the door closed, Meredith turned toward the queen, who was issuing orders to her staff. "For the rest of the morning I shall be indisposed. There will be no exceptions."

The reality of what lay ahead caused Meredith's stomach to churn.

Surely in the light of day the queen would see the folly of her plan. It was unthinkable that Mary would permit herself to be abducted by a nobleman for the sake of a romantic interlude. She must realize the risk to her reputation if her secret was discovered. Further, could not the queen see how impossible it was for an imposter to assume the throne? Even for one day?

Meredith's head swam with questions as she turned to watch the flurry of activity. Several servants were busy laying out a gown of regal scarlet velvet, along with a tiara of diamonds and rubies, and a necklace of ornate gold filigree and matching rubies.

Meredith's mouth rounded in an O of appreciation. "Oh, Majesty, it is breathtakingly beautiful. You will look magnificent."

The queen smiled indulgently while her friends giggled like children.

"I will not be wearing it," Mary said without a trace of regret. "The gown is for you, Meredith."

"Majesty." Meredith drew back. "I could not. It is too fine."

"But you will be presiding over Court this day. You must look every inch the queen."

Meredith crossed her arms over her middle, feeling her stomach churn. "Please, Majesty. I beg you. Forget this foolish dream. You must not do this thing you plan."

"But I shall." The queen stood and walked to her, grasping her cold hands and forcing her to meet her steady gaze. "For so long now I have dreamed of being, not the queen, but an ordinary woman. I want to experience what other women have, Meredith. I want to be loved like a woman. And you are going to make this dream possible."

"Majesty," Meredith whispered, forcing the words from a throat that had gone suddenly dry. "What will become of the people who come to the queen for solace, and find me instead? What of the pronouncements I make this day in your name? Are they all to be withdrawn on the morrow?"

"Nay, Meredith. Have no fear." Mary brought her arm about the trembling woman and drew her close. "When you sit upon the throne this day, you speak for the queen. You are the queen. Whatever you declare, it is law. And whatever you rescind, it is rescinded for all time. Is that clear?"

A violent tremor rocked the young woman's slender frame. "Oh, Majesty. That makes it even more difficult to bear. I am not worthy to pass judgment on others. I have not the right."

"I give you the right," the queen said sternly. "Am I not your queen?"

"Aye, Majesty."

"Then kneel, Meredith, and accept the edict of your queen."

Meredith knelt and the queen touched a hand to her shoulder. In regal tones she pronounced, "I, Mary Stuart, Queen of Scotland, do declare you, Meredith MacAlpin, the bearer of my name and seal this day. All that you proclaim on this day shall be law. Let no man rescind your orders."

Meredith swallowed down the little knot of fear that rose in her throat. When the queen caught her hands and drew her to her feet, she was startled to see that the Maries were no longer laughing. For the first time they realized what a dangerous scheme had been set in motion.

"Now," the queen said regally, "go to your sisters and the rogue who carries his heart on his sleeve. Confide in no one. And when it is time to dress for Court, you must do so without drawing undue attention to yourself." As Meredith prepared to make further protest, the queen gave her a friendly shove. "Go. I command you to put aside your fears."

Even though it was a royal command, Meredith knew it was impossible to obey. Her fears for what was to come could not be ignored.

The preparations for Court were a blur of activity. Meredith stood in the queen's chambers, staring at her reflection in a looking glass, while servants dressed her hair and helped her into her gown and jewels. When the crown of diamonds and rubies was placed upon her head, she felt as if the weight of the entire world had suddenly been thrust upon her.

She turned to where Mary stood, surrounded by her Maries. Wearing a flowing gossamer gown of palest pink, with her hair loose and falling in soft waves to her waist, the queen looked for the first time like the young girl she was. Her cheeks were flushed with the thrill of her adventure. Her eyes sparkled. With a little laugh she crossed the room and took Meredith's cold hands.

"Meredith MacAlpin. You have earned the undying gratitude of your queen."

"Majesty."

As Meredith began to curtsy Mary stopped her. "You will bow to no one this day. Remember. You are the queen."

As tears misted Meredith's eyes Mary called, "Flem, take Her Majesty to meet with Lord Aston." To Meredith she said softly, "He will go over your appointments this day, which have already been scheduled. If there is time he will ask you to read the list of petitioners."

So that the others could not hear, Meredith whispered, "Majesty, there is still time to end this charade."

"Look at me," the queen commanded.

Meredith stared into her eyes.

"Would you ask me to give up this one chance to live as others do?"

Meredith slowly shook her head. "I am unworthy to ask anything of you, Majesty."

"God bless you," the queen said with feeling. Then, hugging Meredith to her, she turned away.

Mary Fleming took Meredith's arm and led her to a small council chamber where the queen met daily with her advisers.

The keeper of the gate at Holyroodhouse strode toward the crowd of elegantly dressed men and women who gathered at the entrance of the castle. Unrolling his scroll, he began to read the list of names who would be granted an audience.

From their position in an upper window, Brenna and Megan watched the spectacle with avid interest. When Meredith had told them that they would be permitted to attend Court this day, they nearly fainted. Had it not been for the strong arms of the men who accompanied them, they would not have been brave enough to walk through the hallowed halls and follow the gnarled old man who led the procession to the throne room.

As they were ushered into the elegant great hall, they stared at lush tapestries depicting the royal lineage from the time of the first great Scottish king. The floors were covered with rich carpets bearing the royal seal. Around the room were chairs covered in regal red velvet. And on a raised dais stood a throne, covered in rich scarlet brocade. Slightly behind the throne to either side were chairs for the queen's advisers.

The petitioners were escorted to chairs in a gallery section set on either side of the throne. Brenna and Megan had hoped to find chairs in front, but most of the gallery was already filled. They were forced to take seats in the far corner of the gallery behind rows of spectators. Brice and Angus stood behind them.

A flurry of trumpets heralded the arrival of the queen. Brenna and Megan strained to see over the heads of the spectators, but all they caught was a glimpse of scarlet velvet and the glint of rubies and diamonds that adorned the royal crown.

For his part, Brice was completely disinterested in the pomp of the royal Court. He had had his fill of such things in his youth. His thoughts centered on only one. Meredith. To know that she was safe, and spending the day in the security of the queen's palace, filled his heart with peace.

Their brief meeting after morning meal had been unsatisfying. Though they had talked about her journey from the Highlands, and the perils they had both faced, there had been no time alone.

Tonight, he thought with a rush of heat. Tonight he would go to Meredith's chambers. And at last they would be reunited.

When the queen ascended the throne, Brice glanced at the two young women who actually trembled with excitement. For all his disenchantment with royalty, he realized he would enjoy watching the proceedings through the eyes of Brenna and Megan. If only Meredith could have joined him. Or better, if they could have slipped away during these long hours. But she had insisted that there were pressing matters that she must attend for the sake of the queen.

Brice's eyes narrowed. When he and Mary Stuart were alone on the morrow, he would confide his fears about Meredith's safety. And he would officially ask the queen to look into the mysterious murders taking place along the Border. It had never mattered to him before. Let others think what they wanted about him. But now it was time to clear his name. So that he could ask Meredith MacAlpin to share it.

Meredith's heart swelled as she walked up the aisle and lifted her hand to the masses of people who bowed and curtsied as she passed. She was experiencing her first taste of what it was like to be loved and revered by so many. And yet the nagging thought persisted. How could it be that none of them noticed that she was an imposter? Even Lord Aston, the queen's aide, had gone over the list of activities without so much as a pause to glance directly into her face. Did she dare to hope that she could get through the entire day without being found out?

As she took her seat upon the throne, she cast a benevolent smile over the crowd.

Lord Aston began reading the first petition. As he read from the scroll, Meredith allowed her gaze to scan the spectators. They were staring at her with such awe, she felt her throat go dry. What was she doing here? God in heaven. This was not some silly game being played out so that the queen could experience romance. This was, for many of the people seated before her, a matter of life and death.

As Lord Aston's voice droned on she lost her sense of concentration. It no longer mattered what the petitioner was requesting of his queen. She was an imposter. An ordinary woman who was being asked to make decisions that would affect the lives of the people she loved.

As Lord Aston finished his speech, Meredith waited for the voice of doom. Surely God would strike her down for such arrogance. She waited for the sound of thunder. Instead there was an ominous silence.

Meredith felt Flem's hand upon her arm and gave a guilty start, bringing her out of her reverie. What had just been requested of her? She couldn't think. Could not even recall the words that had just been spoken.

The crowd shifted uneasily as Lord Aston repeated the petition a second time. Forcing herself to pay attention, Meredith spoke in halting tones.

"I shall take the petitioner's request under advisement. Proceed with the next, Lord Aston."

The crowd gave a murmur of disapproval. They had come here to watch the high-and lowborn among them spar with the queen. They did not wish to have any controversial topics set aside.

Her aide seemed perplexed as he uncurled the second scroll and began to read. This one was easier. A petitioner requested that his neighbor's land be given to him because the neighbor had allowed the land to go fallow.

"What would you do with the land if I were to give it to you?" Meredith asked.

The portly man stood and bowed his head respectfully. Beside him, his wife beamed with pride at her husband's moment of glory.

"I would plant it with crops, Majesty. I have a fine, healthy herd and they have need of more food."

"And who would do this planting?"

"I have four strapping sons."

"You are truly blessed," Meredith said. She looked into the crowd. "Who owns this land?"

A plump woman, her gray hair pulled into an untidy knot, stood. "I do, Majesty."

"Do you have a husband?" Meredith asked.

"He died a year ago." The woman fingered a sash at her waist, too humble to look at the regal figure on the throne.

"Are there any sons who can work the land?"

"I have a son, Majesty. A bonnie lad he is. But he is off fighting the English who raided our Border."

"No other children?"

"There is a daughter, Majesty. Her husband was killed by the English, and she and her three bairns are now living with me. She and I have tried to till the soil but it is more than we can manage."

Meredith studied the woman, then glanced at the neighbor who desired her land. If only, she thought, life could always be equitable. But some were born with health, or acquired wealth, while others seemed always beaten down by the trials of this life.

"Until this woman's son returns and is able to work the land I will grant you permission to plant your crops on her land."

The man smiled, enormously pleased at his good fortune.

"Provided you give half your crops to your neighbor in payment for the use of such land."

The man's mouth dropped open. "But it is my labor, Majesty, that produces the crops."

"Aye. And her land. Furthermore, when her son returns, the land reverts to him and his mother."

"But, Majesty…"

"That is the judgment of your queen."

During this entire exchange, the crowd had grown very quiet. It was obvious, from the smiles on many of the faces, that they were pleased with the queen's decision.

At the queen's first words, Brenna and Megan stared at each other in shock. Though the clothes and jewels were those of a queen, the voice was Meredith's. There was no mistaking it. But though both girls craned to see over the crowd, they could not see their queen's face.

As distracted as Brice was, he, too, knew that the voice he was hearing was not that of Mary. From his position at the back of the gallery he studied the regal figure upon the throne.

By all that was holy. Meredith. Disguised as the queen.

A smile touched his lips and crinkled the corners of his eyes. So that was why she had been so unnerved this morrow. The rumors about the queen's tryst with Lord Bothwell were the truth. And once again his little firebrand was being shamelessly used by Mary.

Brenna and Megan tugged at his sleeve, eager to share their secret. But he put a finger to his lips and nodded. Puzzled, they turned around and continued to watch as this amazing charade was played out.

The petitions dragged on and Meredith handled those that were within her realm. Any that seemed too complicated, or too politically explosive, were "taken under advisement." Each time Meredith made a decision her voice grew stronger, her mannerisms more regal, until she found herself thinking and acting like the queen.

When a nervous old woman in a shabby dress petitioned to force a nobleman to pay her for the clothes she had made him, Meredith turned to study the finely attired man.

"Did the lady make the clothes you are wearing?"

He bowed slightly before his queen. "Aye, Majesty. But one of my own servants had to strengthen the seam here," he said pointing, "or I would not have been able to wear it."

"Has she made other clothes as well?"

"Some, Majesty. But all of them needed additional work."

"And you have paid this woman nothing?"

"Her work was shoddy."

"Yet you continue to wear the clothes she made."

The man fell silent.

"You will pay her the sum you promised her, and ten gold sovereigns more."

"More! Why, Majesty?"

"Because you did not live up to the terms of your agreement. If the clothes needed further sewing, they should have been returned immediately for repairs. The fact that you accepted them, and wore them, proves that they were adequate."

The look on the man's face told the spectators that he was not happy with the judgment. But the dressmaker saw the smiles on the faces of the crowd as she passed.

"I would take a moment," the queen said to Lord Aston as he prepared to read the next petition.

He paused.

Seeing the dressmaker's dilemma had reminded her of a debt she owed. This may be her only chance to repay it.

In regal tones Meredith said, ''I decree that the official dressmaker to the queen shall be Rowena, a woman from the Highland clan Mackay. See that she is brought to Edinburgh this day in the queen's own carriage.''

Lord Aston recorded the edict on a scroll, then stood and cleared his throat before proceeding with the next petition.

In the back of the gallery, Brice watched the woman he loved with a mixture of humor and awe. What an amazing woman she was. She was handling affairs of state as if she had been born for this task alone. He chuckled. Mary Stuart would feel the results of her charade for many years to come.

Lord Aston's voice rang through the chambers.

''Gareth MacKenzie of the Borders, in the matter of the death of Meredith MacAlpin.''

At his words Meredith felt her throat go dry. At the sudden movement in the gallery, she turned to watch as the figures parted and one stepped forward. As she sat on the throne, she found herself face-to-face with the man she most feared and hated. Gareth MacKenzie.

Chapter Twenty-Four

Gareth was feeling supremely confident. Standing in the presence of the queen, with his men around him, he intended to paint a heroic picture of himself. He was aware, of course, that his golden hair and handsome face endeared him to most people. And in front of this young queen he would be the most charming man in all of Scotland.

He had rehearsed his speech until he was certain there was nothing he had forgotten. With characteristic boldness he began.

"My younger brother, Desmond, was to have wed the lady Meredith MacAlpin. On his wedding day Desmond was brutally murdered by the Highland Barbarian, Brice Campbell. His young bride was carried off to Campbell's Highland castle."

Meredith was aware of the gasps from many in the crowd. Scant months ago she, too, would have feared for the life of anyone abducted by Brice Campbell. His reputation as a scoundrel and murderer had been carefully established throughout the land.

In the back of the gallery Brice listened with a look of intense concentration to this man who had set out to destroy his reputation and who had nearly succeeded in ending his life as well.

"To avenge my brother's death and to save the young innocent from this savage, my men and I attacked Campbell's

Highland home, Kinloch House, and though we were outnumbered, managed to kill Brice Campbell. But the lady, probably fearing for her life at the hands of that barbarian, fled into the Highland forests. My men and I searched for days but found no trace of her. It is our belief that the lady perished in the Highlands."

"Could she not have taken refuge in a cottage?"

"We inquired of many Highlanders, Majesty. No one has seen her."

"But if you have no proof of her death, why do you wish to have her declared dead?"

"Her clan is left without leadership or protection, Majesty. There are but two helpless maidens left to lead the MacAlpin clan." Gareth puffed up his chest and stood straighter. "I would be willing to wed the next eldest, Brenna, and offer the protection of my men."

"How very gracious of you." Meredith's tone frosted over. "If I grant your request, and you wed Brenna MacAlpin, you will claim her land as your own?"

"'Twould be my right, Majesty. But in return I would pledge my armies to the protection of her people."

"So, if you were to acquire the MacAlpin properties there would be no more lads murdered in the night, my lord MacKenzie? There would be no mysterious visits from this Highland Barbarian, who has been blamed for the deaths of every man, woman, child and sheep in Scotland?"

At the queen's sarcastic outburst Gareth felt the first tremor of alarm.

"The Highland Barbarian is dead, Majesty. Have you forgotten that I killed him?"

"I have forgotten nothing. This occurred during your attack upon his home, I believe."

When Gareth nodded she asked innocently, "With this Brice Campbell dead, why would the MacAlpins need your protection?"

He paused. He had not expected this question. "There are others who would prowl the darkness in search of those weaker than they. It has always been thus."

"Others? Are you suggesting that some of the murders

along the Border may not have been committed by Brice Campbell?''

He was taken aback by that. "I—would suppose that is true."

"Some murders of Borderers may even have been committed by Borderers?''

Where was the queen leading him? "I do not know, Majesty."

"Come now, my lord MacKenzie. Have you no idea who might have gone about murdering innocent lads?''

"Nay. I know not."

"But I know." She got to her feet and stood facing him, small, elegant, regal. Her voice rang with authority. "Your queen must care about all the people in her realm. Even an insignificant Border lad who dares not walk about a darkened lane lest he be put upon by those bent upon destruction."

Gareth shivered. She knew about Duncan's grandson. His mind raced. "Young MacAlpin was murdered by the Highland Barbarian. I myself witnessed it."

"What an amazing man this barbarian is," Meredith said, her voice like ice. "He can be in two places at once."

Gareth began to protest, but her next words stopped him.

"When you were witnessing this murder, Brice Campbell was entertaining your queen at his Highland castle."

A loud murmur rippled through the crowd.

Gareth's mouth opened but no words could come out.

"Do you still wish to state that you were there when the lad was murdered?''

"Perhaps I was mistaken." Gareth, feeling a sheen of moisture on his forehead, stumbled about for some explanation to smooth over his awkward situation. "Perhaps I came upon him moments after."

"And you did not actually witness his murder?''

"I…" He stared at a spot on the floor. "Nay, Majesty."

"But it was your knife that was found bloodied. A knife you said was taken from you and plunged into the lad's heart. You told all who would listen that the blame lay with the Highland Barbarian."

Gareth was stung by her harshness. The woman was publicly humiliating him.

"I—did not recognize the men who murdered the lad, Majesty. But I thought one of them to be the Highland Barbarian."

"As you thought many times, my lord MacKenzie. Have you not accused Brice Campbell of every Border incident for the past two years?"

There was a long pause, and Gareth felt the monarch's gaze leveled on him. He chose not to respond to her attack.

"Now about this matter of Meredith MacAlpin."

Gareth stiffened at the dark mood of the queen. "I request that your Majesty declare her dead."

Meredith pointed a bejeweled finger at the man who stood trembling before her. "I declare that Meredith MacAlpin is alive."

The crowd leaned forward, their murmured words nearly drowning out her voice.

In the back of the gallery, Brice tensed, wishing he could inch his way through the crowd and get closer to Meredith. MacKenzie had many men here with him. Backed into a corner, he would be like a vicious dog.

"Why would you declare her alive, Majesty?" Gareth's voice rose in anger.

"Your queen has seen her."

"That—that is splendid news," Gareth said in halting tones, trying vainly to salvage his image.

"Aye. Splendid." Meredith was beginning to enjoy herself. "In fact, the lass visited your queen here in Holyroodhouse this very day."

"She is here?" Gareth's eyes narrowed. Without realizing it, his hand went to the sword at his waist.

"She had me spellbound with her stories." Meredith paused for dramatic effect, then said in a voice that carried through the hall, "Meredith MacAlpin overheard you plotting her murder."

For a moment the crowd fell silent, then many stood and began craning their necks for a better view of this unexpected confrontation.

"The woman lies, Majesty."

"Why would she lie about this, my lord?"

"Perhaps she took a blow to the head during her abduction by the Barbarian." Gareth was now sweating profusely, and he wiped a hand across his brow. "I would ask to be allowed to confront the woman who spreads such lies about me."

"You are confronting the woman…" Meredith began, then caught herself. How could she have forgotten who she was supposed to be? "Who speaks for her." She prayed her attempt at a regal tone would cover her lapse. "This day I declare that all lands now held by you, Gareth MacKenzie, shall be equally divided among those clans who have suffered the loss of loved ones by your hands. You will be stripped of all titles. And you shall be banished forever from Scotland. If you return, you will face imprisonment in Tolbooth."

The crowd came to its feet in a frenzy of excitement. How could they have known that an audience this day with the queen would offer such an adventure?

Gareth, standing in front of the queen's throne, appeared stricken. Then, taking advantage of the confusion, he darted past the throne and disappeared through an open doorway.

"Seize him," Meredith shouted to the guards who stood on either side of the throne.

Before the guards took a single step, Brice had vaulted over the railing that separated the gallery from the throne. Sword in hand he followed Gareth in hot pursuit.

Still wearing the queen's gown, Meredith sat in the guest chambers with her two sisters and Mary Fleming.

The crowds of spectators had been disbursed. Soldiers were busy combing every inch of the palace. Angus had gone off in search of Brice.

"We are safe here," Fleming said softly. "That horrid man will soon be found and punished."

"I fear for Brice." Meredith paced, unable to sit.

"Brice Campbell is the most dangerous warrior in all of Scotland. Why should you fear for his safety?"

"He is weary from his long journey. He may grow careless."

"Aye. And he is drained, having suffered a wound at the hands of a Highland enemy, Holden Mackay." Brenna's soft voice trembled.

"Mackay?" Meredith whirled on her sister. "What are you saying?"

"Brice told us that he and his men attacked Mackay's fortress searching for you. But you had already escaped in disguise."

"God in heaven." Meredith slumped into a chair. "And what of Mackay?"

"Mackay is dead. But in the battle, Brice was wounded."

Meredith pressed her fingers to her temples to ease the terrible throbbing that had been building throughout the day.

"You should rest," Fleming said softly.

"I will rest when this is over."

They looked up expectantly at the sound of hurried footsteps. At the sight of the queen, Meredith could hardly hide her disappointment. She had hoped it would be Brice.

"Oh, my darlings, you must gather around me and hear about my wonderful day." Mary gave Meredith a quick appraisal, and noting her obvious distress, murmured, "So now you have had a taste of what it is like to be ruler. Was she a good queen, Flem?"

"She was most fair, Majesty. And very quick of mind. You will be receiving congratulations on your wise decisions of today for many weeks to come."

"Ah. That only adds to an already perfect adventure."

"You were happy with your—abductor?"

The queen blushed. "The Earl of Bothwell is an exciting suitor. And a wicked rogue, much like your Brice Campbell," she said to Meredith.

"Will you tell us everything?" Flem asked.

Mary laughed. "You know I will, Flem. Now let me begin with the very first moment my lover arrived at my chambers."

Brenna glanced at Meredith's pale face. With calm assurance, she surprised the queen and her Maries by taking Meredith by the hand. "Please excuse us, Majesty. Meredith must rest or she will make herself ill."

Though she protested, Meredith allowed herself to be led to the sleeping chamber.

"I will help you change into something comfortable." Brenna reached for the buttons of the scarlet gown.

"Nay." Meredith stopped her. "Until the queen gives her permission, I must continue the charade."

"Aye." Brenna removed the crown and unpinned Meredith's hair. "But at least you can be comfortable."

"I will not sleep. I will merely rest for a few minutes."

"Rest then," Brenna whispered, helping her into bed. "We will be just outside the door in the sitting chamber."

Meredith's weak smile revealed her exhaustion. "I am so glad you are here."

"Then you do not mind that we disobeyed your orders?"

"Nay." Meredith opened her arms and embraced her sister. "Rest now. Soon enough we will be home."

Home. Meredith watched as the door closed. It had been such a long time since she had enjoyed the simple pleasures of home.

Her lids fluttered. With a sigh she gave in to the overwhelming feelings that swamped her. Within minutes she was fast asleep.

The sun had made its arc to the western sky. Evening shadows drifted across the grounds of Holyroodhouse. Meredith heard the door to the outer chamber open, and heard, from the sitting chamber, the sounds of her sisters chatting with the queen. The servants had apparently brought an evening meal. From the peals of laughter that could be heard, it was obvious that the queen was still regaling them with tales of her adventure. What a delightful surprise to know that her sisters were here to share this.

At the muted sound of footsteps Meredith sat up, a bright expectant smile on her face. "Brice..."

The man who appeared beside her bed was not Brice. His golden hair and evil, dangerous smile made her heart stop.

"So, my lady. At last I find you."

As she opened her mouth to scream, he covered her mouth with his hand. In his other hand was a small, deadly knife. "If you summon the others, they will die as well. The choice is yours."

Meredith thought about the two sisters she adored. She would rather die at the hands of this monster than give him

the chance to harm Brenna or Megan. She nodded her agreement. When he removed his hand she sucked in several deep
breaths and fought to control her terror.

Roughly he threw back the bed covers and dragged her to
her feet. The moment the bed linens fell away, he stared in
openmouthed surprise.

"That gown… You…" His eyes narrowed. "You! It was
not the queen who publicly humiliated me this day. It was
you."

"Aye. And it was nearly as satisfying as seeing you dead."
She tossed her head, striving for courage she did not really
feel. "You cannot hope to kill me and escape this palace.
There are guards everywhere."

"I have evaded them for hours," he scoffed. "When darkness covers the land I will join my men who wait for me
beyond the city."

"But where can you go? You cannot hide forever. You have
been banished from Scotland."

"By you. Not by the queen."

"I speak for the queen." With her hands at her hips she
met his level look. "The words I spoke this day are already
law."

"There are ways around the law." He spoke quickly, as
though he had already given this some thought. "There are
many countries that would welcome a man who can command
armies."

"You would ask your men to leave their homes and follow
you?"

"They will go where I lead them." He moved closer. "The
French queen hates Mary Stuart. She would pay me hand-
somely to fight for her cause."

"That would make you a traitor as well as a murderer."

"You are a fool." He studied the firm young body beneath
the elegant gown. "Together we could have owned all of the
Borderland."

"Then you are the bigger fool. I would have rather died
than permitted you to touch me."

His hand snaked out, catching her roughly by the shoulder.
"Then you shall have your wish." His gaze pinned her.

"From the beginning you were the problem. But you will be a problem no more."

"What do you intend to do with me?"

His breath was hot against her temple as he dragged her toward the door. "I had hoped to kill you. But now you will be my assurance that I leave this prison. If any of the queen's guards stop us, you will be as convincing as you were this day. You, little witch, will help me reach my men safely. And," he added with a cruel laugh, "if you prove useful enough, I may even take you all the way to France with me."

As he dragged her toward the outer door, the inner door between the sitting chamber and sleeping chamber was suddenly thrown open. Brice stood framed in the doorway. Beyond him stood the queen, her face aglow, her Maries surrounding her like fluttering birds.

At the sight of Meredith being held at knife point, Brice's blood froze.

Gareth found himself staring at a ghost.

"You are dead. I killed you."

"And I have come back to haunt you," Brice said through gritted teeth.

"Nay. It cannot be. I plunged my sword through your heart. I watched the lifeblood spill from you. As my father did before me with your father."

At his words everyone went deathly quiet.

It was Brice who broke the silence. "Was it also your father who spread lies about my father?"

Gareth gave an evil smile. "Aye. He coveted his wealth and titles. And he taught his sons well. Once a man's name is muddied, it is never clean again."

"And the lies spread about me in the French Court?"

Meredith suddenly realized what heartache Brice must have suffered in a foreign land, with enemies such as the MacKenzies.

"Aye." Gareth laughed. "The queen mother felt that you were exerting too much influence on the young queen. It was my task to see that you were—encouraged to leave."

"Release the woman." Brice's words were deadly soft. "This fight is between the two of us."

Gareth tightened his grip on Meredith's throat. "You will drop your weapon or my dirk will find the woman's heart."

The other women stood in stunned silence in the doorway. Their faces mirrored their shock as they watched and listened.

For a long moment Brice's gaze held Meredith's. He thought of all the battles he had fought, the victories he had savored. How simple life had been when he'd had nothing to lose except his own life. But it was Meredith's life that hung in the balance. And he would gladly pay any price, even death, to save her.

He made a move to toss aside his sword.

As his hand moved to his scabbard Meredith gave a cry. "No, Brice. I cannot let him kill you."

In a panic Gareth pressed the blade tightly to Meredith's throat. She gave a sudden cry of pain. Blood spilled down her bodice.

At the sight of her blood Brice lost all reason. Like a man possessed he lunged, catching Meredith by the arm and yanking her free of Gareth's grasp. With one fluid movement he plunged his sword through Gareth's heart.

For a moment Gareth stared at his assailant, his eyes round and unblinking. Then, with a cry bubbling in his throat, he dropped to the floor.

As Meredith slumped to her knees Brice caught her and lifted her in his strong arms. With blood streaming from her wound she clung to him and whispered, "Oh, Brice, hold me."

Before he could respond she sank into a sea of darkness.

Meredith drifted in and out of consciousness.

Through a blur of voices she heard Brice's voice, low and troubled. "She should have responded to your physician's potion by now."

She thought she heard Brenna calmly stating, "It is exhaustion. She has been through too much these past months. She must be returned to MacAlpin Castle. There she will rest and grow strong."

There was another voice, regal, haughty. "You will take

my carriage and a company of my soldiers. She can be home by morning light.''

And Megan's voice, high-pitched in agitation. "If anything will give her the will to live it is home."

"Home." Though Meredith's mouth formed the word, no sound came out.

She felt Brice's arms around her, cradling her against his chest. She breathed in the familiar scent of him and sighed as sleep once more overtook her.

Meredith lay very still, listening to the sound of birds on the sloping lawns of MacAlpin Castle. She snuggled deeper into the furs surrounding her and breathed in the fragrance of roses that wafted from the cultivated gardens below her window.

Opening her eyes she saw the figure in the chair beside her bed. Brice, his chin rough and unshaven, his eyes red rimmed from lack of sleep, sat watching her.

"At last you are awake." He sat forward and caught her hand.

"Have I slept long?" Her words were wrenched from a throat that felt raw.

He nodded. "I feared you would never wake." He smiled, causing her heart to tumble wildly. "I remembered that other world that once held me in its spell, and thought it had claimed you instead."

"How long have I been home?"

Home. The word caused a terrible pain around his heart. How long had he denied her the comfort of her home?

"For three days now you have slept in your own bed. But you were not here. You were somewhere else. I could not reach you. No one could."

Meredith remembered the way she had suffered when Brice had lingered near death's door. Seeking to comfort him she placed her hand over his. "You need worry no longer, my lord. I am home now. And I am here to stay."

A look of pain crossed his handsome features and she longed to draw him close and ease his suffering. Instead she asked, "Why is my throat so constricted?"

"You do not remember?"

At her arched brow he said softly, "Gareth MacKenzie cut your throat."

She touched a hand to the dressing that covered the wound. "And Gareth?"

"Dead."

She seemed to take a long time to let that fact sink in. She remembered the horrified look on Brice's face as he yanked her free of Gareth's grasp. But nothing more. Neither the pain nor the panic. In a voice still softened by sleep she whispered, "Leave me, Brice, and take your rest. 'Tis over at last. Now we can all live in peace."

Peace. He watched, tormented, as her lids fluttered, then closed. How could he have forgotten her position as leader of her clan? He had foolishly nurtured the dream of making her his bride and uniting their clans. But she was a Borderer, whose gentle, rolling countryside was a battleground that divided Scotland and England. And he was a Highlander, whose people depended upon his leadership for their very survival in a harsh environment. His father had been brutally taken from them. It would not be fair to leave them without a leader again.

Neither of them could go with the other and leave their people leaderless.

Brenna, who had paused in the doorway, reluctant to intrude, now walked to the bedside and touched a hand to her sister's forehead.

"Already the healing has begun. With rest she will soon be as strong as before."

She was surprised to see the stricken look on Brice's face. "I thought that would make you happy, my lord Campbell."

"Aye. I am delighted that Meredith is regaining her strength." He stood wearily. "But now that I know she will survive, I must leave."

"Rest here a few days, my lord, until Meredith is strong enough to speak with you. From what I know of your time together in the Highlands, you have much to talk over."

So she had confided in her sisters.

He shook his head and ran a hand over the beard that darkened his chin. "She has already spoken. She desires to live in her home in peace."

"I heard her words," Brenna said softly. "But when she is stronger…"

"When she is stronger," Brice said firmly, "she will unite her people and rebuild that which Gareth MacKenzie sought to destroy. And I," he said, strapping on his sword and tossing a cape over his shoulder, "have a clan depending upon me as well. I have left them leaderless long enough."

"Meredith will wish to thank you, Brice."

He took Brenna's hands in his and kissed her cheek. "Thanks are not necessary. It is my fault that she has been denied her home for so long now. Tell her only that I…" He stopped abruptly as Angus and Megan walked into the room. With a wry smile he said, "Tell Meredith that I wish her every happiness."

In a low voice the others could not hear Brenna asked, "Do you love her, Brice?"

"Aye. With all my heart. And for that reason I must leave her. She has a duty. As do I."

"You once said that you would even risk losing her if it meant her happiness."

He said nothing.

Brenna and Megan watched as Brice strode quickly from the room without a backward glance. Within minutes he and Angus could be seen urging their mounts into a gallop toward the river Tweed.

With a heavy heart Brenna draped an arm about her sister's shoulder. The two sisters stood at the balcony window and watched until both figures disappeared into the Highland mists.

Chapter Twenty-Five

Brice leaned a hip against the window of his balcony and watched as a falcon slowly circled, searching for prey.

From below stairs came the sad, sorrowful sounds of Jamie's lute. For days now the lad's music seemed to mirror Brice's feelings.

What had he once told Meredith? That he had never felt lonely in his Highland fortress. He gave a bitter laugh and lifted his face to the sky, seeing the falcon's mate suddenly appear. The two birds soared together, looking as though they could touch the sun. Then they suddenly swooped, skimming low to the ground before once more lifting, soaring, until they were lost from view.

He felt a terrible, aching sense of loss.

Ever since he had returned to Kinloch House he had felt restless and irritable. In his absence the great hall had been restored. The women had completed the new tapestries, relating the proud history of the Campbells. Tradesmen in the villages had made new chairs, tables, and settles. Weavers had provided fresh linens. The castle sparkled under the loving care of Mistress Snow and the servants, who filled it with the fresh scents of mint and evergreen.

It was so empty.

Though it resounded with the voices of the serving girls, and the laughter of Brice's men, it no longer brought him joy to walk the halls of Kinloch House.

In every room he saw her. In the refectory, sitting beside Jamie, listening to the booming voices of his men while she quietly ate. In the great hall, warming herself before the fire. In his sleeping chamber, lying beside him. Thoughts of Meredith tormented him.

He had never dreamed it would be so painful to let go.

He had waged terrible, bitter arguments with himself. If he were half a man he would ride to the Borders and take her. It had always been the Highlanders' way. But her plea, in her moment of pain, had touched him deeply. Home. For too long she had been denied the comfort of her home. Because of him. If he truly loved her, he had to give her what she most craved. And in that moment he had seen with perfect clarity. Meredith needed her home. He had no right to deny her her heart's desire.

If she loved him, he thought with growing resentment, she would come to him. She would leave her people without a leader, without protection from the invaders to the south, and come to him. She would leave her gentle rolling hills behind and make her home with him. He studied the land, trying to see it from her eyes. Where he saw shady glens and waterfalls, she would see dark forests where the sun never penetrated. Where he saw wide, peaceful vistas she would see a harsh, primitive wilderness.

What foolishness. She had a duty to her people. And he had a duty to his.

He frowned, cursing the day he had seen her standing at the altar, looking like an angel from heaven. If he had never met her, had never allowed himself to love her, he would not now have this terrible aching void in his life.

He cursed himself for wallowing in self-pity like some love-sick lad. Pulling on his tunic he strode down the stairs and picked up an axe. There were trees to be felled. He would feel better after a day of punishing physical labor.

Darkness spread over the land. In his chambers Brice turned away from the balcony window and sprawled upon a low bench pulled in front of the fire. Below he could hear the sound of his men's voices, low, muted, as they discussed the events of the day. He had no desire to join them.

He heard the sad, haunting notes of Jamie's lute and felt a wave of regret. The lad missed her. Almost as much as Brice did. Jamie had blurted the truth earlier today while they had worked together in the forest. He'd admitted that when Brice returned without Meredith, he had felt as if he'd lost his mother again.

It had been a blow to Brice. But he vowed to spend more time with the lad to ease him through this sense of loss. In time the pain would cease. For both of them.

He lifted a half-filled tankard and drank. At a knock on the door he called, "Enter."

Angus entered, then beckoned for Mistress Snow to follow.

"Do we disturb you, old friend?"

"Nay."

Brice stood and indicated the settle. The housekeeper took a seat but Angus preferred to stand.

Brice glanced from his friend to the woman. Both of them were grinning and looked as if they would burst if they did not soon share their news.

"Mistress Snow has consented to marry me," Angus said.

Brice caught his friend in a great bear hug. "I am happy for you." He turned to embrace the blushing woman. "For both of you."

"Thank you, my lord."

Brice turned to Angus. "When will you wed?"

"We will speak to the rector on the morrow. I would prefer it yesterday." He and Brice shared a laugh. "But my bride would like a fortnight to return to her cottage in yonder forest and prepare it properly for our dwelling."

"The cottage." Brice turned to Mistress Snow, then clapped a hand on his old friend's shoulder. "I do not think a humble cottage would be the proper dwelling for the leader of the Mackay clan."

Angus stared at him without comprehending.

"With Holden Mackay dead, we must find a way to unite his clan with ours. I have been thinking that you would be the perfect clan leader, my friend. Though I was loath to send you away when I knew that your heart was here with Mistress

Snow." Brice gave them both a knowing smile. "But now that you are to be wed, you have solved my dilemma. Would you and your bride be willing to live in the Mackay fortress and help me bring peace to these Highlands?"

Angus stared at Brice for long minutes, then turned and lifted Mistress Snow into his arms. "What say you, lass? Would you be willing to give up your duties here at Kinloch House and live like the lady of the manor?"

"Oh, Angus." As he lifted her high in the air she laughed in delight. "I cannot believe it."

"Nor can I." He set her on her feet and, keeping one arm draped about her, extended his other arm toward his old friend. "I would like Alston as my right hand. He is good with people. Mackay's men will take to him."

"He is yours."

"We must go below stairs and tell the others." Angus turned to Brice. "Will you join us?"

"In a while."

When they had left, Brice turned to stare thoughtfully into the flames of the fire. He would miss the company of Angus and Alston, the red-bearded giant. And the loss of Mistress Snow would surely be felt in Kinloch House. But he was happy for his friends.

If only he could shake off this heaviness around his heart.

The hounds set off a wild frenzy of barking. He heard the babble of voices and the sound of Jamie's lute. They would no doubt celebrate long into the night. This sad place badly needed a celebration.

Picking up his tankard he drained it and set it on the mantel. At a sound from the doorway he turned.

His mind was playing tricks on him. He was seeing her again, looking far lovelier than she had ever looked before.

She wore a hooded cape of lush green velvet, lined with ermine. Her cheeks were flushed, and her green eyes sparkled with a light that he had seen before, on that first night they had loved. She slid the hood back to reveal a mane of mahogany hair that tumbled down her back in a riot of curls. Entwined in her hair were ivy and wildflowers, their sweet perfume filling the air.

He blinked. The vision did not vanish. Instead she took a step closer. Her lips parted in the sweetest smile.

"Meredith." His heart stopped.

"Aye."

He felt his throat go dry. "You are not a vision?"

"Nay, my lord." She laughed and crossed the room until she was standing in front of him. "Touch me. I will not vanish."

Touch her? He wanted to crush the lady to him. Instead he reached a hand to her and felt his fingertips gently brush her cheek.

"How did you get here?"

"I rode."

"Alone?" His eyes narrowed.

"Nay, my lord. I brought a company of my men."

"Ah." At last his senses were returning. The floor, which for a moment had tilted dangerously, was now steady once more. He brought his other hand to her face and stared down into her eyes. "Why have you come, Meredith?"

"To invite you to a wedding."

"A wedding?" His heart tumbled. His brows drew together in a frown.

"Aye."

"Whose wedding?"

She smiled. "Mine."

His frown became a scowl. She felt his battle for control as he dropped his hands to his sides, where they curled into fists. "You did not wait long to wed."

"I have waited long enough." When she saw the look of pain that crossed his features she could no longer carry on the charade. "Oh, Brice. If you could but see your face." She reached up to touch him and the cape slid from her shoulders, revealing a white gossamer gown that skimmed her breasts and fell in soft folds to the tips of kid slippers.

His hands grasped her shoulders so tightly that she gasped. "You look," he whispered, "as beautiful as you did on that morn when first I saw you in the cathedral."

"This time," she said, looking up at him with love shining in her eyes, "I dressed for you."

"For me." He allowed his gaze to travel slowly over her, devouring her.

And then he knew.

"You've come to stay?"

"Aye. If you'll have me."

"Oh, Meredith." He drew her into the circle of his arms and kissed her with a savageness that left them both dazed and reeling.

He lifted his head and touched a fingertip to the tear that squeezed from her eye and coursed down her cheek. "Tears, firebrand?"

"I was so afraid, Brice."

"Of what?"

"Afraid this was all a terrible mistake. Afraid that when I reached your beloved Highlands you would not want me."

"Oh, my love. You are all I want."

"Then why did you leave me without a word?"

"I had no right to ask you to give up your title, your power, your home, for me."

Another tear spilled over, and then another while she wrapped her arms about his neck and clung to him. So Brenna had been right. She would be forever thankful to her sister for urging her to take the risk.

Against his throat she whispered, "You are all I want, Brice. Without you it is empty."

"Oh, little firebrand." He buried his lips in a tangle of her hair and crushed her to him. "What arrangements have you made for your clan?"

"Brenna will be the MacAlpin." She smiled. "Without Gareth MacKenzie to divide them, the Borderers have united to stand against any English attack. Though I fear Brenna's greatest challenge will not be with the English, but with our sister, Megan."

Brice laughed. "Aye. The lass is like another I know." He kissed the tip of her nose.

"Be very careful, my lord. We are not yet wed."

"Nay. But Angus and Mistress Snow are below stairs now planning their wedding. And if we are wise, we will ask to share their ceremony on the morrow."

"Oh, Brice. Could we?" She caught his hand. "Let us go below and speak to them."

She was surprised when he resisted. Before she could tug again on his hand he dragged her roughly against him and covered her lips with his. Instantly she felt the rush of desire that begged for release.

"We will talk with them later." The words were ground against her lips.

They sank to their knees on the fur throw. His fingers moved to the buttons of her gown.

"My men…"

"Will be invited to a wedding on the morrow. But for tonight, my beloved, just let me love you."

Love. "Oh, Brice," she breathed against his lips. "I love you so."

"And I love you, Meredith. So much." His fingers began to weave their magic. His lips moved over her, igniting little fires wherever they touched. "Welcome home, little firebrand."

Home. Aye. These Highlands were now home. This man, this Highland Barbarian, held her heart.

She felt a welling of so much love. A love that would endure even beyond this lifetime. A love to last an eternity.

*   *   *   *   *

Author's Note

A quotation from John Fordun's "Chronicles" in Skene's *Celtic Scotland*, from 1363 to 1384, states:

The highlanders…are a savage and untamed nation, rude and independent…comely in person but unsightly in dress, hostile to the English people and language…and exceedingly cruel. They are, however, faithful and obedient to their crown and country….

That quotation fascinated me. And as I researched, I discovered some who could have been my ancestors. I admit that I fell in love with these highland barbarians.

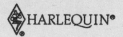

Not The Same Old Story!

 Exciting, glamorous romance stories that take readers around the world.

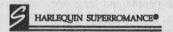 Sparkling, fresh and tender love stories that bring you pure romance.

 Bold and adventurous— Temptation is strong women, bad boys, great sex!

 Provocative and realistic stories that celebrate life and love.

HARLEQUIN AMERICAN ROMANCE® Contemporary fairy tales—where anything is possible and where dreams come true.

HARLEQUIN® INTRIGUE® Heart-stopping, suspenseful adventures that combine the best of romance and mystery.

LOVE & LAUGHTER™ Humorous and romantic stories that capture the lighter side of love.

Look us up on-line at: http://www.romance.net HGENERIC

Take 2 bestselling love stories FREE

Plus get a FREE surprise gift!

MEN at WORK

All work and no play? Not these men!

April 1998

KNIGHT SPARKS by Mary Lynn Baxter

Sexy lawman Rance Knight made a career of arresting the bad guys. Somehow, though, he thought policewoman Carly Mitchum was framed. Once they'd uncovered the truth, could Rance let Carly go...or would he make a citizen's arrest?

May 1998

HOODWINKED by Diana Palmer

CEO Jake Edwards donned coveralls and went undercover as a mechanic to find the saboteur in his company. Nothing—or no one—would distract him, not even beautiful secretary Maureen Harris. Jake had to catch the thief—*and* the woman who'd stolen his heart!

June 1998

DEFYING GRAVITY by Rachel Lee

Tim O'Shaughnessy and his business partner, Liz Pennington, had always been close—but never *this* close. As the danger of their assignment escalated, so did their passion. When the job was over, could they ever go back to business as usual?

MEN AT WORK™

Available at your favorite retail outlet!

HARLEQUIN® **Silhouette®**

PMAW1